IN THE S

Part I:
Capricorn–Gemini

Hiding Behind The Couch Series
Book Four

by
Debbie McGowan

Beaten Track

www.beatentrackpublishing.com

ALSO BY DEBBIE McGOWAN

Champagne
(1st Edition: highblue, 2004;
2nd Edition: Beaten Track, 2012)

'Time to Go' in *Story Salon Big Book of Stories*
(Edited by Joseph Dougherty; iUniverse, 2006)

And The Walls Came Tumbling Down

No Dice

Double Six

HIDING BEHIND THE COUCH SERIES
(in chronological order)

Beginnings (Short Story)
Hiding Behind The Couch (Book One)
No Time Like The Present (Book Two)
The Harder They Fall (Book Three)
First Christmas (Short Story)
In The Stars Part I (Book Four)
Breaking Waves (Short Story)
In The Stars Part II (Book Five)
A Midnight Clear (Short Story)
Red Hot Christmas (Short Story)

For more information about Hiding Behind The Couch, visit
www.hidingbehindthecouch.com

www.debbiemcgowan.co.uk

Beaten Track

First published 2014 by Beaten Track Publishing
Copyright © 2014 Debbie McGowan

A CIP catalogue record for this book
is available from the British Library.

ISBN: 978 1 909192 31 7

Zodiac Illustrations: Emma Pickering
www.noirestudios.co.uk

Cover background stars taken from
FootageIsland Sparkling Stars animation
www.youtube.com/footageisland

Beaten Track Publishing,
Burscough. Lancashire.
www.beatentrackpublishing.com

ACKNOWLEDGEMENTS

Thank you to my wonderful proof-readers, Tracy and Andrea, for your persistence in / insistence on finding and then laughing at my dreadful mistakes, not to mention your extraordinary expertise in all matters, but in particular, those of bingo and healthcare! The Circle thank you, too!

"Love Hearts" used with kind permission:
Swizzels Matlow Ltd.
www.lovehearts.com

Excerpts from:

"The Signs", by Henry Van Dyke
The Project Gutenberg EBook of The Poems of Henry Van Dyke.

Hamlet, by William Shakespeare.

Reproduced under the terms of the
Project Gutenberg Licence.
www.gutenberg.org

"Footprints In Your Heart", by Eleanor Roosevelt;
also attributed as
"Today is a Gift", by Laszlo Kotro-Kosztandi.
Further bibliographic information unavailable.

For my friends on the flat roof:
we steered a wayward ship,
lost and found God, glimpsed Satan,
didn't learn a lot of Latin.

And for Powelly, rider on the storm.
Elf people, though, dude. Seriously?

"In the magical universe there are no coincidences and there are no accidents. Nothing happens unless someone wills it to happen."

William S. Burroughs

CONTENTS

Capricorn

The goat looks solemn, yet he likes to run,
And leap the rocks, and gambol in the sun:
The truly wise enjoy a little fun.

MARIGOLD
Friday 6th January

Rank mops and disinfectant. The stench clung to every grubby cubic inch of air. Metal clanged loudly against metal; the jangle of keys echoed around the corridors and up through the levels, ricocheting along landings and up into the void above. It was a grey, grey world. The steel doors were painted in industrial grey; the bars were Hammerite grey; the walls, perhaps a shade lighter than the doors, still grey; the skylights up above showed nothing but grey sky. Even the uniforms and overalls were grey. Everything: grey.

Well, almost everything.

"Eh, it's our turn," a voice shouted from across the void. "This is fucked up."

"Yeah," another voice agreed from behind. "Oy! Marigold! Get a new fuckin' mop, you cunt. It stinks to shit."

'Marigold' continued along the corridor, trying to ignore the multiple complaints as he passed each cell. They had every right. No supplies, the mops hadn't been changed in all the time he'd been in here, which was five months, two weeks, four days and three hours. Seventeen days to go. Then he'd be out. He glanced up and spotted Darren ahead of him.

"Alright?" he greeted, wheeling the stinking, grey mop bucket behind him.

"Yeah. Noisy today."

"Third's not been cleaned this week. That's why," Marigold explained. Hardly anyone here called him by his real name, not even his fellow wing cleaners.

"So why're we doing Second?"

"Don't ask me. Anyway, sooner we get on, the sooner we'll be done."

Marigold wheeled his bucket on along the filthy concrete third floor of C-wing. Darren followed with the trolley, past the rest of the cells, to the lift, where they waited whilst the screw unlocked the gate. Marigold let Darren enter first, then dragged the mop bucket in and turned to watch as the gate was locked again. The lift started to descend.

"Not long now, huh?" Darren said, gnawing at the grotty stubs of his fingernails.

"Nope. Two weeks, three days."

3

Darren changed hands. "Wish it was me."

"Yeah," Marigold replied absently. The lift came to a stop and the gate procedure was repeated, in reverse, to the accompanying shouts of the third landing prisoners tumbling from above. The second landing was empty, with everyone out for exercise, not that it would have mattered, as they only cleaned the corridors. Darren pulled the wide floorbrush free of the trolley and flipped it up the right way.

"Gonna start at the other end," he told Marigold and headed away from him.

"Right. I'll just get this shit off the wall first."

The second landing was where they put the weirdos, not the pervs—they were on the fourth floor—the ones that were a bit loopy but not loopy enough to be in K-block. It was closer to the screws' station, just in case anything kicked off, which it didn't very often. In fact, most of the time there was just this line of shit along the wall, from the showers to C221. And they wondered why he'd asked for rubber gloves? Doctor Sheridan got him permission eventually, but he had to hand them in at the end of every day. Sometimes he wondered why he wasn't in K-block himself. Obviously he wasn't loony enough, or maybe just not the right kind of loony. He was never the right kind of anything.

He squirted dilute disinfectant over the trail of faeces, breathing through his nose, which might seem counter-intuitive to the uninitiated, but for as much as it stank worse when it was wet, he'd once got hit in the face by sprayback and swallowed it; he wasn't making that mistake again. Back to the start of the line, he retraced with a rancid, damp cloth, pushing the brown smudge around until it disappeared through absorption or dissipation, then went to join Darren down the far end.

"So what's this job then?"

"Don't wanna say," Marigold mumbled quietly.

"Suit yourself."

Darren continued along with his brush, missing the edge of the corridor all the way, leaving a grey ridge of dirt and dust.

"You gonna go back over this then, yeah?"

"Nah. The mop'll get it."

Marigold closed his eyes as he wrung out the mop and plonked it down dead-centre of the corridor, then swooshed from side to side, swirling it to pick up the debris Darren had left behind. The mop beat a rhythm as it hit against the walls and the doors, and he started to sing along in his head. Freaking weird choice too: "Message in a Bottle". It was a song that he sometimes heard on the radio when he was little, but not one he'd heard in a while. Up ahead, Darren had stopped to engage in a shouted dialogue with a prisoner on the landing below.

4

"Tomorrow," he repeated.

The prisoner swore and disappeared from view.

"What was that?" Marigold asked.

"He wanted to know when First was being done."

"Some time never, did you tell him?"

Marigold waited. He couldn't go any further until Darren moved on, so he leaned on the railing and returned to the song, escaping into the thoughts that went with it. They were nothing exciting: just daydreaming about getting out and wondering what the job would be like: cleaning offices wasn't going to be much more interesting than cleaning prisons, but there would hopefully be less shit and maybe even some cleaning stuff. That would be a luxury.

And he'd be free.

"What d'you think that is?" Darren called. He'd stopped again, just a couple of cells down. It really was no wonder that Third never got done.

"What what is?"

Darren pointed up. Marigold's gaze settled on the dirty bitten fingernails, his lips pursing in disgust, then followed the direction of the finger, up to the top of the door of C208, where a small, crumpled triangle of light grey stood out against the darker grey of the heavily scarred paintwork.

"Dunno." He moved closer to inspect it. "A sheet, maybe?"

"Huh." Darren shrugged and leaned on his brush. "When you get out, see if there's any jobs going for me, will ya?"

"I could be working down the sewers, for all you know."

"It'd still beat cleaning this shithole." They both started laughing, but then stopped dead at exactly the same time. "You hear that?" Darren asked. Marigold nodded and moved towards the door, holding his breath, his ear turned towards the barred square aperture. He stood on tiptoes and cautiously peered into the cell.

"Ring the alarm!" he shouted. He dropped the mop and tripped over it in his haste, falling against the door. Darren was still standing staring. "Ring the fucking alarm!" Darren shook himself out of his trance and ran down the corridor, thumping the nearest button.

Marigold reached through the bars and grabbed the twisted sheet. It came loose in his hand and he watched in horror as the body dropped from view, slumping to the floor with a thud. The door moved a little and he pushed against it, but he was slightly built and Callaghan was much bigger and heavier. With a mighty shove, he wedged himself between the door and the wall and slowly eased through the gap, his back scraping painfully against the lock. The door slammed shut with him on the inside, looking down on the blue-grey dead man, the sheet now forming a loose coil around his head, not the tightly twisted noose it had previously been. Marigold didn't know what to do. He reached out and touched the flayed-out fingers: icy cold. He was definitely very dead. Marigold started to laugh at how ridiculous that was. You're dead or you're not. You can't be more or less dead. *Very* dead. It was hysteria.

The alarm was now joined by rapid-fire bootfall and clanging bunches of keys. About time, he thought, and stepped back out of the way. He'd been in the cell with Callaghan's corpse for less than a minute, but it was long enough.

The body doubled up and fell into a most unnatural position, the force of two burly screws more than a match for a dead man. As his legs slid outwards, Marigold spotted a small square of white, so incredibly bright against the grey of everything else. He bent down, reached out a yellow-gloved finger and spun the square the right way around, squinting at the single word written on it.

"Hadyn."

Marigold picked it up and quickly shoved it inside his overalls.

HAIR
Friday 13ᵗʰ January

"Is my hair receding?"

Josh pulled back his fringe and shoved his face right into Eleanor's. She backed off, in part because he'd invaded her space, but mostly because she couldn't focus on him that close up.

"A bit—maybe?" she answered cautiously. He let go of his hair and sighed. George shook his head in exasperation.

"He's been on about it all week," he complained, which was entirely true; Josh had voiced his anxiety regarding his receding hairline a minimum of once a day, every day, since Sunday, when they'd been watching a TV programme about alopaecia. Now it was Friday evening: Kris's birthday, and the usual joint 'celebration' of Jess's too, not that she appeared to be in a particularly celebratory mood. They were all out together at their favourite Chinese restaurant, and George, reluctantly, was driving, hence Josh's alcohol-induced openness about his current major concern.

"I don't want to go bald," he lamented, lifting a wonton from his soup bowl and pulling a face. "I'll end up looking like this." He examined the pale, doughy ball on his spoon sorrowfully. Eleanor tutted and raised her eyes.

"I wonder about you sometimes."

"I like my hair. It's very important to me."

"We know!"

"George said it's one of the things he loves about me."

The beer was making Josh more candid than usual, given that his general disposition was one most accurately to be described as aloof. He realised this for himself and quickly swapped his beer bottle for a glass of water. The alcohol was going straight to his head.

"I wouldn't mind," George said, "I've been going bald since before I turned thirty. And so's Kris."

Kris glowered at him, but didn't argue to the contrary, although in his case his hair was thinning rather than receding, which meant the transplant had gone unnoticed. Shaunna knew about it, of course, because she did his highlights and haircuts. In fact, it had been her idea. Now, with all of their friends staring at him, trying to comprehend the contradiction presented by his full head of hair and George's undisputed assertion, Kris figured he may as well come clean.

"It's still all my own," he said, running his hand through it by way of illustration. Adele, who was sitting to his right, repeated the action and squinted at his scalp.

"Did it hurt?" she asked, giving his hair a tug to see if it was attached.

"Yes!" He pushed her hand away.

"Sorry," she said, although she was still staring at his head. He moved his chair back a little to try and get out of her way, but she was enraptured.

"Oh, for heaven's sake!" He allowed her to continue examining his hair, like a chimp grooming another chimp, whilst the conversation, remaining on the hair theme, moved on.

"You know, Josh, we are thirty-eight now," Dan pointed out.

"Ahem!" Kris said loudly. "Birthday boy here!"

"All right," Dan laughed. "Some of us are thirty-nine. It's to be expected."

"Ha! Speak for yourself," Josh protested. "*I'm* still thirty-seven!"

"For all of..." Dan paused to calculate how long it was until Josh's birthday, "...another five weeks."

"How nice of you to remember," he retorted. "And anyway, *you're* nearly thirty-nine, so I don't know what you're being so smug about."

"Not for four months, but I don't care, unlike some people."

"I don't care!" Josh snapped. "You're the one who brought age into it!"

"Actually," Andy interrupted, hoping it would stop the pair of them from going at it full 'tooth and nail', "I think he was talking about me."

Murmurs of 'the big four-oh' and 'life begins at...' sounded from all around the table. Andy folded his arms and studied the ceiling, waiting for them all to quieten down. He didn't care about his age either, although he was aware that his recent actions might imply otherwise, should they ever come to the attention of his seven closest friends and his brother.

"You and Dan aren't going to go bald," Shaunna stated authoritatively. They both had thick, brown-black hair that was showing no signs at all of receding or thinning, a sprinkling of silver starting to seep in at their temples, giving both men a more distinguished profile. They were sitting side by side and turned face-to-face at the same time, mirroring each other's gestures and facial expressions as they examined one another.

"You're definitely more grey than me," Dan said.

"Probably," Andy agreed. "But then you won't find any Just for Men in my bathroom cabinet."

Dan's nostrils flared, but he chose not to retaliate at that moment. He was saving it for another time, when he'd gathered all the ammunition he needed.

"Does that mean I *am* going to go bald?" Josh asked Shaunna.

"Not necessarily," she replied cagily. "It just means they definitely won't."

"But I probably will," he persisted.

"I didn't say that. I said they won't. That's not the same as saying you will. It's just that—oh, never mind." Shaunna went to dip a prawn cracker in her bowl and dropped it. For a moment it bobbed around hopefully, like a little white lifeboat, then it started to take on soup and sank. It was a disaster.

"Couldn't you just lie to me?" Josh suggested.

"Really, what point would there be?"

He shrugged. "I could pretend I believe you." He blew up at his fringe and made a sad face. "It's so unfair. They..." he waved his arm at Dan and Andy, "...they don't even care whether they've got hair or not."

Shaunna finally pulled the limp prawn cracker to shore and lifted it gently onto her side plate. Andy patted her arm.

"You tried your best," he said. "It just wasn't meant to be."

She grinned at him. "You should let me style yours for you."

"Nah." He pulled his fingers through the locks curling up behind his ears. "I don't do hairdos. Dan might let you give him a blue rinse though, if you ask nicely."

Dan stamped on his brother's foot under the table, for his and Shaunna's conversation had not gone unnoticed.

"So why have you got a hair piece?" he asked Kris.

"Not a hair piece! Transplant."

"All right, keep your wig on!" Dan came back at him, receiving multiple groans from around the table. "Still, why go to all that trouble and expense? You're a radio actor."

"I've started auditioning for TV again. I'm bored with doing adverts for pointless stuff that no-one wants."

"Da-a-ad," Shaunna began in a high-pitched, childlike voice, "why are we parked on the motorway again?"

"Oh God, here we go," Kris said, rolling his eyes.

George picked up the next line, in his best radio voice: "Car trouble?" he said.

"Always breaking down?" Eleanor continued.

"Time for a change?" Adele added.

"Our cars come with nought percent finance, three year conditional warranty..." Dan said, leaving Josh to finish off with 'his bit'.

"Duh-buh-duh-buh-duh, duh-buh-duh-buh-duh. Terms and conditions apply." Everybody started laughing—well, nearly everyone—and Kris huffed.

"I hate you all," he said, "but that's exactly what I mean. So anyway, I went for this audition last week, for a new crime series. They reckon it's gonna be huge—prime time slot, loads of advertisers interested, two seasons lined up—and guess what? I got a callback!"

9

"Nice one, mate!" Dan congratulated. Everyone else followed suit with utterances of 'well done' and the like.

"Yeah," Kris said thoughtfully. "The only problem is, they wanted someone who could speak Swedish and do British regional accents, and I said I could, which I can—Glaswegian, London, Brummie, Northern Irish—but it's set in Manchester and I can't do Mancunian." He sighed dejectedly.

"Why not?" Adele asked.

"I learn accents by listening to them and I don't know anyone from Manchester."

"Why don't you just watch *Coronation Street*?" she suggested.

"I tried that, but I need to listen to everyday conversations."

"Or maybe you could…" Josh began, then stopped and quickly changed what he had been about to say. "…go on YouTube? There's bound to be loads of clips on there of people just talking."

"Hmm, that's not a bad idea. Why didn't I think of that?" Kris said. "It just goes to show that it pays to have friends with brains. Thanks."

"No problem," Josh muttered, quickly shoving the last wonton in his mouth. The conversation had once again shifted around the table.

"Nice recovery," George said, squeezing the hand he was holding.

"Thanks." Josh blushed under his hair. "Does that mean I can buy the paper for the spare room?"

"Nope."

"But I've not mentioned it at all."

"It's not even been two weeks!"

"George."

"Nope. You said it could wait till Easter."

"But what if it sells out and they don't get any more in? Then I'll have to choose something different. I really liked that paper as well. Picture it: that paper, with a dark blue shagpile rug…"

"All right. I'll meet you halfway. See if you can manage until after your birthday."

"Another five weeks? Seriously?"

"Yep." George turned his attention to his food and ignored all further protest, which by and large consisted of Josh staring at him and huffing, but not much else, because there wasn't any point.

They'd already been here for more than an hour and still not got past the starters, which was always the way. They spent so much time talking that it took them the best part of the evening to finish a meal, but they bought plenty of drinks between them, so the restaurant staff didn't mind at all. The waiter smiled politely and checked if they were finished with their soup bowls to make way for their main course and they all went off to make their selections from the 'all-you-can-eat' table, with the exception of Kris, whose food was prepared separately to ensure it wasn't contaminated with shellfish, although the desensitisation had definitely reduced the severity of his reaction. The treatment consisted of him receiving fortnightly 'incremental updoses' of the protein that caused his allergy, and he was about to enter what the doctors running the trial referred to as the 'maintenance stage', whereby the treatment would stop, but they would continue to monitor his tolerance of the allergen, and it was looking good so far. Nonetheless they had advised him against eating food fried in the same pan as real prawns, but even with the added cost of special preparation, the Chinese restaurant was still a cheap night out, and he'd finally persuaded Shaunna that it was safe for her to enjoy the occasional prawn cracker, although prawn cocktail crisps were still banned from the house, regardless of the number of times he pointed out the seafood-free ingredients list on the backs of packets in the supermarket.

Jess was first to return to the table, with her very meagre pile of noodles and a singular sweet and sour pork ball.

"You not hungry?" Kris asked her.

"Hmm?" she said. She hadn't heard the words.

"What's up?"

"Oh. Nothing. Just not feeling much like eating tonight." She smiled quickly and picked up her fork, spinning some of the noodles onto it. The waiter brought Kris's food and deposited it in front of him; one by one the others returned to their previous positions around the table, and the conversations started up once more.

"Did you get a reply from Stas?" Dan asked Andy through a mouthful of blackbean sauce.

"Yeah. One of the trucks got stuck at the border, apparently," he responded. A couple of the others heard this conversation, but didn't bother asking what it was about. Their business was flourishing, providing a much-needed logistics service, coordinating the supply, ordering and delivery of anything from singular catering ovens to dozens of five tonne concrete slabs for sea walls. However, it wasn't especially exciting work at the best of times, and the project Dan was referring to was even more mundane than usual, involving the shipment of steel components for a retractable football pitch, from Mariupol, a large city in south-east Ukraine, back to London. Unfortunately, one of the truck drivers had got himself arrested and was being detained whilst the authorities checked his documentation. Meanwhile, the other trucks were being stopped at any and every given opportunity, for no reason other than that they were associated with the man in custody. Stas was the Jeffries brothers' point of contact in Mariupol, and he was doing an excellent job of keeping them updated, which was what the rest of their conversation was about.

11

"How're you feeling Adele?" Eleanor spoke across the table. "Has the morning sickness eased off any?"

"Yes, thank goodness," Adele said, prodding at a piece of green pepper and sending it shooting towards Dan. He picked it up and ate it without even looking. She glared at him and Eleanor snorted with laughter.

"He must have a death wish," she joked. "So what are you now? Fifteen weeks?"

"Just past," Adele confirmed, trying her luck with a second piece of pepper and this time succeeding. "It's weird. I'm nowhere near as worried as I was the last time."

"Thank God," Shaunna muttered. She was sitting next to Eleanor and a couple of places round from Adele. Since they'd returned from the 'holiday' in Wales, they'd shifted positions so that now when they were out as a group, they more often than not ended up with the same people they had shared a cabin with. Thus, to Shaunna's left was Andy, who was sitting next to Dan, with Adele to his left. Across the table, Kris and Jess were seated together, as were George and Josh. Eleanor was sat on Josh's other side, which she was finding a little strange. She'd spent so many years sandwiched between the pair of them, trying to sustain conversations and avoid uncomfortable silences, that she felt a bit of a spare part, especially with James staying home with Toby. George picked up on this, and reached across Josh, lightly tugging her sleeve to get her attention.

"Did you get that link I sent you?" he asked.

"Yes, thanks," she confirmed. "I'll have a proper look at it tomorrow."

Josh eyed them both suspiciously.

"It's nothing to do with you," Eleanor told him.

"What are the pair of you scheming?"

"I said, it's nothing to do with you, nosey parker." She gave George a knowing wink, then busied herself with her food. Josh blew air out of his nose and turned to George.

"I can still get into your email, you know."

"Can't. I changed the password." George scooped up a forkful of rice and quickly stuffed it in his mouth. Josh examined him for a minute and grinned smugly.

"Got it," he said.

"Yeah, right!"

Josh took out his phone and started tapping at the screen.

"So when's Ollie next visiting?" George asked Eleanor, trying to ignore Josh's antics.

"February half-term," Eleanor said, "the week after somebody's BIRTHDAY, which might not be quite so much FUN if they persist with what they are DOING!"

"Oh, fine," Josh huffed. Just to prove his point, he showed George the display on his phone and stuck out his tongue. He closed the email app and put his phone away. George shrugged.

"I'll just change it again."

"And I'll guess it again." Josh grinned wickedly. George turned and grabbed him by the scruff, pulling him close.

"So I'll change it to something completely random."

"And then you'll forget and won't be able to get into your email," Josh said, moving in and licking his nose.

"I'm going to get you back for that. You know that?"

"Promises, promises."

"For God's sake, get a room," Kris scolded them, in jest. He was as happy as all of their friends were that they were finally together, and it also meant they left him and 'Ade-wee-an' alone for a while, although for obvious reasons Adrian had always been known as Ade, and it was only really Shaunna who made fun of his speech impediment—not maliciously. She liked him; they got on really well, and she could see how much he and Kris loved each other. Nonetheless, Kris's comment prompted a further round of banter, with George ribbing him, and by extension Shaunna, for the fact that the two of them had spent the best part of the last two decades like a 'pair of mating snails'. This remark set Andy and Dan off into hysterical (and loud) fits of laughter, while Adele looked set to throw up. Jess didn't react.

Earlier in the evening, when the conversation about hair had been taking place, Josh had noticed that she was quieter than usual and a little withdrawn, even taking into account the disharmony created by her short and very badly judged fling with Rob Simpson-Stone. She and Andy were back on speaking terms, although he was still staying at his mum's and saving up a deposit for his own place. He'd lost a significant amount of money when Rob defrauded Jess, but he didn't hold it against her. It was only money, after all; what she'd done to their friendship hurt far more. What Josh had picked up on, therefore, was not so much that she was quiet and distracted, but that she was twisting her hair around her fingers, examining it closely as if checking for split ends—not a behaviour that she was given to displaying in public.

Then, when the conversation moved on and Eleanor was asking Adele how she was feeling, again he saw a flicker of something and soon after she quietly departed for the Ladies', returning ten minutes later with no evidence to suggest she'd been crying. A sadness beyond tears: it was tangible to him and he had raised his shield to protect himself from the shockwave, because that was how he felt it. Now, as they ordered desserts and coffees, Josh continued to watch her in his peripheral vision, taking note

13

of the tiniest movements of her lips, the occasional unchecked frown, the distance in her eyes. Being confident in the accuracy of his interpretation had never felt so awful, and he was wishing desperately that she might prove him wrong. At the end of the evening, when she was waiting for her credit card to be returned and everyone else was making their way outside, he asked George to go and get the car, whilst he stayed back to talk to her, waiting by the door, patiently observing as she pulled on her coat, unaware that he was there. She picked up her bag and started walking towards him, her eyes to the floor. She still hadn't noticed him and jumped when he stepped in front of her.

"You startled me," she said quietly.

"Sorry. I didn't mean to. What's wrong?"

"Nothing," she answered dismissively, knowing all the while that he had already seen straight through the lie.

"It's not nothing," he said, taking hold of her hands. She closed her eyes, then squeezed them tightly shut. He put his arms around her. She didn't move. "Shall I ask the questions?" he suggested. She nodded. "Have you seen a doctor?" She gave no conscious response. "And did they send you for tests?" She swallowed and bowed her head. "Are you waiting on results?" She pulled her hand free and covered her face. "When's the appointment? I'll come with you." Her breaths were heavy and shaky and a tear seeped its way between her fingers.

"Don't tell anyone," she beseeched, her voice muffled by both her hand and the sorrow. "Please?"

"I can't promise that, Jess, I'm sorry, but I'll only tell George, and you can trust him not to say anything."

"Why?" she asked.

"Why do I have to tell George?" Again, she didn't respond, but he knew that was what she meant. To explain would take too long and anyway was an attempt to waylay him. "So when's this appointment?" he asked again. She delved into her bag, pulled out a tissue and blew her nose. He waited for eye contact, yet it was fleeting, evasive.

"It's fine," she said. "I'd rather go on my own."

"OK, so where do you want to meet up after?" He wasn't taking no for an answer. "We'll go for a coffee, maybe something to eat."

"Monday," she relented. "My appointment's at one-twenty."

"I'll be waiting outside."

EXTERMINATION
Saturday 14th January

"Mouse!"

The cat darted past in pursuit of the previously announced rodent, which duly squeezed itself through the narrow space between the floor and the kickplate of the cupboard that Sean was squatting on top of. His legs were already starting to ache and he had a crick in his neck from keeping it bent so as to avoid bashing his head on the shelf above. Sphinx prowled back and forth along the expanse of cupboard for a couple of minutes, then lay down, positioning himself at what seemed the most likely exit route his prey would take. Sean wondered how long he could maintain his own position before he lost the feeling in his feet and fell off, headfirst, knocked himself unconscious, later to be found eaten alive, his gnawed, rotting corpse teeming with tiny, fat mice. He could hear it scurrying about below him, and much as he wasn't really that frightened of them, the sudden movement was why he was in his current predicament. Carefully, he moved first one leg, then the other, and kind of bounced his way towards the edge of the cupboard. He lost his balance, toppled and cracked his head on the edge of the shelf.

"Bollocks!"

Sphinx started purring and made himself comfortable. It looked like he was in it for the long haul.

The phone started ringing. Sean cursed under his breath and decided to brave the drop to the floor, even though the pins and needles were unbelievably painful. He hobbled down the hallway and into the lounge, typically reaching the phone just as it stopped. He waited, picked it up and checked for messages: they'd not left any. Last number called: they didn't leave that either. He hung up again and rubbed the bump on the back of his head. It felt sticky and wet and he instinctively brought his hand down in front of his face. Blood: not much, though. He went up to the bathroom to try and get a better look at it, although it was too far down the back of his head to see. He glanced around the bathroom, spotting the silver cosmetics bag Sophie kept here for when she stayed over. There was bound to be a compact mirror in there. He unzipped the top and duly located a little round mirror, lifting it so he could see the reflection of the back of his head in the mirror on the wall, which kind of worked. He turned around and tried again, this time looking in the small mirror and immediately spotting the gash, even though it was mostly concealed by his hair and he probably wouldn't have spotted it at all, were it not for the blood. It was hardly worth worrying about. He gave it a quick wipe with a dampened facecloth and went to put Sophie's mirror back, her washbag tilting and spilling some of its load. Fortunately the toilet seat lid was down and the array of metallic, cylindrical objects landed on the floor, where they rolled around, then came to a rest at the base of the pedestal. He stooped to retrieve them, marvelling at all the different products: an eye liner, an eyebrow pencil and a lip pencil that looked identical but for the lettering identifying their function; a round pot of creamy coloured cake, now fractured across its centre. It was fascinating to behold the lengths to which women would go to enhance their looks, to make themselves more appealing, or so they believed. Sean scooped the cosmetics together and shook down the rest of the contents of Sophie's bag to make room for the escapees.

It would be a good two hours later before he was able to fully comprehend the series of events that unfolded next, for at the exact moment that the phone started ringing again, the cat emitted an ear-splitting screech and a pink box slid from inside the bag, right onto his waiting palm. Pregnancy test: times two; box open; one missing.

Sean made a pot of tea. Another pot of tea. The third pot of tea, in fact, that he had made since this morning, when he banged his head fleeing from the mouse that he presumed to be one and the same as the owner of the decapitated, mauled remains strewn across the red tiles of his kitchen floor. The third pot of tea since Diane Sheridan had called to request his assistance as an independent character witness; since he discovered the pregnancy tests. Test. Singular.

Now he was waiting for something to happen. He'd called Sphinx in from the garden, in the hope that he might, for once, clean up his own crime scene, although the cat seemed rather more concerned with removing all traces of the victim from his front paws. And Diane should by now have received an email asking that she explain herself. But he hadn't called Sophie. He'd pulled up her number on his mobile phone multiple times. Unlocking the screen now would reveal that it was still on display, but he couldn't bring himself to press the 'call' button. As if a prompt to action, his phone bleated against his hand to indicate the arrival of email. He swiped his thumb across the screen and stared at the tiny picture of Sophie. It was taken when they were away in Italy last summer; in it, she was wearing a red suntop, a vast cocktail of graduated peach-orange in her hand, her mouth oohed around a straw, her eyes laughing. It had been a fun holiday. Sun. Sea. Sambuca. Far too much Sambuca. Sean pressed the back button and loaded his email.

16

Sean,

Apologies for the rather vague message. Can you give me a call to arrange to meet? I'll come to you if that's more convenient. It is rather urgent, but I appreciate you're busy.

Diane

Sean copied the number from the footer of the email message and was all set to call her back when he heard the front door open.

"Hi," Sophie called from the hallway. "Oh. Ew. Yuck, that's revolting." She stopped by the living room door, her eyes trained on the sinewy viscera still adorning the kitchen floor.

"Mouse," Sean stated. Sophie nodded her understanding. She went upstairs, taking her coat off on the way.

"I'm gonna have a bath, I think," she said. "I'm freezing and feel really grotty. Those goats stink. They're cute though." She continued talking as she wandered between the upstairs rooms. Sean heard the bath taps start to gush, then the bedroom door open. "Jake's had to put up a sign to tell people not to pick them up—utterly ridiculous, but it had us all laughing. Of course, I can kind of see why they'd want to, but they don't like it at all, except for little Bo. She loves being cuddled, which is quite strange. You wouldn't think goats would like that, would you?" She came back down the stairs and stopped again in the hallway, this time looking directly at Sean. "What's the matter?"

"I was going to ask you the very same thing, but that you'd keep still for a minute and stop talking."

"Why? There's nothing the matter with me. Are you sick?"

"No. Are you?"

"What are you on about?" She walked through to the kitchen, dodging around the entrails, and filled the kettle. Sean appeared behind her.

"Is there anything you need to tell me?"

She returned the kettle to its base and swivelled to face him. "You seem to think there is. Care to enlighten me?"

"I knocked your make-up bag over," he explained.

"Right?"

"And stuff fell out of it."

"OK."

"Eye liners and what have you, you know?"

"Yes. That's what us women keep in our make-up bags."

"And pregnancy tests."

"Oh."

17

Silence, other than the sound of the bath filling, the water molecules inside the kettle becoming excited. Sophie stared at the kettle and sucked her teeth. Sean stared at Sophie, motionless.

"I need to go and turn off the taps," she mumbled and shuffled past him. He stayed where he was. He couldn't think what to say, had hoped that she would just volunteer the information. "Come talk to me," she shouted from the top of the stairs. He did as he was told, trailing around after her while she undressed, added bubble bath, climbed into the steamy water. He sat on the toilet seat and trained his eyes on the door.

"OK, so," he said.

"So?" she repeated.

"Are you pregnant?"

"Yes."

"Right."

He pulled a piece of toilet paper from the roll and began folding it in half and half again, and again.

"I'm going to the hospital on Thursday," she told him.

"To confirm the result."

"For a termination."

"A termination," he echoed.

"Yeah." She slid down into the water, submerging her hair, and her ears. It wasn't necessary. Sean was at a loss. She pulled herself up to a sitting position again. "Damn. Can you pass me the shampoo?" Sean did so. "Thanks." She tipped some into her hand and rubbed it into her wet hair. "Is that a problem? I mean, it was an accident, so I thought..."

"I'm sorry, Soph," Sean interrupted, "but can you talk me through this? You're pregnant. You didn't tell me."

"We discussed it last year, didn't we?"

"We discussed not wanting children, not what we'd do if this happened."

"It's all the same. We don't want children; the sensible thing is for me to have a termination."

"Sensible, yes. But is it really so simple? You're pregnant, Soph. It's not like getting antibiotics for a chest infection."

"Did you want me to keep it?" Sophie's voice was calm, but he could tell she was getting angry.

"It's not my decision to make. But an abortion, Soph. Are you sure it's what you want?"

"I know what I don't want," she snapped. "I don't want the third degree off you! And I don't want to have a baby, just because you think abortion is immoral."

Sean got up and left the bathroom without another word. She was right. He didn't agree with abortion, but he didn't want to be a father, either.

Whatever she decided he wouldn't be able to reconcile it, and he knew that his response was selfish. After all, she was the one who was pregnant—the one who was facing a traumatic and potentially invasive medical procedure. He should be supporting her through it, not adding to her troubles. He returned downstairs and waited until he heard the bath emptying, then made her a cup of hot chocolate, took it back up and waited in the bedroom for her. She came in drying her hair.

"Sorry," he said.

"So am I."

"You do what's best for you. I'll support you."

"Thanks. I should've told you. After all, it's your decision too, but I just thought…"

"No, Soph. It's *your* decision, because it affects you, not me."

"And what if I'd decided to keep it?"

"Well, obviously that would have been different, in the longer term."

"Are you OK with it?"

"Yes. It's not ideal, but, you know, it's not the right time for us to become parents. I don't suppose it'll ever be the right time, if I'm truthful."

"I just wanted to get it sorted with the minimum of fuss, you understand?" Sean nodded to show he did. "So," she said, "you're gonna have to clean up the dead mouse, unless you want to add vomit into the mix."

She didn't need to tell him twice. It had been the morning sickness that alerted her, not the sudden drop in blood pressure before Christmas, nor the lack of menstruation. She'd always been irregular and she'd felt fine since the trip to the health spa, so didn't bother her GP about it; she just got on with the festivities, then work, then uni, but the nausea almost finished her off last weekend, especially once she saw the result. The sickness would generally ease as the day progressed, occasionally re-triggered by particularly pungent smells—like the pygmy goats at the farm, and, she found out a few minutes after Sean finished clearing the kitchen floor, fresh coffee. And much as it was awful, it was entirely manageable, so she was treating it as nothing more than a relatively minor ailment that would soon be cured, because that was as much as it meant to her.

Sean was having a little more difficulty seeing it that way. He wasn't 'pro-life' as such, but he certainly wasn't 'pro-abortion'. He'd once counselled a young woman from a strict Irish Roman Catholic family and she refused to consider termination as an option at all, yet referred to the baby growing inside her in the most hateful terms—the spawn of evil, the demon's bastard, and so on—and the damage caused by continuing with the pregnancy by far outweighed that which would have resulted from ending it when she could. Ultimately, her body made the decision that her mind could not, as the rape had been so violent that it damaged her cervix. So, yes, he could see that in some circumstances an abortion was the right and only course of action. But this time? It seemed selfish and irresponsible; neither of them would suffer particularly for bringing this child into the world. His job was well-paid and secure. Sophie could easily move in here. As their child got older, they could expand the second floor above the kitchen extension, and build him or her their own bedroom. On a purely financial level, there was no reason why they couldn't do this. On a practical one, he'd calculated that the baby would be due some time in August, which might delay Sophie starting her Masters, but again, the disruption to their lives would be minimal. As for the emotional impact: herein lay the problem. Problems. Multiple.

Neither of them wanted children. They were quite certain of this. Their relationship suited them both; Sophie came and went as she pleased; Sean worked and went away to conferences and courses as and when he needed to. There was no requirement for one to check that any arrangements they made were acceptable with the other. Up until three months ago, it wasn't unusual for several weeks to pass by without seeing each other at all, outside of the counselling course. Three months: he'd been dry for that long and until today thought he'd well and truly nailed it. Now he wanted a drink.

It was a little after nine in the evening when Sophie decided to go home. She was tired and irritable and Sean was trying to ignore the reasons why. After she'd left, he made a cup of tea and turned on his computer, not that he had any work to do. He opened his web browser, checked for new messages or updates from 'friends'. He closed his web browser and looked through his email. He clicked listlessly on document icons, opening and closing them again. He drummed his fingers on the desk, then pushed his chair away and slung his feet up. Sphinx hopped up on his lap and kneaded at his thighs for half a minute or so before he curled up, purring and training his head against Sean's palm. Some time soon after, they both fell asleep in the chair; Sean's neck would suffer for days to come.

SWEET LITTLE LIES
Monday 16ᵗʰ January

Josh had only just parked up when he spotted Jess at the hospital's main entrance; he pulled away from the kerb and tooted his horn. For a moment it looked as if she hadn't heard him, but then she turned and glanced around, saw him coming towards her and walked over.

"Hi," she said breezily, climbing into the passenger seat. He nodded and smiled, but didn't speak, only moving off once she'd fastened her seatbelt. The radio played quietly; the weather and traffic report, followed by the news, into an unremarkable chart hit, then another and another.

"I thought we could try the new coffee shop on the high street," Josh suggested.

"Fine by me." She sniffed. "Have you started smoking again?"

"No. Why?"

"I just caught a whiff of smoke."

"Not me."

"It must've been when I shut the door."

"I imagine so. How was your weekend?"

"Not too bad. I went to my mum's yesterday. She's bought yet another new sofa."

"Really? Didn't she buy one just before Christmas?"

"Yeah. She didn't like it. Too big, she said." This mundane conversation was normal; the sort of thing friends chat about on a daily basis, or when there are other things that need to be said.

"How did it go?" Josh asked.

"The tests? Oh. Fine, fine."

"That's good. So what now?"

"Nothing. They'll send me another appointment for a check-up in a couple of months."

They turned onto the high street and drove up and down, looking for a parking space. On the second pass, a car pulled out; Josh quickly dodged in behind it.

"I'll get a ticket," Jess offered. Josh watched her make her way to the Pay and Display machine; Fleetwood Mac's "Little Lies" started up on the car stereo. He listened a moment longer than necessary and switched off the engine. Yes, she was lying, that much was clear; about what, he did not know. She reached across and passed the ticket to him, closed the door and turned away, releasing her hair from where it was caught in her coat collar. Josh stuck the ticket on the windscreen.

"Aren't you working today?" she asked. He pushed the button on the key fob. The locks clicked.

"No. I only had three booked in and I moved them to tomorrow. They were all right with that."

Jess nodded. Josh opened the coffee shop door and allowed her to enter first.

"What would you like?"

"Just a flat white, thanks."

"No cake?"

"Erm…" She thought for a minute and scanned the glass counter, shaking her head. "Oh, actually, I'll have one of those muffins." She pointed at the large, domed chocolate cakes.

"I think I'll join you," Josh said. "I'll get them. You find us somewhere to sit."

Jess spotted an empty sofa right against the back wall, far away from foot traffic and the outside world. She went over and took out her phone. Nothing there to distract, she picked up the copy of today's *Telegraph* that was on the low table next to the sofa.

"He's bringing them over," Josh explained. He sat down and took off his coat.

"When did this place open?"

"Just before Christmas, I think. I've only been in here once, for take-out. The coffee's all right—better than the one by us, that's for sure, but a bit far to come on a work day."

"Yeah." Jess turned the page of the newspaper and pretended to study the articles within. She wasn't wearing her glasses, so there was no way she could read the tiny print. Josh leaned back and watched the couple sat on the only other sofa in the place; it was just for something to do, because they really weren't that interesting, both so engrossed with their phones that they were paying little attention to anything else, including each other. Without moving his head, he glanced at Jess, who was still 'reading' the paper. The barista brought over the tray with their drinks and muffins.

"Thanks," Josh smiled. Jess uncrossed her legs and crossed them the opposite way. The barista left with the empty tray. Jess put the newspaper down and picked up her cup, carefully balancing it on her knee, her eyes trained on the gentle sway to and fro of the coffee's meniscus.

"How long did it take you to get over your depression?" she asked. It was so out of the blue that Josh was completely thrown.

"Erm," he said. *Think! Come on, brain.* "I'm not sure. Why?"

"I always wanted to ask, but it never seemed a good time. You were—how to put it? Cut off, emotionally. Not cold, as such, because you've always been there for me. For us all, in fact. But you always kept your distance and I wondered if—I'm sorry. I'm prying."

"No. It's OK. I don't mind you asking. Well, I do, because we've never talked about it, and I should've said thank you a long, long time ago."

"Is that why you're here, now? You think you owe me?"

"Hardly! Or at least I do owe you, big time, but that's not why I'm here. Although I'm also not here to talk about me."

"That's true." She sipped at her cup and returned it to the saucer, exchanging it for her muffin. "I must say it's lovely to have the old Josh back."

"The what now?"

"You know, the gushy clever-clogs I went to school with?"

"I was never gushy!"

"Yes, you were. Or have you conveniently forgotten crying over Ophelia's sorrow at Hamlet's rebuttal?"

"Ah, hmm. You got me." Josh laughed. Jess laughed too.

"It is very sad, I'll admit," she said.

"You know what's sadder than that? I can still remember most of it!"

"Not surprising! How many times did you make us read through Act Three, Scene One?"

"And weren't you glad I did?"

"Ha ha, yeah! That exam question was a gift. O heavenly powers, restore him!" Jess put her hand to her forehead and flopped back dramatically against the sofa. Josh turned to her with a troubled frown, also hammed, and took up the role of the Prince of Denmark.

"I have heard of your paintings too, well enough. God hath given you one face, and you make yourselves another. You jig, you amble, and you lisp; you nickname God's creatures and make your wantonness your ignorance. Go to, I'll no more on't! It hath made me mad. I say, we will have no more marriages. Those that are married already - all but one - shall live; the rest shall keep as they are. To a nunnery, go."

Jess's mouth dropped open. "Oh my word! How on earth do you remember all of that?"

"It's an affliction," Josh said ruefully.

"You'd make an amazing lawyer."

"Maybe you're right," he said, rubbing his chin thoughtfully and with an entirely faked arrogance. She elbowed him and he grinned. "But nowhere near as amazing as you."

"Thanks. And I suppose if you're saying it, then it must be true."

"Absolutely." He picked up his cappuccino and scooped out some of the foam with his finger. "Here's an idea," he said. He put his finger in his mouth. She turned and placed a knee up on the sofa, immediately creating a barrier between them. He glanced down, then looked her in the eye again. "I'm still going to suggest it anyway."

She shrugged; she wasn't going to agree to anything until she knew what it was, but she kept the eye contact.

He went on: "I'll answer your question, *truthfully*, and you pay me the same courtesy. How about that?"

Jess thought for a moment and shrugged again, this time by way of consent.

"You want to know how long my depression lasted? Nearly two years." It was kind of the truth. She didn't specify *which* depression. "And you were a massive help to me," he continued, "not that I imagine I was particularly gracious about it at the time. Mental illness makes you terribly selfish."

"Yeah, tell me about it." Jess rolled her eyes. She was tormenting him, making light of how difficult it been to support him at the same time as trying to complete her own studies.

"I hugely appreciate you being there for me," he said.

She waved her hand dismissively. "I didn't do that much. I mean, I was only across campus, so it really was no hardship."

"Just accept my thanks, OK?"

She smiled. "OK. Accepted."

"Of course, Sean's appreciation was much, *much* huger than mine," he added with a smirk.

"Ah, I wondered when we'd get around to that." She giggled and blushed a little.

Given their gregarious nature, plus the amount of time she spent in his company when Josh was depressed, it wasn't especially surprising that Jess and Sean had, on more than one occasion, ended up sleeping together. Neither of them had mentioned it since, and Josh had also kept it to himself, because it was just one of those things that happened at uni, or so he'd been led to believe, for it had never happened to him.

"How is Sean these days?" Jess asked.

"Same as ever. Full of his own self importance. Charming the pants off all the females on campus."

"He never married?"

"He did. And divorced. Now he's in a very strange long-term relationship with someone he doesn't even seem to like that much."

"Why?"

"I think he loves her."

"Oh, well, tell him hi from me," she said, then became very quiet and still. She knew her turn had come. Josh looked at her expectantly, but didn't prompt or push. She needed time to put the words together.

"All right," she said. "I'm going to say this once and once only and I don't want to analyse, or examine, or discuss it. I'm going to tell you how it is and leave it at that." She stared into his eyes, awaiting his acceptance.

"OK," he granted.

"I'd been having horrendous abdominal pain on and off all last year, and it got so bad that back in October I went to the doctor. She did an internal exam, sent off blood tests. They indicated abnormalities—too much CA-125, or something like that—so they sent me for an ultrasound in November. They called me back in for a CT scan just before Christmas, and phoned me the day after Boxing Day. I told them I was away on holiday, and they said to call the hospital as soon as I got back. I didn't call and I didn't have an appointment today. I made it up. And I'm really sorry."

Even if she had not demanded it in advance, Josh would have had no words to give back. Jess took his hand. They sat still and silent for many minutes; she wished she hadn't imposed this muteness upon him, and now she searched her memory. Somewhere in there were the lines that she could use to help him understand. She found them, reached around her for imagined objects and passed them to him, one by one.

"There's rue for you, and here's some for me," she recited. "We may call it herb of grace o' Sundays. O, you must wear your rue with a difference! There's a daisy. I would give you some violets…"

Josh smoothed his thumb across the back of her hand and spoke so quietly she could only just make out the words.

"Do you see this…" He paused and came out of character. "Oh God." He closed his eyes.

He had so many questions, so many placations. If she hadn't had the results, then everything might be all right. There was hope. Yet the urgent recall to the hospital indicated otherwise. And he had promised. No analysis, no examination, no discussion.

"If you choose to research it," Jess interrupted his terrible silence, "which I know you will, then I don't want to know what you discover. Unless…" She picked up her coffee and emptied the cup. "I have an appointment at…" checking the time on her phone, "…four."

Josh finished his own coffee and pulled her close. She was lying again. He kissed her cheek and whispered into her ear.

"The time is out of joint. O cursed spite. That ever I was born to set it right. Nay, come, let's go together."

U-TURN
Thursday 19ᵗʰ January

Seven-thirty in the morning. It was bitterly cold, with thick ice coating the night shift cars, a landscape of randomly placed, frost-faded blocks dotted around the vast and extortionate hospital car park. George reversed back and attempted again to pull up close enough to the machine to extract the ticket. Still unable to reach, he popped his seatbelt and opened the door; the Siberian blast of air took his breath away. Sophie retched over the bowl on her lap. George tugged the ticket from the machine and closed the door again, silently cursing the conspiracy that kept putting him behind the wheel. He fastened his seatbelt and breathed through his mouth. The smell of vomit in an enclosed space versus an outside temperature of minus seven degrees Celsius, according to the dashboard thermometer: he decided to put up with the vomit.

They parked in a space on the far edge of the car park and Sophie left the bowl in the passenger footwell, smiling apologetically at George as she looped her arm through his and they walked towards the main building. The letter had stated she needed to arrive by 7:45; she hoped she was at the top of the day's list. Anything to get rid of the horrendous nausea, which presently stopped her in her tracks. George turned, watched her puff out her cheeks and swallow. She turned grey, pinked up again and nodded. They continued.

The woman on the reception desk had a lemon-sucker face and acknowledged Sophie's arrival with no more than a sideward flick of the eyes, the hand idling on her computer mouse lifting a micron at most.

"Name." she said.

"Sophie Spyris."

"Postcode."

Sophie ran for the toilet.

"I'm sorry. I don't know," George told the woman. She sneered at him. "I can give you her address, if that helps?"

"Date of birth," she commanded.

"Erm, her birthday's the twenty-first of April. That's all I know. I can probably work it out, if you like."

The woman tapped at her keyboard. Sophie returned.

"Sorry," she said.

"Take a seat," the receptionist ordered. She did so, glancing around her at the other women, none of them what she would have expected in an 'abortion clinic', prior to falling foul herself. As she turned her head to get a better look at the closest of her fellow patients, the woman bolted across the waiting room and, without the luxury of time to shut the door behind her, shoved her face into the toilet bowl. George yawned.

"Tired?" Sophie asked him.

"Reflex, I think. I'd have already been at work an hour by now."

"I'm sorry," Sophie apologised again. She lowered her eyes and examined her hands.

"Hey, I didn't mean it like that. It was just to explain why I wasn't tired."

"I know."

The woman returned from the toilet and took her seat once more, making eye contact with Sophie. She smiled sympathetically.

"It's awful, isn't it?" the woman said.

Sophie nodded. "The pits."

A nurse emerged from a corridor to their right and picked up a set of notes from the reception desk. She called a name and stared out across the waiting room. One of the other women picked up her bag and she and her companion—an older woman, perhaps her mother—followed the nurse along the corridor. The other patients and their abortion partners watched on in envy.

"I've left my bag in the car," Sophie thought aloud.

"I'll go get it," George said. He was out of his seat before she had a chance to protest, already bored with waiting and they'd only been here for fifteen minutes. It didn't bode well for the rest of the day. The automatic doors parted and once again the icy wind rushed him. He drew in breath and shivered, pulling his hood up and his sleeves down. With head bowed, he marched across the car park, only looking up when he reached the car. He opened the door and bawked. The smell was horrendous. He grabbed Sophie's bag from the back seat and closed the door, then, as an afterthought, took the bowl out and hid it under the front of the car, against the line of trees along the edge of the car park. No-one would see it there— with any luck he'd have forgotten about it himself by the time they were ready to leave. He locked the car and started making his way back.

There were a few more cars and people about now; he assumed it was opening time for outpatients and the like. He stopped for a man in a wheelchair to be brought down the ramp on the back of an ambulance. The poor old guy was wearing only pyjamas and a dressing gown and complaining loudly that he'd wet himself, opening his dressing gown to demonstrate. The front of his pyjamas was gaping wide open and doing nothing to protect his dignity, and George looked away into the distance, banging his sleeved hands together to try and keep the circulation going. There wasn't much of interest to look at, for this was a new hospital, with small triangular areas of grass, surrounded by currently barren bark-mulched borders, benches placed here and there. At this time of the morning, on a bleak winter's day, the benches were vacant. Except for one. George watched him for a while—long enough for the ambulance to have departed—before he went over.

"Dan?" he called out, more to announce his imminent arrival than to check he had made a correct identification. Dan had his head down and was kicking a piece of gravel from one foot to the other. He acknowledged George with no more than a slight crinkling of his brow. George sat down beside him, starting at the coldness of the bench against the back of his legs.

"Dan. Is everything OK?" he asked.

Dan continued to kick the stone and remained silent. A tear dropped from the end of his nose and he sniffed.

"What's happened?" George tried again.

"Err…" Dan wiped his nose on his sleeve. He stopped kicking at the stone, but kept his face turned down. "Adele," he said. "She's…they think she probably…" He couldn't go any further, because saying it would make him accept it as the truth, and he wasn't ready to. Not yet. George understood. He put his arm around his friend. There was nothing more he could do and even this he couldn't do for very long. Sophie was waiting inside and it was freezing. *They* were freezing.

"Aren't you cold?" he asked, noting that Dan's hands were blue.

"Not really." He sat up and stared across the car park.

"How long have you been here?"

"A couple of hours? What time is it?"

"Just after eight o'clock."

"Yeah. Couple of hours," Dan repeated vaguely.

"You need to go inside," George told him. He received nothing in response. "Come back with me now," he suggested.

Dan shook his head. "I'll be OK. You go do what you need to—actually, why are you here?"

"Oh," George thought quickly. "I'm just here with a friend who's having day surgery. Nothing serious."

Dan gave a half nod of his head in response.

"Yeah. I'm gonna have to go back to her."

"No worries. See you later."

George frowned. He was worried. Very worried, in fact. As he returned to Sophie, he tried to call Andy on his mobile phone several times, but it was going straight through to voicemail. On the final attempt, he left a message to ask him to call as soon as he could, then sent Josh a text asking him to call too. He put his phone away and continued along the corridor to the waiting room where he had left Sophie. She wasn't there.

"Room two," the sow on the reception desk said without so much as a glance. George walked over to the desk and stared down at her, waiting for her to look up from her screen, which she had to do eventually. She examined him disdainfully. He smiled, and noted the crucifix on the chain around her neck.

"I'm sorry to say this," he said in a polite, measured tone, "but I find your attitude quite appalling. In fact, I'm so appalled that I'm considering making a formal complaint about you."

The woman blinked slowly at him and sneered. George's phone vibrated against his thigh. He reached into his pocket and pushed the button to dismiss the call.

"What's the problem, exactly?" the woman asked him.

"The problem is you. You are extremely rude. This is a traumatic enough experience for these women, without you treating them like they're irresponsible teenagers who did this on purpose. And so what if they were? It's not your business to judge them. You only work here, so do your job and do it properly. Would it cause you any hardship to treat them with a bit of respect?" He turned to walk away, but then turned back again. "Oh, and if you don't agree with abortion, then go work somewhere else."

"Is that all?"

George could feel his temper fraying past the point of return and backed off.

"Room two, did you say?" he asked quietly. She nodded. He walked away through the double doors and located the room, peering through the door's glass panel to see if it was safe to enter. Sophie was sitting on the edge of the bed, swinging her legs. George knocked lightly and went in.

"Hey," he said. She smiled at him, but didn't speak, the nausea too much to cope with just at that moment. George put her bag down on the chair and took his phone out of his pocket. It was only then that he discovered he'd answered Josh's call rather than dismissing it.

"Hello?"

"George! What the hell was all that about?"

"Oh, the receptionist is a complete cow."

"Yes, I got that much. What am I? A witness in case she has you arrested for verbal abuse? It was a most impressive bollocking, incidentally."

"I've just bumped into Dan, outside."

"And?"

"Err, well," he glanced over at Sophie, "it's a bit tricky to explain, but Adele's here, and…"

30

"I understand. Can you do short answers?"

"Yep."

"How's Dan?"

"A mess."

"And Adele?"

"Don't know."

"OK. I'll give Andy a call."

"No response."

"Shaunna?"

"Didn't try."

"You OK?"

"Kinda."

"Soph OK?"

"Green."

"Nice. All right, I'll phone Shaunna and Kris, see what I can sort out. How long will you be there, do you know?"

"Not sure."

"Ring me when you're leaving. OK?"

"Will do."

"Love you."

"Love you too." George hung up. Sophie had been watching him throughout the call. Just as she opened her mouth to speak, a nurse came into the room and greeted her with a friendly smile.

"Sophie Spyris?"

"Yes," Sophie confirmed nervously.

"I'm just here to have a chat with you and make sure you understand what's going to happen today. Is that all right?"

"Err, yeah, OK," Sophie replied absently. She was still watching George.

"I'll wait outside," he said and left.

The nurse quickly ran through questions to check Sophie's address and date of birth, and she gave all the right answers, but she wasn't really listening.

"OK, now," the nurse continued, "because your sickness is quite severe, you've decided to have a vacuum aspiration. Is that…"

"Actually," Sophie interrupted her, "I'm really sorry to mess you about, but I'm not sure I want to go through with this."

"That's absolutely fine, Sophie. I can give you a little time now to have a think about it, perhaps talk it through with your partner. I'll come back in twenty minutes or so and we can chat again. How does that sound?"

"Erm, yeah, thanks. That'd be great."

The nurse nodded and left her alone in the room. Sophie closed her eyes and took a deep breath, then she called George back in.

"Your friend, Adele," she said. "She's had a miscarriage, hasn't she?" George looked away. "How many weeks was she?"

"Why?" he asked.

"I want to know."

"What difference does it make? That's her, not you."

"I just—I need to know."

George sat on the opposite end of the bed and rubbed his belly in an attempt to stop it from rumbling. He hadn't thought to have breakfast, hadn't even felt like eating, until now. It rumbled anyway. Sophie raised an eyebrow.

"How many weeks, George?"

"Sixteen." His belly rumbled again, even more loudly than before.

"Sixteen? That's awful. She must be devastated. That's a long way on to miscarry, and yet, it's only seven weeks further…"

"Don't do this to yourself, Soph."

"I can't help it. It changes everything." She watched him. He was worried about Dan; she could see. "Go," she told him. "I'll get a taxi home."

"No. It's fine. Josh is dealing with it, and anyway it's your car. What d'you mean, it changes everything?"

"Because until now it was just this 'thing' making me feel bad-tempered and sick, but I hadn't really thought about it. Not *really* thought about it."

"But you were so sure."

"Yeah, and maybe I'm making a big mistake, but I've still got time to change my mind. If I go through with this today, though, then that's it. Done."

George didn't respond. He was her friend, not her conscience. She had to make the decision for herself. His belly, however, had even less tact than the sour-faced receptionist and protested loudly. George squirmed with embarrassment and Sophie laughed.

"You hungry, by any chance?" she asked.

"Starving."

"Me too. Let's go get breakfast."

HANKERING
Thursday 19ᵗʰ January

The journey back from Euston always reminded Andy of one particular occasion he'd taken this trip when Dan and Kris were at university. He'd travelled down on the Friday night and met up with them at a pub in King's Cross, where the beer was flat, warm and (by London standards) cheap, the music too loud and the staff too few in number to cope with the pre FA Cup Final rush of customers. However, what struck him first and hardest was just how rude people were. Of course, he'd been warned in advance to expect none of the congeniality of their home town, but even so, he was ill-prepared for the level of anti-social and generally ignorant attitudes he experienced during the course of that weekend. Case in point: they stopped off at a fish and chip shop near Wembley on the Saturday evening, whereby the act of holding a door open resulted in him being told to "go fuck himself", for he had been fooled into believing that the recipient of his consideration was an ally, on account of them both wearing the same team shirt. Needless to say, since then he'd learned to kept his head down, like the rest of the people in the city, and tried not to take it too much to heart when they not only failed to thank him for stepping out of their way, or any other courtesy he extended, but more often than not treated him with a level of contempt beyond that which he would expect if he had accidentally killed their favourite pet.

That first trip down to the capital had certainly been an eye-opener, and much as he felt unpatriotic saying so, London ranked highly amongst the worst cities he'd visited, not just because the population were by and large rude, greedy and self-centred. He didn't even mind the London Underground, although it was far more efficient now than when Dan and Kris had lived there. No, what he hated the most was the materialism of its citizens and visitors, for whilst trying to engage people in polite conversation was virtually impossible, they could wax positively lyrical when it came to discussing money and investments, seemed to take an almost masochistic delight in bragging about how the cost of living was so massive in the city compared to elsewhere, and as such perceived themselves to be superior in virtually all aspects of life. He didn't like to tell them that their bare and meaningless existence of commute-work-commute-sleep was neither big nor clever.

But all of this was very much beside the point. The football had been the reason for his first and many subsequent visits; likewise for this trip, although not as a fan on this occasion. Business matters prevailed and it hadn't been much fun, other than for the unofficial guided tour of the stadium, which was impressive in its own way, but he was bored and wanted to leave almost as soon as he'd got off the train. Now, twenty minutes north of the city, whistling through the countryside at over a hundred miles an hour, he realised he'd let the opportunity to do something he'd wanted to do all of his life pass him by. And why? Because of a girl.

Note: girl. Not woman. No, she was a woman, but a young woman, petite, slender, tough as hobnail boots—and she had the most ridiculous name; well, Andy didn't think so, and much as he hoped that their long-distance relationship might last a while, he was also dreading telling his brother. In fact, he could hear him now: "She's called what? Isn't that the name of a liquorice allsort?" Worse still that he should have to introduce her to everyone else. Last time he saw her, her hair was kind of normal, if normal includes fluorescent orange, but at least it was all one colour, unlike the first time they met (the less said about that, the better), when it was bright-white and purple in daylight, ultra-violet by night. It was cropped shorter than his, and gelled to a point at the front, going before her like the spikes on the toes of her boots. Krissi once had a pair just like them and he wondered if they had other things in common too. Perhaps the same taste in music? Men? Oh.

That one sneaked up all of a sudden. Yes, she was a girl. Younger than his daughter. *Younger than his daughter...* but he was young himself, so it wasn't that great an age difference. Just as he was recovering, a second shockwave hit. *What would Shaunna think? Would she be jealous?*

"Tickets, please," the inspector called from the far end of the carriage. Andy searched his pockets in relief, pushing the thought deep down with the loose change and receipts. When he pulled his ticket free, it brought pocket flotsam up with it, the inspector now upon him. He dumped the stuff and passed his ticket over.

"Glasgow?" the inspector queried with a frown. "You need to change at Manchester."

"Thanks." Andy responded as if this was news to him and took his ticket back, returning it to his pocket along with the receipts and change. *Will she think I'm an idiot?*

"Is anyone sitting here?"

He looked up into the face of an older woman. "No, no. It's a free seat." She smiled briefly in thanks and sat down. *Maybe I should explain.*

"I'm sorry," the woman said, catching the bottle of water as it rolled across the table towards him.

"Hmm?"

"I said I'm sorry." She held up the bottle of water by way of explanation. He nodded to imply he had understood, but his mind was very much elsewhere. He needed a distraction; music. That always worked. He took out his phone and pressed the button to wake it up. No response. Dead as the proverbial dodo. He glanced at the arm of his seat, grateful to find that this was one of the newer trains, dug out the power adaptor and plugged in his phone.

"Oh, I really am so very sorry," the woman said again; this time the water bottle landed in his lap. He picked it up and passed it back.

"If you don't want it, you only have to say," he joked, making her feel a little more at ease. She smiled.

"Thanks. I'll keep hold of it." She popped the lid and swigged. "I've just left my husband."

Andy nodded. There wasn't a whole lot he could think of to say to that.

"We've been married for twenty-seven years."

"Long time." He poked at his phone. Still it wouldn't start up and he needed an escape route.

"Yes, and we've been very happy for most of it."

"Right." *Bloody phone!*

"Now I've made you feel really uncomfortable. I'm so sorry. I don't know what came over me." The woman said all of this in one breath and turned to stare out of the window at the fast blur past of too-close trees. Andy watched her.

"No worries," he said. Finally his phone screen lit up, although it took several minutes more to properly load all the apps and everything else. The woman opposite was clearly done baring her soul, so he took out his earphones and stuck them in his ears. No sooner had his music loaded, than several text messages came in at once: all missed calls; six from George, three from Josh, three from Ellie and the most recent one from Kris. Andy glanced across at his companion, who was lost in her own thoughts. He returned Kris's call.

"Alright, mate? It's Andy."

"Hi. You OK?"

"Yeah. What's up?"

"Sorry to do this over the phone, but Adele's lost the baby."

"Crap." Andy paused to think. "I'm on my way back from London. How's she doing?"

"Pretty well, considering."

"And Dan?"

"That's why I've been trying get hold of you. He's in a bad way."

"How bad? Arrested bad?"

"Oh, no, nothing like that."

"Well, I'll be back…" he mentally calculated how long it would take to get home, "…in about three hours. I'll give you a call then, all right?"

"OK. Speak later." Kris hung up. Andy frowned and rubbed his chin. The woman opposite was still looking out of the window, but she'd clearly heard his end of the conversation. She remained with her head turned towards the window, but shifted her gaze so she could see him. He threw his phone on the table and flopped back in his seat.

"Bad news?" she observed. "I ask in case you needed to share. Don't feel you have to."

Andy examined her for a moment and accepted her offer. "My sister-in-law's just lost her baby," he said. The woman turned and smiled sympathetically.

"So sorry to hear that."

"Yeah. Me too." Andy picked up his phone and rubbed at the screen with his thumb, trying to smudge away the fingerprints. "I was looking forward to being an uncle again."

"Again? What've you got?"

"A niece. Shaunna. She's two and a bit." He opened his photos and passed his phone across. The power cable didn't quite reach far enough and she had to lean forward to see the screen.

"Wow, she's gorgeous," she said.

"There's a couple more on there. Feel free to have a browse."

She thumbed through to the next photo, glancing up to compare him to the picture of little Shaunna. "No missing the family resemblance, is there?"

"No, me and my brother are very alike." It was a statement confirmed by the next photo, which was of him, Dan and their mother, taken last Christmas day, just before Michael arrived and ruined the festivities.

The woman passed his phone back. "It's so sad when someone loses a baby," she said. She picked up her water bottle, repeatedly flipping the lid open and shut as she spoke. "My daughter had a miscarriage a few months ago. She's still not really recovered. I don't suppose you ever do." She returned to staring out of the window. Andy waited for a few minutes, to see if she was going to say anything else; when it was apparent she was definitely done this time, he put his earphones back in and hit the 'play' button, then sent a message up to Glasgow to explain, without going into detail, his sudden change of plan. She'd understand. He settled back in his seat and closed his eyes.

Back to Manchester, then a connecting train home; it was a little after midday when Andy walked out of the station. He picked up a cab and went straight to the hospital, where he found Dan, still sitting staring at the floor, but thankfully inside and in the warmth of the hospital coffee shop, the last two inches of a not so warm latte in front of him. Andy bought one for himself and a fresh, hot one for his brother, then sat down on the chair opposite. Dan registered his presence with a faked smile.

"Alright, bro? Thought you were gonna be away until Monday."

"Changed my plans," Andy told him. Dan acknowledged with a passive nod. "How're you doing?"

Dan shrugged dismissively. "Fine. The doc said we should leave off trying for another couple of months, but it's one of those things. Just bad luck."

"Is Adele OK?"

"Yeah. They're doing some medical procedure to make sure there's nothing that can cause an infection. She's sat up there, reading magazines and gossiping with the other women. You know how she is."

Andy instantly picked up on the hostility behind the words, the anger towards Adele, although it was unclear what Dan was angry about. Surely he wasn't blaming her for the miscarriage? She'd been so obsessively careful about what she was eating and drinking, the amount and type of exercise she was doing. She'd even stopped using fake tan, 'just in case'. She really couldn't be faulted in any way at all. Perhaps it was a grief thing, although he was himself, thankfully, somewhat inexperienced when it came to bereavement. In fact, the closest he'd come to losing anyone was the break-up with Jess last year, which still hurt now, because they had been such good friends for such a long time, and whilst he hadn't quite yet forgiven her, he had put it behind him, and they were back on speaking terms. However, his good fortune was leaving him feeling somewhat inept when it came to supporting his brother, who had picked up his latte and examined it, but was once again staring at the floor.

"Where's Shaunna?" Andy asked. "With Alice?"

"Yeah. She's got a dentist appointment this afternoon, she said." Dan remembered his drink and took a mouthful. "Alice, that is."

"Yeah. I figured. What time? I'll go and take over, if you like."

"Two o'clock. What is it now? Half ten?"

"Err, no. Nearly half twelve."

Dan nodded.

"OK. Is there anything else you need me to do?"

"Stay here a bit longer? I've got to go back up and see her, and…" Dan stopped mid-flow, needing his brother to stay but too proud to say so.

"No worries." As Andy said this, his phone started vibrating in his pocket. He pulled it out, checked the screen and decided to ignore the call. Dan didn't even notice, or if he did he didn't pass comment. Now there was nothing left to talk about. They sat in silence, each sipping at their coffee, not uncomfortable, exactly, but a little uneasy simply because of the situation. Andy's phone began to vibrate again, amplified by the coins in his pocket. Dan raised an eyebrow in query.

"Just a friend," Andy said dismissively, feeling his cheeks start to glow. Dan rubbed his eyes. The silence resumed, broken only by the comings and goings of the hospital around them, staff quick-marching to and fro, visitors arriving and leaving, a woman in a wheelchair getting stuck on their table.

"You need any help?" Andy asked her. She gave him a directionless smile, which he assumed to mean 'yes', and gave her a hand with manoeuvring the handles of the chair through the too-narrow gap between the tables.

"Thanks," she said, as she finally made it to the counter.

"No problem." He turned his attention back to Dan. "You eaten?"

"Nah. Don't feel much like it."

"I'll get us something." He didn't bother waiting for a response. He returned with two sandwiches and handed one to Dan, who took it and ate it without comment, which meant he hadn't eaten at all today and wasn't really aware of what he was doing, as the café only had cheese, and usually he would've complained about the fat content.

"Everything's set for the London job, by the way," Andy attempted by means of a distraction. It worked, for a little while.

"Good stuff. Have they signed on the dotted line?"

"They have. They didn't even try and bargain, so we're up about four grand on last month."

"Bloody hell! We'll be retired by fifty at this rate." Dan got up and put his sandwich wrapper in the bin. "I'm gonna get a bottle of water and head back to the ward."

"OK, bro. You need me to come?"

"Not unless you want to. Shaunna's up there. As in grown-up, not baby." A vacant glaze came over his eyes once more.

"I'll leave it then," Andy said. "They won't want too many visitors at once." It wasn't that he didn't want to see Shaunna as such, but he was still beating himself up about the weird thoughts he'd had on the train. "I'll go to yours and take over from Alice, OK?"

"Sure. See you later." Dan paused as he passed Andy on his way out, and put his hand on his shoulder. "Thanks."

"See you later," Andy replied. He turned to watch Dan leave, then went to pick up a taxi.

ROBERTA
Thursday 19th–Friday 20th January

21:18, BB [mobile]
just about to get off the train - what number bus? b x

"Ah, fuck." Andy pressed on the phone number displayed above this last entry in the text message dialogue and put the phone to his ear.

"Ah foo," Little Shaunna said. Andy shook his head and mouthed 'no' at her. The phone rang a couple of times and then picked up.

"Hallo?" the voice at the other end responded.

"Hi. What d'you mean what number bus? Where are you?"

"At the station. I thought I'd surprise you."

Andy ran his free hand over his hair. Yes, she'd certainly achieved a Grade A on that score. Not much he could do about it now.

"I'll text you the address," he said. "Get a taxi."

"I haven't got a lot of cash on me."

"I'll pay when you get here," Andy told her. "See you soon, bye." He hung up and sent Dan and Adele's address via text message, hoping he could come up with an idea for what he was going to do—actually, what the hell *was* he going to do? His *girl*friend was on her way to his brother's house. Dan didn't even know there was a girlfriend!

"Addy. Up, up," little Shaunna said. Andy looked down at his tiny niece, her little arms stretched above her head. He picked her up and she snuggled into his neck.

"Time for bed, chicken," he said. She flopped against him and he turned so he could just see her sleepy smile under his chin. He kissed her on her delicate, soft forehead. With any luck she'd be out for the count before his visitor arrived.

"Here we are," he said, laying Shaunna down and pulling the little pink duvet over her. She looked even tinier than ever, with her black curls forming a dark halo around her rosy round face. He knelt by the bed and put his head next to hers.

"Night, night," he said. He kissed her forehead again.

"Night, night," she echoed and closed her eyes. He got up and crept to the door, dimming the light. As he stepped outside, she called his name and he turned back. She scrunched her fingers to wave at him and he smiled and

39

waved back, then returned to the lounge, perching on the edge of the carp pool, absentmindedly watching the fish bob to the surface. This was the worst timing in the world. Dan was going to be an emotional wreck, and certainly not receptive to visits from strangers, although knowing his brother the way he did, it was perhaps marginally preferable to visits from friends. And then there was the issue of where she was going to stay. Andy was still living at his mum's and, much as she wouldn't see her out on the street, she wouldn't look too favourably on her being there either. The only thing for it was to pay for a hotel room, although he was still trying to make back what he'd lost to that scumbag, Simpson-Stone; even the thought of his name got him raging again.

The sound of a car pulling up outside brought him back to his senses, and he glanced furtively out of the window. It was Dan. Well, at least he had some time to warn him. Alas, fate didn't even allow that thought to settle in his mind, as just as Dan stepped out of his car, a taxi pulled up alongside. Andy watched from behind the blinds, his brother paused halfway between the road and the building, the taxi door opening and closing. She moved towards Dan, grinning broadly, her hand outstretched. His back was to Andy, so he couldn't see his expression. Dan shook her hand and took her large holdall from her as they walked up the path together. Andy gulped and prepared himself for their entry.

The front door opened.

"Glasgow, you say? How long does that take? Must be pretty exhausting."

"No, not really. It's only a few hours, although it'd be a heck of a lot quicker if the train didn't stop at every wee village along the way."

They came into the lounge and stopped in front of Andy, both smiling. Andy wasn't smiling.

"Everything alright, bro?" Dan asked, his face suddenly ashen.

"What? Oh. Yeah. Sorry, everything's absolutely fine," Andy assured him, having realised how his reaction would have been interpreted. "I've just put Shaunna to bed. You OK?"

"Yeah. I'm gagging for a beer." Dan put the bag down and wandered through to the kitchen. "You two staying for one?" he called back. They looked at each other and shrugged.

"Please, bro," Andy replied. He didn't know what to say.

"I'm sorry," she whispered.

"It's OK, I think," Andy smiled quickly. "It's just not the greatest timing."

"I know. Dan just told me about his wife. It's tragic. My aunt lost a baby a couple of years ago."

"Oh!" Andy failed to hide his surprise at his brother's candidness. He indicated for her to follow him over to the sofa.

"Here you go, Bertie," Dan said, passing her an open bottle.

"Cheers, Dan." She swigged half of it right away and sighed loudly. "That hit the spot."

"Bro." Dan handed a bottle to Andy.

"Thanks." He put it on the low table in front of the sofa and sat down. Bertie remained standing, slowly spinning around and surveying her surroundings.

"You want the tour?" Dan asked. She nodded and followed him over to the carp pool, where they stopped so he could tell her about the dozen young fish lazily drifting in the LED illuminated water. Andy picked up his beer bottle and drained it in one go, then went to get himself another. He needed it. He stayed in the kitchen, watching on as Dan and Bertie disappeared back out to the hallway, listening to her enthuse about the bathroom. A door closed; another opened. Andy wondered what Adele would make of Dan showing another woman their bedroom, as it was apparent from the dribs and drabs of conversation wafting his way that this was where they were currently.

He had to admit that his brother's flat was probably quite impressive for first-time visitors. Much of it was open-plan, with a long through-lounge-diner, spanning from front to back of the building. In the centre of the front section was the vast carp pool, rising to a metre above floor level and a little over two metres in diameter. The middle section consisted of plush, black leather seating, arranged around a low, rectangular table of Japanese origin, a massive plasma screen taking up all of the facing wall. Beyond that was an enormous dining table with eight chairs. As they returned to Andy, Dan was explaining that the flooring was relatively new (although not why) and that there was under-floor heating throughout the apartment.

"Wow, that must cost a fair bit to run," Bertie said.

"It doesn't, as it goes." Dan indicated with his arm. "And this is the kitchen, obviously." He stopped his narration, while she slid the black high-gloss drawers in and out, enthralled by the slow-close mechanism. Andy was peeling the label off his beer bottle, feeling terribly self-conscious. He glanced up and Dan winked at him.

"Ace," Bertie said, prodding at the buttons on the front of the fridge. "What's this do?" She indicated to the grey square on the opposite door to the water and ice dispenser.

"It's a touchscreen," Dan explained, turning it on. The start-up screen displayed. "TV, internet, security camera…" Dan talked her through the various icons, pressing each in turn.

"That's brilliant."

"And this is the garden," he said, switching on the external lights. It was too cold to go outside, so he just showed her through the patio doors, giving her a moment to admire the uplit trees and illuminated patio, with its stylish table and chairs, terracotta pots and windchimes.

"I don't wish to be rude," she said, "but are you loaded?"

Dan laughed. "Put it this way, we're comfortable, although a lot of this stuff came from business deals. Like the fridge, for instance, was a prototype from a show home project that I worked on, and when they shut the place down, they sold it to me for the same price as a normal one. And the heating I got as payment for a job I did for a builder in London."

"Uh-huh," Bertie nodded.

Andy hadn't said a word since he accepted the bottle of beer; he couldn't decide whether Dan was just being polite, or if he and Bertie really had hit it off. Maybe she was no more than a useful distraction from losing the baby. Whatever, this was a very different first meeting to that which Andy had anticipated and he was utterly at a loss as to how to deal with it.

"More beer?" Dan asked her.

"If that would be OK?" She glanced at Andy and he nodded. "Cool," she said. "I'm just popping to the loo." She smiled and wandered off to the bathroom, leaving him at the mercy of his younger brother.

For a minute or so neither of them spoke, then Dan took a breath in. Andy knew what he was about to say; it was exactly as he'd predicted.

"Bertie Barrett. Isn't that the name of a liquorice allsort?"

Andy blinked slowly.

"She looks like one of the round ones you get. You know what I mean? The pink things with the black middles?"

"Yeah, I figured," Andy said. "That's Bassett, not Barrett. Look. I'm sorry, bro. I didn't ask her to come."

"I know. She said. She wanted to surprise you."

"Yeah. She did that, all right."

"It's fine."

"Are you sure? We can be out of your way as soon as. Just say the word."

"Nah. I like her." Dan patted Andy on the arm. "Besides, I need the company."

As he said this, Bertie came back through from the hallway, her face turned away from them and peering down.

"Here's Daddy, sweetie pie," she said. She came into the room, with little Shaunna holding her hand, and led the sad looking little girl across the room; Dan went over.

"What's the matter, baby girl?" He scooped her up in his arms.

"She was standing in her bedroom doorway, crying," Bertie explained. "And calling for her mammy."

"Ah."

"Mummy?" little Shaunna said, by way of asking where she was; although she was now twenty-seven months old, her premature birth meant her language development was delayed, but she was very expressive with her single words and had just about mastered the distinction between 'Daddy' and 'Addy', which was more than most people could manage.

"Mummy will be home tomorrow," Dan comforted, gently brushing the hair back from her face. "Look at that snotty nose! Yuck!" She giggled, but she was still very tired and sad. Dan gave her nose a gentle wipe with a tissue.

"Addy," she said, reaching across to Andy. He took her from his brother.

"Wanna go bed?" he asked her. She put her hands either side of her head. "That's a yes, then. Come on, trouble." He carried her back towards her room.

"Dat?" she asked, pointing at Bertie.

"That's Bertie." Andy paused so she could look.

"Birdy," Shaunna tried to repeat.

"Close enough," Dan laughed.

"Night, night," Shaunna called, waving over Andy's shoulder as they disappeared through the door.

"Night, night, baby girl," Dan called after her. Bertie watched on, smiling.

"You two are so alike, it's scary," she said. Dan indicated for her to follow him and they went to sit in the lounge.

"Yeah. You're not the first person to say that," he remarked with a grin. "People generally assume we're twins, which we're not. Andy's a year older than me."

"OK. You get on really well with each other, though. I guess you have a lot in common?"

"Kind of. I'm not quite so much of a lunatic as he is."

"Meaning you don't go out with girls half your age?"

"Meaning I'm not into leaping out of planes and diving with deadly fish."

"Ah, I get you," Bertie said.

"Are you really half his age?"

"I'm twenty."

Dan was taking a swig of his beer and miraculously swallowed it without showing his surprise. However, it did create a lull in the conversation, and they both sat drinking in silence for a moment or so, before he switched on the TV. As usual, it was showing children's programmes, and he left it until they could take no more, at which point he tuned it to a music channel. Andy returned and sat on a chair.

"She's asleep again now," he said. "I read her a story."

"Cheers, bro." Dan stifled a yawn. He was shattered. "So, Bertie, what do you do? Are you at uni, or…"

"Yeah. Well, I was, but I'm deferring the rest of this year to go and do voluntary work."

"Oh, right. Doing what?"

"I'm not sure yet, but probably teaching English in an African school."

Dan nodded, his eyebrow raising by itself at the thought of lots of small African children speaking with a broad Glaswegian accent. Andy burst into fits of laughter.

"You really are way too much alike," Bertie said, shaking her head, because Andy's response had been exactly the same.

"You figured out where you're staying?" Dan asked.

"Not sure, yet." She glanced at Andy.

"Hotel, I think," he said.

"It'll cost a fortune," Bertie protested. "Are there no hostels around here?"

"I think there's…" Andy began, but Dan interrupted him.

"You're welcome to stay on our sofa, if you like?"

"Oh, I don't want to be any trouble."

"It's no trouble at all. And it'll give Andy a chance to sort something else out, hey, bro?"

"Yeah. If you wouldn't mind?" Andy looked from one to the other, and they gave him their mutual approval.

With that sorted, they finished their beers, and Dan went to bed, leaving his brother to sort out a duvet and pillows.

"I'll be back first thing," Andy said. He gave Bertie a peck on the cheek and she waited for more. When it wasn't forthcoming, she saw him to the door and locked up after him, as instructed.

Next morning, at a little after six, Shaunna went to wake her dad, pausing in puzzlement at the heap of bedding with the pink shock of hair spiking out of one end.

"Birdy," she said to herself and continued her journey to her parents' bedroom. It was a bit of a struggle, but eventually she climbed up onto the soft mattress and crawled up to the top, snuggling into the warm space next to Dan. He stirred and opened one eye.

"Hiya, baby girl," he smiled.

"Hiya," she replied, then pointed at the door. "Birdy?"

"Huh?" he asked, then remembered their house guest. "Ah, yeah, Bertie's sleeping."

"Shh," little Shaunna said, and wriggled closer. Dan encircled her with his arms. It didn't hurt quite so much this morning, so long as he stayed focused on his tiny girl, who buried her head under his chin, her hair tickling his nose. He smoothed it down and drifted back to sleep.

Andy arrived at Dan's flat a little before nine o'clock, and soon after concluded that whatever he'd thought might happen next, and he didn't think that his level of expectation was particularly restrictive, was in fact, based on the general scheme of things, the least likely course of events to follow. Thus, he knocked on the door and waited. He knocked again. A minute or so later, by which point he had the spare key ready in his hand, Bertie opened the door. Andy opened his mouth to say 'hi', but got no further than this, before Dan appeared in the hallway behind Bertie and chucked his car keys over her shoulder. Andy caught them and shook his fingers.

"Do us a favour, bro? Can you go and pick up Adele? Alice has phoned to say she's sick and I need to get Shaunna to playschool."

"Why don't I take her?"

"Well, that'd be great, but they have a policy about nominated adults, so it's got to be me, Adele or Alice."

"Ah. Fair enough."

Throughout this interchange, Bertie had been watching Andy. She didn't know what to do for the best. She couldn't really go with him to the hospital, in the circumstances, and she couldn't stay in the flat on her own. It was a stupid idea to come visiting unannounced. Andy gave her a smile to try and comfort her.

"Come with me. We'll figure something out on the way," he suggested. She nodded in agreement and went back inside to collect her bags.

"Thanks for the loan of the sofa, Dan," she said as she bounced past and out to the 4x4.

"No worries. See you later."

"Right," Andy said, as they belted up and he started the engine. "So our options, then. I could drop you at my mum's, but I'd rather be there with you, if you have to meet her now."

"Is she that bad?"

"No. She's OK, actually. It's more our Mike who's the problem. That's mine and Dan's older brother. He's, erm, well, a bit of a knob."

Bertie giggled.

"OK, so if not your mam's then?"

Andy's next thought was to leave her at The Pizza Place for an hour or so, but it wouldn't be open yet, aside from which she didn't know he had a daughter who was older than she was, not that he'd been lying about it. They just hadn't got that far into their relationship.

"Tell you what." He fished his phone from his pocket and passed it to her. "On there you'll find someone called Josh."

She went through his contacts list, until she found the number.

"OK. Got it."

45

"Dial it," Andy instructed.

"And put it on loud speaker?"

"Nah. When he answers, explain what's going on and ask if he minds having a visitor."

Bertie looked at him incredulously.

"It'll be fine, honestly," Andy assured her. "Just check to see if he's at home or at work."

"OK." Bertie dialled the number and waited nervously for a response.

"Hey, Andy. It's George. Josh is in the shower," the voice said.

"Ah, err, hold on." Bertie turned to Andy. "Somebody called George answered."

"Yeah. They do that. Just tell him what I said."

Bertie shrugged and put the phone to her ear again.

"Hi, George," she began, "Andy said to ask if you mind having a visitor?"

"Um, sure," George said. "Who are you?"

"Bertie. Andy's girlfriend."

"Oh, right." The line went quiet. "Sorry, Bertie, but I'm not really following?"

Bertie put her hand over the phone. "What do I say?"

"Just tell him what's happening!" Andy said, getting exasperated. "Oh, forget it. Just stick it on speaker."

Bertie did as requested.

"Alright, George? I'm driving, so I'll have to be quick, mate. Basically, I've got to pick Adele up, and Bertie needs somewhere to be for a couple of hours. Would you mind?"

"Ah, gotcha. Yeah, that's fine," George said. "How long you gonna be?"

"About ten minutes?"

"Righteo. See you in a bit."

George hung up. Bertie looked bewildered. They pulled up at traffic lights and Andy glanced at her.

"Sorry," he said.

"It's OK. It's my fault," she responded quietly. "I didn't mean to be a pest. I'll head home again this afternoon."

"No. Why don't you stay for the weekend?"

"If you're sure?"

"I'd like you to."

"OK, I guess," she agreed. She was still feeling a bit worried about where she was heading next, and as they drove out to Josh and George's place, Andy gave her the potted history of The Circle, in an attempt to explain why what they were doing was entirely normal for them. She wasn't convinced by what he was saying, because it sounded like he was only saying it to make her feel less guilty.

When they arrived, Josh was standing at the gate, with his arms folded, watching the house next door but one.

"Hi," Andy greeted him, turning to look in the same direction. He could hear the conversation taking place on the neighbour's doorstep. It was about a parish magazine. The woman standing outside was laughing and joking, and the man standing in the doorway was talking into her ear, a wide, cheeky grin on his face. She patted his arm, turned and walked away. The man turned and winked at Josh. Josh grunted.

"Smarmy git," he said. He glanced at Bertie, then at Andy.

"Bertie. Short for Roberta?"

"You got it," Bertie grinned. She held out her hand. Josh shook it.

"Come in. It's bloody freezing," he said.

"Cheers for this, mate," Andy called. "I'm heading off. Catch you later."

"OK. See you."

Andy hopped up into the 4x4 and was almost out of sight before Josh and Bertie made it inside.

"Oh, look at you!" Bertie said, stopping in the hallway. She waited for Blue to come to her, then carefully knelt down so the young dog could get a good sniff of her. "He's gorgeous." George was watching from the kitchen doorway.

"You obviously know your way around dogs," he said.

"Yeah, a bit. We've always had dogs at home. Irish Wolfhounds, mostly."

"Oh, well, no wonder you didn't freak out about him being a Shepherd, then!" George laughed.

"He's just a wee baby. How old is he?"

"Four months, give or take. Would you like a drink?"

"If you're making one, that'd be great." She was scratching Blue's ears, and it was difficult to judge which of the two of them was enjoying it the most.

"What would you like? Tea, coffee, a cold drink..."

"Coffee, please."

"Instant, filter, cappuccino, latte..."

"Oh! Erm, latte, if that's OK?"

"Plain, vanilla..."

"George!" Josh stopped him mid-flow. "We're not running a bloody café!"

Bertie laughed. "Plain is just fine, thanks. No sugar."

"Coming right up," George said.

Josh ushered her into the lounge and she sat on the end of the sofa, Blue having followed her in, now standing in front of her, with his head on her knee. Josh watched her carefully. She didn't seem too bothered, even though she'd clearly noticed that this was what he was doing.

"My mum's a therapist," she said eventually.

"Ah, I see." That explained it then.

"So, what do you see?" she asked him.

"An only child, in her early twenties, who really wishes she wasn't so impulsive."

"Uh-huh." Bertie smiled. "Maybe I'll learn one day."

"Here you go," George said. He placed the latte glass on the table in front of her.

"Thanks, George."

"Right. I'm going," Josh announced. He grabbed his keys and kissed George. "See you about three, hopefully."

"OK. Have a nice day," George said. Josh rolled his eyes. It was Friday: uni day.

"Nice to meet you, Josh," Bertie called after him.

"You too," he replied.

The front door closed behind him. It was really warm in their house, and Bertie stood up to remove the thick, home-knitted sweater she was wearing. She pulled it over her head, at the exact same moment as Josh came back in, having realised that he'd left his phone on the table, and just in time to catch an accidentally topless Bertie. She pulled her t-shirt out of her jumper and quickly put it back on. George turned away. Josh tried not to laugh.

"Oh God, I'm so sorry," she said. She'd blushed almost as bright a pink as her hair.

"Don't worry," Josh grinned. "Bye, again." With that, he was gone a second time.

"I'm so embarrassed," she told George. He didn't know what to say, so he said nothing for a while, then figured it out.

"So, how did you meet Andy?" he asked. She blew air out of her mouth, her usually gelled fringe rising with the breath.

"Interesting you should ask…" she began.

By the time Andy returned from dropping a very delicate Adele back at home, George and Bertie were well acquainted, and both a bit giddy, having consumed far too many lattes between them during the course of the morning. George opened the door, took one look at Andy and started giggling. Andy raised his eyebrows.

"She told you, didn't she?"

George nodded, trying very hard to contain his laughter.

Andy turned bright red—not something that happened very often, given how confident and unashamed he was, always prepared to have a go at something new. "Do me a favour and don't tell anyone else?"

George couldn't speak in order to agree to this, but put his hand over his heart. Andy shook his head, although he was smiling too. Yes, it had been embarrassing, but it was also kind of funny to look back on. George walked away, singing "Love in an Elevator" under his breath, deliberately loud enough for Andy to hear.

"Funny," he called after him.

"I thought so," George called back, still struggling to control the giggles. "I totally empathise, though—well, not totally," he added with a chuckle, having once got stuck in the tower block lift, although it had been rather cold and draughty, and thankfully only for twenty minutes, as opposed to the two hours Bertie had reported that she spent with Andy on their first encounter.

"She did tell you it was all her doing, didn't she?"

"Aye, I did," Bertie appeared in the hall and smiled. "Everything OK?"

"Yeah, not too bad." Andy returned the smile, but he was still keeping his distance. This wasn't like him, and it was making her feel even more guilty about having landed on him the way she had. "You ready?" he asked. She nodded.

"I'm gonna take the six forty train home," she told him. "George booked me a ticket."

"OK. If you're sure that's what you want to do."

"It is."

George came back into the hall and stood watching them. They needed to talk, for Bertie hadn't just told him about how she and Andy met.

"Me and Blue are off for a walk," he said, "give you guys some time." Neither protested and a couple of minutes later, they were alone.

"I told you I was waiting on the agency to contact me?" Bertie asked. Andy nodded to confirm that this was true. "They sent me an email yesterday, just after I got your message. There's a flight on Monday, if I want it. I've got everything else sorted—my jabs, passport, and they'll sort the visa—but if you want me to stay…"

"No. Go for it. You've got to."

"Cool. Thanks." She stood on tiptoes and kissed his cheek. He smiled and put his arms around her.

"You don't need to thank me. When I—" he stopped abruptly. What he'd been about to say was 'when I was your age', with an elaboration on how he'd always gone off on a whim. Granted, the fact that he was only five months away from turning forty hadn't changed anything, but nearly saying those words had. For her part, Bertie sensed his unease.

"George told me about Krissi. By accident, I think. He assumed I'd already know."

Andy frowned.

"You know the age difference has nothing to do with it, don't you?" she asked, trying to reassure him.

"Yeah. I've never really thought about it, to be honest. You and me—we just hit it off, although next time I'll think twice about getting into a lift with a strange woman." They both laughed at this. "As for Krissi," he continued, "I was still at school when…it happened. And I didn't have much to do with her growing up, because I didn't know."

"She's older than me?"

"Yeah. Twenty-three. And mega-successful. She manages a pizza restaurant—been offered promotion too. Meanwhile, I'm still here living like a student, dating a student."

Bertie pulled away and took hold of his hands, squeezing them tight. "Don't change for anyone," she said. He smiled.

"So, we've got a few hours before your train. I guess I'd best show you the sights, not that there's much to see."

"Brilliant," she said. She reached up and kissed him again, this time on the lips, but it was still no more than an innocent peck. Meeting his brother and some of his friends had made her realise that however 'young' Andy was in his attitude and his behaviour, he had a whole lifetime of experience, both with these people and without. She had a lot of living to do and was so excited to be flying to Mali on Monday that she was fit to burst.

"And you can rave away while I show you boring things," Andy laughed, sensing in her the tingle of a new challenge he had so often felt himself. No hard feelings; no regrets. They'd had a fun couple of months, but a few hours from now they would each head off their own way, maybe catch up again at some point in the future, if time and opportunity allowed, but they had no firm plans.

Not long after, George returned with Blue, and Andy and Bertie left for one last afternoon together, stopping off briefly so that she could say goodbye to Dan. Andy borrowed the 4x4 to take her to the station. A final, emotional hug, then she was on her way back to Glasgow, and Andy was single once more.

KID GLOVES
Friday 20ᵗʰ January

Sean hung up and flopped back in his chair. He was sitting at his desk, in his office at the university, having spent the past two hours staring at the bleak, naked skeleton of the cherry tree in the courtyard outside his window, trying to come up with a foolproof means of distraction; Diane Sheridan's call had afforded him what he hadn't been able to find for himself. Now it was just a case of passing the time until she arrived. An hour, she said. Sean glanced at his computer screen—the floating, gloating fraud of an analogue clock that he'd chosen as his first screensaver and insisted on reinstalling on every new computer he'd had since. Ten to eleven: by 'his' standards, he was late, which is to say, he was less than fifteen minutes early. Sean sighed and turned his attention back to the cherry tree.

They'd developed a rather effective mutual support strategy over the past three months. Indeed, last October could have ended in something akin to a mass mental breakdown, had it not been for the four of them working together to jolly each other through the worst of it. Eleven years working as a clinical psychologist: it had taken all that time for him to finally accept his own advice. Everybody needed somebody sometimes, even he: the invincible, happy-go-lucky, ever-optimistic Doctor Sean Tierney, always armed with a cheeky grin and a sprinkling of Irish good humour. Was it faked? He began pondering on the possibility just as the knock came on the door. He didn't bother to answer. There was no need. The door opened.

"Morning," Josh greeted him with light inflection and a smile.

"It's as well you didn't use the word 'good' in that statement," Sean responded. "It is morning, though, for what it's worth." He briefly returned his gaze to the drab wintry world outside.

"Was my attempt at affecting 'couldn't-care-less' as unconvincing as yours?" Josh asked, propping himself on the corner of the desk and picking up a copy of a journal bent open at an article about cognitive behavioural therapy and male psychological distress. Josh turned back the cover. "*Psychology and Psychotherapy: Theory, Research and Practice.* Do they publish anything other than reviews of CBT these days?"

"Not often. It's that or social support networks. Common sense, no?"

Josh put the journal down without comment and folded his arms. He wandered over to the bookshelf and scanned the spines. Nothing new.

"Your turn today, then," he said.

"If you wouldn't mind," Sean replied.

"Fine. Grab your jacket. We're going off-campus."

Sean swivelled his chair around, away from the window, his eyebrow raised in query. Josh wasn't intending to explain, that much was clear, so Sean did as advised.

"You know it's not going to get above zero today?" he said as they descended the stairs. Josh continued to march ahead, hands in pockets, leading the way back to his own office, or what was his office for now. He was being moved out, at some point, when the powers-that-be got around to it. He unlocked the door, grabbed his coat from the standard coat-rack and locked the door again. Sean followed, his expression shifting through curiosity, puzzlement and confusion, eventually resting on bemusement as they walked past the library and down towards the road. He knew where they were going, or at least, he knew how they were getting to wherever they were going and beyond that he didn't care. They climbed aboard the bus idling at the stop and Sean took a seat on the left; the only other passengers were two students, huddled together near the back, on the right. A few seconds later Josh sat down in front of him and turned sideways, his legs up on the seat, feet dangling over the aisle.

"No appointments today?" Sean asked.

"Nope. They cancelled them all on my behalf, apparently."

"That was nice of them."

"It'd have been nicer if they'd told me. I could've come in a bit later. What about you? Busy day?"

"I've got to be back in an hour," Sean informed him. "Diane Sheridan's coming down."

"Vera?"

"Yeah." Sean laughed, in spite of his misery. Josh had always called Diane 'Vera', on account of her Antipodean heritage and scraped-back blonde hair that he said always put him in mind of the prison warden 'Vera Bennett' in the long-finished soap opera *Prisoner: Cell Block H* that they had wasted many late nights on as undergraduates, although whether he would have made this association had she not worked for the prison service, it was difficult to say. Whatever, she came across as harsh and brash and Sean could tolerate her only slightly more than Josh could, thus it was immediately apparent that this was not a social visit.

"What for?" Josh asked.

"Something to do with an inmate dying and a formal inquiry," Sean explained. Josh didn't respond, instead reaching up to ring the bell. Ten seconds later the bus decelerated, the doors hissed open and the cold air came rushing up the steps. Josh fastened the top button on his coat and pulled his scarf tighter; Sean zipped his jacket right up to his chin and they made a dash for it, across the short expanse of pavement to Cordelia's Aquarium, through the lines of vast glass tanks filled with coral, anemone and myriad other marine life-forms, and onwards, to the café at the back. Cordelia was sitting behind the counter, crocheting a circle. She glanced up from her work, her eyes settling on her two newest, and only, customers.

"Good morning. Cafetière for two, please, Miss," Josh grinned.

"Joshua Sandison. How wonderful to see you!" She poked the crochet hook through a hole in the ambiguous garment and pushed it under the counter, then swooshed her way around the glass cake cabinet to hug him. "You look very well," she said, standing back to get a good look at him. She was the same as ever: a swirling, floral skirt that swept down almost to the floor, revealing no more than an inch or so of bony ankles and below these flat, buckled shoes.

"You too, Mrs. Kin..." He automatically corrected himself. "Cordelia."

"And this is—" She put up a hand in advance, to silence any prompts, examined Sean momentarily, then closed her eyes, searching for his name in amongst those of all the other people—children, mostly—that she had ever known. "Sean?"

Sean nodded dumbly, impressed. They'd met once in Josh's company and once since without, both occasions over a decade ago. Now that was advanced, almost magic trick level recall.

"Go and sit down, boys," she told them, motioning with her hand, "and I'll get that coffee for you." Josh and Sean did as they were told; Cordelia Kinkade still had far too much of the schoolteacher about her for there to be any choice in the matter. Josh checked the tanks running alongside the tables, squinting to read the signs underneath, before choosing their seats. Sean sat down and glanced at the sign.

"Hippocampus Zosterae?" He peered in amongst the swaying seaweed.

"Dwarf seahorse," Josh said knowledgeably, as one of the tiny, white creatures bobbed out from its hiding place behind a rock.

"Do you remember that idiot postgrad who dissected the sheep's brain in front of all us first years?"

"Yes, unfortunately. I think of him every time I smell vomit."

Sean laughed, although it hadn't been funny at the time, with several of the students behind them throwing up over the course of the ten minutes it took for the campus cleaning squad to arrive with the sawdust and mop bucket.

"He was one of Harrington's disciples, wasn't he?" Josh asked.

"He certainly was," Sean confirmed distractedly, watching the little seahorse slowly progress to the front of the tank. He shook his head in wonder. "God, they do too."

To anyone else, he probably would have needed to explain this statement, but both Josh and the aquarium proprietor were already on his wavelength, as was evidenced by what she said when she delivered their coffee, along with two slices of homemade Bakewell tart.

"I still recall our chat as if it were only yesterday," she said to Josh. "You thought I was spinning you a yarn when I told you that part of the brain was named after the seahorse."

Josh nodded and smiled. "I thought seahorses were mythical, that's why," he justified, not for the first time. The conversation to which she was referring took place thirty years ago and she'd mentioned it on almost every occasion they had seen each other since, for she was secretly very proud to have been an inspiration, perhaps *the* inspiration, for the academic path that Josh had chosen to pursue.

Sean sat back with his arms folded, looking both amused and smug. The rarity of hearing Josh admit he was wrong about something made it all the more enjoyable an experience, and Cordelia appreciated her audience.

"It was only when I brought the children to visit the aquarium that Joshua realised they were real aquatic creatures," she explained. Sean chortled.

"Every year," Josh groaned.

"I recall you being a very willing teacher's helper," Cordelia reminded him.

"That's true. I'd do anything to get out of art lessons."

"You weren't so fond of the more creative subjects, were you, dear?" She said this to Josh, who shook his head, then she addressed Sean. "Although it has to be said that some of the paintings Joshua completed as homework were outstanding." She gave Sean a wink and turned her attention back to Josh. "And what is George Morley up to these days? Are you still in touch with him.

"Yes, you could say that," Josh grinned. "He's fine."

"Is he still in the USA?" she asked.

"No. He's been back a couple of years, or so."

"Gosh! It only seems that long since he emigrated."

"That was over twelve years ago now."

"Gracious me. Time really does march on," she said, wandering back over to her counter. "Do give him my regards next time you see him."

"I will."

Sean frowned, puzzled as to why he hadn't told her.

"Any second now," Josh whispered. "Just wait."

"So, did George bring a fellow back with him?" Cordelia called, picking up her crocheting again.

Josh nodded a tacit, "I told you so," at Sean.

"No," he said, in answer to her question.

"You're not telling me he's stayed single all this time?"

"No," Josh said again.

"Good. He deserves to have someone special in his life. Such a lovely boy. Of course, you both are."

Josh wasn't giving anything away, for as much as she was his favourite teacher, she was still a teacher, even if she was long out of the profession. This aquarium had belonged to her late husband, who died at the age of sixty-five, from early onset dementia. His illness dictated the point at which she decided to retire from teaching, firstly to care for him while she was still able, then to visit him in the hospice, and finally, to take on the day-to-day running of the aquarium—a curious establishment for a town like theirs, but always popular with local schools and colleges. How fascinating it was to look back with adult eyes on the falseness of childhood perception: Mrs. Kinkade had seemed so *old* when they were so young themselves, yet she must only have been in her early forties. Now in her early seventies, she looked no different to Josh than she did when he was at school.

Cordelia made no further queries regarding George, sidetracked by several more customers, thereby granting Sean the chance to speak to Josh. As usual, he headed right into it with no preamble. They didn't need one.

"You know about Soph?" he asked. Josh nodded to confirm he did. Sean sighed and broke a chunk off the Bakewell tart. He put it in his mouth and chewed laboriously, even though the sponge was light and moist and the pastry crisp. Eventually he swallowed and slurped a mouthful of coffee. "It's making me want to drink again," he confessed.

"Understandably," Josh said.

"How so?"

"It's a big thing to cope with emotionally, a pregnancy."

"For Soph."

"And for you too," Josh argued. "One of my friends had a miscarriage yesterday. She was sixteen weeks pregnant."

"Oh, no. That's terrible news."

"Yes, it is. But it's not just her who's feeling it. In fact, from what I hear she's coping very well, considering. The dad, however, is a different story."

"Maybe you shouldn't be listening to me harping on, then."

"He won't want to speak to me today," Josh assured him. "Come Monday, I envisage he will burst into my surgery in a rage, wanting to off-load. Today, he'll want nothing to do with me or anyone else. The only one he might put up with is his brother."

Sean accepted this justification for the continuance of their 'therapy session'. He rested his head on the back of the chair and watched the seahorses—two of them now—curled tail-to-tail.

"They're mating," Josh explained.

"Impeccable timing," Sean said wryly.

"And have you had a drink?"

"No."

"Good, because you're driving us home. I'm doing trial by Sauvignon Blanc this afternoon."

"You're not going to take the post, are you?" Sean asked, now realising why Josh's appointments for the day had been cancelled, and he was truly astonished. The university had been pestering them both about teaching on the postgraduate psychology modules for years; until now, Josh had absolutely refused to involve himself in so much as a tentative discussion.

"Not unless I get what I ask for, I'm not," he said. "But if they want to give me free wine and gateau—well, it would seem rude not to indulge!"

Sean smiled. "Thanks," he said, and he meant it. He knew Josh rarely drank during the day, but the possibility that he might be needed to drive later was enough reason to stay sober.

"A day at a time, *Seany*," Josh said, the most fleeting smirk passing over his lips.

"I don't care."

"I know." Josh picked up his untouched Bakewell tart and bit off the point, the pleasure immediately registering on his face. "This is fabulous," he said, turning on his chair to give a thumbs-up to Cordelia.

"Thought you'd approve," she smiled.

He turned back to Sean. "I'm going to tell her about George and me before we go," he explained quietly. "I'm very nervous about it."

"Why?"

"I don't know. Because she's known me since I was four, I think. And she's a teacher."

"She'll be pleased for you," Sean asserted.

"I hope so." Josh breathed out heavily. "Anyway, you wanted to talk? Talk."

The bus back up to the campus was due in just under thirty minutes, and there was enough coffee for another cup each, which Josh duly poured, then listened as Sean talked, about him and Sophie and how they'd decided they didn't want to have children. He still felt the same way about it, but he was angry that she hadn't discussed the termination with him, yet at the same time he believed it was not his business. Their relationship was long-term and monogamous, but there was no intention of committing to marriage or anything like that, from either side. He thought he'd got past feeling jealous of how close Sophie was to George, rationalised how ridiculous it was; however, the fact that she'd arranged to go to the hospital with George and hadn't even told Sean about the pregnancy was like a kick in the teeth. He hadn't heard so much as a whisper from her since, and she wasn't returning his calls. Josh didn't pass comment on any of this, because that wasn't the point of their 'therapy' sessions. They each needed someone to talk to who knew them, their weaknesses, their history; someone they trusted. For Josh, this did sometimes mean Sean offering real therapeutic interventions; for Sean, most of the time he just needed an ear and that was what Josh gave him, whilst also appreciating the significance of the dilemma it put him in as regards knowing that Sophie hadn't gone ahead with the termination after all, a fact of which, seemingly, Sean was ignorant.

It was nearing the time to leave; Josh decided to wait until they were back on the bus before he told Sean about Sophie, and not because of his own requirement now. Rather, he knew that the distraction of dealing with Diane Sheridan would give Sean time to absorb the news slowly and was less likely to result in him heading straight for the nearest pub. But first Josh had to deliver his own news, and spent a moment calming down as he prepared to pay. He walked over to the counter, wiping his sweaty palms on his thighs.

"It's been lovely to see you again, Joshua," Cordelia smiled warmly as she gave him his change. She took his hand and gave it a squeeze. "You seem so much happier than when I last saw you."

"I am, Cordelia," he said. His stomach was churning and he swallowed, trying to find a best way to tell her, ordering and reordering the words in his head. She gave him a foot-up.

"There's someone special in your life too," she stated.

"Yes, there is," Josh confirmed. "It took me a while to realise, but there always was."

For a few seconds her brow creased, intrigued, but then a wide smile spread across her face.

"I'm sorry, Miss," he said in a small voice, "but we don't care that it's— how did you phrase it?"

"Frowned upon," she reminded him.

"That's right," Josh laughed. "We don't care that it's frowned upon for little boys to hold hands."

She turned his hand over in hers and ran her finger over the surface of his engagement ring. When her eyes met his again there were tears in them.

"Congratulations," she whispered. She leaned across the counter and patted him on the head, the way she used to when he'd got all of his spellings correct.

"Thanks, Miss," he beamed. "I'll bring George with me next time."

"I should jolly well hope so too," she said sternly. "And you'd better make it soon. I'm an old lady."

Josh shook his head. "You'll never be an old lady, Mrs. Kinkade, but we'll call in very soon, I promise." He moved away, following Sean towards the exit.

"I won't forget," she called after him, "not with all of these hippocampuses around."

"Hippocampi," he called back as he waved and disappeared through the door.

"Hippocampi," she repeated with a chuckle. She sighed and wiped away a tear. "So proud of my little ones."

Diane Sheridan was having an argument with the campus security guard, who was trying to explain, as politely as possible after five minutes of already having explained, that there was no VIP parking available, and even if there had been, she wouldn't be getting it, because she wasn't a VIP. To cap it all, he'd had no prior notice of her visit, thus refused to give her a visitor's permit, and was adamant that he wouldn't be lifting the gate to let her drive on-campus and risk running the gauntlet with the private wheel-clamping firm that the university sub-contracted in. Furthermore, as there was no answer on Sean Tierney's office phone and he hadn't told the faculty secretary that he was expecting a visitor, she was, the security guard explained, in essence a trespasser.

"All I can advise, madam, is that you park as close to the main entrance as you can," he smiled through gritted teeth. She swore at him, stormed out of the security hut and climbed back into her car, parked on double yellow lines and blocking the passage for the campus bus, on which Sean was currently a passenger. She sat, stubborn and resolute, in her car, repeatedly calling Sean's mobile phone and hanging up each time it went through to voicemail. Alas, he had switched it to silent and the vibrations emanating from the wheel over which he was seated meant he remained unaware that anyone was trying to call him until he and Josh got off the bus only a few yards from where Diane was parked. She called again and he answered it.

"Ah, good. One moment," she said. She got back out of the car and returned to the security hut. Josh spotted her and nudged Sean.

"Hang on. I'm just on the phone to—Oh!" he said, as he watched her disappear inside.

"Can you tell this...man that I'm here on official business," she demanded. She passed the phone to the security guard.

"Doctor Tierney?" he asked uncertainly.

"Hi, yes. Sorry. I've been off-site for the past hour. Doctor Sheridan is here to see me."

"Cheers," the security guard responded and passed the phone back. She hung up.

Sean shrugged and put his phone away. "I'll cadge a lift with her."

"OK. I'll catch up with you later," Josh said and headed off in the direction of his own office, which wasn't that far from Sean's.

"Come with me, if you like," Sean shouted after him.

"No, no. You carry on," Josh called back. Sean sighed and stepped into the road, in front of Diane's car. She squinted under her sun visor and scowled at him. He gave her a cheesy grin and walked around to the passenger door. Begrudgingly, she cleared her bag and phone from the seat, then put her foot down almost before he'd shut the door. Neither of them spoke until she'd parked up in a location marked as a box junction in the absence of any real spaces, and made the lengthy walk to Sean's office, where she pirouetted on the spot, eyeing the academic clutter with disdain. Sean smiled apologetically and removed the pile of books from the least full of the two chairs that weren't his own. She perched uneasily on the edge, the strap of her bag still on her shoulder, the giant satchel resting on her lap, her nose wrinkled into a half-sneer, as if there were a bad smell in the room. Sean ignored all of this. He was doing her a favour, after all, but then she'd always been ungracious.

"So, Diane," he said, settling into his seat. He'd loosened the backrest and ended up a little more reclined than he'd intended. She didn't notice.

"Sean," she grimaced, or smiled, possibly.

"What can I do for you?"

"Quite frankly, the situation is ridiculous," she began. He shifted position and tried to look attentive. "I don't know if you read our last HMI report?"

"Can't say I did."

"Well, on the whole it was good." She paused.

"But?" Sean prompted, knowing there was one coming.

"But it did mention a little bit of an issue with prisoners at risk of suicide and self-harm not being monitored closely enough."

"OK."

"And now one's gone and hanged himself."

"OK."

"His records will show he was known to be at risk."

"And?"

"There was a—communication error," she said.

"You mean you forgot to tell the screws?"

"Not so much forgot, as, erm…" She looked down and unclasped her bag, took out a file and passed it across. "This is Kevin…"

"Callaghan," Sean finished. "I know who he is." He stared at the photograph attached to the front of the file, the lifeless eyes, the hollow cheeks; not the same Kevin Callaghan he saw sprawled face down on the pavement a little over a year ago, or at least, it was the same man, but he looked—dead.

"Was he still alive when this was taken?" he asked, intending it as a joke. Diane glowered at him. "Sorry. That was a bit insensitive." He lifted the cover page and read Callaghan's profile: psychotic episodes, depression; nothing damning there. He turned the page and skimmed through Diane's notes from one-to-one sessions. "These only go back three months," he said, flicking through the pages to double-check.

"Yes," she confirmed. "Before that, you may recall, I had one of your students on placement?"

"Meaning?"

"That their notes are inadmissible."

"Because they shouldn't have been working solo."

"That was not made clear. Your placement handbook states…"

"Our placement handbook is intended as a general guide of our expectations and the course requirements. It doesn't supersede the structures institutions already have in place. He should not have been working one-to-one with prisoners, certainly not unsupervised."

"He turned out to be very unreliable. You know he just left? No notice whatsoever."

Sean closed the file and put it down on his desk. He was getting angry. Correction: he was angry. Very bloody angry. However, he wasn't about to relinquish the upper hand. He studied Diane's face for a moment, waiting until she broke eye contact, just for the satisfaction of the experience.

"Let me lay it on the line here, Diane. I'll start with your treatment of George Morley when he was on placement with you. There are several things you need to know about George. First and foremost, he is highly dependable, and was one of only three students on the diploma course set to achieve a distinction. Second, the failure of his placement at the prison led to him leaving the course." This wasn't true, but Sean had always questioned whether it was a contributing factor. "Third, he is the only student I've lost, and as such your action, or inaction, has been detrimental to the course's performance, for which I will be held accountable."

"Let me just interrupt…" Diane started.

"No!" Sean cut her off. "Kevin Callaghan was the ex-husband of one of George's closest friends. He held her hostage, at knifepoint. It was George who challenged him, and saved her life, putting himself at great risk."

Diane appeared suitably taken aback by this. It was obviously news to her. Sean shook his head.

"You didn't read up on Callaghan's offences properly prior to his treatment. You ignored George Morley when he informed you that he knew him. You didn't tell the prison staff that Callaghan was a suicide risk."

Diane extended a leg, twisting it from side to side and examining her shoe.

"You're in deep shit," Sean said. "And you have the audacity to come here, asking for my help? I think it might be time for a little humble pie, don't you? Rather than ripping into *my* students?"

"I was personally involved with Kevin Callaghan," Diane said, quietly, talking to her shoes.

"Sorry? Did you say *involved?*"

"We weren't having a relationship or anything like that, but I liked him and believed him. I tried to distance myself, but it didn't work. He asked me to keep quiet about how depressed he was, and I could understand why. He was a doctor. Did you know that?"

"Yes, I did. He had his licence suspended."

"Of course," Diane nodded. "You worked with him at the hospice."

"Where he was practising without a licence," Sean pointed out.

"Yes," she conceded. She was crying. He could see a drip of snot hanging from her nose. She sniffed loudly and the snot shot back up her nostril. Sean looked away and tried not to laugh, while she fished a wad of tissue from her satchel. He picked up Callaghan's file again, more for something to do, so that she had time to recompose. He didn't like her enough to offer comfort.

After several more minutes spent sniffing, Diane pulled another folder from her bag and placed it on the desk.

"I'm going to lose my job over this," she said. "There's no point in me even fighting it, but I made Kevin a promise. His ex-wife, Ellen, is it?"

"Eleanor," Sean corrected.

"That's right. He wanted her to know the truth. I was trying to persuade him to put together an appeal, but he refused. He said there was no point; he'd never get his career back."

"He got that much right," Sean said scathingly. "Looks like he took yours with him along the way. How could you have been so stupid?"

"I know that's how it seems." Diane sighed and dabbed at her eyes. "Look, Sean, I'm not going to ask you to act as a character witness. It's too late for anything like that. But I do need you to do a couple of things for me, or not for me, as such. For Kevin."

Sean put the file down and scanned his bookshelf, trying to tap into some level of empathy for his colleague. His gaze drifted and came to rest on the journal article Josh had been looking at earlier; he smiled to himself, imagining what Josh would have to say to Diane if he were here right now.

"Go on," he said, instead of laughing in her face, which was more what he felt like doing.

"There's a young man due to be released next week. He's not a bad lot, and he has employment lined up, a place to live and so forth."

"I thought you said this was a favour to Callaghan."

61

"Indirectly, it is. See, Kevin befriended Hadyn—the inmate I just mentioned—gave him a lot of help with his OCD. He needs follow-up for his treatment and some general support. He's taken Kevin's death very badly." Diane looked up and made eye contact. "I can think of no-one I trust more to give him that support," she said. Sean nodded, acknowledging the sincerity of this statement.

"And the other favour?"

"All I ask is that you read my notes." She indicated with her eyes to the second file she had placed before him. "And keep an open mind, because in my opinion, misguided or otherwise, they got the wrong man. Kevin Callaghan is innocent."

Aquarius

"Like water spilt upon the ground,"—alas,
Our little lives flow swiftly on and pass;
Yet may they bring rich harvests and green

CORRESPONDENCE
Saturday 21ˢᵗ–Sunday 22ⁿᵈ January

06:15, Dan [mobile]
You up bro?

06:20, Dan [mobile]
Andy?

06:31, Dan [mobile]
Lazy arse. Call when you get this.

***

Andy trudged, scuffing his feet through the gravel down towards the gates, eyes half shut, each out-breath a miniature cloud suspended before him in the crisp, dark January morning. He checked the weather app on his phone: minus four. And it felt like it. He arrived at the gate and braced himself for touching the icy wrought iron, opening it just enough to squeeze through. He pulled it to a close behind him and turned to watch the road: not a car in sight.

"Awesome," he muttered sarcastically, trying not to take in too much of the frigid air. He checked his phone again: 06:50; the gym wouldn't even be open yet. And it was Saturday. What the fuck was he doing? He should've just told Dan straight: go back to bed. Stay with Adele. Look after each other. Just as he reached into his pocket for his phone (an action that, if completed, would have confirmed only a minute had passed since the last time he did it, but it was too cold for patience), the sound of an approaching vehicle distracted him. Diesel. Big engine. 4x4. Thank fuck.

"Alright, bro?" Dan said. He waited until the door was shut before he slowly pulled away. The roads were slippery enough to require caution, even in a four wheel drive that could probably have hammered its way up and down the Himalayan pass between Syabru and Kathmandu, no problem at all. Andy grunted a greeting and plugged in his seatbelt.

"Bertie get off OK?" Dan asked.

"Yeah." Andy settled back into the seat and closed his eyes.

"Tired?"

"What do you think? It's not even seven yet. I've had four hours' sleep and it's pitch-bloody-black."

Dan focused on the road ahead and didn't say anything else for a few minutes, then, "Sorry, bro."

Andy sighed. "No worries." He opened his eyes and gave them a good rub. After that, neither spoke again, until they were inside the gym, warming up on adjacent bikes.

"When we're done," Andy said, in time with the swishing rhythm of the rotating rubber belt, "I'm gonna buy us breakfast." He waited to catch the up-beat. "And you're gonna talk to me."

Dan cycled on silently. Ten minutes. Warm-up complete. On to the treadmills, set to a nice leisurely jog. Thump thump thump thump.

"Failing that," Andy continued, adjusting in accordance with his new rhythm, "you're gonna talk to Josh."

"What for? I'm fine." Dan's syncopated protest fell on deaf ears. Andy had inserted his earphones.

***

08:53, Shaunna [mobile]
Morning hun. How you feeling? x

08:55 Adele [mobile]
AM OK THANKS. WHAT YOU UP TO TODAY? X

08:57 Shaunna [mobile]
Not much. In work at 12. Kris is out with the dog. Ade's still in bed. Bored! Might have breakfast and pop round to yours? x

08:59 Adele [mobile]
GET BREAKFAST ON YOUR WAY - IN THE MOOD FOR A QUASSON. CANT SPELL IT SORRY. :) X

09:00 Shaunna [mobile]
LOL. OK hun. Be about 20 minutes. Get the kettle on! x

***

"Your croissants, ma'am," Shaunna said, holding up the bag of pastries as if they were an entry requirement. She stepped into the hallway and followed her friend to the source of the smell of the freshly brewed tea in the lounge.

"Hiya," little Shaunna said, handing grown-up Shaunna a very small bear.

"Hiya," grown-up Shaunna replied. "Ta." She accepted the tiny teddy. "I bought some pain au chocolat too—wasn't sure what Missus here would eat."

"Anything at all. She's got past that fussy stage," Adele said. "Although she's already had breakfast with Dan, a couple of hours ago."

"Blimey! Has he gone to work?"

"Nope." Adele breathed out loudly and set about pouring the tea; since Alice had been child-minding for them, she'd discovered that tea from the pot was her preference, although didn't usually bother, but it seemed a good morning for it.

"Oh." Shaunna frowned. "Gym?"

"Yep." Adele sat down and waited for grown-up Shaunna to dish out the pastries.

"On his own?"

"With Andy."

"That's something," Shaunna said. She took a bite of her croissant and chewed thoughtfully. "Isn't he talking to you?"

"Yeah, he's talking. Sort of. He keeps snapping at me, like it's my fault, but the doctor told us both. There's nothing we did that caused it. He's just being an idiot. I mean. It's not even like I was that far on."

"He's obviously taking it badly."

"Or being a selfish prat." Adele tore a large piece from the croissant with her teeth and chomped angrily. Shaunna watched her friend.

"How are you really feeling, hun?" she asked. Adele shrugged and swallowed hard.

"I'm fine. My hormones are a bit all over the place, but they said they would be. And I've got the worst period pains ever, but I'm coping. And I just don't get it."

"What d'you mean?"

"Well, it's me, isn't it? It's *me* who's had a miscarriage. It's *me* who should be all cut up about it, not *him*."

Shaunna picked up her tea and slowly sipped, planning out her response. Adele didn't understand how Dan was feeling, because she wasn't feeling like that herself, which had always been one of her weaknesses—not so much a lack of empathy, but a lack of forethought, because once she gave herself time to consider it, she was able see things from other people's perspective. However, this was Dan, so it was probably going to take a bit longer than usual, and trying to use an example to illustrate didn't work with Adele either. It just confused her further, so straight-talking was the only way.

"What I think," Shaunna said carefully, "and I might be totally wrong," she paused to make sure Adele was listening, "is that to Dan this feels the same as losing a baby after it's been born."

"But it's not!"

"No, but I don't think most men can get their heads around pregnancy. To them, it's like from the minute you tell them you're pregnant, they've got this image of a fully-formed, newborn baby that's hidden away somewhere. You know, like the way grown-ups told us that babies were found under gooseberry bushes? I reckon men see it a bit like that. They don't connect the bump to the baby."

"That's stupid."

"Maybe, but it must be really hard for them. I don't know about you, but it was only when I started to feel Krissi moving around in there that it hit me that I was going to have a baby. Until then, it doesn't seem real."

"I felt like that too."

"Imagine what it's like for men. One minute they're just going along as normal, the next they're a dad."

Adele sighed. "So, are you saying that to Dan this is like if we'd lost little Shaunna?"

Shaunna reached across and took Adele's hand, for she had spotted the trembling lip. She'd got through to her. "That's exactly what I'm saying."

"Oh, poor baby," Adele said. She started to cry and instinctively reached for her daughter, because seeing it from Dan's point of view had only come from imagining how it would feel to lose little Shaunna, and it hurt so much.

"I'm sorry, hun," Shaunna said, feeling dreadfully guilty. She hadn't intended to upset her like this, even if it did have the desired effect. She moved along the sofa and put her arms around her friend. Little Shaunna looked from one to the other of the two teary-eyed women and held up her chocolatey hand to offer them a bite of her squished-up pain au chocolat. Adele laughed and sobbed at the same time. She withdrew and found a tissue.

"Thanks," she said. "I understand now."

***

"That was disgustingly fat." Dan shoved the empty, ketchup-smeared plate across the table. Andy did the same with his own plate, and belched in satisfaction.

"Nah. We just did a two hour workout. That only put us back where we started, bro."

"True enough. What you up to today? Any plans?"

"Well, I was gonna have a lie-in, but some bastard got me out of bed at six-thirty."

68

"Yeah. Sorry."

"I'm here now, so talk to me."

"What's there to say?"

"I dunno. What's bothering you?"

Dan breathed out through his nose. It was kind of a laugh, but not one of joy. More of disbelief. He picked up the vast mug of milky coffee and held it with both hands. "She's not bothered. Do you know that? She lost the baby and she doesn't give a shit."

"It's probably her way of coping."

"Good luck to her."

Andy couldn't think of anything to say. They were closer now than they'd ever been, but that hadn't suddenly transformed their relationship. They didn't talk about things like this. They fought, or worked out, or got pissed, or ate big fat fried breakfasts—precisely what they were doing now, and it was a good thing, for Dan. It would get him through this in the short term. In the longer term, he needed to talk to Adele. They needed to communicate with each other. That's what the leaflet said. Andy had read it from cover to cover, then read it again, and again. It was why he'd only had four hours' sleep. Well, that and Michael coming in at two in the morning, tanked up and swearing about how shit his life was. What a complete moron.

"Have you tried talking to her?" Andy asked.

"What's the point? In the hospital they were only worried about her, and she's come home all full of her own self-importance, bragging about how well she's coping, how strong she is. As I say, if she's so fucking important, then good luck to her." Dan slurped angrily at his mug and slammed it down on the table. Andy peered inside it.

"I'll get us another," he said. He picked up the mug and took a deep breath. "Then you're gonna go home and talk." He quickly moved away from the table, aware of his brother's snorting exhalations behind him. A greasy transport café wasn't the ideal location for bereavement counselling, surrounded by large, sweaty truckers and brickies and their young apprentices, but it was familiar, normal. Andy chanced a swift glance at Dan while waiting for their mugs to be replenished. He was scowling at his phone. Andy turned away again and took out his own phone. He typed: "Help!" He sent it to Josh. He got a reply.

"With?"

He sent back: "Dan. Won't talk. Angry with Adele. Ideas?"

Josh replied: "Will get back to you…"

***

69

10:05, Josh [mobile]
Hi Shaunna. Hope you're OK. Just wondering if you've heard from Adele today? x

10:06: Shaunna
Just with her now. Why? x

10:08: Josh [mobile]
Got a message from Andy. Dan's not coping, he said. He won't talk about it and he's angry with Adele. Wondered if you knew any more? x

10:11: Shaunna
Yeah. Will give you a call now. x

***

"Hey, Shaunna," Josh answered.

"Hi, Josh. Right, so, basically—hang on."

Shaunna listened quietly. She was sitting on the edge of the bath, and Adele was just outside the bathroom door. She heard her return to the lounge.

"OK. Basically, Adele is doing all right. The doctors told her there was something wrong with the baby, so she accepted it straight away. She couldn't see why Dan was so upset, but I've, erm, explained it to her. I think if he comes home and they talk, then we might get somewhere."

"OK. Are you all right?"

"Oh, I'm fine, thanks. You?"

"Not bad. Just waiting for my client to show, then that's me done for the day."

"That's good."

"Yes, I'll let you know on that one," Josh said doubtfully. "George is in a funny mood."

"Oh?"

"Would you believe me if I said it was complicated?"

Shaunna laughed. "It always is with George."

"Tell me about it! Anyway, I'll leave you to it. Thanks, Shaunna. Enjoy your weekend."

"You too. Bye."

***

"Addy!"

"Hiya, trouble," Andy smiled at his niece and picked her up, twirling her around his head. She squealed and he tipped her the right way up. "Look at all that chocolate! Nmm, nmm, nmm." He pretended to eat her face—it was still covered in the filling from the pain au chocolat—and she giggled and pushed him away with a palm against his nose.

Adele stood watching them. She was smiling, although her eyes were red from crying and she was still feeling quite teary. Dan had gone straight through to the bedroom without a word. Andy gave her a sympathetic smile.

"You OK?" he asked. She nodded.

"I've talked to Shaunna, and she said..." Adele stopped and sniffed sharply. "She helped me to see why Dan was taking it so badly."

"Yeah, he is," Andy confirmed. "I read a leaflet about men and miscarriage, and it said it can be a lot harder for the dad, especially when the hospital focuses so much on the mum. It also said you should talk about it. So, I think..." he tipped his niece upside down again and she let out a shrill squeal. "I'm gonna take Little Miss Chocolate Face to see her nana."

"I'll give her a clean up," Adele said. She took Shaunna from him and gave him a hug. "Thanks, Andy. You're the best."

Andy watched Adele leave the room, crossing paths with Dan in the doorway. They couldn't even look at each other.

"Where're your keys?" Andy asked his brother.

"Why?"

"Gonna take Shaunna up to see Mum for a bit."

"You're not borrowing the car."

"I am," Andy told him firmly. "You're going to talk to each other, whether you like it or not."

"And say what?"

"Tell her how you feel. Get her to tell you how she feels. That's all. Dead easy."

"Yeah, right."

"You've got to do it, bro. It's not gonna go away." Dan sighed and put his head down.

"I s'pose."

"Just remember what I said, yeah?"

Dan managed a laugh. "Yeah. Hiding." He threw his keys to Andy. "Thanks."

Adele came back with a much cleaner looking little Shaunna and passed her back to Andy.

"See you both later," he said.

"Bye, bye," little Shaunna waved over his shoulder with scrunched up fingers. Dan and Adele waved back. The door closed. Dan turned and tried to walk past Adele, his plan being to go and have a shower, even though he'd had one at the gym. He didn't want to talk about it. He couldn't see the point. However, as small as she was, there was no way he was getting past her. She stood, arms folded, right in the middle of the hallway.

"I'm sorry," she said. He stared at his feet. "Dan. Look at me." He looked up, but kept his face turned down. "I really am so sorry." She moved towards him. He allowed her close, then put his arms around her. She held him tight, and he cried; that big, strong, proud man of hers. He cried. And as he cried, his whole body jolted, as the broken pieces of his heart bumped around blindly in the deep, dark emptiness within. For a long time, they remained, standing in the hallway, holding onto each other; her tears fell for him, and his for the baby that was no more. At last, when he found he could stop, he lifted his head and their salty lips met. He moved away and wiped his eyes with the heels of his hands. He looked at her and attempted a smile.

"So glad I don't wear mascara," he joked. She laugh-cried and wiped under her eyes with the edges of her forefingers, transferring the black smudges.

"I never realised," she said. "I didn't know it hurt the dad too. And when the doctor said that there was something wrong with the baby, I thought, well that's OK then. It's better this way, because it would be awful if it had been born and then died, but Shaunna said that might be just how it feels for you."

Dan sniffed back a new round of tears, but didn't say anything, because Shaunna was bang on. That's exactly how it felt, and he couldn't comprehend Adele's acceptance. How could she be so matter-of-fact about it?

"I'm going to make a drink," she said. "Then we can sit and talk." He followed her through to the kitchen, passing her the cups and the milk, so that they were doing it together, because it seemed right to do that. Then he followed her through to the sofa and lay down, with his head in her lap. She stroked his hair. He chewed on his thumb.

"Can we try again?" He sounded so small, so helpless.

"The doctor said…"

"I mean when we're allowed to."

"I'm not sure that I…" She paused, sensing the tension in his shoulders. "Can we talk about it another time?" she suggested. "We need to heal a bit first."

"OK," he agreed shakily. He sat up and pulled her to him. She snuggled into the crook of his arm.

"Do you want to talk about how you're feeling?" she asked.

He shook his head.

"Do you want me to ask how you're feeling?"

He shook his head again.

"What then?"

"Tell me why you don't feel like this."

"I said already. If there was something wrong…"

"But our baby died."

"It wasn't a baby. Not really. Not yet."

He sighed heavily. She laced her fingers through his.

"We're so lucky, Dan. We've got little Shaunna, haven't we?"

"True."

"And we went through so much stress and worry."

"But we got there in the end. She's healthy, and she's beautiful."

"And that's all that matters." She looked up at him and smiled. "When Andy brings her back, we should go out somewhere, just the three of us. What d'you think?"

"Yeah, OK."

"George said Farmer Jake's have made one of the barns into a huge playroom with a ball pool and sandpit and stuff. Maybe we could go up there." She sat up and kissed him, and he ran his hand across her belly. She covered it with her own hand and met his sorrow-filled gaze. She sighed in pretend exasperation and bit him gently on the chin.

"It'll soon be all better," she promised.

***

From: Ellie
Sent: Sunday 22nd January, 10:04
Subject: A bit sensitive

Hi Adele,

Hope you're OK and this message doesn't upset you, but I need to ask, as I'm just on my way to meet my mum at church.

As you know, I booked Toby's christening for April the 9th and I wanted to check that you're OK with that.

If not, let me know, because I really don't mind changing the date and moving it to later in the year.

Speak soon,
Ellie x

From: Adele
Sent: Sunday 22nd January, 10:41
Subject: Re: A bit sensitive

Hi Ellie,

Awww, that's so nice of you. It's totally fine. You go ahead with the christening. I'm looking forward to it. I've never been to one before! See you on Tuesday?

A x

From: Ellie
Sent: Sunday 22nd January, 13:25
Subject: Re: A bit sensitive

Thanks, honey. I'll stick with the 9th of April, if you're definitely definitely sure you (and Dan) are OK with it.

And yes, Tuesday. Shaunna's going to try and pop out for half an hour if the salon's not too busy.

Did we say 11 o'clock? I can't remember.
x

From: Adele
Sent: Sunday 22nd January, 14:16
Subject: Re: A bit sensitive

Yeah, it was 11. See you then. And it's fine I promise!

A x

***

14:25, Dan [mobile]
Stop stressing - looking forward to wetting the head of that littlun.

14:26, Ellie [mobile]
OK. Thanks Dan. x

14:28, Andy [mobile]
Me too! See you Tues. x

14:29, Ellie [mobile]
Hmm. It's a christening Andrew, not a stag do! 11 on Tuesday - don't be late! x

14:31, Andy [mobile]
OK boss :) x

ROOMS WITHOUT VIEWS
Monday 23rd January

They stood, arms folded, yellow hard hats propped casually on heads, rigger booted feet almost a yard apart, the two of them. Identically posed, like figures in a life-sized Lego construction scene, they watched from the other side of the street, as the crane swung away from the warehouse and came to rest. Dan took his hard hat off and scratched his head. He looked at his brother; each nodded and smiled. They crossed the road and began unclipping the wire fencing.

Inside, they were stood, arms folded, rock band t-shirt hems scrunched up around hands in black jeans pockets, New Rock booted feet with heels together, baseball booted feet below crossed ankles; the two of them. Not identically posed, indeed, more like an audience at a very poorly attended gig, they watched from across the studio, as the cables dropped down between the iron girders and coiled into a vast, industrial, rubberised sleeping snake on the stage. Krissi pushed her hair behind her ear and glanced sideways. Jason pretended not to notice, but his smile gave him away. Seconds later a third person appeared on the stage.

"If we run these along this wall," he called across, "and then back to the control room behind there, yeah?"

"Cool. Cheers, Stu," Jason said. Stu—the guy on the stage, who was also dressed in black t-shirt and jeans—nodded and rooted out a cable end from the heap.

"I still think this is completely insane," Krissi said, shifting her weight from one leg to the other. "It's gonna cost a fortune to heat, and what about sound-proofing? There's no way…"

"Listen to Miss Negativity there," Andy said, coming up behind them. She shoved with her elbow and caught him in the solar plexus.

"Well, it's true," she defended. "This place is massive, and in all honesty I'm struggling to think of three local bands, never mind, like, the hundred a month you're gonna need to keep things ticking over."

"Three?" Jason said incredulously. "I can name at least twenty off the top of my head!"

"Go on then," Krissi challenged.

"Crimson Cemetery, James Dean's Not Dead, Raven Heartspill, Roach Reunion, Gods of War…"

"Yeah, all right. I stand corrected."

"Hey, I only got to five!"

"Yeah, but it's actually only the same five musos who all swap instruments and clothes. You know, like Slipknot is the same band as Stone Sour?"

"It's not! It's only Corey…"

"Not interested," Krissi cut him off.

"Plus there's all those cheesy indie bands you're mates with."

"They're not indie!" She walked away before there was any further argument. Jason turned and looked at Andy. He shrugged.

"I did do my research."

"You don't need to convince me," Andy said. He could get a basic rhythm out of a drum kit, but that was more or less the limit of his musical knowledge. Oh, and he could name pretty much every member of every early nineties BritPop band.

"Right, Jay," Dan appeared in the doorway. He strode across the vast, dark studio. "That's the last of the ventilation pipes in situ. The crane's gone, so we'll tell them to crack on with the tarmac."

"Awesome," Jason said, shaking Dan's hand, then Andy's. "Thanks, both."

"No problem," Dan smiled. "And we're on schedule to be done well before the fifteenth of April."

Jason nodded, impressed.

"You can expect the heating guys to be done by the end of the week…"

Dan continued, as Krissi came back into the studio, two paper cups clasped by their rims between a finger and thumb of each hand. She just caught the end of Dan's detailing of who was coming in and when.

"Shit," she said. Andy grabbed two of the hot cups from her and passed one to his brother. Krissi gave one of the others to Jason and shook her burning hand. The three men glanced into their cups and started to laugh.

"What's funny?" Krissi asked.

"Nothing," Dan said, rubbing her head paternally. "Your mother must be very proud."

"I'd wait till you taste it first. That machine's definitely not working right." She nodded towards the door, outside of which a vending machine, installed the previous week and currently producing highly variable facsimiles of the hot beverages it portended. Andy sipped carefully at his cup.

"Not up to Shaunna's or Alice's exacting standards, I'll admit, but it tastes fine to me."

"I'll give the company a call later," Jason said. "Get them to come and check it over—again." As he said this, his phone started up. He groaned and took it out of his pocket as he walked away.

"Faith No More," Andy observed. "Cool ring tone!" Krissi raised her eyebrows in query. "I can play the drum riff from 'Epic'," he explained. Krissi nodded and said nothing, continuing to watch Jason just outside the door.

"He doesn't look very happy," Dan observed.

"How can you tell?" she joked, as her friend's moody 'goth' demeanour didn't fluctuate much in company. "That's the ring tone for his dad, and they've been at it for weeks. Apparently, he was gutted that Jay didn't ask him to be a trustee, so then he did ask him and he refused. Told him he was in retirement."

Dan nodded. "Yep, sounds just like Bill."

Andy was standing quietly, staring up into the girders.

"What's up with you?" Dan asked him.

"Huh? Oh! Nothing. I was just going through the lyrics in my head."

Dan and Krissi made eye contact and then both rolled their eyes at the same time. Yes, the Jeffries genes were strong, just like the personality and wilfulness that went with them.

"Awesomely," Jason said as he walked towards them, although stormed may well have been a better way to describe the motion, "he's coming down to check on how *we're* doing. We! He's winding me up, right?"

"Yeah, probably," Krissi consoled.

"Well, *we* are gonna leave you to it," Dan said. He and Andy finished the last of their tea.

"It wasn't that bad," Andy said with a shudder. Krissi laughed and shook her head.

"Maybe I won't be inviting Mum down just yet," she grinned.

"Any problems, give us a shout, all right, Jay?" Dan said.

"Yeah, thanks again." Jason and Krissi watched Dan and Andy leave.

"Indie," Jason muttered.

"Not indie."

"It is."

"Not."

"Is."

"Not playing." Krissi walked away. Jason smiled and followed.

***

Dan and Andy climbed into the 4x4 and sat in silence, looking back at the warehouse. It was really starting to take shape, and Dan was thinking he might just have to eat his words. When Jason first asked him to be a trustee, he'd been reluctant, but agreed, because he wouldn't have been anywhere near as successful in his business without Alistair Campion's support and felt that he owed him. He'd been waiting ever since for Jason to offload the money and the responsibility, all the while listening without comment to what seemed like pipe dreams of 1950s diners and music studios. But credit to him, he really had done his homework. The diner had opened just before Christmas and seemed to be off to a decent start. Now the studio was past the halfway mark. It looked like Campion Community Trust was a runner after all.

"You're miles away there, bro," Andy said.

"Yeah. I was just thinking about Alistair and Jason."

"What about them?"

"I never thought he'd do it. Get the Trust up and running. But the more time I spend with him, the more I come to realise how like his father he really is." Dan put his seatbelt on and Andy followed suit.

"I didn't know Campion well enough to comment," he said.

"No. I'll tell you what, though. Krissi freaks me out a bit these days."

"Why?"

"I dunno. She's like a mix of you, Shaunna, Kris, me…"

"And the rest of them."

"Them?"

"The Circle?"

"The bloody circle." Dan started the engine and moved off. "I'll swing for Tom Kerry the next time I see him."

"Yeah. Maybe that's not such a wise move, considering you stole his wife."

"He stole my girlfriend, you mean."

"Whatever."

"Meaning?"

"Nothing, bro." Andy turned away and looked out of the passenger window. Neither of them spoke for the rest of the journey back to their mother's house, where Dan pulled up outside the gates.

"You coming in?" Andy asked.

"Nah. I need to get home and shower. Apparently we're at the out-laws' this evening."

"Nice. Well, I'm gonna shower and get an early night—see if I can fit a workout in before I meet Ellie in the morning and get the 12:30 train."

"You want some company?"

"If you like. It'll be an early one."

"I'll give it a miss then, if it's all the same to you."

"OK. Have a good evening."

"Cheers, bro. See you when you get back."

"Yeah." Andy climbed out and turned back to close the door. "Friday."

"Friday?" Dan queried.

"I'm gonna catch up with some friends while I'm down there."

"Ah right. Enjoy. Love to Mum."

Andy slammed the car door shut and waved briefly. Dan raised a hand in response and reversed back onto the road. Friends, he thought. That's what he'd said the last time, when they dropped him off after the Chinese meal, then gossiped about it all the way home. The kind of friends, Adele had analysed, who wear patchouli oil based perfume and, Alice later observed, made his brother's scent turn sky blue; the kind, Dan had noticed, without comment, who left shocking pink lipstick on collars, and lovebites on necks. Young, unconventional and adventurous: that was the profile Josh had given and once again he'd been spot on. This time though, with Bertie having departed for Mali that morning, his brother's cryptic response left him mystified. It had been four months and three girlfriends since Andy and Jess split up, each one less conventional than her predecessor, and none of them formally introduced. But then, Dan thought, he shouldn't really be that surprised. He parked up outside the flat. Time to find out what Adele thought. He opened the door. All was quiet.

"Adele?"

"In here," she called from little Shaunna's room. He frowned and went in.

"What's up. Ah." He looked down at his daughter. Very spotty.

"Chicken pox," Adele said.

"Guess we're not going anywhere then."

"Guess not."

"Shame."

"Yeah." Adele sighed. "Shall I phone for a curry?"

"Sounds good," Dan said. "I'll stick some drinks in the fridge for later." He grabbed her from behind and kissed her neck.

"Must be all that thinking about Sally-Anne," she teased. Dan released her.

"Yeah. That'd be it. Best not tell my mother you've got the hots for Len, either," he said. Adele let out a high-pitched 'ha' and followed him out of the room.

***

"What do you want to eat?" Krissi shouted from the kitchen. Jason was lying on the sofa, reading a music magazine.

"Dunno. Are you cooking?" he shouted back. Krissi came through and shoved his legs up so she could sit. He put them over her lap, big heavy boots and all. She pushed them off and they fell to the floor with a thud.

"Ouch!" Jason sat up and rubbed his lower back.

"Do you want me to cook?"

"Isn't it your turn?"

"Yeah, but…" She stopped, uncertain how best to go on. He put down the magazine and scrutinised her face. She smiled, but it didn't disguise her anxiety. "It's just that, well, you've not eaten properly for weeks, Jay."

"I am eating properly."

"You're losing weight again."

"No I'm not," he protested. He stood up and lifted his baggy t-shirt, showing off his tiny waist, his ribs visible through his pale skin. Krissi poked his hollow belly.

"Yes, you are."

He sat down again and sighed.

"D'you want to talk about it?" she asked.

"No."

"OK. But will you try and eat with me tonight? You don't have to eat very much. Just a little bit, to make sure your tablets work."

He inhaled, getting ready to protest, but noticed the continued concern in her eyes. She was a good friend and she didn't nag, much.

"All right," he said. "After all, I don't really want to start having fits again, do I?" He swung his legs back over her lap.

"Thanks!" she said, shoving them off again. She knew that really he was doing it for her. "So, what would you like?" He shrugged. "Something simple and easy on the tummy—how about egg, mash and beans?"

"Yeah, cool." He picked up his magazine again, following her with his eyes as she got up and walked across the room. He waited a couple of minutes and then went to join her in the kitchen.

"Need any help?" he asked, picking up one of the potatoes she had just put next to the sink. She handed him a vegetable peeler, took a knife from the drawer and began on another of the potatoes.

"I'm sorry I keep going on," she said, keeping her eyes focused on what she was doing. "I worry about you."

"I know."

"And sometimes I think—well, that you use being veggie as an excuse."

"That's so not true," he said in a tone that was supposed to be a pretence of being offended, although his potato peeling had become a little more sharp and jerky.

"Jay." She stopped and put her hand on his arm. "I'm not going to have a go, but you know my mum's friend Josh is a counsellor?"

"Yeah, obviously." He was getting defensive now. She needed to say it and move on before he shut her out.

"That's all really. If you decide you need to talk to someone about whatever it is that's bothering you, he's a good listener. And he won't tell anyone anything you've said."

He'd finished peeling the potato and held it out to her. She swapped it for one with its skin on and he huffed.

After they'd eaten, Jason lay with his legs over her once again, and this time she kept hold of them. She was pretty sure he didn't go and vomit after he'd eaten. In fact, she didn't really think he had an eating disorder. He just didn't eat. Even so, she wasn't taking any chances. Jason knew what she was doing and spent the rest of the evening switching his attention between the appalling film they were watching, which was some kind of action hero nonsense with Bruce Willis, and watching Krissi's facial expressions change without her conscious knowledge. Every so often, she'd glance his way and smile, but no words passed between them. He wasn't going to speak to Josh, not yet. Maybe a time would come when he wanted to talk about it, but he wasn't ready. Still, he made a silent promise to himself and to her in that moment: he would start eating properly, and regularly. At least that would be one less stress in his life.

RELEASE
Tuesday 24ᵗʰ January

The room in the 'halfway house' was all right, Hadyn supposed, now that he'd cleaned and put a dust cover on the mattress. And the other people staying there were so-so. The bloke in the room below his was schizophrenic, although he didn't hear voices or see things and that made no sense. In the room next door was another bloke of his age, with the same ABH conviction, but not much else. He couldn't read or write and said he had ADHD. That's what they all said inside. The other room was empty, and Hadyn was optimistic that they'd fill it before Darren got released. He really didn't want to be reacquainted. Even the thought of it made him feel a bit sick.

It was just a little before 6 a.m. and his first morning of waking up on the outside. He'd imagined he would be elated, but he felt nothing. That wasn't true; he felt something, but he couldn't pin it down. It was the same feeling he'd got each time they moved to a new flat when he was younger, so he guessed it was just a sense of displacement. Anyway, today he was meeting with the psychologist, so maybe he'd ask about that, see what he thought. But that wasn't until eleven o'clock. He lay there a moment or so longer, waiting on...

No prison bells here, Marigold.

He got up, stretched, lifted the curtain. Dark. Wet. Dirty street. He dropped the curtain again and put on his shoes, to go to the bathroom. He was going to try and get rid of that habit, because the floors here looked clean, yet he just knew they weren't, and what if, so soon after release, he stood on a piece of glass or a nail or something, and got an infection? He might not even notice, and it would get worse, become gangrenous. Shoes. They were sensible, not irrational. He tiptoed, as quietly as he could, to the bathroom, locked the door behind him and washed his hands. He took a pee, flushed the toilet, washed his hands. He turned on the shower, ran his hands under the light sprinkling of the water.

To check the temperature.

The shower was warm. He stripped off and stepped underneath. Warm, but weak. It would take an age to get washed properly, to get thoroughly clean, in this. He closed his eyes, soaped his body with shower gel, and again, and again. The suds were soft and plentiful. He opened his eyes and studied in wonder the inches of white bubbles piling up around him. He could barely see his feet. He was clean. He knew, yet he would need to touch the shower dial to switch it off, and then he would be dirty again. And what about the lock on the door? He should've bought gloves yesterday.

You can't wear gloves in the shower.

Once the bubbles had run away a little, he carefully stepped out, using his towel as a shield to turn off the shower. It got wet. He did his best to dry himself, used the towel again to unlock the door, opened it slightly, wrapped the damp towel around his waist and stepped onto the landing. His shoes. He'd forgotten his shoes. Now his feet would be dirty. He returned inside the bathroom, pushed the door shut with his bottom, washed his feet in the sink, dried them with the towel, struggled to push his damp toes inside his shoes, repeated the open the door with the towel and wrap around waist procedure and stepped outside once more. It was exhausting.

Back to his room: he heard the bloke in the next room moving around, a door open and close, a low grumbling voice, swearing, fading from hearing, another door open and close, silence, a toilet flush, the voice getting louder again. A knock. He jumped.

Cautiously, he opened his door a couple of inches and peered through the gap.

"Alright?" his neighbour smiled, showing off the dark space of his missing front tooth.

"Alright?" he answered.

"Can you close the bathroom door after you, ta." The bloke plodded back to his room. The door opened, and closed.

He's just like me. But I know and he doesn't.

Clothes on, hair towel dried, still crew-cut short. He went downstairs to eat breakfast. Another trial to behold. He searched through all the bowls until he found one he thought he could stand to use, then the same for the spoon, washed them both, dried them, washed them again.

Just fucking stop it, Marigold.

He put them down, spooned bran flakes in, for fear of the dirt on the outside of the box getting inside the bowl, inside his body. This was worse. Far far worse than it had been for a good few months now. Four hours until he saw the psychologist. He'd tell him all about it. Doctor Tierney, that's what Doctor Sheridan had called him. He worked at the hospital and the hospice, but he was to go to the university. He'd never been to a university. They were big and full of people, and dust and dirt. Maybe there would be automatic doors. There would be toilets he could use, where he could wash his hands. Wash off the dust and the dirt. He could get some gloves on the way there. Go and see Doctor Tierney, tell him all about it.

Get cured. Ha.

Breakfast done, he poured himself a drink of orange juice, into a newly washed and rewashed glass, washed and put away his breakfast things, returned to his room, and sat, watching the daylight growing outside. It was a dark, gloomy morning and he didn't want to go out there, into the dirty world, but he had to. Today was the first day of the rest of his life. Free.

Except I'm not.

Free from prison he might be, but this OCD was a prison in itself. He was determined to beat it. Once and for all.

At ten minutes to nine, Hadyn stepped out of the front door, pulled it closed behind him and walked, without looking back, even though every part of his being was screaming, his heart banging faster, faster.

People don't wash their hands. They go to the toilet, then touch the door handle.

He pushed on, breathing. Deep breath in. And out. He kept walking, walking, the shops coming into view up ahead. Walking, walking.

They put their hands down their pants, then touch the door handle. I touched the door handle. I need to wash my hands.

He would not give in to this. He had to make it. What was it Callaghan had said? Baby steps. He looked in front of him, towards the corner of the street. If he could make it to there, that was success. He made it, stopped, exhaled slowly. Next: across the road. The panic was flowing away from him, almost as if he had loosened the drawstrings around the bottoms of his pants and it had all swooshed out onto the pavement. He refused to look down, to see the disgusting, discarded chewing gum, the smudges of dog turd. He would not look down. Onward to the next corner, across another road.

Nailed it, Hadyn!

He smiled and nodded to himself, remembered he had his MP3 player and batteries. And money to buy more. What a luxury! He stuck the earphones in his ears and pressed play. Metallica. Great times. He felt his feet fall in time with "Wherever I May Roam".

Free.

Not entirely free, of course. The meeting with Doctor Tierney was a couple of hours away, and he was looking forward to it, although he was nervous. He imagined that if he refused to go, he'd be in breach of his licence and end up straight back inside. Then this afternoon he was meeting with Stella, his probation officer. She'd called him yesterday, to make sure he was settling in. She seemed nice enough, if not a little abrupt. Then to work this evening: only three hours this first time. They were going to show him around, how to work the floor buffers, what he had to do. He'd reached the shopping centre. Now to get inside. He approached, hesitating just outside the doors, optimistic that a sensor would pick him out and the doors would swing open accordingly. When this didn't happen, he tried to think what to do. He could pull his sleeve over his hand, but then his coat would need to be washed and it was easier to wash his hands. As he was in the process of talking himself into this option, another person exited via the door in front of him. He quickly sneaked past, just making it through the gap. He was in! He glanced around, trying to orientate himself to this new place. They'd said he could go home, if he'd wanted to, but he didn't.

Not back to him!

He moved forward, almost gliding, towards the escalator positioned in the centre of the concourse, dead ahead. All he needed was a discount shop, or a supermarket, or a hardware store—anywhere that sold latex gloves. At the top of the escalator, he spotted it. A chemist. They would sell them, he was sure. Pleased he had reached his destination so quickly and with relatively little distress, he allowed himself a quick smile and stepped off the escalator, to be intercepted by a man selling cable TV.

"No thanks," he mumbled quickly and kept moving. That's what they'd taught him.

He's not deliberately trying to wind you up.

Still the man persisted.

"No. Thank you!" he repeated, put up his arm to block the intrusion.

"Alright, pal. There's no need to get shirty."

He's not deliberately trying to wind you up. Keep moving.

He stepped inside the shop, panting, shaking.

"Are you OK, son?" The woman from behind the counter advanced on him. He took a breath, shook his head frantically.

"Don't touch me!"

She backed off. He nodded his gratitude.

"Need some gloves. Latex gloves."

"We're waiting for a delivery, got none in, sorry. The discount shop just across the way has them." She stepped slightly closer. "You don't look so well, son. I can go and get them for you, if you like?"

"No, I'm OK." He steadied his breathing. "Thank you." He left.

"What was that about?" the pharmacist asked.

"Agoraphobia, I reckon."

The cable TV man left well alone this time, and Hadyn made it all the way to the discount shop without further intervention. The door was wedged open. He went in, wandered the aisles, unseeing, unsure where he might find the gloves, not wanting to ask anyone, not quite convinced he was in control. Up and down, up and down. No gloves.

Ask for help.

"Excuse me. Do you sell latex gloves?"

"Yep. Just up there." She smiled and pointed past him. He followed the arm to the end of the finger—manicured, neat, clean—to the place indicated.

"Thank you." He found the gloves, paid for them and fled, searching now for a public toilet, where he could wash away the dirt from the coins in his pocket. Up another floor, so many people, too much dirt, pursuing the signs. Female cleaner.

You call that cleaning?

He stood in front of the sink, pushed on the tap. A slow trickle of water. Soap: none. He used the water, rubbing and scrubbing with his thumbs and fingertips, into every crease between his fingers, around his nails, rubbing and scrubbing, scrubbing and rubbing.

Just fucking stop it, Marigold.

He stopped.

Like he had fought to shove his wet feet into shoes, so now did he push and pull at the gloves, ripping holes in and fingers off three, before he got a full pair over his hands. He let out an enormous sigh and walked away, finally calm. The shopping centre clock said it was just coming up to ten: time, then, to take a slow, leisurely walk up to the university and find Doctor Tierney's office. Now he had gloves it was easy.

***

Sean finished off the academic reference he was typing before he answered the knock at the door. He wasn't sure why. Nothing Diane had told him suggested he needed to start the session with a deliberate move to get the upper hand. Psychologist's instinct, maybe?

"Come in," he called.

The door handle turned very, very slowly. Sean watched, bemused. The door opened and a young man came into view. He stepped inside and quietly closed the door. He turned back to face Sean and smiled. Sean returned the smile.

"Hadyn?" He stood, held out a hand, saw the gloves. Hadyn shook the offered hand. "Have a seat, there," he said. He indicated to the chairs—cleared of books, journals and paper, for once. In fact, his office was far less cluttered than usual, because for some reason he'd considered that an OCD sufferer wouldn't cope so well with the amount of junk he lived and worked with. Josh had enough trouble, and he wasn't OC. Well, he wasn't diagnosed, but it was safe to say that he fitted most of the criteria. There again, so did most people, to varying extents.

"Doctor Tierney," Hadyn responded. "Thank you for agreeing to see me."

"Oh, it's no trouble at all. I'd offer you a drink, but I don't think I've any clean mugs." He knew he didn't, and even if they were 'Tierney clean', they wouldn't be up to scratch for the gloved young chap sitting before him, perched on the very edge of the seat, a look of moderate disgust etched on his face. "Perhaps," Sean suggested, "we could have a chat and adjourn to the café in a while. Let's see how we go."

Hadyn nodded his acceptance—of the suggestion, at least. They were still both eyeing each other up, trying to work out what it was they were dealing with. Another knock at the door broke the silence.

"Come in," Sean called warily. He was uncertain how Hadyn would react to an immediate interruption to his first session. The door opened and George came in.

"Hi, Sean. Sorry to disturb you, but I was wondering if you've seen Josh this morning?"

"Is he not in the lecture theatre? L2, I think it is?"

"Ah. OK. I just tried everywhere but there. Cheers." He turned to leave and spotted Sean's visitor.

"Hello, Hadyn," he said, his surprise apparent. He held out his hand. "I've washed them, just," he added. Hadyn stood and shook hands again, feeling very happy with himself for doing so.

"Hello, Mr. Morley," he smiled, pleased to see a face he recognised.

"You're looking good, man. When did you get out?"

"Yesterday."

"And how's it going?"

"Not so bad. You'd be proud of me."

"OK?"

"A bloke in the shopping centre tried to sell me cable TV and I freaked out at first, but then I walked away."

"Well done, Hadyn. That's great."

Sean was watching this whole interchange in total wonder.

"Thanks," Hadyn said. He noticed Sean's attentiveness and felt he should explain. "Mr. Morley took most of our anger management sessions in prison. They've helped me loads, because I'd always get so worked up before, thinking people were getting in my face on purpose."

"Oh, right," Sean said, as if the information was entirely novel to him. In his head, he was calling Diane Sheridan every name under the sun, for her role in losing him his star pupil.

"But now I can think, and I keep reminding myself that they don't know about my OCD."

"How is it, Hadyn?" George asked. "I'm guessing it's pretty bad." He indicated to Hadyn's gloved hands with his eyes.

"Yeah. I think it'll settle down, though, once I'm used to being on the outside again."

"You're probably right," George agreed. "Anyway, it's great to see you."

"You too, Mr. Morley. And thanks for all your help."

"No problem." George smiled, then thought for a moment. "You know, I'm not a counsellor anymore, but if you like, we could stay in touch, and I can be around to help you out, while you adjust." He looked to Sean as he said this. Sean shrugged.

"Oh, you don't have to do that," Hadyn said.

"No, but I'd like to."

"OK, then. Thanks." Hadyn smiled—a big, genuine, beaming smile.

"Cool," George said. "I'll get your address off Doctor Tierney—and you call me George now, you know. See you soon." He left. Sean watched Hadyn and then sat back in his chair.

"Well, I suppose we best have a think about where we go from here," he said thoughtfully. "Why don't you tell me a little bit about yourself, Hadyn."

"OK, Doctor Tierney," he said. He turned so that he was sitting bolt upright and directly facing Sean. "Erm, I've got OCD about things being dirty and it gets worse when I'm stressed. I got done for ABH when I attacked a debt collector who came to our house, looking for my stepdad. He's a big, ugly bastard, my stepdad, and beats me and my brother up. He's not very nice to my mum either. I passed all my GCSEs, but got kicked out of school for fighting, and I was still on a two year suspended for assaulting my boss at the factory, which was why they sent me down. And, well, that's it really."

"All right, now, that wasn't quite what I had in mind," Sean said. "Tell me about *you*—your interests, hobbies, things you like, things you don't, what you want to do with your life—that kind of thing?"

"Oh." Hadyn thought for a moment. "I love music. Listening to it, writing it. I write songs, not proper music, just chords and stuff, and lyrics. I hate having OCD and want to get better. Then I'll think about the rest of it."

"Goodness. I'm impressed. Thanks for being so open with me. I quite often have to prompt people a fair bit."

"I bet you don't usually work with cons, though. We only got twenty minutes on our own, and Doctor Sheridan said we just had to get it out in the open."

"Ah, I understand." Sean didn't imagine Doctor Sheridan had imposed the same time restrictions on a certain GP inmate. At some point, he was going to have raise the matter of Kevin Callaghan with Hadyn, but not just yet. He needed to build his trust first.

"She was nice to me, Doctor Sheridan," Hadyn continued. "All the others, including the screws, called me Marigold, cos of the gloves, but she didn't. She always used my name."

"You didn't like them calling you Marigold."

91

"No. I hated it. Made me angry, and they knew that. Cos it was fun to wind me up. Not that they were picking on me especially. Everyone does it to everyone else inside, cos there's not much to do, is there? And then I'd just fucking lose it and they'd do it even more. The screws'd take my gloves away and then I'd be stressing about the dirt. And Callaghan, he said…" Hadyn stopped talking. He wasn't sure if he was allowed to mention Callaghan in these sessions.

"What did he say, Hadyn?" Sean asked, hardly able to believe his luck, that Hadyn had brought him up without prompting, but he needed to stay professional. The point of this session was to assess where his new client was up to in his treatment, not to satisfy his own curiosity. Hadyn was frowning. Sean shook off the temptation. "Did you know him well?" he asked.

"Sort of. As well as you know anyone. He was on a different floor to me. The loony floor, although he wasn't that mad, not like some of the others. Like when I'd say to him about the shit on the walls, and I knew there wasn't any there really, but I just felt like there was all this dirt there you couldn't see, and there's a bloke in C221 deliberately gets it on his hands and rubs them along the wall, just to piss me off, so I could see it there even when I knew it was gone. The germs. All that bacteria. Nasty stuff, shit. So Callaghan'd say it's real to you, and that's what counts. He saw some crazy things, though."

"Hmm," Sean said, rubbing his chin, his fingers rasping against the stubble. He hadn't shaved since Friday and probably looked rough as hell. He felt rough as hell. He resisted the temptation yet again. "Maybe we can talk a little more about Kevin Callaghan next time we meet," he suggested. "Today, we need to sort out where you're up to with your treatment."

"What about the anger management?"

"Well, from what you're telling me, I think if we can get your OCD in order, then the anger will sort itself, with a little help from George. I'll chat to him about that later."

"It's weird, all this openness," Hadyn said, playing with the cuff of one of his gloves. His hands were getting sweaty and it was starting to agitate him.

"There's a bathroom just across the way out there," Sean told him. Hadyn nodded and left the room, giving Sean a few minutes to think over what he'd heard and seen so far. Hadyn certainly did seem to have his head screwed on, and demonstrated significant insight into his own problems, which was a big part of the battle already won. Whatever Diane had been doing was working, and it was, as is often the case, a mix of a variety of therapeutic interventions. The door opened quietly and Hadyn returned, smiling briefly as he resumed his seat.

"Tell me," Sean said, "how would it have felt if I'd asked you not to put another pair of gloves on?"

Hadyn became flustered and started fidgeting.

"It makes you anxious to think about it, doesn't it?"

He nodded.

"It's OK. We're going to aim to do that in a few sessions' time, but not yet, so don't panic."

"Doctor Sheridan said that I needed to stop wearing gloves once I was released, although I've got a cleaning job, so it will be OK to wear gloves for that, won't it?"

"Of course, Hadyn. A very sensible move, for sure. The thing is, I know my office isn't the tidiest of places, but it's clean enough."

"I know. It's not about the dirt, is it Doctor Tierney?"

"It's not. You're quite right." Sean waited, for he could feel that Hadyn was about to give him the full autobiography. What he wanted to hear was *his* story, rather than the one which Diane, or any other well-meaning professional, might have fed him. He wasn't very optimistic, so Hadyn's next words took him pleasantly by surprise.

"Callaghan—he was a doctor once—said that I needed to be honest with Doctor Sheridan, tell her everything that I told him, about how my stepdad made me feel, because that's when my OCD started. When I told her, she said I should write it all down, before I started talking about it, because talking about it plants ideas in your head that aren't yours."

All right, so maybe he'd misjudged Diane. No, he hadn't. She was still an obnoxious, self-serving bitch, but she could be good at her job, when it suited her.

"Did you write it all down?"

"Yeah." Hadyn reached inside his coat and pulled out a wad of dog-eared A4 lined paper. He passed it to Sean. "Nobody's ever read it, though. Except Callaghan."

Sean paused in his careful unfolding. "Are you happy for me to read it, Hadyn?"

He nodded. "That's why I brought it. Got to get better, Doctor Tierney. I'm not going back to prison."

"OK, so shall I read it now? I ask only because there's an awful lot to read and it will take up much of our time today."

"What do you think would be best?"

"I think we should use the time to draw up a draft schedule, to help you keep some routine. I'll read this before I see you next. How does that sound?"

"Great, Doctor Tierney."

"Good stuff." Sean loaded his calendar on-screen. "Now, Hadyn. It's perfectly acceptable for you to call me by my first name, OK? And that's Sean."

"All right, Sean," Hadyn smiled. He was still fidgety and anxious, but for the rest of the time they chatted in broad terms about when his sessions would be, what they would cover in each one, and how they fitted into his day-to-day routine. Sean set him homework, initially consisting of not wearing gloves whenever he was in his own room, and if he felt he could cope, leaving them off whenever he was in the house. Diane had taught him some relaxation techniques to help with this too.

"Thanks, Sean," Hadyn said, shaking hands at the end of their time together. "It's been really helpful talking to you today."

"No problem, Hadyn. It's been good to meet you. When you're a bit better, you should have a think about careers, because you're quite a bright feller, you know."

"Yeah, that's what Callaghan said too." He had the other letter in his pocket and was desperate to share with Sean, but not today. He wasn't sure he could trust him. Not just yet.

STRANGERS
Thursday 26th January

Jess stepped out of the hotel bathroom and squeezed the excess water from her hair, trying to ignore her mobile phone ringing away on the bed. It would be her clients; it always was. The mediation process was a complete travesty, not least because she felt utterly inept undertaking it in the first place. As she'd told them, just because she'd done the training didn't necessarily mean she was an expert, and try as she might not to let them, she knew her own personal biases were influencing where things were heading.

Her clients: Beth Shipley, a thirty-six year old woman, who had left her husband of twelve years to cohabit with another woman in Reading, taking her two children with her, and her husband, Jonathan, whom Jess had known since primary school, and who wanted custody of the children, as did Beth. The reasons they had asked Jess to mediate were many. Her acquaintance with Jonathan was top of the list: he knew her well enough to feel comfortable talking to her, which was an important consideration, given that, like many of those who worked in IT, his social skills were significantly lacking. Second, it was assumed that her friendship with Kris and Shaunna meant she'd take a sensible stance on same sex parenting, which was true enough. The children's feelings were paramount, of course; however, they wanted to live with Mum *and* Dad, although in spite of their rather tender ages of eleven and nine, they had readily grasped the concept of joint custody and the benefits it would afford. Two lots of Christmas, birthdays, holidays; clothes and toys at both homes. It was an acceptable compromise, the children had said, trying to look suitably disappointed that their parents didn't love each other anymore. However, on the matter of joint custody, Beth and Jonathan didn't agree. Beth believed that the best place for children was with their mother; Jonathan contended that their mother was a harlot—yes, he actually used that word to describe her. How do you mediate that?

The phone had stopped ringing now, and Jess picked it up, glancing at the darkened screen. Just as she was considering whether it was worth checking to see if the call actually was from the Shipleys, it started ringing in her hand and made her jump. Not the Shipleys: she answered it.

"Hello?"

"Hey. You OK?"

"Yeah. Not bad. Bored out of my skull. You?"

"Yep. I'm fine. And I have the perfect antidote to your boredom."

"Which is?"

"Dinner."

Jess sighed and absently pushed at her cuticles with her thumbnail. "I'd love to, Andy, but I'm in Reading, remember?"

"What a coincidence! So am I."

She could feel herself smiling.

"Where would you like to meet?" he asked.

"Where are you now?"

"In the bar of your hotel."

"Give me ten minutes," she said and hung up.

Twenty-five minutes and another bottle of beer later, Jess arrived in the hotel bar, her hair still slightly damp. She was wearing grey jeans and an orange, cowl neck, mohair sweater. Andy watched her approach the bar, eyeing her up and down. She leaned across and kissed his cheek.

"Hi," he said, trying to sound casual, but not achieving it.

"Hi," she replied. She slid onto the barstool next to his and he handed her a beer. "Thanks."

"Surprised?"

"Yeah, you could say that," she said, swigging at the beer. She looked at him enquiringly.

"I was in London," Andy justified, "and I figured we might as well meet up while I was down this way."

She accepted his explanation with a shrug. He was still looking her over. He had done it a thousand times before, but this time it was making her feel uncomfortable.

"How's the case going?" he asked.

"Not well. Jonathan is one of the most stubborn, pigheaded, arrogant men I've ever come across. He was never this bad when we were younger."

Andy laughed. "You're kidding, right?"

"No. I'm serious. OK, I know he was a bit of a pain in the ass in sixth form, but that was nothing—not compared to the way he's acting now."

"Why? What's he up to?"

"The house they've got, back home? It's a four-bedroomed detached. It's huge. Obviously, Jonathan's living there on his own at the minute, because Beth brought the kids down here, but even when they were together, they were thinking of selling it and getting somewhere smaller. Jonathan's business isn't what it was. I've seen his accounts, so I know. But now, with the divorce going through and whatnot, he absolutely flat out refuses to put the house on the market—says he'd rather watch it get repossessed and lose everything than give Beth any more money."

96

Andy nodded thoughtfully. "You can't blame him for that. She did leave him for somebody else."

"I think he's more bothered about the fact that Lynette is loaded."

"That's Beth's girlfriend?"

"Yeah. And due credit to them, those children have really got their heads around it all. They can see the benefits of living with both parents. They don't even care that Lynette has children and they'd have to share with them. I think they just want it over and done with now, get a bit of normality back."

"I'm guessing you'd be pretty pleased too?" Andy said.

"Hmm," Jess sounded ambiguously.

It wasn't the specific request for her services, nor the flattery, nor the payment in advance; none of these factors in themselves would have been sufficient to persuade her to take on this job. She was doing it for distraction, and that was all there was to it. For whilst she was down in Reading, she didn't have to think about the tests, or the hospital, who kept calling and sending letters, reminding her that she had yet to go for her results. No doubt when she got home, there'd be a ton of missed calls and messages on the house phone.

"What are you thinking about?" Andy interrupted her train of thought.

"What? Oh, nothing much. Just pondering ways of convincing Jonathan to sell up."

And so, the conversation continued along these lines for the better part of the evening, but Andy knew there was something wrong. When she had walked into the bar, he couldn't take his eyes off her, and it had nothing to do with desire. She looked—sick. Her skin was dull, she'd lost weight, her hair, even taking into account that it was damp, was hanging lifelessly around her shoulders. There was something wrong, and he couldn't figure out what it was. Even if they'd still been on the same over-familiar terms that they'd enjoyed in the past, it was the kind of something she would never have shared with him. He could perhaps take some solace from that. Instead of attempting anything so complex as asking what it might be, they left the hotel and headed for a pizza restaurant, where he ordered a large 'house special' with eight different toppings, including very spicy beef and chorizo, whilst she picked at a small ham and pineapple thin crust, just about managing to eat half of it, before he ate the rest of that too, and then they moved on to the cinema, which was massive and modern, compared to their local one, although there were very few people around.

"Where are you staying?" Jess asked, as they walked back to her hotel afterwards.

"I'm not. I'm getting the last train back into the city, in..." Andy checked the time on his phone, "...fifteen minutes."

"Ah, OK." They stopped walking as they approached the hotel's front entrance. "Thanks for this evening. It's been really nice to spend some time with you again, after—"

"Yeah," Andy cut her off quickly. She reached up to give him a peck on the cheek and he looked down at his feet. He frowned.

"I'm sorry," Jess said. She stepped away from him. He shook his still downturned head. She followed the direction of his gaze, saw what he saw and closed her eyes.

"Jess?"

"Heavy period," she said dismissively. "I need to get to my room." She backed away quickly. "I'll give you a call when I get home, OK?" She ran up the stairs and in through the hotel door; a quick wave and she was out of sight. Andy stayed where he was for a minute longer, then jogged back to the train station.

BINGO
Saturday 4th February

They met up for their usual weekly walk through the woods. It was a bright and peaceful February morning: misty, with a light frost on the ground, but nothing too extreme and certainly nowhere near as cold as it had been over the previous few weeks. Even so, George was wearing a thick woollen coat and a beanie hat, as well as woolly socks, thermal underwear and jogging pants—so many layers, in fact, that he looked twice the size, and may well end up losing half a stone through perspiration alone. Kris was wearing a full set of Scandinavian layers—denim parker, hat, scarf, the most outrageously colourful stripy jumper, jeans over long johns, boot socks and hiking boots. George looked him up and down and burst out laughing.

"Hey! At least we'll be warm and toasty!" Kris said, as they watched a man in a light anorak march past, puffing and panting, his cheeks reddish purple with cold. His two greyhounds, suitably coated up, slinked along behind him.

"You look like a kids' TV host," George said, as they set off along the path between the barren, leafless trees.

"Don't say that," Kris groaned. "That callback I had?" He let Casper off his lead and watched as the Labrador tore off along the path ahead.

"That bad was it?"

"No. It went really well."

George frowned. "So why the long face?"

"She wants me to do a second one. The casting director, that is."

"Right. That's a good thing, surely?"

"Well, kind of. Mia—the casting director—bought me lunch the other day. She said I was perfect for the role. Exactly what they had in mind."

George winced and stopped walking. In spite of the socks, a stone had still flipped into his boot; he leaned on Kris to steady himself. Kris staggered, then grabbed his arm and they both nearly fell over.

"So what's the problem?" George asked, still standing on one foot, shaking his up-ended boot and waiting for the stone to fall out. When nothing happened, he tipped it and peered inside. The tiniest piece of gravel rolled out, hit him on the chin, and dropped to the floor.

"The producer and the writer are a husband and wife team."

"And?" George put his boot back on and they set off once more.

"Mia asked on my behalf if the character could come from somewhere else, but the writer's dead set on him being from Manchester. Apparently there's loads of flashbacks to the gay club scene in the 1990s."

"I didn't think it was a gay character."

"Ah, well, they gave us a section of script to run through in the callback. You won't believe this," Kris said dramatically. He put his gloved hand on George's arm, stopping him in his tracks. George turned slowly and looked at him. "DI Mark Lundberg—that's the character—has been happily married for years, but he's got a hidden past."

George started laughing again. Kris glared at him.

"That's hysterical."

"I haven't told Shaunna, yet."

"Hmm. Good luck with that one."

"It's not going to happen," Kris said, sounding only slightly disappointed. "I can't get the accent right."

"So have they knocked you back?"

"They want to run the scene, in character."

"When?"

"Tuesday."

George nodded and walked on. Kris followed.

"I'm screwed," he said.

"Is your Manchester accent really that bad?"

"It's shit," Kris sighed, then, by way of illustration, called Casper. "Come 'ere, Casper, lad. Eee, it's friggin' Baltic, innit?"

This time George ended up laughing so much he was nearly choking. "Yeah, that's pretty shit," he said, when he finally stopped, several minutes later, and with tears streaming down his face.

They'd reached the spring at the end of the woods, but it was too cold for the dogs to play in it today, with icicles along the banks, suspended from long fallen branches and decaying clumps of leaves and grass. Instead, Blue went off to greet a border collie that was lying low, in wait, eyes fixed on a tennis ball thrower in its owner's hand. The woman extended her arm and the tennis ball catapulted through the trees. The collie shot off like a bullet and caught it on the bounce. Blue stood and watched, fascinated, then lolloped off after the collie to watch the whole process again, standing nearby, his eyes flitting between dog and owner. Casper, meanwhile, was rolling in something stinky on the path up ahead. It turned out to be fox excrement.

A little while later, they met a man with two black retrievers, both elderly and ploddy with wobbly back legs. They always saw the same people and dogs, amongst them the man with the retrievers, the woman with the collie, the old guy with the old English sheep dog that stank to high heaven, although they hadn't figured out if the smell was the dog or his owner; looking at the pair of them, it could well be both. There was also a woman with spaniels, with whom they frequently stopped to chat, but she wasn't out this morning. After the black retrievers, they saw just one other person: a bent over older woman with a Westie in a tartan coat. It set George off pondering over whether he was brave enough to do what Josh had almost accidentally volunteered him for a few weeks ago, when they were at the Chinese restaurant. He'd been thinking about it a lot since, and had come to realise that sooner or later he'd have to do it anyway.

They'd completed the circuit of the woods and the day was becoming increasingly damp and dreary, with that curious weather phenomenon sometimes referred to as 'mizzle' setting in around them. Kris had left Shaunna and Ade at home, both of them lamenting their terrible colds. Josh was due back from work in half an hour, so they agreed to call it a morning.

As they reached the gate, they both paused to clip leads back on collars.

"What you up to tonight?" George asked.

"Nothing. Why?"

"Do you fancy going out?"

"You and me?"

"Yeah. Just the two of us. There's some people I want to introduce you to."

Kris examined him suspiciously, but George wasn't giving any more than this away. "OK, I think," he agreed, although still looked a little doubtful.

"Cool. I'll come to yours for half six," George confirmed, before he headed for home. No need to bath Blue today; the earth was frozen solid. He arrived back just before Josh did, and was busy peeling off his multiple layers. Josh put his hands up inside George's jumper and he squealed at how cold they were.

***

That evening, dead on six-thirty, George knocked on Kris and Shaunna's front door, as arranged. Shaunna answered. Kris was still in the bathroom, having decided at the last minute that he needed to shave. George had to admit that Shaunna didn't look very well, her nose shiny and red, her voice croaky. He heard coughing from the lounge.

"Maybe I should've worn a surgical mask," he joked, as he stepped into the hallway, taking the tea towel from Casper and hanging it on the end of the banister.

"Hey, George," Ade waved at him, as he wandered out of the lounge on his way to the kitchen.

"Hi," George waved back.

"You going straight out?" he asked.

"Yeah, I hope so." He glanced up the stairs optimistically. The toilet flushed and Kris appeared on the landing a moment later.

"Won't be a sec," he called, then disappeared again. Shaunna sneezed.

"Sorry," she croaked at George.

"It's OK. You sound terrible."

"I feel terrible," she confessed. She wandered off after Ade, and George listened as the pair of them coughed, sneezed and wheezed their way through an exchange in the kitchen. He chuckled to himself. Kris came bounding down the stairs, pulling his jacket on along the way. He stopped by George and rolled his eyes.

"It's like a school sick bay in here. You ready?"

"Yep."

"See you invalids later," Kris called and opened the front door, ushering George outside. "Mmm. You smell good."

"Thanks. It's Josh's aftershave. Not sure what it is, but I couldn't find mine."

"Well, it suits you, whatever it is," Kris said, sniffing him again appreciatively. George glanced sideways at him. "What?" he asked.

"Nothing."

"I'm not allowed to pay you compliments anymore?"

"Yeah, all right. Maybe I'm being a bit paranoid," George admitted apologetically. Kris always did gush like that—telling him he looked 'fab' in whatever he was wearing, how 'fit' he smelled, and so on. He also knew why he was starting to get jumpy.

"So, where are we going?" Kris asked.

"Bingo."

"Bingo?"

"Yeah, you know, that game where they call out numbers and you mark them off on a..."

"I do know what bingo is, thank you. I used to work in the bingo hall, you may recall."

"Well, where we're going is nowhere near as classy as the place you worked, believe me." Stage one of the preparation complete.

After that, Kris made no more queries about their destination. They took the bus from the end of the road, staying on it as it sailed through the town centre, headed out past the new housing estate and onwards. It wasn't an area Kris was familiar with and he was becoming increasingly curious. He cleared a patch in the condensation on the window and peered out into the dark streets beyond. They were coming up on a small precinct of retail buildings, all constructed from the same pale tan brickwork, and consisting of a pub, an off licence, a takeaway, several small shops in darkness, a convenience store, and, just a little further on, a bingo hall. They stepped off the bus and strode past the pub, where a group of lads were standing in the doorway, sharing a joint. George tugged at Kris's sleeve to stop him from staring.

"Where the hell are we?" he whispered in wonder.

"The edge of the council estate. Behind there," George pointed beyond the row of shops, "is where I grew up."

"You lived here?"

"Yep. See that tower block?" George nodded towards the top two floors of the block of flats just peeking over the bingo hall, illuminated squares in a black hulk against the star-strewn sky, partially eclipsing the almost full moon.

"No way! You did not live there!"

"My mum still does."

"I thought..." Kris stopped talking. He didn't know what he thought, because he'd not actually ever given any consideration to where George lived. It simply hadn't occurred to him before. Back when they were at school, they used to go to Kris's house, because it was 'the place' to be. Prior to his parents' return to Sweden, they had lived in a significant, Victorian detached property in one of the older streets on the outskirts of the town, with six bedrooms, a vast attic and an enormous, rambling garden, taken up by a pair of two hundred year old oak trees, complete with a 'treehouse', where they used to spend hours together, doing what teenagers who are 'going out with each other' do when they find themselves fortunate enough to be alone somewhere for any length of time. All of his friends, with the exception of Dan, preferred to come to his house, rather than invite him to their homes, because his family were easy-going, if not a little odd, and always welcomed his and his brother's friends. They were also completely uncaring about whether the friends were male, female, gay, straight or otherwise. If they stayed over, they slept in the same room regardless, and Lars and Kris knew better than to abuse this trust by doing anything stupid, which was why his parents were initially so devastated to hear that he had got Shaunna pregnant. Once he told them the truth, they were more supportive than he would ever dared to have hoped.

They had now arrived at the front desk of the bingo hall, and filled in membership forms, then George exchanged cash for two books of tickets.

"You playing the national, love?" the woman on the counter asked. He ummed and ahhed, confused and unsure how to answer.

"Yes, please," Kris said, taking over. This bit he understood.

"And the lates?"

George shrugged.

103

"And the lates," Kris confirmed. He paid for the rest of the tickets and passed a set to George. "Can we have two pens, as well?"

"Pens?" George asked.

"Dabbers," Kris explained. "For marking off…"

"Yeah, I know what they are," George cut him off, then smiled an apology. There was always at least one on his mother's coffee table. In fact, a few years ago, there was a bit of a hoo-hah over a fruit-scented edition of the very wide felt-tipped pens favoured by bingo fanatics, and he'd been steadily building a collection of this particular version, which, it turned out, exploded when shaken, creating ink splats that didn't wash out of clothes. His mum had been furious at having to buy him a new school shirt when she'd not long bought the one he'd ruined, and in the end he felt so guilty that he put his paper round wages in the jar she used for money for the meter. He got away with it for a few weeks before she noticed.

They went up the stairs into the main hall, the drone of the caller on the early session audible as they approached the walkway around the edge of the large room, in which the scent of long-ago smoked tobacco still lingered.

"Let's get a beer," George suggested quietly, heading off in the direction of the bar, scanning the rows of tables on his way. There were quite a few people dotted around the place, some chattering away quietly, while others huffed, flustered by the noise. A woman over in the corner shouted 'shut up' at the people on the next table along. George smiled to himself and continued with his search. Just as they reached the bar, he located her, sitting in the middle row of tables, with another woman, heads bowed over tickets, both squinting hard in concentration.

"You're stressed," Kris observed, circling his thumbs on the back of George's shoulders. George glared at him and shrugged him off.

"What can I get you?" the barman asked.

"Lager?" George asked Kris.

"Fine," Kris confirmed.

"Two pints of lager, please."

The young guy behind the bar nodded and proceeded to pull their pints.

"What's the matter?" Kris persisted.

"You'll find out in a minute," George said. He paid for their drinks and passed one over. They were going to have to wait until the current session was finished before they approached.

"I must say," Kris whispered, "I didn't really take you for a bingo man."

George laughed quietly. "I'm not. We're here for your benefit."

"Right?"

Before George could respond, a woman over to their left called 'house' and multiple groans of 'only needed number X' were heard from all directions.

104

"Come on," George said, moving off and beckoning Kris to follow. Kris did as directed, still looking decidedly bemused by the whole affair.

She had her back to them as they approached the table, and the other woman glanced up, nudging her companion's arm and nodding towards them. She turned around.

"Aright?" she said. "What the fuck're you doin' 'ere?"

"Hi, Mum," George said, leaning over and kissing the proffered cheek. Thankfully, she was without rollers and headscarf, because bingo nights were an 'occasion'. "Hello, Pauline," he greeted the woman sitting opposite his mother, of the same type, but a little larger all round.

"Evenin', Georgie. How are ya, love?"

"I'm very well, thanks, Pauline. You?"

"Aye, can't complain," she said, smiling and eyeing up Kris. "Who's yer mate?"

"Mum, Pauline, this is Kris," he said, turning to Kris, who was standing completely still, utterly dumbfounded, but quickly rallied. "Kris, this is my mum, Iris, and her friend, Pauline."

"Kris," George's mum nodded at him by way of a greeting, a glint of suspicion in her eye. Kris stepped forward and turned on his best smile. He took her hand and shook it gently.

"Lovely to meet you, Iris."

"Yeah, leave it out," she replied, pulling her hand away. Kris frowned and looked to George for guidance.

"She thinks you don't mean it," he translated. Pauline chuckled.

"Oh, right," Kris said. Iris glared at George.

"Are ya stoppin'?" Pauline asked, shifting her handbag from the chair next to her. Kris correctly took this as an invitation to sit down. George picked up his mother's coat from the vacant chair next to her and hung it on the back.

"'Sup wi'ya?" his mum asked.

"Nothing. Why?" George said, pulling his chair in.

"You fell out?"

"Who? Me and Josh? Don't be daft."

"So what's soft lad 'ere for?" She nodded at Kris as she said this.

"He's one of my friends. Thought it'd be nice to come over and introduce ourselves, seeing as we were here, anyway." He glanced at Kris, who was following the conversation quite well, all things considered. "Kris is an actor," George continued, "and he's gonna be in a new series on telly."

"Oh aye? What's tharabout? Another of them fuckin' queer eye thingies, is it?"

George blushed and looked away.

"It's a crime series," Kris said. "I'm playing a detective inspector from Manchester."

"Right," George's mum said. "Am a meant to be impressed?"

"No, Mam. Just try not to be too insulting," George suggested, pointlessly, as she'd take no notice whatsoever.

"Aright, mardypants," she muttered. She glanced up at the clock: another ten minutes before the main session started.

"Goin' for a cig. Comin', Paul?"

"Aye, may as well," Pauline replied. She shuffled around Kris. "Budge in a bit, love, ta," she said to him. He did as requested and watched on, grinning like an idiot, as Iris and Pauline waddled off towards the exit.

"Oh my God, your mum is amazing!" he said to George, once they were out of earshot.

"Hmm, if you say so." George took a swig of his beer.

"I'm guessing they come from Manchester?"

"Mum does. Pauline's from Altrincham, which is good enough for your purposes."

"Fab," Kris gushed. "So she figured I'm not straight, then?"

"Yeah. She's got the most accurate gaydar in the western hemisphere."

Kris smiled and let the 'gaydar' comment go. George continued.

"The first time she met Josh she asked him if he was 'another one of them fuckin' woofters'."

"She didn't? How funny. What did Josh say?"

"Nothing. She completely knocked him for six."

"God, I'd have loved to have been there."

"Yeah, well, he's won her round since. She came to ours for Christmas dinner, which was a bit weird."

"Why?"

"Dunno. They talk in this kind of clipped form of English, where she tries to come over all posh, and he tries to sound down to earth."

"Aww, bless them. Just shows how much they love you."

"I guess so," George said bashfully. He hadn't thought of it like that.

"Your accent's gone a bit Mancunian since we got here, by the way," Kris observed. "Did you know that?"

"Seriously?"

"Yeah. You sound totally different."

"Do I 'ecker's, like," George said.

"Sorry?"

"It means 'no I don't'."

Kris mouthed an 'oh'.

"Although you probably won't hear many people say it for real, and you definitely won't hear my mum say it. She's, err, well, she swears. A lot."

"Say it again."

George did as requested. Kris tried to repeat it and failed.

"And again."

"No! I don't even have a real accent!"

"Please?"

"No, lad! It's bobbins."

"Huh?"

"Rubbish. Bobbins."

"Ah. OK." Kris laughed. "I should maybe write all this down."

"I wouldn't, unless you fancy a clout round the ear 'ole." George grinned.

"George! That's fabulous! You're so going to give me lessons."

"I'm so not."

"So are."

George's mum and Pauline were heading back, so the men stopped talking and shifted their chairs in to let them pass.

"Bit nippy out there," Pauline said, rubbing her hands together.

"Nippy? It's fuckin' Baltic, Paul!" George's mum said. Kris was drinking his beer and had to spit it back into the glass. George exploded with laughter.

"Did I say somert funny?" his mum asked curtly.

"Erm, no." He was still giggling. His mother eyed him carefully.

"You're a bloody barmpot, you are," she said. "Anyhow, as I were sayin'…" She turned her attention back to Pauline and continued the conversation that they had apparently been having outside—something about a residents' association on the estate, which some of the younger tenants were in the process of setting up to try and prompt action from the council on the tower block. Kris sat listening in awed silence, as the two women conversed in a curious language vaguely resembling the one he understood and spoke on a daily basis, but alien in many ways. Meanwhile, George doodled on the back of a gambling awareness leaflet he'd found on the table; he was feeling very out of place. The first game kicked off and the women fell silent while the four of them sat, marking off their numbers. After three minutes or so, someone at the table behind them put her hand up.

"Claim in the centre. Thank you, Trisha," the caller announced. A young woman with her hair scraped into a harsh pony tail high on her head came trotting across. George watched on, mildly intrigued.

"Thank you, Sheila," she said. "Checking a claim on the green page, seventeen is on the claim, security number 3-4-7-6. Membership seen."

A few seconds of murmuring followed.

"Thank you, Trisha," the caller drawled nasally. "That's a good claim. Any further claims?"

A pause.

"Don't forget to shout when you claim," the caller said in a weary tone, evidently sick of repeating herself. "Carrying on for your full house…"

The procedure was repeated again for the full house, then on through another five tickets, with George becoming increasingly bored by the whole affair, whilst Kris seemed to be having a great time. On the last game, the woman at the next table along called 'house' and Trisha The Checker came over.

"Jammy bint," George's mum muttered. "Second she's won and we've not fuckin' bin 'ere an hour yet." She swigged the rest of her half-pint in disgust. Kris was immediately on the case.

"Let me get you another one," he smiled, picking up the four empty glasses. "What're you drinking?"

"'Ere, love." She opened her bag to get her purse out. George felt his shoulders tense. This was where things could turn nasty. Kris spotted it in an instant.

"Sort it out when I come back," he said. "Lager, is it, Iris?"

"Aye, love, ta."

"Pauline?"

"Bitter, lad, if yer gettin'," she said, nodding after him.

"I'll give you a hand," George suggested, but Kris shrugged the offer away. George turned back and smiled at his mum.

"Right, you. What's this about?" she asked.

"Can't we just come and join you for a game a bingo?"

"Where's Josh?"

"At home. He's not a big fan of bingo."

"And soft lad, there, what's-his-name, Kris? He's into his bingo, is he?"

"He is, actually." George folded his arms indignantly. "He's a dab hand." He registered the pun, but said nothing. "I bet he wins more than you do tonight."

She didn't say anything else, until Kris returned from the bar.

"There you go, Iris." He carefully placed her drink down in front of her. She nodded an acknowledgement and pushed a pile of coins towards him.

"Have that one on me," he smiled.

"Why?"

"Because I said so."

She shrugged and took her money back. George couldn't believe what he was seeing. Normally she'd have kicked up a fuss about accepting a drink off him or anyone else, so this was somewhat out of character.

"And how d'you two know each other?" she asked Kris.

"We went to the same high school."

"With Josh?"

Kris nodded. "Yes. We're all very good friends."

"You comin' for a smoke, Iris?" Pauline interrupted, sensing George's discomfort.

"Aye, alright then." She got up and shuffled past George. "I'm not done wi'ya yet, lad," she said, glaring at him. The two women waddled off again and George pulled a face behind her back. Kris giggled.

"I'm glad you think it's funny," George grumped.

"Sorry, but she's just so…down to earth."

George frowned and picked up the leaflet he'd been doodling on.

"What did I say now?"

"Down to earth. Can you imagine what Ellie, or Jess will think of her? Or Adele, for that matter?"

"So what?"

"You know, she usually swears a lot more than this."

"Well aren't I honoured!"

"Yeah." George took another swig of his beer and spent a few minutes looking around at all of the people playing bingo with the plastic slotted numbers on their tables. "I think we might've cramped their style a bit," he said.

"Probably."

"And it's really bloody boring."

"You could always teach me some more phrases."

"No!"

"Please?" Kris fluttered his eyelashes.

"Don't do that in here!" George snapped.

"Why?"

"Let's just say it's not the most gay-friendly estate on the planet."

"Oh really?" Kris looked up at the bartender.

"One gay guy working the bar is not gonna prove your point."

"Ooh. That sounded just like Josh."

"Did not."

"Did too."

George stuck his tongue out at him.

"And that's Josh."

"Is not."

"It bloody is!"

"Not," George said, laughing as he knew it was true. He and Josh spent so much time together that it was inevitable they would pick up some of each other's ways and he loved that this was so. However, his mother was on her way back again, so they put their conversation on hold once more. She pushed past and gave George a quick, half-smile. He returned the gesture.

"D'you need another drink yet?" he asked.

"No," his mother replied briskly, then turned her attention back to Kris, picking up where she'd left off earlier. "So Josh knows you're out together tonight, does he?"

"Yeah, I think so," Kris said, looking to George to confirm that this was the case. George nodded once.

"And he won't mind then, Josh?" she persisted.

George sighed. "No, Mum, he doesn't mind at all."

"Right," his mum said dubiously.

"Eh, Iris, did that council bloke come to yours yesterday?" Pauline asked. It was an appallingly disguised change of subject, but it worked.

"The leccy feller, you mean, Paul?"

"Aye, that were 'im, I think."

"Yeah. What were that for?"

"Well…"

They were off again. Kris folded his arms and sat back listening, affecting an interested nod as appropriate. George re-read the gambling awareness leaflet.

"National next," Kris told him excitedly. George had no idea what that meant and didn't really care, but played along for the sake of filling the time, for what it was worth. He could hardly keep up with how quickly they called the numbers out, although his three companions were having no trouble at all. No-one in their hall won anything of significance. Another lull ensued. George drew snakes and ladders on his used tickets.

"What's Josh up to this evenin'?" his mother started again, seemingly intent on filling every short interval with further interrogation.

"Dunno. He's probably reading a book, or writing up his research, or whatever."

"That's right," Pauline said. "He's one of them psychos, in't 'e?"

"Erm, yeah," George laughed.

"Psy-cho-lo-gist, Paul," his mother corrected, pronouncing it very slowly.

"Aye, them as can see inside yer 'ead," Pauline said, by way of confirming that she was right in the first place.

"So he'd know then, eh?" George's mum nudged him with her elbow, "if you was up to anythin' with laughin' boy there."

George shook his head disdainfully and studied the ceiling. Soon after, the second half of the main game began, saving him, for now. Much as it was infuriating, getting the third degree, it was also endearing, and showed how much she cared about Josh, to be worrying that he was up to stuff behind his back, although he was a bit upset that she thought he'd do something like that. Presumably it was one of those 'like father, like son' things.

The games progressed with the same rapidity as before, George now so disinterested that he started to try and predict what number would be called next. With a zero success rate, he switched to guessing higher or lower, and got a few correct in a row. These antics took him through the first three of the five games. Two more to go and then only the late session to endure. He glanced at the booklet, pleased to see that it contained just three tickets.

"Line!" Kris said and put his arm up. A lull in number calling proceeded as Trisha The Checker came over to check his card. She gave him his winnings and they continued with the game. Someone over the other side of the room called 'here' for a full house. It turned out to be a false claim, and the calling temporarily resumed, ending a couple of numbers later. George's mum shoved her tickets away in disgust.

"Told you," George said, then immediately wished he hadn't, because it was essentially permission for her to continue her cross-examination. On the plus side, Kris seemed more than happy to field her queries, even though they took a somewhat more personal path next.

"So, you and George, then? You ever bin an item?"

"Yes, when we were at school."

"How come we never met?"

"Well, I guess, because my house was closest?" Kris suggested.

"Hmm. Probably as well, mind, terrible buggers round ours, eh, Paul?"

"Eh?" Pauline hadn't been listening.

"I say, they're terrible up our way. Fuckin' 'omophobes."

"Oh, yeah," Pauline agreed. She hadn't a clue what Iris was talking about. George picked up his glass and sipped at it, for something to do. He really wasn't in the mood for drinking and the lager was pretty awful—flat, with a kind of stagnant smell to it. The last game was soon underway and gave him temporary respite. This was won by a woman who was younger than he and Kris, and accompanied by her mother, by the looks of things. They were an odd pair, both with the same style of little round, thick-lensed glasses and basin haircuts.

His mum started up again, "So, Kris, are you…you know?"

"What's that, Iris?"

"Seeing anyone?"

"Yes, I am."

"Right," she said. "Nice, is he?"

"He's OK," Kris replied cagily. There were things going on at home that no-one else knew about, and that he certainly wasn't about to share with George's mother.

"Only OK? You can do better than that, lad." She didn't pursue this any further. "What about this telly programme?"

"Well," Kris began, his eyes lighting up.

111

George decided to take the opportunity to go off in search of the toilets, partly because he'd already heard more than enough about the crime series, but mostly because he wanted to phone Josh. It took a couple of attempts for him to answer.

"Hey, you," Josh said. "Everything OK?"

"Yeah. Did I wake you up?"

"No. I was making coffee and didn't hear my phone. How's it going?"

"They're getting on like a house on fire."

"That's good."

"Hmm."

"What's the matter?"

"My mum keeps asking about you—wants to know why I'm here with Kris and not you."

"Oh, right."

"You don't sound surprised by that. Thanks!"

"Sorry. I'm not following why that's a problem."

"She thinks I'm seeing Kris behind your back."

"Ah, I see." Josh paused. "That's actually quite nice of her, don't you think? To worry about us like that?"

"Well, yeah, I suppose. But it means she doesn't trust me." The line went quiet for a while, because Josh didn't know what to say. Eventually he found his tongue.

"Why wouldn't she trust you?"

"Because of my dad."

"Did he have an affair?"

"He had lots of affairs."

"Right, well that makes sense."

"I'm not like him," George said. He sounded angry and upset.

"No, you're not," Josh assured him, "but you can see why she'd worry." George didn't respond. "Listen, I'm going to come and pick you guys up. What time will you be finished?"

"Dunno. About another half an hour, probably. You don't need to."

"I do. If only to reassure your mum that everything's all right between us. I'll see you at nine-thirty. OK?"

"OK. I love you."

"Love you too. Bye." Josh hung up. George returned to the table, where Kris was sitting on his own, tapping away at his phone.

"They've gone to smoke again," he explained without looking up.

"I gathered."

"Just telling Shaunna about your mum. She's dead excited to meet her."

No response.

"Sorry. Shouldn't I have done that?"

George shrugged. He was past caring. Of all the reasons he had worried about introducing his mum to any of his friends, this had definitely not been one. To have her ask them outright if they were gay? He knew Kris could handle that, and he didn't seem to care about his mother's appalling language, either. Of course, she was in her best togs, because it was a night out, so she looked a lot more presentable than usual, but somehow he thought that Kris would've found her just as charming if she had been in her rollers, jogging pants and tatty old slippers. He'd misjudged his friends yet again, and made a huge deal out of something that didn't even matter to them. However, to have her accuse him of cheating on Josh? That really hurt.

When the two women returned, George went to the bar with Pauline, leaving his mum and Kris to further converse about Kris's starring role on TV, or anything else that took their fancy.

"What's up, love?" Pauline asked.

"Ah, nothing really," he said.

"Yer mum upset you, didn't she? Thinkin' you was seein' yer mate on the side?"

"Yeah, a bit. She didn't mean to, I know. It's just…"

"I know, love." She rubbed his arm gently. Pauline was one of the first people his mum became friends with after they moved to the flat, so didn't know everything that had gone on with his dad, but could figure out most of it, because a lot of the men around their way were just like him. Or the older ones were: anything pretty in a skirt that showed them the slightest bit of interest and they were off. Pauline's husband had been no different.

"You're special," she said to him, as they headed back with the drinks. "She loves you and wants the best for you. That's all."

"Thanks, Pauline," George smiled. She was right. His mum wasn't really accusing him of anything. She was warning him not to make the same stupid mistakes his dad did. Like that was going to happen.

The last three games went by quite quickly for everyone other than George, who, during the course of the evening, had come to realise how much he hated bingo, so just dabbed away half-heartedly at his cards, not really paying attention to what he was doing, thus not noticing that on the final game he had completed a line, until someone leaned over his shoulder.

"You've won, there, haven't you?" Josh said, pointing at the ticket.

George felt his heart speed up and his skin tingle at the light touch of Josh's chest against his back, his hair tickling the side of his face.

"Ah, yeah. So I have. Mam, call it."

His mother shouted and waved her hand, and Trisha The Checker came over. Josh pulled up a chair and sat down next to George.

"You OK?" he asked. George took hold of his hand under the table.

"I am now."

The young woman finished checking George's ticket, and the last few minutes of the game proceeded. Someone called for a full house and George's mum slammed her pen down.

"Every fucker but me," she snarled in disgust.

"You can have mine," George said, pushing his winnings across to her. She pushed it back.

"You paid out, dint ya?"

"Yeah, so?"

"So you take it. It's only a tenner, anyhow."

George pushed the ten pound note across to her again. She glared at him and folded her arms, but left it where it was and instead turned her attention on Josh.

"A bin chattin' to your mate Kris 'ere, about his telly show," she said.

"Have you, Iris?" Josh had a good idea where she was going to take this, and couldn't decide if he should just try and nip it in the bud. With anyone else, he probably would have done, but his verbal sparring skills were no match for Iris Morley.

"Aye. We had a good old chat, dint we Kris?"

"Yes, Iris, we did. It's nice to finally meet you, after all this time."

"I was sayin', Josh," she continued, "I was surprised you was mates with each other, what with George…"

"Right, Mam, that's enough," George interrupted. She took a breath in to say something else, but Josh caught her eye. Incredibly, she took notice of the unspoken message and said no more. George squeezed Josh's hand and he squeezed back.

"We best be on our way, Paul," Iris said. Pauline nodded and stood in preparation of putting on her coat.

"Would you like a lift?" Josh asked. Iris dismissed the offer.

"You're alright, ta, bein' as 'ow we only 'ave to bob through the ginnel." Kris had no idea what anything she'd just said meant.

"Alley," George and Josh explained in unison.

"You comin' fer your dinner tomorra?" George's mum asked as they made their way outside.

"Yeah, will do. I'm working earlies, so it'll have to be tea. About three?"

"Alright, love," she said. He gave her a hug and a kiss. "Ta-rah, love," she waved at Kris. "See yer tomorra," she told Josh.

"You will. Night, Iris," he responded. He, George and Kris watched on as the two women trudged away, pulling on plastic rain hats and getting their cigarettes out of their bags, ready to light up as soon as they stepped outside. George heaved an enormous sigh of relief. Kris patted him on the back.

"Thanks," he said, appreciating, although only partly understanding, how much George had suffered on his behalf tonight.

"Did it help?"

"More than you'd believe."

They stepped off towards the exit, Josh walking slightly in front. He opened the door ahead of them and shivered.

"Brr. It's a bit chilly," he said, rubbing his hands together.

"Chilly?" Kris said. "It's friggin' Baltic!"

And this time he got it right.

BIRTH PLAN
Thursday 9ᵗʰ February

No nasty receptionist in the antenatal clinic: George waited with Sophie, behind two other women who looked like they were not that far off giving birth. He was trying not to listen to their conversation about heartburn, and backache, and due dates, and bladder control, or lack thereof, even though it was all so very fascinating—and also making him glad that he was a man. On the plus side, since Sophie had made the psychological adjustment to staying pregnant, her morning sickness had eased off considerably, and better still, the 'forgotten' vomit bowl had gone from the hospital car park.

"Good morning," the receptionist smiled at Sophie. "Can I take your name please?"

"Sophie Spyris," she replied. The usual date of birth and address questions followed.

"And are you Mr. Spyris?" the receptionist asked George.

"Um, no. I'm George Morley, but I am the birth partner."

"That's fine. Can I just jot down your details, Mr. Morley?" George obliged. "Please take a seat, and someone will be out to see you soon." They went and sat down.

This was what they called the 'booking appointment', where they took blood samples to screen for various conditions, and would talk them through pregnancy. In preparation, George had been ploughing his way through library books like a man possessed, and he already had quite an extensive knowledge of childbirth—admittedly of the large mammal variety—before he began. However, he definitely wasn't someone to be accused of complacency, and regardless of how much he knew it would never be enough, as far as he was concerned. Now, he was trying to be calm and sensible, even though he was so excited about Sophie's ultrasound scan that he could barely sit still. She was pretending she hadn't noticed, whilst at the same time hoping the novelty would wear off soon.

"Sophie Spyris," a midwife called. Sophie and George stood up together.

"You want me to carry your bag?" he asked.

"Pregnant, not disabled, George," she reminded him again. He smiled apologetically. "But I reserve the right to change my mind on the bag carrying," she said as they followed the midwife to the indicated cubicle.

"All right, Sophie, my love," she instructed, "if you can just take off your trousers for me and make yourself comfortable. There's a blanket on the bed. I'll be back in a second to have a feel of your tummy." The midwife left them alone again.

"I can wait outside, if you like?" George offered.

"You might as well get used to it," Sophie said, unzipping and removing her jeans. "You're gonna see a whole lot more of me than my legs."

"Ah, yeah. That's a good point." George went red. "You know I've never actually, um…what I mean is that…"

"The last woman's bits and bobs you saw were your mother's when she gave birth to you," Sophie finished for him. He went even redder. "It's OK, George. I don't think you're required to label them or anything."

"I could probably do that," he joked, trying to make light of his embarrassment. "I've seen pictures and stuff."

"Maybe we should watch some of those childbirth videos," she suggested.

"Maybe we shouldn't," George said quickly, his cheeks now demonstrating that it took far less time to drain the blood away from them than it did to pump it up there to begin with. Sophie laughed and settled back on the bed.

"How are you feeling?" she asked. She knew he was excited, of course, but she was wondering about everything else, particularly the fact that Sean wasn't a part of it.

"I'm OK," he answered, understanding immediately. "Don't worry about Sean. Josh is working on him."

"What's he said? Only he's not really talking to me. Well, he is talking to me, as in his mouth keeps on opening and closing and the words keep pouring out, but he's not talking to me about this." She pointed at her belly.

"Not much, to be honest. He's apologised to me, which I thought was rather funny, as he's nicer to me than you are."

"Thanks! I'll try not to take that to heart."

George grinned at her.

"Have I been that horrid?"

"Not really. Anyway, it's not about me. How are *you* feeling?"

"OK." She nodded thoughtfully. "Glad you're here." She held out her hand and he took it.

"Me too."

A short while later, after Sophie had been prodded with fingers and needles, and sworn at George profusely about how desperately she needed the toilet, with a threat to leave a puddle in the reception area if they didn't get the scan over and done with soon, they were taken into a darkened room, where a radiographer performed the ultrasound scan, turning the screen for Sophie and George to see.

"There's the heartbeat," she said, pointing to the rapidly pulsing point in the middle of the display, "and there's baby's head." The rest of the description wasn't needed, because the image was amazingly clear. George was so completely enthralled that he didn't notice Sophie crying, until the radiographer gave him a nudge.

"Oh, Soph. What's the matter?"

"I just…" She started to sob and he held her close.

"I'll get you cleaned up now," the radiographer said, working around George to wipe the gel off Sophie's belly. She left the room for a couple of minutes.

"I'm trying not to think about it, George, but it's only three weeks since we were here, and…" She looked at the still image on-screen, left there so that a printout could be made. George pulled some of the blue paper towel from the roll next to the bed and gave it to her. She blew her nose loudly and tried to get the tears in check.

"I don't know what to say, Soph, because I can't understand how this feels for you."

"I'll be OK," she said, patting his hand.

The radiographer returned and handed George the ultrasound image.

"Baby's first photo. When you come for your next scan, it will be done using the 3D machine."

"Cool," George said.

"It is." She saw them back out to the waiting room and called in her next 'patient'. That was them all done for today.

Sophie drove back, and they discussed names, none of which struck either of them with any great sense of being the 'perfect' name, boy's or girl's. After that, George made them lunch, whilst Sophie made a copy of the scan image for him, then they went on the NHS website to start writing up the birth plan. There was a section about the birth partner, with questions to help them decide if Sophie wanted George there in the event of a caesarean, or if a forceps delivery were needed.

"I don't want you to feel under pressure," she told him. He sighed and shook his head.

"See those questions?" he said, pointing at the screen. "They ask what *you* want, not what I want, and if you want me there, I'll be there."

"I want you there," she confirmed.

"Good. That's sorted then. Whatever happens, I will be there."

When Josh arrived home from work, Sophie said her goodbyes and went to show Sean the still from the ultrasound scan. He was politely interested, but otherwise didn't say much, and they ended up having the usual non-argument relating to her only involving him because she felt she should, rather than because she needed him. Unfortunately, right at that moment, it was the truth, and in many ways they were both grateful for this. Maybe in time things would change. For now they were just taking each day as it came.

Had they gone to visit their neighbours next door but one, they'd have heard a very different conversation taking place.

"George?" Josh called from the kitchen.

"Yeah?"

"Why is there a foetus on the fridge?"

George came into the room and grinned all dewy-eyed at the picture. "Look," he said, pointing to the tiny bud of a hand. "He looks like he's sucking his thumb."

"He?" Josh shuffled George sideways so that he could put the milk away.

"I've got a gut feeling."

"You know that's the umbilical cord, not a…"

"Yes, Joshua, I do. I just have this really strong sense that it's a boy. I can't explain it. We were discussing names on the way home, and…"

George continued to ramble on, and Josh was listening, but he was thinking at the same time, trying to come up with a way of getting through to Sean, before it was too late.

"…confirmed the due date as August the twenty-fourth, and Soph's mum said she was born exactly on her due date, which I know all pregnancies are different, but there's got to be something genetic to it, don't you think?"

"Erm, yes, I suppose," Josh said. "Can you shush a minute. I have an idea."

"What?"

"Will you talk to Sean?"

"About?"

"The baby."

"I can try."

"OK. Good." Josh nodded and continued to look at him.

"What, now?"

"It's as good a time as any."

George sighed. "All right. I'll see you in a bit." He left the house.

Two minutes later, he came back.

"Isn't he home?" Josh asked.

"Um, no. What I mean is yes, he is, but he's pretending not to be."

Josh chewed his lip thoughtfully. "August the twenty-fourth, did you say?"

"Yep."

"OK. That gives us six months to talk him round. What do you think?"

"I'm the birth partner."

"I know."

"I'll think about it," George said very seriously. He went upstairs and started running a bath.

"It's not your baby," Josh shouted after him. He came back down, collected the ultrasound image and went back up the stairs again, holding it against his chest.

"Poor little fella. Did that mean man frighten you?"

"Still not your baby," Josh called.

"Don't care." George closed the bathroom door. Josh shook his head and went to sit down, muttering under his breath.

"Just be careful that you don't throw the baby out…"

The bathroom door opened again.

"And I don't want to hear any smart remarks about babies and bathwater."

Blue put his head on Josh's knee and looked up at him.

"Yes," Josh said, "looks like you're getting a baby brother."

BLOODY VALENTINE'S
Tuesday 14ᵗʰ February

Josh smiled, trying to disguise his unease with his current client—a man in his late fifties who, after twenty minutes of waffling about deaths in suspicious circumstances and violent gangland killings, had declared that he could see ghosts. But not any old ghosts. Oh no. Obviously these were the ghosts of the victims, and in Josh's head, he could hear them calling 'Avenge my death!', although these words had yet to pass the lips of his newest client. And he'd said he wasn't going to take on any more. His phone vibrated against his leg for about the twentieth time in the past hour and he shifted position. Ghosts. Good grief.

"When you say 'see', can you explain what you mean by that?"

"I don't understand the question," the man said. Mr. R. Forster. That was his name. No clues as to what the 'R' stood for.

"When the 'ghosts' make themselves visible to you, do you see actual people? Or do you just see lights, or…"

"Actual people," Mr. Forster confirmed. "Full bodied, a bit wispy around the edges, but definitely people."

"I see." Josh's phone vibrated again.

"Did you need to get that?" Mr. Forster asked.

"Oh, no. Sorry. It's nothing important." Josh smiled apologetically. He usually turned it off and put it away in the drawer, or left it in his jacket and hung that in the closet across the room, but today he'd been typing a text message when Mr. Forster arrived, so hastily shoved it in his trouser pocket, where it had been buzzing away ever since. "OK," he said, "do these 'ghosts' talk to you, or can you just see them?"

"I can't hear them, but they are talking. I can see their mouths moving." Mr. Forster suddenly covered his face. "Oh God, it's so terrible, the things these poor souls endure." He uncovered his face again. "They're screaming, crying out, unheard, across the void, calling for help."

As a fruitcake, Josh thought to himself. His phone vibrated again and he took it out, turned off the notifications and put it down on his desk. He glanced at the clock. Five minutes of this craziness left.

"Can you recall when these experiences first started?" he asked.

Mr. Forster pondered for a moment before he answered. "It's been since the death of my wife."

Josh started to make a note of this. "And when was that?" His phone screen lit up: call from Ellie. He turned it face down.

"Five years ago. Are you sure you wouldn't like to answer your phone? It must be quite important, if they keep trying to call."

"It's not, I assure you." Josh smiled—again. He was starting to get cramp in his jaw. "I understand this might be painful, and if it's too painful, please don't feel you have to answer. May I ask how your wife died?"

"She was killed in a car accident."

"I'm sorry to hear that."

"Drunk driver, hit the back of her car."

Josh frowned and nodded sympathetically.

"She's been visiting me ever since."

"Did you ever have any bereavement counselling?"

"No. My doctor suggested it, but I told him I didn't need it. She's still with me, isn't she?"

Josh shrugged. "Depends on your beliefs."

"Do you believe in an afterlife?"

"I'd prefer not to comment. This is, after all, about you."

"I do. And I believe that troubled spirits—the ones who were not ready to leave—get lost in between this world and the next. That's where my wife is, and all the others calling out to me. I think she may be directing them towards me."

Josh glanced at the clock again. Time up. He slid forward on his seat and uncrossed his legs.

"That must be some solace. That you feel your wife is helping other lost souls?"

"Yes," Mr. Forster nodded, "I do take some comfort from it. However, I'm exhausted. I need to block them out, silence them. I've asked them to leave me alone, but they won't listen. They just keep coming, again and again, 'Avenge me! O, avenge me!'"

And there it was. Josh rubbed his nose, trying hard not to laugh. He cleared his throat.

"All right, Mr. Forster. We have another appointment booked for the same time next week, don't we? That will give me time to consider our options, which we can discuss then. How does that sound?"

Mr. Forster nodded and stood up. He was distracted, as if watching something going on across the room. Josh couldn't help himself and glanced in the same direction, then back at Mr. Forster. The man smiled and shook Josh's hand.

"Thanks," he said, then indicated with a nod across the room. "My wife," he explained. "She's blowing out the candles on a birthday cake."

"OK." Josh could feel his eyes growing wide of their own accord.

"Is it your birthday?"

"Err…"

"She's nodding to say it is."

Josh laughed in disbelief and combed his fingers through his hair.

"Yes," he confirmed, "it's my birthday."

"Have a good one," Mr. Forster said. "See you next week."

And then he was gone, leaving Josh standing in the middle of his surgery with his mouth hanging open and wondering if he was staring rudely at (or right through) the invisible, late Mrs. Forster. He shook himself out of it and picked up his phone: lots and lots of text messages, missed calls, emails and online notifications; there's nothing like social networking to make one feel extraordinarily popular. He ignored all of the online stuff and went straight to his text messages.

12:52, Dan
Happy Birthday mate!

13:01, Adele
HOPE UR HAVING A LOVELY DAY C U LATER. A X

13:16, Kris
PLS tell me ur not working on ur bd! catch u later. x

13:31, Tierney
Have one for me!!! ST xx

13:45, Andy
Happy Birthday mate! x

13:54, Shaunna
Happy Birthday to yoo-oo! x

13:56, Ellie
What time are you home? About four? Let me know. x
13:58
Oh yeah and Happy Birthday! :) x

14:19, Jess
happy birthday josh. jess x

14:23, Unknown
How do you know he's veggie?

125

Josh went through each of the messages, returned a 'thanks x' to those offering a general birthday wish, confirmed for Eleanor that he would be home just after four, and then clicked the 'call' button on the last one— number unknown, but the content of the message meant the sender was obvious to him. She answered straight away.

"Hey, Krissi."

"Hi, Josh. How are you?"

"Fine, thanks. You?"

"Yep. Same. So? How did you know?"

"It's obvious, isn't it?"

"Is it? I mean Jay's never said anything, cos he doesn't want to upset Mum, not when she's been feeding him meat all this time."

"Ah." Josh laughed. "I understand. Well, I won't say anything, but he probably ought to tell her at some point."

"Yeah. He probably ought, but he probably won't." Krissi went quiet and Josh pulled his phone away from his ear to check that the line was still active.

"You still there?"

"Yeah."

"What's the matter?"

"I can't really say anything, but…" She stopped again. "Forget it."

"OK," he said. "But it can easily be remembered again, if need be."

"Thanks," she said.

"So, are you coming?"

"Yeah. Looking forward to it. It'll be about eight-thirty, though, if that's OK?"

"Good stuff. See you later."

"Bye." Krissi hung up. Josh tapped his phone on his teeth. So, why hadn't Jason told anyone he was vegetarian? It wasn't as if it was something to be ashamed of; indeed, many would consider it admirable. Oh well. It was another minor mystery that would undoubtedly solve itself in time. Josh checked the clock: another half an hour until his next client, which was just long enough to head down the road to the coffee shop, except…

"Someone order a cappuccino?"

A cup appeared around the door.

"Nope. You got the wrong office, sorry."

George came into view, grinning broadly. He put the cappuccino on Josh's desk and gave him a kiss.

"Hi."

"Hi, yourself. What are you doing here? I thought you were working."

"Late lunchbreak. Kind of." He sat on the couch. Josh picked up the cup and sucked a mouthful of the thick, frothy coffee through the hole in the lid.

"But that we all had jobs like yours."

"It won't be like this in summer, though, will it? When I'm working fourteen hour days, while you're sitting at home, researching and planning lectures, or whatever it is you academics do."

"Hey, I still haven't signed the contract!"

George looked at him and said nothing. Josh nervously bit the inside of his cheek.

It was almost a month since he had wowed the director of social sciences, a man who wasn't easily impressed, although the rest of his faculty had been on at him and his predecessor for years about making both Josh and Sean offers they couldn't refuse so that they would take full time positions at the university. Neither was keen to be tied down, and the money alone wasn't enough, for their current arrangements gave them far greater flexibility to do their own thing. At present, Sean lectured on the nursing and counselling courses over two days a week; Josh did a day of student counselling, plus half a day on the counselling diploma, and they were both on the ethics committee. The rest of Josh's work was his private clients, and he had started to reduce this in preparation for introducing the Masters in Counselling and Psychotherapy in the new academic year, but that was only a further day of commitment—still a long way off working full time for the university. And, truth be told, he really didn't enjoy the counselling job much. In fact, since meeting Iris Morley, he had come to realise that most of what he did was meaningless and trivial, and he had always been an academic at heart. But both he and George knew why he was delaying signing the contract, and it was for one reason only, albeit a fairly significant one. For, with the contract came a confidential health questionnaire, which bore the instruction:

> If you have any medical condition that would require reasonable adjustment to be made to your workplace or working practices, please provide further information.
>
> Examples include…nervous or psychiatric conditions, etc.

Accompanying the questionnaire was a leaflet on government help with 'Access to Work', which George kept leaving out on the coffee table, by way of subtly prompting Josh into action. The fact that the university had hounded him for the past ten years was a good indication that they wanted him desperately enough to be as flexible in his terms and conditions as he dictated. So all that was left was for him to tell them the truth, and it was a truth he continued to deny. He had a form of bipolar disorder. Granted, it didn't fully fit the criteria, and it was mostly under his control, but, for those few days when he was 'sick', there was no way that he could work, certainly not for anyone but himself. Still, today was not the day to ponder over such possibilities, perhaps.

"Right," George said. He got up again. "I'm going back to work."

"How did you get here, by the way?"

"Borrowed Soph's car."

"That's very brave of you."

"It was for a good cause." He put his arms around him. "I'll be home about six."

"When I'll get my birthday present?"

"Hmm, maybe." George grinned and released him. Josh watched him leave, wondering again what his present was. He hadn't ruined his surprise by logging into George's email, even though he'd successfully guessed every new password he'd set. His patience had lasted this long, it could last another few hours, surely?

Josh's final session of the afternoon was just as entertaining as the previous one had been and was what could only be described as a catch-up session with Alex the vampire, who popped in once a month 'for a chat'. Today being St. Valentine's Day and all, it was a very fitting and interesting session to conclude with, because Alex and the once-mysterious Lileth, AKA Lucy and now his "beast fiend", were going to a "Vampires' Anti-Valentine Ball", which was some kind of protest against romance and included as part of the ticket price an utterly bizarre menu of cocktails called things like 'Love Kills' and 'Blood Lust'. Josh had yet to figure out whether his client's contentment with all other aspects of his life constituted successful treatment, but the repeat custom was Alex's doing, not his—not that he was complaining.

And so to home. Josh parked up outside the house and paused to listen to the end of a song on the radio. They were all out on the timeless, soppy ballads and currently playing was "I Think I Love You", by David Cassidy, which made him smile, to think back now. It was a song his dad had on a cassette that he played on perpetual loop in the car, and came to have its own significance when, years later, they played a cover version of the song at the sixth form ball. He turned off the engine and remained in the car a while longer, sitting in silence but for the song still playing in his head, cross-fading into his memories of the morning after, the blackcurrant stained tuxedo hanging on the back of the door a painful spectre of the night before. He'd shoved it in the wardrobe, behind everything else; out of sight, out of mind, the saying had whispered deceitfully in his ear, and kept whispering for three long years, until finally it was *he* who went out of *his* mind.

The whispering had stopped long before he came home from university, but it was never far away, hiding behind his books, under his bed, in the suit bag with the blackcurrant stained tuxedo, in his dreams. *In his dreams*—not the scariest thing in the world, a waterslide. Some of his clients told of nightmarish chases, being pursued by fantastic and deadly creatures, or of being buried alive, or falling forever. Others, like Mr. R. Forster, weren't even safe during the hours of wakefulness. *A waterslide, Joshua? Must do better.*

And he *had* tried to make sense of it, *before* he'd called George in the early hours of the morning. If it symbolised fear, then what was it he was actually afraid of? That he had misinterpreted his own feelings? That he had misunderstood when George told him he was in love with him? That he would fall apart again if he dropped his guard? Terrified, more like. After all, he'd finished his training, engaged the professional switch, and left it in the 'on' position, right up until last year, when he'd unzipped that suit bag and set the whispering free. Neither auditory hallucination, nor disembodied spirit; it was the whispering of his own subconscious and he alone was responsible for its liberation. Now the switch kept tripping, and each time it did, he got a little more used to feeling. It was strange and disorientating, but no longer terrifying, which didn't at all explain why he had decided on a meal out at a vegetarian restaurant with everyone else, when they could have been enjoying a romantic dinner for two. Because it was the way they did things, that's why, and he was looking forward to it, if for no other reason than that it was something different. OK, so the choice of venue was due to everywhere else being booked solid. Of course, they could have talked the Chinese restaurant into accommodating them, but they'd done that for last month's birthdays, and he fancied a change.

He unlocked the front door and sniffed. Coffee. Interesting, as he was supposedly first home. Slowly, he pushed the door open and listened. Vacuum cleaner. Either George had upped the ante on the dog training, or he'd been telling fibs when he said he wouldn't be home until six. He stepped into the hall and closed the door. The vacuum cleaner powered down. He glanced up.

"What are you doing vacuuming my stairs?" he asked. Eleanor pretended she hadn't heard him and proceeded to unplug the power cable and wind it up.

"Yay!" he heard from the kitchen. He walked through, arriving just in time for Adele to hand him a cappuccino.

"And who let you loose on my coffee machine?"

He heard the front door open again and turned, catching a glimpse of Andy as he disappeared from view.

"Just how many of you are here?" Josh asked. Adele giggled but didn't answer his question.

"OK. I think that's all the sawdust gone." Shaunna dumped a full, black bin bag by the back door.

"Stairs are clear," Eleanor said, walking right past him and heading for the kitchen sink.

Josh waved his hand in front of Shaunna's face. "Hello? Can anybody see me?" he asked.

Adele, Shaunna and Eleanor all looked at each other and shrugged. Josh huffed impatiently. Andy came back in.

"Alright, mate?" he smiled.

Josh grunted. "Where is he?"

"Upstairs," he said. Josh pushed past. They arrived in the hallway at the same time.

"Hi," George greeted him breezily.

"What's going on?"

"It's, um…"

"A bit complicated," Shaunna and Eleanor finished in unison, laughed and high-fived each other.

"Yeah," George grinned. "What they said."

Josh drew breath in readiness to rant and George shushed him.

"Come and see," he said. He took Josh's hand and led him to the stairs.

"Hold on," Adele called. She grabbed a tea towel and came up behind Josh, covering his eyes and loosely knotting it behind his head.

"This had better be worth risking broken limbs for," he grumbled, grasping blindly at the banister with his free hand. They stopped at the top of the stairs and he heard the sound of a key turning in a lock: the spare room, out of bounds since New Year. George took his hand again and steered him in that direction, then stepped to his side and pushed him forward. He could hear everyone else drawing to a halt behind him. Slowly, George pulled the tea towel from his eyes.

"Your birthday present," he said.

Josh blinked hard a couple of times, in an attempt to de-blur his vision and also by way of checking that he wasn't seeing things.

"What's this?" he asked, pointing to the corner of the room.

"A computer," George said matter-of-factly.

"Well yes, George, but where did it come from?"

"Dan got it off a guy in…"

"OK, I don't want to know," Josh interrupted. "And this?" He pointed to the miniature filing cabinet next the computer.

"A miniature filing cabinet."

"Which contains?"

"Your books."

"Come again?"

George stepped forward and opened the top drawer, revealing multiple memory cards, stacked on their edges, with clips across the tops so that they were suspended and hanging free. He closed the drawer and opened the one below, and then the bottom drawer, each filled with more of the same.

"All of them?"

"Every single last one. If we couldn't find it, we scanned it."

"I see. And what do I do with those?" Josh nodded at the memory cards.

"Put them in here," George said, pointing at the slot in the computer, "or in your tablet."

"Right. And my actual books?"

"In the loft."

"OK."

Josh didn't want to seem ungracious, and was, in fact, completely overwhelmed. The spare room had been transformed into an office, for him. And it had been decorated, with the wallpaper he'd said he liked when they were in the DIY store, with a matching rug and huge, plush office chair. There was a corner desk, underneath which was a full-sized, two-drawer filing cabinet. However, this was where his bookshelves and books had been, and much as he was impressed by the all-new, space-saving digital editions, he liked books—proper, paper-based, physical, *real* books.

"Any further questions?" George prompted.

"Erm, no, I don't think so," Josh said, trying to rally.

"Are you sure?" George asked, a twinkle of mischief in his eyes.

"No," Josh repeated cautiously. There clearly was more to this, but he couldn't figure out what it was he needed to ask.

"All right, then." George grinned and stepped out of the room, switching off the light on his way, leaving Josh standing in the dark.

"George, what did you do that f…" Josh was silenced when he went to flip the light switch, only for the room to remain in part-darkness because it was now a dimmer switch, whilst the sound of a motor started to quietly whirr from somewhere within. George turned the light back up to full and watched Josh as his eyes followed the stairs slowly descending from the ceiling and unfolding themselves. He turned and walked out of the room, muttering 'excuse me' a few times as he pushed past his friends, before disappearing into the bedroom.

"I'm just getting changed," he managed to explain as the door closed. "Won't be long."

Eleanor shook her head. Andy shrugged. Adele and Shaunna looked at each other in puzzlement. George shooed them away.

"It's OK," he whispered. "Just give him a few minutes."

George waited until they were all downstairs, then knocked on the bedroom door.

"Can I come in?"

"Erm…" Josh's voice was very quiet. "Yes, of course you can," he said.

George opened the door slowly and stepped inside. "You OK?" He watched Josh pretending to search through his wardrobe.

"Yes. I'm fine," he said assuredly, then gave himself away by sniffing. He started to laugh and turned around, wiping his eyes as he did so. "A bit surprised, and erm…"

George moved towards him and he looked up, studying the ceiling as he tried to blink away the tears.

"The wallpaper. Who…how…" Josh shrugged.

"Yeah. That was Shaunna. She's almost as good as you."

"Fixtures and fittings?"

"Adele. And the loft stairs were Andy's doing. He pulled in a favour."

"Bloody Jeffries and Associates," Josh laughed and cried at the same time. "I bet their 'associates' wish they'd never had anything to do with them!" He put his arms around George and kissed him. "It's incredible. I don't know what to say."

"Thank you would be just perfect."

Josh nodded. "Thank you."

"Want to come and see your real library?"

Josh took George's hand and followed him back to the spare room, where the steps were still extended. He examined them, a little reticently as they were quite steep, but there was a rail running up either side and they seemed sturdy enough.

"I'll be just behind you," George reassured him.

Cautiously, he put his foot on the bottom step.

"We can always put some cushions on the floor," George suggested. Josh let go of one of the rails and poked him. He grinned. "Or get Andy to fit a safety harness?"

"OK, I think you've made your point. I'm doing it." Josh lifted his other foot and put it down firmly on the next step. It shifted slightly, but he ignored it and continued upward.

"There's a pull-cord, just to your—ah. You found it," George said, as the loft above illuminated.

"Wow!" Josh uttered. He'd yet to make it off the top of the steps, and wasn't entirely sure he'd be able to get down again unaided, but just now that didn't matter, because he needed a few moments to take it in. What he'd been expecting to find was his bookshelves positioned around the new loft hatch, within easy reach. What he was looking at was a grown-up reproduction of the reading corner from Mrs. Kinkade's classroom. The bookshelves were arranged around the walls at this end of the loft, with two beanbags in the centre of what could well have been the rug from primary school, other than that this one was not in the slightest bit threadbare.

"How is this even possible?" he asked, once again awestruck.

"Ellie had the spare key and she's been overseeing things while I've been at work," George explained. "Once we build the extension, you can move out there, but whatever, you needed to be able to get up into the loft, and that was the main objective, really—getting the steps put in."

Josh shook his head in wonder. "I'm not going up just at the moment, but I will. I promise."

"I know you will," George said, affecting a stern tone. He made his way back down and stepped to one side.

"Thank you, again," Josh said, taking the offered hand as he came back to floor level. "Now to face the rest of them." He took a big breath and swallowed hard. "I will not cry, I will not cry," he repeated to himself as they left his 'office' and headed downstairs. He was lying.

"I just wanted to say…" was as far as he got before the tears started up again. He turned away, embarrassed, because he didn't do open displays of emotion in front of other people. Not for real.

"I'm gonna guess that means you're pleased with it?" Andy hedged.

"Yep," George answered on his behalf, "he's very pleased with it." Josh nodded.

"Great. Right. I'm off," Andy said. "I need to go home and shower. I smell like a skunk's armpit."

"Yeah, you do," Shaunna agreed, holding her nose and backing off.

Adele looked confused. "What does a skunk's armpit…oh!" She figured out the joke and giggled.

Eleanor tutted and gave Andy a hug.

"I don't care if you stink or not. Thanks." She stood on tiptoes and kissed his cheek. "Although you're right. You really do need to shower."

He pretended to be offended, then continued on his way, giving Josh a pat on the back as he passed.

"See you in a couple of hours, yeah?"

"You will," Josh managed to mumble. "And thanks for…" He waved his hand in the direction of the stairs.

"No worries," Andy smiled.

"Yeah, cheers, Andy," George said, seeing him out.

Josh had pulled himself together a bit now, and went to the kitchen to get the cappuccino Adele had handed him when he came in. It was still just about warm enough. He gulped it down in one go and was about to ask if anyone wanted a drink, when Eleanor appeared next to him.

"Hey," she said, rubbing her hand across his shoulders. "Are you all right?"

"Yes, I'm fine," he smiled. He gave her a hug. "Totally blown away, but fine."

"I've never seen you cry."

"No. I try not to." He kissed the top of her head. "Thank you so much. It's really bloody awesome."

"Oh, I didn't do much," she dismissed. "Just my usual bossing people around."

"Yes, well, someone's got to. Are you staying for a coffee?"

"No. We're going to leave you to it. See you later." She hugged him again. He followed her into the hallway and hugged Shaunna, then Adele.

"It's amazing. Thank you so much," he said.

"Aww. That's OK," Adele smiled. She gave him a peck on the cheek. "Happy Birthday."

"Yes," Shaunna said, kissing his other cheek. "See you in a couple of hours."

Josh waved them off and shut the door, then turned to George.

"So. No more lies and secrets?" he said, advancing on him. George backed away, against the wall. "That's what we agreed, I recall?"

"Well, yeah, but…"

The rest of the words were lost in a kiss that outlasted the memory of what he'd been about to say. Josh released him.

"I think I love you," he said.

"Uh huh?"

"It was on in the car."

"Ah. They played that at the sixth form ball."

"Did they?"

"Yeah. It was stuck in my head for ages. Don't you remember?"

"Of course I remember. It was stuck in my head too. I can't imagine why. Can you?"

George smiled. "So, do you still think you love me?"

"After all the lies and secrets?" Josh paused, as if he needed to consider the answer. "Yes," he said. "And I don't think. I know."

THE GODFATHER
Tuesday 14ᵗʰ February

"What does bean curd taste like?" Dan asked, the question not aimed at anyone in particular.

"Whatever you want it to," Andy replied cryptically. Dan turned and gave his brother a look that would have frightened most mortals away. Andy just grinned.

"Which dish are you looking at?" George asked.

"Dunno. Err. Lime marinated tofu? What's that like?"

George studied the description for a moment. "Lime, garlic and black pepper. That's what it'll taste like."

"See?" Andy said. "Told you."

"Yeah, he does have a point," George agreed. "Basically, tofu—bean curd—is bland, rubbery stuff that takes on the flavour of what it's cooked with. It's quite nice if it's done properly."

Josh mimed throwing up. He hated tofu with a passion. Shaunna laughed at him.

"You chose this place. Didn't you check the menu first?"

"Well, yes, but…" Josh glanced over the menu again. "Actually, no. I didn't." He wrinkled his nose. "Sorry." He smiled guiltily.

Dan frowned. He wasn't having a lot of success finding anything that he remotely fancied the sound of. He was a steak man all the way.

"Well, I'm going with the goat's cheese and rocket," Josh said and closed the menu decisively.

"Ooh, I like the sound of that too," Adele lamented. She was struggling to settle on one main dish, currently torn between the pan-fried butternut and sweet potato medley, the four cheese stone-baked pizza, and now the goat's cheese and rocket risotto. "What are you having, Ellie?" she asked. Eleanor shrugged.

"Not sure yet. I'm thinking I might have that lime marinated tofu?"

James nodded his approval. He'd been to Green Days restaurant before and tried quite a few of the dishes, including the lime tofu. It was a good choice, but he was going with the mushroom and courgette lasagne, as was Shaunna. Kris and George had both decided on the brie and wild mushroom potato cakes. Krissi and Jason were yet to arrive, but had sent their orders to Kris via text message, both opting for the butternut and sweet potato.

"Did you like your present?" Dan asked Josh, once the waiter had departed from their table. In the end Dan had settled on the goat's cheese and rocket too, because he at least knew what they were and risotto had a bit of texture to it.

"Yes, I did." Josh nodded enthusiastically to ensure that no-one was left in any doubt that this was so. "Once I got past the shock, that is. You are all far too devious for my liking these days. There was a time when I could see right through the lot of you."

"You know what they say?" Shaunna said. "Love is blind."

"I don't think they quite meant it like that, whoever 'they' are," Josh contended. "Although they do have a point." He grabbed George's hand and kissed it. George looked taken aback.

The waiter brought their drinks order over and spoke into Eleanor's ear, while she nodded in agreement with whatever he was saying. Josh watched in suspicion. The waiter left and she turned away so that Josh couldn't see her face.

"What are you scheming now?" he asked.

"Nothing." She reached across the table and selected a roll from the bread basket.

"Oh, really?" He poked her arm.

"Really," she said with a wink. However, she did need to talk to him about something else and had been intending to do so earlier, when he came home from work, but hadn't anticipated his response to his birthday surprise and didn't get the chance as a consequence. Now she cupped her hand around his ear and whispered. He nodded. She continued. He smiled.

"Yes!" He started to jiggle with excitement.

She whispered some more.

"No, of course not, you goon," he said and hugged her. "It's only right, isn't it? I mean, he's…"

She whispered one final thing.

"Yes, now," he agreed.

"OK," she said. Only James, to her right, and George, to Josh's left, had been paying any attention to their bizarre dialogue. She looked George in the eyes.

"What?" he asked.

"I want to ask you something."

"Right?"

She looked at Josh, a worried expression on her face. "What if he says no?"

"He won't. Just do it!"

"OK," she said again. "George?"

"Yep?"

136

"Do you believe in God?"

"Um, I guess. Maybe. I can't say I've thought much about it."

"But you're open to the possibility that there is a God, unlike someone else not sitting a million miles away." She smiled quickly at Josh. He turned and looked at George.

"Which has no bearing on her next question, incidentally," he told him.

"Confused," George said, crossing his eyes and scratching his head. Eleanor laughed.

"Would you like to be Toby's godfather, George?"

"Really?"

"Of course really."

"Oh my...no way!" He leapt up and pushed past Josh's chair, then grabbed Eleanor and hugged her tightly, kissing her all over her face. "I would be so honoured to be—oh wait. Am I allowed?"

"Yes. Well, I haven't told the priest that bit, but it's not relevant, is it?"

"OK, if you're sure."

She shrugged and looked to James. He nodded. "We're sure."

"Well, then, the answer is—yes!" George said. He almost hugged James, but thought better of it and shook his hand instead, then hugged Eleanor again. "How exciting! I can't believe it. I'm going to be a godfather!"

"George, sit down," Josh said, tugging at his t-shirt. "You're making the place look untidy." George's antics had attracted the attention of a few of the other customers, but he was oblivious. He giddily returned to his chair.

"I'm going to be a godfather," he told Josh.

"I know. What happened to your usual 'um, OK'?"

"Too excited!" He couldn't stop smiling. He poked Adele, who was sitting to his left. "I'm going to be a godfather," he said.

"Who to?" she asked. Everyone else groaned. "Oh!" She giggled. "Yay!" He hugged her and she squeaked.

"Oh, that reminds me, George," Shaunna said. "I needed to speak to you about something."

"Sure. Go ahead," he smiled happily.

"Are you going to be a godfather?" she asked.

"Why, yes, I am!"

"That's awesome," she laughed.

"Good grief," Josh said.

Their food was delivered soon after and they continued in this vein throughout the meal, pausing to welcome Krissi and Jason, who quickly caught up with the news and the eating. As well as George, Eleanor and James had asked Ben, the eldest of Eleanor's younger siblings, to be a godparent, because it was easier than not asking him. The priest was prepared to compromise on George's not being a Catholic, if the other two were confirmed and had received Holy Communion, but even if he had not made this stipulation, the choice was obvious, and now that George had got over his initial excitement, the time was right. Eleanor and James nodded at each other and looked across the table, waiting for the current conversation to reach a suitable pause.

"Veggie?" Shaunna said loudly. "Since when?"

"Erm." Jason turned even paler, if that were possible.

"Always," Krissi stated.

Shaunna looked from her daughter to Jason and back repeatedly. She flicked her hair over her shoulders and turned away. Then she turned back again.

"I'm not cross with you, Jason," she said.

He swallowed hard.

"Really, I'm not, so don't you go getting upset now." She gave him a smile and patted his arm. "However, it would've been nice if *someone* had told me—Missy!"

"I know. Sorry, Mum," Krissi mumbled. Twenty-three years old and still a ticking off from her mother could silence her in an instant.

Eleanor watched the two women trying to ignore each other, picking at their meals, now rather less appetising than they were a few minutes ago.

"I'm surprised you're not vegetarian," Kris said to George.

"Why?"

"Well, with your whole animal thing going on…"

George shrugged. "If I could kill it myself, I figure it's OK to eat it."

"Hmm. Interesting philosophy."

"And complete tish," Josh scoffed. George turned and looked at him.

"Just because it's your birthday…" he started.

"If you could kill it yourself?"

"Yeah? What's wrong with that?"

"What, like cows, you mean?"

"Ah." George grinned.

"No more roast beef dinners for you!"

"Nor you!"

"Oh, I can still have them," Josh said, moving his face up close to George's, "because I don't need to justify my right to eat them."

George was staring right into his eyes. "No, but you do need to cook them."

Josh smiled. "OK. You win."

"That easily?"

"For now," he teased.

"So, anyway," Eleanor interrupted. "Shaunna."

Shaunna, who was currently trying to spear a very wayward sliver of courgette, just said, "Hmm?" without looking up. Eleanor waited for eye contact and as soon as it was granted, the request made itself without the need for words. Shaunna's face broke into a wide smile.

"Me too?" she asked.

"Yes, you too," Eleanor confirmed. "That's if you…"

"Yeeeeesssss!" Shaunna punched the air and then reached across the table to bump fists with George.

"Yo! Fellow godparent!" she said. He laughed. "We're gonna be an awesome team."

Dan shook his head. "Poor kid."

"Yeah," Andy agreed.

After that, things settled down a little and when they'd finished their main courses, Krissi passed a small, cylindrical gift to Josh. It looked like a poster tube, but was much heavier. He frowned in puzzlement as he opened it, poked his finger inside and then quickly withdrew it, looking a bit concerned as to what he might find.

"It's all warm and furry," he explained, as he tipped the tube and shook it, the item inside slowly working its way free. It fell onto his hand and opened out, revealing itself to be a mouse mat that was a tiny, yet exact replica of the rug on the floor of Freud's study.

"That's really awesome! Thanks," he gushed, once again overwhelmed. This wasn't the first time they'd gone all out to spoil him on his birthday, but it was a long time since it had affected him like this. Perhaps Jess was right: the old Josh was back, not that he'd been aware that he was acting any differently, until last September. He could feel the tears coming on again and used the mouse mat as a distraction, positioning it on the table and his knee, and generally admiring it, but then nearly knocked his drink over it, so rolled it up again and returned it to its tube, turning away to stow it safely in the pocket of his jacket, hanging on the back of his chair. When he turned back, there was a cake on the table, complete with candles.

"A cake? At my age? Are you serious?" He glared at Ellie and she tried to act innocent.

"Don't forget to make a wish," Adele said. Josh sighed and shook his head.

"I really am too old for this, but here goes." He thought for a moment, settled on a wish and blew out the candles. The flames flickered away then relit themselves.

"Oh, what a surprise," he said dryly. He blew them out a second time, and once again they re-ignited. "Do I get a wish every time?" he asked.

Shaunna shrugged. "Why not?"

Josh laughed, blew them out one last time and quickly extinguished the wicks with dampened fingertips. Everyone clapped and before he got as far as saying, "Don't you dare sing Happy Birthday," they were all doing it. When they were done embarrassing him, he sliced up the enormous cake and handed it around. It was delicious—coffee cake, with a vanilla buttercream topping, baked by Shaunna, and with just one thing missing. The waiter wrapped the remaining slice of cake in foil for him to save for Jess, when the Reading case was over, or when she ran out of excuses for not coming home. Josh hugged and thanked everyone and carefully carried the slice of cake out to the car. He'd had a fantastic evening, even if he did find the whole notion of celebrating a thirty-eighth birthday a bit ridiculous.

Back home, George made coffee for Josh and poured himself a glass of squash, taking them upstairs to the 'office', where Josh had been playing with the remote control for the stairs ever since they got back, Blue sitting next to him, the pair of them following the movement with their heads. When the stairs next came to rest against the floor, George went up into the loft and turned on the light.

"Come on," he called down.

Josh and Blue gave each other a look.

"I guess we'd better," Josh said to the dog. Blue put his ears down. Josh patted him reassuringly, took a deep breath and started climbing the stairs, although he was more worried about the downwards than the upwards, but they were sturdy and not that steep really. He stepped off the top, into the loft and breathed out, panting, as he'd held his breath all the way up. He turned and looked down through the hatch, keeping a tight grip on the top of the handrail. Blue was still at the bottom of the stairs, with a paw on the first step.

"You can do it, Blue," he coaxed. The dog tried a couple of steps, then gave up and walked away.

"Never mind," George said, "he'll do it in his own time, but here *you* are." He flopped into a beanbag and his legs went up in the air. Josh laughed, then did exactly the same with the other beanbag. Eventually they both righted themselves and got into something of a more comfortable sitting position.

"This is amazing," Josh said, glancing over his bookshelves then attempting to shuffle closer to George.

"I'm so pleased you like it. I wasn't sure how you'd feel about having everyone traipsing around, and not knowing about it, and, well…anyway. I'm glad you like it."

"I do." Josh reached over and attempted to kiss him, but only managed to graze his cheek with his lips.

"Was Ellie OK with you saying no?" George asked.

"No to what?"

"Being godfather."

"She didn't ask me."

"Oh." George frowned. "I thought she'd asked you first."

"Why? You're the perfect choice."

"I don't know about that."

"Hmm. Whatever, George."

George frowned, not really following what Josh meant.

He explained: "Firstly, there's the way you and Ollie just kind of bonded. And then there's the fact that you completely ignore all us adults every time we go round to visit. You love Ollie and Toby, and they totally adore you too. You're already doing it!"

"OK," George accepted bashfully. "If you put it like that." He wriggled about, then reached across to the bookshelf and pulled out a slim, paperback volume. Josh squinted at the cover and grinned.

"We can read a paragraph each," he suggested.

George shook his head and laughed. "I don't think I've ever got past the first couple of chapters," he said, flicking through the pages of the book— Charles Dickens' *Great Expectations*. It was a book they had partly read together at primary school. He put it back on the shelf and shuffled round so that he was facing Josh, although he wasn't making eye contact.

"I need to, err," he began hesitantly. He took a breath and started again. "Well, it's like this. I know you're a grown-up and everything, but it took us so long to get together that I really don't want to lose you now. And it's your choice I guess. I can learn to live with it if I have to. But I really…"

"George. What are you talking about?"

"Smoking."

"Pardon?"

"As I say, if you…"

"I'm not smoking."

George looked at him doubtfully.

"I'm not. I promise."

"OK. I just got a sniff of smoke on your sweater this afternoon and— forget it then."

"I'm never going to smoke again, not after seeing the state of your mum's flat." He used his whole body to shift himself and puckered his lips. George leaned across and kissed him. "See? No nasty cigarette breath."

George nodded to show he believed him.

"Right. I'm going down. Do you want to call the fire brigade now? Give them advance notice?"

George tutted. "I'll help you to get down. I'm very proud of you."

"Me too!" Josh said. "Your turn tomorrow."

"Oh no."

"Oh yes. Today lofts, tomorrow cows."

It took a couple of attempts for George to get up out of the beanbag, after which he went part-way down the loft stairs and turned back, with his arms out, more for security than anything, although he could probably have held Josh's weight if he did fall. Josh stepped down, his face serious and pale, but he made it to the bottom.

"See? Not so hard at all," George said.

"No, piece of cake!" Josh retorted sarcastically, although he was laughing, but then he recalled the cake he had saved for Jess, and his birthday wish.

"Hey." George took his hands.

"I'm OK. Just thinking."

"I know. Your wish?"

"Yes." Josh closed his eyes and snuggled into George's shoulder.

"Let's not worry about it now. Have you enjoyed your birthday?"

"I have. Thank you."

"And I really am so proud of you. You went up and all the way back down again, by yourself."

"Yes, I did. So, definitely the cows tomorrow."

"Maybe not."

"I can give you until Easter."

"Make it summer and I'll think about it."

"We can start with calves, work our way up."

"Cows on hills?" George suggested with a grin.

"I dare you."

"You're on!"

WHEN HARRY LEFT SALLY-ANNE
Thursday 16th February

"Adele! Daahling! Mwah! Mwah!"

Her stepmother embraced her swiftly and released her.

"Come in, daahling," she said, stepping aside. She attempted a smile in Dan's direction, although it was far more sultry than that. "Henry's in the den," she instructed him.

Dan nodded and headed straight down the hall, through the kitchen and out to the shed, where, sure enough, Adele's dad was sitting, watching a fishing programme, on the tiniest TV screen.

"Alright, Harry?" Dan greeted his 'father-in-law'.

"Dan," Harry replied by way of returning the greeting. Without getting up or looking round, he reached into a small fridge to his left and extracted a can of lager.

"Cheers." Dan opened out a canvas camping stool and perched alongside.

"I'm leaving your father, daahling," Sally-Anne declared, viciously thrusting the cafetière plunger down into the glass vessel.

"Again?" Adele muttered under her breath.

"What, sorry, pardon?"

"I said 'oh dear'," Adele lied. "Why? Has he upset you, Sally?"

"Sally *Anne*, daahling," Sally-Anne decreed. She knew Adele deliberately missed off her middle name to spite her, but always went along with the pretence that the girl knew no better. She was barely a decade older than Adele herself, which was, of course, why they despised each other so thoroughly. For *Henry*, though, they could put their differences to one side. Most of the time.

"The thing is, Adele, sweetie, he's just so dreadfully selfish. Did I tell you about the fishing trip?"

"No?" Adele didn't really want to know about the fishing trip. It would be the same story as the last fishing trip, and the one before that, and the bowling competition in Cumbria, and the free tickets he won to the World Snooker Tournament finals.

"Well!" Sally-Anne began dramatically, then paused, her mouth poised in an upside-down smile, her breath held with it. She exhaled, "Eau," and turned the smile the right way up. "Shall we go and sit, daahling? Then I'll tell you all about it."

Adele briefly smiled back and followed Sally-Anne into the living room, balancing on the edge of the cream damask armchair. No way were there this many plants here the last time, she thought, poking a pointy leaf away from her face. Little Shaunna climbed up onto the sofa and stuck her thumb in her mouth. It was past her bedtime.

"So," Sally-Anne began again, "last weekend, your father announced he was going night fishing, insisting that he'd told me weeks ago. Well, I said, Henry, dear, you did absolutely nothing of the sort, or else I would have known. And, I said, had you told me, I would, obviously, have bought in supplies for your trip."

She paused to listen, as the patio door slid open, her face morphing into an expression somewhere between dismay and disgust, as her husband used the toilet with the door open, farted loudly and flushed. Adele tried not to laugh, but little Shaunna noticed and started giggling.

"Do you see what I have to put up with?" Sally-Anne sighed dramatically. "And it's not just the fishing trip. Oh no. He snores like, like…a giant snoring whale."

"Do whales snore?" Adele asked. "Where do they sleep? Do they even go to sleep?" Sally-Anne's eyes rolled in their sockets, and she flopped back into the sofa. Shaunna watched her and looked at her mother, raising her hands as if to say, "I don't know why."

"And, of course, there's the Viagra saga." Sally-Anne picked up a copy of *Cosmopolitan* and fanned her face.

"Oh!" Adele was too shocked to say anything else. She took a mouthful of her coffee and swallowed quickly. It was *disgusting*!

"I did tell you about the Viagra saga?" Sally-Anne asked. Adele shook her head dumbly.

Oh please don't tell me about the Viagra saga.

"Well," Sally-Anne said, waving her arm. She struggled to pull herself upright, her legs lifting into the air with the effort. She was wearing electric blue mules with three inch heels, her matching blue painted toes hanging over the ends of the open fronts, and sunshine yellow skinny jeans. It was most unbecoming. "With Henry's ED being down to the diabetes," she pronounced the word 'diabeats', "he's entitled to the treatment on the NHS, but he won't see the doctor about it. Too embarrassing, he says. But you know how it is, daahling, there's only so much Mr. Duracell can do for a gal."

Adele wanted to be sick. Sally-Anne always had this effect on her. Twenty-five years: that's how long she'd endured these laments. Twenty-five years, and it still made her want to vomit.

"So, I told him: Henry, dear, you simply have to see Doctor Walker, or else we're done for. And do you know what he said?"

"No?" Adele asked, even though she didn't want to know at all what her father had said, but was very much hoping it was along the lines of 'go boil your head, you crazy bitch'.

"He said, 'I'm going to bed. Good night.' And that's just what he did. Left me here, sitting all alone, our marriage in tatters, while he snores away like a, like a…"

"Snoring whale?" Adele suggested.

"Quite," Sally-Anne agreed. "A snoring whale." She fanned herself again with the magazine. "And I'm having terrible hot flushes. They make me come over all bilious."

She got up and made a tremendous deal of staggering from the room and up the stairs, from whence the sound of aerosol spraying could be heard for several seconds.

"Dat?" Shaunna asked, pointing in the direction of the noise. Adele mimed spraying deodorant to her daughter.

"Sally-Anne stinks," she said. "Pooey."

Shaunna giggled and pinched her nose.

Sally-Anne returned downstairs and resumed her position in the middle of the sofa.

"I'm afraid, daahling, that your mother was right all along. Your father is a swine."

Meanwhile, out in the 'den', Harry was on his third can, Dan on his first and only, because he was driving.

"Women are like that," he was telling his 'father-in-law'. "But you know what they say. You can't live with them…"

"You're not wrong there."

Neither spoke again for several minutes, instead tuning their hearing to the quiet ruminations of the man on the telly, who was sitting in amongst a clump of bull-reeds, an orange float bobbing on the lilypad-dotted surface of the lake before him.

"One of these days I'll say bugger off then," Harry said, flicking the ringpull on the top of his can. "When she starts up with this 'I'm leaving you' crap. I'll just say, 'Off you pop, petal.' God, I'd bloody love to have the balls."

"How long you been married now?"

"Twenty-five years. You get less for murder. A bit of plea bargaining, keep your head down, you could be out in half that."

Dan laughed. True: Sally-Anne was hard work, but he didn't imagine Harry was a whole lot of fun to live with either. He loved his daughter, and would do absolutely anything for her, which was really the cause of his marital difficulties. Sally-Anne was jealous. Even Dan could see that, for Harry did like to share, whenever he deigned her worthy of listening to at all. She'd said some pretty horrendous things about Adele over the years, behind her back and to her father, but never to her face. She wasn't a very nice person and they were well suited, but Dan did feel a little more sorry for Adele's dad.

"We should go inside," he suggested. He swigged the last of his beer and stood up.

"You go on," Harry told him. Dan shrugged and left him to his fly-fishing programme. Sally-Anne was in the kitchen, preparing 'canapés', or, in fact, Ritz crackers with cream cheese and smoked salmon of the supermarket value variety, not that there was anything particularly wrong with that, but it was the passing it off as something better that epitomised the kind of woman she was. Adele was slowly winning her battle with herself not to emulate this, for much as she disliked her stepmother, she was the closest she had to the real deal.

"Hi," Sally-Anne breathed at Dan as he stepped in through the patio door.

"Everything all right?" he asked.

"Oh, yes. Adele and I have been having a lovely chat." She moved as if to pass him, then deliberately fell against him. "I'm terribly sorry," she gushed, fluttering her false eyelashes.

Dan gave her a brief smile and backed away as far as was possible in the narrow kitchen. She stank of alcohol: vodka, at a guess.

"These heels are such a nightmare," she explained, tottering artificially and giggling—her usual performance. She grasped him by the left bicep as she shimmied past. He tried his best to relax the muscles. She wasn't a bad looking woman really, but he'd learned long ago that most beauty was only skin-deep, *and* she was his 'mother-in-law'. Eventually she made it to the door, but not without scraping her fingernails the breadth of his chest. He followed her, at a safe distance, to the living room, stepping around a giant parlour palm and still getting slapped in the face by a huge, hand-shaped leaf. He glanced at Adele, ignoring Sally-Anne's deliberate preparation of the centre cushion of the sofa—between her and Shaunna—and sidestepped across the cluttered room to the other armchair.

"Canapé, anyone?" Sally-Anne offered, smiling brightly and trying to hide her obvious disappointment at Dan's choice of seating. Little Shaunna climbed down from the sofa and went to sit on her dad's knee. Adele took one of the small biscuits, for the sake of politeness. They were already starting to go soggy, and the smoked salmon was tasteless.

"I was explaining to Adele before," Sally-Anne addressed Dan, "I'm thinking of getting some wallpaper for in here." She indicated to the walls, as if he wouldn't know where wallpaper should go. Adele's mouth dropped open. This was absolutely *not* what Sally-Anne had been explaining, unless the wallpaper had a purple diamond pattern running through it! She didn't say anything, though. God forbid that she should inadvertently encourage her to further divulge details about the sex she wasn't getting from her father. It really was all a bit too much.

"And you see," Sally-Anne continued, "Henry's health just isn't up to interior design these days."

Dan nodded once.

"So, if you've got a little time for me, in your terribly busy schedule, sweet, I'd be ever so grateful." She blew him a kiss, the newly applied lipstick transferring from her lips to her fingertips. Adele folded her arms and looked the other way. Dan smiled awkwardly. His phone vibrated against his leg.

"Gotta take this," he said, and made a hasty exit, taking his daughter with him. Sally-Anne turned and blinked meaningfully at Adele.

"Are you planning on going away this summer?" she asked.

"Yes. We're going to the South of France in July." They weren't; they were going to Turkey in August, but if Sally-Anne knew that, she'd be begging to come too, and they'd done that once before. Never, ever again.

"France? Eugh. It's so…full of the French," she said. "I can't stand it. The language, the culture, the wine, the food. All dreadful." She shuddered in disgust, then picked up the silver platter on the table. "Another canapé, daahling?" She thrust the tray at Adele and got up, staggering slightly; this time it wasn't faked.

"Just popping to the powder room," she said, wobbling on her heels as she exited, passing Dan in the doorway. He watched her leave and mimed drinking to Adele. Adele nodded.

"Can we go soon?" he whispered.

"Yes," Adele whispered back. "Just need to go and see my dad's OK first."

"He's fine," Dan assured her, "but he's miserable as sin."

"He's always miserable as sin."

"More than usual."

The toilet flushed and a moment later Sally-Anne came back into the room, minus one of her shoes yet continuing on her trajectory as if she hadn't noticed it was missing. She fell onto the sofa and hiccupped.

"I'm popping out to see Daddy," Adele said and left, knowing that Dan was in danger of being attacked, but in her present state Sally-Anne would be easy enough to fight off and wouldn't try anything too risky with little Shaunna there. At least, that's what Adele hoped.

"Hi, Daddy," she called, as she pulled open the shed door. It was quite a cosy set-up, with the chair, and the TV and the fridge. He was smoking a cigar.

"Hello, girlie," he smiled and lifted an arm so she could snuggle close and give him a hug.

"You OK? Dan said you were fed up."

"Oh, nothing to worry about. Just getting used to this being retired malarkey. Settling in, they call it." He'd turned sixty-five the previous September and wasn't much enjoying the copious leisure time it afforded him. His health wasn't good enough to make the most of it, and his wife was too demanding. "Are you all right now?" he asked.

"Yes. I'm all better. Dan took it hard, but I think he's getting over it."

"That's good," he replied vacantly. He was staring into the mid-distance and Adele glanced across the shed, spotting the photo album. Her mother: she hadn't seen her since the wedding, when she'd turned up in a short, white dress with a red ribbon around the waist, red shoes and a hat with an enormous red bow. Trailing behind her was a little man, possibly of Italian origin, who went by the name of Paolo, had a Geordie accent and a lisp and called her 'Meethelle'. At one point, just before Adele and Tom left the reception, Paolo was singing to her mother: The Beatles' song of the same name; no easy feat with his lisp and dreadful accent. Her mother had said something to him, in French, assuming that no-one else would understand. However, Josh had heard and understood enough of it to pull her to one side and tell her how inappropriate it was for the mother of the bride to behave the way she was behaving. Adele refused to speak to her, for if there was one thing she and Sally-Anne had in common, it was an utter despise of her mother. Unfortunately, the same was not true of her father.

"We're going soon," she said to him, her mind drifting back to the present. "Why don't you come round at the weekend, on your own, and watch the football?"

"No—thanks. I don't want to be in the way."

"You won't be in the way."

Dan was right. He was even more miserable than usual, and she hated to think of him sitting out here, alone, depressed, while Sally-Anne was in his house, getting tanked up on vodka, or gin, whatever her currently preferred poison. And that was why the living room was full of plants: Adele had seen the bottles stashed in the pots. There was one in the toilet cistern, another under the kitchen sink, two behind the fridge. Sally-Anne needed professional help. She'd quite possibly go to her grave before she accepted any.

"So are you going to come?" Adele tried again. He got up, gave her a hug, and kissed the top of her head.

"I'll think about it. How's that?"

"OK," she accepted. "Night, Daddy. Love you."

"Night, girlie. Love you too."

***

The next morning Sally-Anne found him, cold and blue, propped in his chair, burned down cigar in the ashtray, empty can fallen into his lap. He looked ever so content. The fly fisherman mumbled on.

Pisces

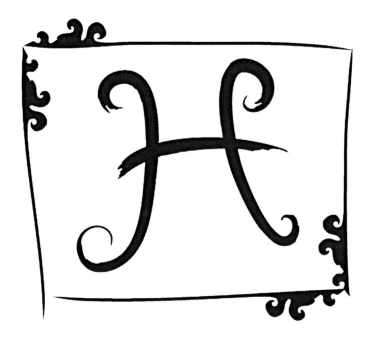

Last of the sacred signs, you bring to me
A word of hope, a word of mystery.—
We all are swimmers in God's mighty sea.

WHODUNNIT PART ONE
Monday 20th February

The woman who brought the trolley smiled and left; Sean acknowledged her with a polite nod. He'd asked for coffee and tea, thus there were two mini-urns, paper cups, and a basket filled with clear plastic packets, each containing three digestive biscuits. Not bad, really. The hospital were usually a little less forthcoming, but this was the only place with a room large enough for a 'case conference', which is what he'd booked it in as, and it was a case conference—of sorts, albeit a very small one, but still too big for his office, here or at the university, and also not strictly hospital business. Now to wait for everyone to arrive; he checked the time: still another fifteen minutes to go, which meant…

"Afternoon," Josh greeted him, already with eyes narrowed in suspicion.

"Josh," Sean nodded. "Thanks for coming." He shook his hand and indicated to a seat at the top end of the conference table.

"What's this about?" he asked. He sat down and checked his phone.

"A case of wrongful imprisonment."

"Of whom?"

"I'll explain when everyone else gets here."

Josh accepted this and got up to pour himself a coffee. He returned to his seat with his paper cup and took a sip.

"Ugh, that is revolting." He put the cup down and peered into it with a grimace.

"Yeah, it's pretty bloody awful stuff they serve in here. Pity the patients, I do, having to endure that muck."

"Think I might swap it for tea," Josh suggested.

"I wouldn't go to the trouble if I were you."

Josh nodded and instead took out his tablet, turned it on and opened a game.

"You're restless today," Sean observed.

"Hmm? Not really. I just hate this place." He closed the game and put his tablet down on the table, almost to prove the point. There was a knock at the door and one of the nurses poked her head into the room.

"Doctor Tierney? Are you expecting someone called Hadyn O'Farrell?"

"Yes, Kate. Is he here?"

153

She disappeared from view. Voices were heard outside, then Hadyn came in. He smiled at Sean and held out a latex gloved hand.

"Hi, Doctor Tierney," he said. Sean shook the offered hand.

"Hello, Hadyn. You're looking well. Thanks ever so much for coming along today."

"Oh, it's OK. I've got to be at work in an hour and a half."

"We'll be finished long before then, don't you worry. This is my colleague, Josh Sandison," Sean introduced. Josh stood and shook Hadyn's hand.

"Hi," he said. There wasn't much else he could say, as to do so would be to betray George's confidence. Instead, he prepared himself for acting out the novelty of their meeting. He was fairly certain that he wouldn't have reacted to the gloves, even if he hadn't known the reason for them in advance, so he continued the charade of ignoring them. Hadyn retracted his hand from Josh's.

"OCD," he explained. Josh mouthed an 'oh'.

Hadyn took a seat on the other side of the table to Sean and Josh, perching himself on the very edge and trying not to fidget.

"How's it been going?" Sean asked to keep him distracted, even though he'd seen him only a few hours ago.

"Very well," Hadyn nodded. They set off on a conversation that Josh found extremely uninteresting, and once again picked up his tablet. He reloaded the game. He was curious about why Sean had invited him, but there was no point in asking, because he was evidently playing the suspense card.

"So, who else are we waiting on?" Josh tried as a subtle probe in the next pause in Sean and Hadyn's dialogue.

"Just a couple of prior employees of Campion Holdings PLC, and a GP."

Josh nodded without looking up from his game. The door opened again. Josh still didn't look up.

"Ah, Doctor Brown. Glad you could make it," Sean greeted the newest arrival. "This is…"

"Josh?"

Josh paused with his finger on the screen.

"Ellie? What the hell?"

"Doctor Brown, please help yourself to tea or coffee. It's not great, I'm afraid, but it's the best I can do."

"I'm all right, thanks, Doctor Tierney." She sat down next to Josh and took a water bottle from her bag, along with a note pad and pen.

"This is Hadyn O'Farrell," Sean said. Eleanor smiled at the young man sitting three seats to her left.

"Hello," he muttered awkwardly.

"We're just waiting on Bill Meyer, your husband and Alice Friar now," Sean explained—to Eleanor. Josh glared at him. "Everything all right?"

"Fine. Everything's absolutely fine," Josh smiled. "Actually, I've just remembered, I needed to talk to you about something—in private." He indicated toward the door with his head. "It's quite urgent," he said. Sean's right eyebrow went up involuntarily and he gave Hadyn and Eleanor a quick smile.

"Excuse us," he said. He got up and made his way across the room, Josh following. They stepped outside and Josh closed the door.

"Just what is going on, Sean?"

"Fun, isn't it?" Sean grinned at him.

Josh breathed out of his nose, hard. "Whatever 'it' is, you're turning it into a bloody circus. Now, if you don't start talking, and soon, I will start walking."

"No you won't."

"Watch me." Josh pushed down on the door handle, keeping eye contact with Sean.

"OK, OK," he said. "I'll tell you this much." He paused, trying to decide on the least exciting aspect he could so as to not spoil his great reveal. Josh watched on impatiently. Sean's lip twitched. Josh opened the door an inch. That was enough.

"Kevin Callaghan, in my learned opinion…" Sean paused again. Josh snarled.

"Security cameras or not, so help me, in a minute I'm going to…"

"Didn't kill Campion," Sean finished off quickly.

"I see," Josh said, predictably. "And from where did you learn this opinion, precisely? Vera Bennett?"

"Erm, well…"

Josh shook his head. "So why are we all assembled here? What's it got to do with any of us?" The sound of approaching voices stopped him from going any further, as Alice Friar and Bill Meyer rounded a corner and came into view.

"Miss Friar," Sean smiled and held out his hand. She backed away. "Ah, of course. The synaesthesia," he acknowledged courteously. "My apologies." He kept smiling and shook Bill Meyer's hand instead. Eleanor stuck her head out through the door.

"James is caught in traffic. He said he'll get here as soon as he can."

"All right, so I guess we can make a start. Shall we?" Sean signalled towards the room, and Alice and Bill went inside, looking distinctly bemused. Sean stepped aside to allow Josh to pass, but instead he indicated with his arm.

"After you, Ringmaster," he said. Sean mimed taking off a top hat and bowed, which only riled Josh more.

"Good afternoon," Sean smiled at the people gathered within; he waited until they were all seated before he sat himself. "Thanks, all, for coming today. I felt this was the most efficient way to try and establish some facts. First, if I might introduce you all to each other on your behalf, which isn't to say you don't know who you are yourself." He stopped and smiled again. His audience was not impressed. "However, there are certain aspects of who you are and what you do that are more pertinent than others, as regards to why you're all sitting here now.

"First off, I'm Sean Tierney, a clinical psychologist, here at the hospital, but more importantly, also at the hospice, where the late Mrs. Jenny Campion spent her final days. To my left is Josh Sandison, a psychotherapist and close friend of both myself and Doctor Eleanor Brown—to his left. Eleanor is a general practitioner and was previously married to the late Kevin Callaghan. Next to Doctor Brown is…"

"Pardon?" Eleanor interrupted. "Did you say *late* Kevin Callaghan?"

"Ah." Sean had assumed that someone in the prison would have informed her. "Yes," he said. "I'm sorry. I thought you knew."

Josh examined him closely, but Sean wasn't letting anyone in, not while he was performing. He'd deal with it later.

"Eleanor," Sean continued, "if you'd prefer, we could pop outside and have a chat before we go any further?"

"Err, no, it's fine," she said, nodding to confirm. He accepted this and went on with his introductions.

"To Doctor Brown's left is Mr. Hadyn O'Farrell, who was an acquaintance of Kevin Callaghan, and has what we might call 'inside information'. Around from Hadyn is Miss Alice Friar, a longstanding employee of Campion Holdings PLC. Prior to Mr. Campion's death, she was his personal assistant. Next to Alice is Mr. Bill Meyer, previously chair of the board of directors at Campion's. We are also expecting Mr. James Brown, managing director of The Pizza Place and a close friend of Mr. Campion. As some of you will already know, he was the lead suspect in the investigation of Mr. Campion's murder, a crime for which Kevin Callaghan was later found guilty.

"I'd hoped the psychologist from the prison where Callaghan was serving his sentence would be here, but she has been suspended from duty, pending an investigation into her conduct involving, would you believe, a certain Mr. Kevin Callaghan. Intriguing, is it not?" Sean smiled again. Still his audience remained straight-faced, but they did at least seem curious.

"By now you'll all be thinking to yourselves this is a waste of a perfectly good Monday afternoon, and you'd be right. But our choice here is quite simple. As easy, you might say, as the decision of what to have for breakfast, or…"

"Doctor Tierney," Josh interrupted, "some of us have other duties to attend to, so if you could please cut to the chase."

Sean nodded graciously.

"Of course, Mr. Sandison." Sean picked up a pile of papers and handed them to him. "Please help yourself to a copy and pass them along."

Sean watched as the papers circulated around the table, each person examining the two page printout carefully. Some were frowning, others squinting, all trying to make sense of the information they were reading. Alice was the first to realise what it was.

"This is the series of events leading up to Mr. Campion's death," she said. Now he'd got her attention. She continued onto the second page, nodding her head and intermittently tapping at the sheet with her finger. "Yes," she said and nodded a little more enthusiastically, "and yes. Of course!" Bill Meyer leaned across and asked her a question. She pointed to something on the list and he nodded. Josh looked to Eleanor to see what she thought. She looked as confused as he felt. There was a firm knock at the door and Sean went to open it.

"Ah, Mr. Brown. Glad you could make it. Come in, come in." He stepped to the side. James came in and looked around the room.

"Eleanor? Josh?" His eyes traced the circumference of the table. "Miss Friar. Mr. Meyer." He looked to Sean.

"I'm about to explain." He gave James a copy of the document everyone else already had. "Ladies and gents, I would like, if you'll permit me, to take you back in time, to the hours preceding the death of Alistair Campion."

"Why?" Josh asked.

"Because…" Sean began, but Josh cut him off before he got any further.

"See, much as I'm sure everyone's enjoying the whole *Columbo* routine, it would be far easier if you just tell us what you know, or ask us questions—whatever the reason is that you've gathered us here today."

"True enough, Josh. But I'm sure you can appreciate better than most how easy it is to inadvertently lead a witness."

"OK," Josh conceded. "Get on with it, then."

Sean smiled at him and he fake-smiled back. By this point James had caught up with everyone else and now turned to Sean.

"Kevin Callaghan didn't murder Alistair," he said, then to Alice: "Perhaps our suspicions were correct, after all."

"I believe you are right, James," she said.

Everyone else in the room was silent, their eyes flitting from one to the other, awaiting further explanation.

"James?" Eleanor queried.

"You may recall from our evening in the jazz bar," he looked from Eleanor to Josh as he said this, "that I mentioned one of the offenders Alistair had supported? Alice and I were both of the opinion that it was he who was responsible, but we could think of no motive."

"So why did you suspect him?" Josh asked.

"For the same reason the police suspected me," James said. "It had to be someone with access to Alistair, who would not have looked out of place on the directors' floor, which meant it had to be a director, or a close associate."

"However," Sean said, "let's not forget that Callaghan was working at the hospice at the time, so could potentially have gained access that way, which is why the police were happy to accept his confession."

"Indeed," James agreed.

"But he would have had to come through me," Alice said. "And he didn't."

Josh examined her for a moment before he spoke, choosing his words very carefully. "Alice, can I ask why you didn't say anything at the time?"

"I tried, but the police weren't interested in listening." She smiled sorrowfully. "I was just the mad old secretary who saw things that weren't really there, as far as most of the staff were concerned. And then Callaghan confessed, so there seemed little point in saying anything. I just assumed I'd got it wrong."

"But you didn't ever believe that, did you?"

"No. You're quite right, Mr. Sandison. My synaesthesia allows me to see things other people can't see." Now she studied him, or rather, the space around him, and made eye contact once more, her brow creased slightly with concern. Josh nodded.

"I understand," he said.

"The day Mr. Campion was murdered, I could see *his* scent—the man James and I suspected. And he shouldn't have been there at all, because Mr. Campion had dismissed him a month before. But he'd been in the coffee room, and then, when I went up to the boardroom, I could see that he'd been in there too. I met Doctor Callaghan just once, and I was quite certain he had never been to the offices, but the police—well, they had their man, so what did a crazy old crone who…" She stopped, but what point was there to continuing with the secret now? She had nothing left to lose. "They found out about our affair, and our son, and they started to pursue him. When they arrested Doctor Callaghan I dared not say anything, for fear that they would interrogate Jason further."

Throughout Alice's explanation, Bill Meyer had sat, quiet and still, with his head bowed. Now he looked away. To his credit, he would have offered comfort, were it not for the synaesthesia, like he had tried to offer it so many times before.

"What is it, Bill?" Sean asked.

"As you are no doubt aware, my wife and I adopted Jason, thus I share Alice's concerns regarding his welfare. If you tell the police about any of this, they will re-open the investigation, will they not?"

"Quite possibly."

"And Jason will immediately become their prime suspect."

"I find that unlikely. He wasn't aware he was adopted until after the murder."

"Do you honestly believe that will stop them from interrogating him? After all, they accepted Kevin Callaghan's confession without question."

"And the eye witness identified a black man, which Doctor Callaghan was not," Alice said.

"Then we must ensure that you are given the opportunity to make a statement this time," Sean told her.

"Skin colour didn't protect Callaghan," Hadyn pointed out. It was the first time he'd spoken.

"Hadyn is right," Bill said.

"We'll seek assurances from the police first," Josh said. "I think that maybe…"

Sean laughed haughtily, stopping Josh mid-flow. "You're telling me you'd trust the police to conduct a fair investigation?"

"They didn't have all the evidence. If Alice…"

"I'm sorry, Mr. Sandison," Alice interrupted, "but for Jason's sake, I must refuse."

Sean exhaled loudly. "When there is still a murderer on the loose?"

"Who has kept his distance," Bill said.

"So far," Josh argued.

"Enough!" Eleanor said loudly. Everyone stopped talking at once.

"My apologies, Doctor Brown. I didn't realise you were waiting to speak." Sean attempted a polite tone, but the discussion was getting a little heated.

"I wasn't, particularly," she snapped. "But Doctor Callaghan," she looked at Alice as she said his name, "held me hostage in his car for two hours. He had a knife. He stalked me for a year. He was mentally ill. Just because you didn't see him doesn't mean he wasn't there."

Alice didn't have anything to say and looked like she was about to start crying. Josh looked at his friend, and, knowing the risk he was taking, decided to speak out.

"I don't think anyone is suggesting Kevin was entirely innocent, Ellie."

"Oh, I'm so glad to hear it!" She got up and shoved her chair in. "Don't forget, while you're getting all excited about your big murder mystery, that my husband was the prime suspect last time. And as Hadyn so succinctly explained, James doesn't even have the alibi of skin colour to protect him. I'm done here." She left the room, everyone stunned to silence for several minutes after she'd gone. Josh was in two minds whether to follow her, as was James, but both stayed. In the interim, it had dawned on Josh that Sean hadn't told them anything. He'd merely set the ball rolling.

"Doctor Tierney, you have yet to explain. Why did you convene this meeting?"

"Because I have been given sufficient reason to believe what James and Alice have said all along. Kevin Callaghan did not murder Alistair Campion."

"And your evidence?"

"A letter from Kevin Callaghan, which I have in my possession, offering an explanation for his actions prior to his arrest." He opened his folder and gave the letter to Josh. "I will leave it with you to read and judge what should be done with it."

"This letter," Bill interjected, "does it contain information that might influence our decision about whether we co-operate?"

"Potentially, yes, but it is a private letter, addressed to Doctor Brown. It is therefore right that she sees it first."

"I have another letter," Hadyn said quietly.

"What was that, Hadyn?" Sean asked. Hadyn coughed to clear his throat.

"I have another letter from Callaghan," he said, loud and clear this time. He extracted from his pocket the very crumpled, folded up square of lined paper and held it at arm's length. Josh reached across and took it from him, noting the name handwritten on the topmost face.

"It's addressed to you," he said.

"Yes," Hadyn confirmed. "It's OK. I don't mind you reading it." Josh nodded and carefully began to unfold it. Hadyn watched. "It's a suicide note, to say goodbye."

Josh dropped the paper and it fluttered down onto the table. Sean leaned forward to retrieve it, deliberately resting his hand on Josh's shoulder as he did so.

"I'm, err..." Josh swallowed. "I'll leave you with that and go and see if Ellie's all right." He left the room.

Sean waited until the door had closed before he opened out the letter. He scanned over the words; much of it was what he'd expected to find: apologies, lessons for young Hadyn to take from Callaghan's suicide, how he had no other choice—a shorter and more emotional version of what was in the files Diane Sheridan had left with him. However, there was one piece of information that wasn't in the files. Sean re-read it and looked around those who remained in the room.

"Did any of you know Kevin Callaghan, prior to him being arrested for Campion's murder?" People looked to each other, shaking their heads to confirm that they did not.

"No," James said. "Why do you ask?"

"It is apparent that Callaghan's experience of the world was somewhat departed from reality, although it is difficult to establish how far."

"So you are hoping that someone can substantiate what he has written," Bill observed.

"Quite," Sean said, turning his attention back to James. "And ideally without involving Eleanor."

"Your concern for her wellbeing is much appreciated," James said. "However, if it will help…"

"You misunderstand me, James," Sean interrupted. "Of course, I am concerned for her welfare, but—see, Callaghan mentions a name here, of the man he believed was responsible for murdering Alistair Campion."

James and Alice made eye contact across the table.

"He also states that this man visited him in prison on a number of occasions, and was someone with whom he was in contact prior to his arrest."

"Dare I ask?" James said. "Who is this man, Doctor Tierney?"

Sean nodded. "Yes, James. I'm afraid it's you."

MILK BAR
Monday 27th February

She stopped across the street to consider her options: the building on the right was an old pub, renovated and regurgitated to meet the requirements of the modern consumer; in other words, it sold a range of pretentious pre-packed foods, fake gassy beers and fruit-flavoured ciders, and at two o'clock on a week day afternoon was the very last place she wanted to be. Or, to be accurate, the last place she wanted to be next to home. On the other hand, she could see inside the building on the left, and it was chock-full of teenagers, which was a good thing in some respects, as it meant it was well on its way to being a roaring success and was keeping its customers off the streets. As for being somewhere she could pass a few hours alone? Shaunna sighed and crossed the road.

The milk bar was kitted out exactly as she'd anticipated, with way too much chrome and two-tone, and tables in their own part-secluded booths running from the rear wall to the full-front window. To her left there was a bar with high stools (all occupied) which terminated at the serving counter, today being staffed by three smiling student types, all dressed in red and white striped shirts and black pants; over these they wore aprons emblazoned with what she assumed to be (although she was too preoccupied to have noticed on the way in) the milk bar's rather unimaginative logo, consisting as it did of the word "Milky's", in swirly neon style writing. Shaunna took her position in the queue and glanced once more at her surroundings. There were no free tables.

"Yes please?" The voice of one of the young women behind the counter called her back.

"I, err…" She hadn't even begun to consider what she might want to drink and scanned the lit wall menu in panic. "Can I have, err—what d'you recommend?"

"Depends what you like," the girl smiled cryptically. This wasn't at all helpful and Shaunna raised her eyebrows in alarm. Maybe she should have gone to the pub next door after all.

"I like milkshake," she offered. The girl laughed.

"That doesn't narrow it down much in here."

Shaunna looked the menu over again. Fruit Yoghurt Crush: that sounded OK. "What's yoghurt crush?"

163

"It's a fruit and yoghurt based smoothie, with a crushed fruit topping."

"Right. I'll have the blueberry one."

"An excellent choice," the girl said, far too enthusiastically. "I'll bring it over for you. Where're you sitting?"

Oh God! So many decisions! Shaunna swivelled on the spot. The only space was at a table currently occupied by a man on his own and probably the only other person in here above the age of twenty-five.

"Over there," she said, hoping he wouldn't mind sharing his booth. The girl nodded and set about preparing the order. Shaunna loitered a moment longer, readying herself to invade the space of someone who looked even less in need of company than she was.

"Excuse me," she said hesitantly. The man looked up from the book he was reading, or had been, until she disturbed him. She smiled. "Is it OK if I sit here, only…" She looked around the crowded establishment by way of explanation. He shrugged.

"Sure. Be my guest." He turned his attention back to his book. Shaunna mumbled an apology and sat down on the opposite side of the table. The seats were not as comfortable as they looked and she perched awkwardly on the very end, trying to keep as much distance between them as she could, watching the comings and goings of the young clientele, all of them looking very much more at home than she or her new acquaintance.

"I don't bite," he said without looking up, "which is to say I don't mind sharing my table, so feel free to spread out." He turned a page and said no more. Shaunna shuffled a little further along the seat. The waitress brought her drink over and she tacitly smiled her thanks rather than further distract the man from his reading. She leaned forward and sucked gently on the straw sticking out of the glass in front of her, but the thick liquid resisted her effort entirely. She sucked a little harder. Still nothing: she gave up and stirred the purple gloop a couple of times, then tried again, this time getting the slightest hint of blueberry and yoghurt on her tongue.

"It's got a scoop on the other end," the man said, still with his eyes focused on his book. Shaunna frowned, confused at first, but then she realised what he meant and lifted the straw free, examining the scoop cut into the dripping end of the wide tube. He was watching her, she could tell, even though his head was still bowed. And he was laughing. At her.

"There's a bit of a knack to it," he said, positioning a bookmark between the pages and exchanging the book for his own drink: the same as hers, but in pink; strawberry, or raspberry, perhaps. He took hold of the straw, tilting it at an angle as he pulled it from the glass, so that the scoop was loaded with red mush. "Imagine you're eating a dessert," he suggested. She watched him put the fruit in his mouth and chew. She followed suit with her own 'drink' and the silence resumed, as they each repeated the motion several times over. It was hard-going, but a wonderful diversion, because this was the first time she'd thought about what had brought her here. She felt the man's eyes on her and smiled self-consciously.

"I'm not usually so stupid," she said.

"Don't beat yourself up about it. You buy a drink, you expect to be able to drink it. That's not stupid, it's common sense."

"I suppose."

He was still watching her. Why was he doing that?

"Do you come here often?"

And why did she ask that? She blushed. He laughed.

"No," he said. "As a matter of fact it's my first time. You?"

"Mine too." She gave the drink another stir and tried the straw again, with some very limited success. "I half considered going to the pub next door—not a good idea really, the way I'm feeling." What was she doing?

"A lot on your mind?"

"Yeah, you could say that." No way was she going to tell him. Why was she even thinking about it?

"Pretty big stuff too, isn't it?"

She took a breath in. No. Shut up, Shaunna, she said, in her head.

"Say no more," he said gently. "You don't want to talk about it with a total stranger. A wise move, for sure." He busied himself with his drink and she watched him, properly. He was a little older than she was, maybe mid-forties, and sounded like her grandfather, so originating from Derry, or thereabouts. He met her gaze and she crinkled the corners of her eyes in thought.

"You don't seem like a stranger," she said.

"How so?"

She shrugged. "You remind me of one of my friends."

"Oh, so there's two dashingly handsome and disgustingly immodest Irishmen in this town?"

She laughed. "You're from Derry?"

"A long time back, but yes. I came here to study. How about you? Those glorious, fiery tresses of yours are an export of our Emerald Isle, are they not?"

Shaunna nodded. "My mum is—was—Irish. She's dead now. And my dad's dad was Irish too."

"Perhaps, then, we are not strangers, so much as misplaced fellow countrymen, if you'll pardon the outdated and terribly exclusive term."

"Maybe." Shaunna took some more of her drink; the ice was starting to melt now and it was liquefying nicely. It reminded her of…she closed her eyes. She didn't want to think about it.

"The name's Sean, incidentally," he said. She opened her eyes again.

"Shaunna," she replied.

165

"It suits you." He mirrored her actions, intentionally. She wanted to talk; just needed permission to do so. They continued in silence for several minutes, intermittently slurping liquid through their straws, stopping only to deal with fruity obstructions. Her jaw was aching from the effort, both of the drink and trying not to speak. She relented.

"Do you ever feel like you're going crazy?"

"All the time. Why?"

"Just wondered if it was me, or everyone gets like this."

"It sounds like you're a pretty together kind of girl usually."

"Usually," she echoed. Surely she wasn't going to tell him?

"We all go through difficult times and it's no bad thing to admit to it," he said.

The words were ready to fall from her mouth, yet it was almost as if she didn't need to speak them in order for him to understand.

"You read minds," she stated.

"I read people," he corrected. "Minds come with them." She frowned, confused.

"Let me explain," he suggested and continued, assuming permission had been granted. "You took a drink from your straw and registered pleasure that it had melted sufficiently for this to be possible, and yet a further thought trespassed into your consciousness, associated with this very specific act, which you neither wanted to face yourself, nor share with me. So you closed your eyes in an attempt to conceal it from us both."

Shaunna folded her arms. He smiled.

"Even I know this is defensive," she assured him, "although I'd be a lot more freaked out by what you just did if I hadn't seen it done before."

"Well, the choice is yours. Tell me if it will help, or don't tell me."

"I feel bad for disturbing you."

"I was merely passing the time, and, like you, trying to find distractions. You are a more than welcome distraction, believe me."

If he put it like that…

"It's a very long story," she said, once again endeavouring to thwart the desire to purge herself on this man—Sean—whom she had known for less time than it took for a yoghurt crush to melt.

"It's longer still if you don't begin telling it," he laughed, but not at her this time. She joined in.

"You're right. About the drink thing, I mean," she said. He gave her his fullest attention. "I got pregnant when I was fourteen. My husband, ex-husband, not sure which, but whatever, back then he was just a friend. We went for milkshakes and he did what you're doing to me now essentially, until I told him. We sat for hours with those milkshakes. Hours! They were like water by the time we got to them."

166

"Ah. That makes sense." Sean attended to his drink and Shaunna followed his lead, in many ways disappointed that it was all but gone. He read her again and agreed. "Shall we have another, do you think, or is it terribly forward of me to suggest it?"

"No. I'd like that," she consented. He shuffled along the seat, ready to make his way over to the counter to reorder, but the waitress spotted him and came across.

"Same again?" she asked. Sean looked to Shaunna to check this was correct. She nodded.

"Thanks," he said and shuffled back, but not quite so far along this time. "Girl or boy?"

"Girl."

"And she must be about what, fifteen? Sixteen?"

"Ha! I wish. Try twenty-three!"

"You surprise me," Sean said. The mistake was sincere and Shaunna appreciated the compliment.

"This husband-ex-husband of yours sounds an interesting fellow."

"How could you possibly know that?"

"You told me." Sean's eyes twinkled with something approximating to mischief. Shaunna's nostrils flared, but the indignation was short-lived and she felt herself smiling.

"Did I also tell you that I love him with all my heart?"

"Yes you did, even after what he has done to you, and—" Sean watched her a moment and nodded. "And what he has asked of you."

The waitress delivered their drinks and Shaunna busied herself with repositioning the glass.

"That's all I know, incidentally," he told her.

That was enough. More than enough. And yet—

"What he did to me, or for me, was stay by my side for twenty-two years without faltering. But when he fell, it was with an almighty crash. He loves me still. He won't let me go." Shaunna spun her drink between her palms; what she'd said wasn't quite right and she took a deep breath, reloading the words upon it. "He won't let go of me."

"Do you want him to?"

It was a question she had refused to consider. He was her best friend, and if he were to release her, there was a chance that their friendship, like their marriage, would be no more.

"Can I lay it on the line?" she asked. Sean gestured his acquiescence. "He has a new partner who loves him very much. They want to start a family, which, they insist, requires my assistance. And before you ask how I feel about it, I don't know. I can't even start to think about it, when he has betrayed everything we had."

"Your husband is gay."

"He desires men, yes. And he probably does love his new partner, but not enough. Not to bring up children together. Our children."

Sean watched her crumble, although to the rest of the world she would still have appeared whole. She used the scooped straw as a crook, grasping it until it bore the entire weight of her sorrow.

"We never discussed having a baby, not in all the years we were together, married, conventional—a traditional family. Now? Now he wants to discuss it."

"Did you ever tell him you wanted to have a child together?" Shaunna didn't answer. "OK. And do you want to do this?"

She shook her head. "I wish I could be that selfless."

"No you don't." The words were gentle yet accusing. Shaunna started in defence; yes, she was being selfish, but she had every right to be.

"I told him I couldn't be a surrogate, but that's not what he wants. He thinks we can continue the way we are, all three of us sharing a house, bringing up 'our' child together, and you know something? I could go along with that." She stopped speaking, looking for a reaction, a judgement.

"Do you want me to tell you what I think?" Sean asked. Again, she gave no conscious response. "I don't usually, because what I think will take on its own significance. For instance, I tell you to leave him and you do it, which I merely use as an example to illustrate, not an instruction, and then you spend the rest of your life wondering why you followed the advice of an Irish guy you met in a milk bar on a miserable Monday afternoon."

"Do you want to tell me what you think?"

"I'd love to, but heed my warning. For whilst I firmly believe that we are in agreement about what you should do, I have, on rare occasion, been known to be wrong."

It was difficult to decide whether he was as arrogant and conceited as his turn of phrase implied, but Shaunna was curious to know his thoughts, so she allowed him to continue.

"It is entirely reasonable to reject the proposal on the basis that he has betrayed you, by discussing this idea with his new partner and not with you, regardless of how immature and selfish this might seem. Bringing a child into the world requires that the parents who commit to the responsibility do so willingly and with no prior reservations. And whilst your living arrangements are somewhat unconventional, they are of no consequence to the decision you face. If they work for the three of you, then it is no-one's business but yours. And now that I have said too much, we should attempt to drink our fruit yoghurt crush and get out of here."

He stirred the unappealing melted mush in his glass and immediately changed his mind. He pushed it away, glancing at his half-read book.

168

"Is it any good?" Shaunna asked.

"No. It's boring as hell, but that's the thing with academic texts. Dry as a nun's—well you get the idea, I'm sure."

"Yeah," Shaunna smiled. "I appreciate you sacrificing your peace and quiet to listen to me ramble on about my mad life."

"It's no great sacrifice. And I've enjoyed it. You're quite a woman, Shaunna."

"Thanks. For your ear and your company. I'd offer to return the favour, but I have nothing to give."

"Ah, now that's where you're wrong." Sean leaned across and retrieved his jacket from where it was still draped around the impression of where he had been sat when she arrived. "I can think of three things you can do for me immediately."

Shaunna waited while he pulled on the jacket, noticing a slight change in his presentation, no longer quite so cocky.

"Firstly, you can promise me that you'll do what is right for you, and not for your husband-ex-husband."

"OK. Done."

"Secondly, you can come and eat pizza with me, give me a chance to unburden myself of some of my own very heavy, although perhaps somewhat less colourful laundry."

"Now?"

"Yes, now. You've nowhere you need to be, or else you'd have already left."

"Fair enough. I'd really like that, but can we make it something other than pizza? Only my daughter runs the pizza restaurant and I'd rather not over-complicate her already bizarrely optimistic view of her parents' relationship situation."

"Absolutely. Your choice then."

"And the third thing?"

"I'm a recovering alcoholic and I really want a drink. I'd be tremendously grateful if you'd stick around until the urge passes. It's a big ask, of a stranger, I know."

"But not of a misplaced fellow countryman," Shaunna reminded him. He couldn't argue with that.

REDEMPTION
Wednesday 1ˢᵗ March

Josh pinched the inner corners of his eyes. He was getting a headache—not surprising, after six hours straight of appointments. It had been an average day, nothing worthy of any further comment; suffice to say that the cold, damp weather meant the middle class housewives of the world were still out in their full winter blues, and he'd been listening to their misery for the better part of it. Now it was late afternoon; he was hungry; more to the point, he hadn't had a coffee since lunchtime. Another two hours and he could go home. But first he was going to head out for a breath of fresh air, a sandwich and a large cappuccino to go from the coffee shop up the street. He grabbed his jacket from the closet, locked up and swiftly cleared the stairs, keeping his head down, in case anyone tried to intercept him en route to his much needed caffeine fix. And as he walked, he took the opportunity to mull things over.

A week and two days had passed since Sean's appallingly judged meeting to revisit the murder of Alistair Campion. He'd expected a massive fallout, but so far all was quiet. Because of Adele's father's funeral, Alice was completely preoccupied with little Shaunna and anyway had little intention of stirring things up. Sean said he'd spoken to Bill, and he merely reiterated their stance on the day: their primary concern was Jason. James was in Birmingham for The Pizza Place AGM. George had been to see Hadyn to make sure he was coping, and from what he could see, he was actually dealing with the situation far better than anyone else. As for Eleanor? Perhaps the less said about that the better.

Twenty-eight years: that's how long they'd known each other, and for most of those had considered the other to be their 'best' friend. Twenty-eight years.

That equated to twenty-seven years without any major disagreements, followed by two in the space of an afternoon. Indeed, the disagreements were so major that they hadn't even got as far as discussing them, and quite frankly, Josh was still struggling to think of a reason—beyond curiosity—why he should bother. Less than six weeks until the christening: they probably ought to try and sort it out before then, not that he had any intention of backing down. For now though, his foremost concern was to try and get rid of his headache.

"Large one, is it?" The woman behind the counter smiled knowingly as he breezed in (it was a pretty gusty day). He nodded and watched as she set up the espresso glasses and prepared a takeout cup. The coffee shop was quiet—just a couple of women, sitting together, each with a paperback in one hand, attempting to lift a massive, soup tureen style cup of frothy coffee with the other. The woman behind the counter peered into the fridge and frowned.

"Won't be a sec," she said and disappeared through a door out back. Josh examined the various accoutrements of coffee-making behind the counter, in an attempt to discern the problem, noting the almost empty milk carton. He yawned and took out his phone for something to do.

16:41, Dan
Been trying to get hold of you - call when you get this. Cheers.

He closed the message to reveal a screen filled with missed call notifications: four from Dan and two from 'number withheld'. His head really hurt. Maybe he should stop at the chemist on the way back to the surgery and pick up some paracetomol.

The woman returned behind the counter and opened the new carton, spraying herself with milk in the process. She cursed and filled the metal jug.

"You OK?" she asked.

"Yeah. Headache," Josh explained. It was lack of caffeine. He knew it well. George would tick him off later, should he be foolish enough to mention it, although if the barista noticed, then it would be the first thing George would see when he walked through the door. Yes, paracetomol and a large dose should see it off.

"Actually, can you make that two?" he asked the woman.

"No problem," she said. She finished off the first and put it on the counter in front of him, then started on the second. Josh's phone vibrated against his chest. Another missed call from Dan. He pressed 'return call' and waited.

"Alright, Josh mate?"

"Not too bad. What can I do for you?"

"Right, well," Dan paused. Josh flinched as a shooting pain hit the back of his eyes. "The thing is…" Dan continued clumsily. Josh sighed, trying to hide his irritation. He really wasn't up to dealing with any of Dan's traumas today, not with everything else that was going on, and this damned headache. He remembered the cappuccino on the counter and took a quick swig.

"Aitch called me," Dan explained. "Long and short of it, George has been arrested."

Josh stopped breathing for a few seconds.

"My George?" Obviously, he thought, after he'd said it, but the mind misfires when confronted with the incredible.

"Yeah. Apparently he wouldn't give the station your number, but Aitch saw them bringing him in."

"What's he been arrested for?"

The woman placed the second cup in front of him. He couldn't believe what he was hearing. Surely there had to have been some mistake. George? It was ridiculous. Josh passed across a twenty pound note.

"It's tricky to explain," Dan said. "Can you come to the station?"

"I'm on my way." Josh hung up and picked up the other coffee cup.

The woman turned around to give him his change, in time to see him disappear through the door. She shrugged and stuck it in an empty compartment in the till, along with a note which read, "the counsellor guy forgot his change". She cleaned the machine and went back to her crossword.

Josh more or less ran back to his surgery, cleared the stairs in three leaps, grabbed his tablet and set the alarm. Halfway through this process, he remembered to leave a note on the door for his remaining clients for the afternoon, then also called them both from the car. His head felt like it was splitting in half. He drank one of the cappuccinos in one go and was starting the second before he'd reversed out onto the road. This was madness, and he was driving like an idiot, he realised, when the car behind screeched to a halt, the driver banging angrily on his horn. Josh mouthed 'sorry' as the other car tore past; he took a couple of deep breaths and tried to focus. It took quite some effort.

Five minutes later, he pulled up opposite the police station and behind Dan's empty 4x4, drank the other cappuccino, then sprinted across the busy road, waving his key fob over his shoulder on his way. There was no-one on the reception desk, so he rang the bell and waited. He was starting to see flashing lights. Just a migraine, hopefully. It would pass. He pressed the button again. Still no-one came. He took out his phone and brought up Dan's number at the same time as a door opened and a female officer came into view.

PC Granger. Oh, joy.

She pulled the perspex screen of the shutter open.

"Hi." Josh attempted a smile, but winced instead. He groaned and shut one eye.

"Mr. Sandison," PC Granger nodded courteously. "How can I help you?"

"I got a call from my friend to say—actually, is DI Hartley available? He knows what this is about."

"I'll call up and see," she said coolly. She closed the screen, turned away and picked up a phone. Josh could just about hear her speaking, but not what she was saying. She was nodding. She glanced back at him, put down the receiver and opened the shutter again.

"Detective Inspector Hartley is busy. One of his team will be down to see you shortly."

Josh nodded in acknowledgement and sat down. She watched him for a moment.

"Do you know why you're here, Mr. Sandison?" she asked. Her tone was different this time. Quieter. Softer. Concerned. That was far, far worse than the brusqueness he had encountered on the previous occasions they had met, during Alistair Campion's murder inquiry.

"Not entirely, no," Josh admitted. His vision was starting to blur. She must have noticed something wasn't right, as he heard the buzzer sound to release the door and the next minute she was sitting next to him with her hand on his arm.

"Are you all right?" she asked.

"Erm, no, actually." Josh stood up and bent over double. He felt like he was going to pass out. PC Granger knelt on the floor and talked quietly.

"Just take deep breaths. Slow down," she said. Josh tried to do as advised. She kept talking to him, reminding him to breathe slowly. Gradually the dizziness started to subside and his sight partly returned. He sat down again and carefully righted himself.

"OK?" PC Granger asked.

"Yes, thanks," Josh smiled unconvincingly. She gently patted him on the shoulder and continued to sit with him. A minute or so later, Dan came into view, accompanied by a non-uniformed officer, but not Aitch. The officer let Dan through and was about to follow, but Dan waved him off.

"We'll come back later," he said. The officer nodded. Dan went straight over to Josh and sat on his other side.

"Blimey, I know you're fair-skinned, and everything..." Josh's face was colourless. "You OK, mate?"

"I'll be fine. Just a migraine and caffeine rush," Josh explained, hoping to reassure himself at the same time. *It doesn't have to be a symptom*; he heard Sean's voice inside his head. "What's going on?"

"Let's go for a coffee, or something," Dan suggested. Unable to do anything but follow directions, Josh carefully stood up and dumbly followed Dan outside.

"There's a pub across the road," Dan said, steering him diagonally away from the police station and in the direction of a large building that Josh could just about make out in the jagged edges of his peripheral vision.

"Wait," he said, as soon as they reached the opposite pavement. Dan stopped walking, but kept hold of Josh's arm. It was a bit strange, this whole role reversal thing, and he wasn't really sure what to say or do, so he remained where he was, until Josh looked ready to move off again. He was squinting against the streetlights and they really weren't that bright.

"Do you need painkillers?" Dan asked.

"I've got some migraine tablets in the car, but they don't work."

Dan nodded in understanding. He wasn't a great believer in painkillers anyway—better to let nature take its course.

They continued to walk and made it to the pub. Dan went to the bar, returning with an orange juice for Josh, and a glass of Coke for himself. Josh kept one eye shut, which was helping a little.

"What's happened?" he asked.

"I'm not entirely sure," Dan began. "Apparently, George was in the park and intervened in a dog fight. The owner of one of the dogs attacked him, and he defended himself."

Josh blinked hard a couple of times and shielded his eyes with his hand. "That doesn't sound right," he said.

"Tell you what. I'll see if Aitch can come over and explain it when he's finished interviewing."

"Is he interviewing George?"

"As far as I know."

***

George was sitting in a police cell, staring at a blank wall. He couldn't believe what had happened—didn't want to believe, but it was there in his head, on constant rerun, as if he were watching it on a TV screen, rather than having been part of it. He was appalled by what he had done, if he had done what his memory was insisting he had done. He examined his hands, for traces of evidence, physical clues to substantiate the feelings of dread and remorse. He was in shock. He heard a key turn in a lock. The door opened. He followed up from the black shoes, to the charcoal suit trousers, jacket and tie. Aitch.

"Alright, George. Now, listen to me. Do *not* say anything. Nothing at all, do you hear me? I'm going to try and delay taking your statement, say that the duty solicitor is unavailable, but you need to stay quiet, do you understand?"

George nodded. He understood what was being asked of him, but not why.

"Josh?" he asked.

"He arrived a while ago. Dan's taken him over to the pub to explain what's going on. I'll sort out for you to see him when they come back."

George shook his head. "No. I don't want to see him."

"But…"

"Not yet."

"All right. I'm gonna go and sort things out. Just try not to worry, OK?"

"Thanks," George said. Aitch locked the cell again and George flopped back against the wall. He should have asked if the guy was OK. Not that he cared one way or the other. The rage started to resurface. He'd do it again. And that was what was frightening him most.

***

Aitch spotted them sitting in a dark corner of the pub and came over.

"Dan, Josh," he greeted them gravely.

"Aitch," Dan responded. "Can I get you a drink?"

"No—thanks. I'm not staying."

Dan nodded. Josh glanced up. The migraine was fading, thankfully. They were brutal, but short-lived. He swallowed back saliva and attempted a smile.

"You look like death warmed up," Aitch said. He dragged a stool across from the next table along and sat down. "Right, here's what we think's happened, but it's based on what the witness said, and they weren't prepared to make a formal statement, for obvious reasons, as will become apparent.

"There were a couple of lads with a big dog, pit bull type—Staffy-Boxer cross we think. A decent dog in the right hands, that. Anyway, the other bloke—the one George didn't half-kill—scarpered. Their dog attacked another dog, not sure what it was. It's undergoing emergency surgery. It's in a bad way.

"The two lads were goading their dog on, thought it was funny. The other owner was shouting at them to get their dog away, but they took no notice. That was when George arrived. He pulled the two dogs apart, and one of the lads went for him. The other owner isn't really sure what happened after that. He heard a dog yelping and George shouting. The next minute, the lad who attacked him was on the deck, choking. His mate pulled George off, called the police, then did a runner.

"When my colleagues arrived, they called an ambulance, and the lad who attacked George is in hospital. He's regained consciousness and is demanding to make a statement. I'm just on my way there now, to explain to him why that's not a good idea."

"Gotcha," Dan said. "So…"

"Hang on," Josh interrupted. His brain wasn't functioning properly, but he was starting to panic. There was only one reason why George would have been in the park, and it wasn't to play on the swings. "George would've been walking Blue."

176

"Ah," Aitch said. He went quiet. Josh closed his eyes. He didn't want to ask, but he needed to know what had happened to Blue. He was a big dog, but young and good-natured. He wouldn't be able to fend off or outrun a strong, aggressive dog, especially one owned by people like that.

"Is he safe?" Josh asked, praying that the answer was yes.

"I don't know," Aitch said. "He wasn't anywhere in sight when my colleagues arrived."

Josh nodded. That was good news, then. He took out his phone and made a call.

"Sean? Can you pop to the house and see if Blue's there?" He paused to listen to the person on the other end of the line. "I'll explain later." He hung up. Dan looked at him and he held up his hand. Thirty seconds later, his phone rang. "Hi…he is? Thank God," Josh covered his eyes, but this time it was in relief. He checked Sean was OK to look after the dog until later, hung up once more and put his phone away.

"Was he there?" Dan asked.

"Unbelievably, yes," Josh said, his voice trembling. One of the first things George had insisted on doing was teaching Blue how to find his way home on command. Josh had thought it crazy, just George showing off, but now not so much.

Aitch got up and put the stool back where he'd got it from. "Right, I'm going to see that tosser in the hospital. I'll let you know where we're up to as soon as I can, OK?"

"Thanks, Aitch," Josh said. "Am I allowed to see George?"

"I don't have a problem with that, but he doesn't want to talk to you yet. I think he's waiting to see what happens first."

Josh nodded. "All right," he said. "Will you let him know that Blue's safe?"

"Will do."

They watched him leave and Josh sagged in his seat.

"How you holding up?" Dan asked him.

"Ha! I'm not."

Dan smiled sympathetically.

"On the plus side, the headache's nearly gone."

"Well that's something, hey?"

"Yes, I suppose." Josh sipped at his orange juice, his mind tearing around in circles, trying to comprehend what was going on. *George attacked someone.* Strangely, the more he replayed the words, the more sense they made. Dan stayed quiet, watching his friend, his personal counsellor for two decades, and tried to remember the lessons he had learned. Now was his opportunity to repay some of the debt he believed he owed.

"You want another drink?" he asked.

Josh nodded. "Best make it a double," he joked. Dan smiled and went off to the bar, returning a short while later with the same drinks as last time, plus an extra bottle of orange juice. Josh shook his head and laughed lightly. He picked up the bottle and studied the label in order to focus his thoughts.

"George did something like this when we were younger," he said, peeling back an unstuck corner of the label. "We used to go on bike rides all the time, down by the canal, mostly. It was a really nice ride in summer, along the canal to the lock, then out into the countryside for a few hours. We got to see dragonflies and all sorts of rare birds and wild flowers."

"Sounds just the sort of thing you and George would enjoy," Dan said. "Why?"

"It's kind of arty-farty and intellectual at the same time."

"You know, I'd protest if it weren't the truth," Josh admitted. "We always got to see a lot of large red damselflies, which are large and red, believe it or not. Beautiful creatures to look at from a distance, not so pretty up close, but we'd have these—I've no idea why I'm telling you this—we'd have really geeky conversations about the different colouring and size, and whether it was related to how successful they were in mating. Likewise, there was one pure white mallard, a male, and it was always with females, yet there were no white ducklings. You wouldn't believe the hours we spent speculating whether it was albino or just a white duck."

Josh smiled at the memories, then became solemn once more.

"This one time, though, we'd stopped to rest by the lock, and there was a gang of boys, a bit older than us, I'd say, and they were throwing stones at a swan, which is a bit bloody stupid to begin with. And the swan was hissing, on the attack, its wings spread wide open. They can be vicious at the best of times, but this one had babies—three of them, I recall. One of the boys went to kick it and George literally leapt up and was over there before I even had a chance to draw breath. He knocked the lad to the floor and was about to smash him in the face with…"

Josh closed his eyes. George had made him promise not to tell anyone about what happened, but they were young then. And he'd come this far. He had to finish the story now.

"He picked up a length of timber and would've killed him, I'm quite sure of it. He's got a red mist thing going on when it comes to animals. One of the other lads got a hold of the timber and disarmed him, luckily. And somehow I managed to talk him down. It's mental. When you think how peaceable he is the rest of the time, that he can just snap like that."

Dan shrugged dismissively. "We've all got something that makes us lose it," he said. To him this wasn't shocking at all. George could be incredibly sensitive and he was a very measured man, but why would he be any different to anyone else in this regard?

178

Josh took a gulp of the orange juice as if it were whisky. He almost wished it was. "The only person he'll be beating up right now is himself."

"Yeah, that's true. It gets you like that, once the adrenaline's worn off a bit," Dan said, then realised how arrogant he sounded. "But then, you'd know that," he added, a little more humbly this time.

"I don't have a whole lot of firsthand experience, I'm glad to say."

"Surely there must be something that makes you angry?"

Josh thought about it for a moment or so and smiled.

"Yes. You," he said. Dan laughed.

"That's only when we've had a drink."

"Yeah, OK, and it's not angry really, it's stroppy, although you're just as bad! No, what makes me really angry is dishonesty."

Dan picked up his glass and looked away.

"What was that for?" Josh asked.

"I didn't say a word."

"You didn't need to."

"It's just—" Dan frowned. "Well, it's a bit hypocritical. I mean, all those years, pretending you weren't interested in George."

"All those years?" Josh repeated. Dan coughed nervously. "Just how many years are we talking?"

"Err…" Dan was trying to come up with a change of subject, but he wasn't a quick thinker.

"Go on, Dan. The truth," Josh demanded. Dan shifted in his seat. Josh forced a change of posture, to try and let him off. "You're right, of course. I've loved George for a long time, and you don't have to answer, but I'm still interested to know how long you think it's been."

"I can tell you when I first saw it," Dan offered. Josh shrugged by way of giving consent. "That first time, coming back on the plane from the ranch. You looked just how I felt after Adele left me for Gavin."

"Oh, good God. Gavin. He was a complete…"

"Turd."

Josh laughed. "Not the word I'd have used, but accurate, nonetheless."

"I thought me and Adele were done for when he came on the scene."

"Seriously?"

"Yeah." Dan became wistful. "He was like me in many respects—an astute businessman, he really knew his stuff when it came to technology—could be very charming too, and he was…"

"A beefcake," Josh interjected. Dan turned and looked at him.

"I'd never have guessed you were into guys," he said. "Not in a million years. Didn't give it any thought, if I'm honest, until the trip to the ranch."

"Hmm," Josh said, "now that *is* interesting."

"Why?"

"You don't remember calling me queer at school?"

"Can't say I do. You sure it wasn't someone else? Or aimed at someone else?"

"No. It was definitely you, and definitely aimed at me."

"Ah, well. Sorry about that. You know what the banter was like. It could've been anybody. It only took one of the lads to say something a bit soppy and we'd have been calling them that. Always something or nothing."

"Yeah," Josh agreed vaguely.

"Anyway," Dan said, "that was kind of when I knew, on the plane and then for a while after. The others said it was because you blamed yourself for him going OS, but I thought, no. There's more to it. You were really down in the dumps, not eating, hardly talking and I figured—well, yeah."

"It's shit, isn't it?"

"You can say that again," Dan agreed. "But it's all behind us now."

"True enough. And are you recovering? You look a bit happier."

"Yeah. It's not so bad. The doctor reckoned there was probably something wrong with the baby, so it was better that we lost it early on. Maybe we'll try again."

"You don't sound too keen."

"I am. Adele isn't. We'll see."

"How's she coping with her dad?"

"Not great. We're just waiting to see what the fallout is with the will and stuff. Sally-Anne buggered off to a detox clinic the day after the funeral, so we've just got to hang fire for now."

"Detox? Prozac, presumably?"

"Nope. Booze. She made a total idiot of herself at the crematorium— went tearing after the coffin as the curtains closed and pulled them down on top of herself." He started laughing at the memory of it. "She was…" now he'd lost it completely. Every time he tried to start talking again, he ended up giggling instead. He coughed, took a deep breath and tried to straighten his face. "All you could see were these legs sticking out of…" He had to stop again and laughed for another minute or so, then wiped his eyes. "Oh God, sorry," he said, "it was one of those 'had to be there' moments. But can you picture it? A crem full of mourners all solemn and dressed in black, and this bloody loony bimbo, wearing odd shoes, legs sticking up in the air, too pissed to stand and wrapped in a curtain, with the vicar, or whatever he is, trying to untangle her."

Dan's giggling was unusual and infectious, because Josh was laughing now too.

"See," he said, "that's my kind of funeral."

"Yeah. It was interesting, I can tell you!" Dan agreed, finishing the last of his Coke.

"Shall I get us another?" Josh suggested.

"Go on then. Just a single, though."

Josh rolled his eyes and went to the bar. His head had cleared a bit now, thanks to Dan's support. He couldn't have got through the last couple of hours without it. He was also wondering, given Dan's involvement in Campion Community Trust, whether he was aware of last week's events. It was unlikely Alice would have said anything, but Bill Meyer might have, and he needed a way of bringing it up in conversation without revealing what he knew.

"Speaking of funerals," he remarked casually as he put the drinks on the table, "has Alice mentioned Alistair Campion recently?"

"No. I think she's finally over it," Dan said. "She hasn't mentioned Jason for a while, either, I'm glad to say."

Before Dan got any further with this, his phone sounded. He answered it. After half a minute or so of saying 'yep', he hung up.

"That was Aitch. There will be no charges against George."

Josh sighed in relief.

"He said give it another half-hour and he'll be released."

"He's good, Aitch. And I'm really grateful for what he's done."

"Yeah, he is." Dan rubbed his chin thoughtfully. "The guy who attacked George? He's got severe burns to the neck."

Josh frowned. "What from?"

"Dog lead lasso."

"Fucking hell."

***

As they left the station, George kept his head down. He didn't want anyone to know what he'd done and wasn't sure how he was going to tell Josh, but as he kept pointing out, they'd promised: no lies and no secrets. He climbed into the passenger seat of the car and watched on as Josh and Dan embraced swiftly, then Dan nodded in his direction, patted Josh on the back and was gone.

Josh sat down beside him and took his hand. He kissed it. "I love you, George Morley. Even if you are a bit mad in the head."

"I can't believe what I did. If that other guy—"

"You'd have killed him. Yes, I know. But for good reason. You were trying to protect a dog, like you tried to protect the swan."

"And the horses," George said quietly.

"The horses?"

"Joe. He wasn't abusive, or else, well…" George put his seatbelt on. "His methods were a bit heavy-handed, and we came to blows."

"So?"

"I'm ashamed."

"You should be proud, that you stand up for what you believe."

"It's not like that, though, is it? It's a weakness. I just lose it."

"Whatever, the outcome is the same. You have to let it go."

Josh indicated and pulled out into the road, catching a glimpse of George as he did so. He was staring at an indiscriminate point on the dashboard, still torturing himself.

"I can help you with some anger management stuff, if you like?" Josh suggested.

George gave him a sideways look. "Think I'll give that a miss, if it's all the same to you."

CLAIR VOYANT
Saturday 4th March

"So, she says she needs another two people," Kris explained to George, who was pretending not to listen. They were sitting in the back of the car, waiting for Josh, who was paying for petrol, and Shaunna, who had gone with him, to help carry the hot chocolates. George finished prodding at the phone in his hands and glanced across the forecourt.

"They sell those awful microwaved burgers in there," he said, by way of a non-response.

"You do realise that you're only delaying the inevitable?"

"Yep."

George continued to watch out of the window. A minute or so later, Josh and Shaunna came back into view, each carrying two takeaway cups and chatting away, paying little attention to anything else. George followed Josh's movements all the way back to the car, and not out of infatuation, although six months into properly being together, it still hadn't diminished any. The thought made his stomach do a little somersault. Josh opened his door and passed the two cups he was carrying to his backseat passengers. Shaunna opened the passenger door and was about to do the same. She gave one to Josh instead.

"So why are you in the back again, George?" she asked.

"Because he refused to drive," Josh answered.

"I didn't refuse. I just said I didn't want to."

"Amounts to the same thing." Josh sipped at his cup. "Mmm. That's good. And nice and warm. I can't believe the weather's turned again. Bloody March and it's about minus ten out there."

It wasn't quite that cold, but it certainly wasn't very spring-like. He turned the car heater to its highest setting.

"OK. It's all set now," George said, handing Josh his phone back; the screen displayed the route to Manchester, where Ade's 'troupe' was performing. "And I saved it to 'favourites' in case you turn it off again." Josh clipped the phone into the holder on his windscreen.

"Turn left onto Newton Street," the SatNav app piped up.

"Newton Street? Where the hell is Newton Street?" Josh pushed the button to mute his phone and it started to shut down. "Bugger," he muttered under his breath. George tutted.

"This is Newton Street," Kris said.

"Oh." Josh pulled out of the petrol station and turned right.

"It said left," George told him.

"Wanna swap places, Morley?"

"Um…"

After that George stayed quiet. Josh didn't need the SatNav to tell him how to get to the motorway, which was the first part of their not particularly long journey, although it was too far to go for an average night out. However, he'd need it once they neared their destination, so he turned his phone on again and a short while later, the screen lit up. Shaunna swivelled in her seat so she could address George.

"I was just telling Josh about this spiritualist night."

"Oh no," he said and closed his eyes.

Kris laughed. "I told you there was no getting out of it. I think it'll be fun."

"Define 'fun'."

"Some of these mediums are amazing. That guy on TV, for instance. What's his name again?" Kris tried to remember.

"Derren Brown?" George suggested with a smirk.

"He's not a spiritualist."

"No, which is exactly my point. He's pretty much debunked all the psychic stuff. It's all glass and mirrors, that's all."

"Smoke," Josh corrected.

"Huh?"

"You said it was glass and mirrors. It's smoke and mirrors."

"You know what I mean. All that 'does anyone know a John or a William?' nonsense. Of course they do. Everyone knows a John or a William."

"Do you?" Kris asked.

"Well no, but…"

"Well then!"

"Stop ganging up on me!" George protested.

Josh laughed. "I understand what you're getting at. Cold reading, it's called, although I agree with Kris. It could be lots of fun." He looked in the mirror and winked as he said this. Somehow, George got the feeling that the spiritualist believers wouldn't share Josh's perception of why a night with a 'psychic medium' was fun.

"Listen," Shaunna said, "I know you don't believe in it, but Adele's desperate."

"But why us?" George complained.

"Because she's asked everyone else."

"And they all said no, which means not only have we got to endure three hours of some idiot conning people into thinking he's talking to their dead relatives, we weren't even first choice."

"I wonder why?" Kris remarked dryly.

"I'm just going to treat it as research," Josh said. He'd arrived at a large roundabout and everyone stayed quiet so he could safely navigate his way around it and make the correct exit.

"So, shall I tell her you're coming then?" Shaunna asked, once they were on the motorway.

"I will," Josh confirmed. "You'll have to work on misery-guts in the back."

"Hmph," George grumped. "I suppose."

"Excellent." Shaunna took out her phone, sent the text message and waited for the reply; it was a 'yay' with far too many 'y's at the end, followed by 'x'. She exchanged her phone for her hot chocolate and settled into her seat.

The venue was in Canal Street, not surprisingly, given that it was at the centre of the widely acclaimed 'gay village'. This was the opening night for one of Ade's acts—a trio of men who performed a very acrobatic Latin-American dance show, and were about to embark on a 'nationwide' tour. George hadn't been to the village in years. Kris had accompanied Ade a few times recently, under the guise of researching for his TV series, and Shaunna had also visited once or twice, but Josh had never been, and was very excited about it.

"So is it all gay bars?" he asked, as they turned off the motorway and headed into the city.

"Pretty much," Kris said, "although there's probably as many straight people go there these days as there are not straight."

"Awesome," Josh responded, already distracted by the wonderfully colourful display of Saturday night revelry.

"The problem we'll have is that some places are men or women only," Kris continued. They were now waiting in a queue to get into a car park, the music spilling from some of the closest bars and creating a hotchpotch of sound, with out of sync bass beats, and stuttering vocals and hi-hats, like an old-fashioned travelling fair.

"I kind of wish I wasn't driving," Josh thought aloud, his eyes following a group of young men walking past the car. He continued to watch them as they headed away down the street. The driver of the car behind him honked the horn. Josh tutted and moved forward a couple of feet, as that was all the space that had opened up between him and the entrance to the car park. Another group—of indeterminate gender—shuffled sideways through the few inches of space between his bumper and the car in front. He made eye contact with George via the mirror. George was grinning at him.

"What's so funny?"

"Just you," he said.

When they eventually found an empty parking space, with Josh giving the mandatory rant about the cost, they started on their way up to the main run of clubs and bars, and George put his arm around Josh's shoulders.

"Oh, like that, is it?" Josh glanced sideways at him. George just grinned again and kissed him.

"Dunno what you mean," he said. Josh hooked his arm under George's jacket and around his lower back.

"Now, are you sure I'm not being too 'out' for you?" he asked sarcastically.

Kris and Shaunna were walking ahead, arm in arm. They were laughing and chatting, occasionally holding back so Kris could point out different places to Josh, who was looking around him in awe.

"Leather and rubber?" he repeated back, his neck craning so he could continue to examine the aforementioned club. A couple of drag kings walked past and he smiled at them, then turned to George with his mouth wide open.

"It's like a huge big mixing pot of gender," he said. "Like him, her, him—that person over there." He nodded in the direction of said individual, who was a good six and a half feet tall, with platform heels, and sporting a massive peroxide-blonde afro and gold sparkly flared trousers. Josh was right: there was no possible way of knowing if they were male or female, but it didn't actually matter, and that just enthralled him all the more.

"This is the place," Kris called back, drawing to a halt outside a club, live music pouring through its doors each time they opened to let someone else in. The flow was all one-way. The four of them walked up to the entrance, and one of the doormen winked at them, or, in fact, at Kris.

"Hiya," he greeted. "How're you?"

"I'm great, thanks," Kris replied. "You?"

"Yeah. Not bad. How'd that audition go?"

"Got it!"

"Oh? Congratulations!" The doorman leaned in close to speak, although he didn't lower his voice, so it was a bit pointless really. "Anthony went for that part. Did you know?"

"No. I didn't."

"Yeah." He stretched out the word and nodded very slowly. He put Josh in mind of Cissy Braithwaite—the female character Roy Barraclough used to play on *The Les Dawson Show*—and he was having a problem keeping himself from laughing. The guy on the door glanced at their group. "They with you, Kris, love?" he asked.

"Yep," Kris confirmed.

The doorman examined them one at a time, suspicion registering as he cast his eye over Shaunna and Josh. He stopped on George for a while.

George smiled quickly and made an obvious grab for Josh's hand. Josh turned away and giggled.

"In you go then," the doorman commanded. "Silhouetto are on after this lot. I saw them rehearsing earlier. It should be a cracking show, that."

"Ooh, that's good to hear," Kris said. "See you later." The four of them went inside.

Once they'd got over the smack in the face that was the mix of heat, flashing lights and noise, they homed in on the stage, where a 'boy band' drag act was performing. They were called 'Take This', and consisted of five women, in suits and ties, singing boy band hits. They were really very entertaining, and being quite well received, given that it was still relatively early in the evening. Shaunna and George went to the bar, while Kris headed over to see Ade, leaving Josh temporarily standing on his own, not that he'd noticed. He was too busy people-watching to pay proper attention. There was a group of young women in front of him, all dressed in cargo pants and vest tops, dancing along manically to the current song, which he recognised as being by New Kids On The Block, but other than that he didn't have a clue. After that, they did a Boyzone number, and Shaunna and George made it back to him.

"Whatcha doing?" George asked.

"Watching them," Josh said, indicating with his head in the direction of the subjects of his current observation: two men dressed all in denim who were perhaps in their late forties and completely oblivious to everything going on around them, until one of them sensed they were being watched and turned in Josh's direction. Josh smiled and continued to stare; George nudged his arm.

"You're gonna get yourself either beaten up or picked up if you carry on like that," he warned. Josh managed to drag himself away. The 'boy band' had just come to the end of their last song and were bowing to a decent smattering of applause. Josh scanned the room and found Kris and Ade, over to the right of the stage, chatting in a highly animated fashion.

"I like it here," he said. Shaunna nodded.

"Yeah. I've been here before. It's a nice club. Very friendly and open.

"Diverse," Josh remarked vaguely. Without realising, he'd settled his gaze on some new people to watch. George shook his head in despair.

"Come here," he said, taking Josh's hand and leading him over to a recently vacated corner of the club, where there was a high table with stools around it. "Stand, or sit, there," he ordered. "That way, you can look as if you're glancing around the room rather than staring."

Josh was impressed with his cunning. He positioned himself on a stool and sipped at his Coke, taking up his vigil once again. A couple of minutes later, Kris came over to join them.

"Ade's guys are on now. You're gonna love the act that's on after them," he said.

"Really, or are you joking?" George asked.

"Wait and see."

Silhouetto had gone up on-stage, and the lights and music died away momentarily, then spotlights flashed all across the room, and the music began again: a Ricky Martin number, sung in Spanish, to which the three men performed the most bizarre dancing Josh had ever seen. He reached behind him and tugged George's sleeve to get his attention.

"They're very agile," he said, completely entranced by the display of acrobatic skills and shiny buttocks. George started to laugh and put his arms around him.

"I love you," he said. "Sometimes you're so cute."

"Cute?"

"Yeah. Cute." George kissed him on the nose. Josh could go with that, he decided, and they both carried on watching the sleek, half-naked men performing their gymnastic tango on-stage. Every so often, the dancers would swap out a partner, or become entangled in some kind of avant-garde ménage a trois, whereby one or all of them would assume a traumatic facial expression and enact a devastating betrayal, in dance form. When they'd finished their first number, everyone applauded and a few of the men whistled. They were good, but they were very odd, and Josh soon got bored, instead returning to watching the crowd, unhindered now, as they were all too engrossed in the performance to notice.

"What do you think?" Kris asked Shaunna. She shrugged.

"They're OK, if you're into that kind of thing," she said. She thought they were terrible, but she couldn't very well say so, given that Ade had been raving about them all the time she'd known him. That was his job: promoting and arranging tours for gay cabaret acts, and Silhouetto were his latest 'big thing'. Still, she was a straight woman, so who was she to judge what did and didn't go down well in a gay bar? Kris certainly seemed to be enjoying them, or so she thought, until he lifted her hair from her ear and moved closer to whisper.

"I think they're bloody awful," he said. "They're so outdated it's hard to believe Ade thought they were a good signing. What was he thinking?" Shaunna waited for him to move away, or say something else, but he did neither.

"What?" she asked.

"Nothing," he said. Still he stayed where he was. "Your hair. It smells so—of you." She turned and looked him in the eye.

"Of course it smells of me, you weirdo." She laughed, although she was a little disconcerted by his continued proximity.

"Sorry. I just…" He backed off. "I haven't been that close to you for so long and—sorry." He picked up his beer and drank most of it in one go. Shaunna examined him, trying to figure him out. Maybe it was just the alcohol. Whatever, the moment was lost, as Ade came over.

"What d'you think?" he asked nervously. "Are they bad, or…?"

"They're fab, honey," Kris gushed. Shaunna followed his lead.

"Yes, Ade. They're really good." He wasn't convinced.

"George?"

"Um, I'm not sure I should say with my fiancé sitting here!"

"That's a good thing then, surely?"

George blushed. Josh glanced up at him.

"Yes, it's a good thing," he confirmed.

"OK," Ade smiled and sighed in relief at the same time.

"You'd think it was you up there, with your butt cheeks out, shimmying away under the lights!" Kris said. He was trying to make Ade feel better, but it wasn't working. Their recent discussions about starting a family began well enough, but then Shaunna asserted herself and that was the end of the matter as far as Kris was concerned. Ade still wanted children, and they were heading nowhere fast. So, really, the questions about Silhouetto were about him. He wanted the approval of Kris's friends, and of Shaunna. He might as well have been asking for the moon.

"I'd best get back," he said. Kris nodded and kissed his cheek.

"See you in a little while."

Ade flashed him a quick smile and dashed back across the club, where he resumed his anxious watching and taking of photos. Josh had seen what had taken place between them, and whilst he couldn't have guessed at the reason behind it, he could see that the relationship was all but done, and it made him sad. Without realising it, he sighed and slumped his shoulders, an action which George completely misinterpreted.

"I'm sorry," he said close to Josh's ear.

"What for?"

"You know."

"I don't," Josh said. He looked up at him. He was still red and a bit flustered. "D'you want to go and get some fresh air?" he asked. George nodded and started to move away. Josh caught hold of his hand. "Be back soon," he explained to Shaunna, who was closest to him.

"What was that about?" Kris asked her. She shrugged. Silhouetto came to the end of their second dance and again were greeted by a round of applause and whistles, although it was quite contained, considering the place was getting very busy. One more number to endure, Kris thought, turning away and looking to see if he could figure out where George and Josh had gone.

"I'm just popping to the loo," he said. Shaunna gave him a look that showed she didn't believe him, but it was true, even if it was only a means of escaping being alone with her. He didn't trust himself, and was terrified he was going to act on his impulses and destroy any chance he had of fixing this mess with her and Ade.

Out on the balcony, George had mostly got over his embarrassment, although his cheeks were still burning.

"You know," Josh consoled gently, "there'd be something very wrong if you didn't get all worked up over watching something like that. Even I can see its erotic potential."

"But that's just it," George said. "I'm not even slightly turned on by any of that." He waved his hand in the general direction the stage.

"Really? That wasn't the feeling I got, if you know what I mean," Josh grinned. After all, George had been standing right behind him. This only served to make him blush more, however.

"Yes, well, think about it, Joshua," he said. Josh frowned and shrugged.

"Not following."

"I'll demonstrate, then," George said, pulling him close. Josh automatically put his arms around him and pushed his hands into the back pockets of George's jeans. The effect was instant.

"Oh," he said. "I see." He didn't know what to do. "Do you want me to move away?" he asked. George shook his head and pulled him even closer.

"I'm thinking," he said, "I'd like to kiss you right now."

"Is that so?" Josh laughed, bringing his lips up to meet George's.

"Yep." George's voice sounded inside Josh's mouth and then they were kissing, properly, and outside, for the first time since their very first kiss. They continued for a long time, exploring each other's mouths, taking each other's breath, falling into each other. Eventually George pulled away because he was having something of a self control problem, particularly as Josh was now also aroused and was biting his lip self-consciously.

"The shiny bottoms got you too, huh?" George said with a wink, trying to play it down. Josh closed his eyes and leaned his head against George's shoulder.

"We should go back," he suggested, then added: "In a minute or two."

"Yeah," George agreed reluctantly.

Kris was watching them from just inside the door, paralysed by jealousy, though it took him a while to figure out why. These days he had no interest in either of them, not that he'd ever been attracted to Josh. What he envied was their relationship. To see that love, that passion, that spark erupting—it was an incredible, magical thing, and his guilt at his own voyeurism had been entirely cancelled out by how wonderful it was to see George so happy and so in love. And he wanted to feel that feeling again, for himself.

190

George and Josh released their embrace and Kris darted quickly away, out of sight. When they made it back inside, Kris was standing next to Ade, acting as if he'd been there all the while. The three of them had arrived just in time to see the parting shot from Silhouetto. The club momentarily plunged into darkness and then the lights came back up.

"Please give it up for Silhouetto," a disembodied voice announced over the sound system. The guys took a bow to applause, whoops and whistles.

"Well," Josh said, blinking in disbelief, "now we know why they're called what they're called!"

George took a quick swig of his drink and didn't say a word.

"Did you like the ending?" Ade asked Kris.

"Erm, yes," Kris laughed. The three dancers were now covered up again, and even though he was laughing, he was also thinking that their final dance, performed naked and backlit, was really what they should have been doing all the way through. It was far more of a turn-on.

"When we ran the dress rehearsal, they said we couldn't do the whole thing in darkness here, because of health and safety," Ade explained.

"Ah," Kris said. That made a bit more sense. Whatever his current feelings for Ade, it didn't alter the fact that he was really very good at his job.

"Anyway, we know for next time," Ade said. He could see that Kris wanted to get back to the others. "You go. I'll be over in a second."

Kris nodded and gave him another quick kiss on the cheek, then walked back over to stand next to Shaunna. She and Josh had the giggles and couldn't stop long enough to say why.

"All this over the word 'endowed'," George explained, which set them off again. Then, just as they were starting to get it under control, something drew the attention of everyone in the building. They all turned to watch as the crowd parted right across the room.

"This is her," Kris said, "the other act I mentioned?"

"Right?"

"Hello, hello, yes, good evening, darling," she gushed, holding out a silk-gloved hand to people as she passed them by. She climbed the steps onto the stage and waited for her entrance music to stop. It was only then that George noticed what was in her other hand. He glared at Kris.

"I," she declared, "am Clair Voyant," with a huge stress on the '-ant'. "And I bring with me…" she dramatically raised her glittery crystal ball above her, "…news from the future, and messages from loved ones."

Josh was utterly mesmerised. The drag queen on-stage reminded him so much of an aging therapist that he knew—one that George had reluctantly spent some time with during his training—right down to the dreadful put-on accent, over the top eyelashes, badly applied magenta lipstick and exaggerated facial expressions. He nudged George.

191

"She reminds me of Zsa Zsa. Maybe she's moonlighting."

George nodded. He looked repulsed. He hated Zsa Zsa almost as much as he'd hated the prison psychologist, although at least Zsa Zsa—real name Zara Lederman—had an ounce or two of humanity underneath all the layers of make-up and chiffon. George leaned over to Kris so he could speak into his ear.

"Can we go somewhere else?"

"Sure," Kris agreed. "I'll just let Ade know." He wandered over to the other side of the stage, where Ade was chatting to the three members of Silhouetto.

"We're gonna move on. You want me to text you when we decide on somewhere?"

Ade patted his arm. "No, you go ahead. I'm shattered. I'll make sure the guys get paid and then head home, I think."

"OK. See you later." Kris went back to the others. "Ready?"

"Ade not coming?" George asked.

"No. He says he's tired." Kris walked away towards the door. George and Josh looked at each other, puzzled. Shaunna put an arm around each of them and shoved gently to move them on.

"Ask no questions," she said, "and I'll tell you no lies."

THE KISS
Wednesday 8ᵗʰ March

Josh pushed open the door to the building next to his own, a waft of dry, hot, perfumed air blasting him as he entered.

"Morning Lois, Cara," he greeted the two young women sitting at their desks on either side of the reception area.

"Good morning, Joshua," Lois responded with a smile.

"Mr. Sandison," Cara said crisply. She hadn't quite mastered the level of formal informality that Lois had made all her own.

"Is she in?" Josh asked, nodding towards the door of the consulting room.

"Yes, she's in," Cara confirmed, "and she's busy."

"OK," Josh said. "I'll wait." He walked past them, through to the tiny stretch of hallway that doubled as a waiting area, sat on one of the chairs against the wall, and randomly selected a magazine from the rack. He flicked through it, disinterested in what the pages displayed. A couple of minutes passed and a woman exited the room. Josh waited until she was out of sight and went in.

"Hey," she acknowledged, continuing with the task of washing her hands at the small sink in the corner.

He didn't reply. Instead, he walked over to her, put his arms around her and kissed her, fully on the mouth, for a good ten seconds. He released her. She was speechless.

"Just checking," he said. And then he left.

THE CHECK
Thursday 9ᵗʰ March

"What do you mean, 'just checking'?"

More than twenty-four hours had passed since he walked into her consultation room and kissed her without warning or explanation. Until now she'd been too shocked to even work out what she should do about it. Now she had responded in kind, or right up until the point where he kissed her, although he was evidently between clients, as he was in his surgery kitchen making coffee.

"What I said," he replied, getting another mug and putting a tea bag in it.

"What you said does not in any way, shape, or form, explain what you did. What exactly were you checking? Whether I still had tonsils?"

He laughed. "Sorry. I didn't think you'd mind."

"Erm…" She didn't know what else to say. She threw out her hands, her expression one of both frustration and confusion.

"I've never kissed a woman before."

"And?"

"And I was thinking, how can I possibly know that I'm gay if I've never even kissed a woman before, so—"

"You kissed me," Eleanor finished. "We haven't even spoken to each other for two weeks. Are you insane?"

"Possibly?"

She let out a tiny shriek. "I just…I can't…" She threw out her hands again. "I have no idea what else to say to you. If anybody else did that to me, I'd slap them, really bloody hard."

"Thanks, then," Josh smiled and patted her on the arm. She pushed him away.

"Joshua! Will you please explain?"

"Come and sit," he suggested. He handed her the cup of tea and she followed, like a lost sheep, taking a seat next to him on his couch. "The thing is this," he began.

"Hold on," she interrupted. "Does George know what you did?"

"No. Why?"

"Are you going to tell him?"

"When I get round to it."

"OK. Go on." She sat back and sipped at her tea, watching him. He didn't appear to think what he'd done was odd at all, and it was unnerving her.

"See, last week I was talking to Dan, and he said something about not knowing I was into guys, but you may remember me telling you that he called me queer once at school."

"God, that was years ago."

"Yes, it was. Third year of high school, to be precise. Anyway, that's by the by. He doesn't remember saying it, but it got me thinking. I know I'm attracted to men, well, I'm attracted to George, but is that enough to assume that I'm gay?"

"Do you need a label?"

"Not really. Labels are terribly destructive things."

"So why does it matter?"

"It's hard to explain," he said. He turned to face her and smiled again, which only served to unsettle her further. He continued: "Last year, in Wales, when George and I kissed? That was the first time I'd ever kissed anybody."

"Wow!" She was genuinely surprised by this.

"Yes indeed, wow. And it was worth waiting for, let me tell you. However, one kiss does not an identity make, so after what Dan said, I decided that I needed a point of comparison."

"Your first kiss at thirty-seven. That's got to be a record."

"I doubt it. In some cultures people don't kiss at all, but…"

"I mean, I was nearly eighteen, and I thought I was a late developer. Thirty-seven, though."

"Ellie. Are you listening to me?"

"Sorry." She shook the thought from her mind and re-commenced sipping her tea.

"I couldn't exactly warn you I was going to do it, as it wouldn't have had the same impact, and I'm really sorry, but I figured you'd probably forgive me once I explained."

"Right. I still think you're insane."

"But do you understand why I needed to do it?"

"Kind of. And your conclusion, oh freaky friend of mine?"

"Hey! Less of the freaky!" Josh scowled at her and she grinned. "I'm fairly sure I'm gay."

"OK. Good." Eleanor took a slightly bigger gulp of her tea than she intended and choked on it. She continued to cough for a minute or so; Josh waited the time out, sipping his own drink and watching her.

"Done?"

"Ye-es," she spluttered. "I thi-ink so-o."

He smiled and took her hand. "Don't take it personally," he said. "You're very beautiful and everything, but, well…"

"I'm not a man."

"More to the point, you're not George."

"I'm not offended," she said. "You're sexually attracted to men, so I suppose it's almost a compliment to my womanliness."

"That's not entirely true," Josh said and inadvertently upset her again. "Oh, no, wait! I didn't mean that. You are an incredible woman, good-looking, gorgeous figure, but—can I tell you a huge secret?"

"I don't know if I can take any more," she said jokingly.

"I'm serious, Ellie. You have to promise not to mention it to anybody else."

"OK. Now I'm offended."

She was more than offended. She was furious. After being friends as long as they had been, even with their current falling-out, she couldn't believe he had asked her to promise to keep a secret before he'd tell her and she was so angry that she was having to fight to urge to get up and leave.

"I'm sorry," he said quietly. "This is massive to me, and it's not that I don't trust you, because I do, even if we don't agree on—everything. But, this thing…" He tapped his fingers on his cup and chewed his lip. "It's the reason I refused to tell George how I felt, and I've never told anyone other than him about it."

Eleanor nodded slowly. She was still angry, but was prepared to give him the benefit of the doubt. She waited until he looked up at her.

"I promise," she said, holding eye contact to ensure he believed her.

"Of course," he said, returning to his prior skittishness, "now I've made such an enormous thing of it, I'll have only made you more desperate to share."

Eleanor huffed in exasperation. "You just need to tell me now."

"All right," he said, steadying himself. "I'm not sexually attracted to men. Intellectually, emotionally, physically, yes. Sexually, no."

"You mean you're asexual."

"Yes! That's it!"

"So what? I've got a few patients who are asexual."

"Have you?"

"Yep. It's more common than you'd think, in women, at any rate, and I'd guess in men too, but I couldn't say, being as my patients are all female."

"And do they come to you for treatment?"

"Sometimes. Some of them have hormone imbalances, or mental ill-health, or it can be related to medication, or other physical conditions that might resolve themselves. But some of them are there for an entirely different reason and it just happens to come up in conversation."

For several minutes, Josh sipped his coffee thoughtfully, occasionally shaking his head, or smiling to himself. "I wish you'd been my doctor when I was younger," he said finally.

"Why?"

"Because I was nineteen and he decided there must be something wrong with me, what with me not wanting to shag everything on campus, if you pardon my crudeness."

"Not all students are like that."

"Of course, I did go in there telling him there was something wrong with me to begin with, and he sent me to the hospital for tests. They tested my hormone levels and arousal response—that kind of thing. It all checked out."

"That's standard procedure," Eleanor assured him, "although you'd normally have other symptoms if there was a clinical reason for it."

"Yes, I know that now. I didn't then."

She watched him for a little while, as he continued to drink his coffee, quietly mulling over what she had said, no doubt. It must have been such a tremendous burden to him, and he'd never told anyone. It didn't surprise her though, because he was what he was.

"I won't break my promise, Josh," she said.

He nodded. "Thank you."

"But you like kissing?"

He laughed and covered his face. "I could kiss George from the minute I wake up and not stop till I fall asleep again. It is the most amazing feeling in the world, being with him. I never thought I'd get to experience that kind of physical closeness. Although my lips get unbelievably chapped!"

"When he and Kris kissed at the reunion…"

"It tore me apart. But I hadn't really sorted out how I felt. The whole sex thing—in my job it's mostly the opposite. The people I see with sexual difficulties, they're usually down to having an abnormally high sex drive, or being gay and not wanting to be, or even paraphiliac, but not asexual."

"And that's why you didn't tell George?"

"I didn't realise I was in love with him, not until last year."

"Honestly?"

"Honestly."

"Well I could've told you when he went away to uni that you were in love with him."

"Don't be ridiculous."

"It's true!"

"How did you know?"

"It's the closest I've ever seen you get to breaking down—before all that blubbering you did on your birthday—when he left for Aberdeen."

198

Josh closed his eyes and called to mind that day, standing on the platform, watching George through the window of his train, as he settled into his seat, waving, smiling. Eleanor was right. It broke his heart.

"It's done with now," he smiled.

"It sure is." She finished the last of her tea and stood up, as did he. She hugged him. "So, Mr. Sandison, you're perfectly normal. Well, you're not, but you know what I mean."

"Yes, I do. And I promise I won't kiss you again."

"Oh, you can kiss me all you like, but no tongues next time, OK?"

CLAIRVOYANT
Wednesday 15ᵗʰ March

Every time Josh saw a sign advertising a 'Psychic Night', he wondered if the venue had to book in advance, or if they just stuck up the sign, and said psychic medium would arrive accordingly at the pre-designated time. The same thought struck him now, as he parked up the car at the far end of the very full hotel car park. Sean unclipped his seatbelt and leaned forward, expecting George to get out and let him out, but George was in no hurry.

"This is gonna be crap," he said, watching as a group of middle-aged women made their way towards the entrance. He turned and glared at Josh, then Sean. "And you call yourselves scientists?"

"Loosen up a little, George. We'll have a great time," Sean said, trying to jolly him along. George's nostrils flared and Josh grinned at him.

"Come on. Let's do it," he said. "If we're quick, you can get a couple of beers in beforehand. Then you'll have a ready-made excuse to escape." Josh got out of the car and waited for George, then Sean, to climb out and shut the door. He locked up.

"You know what's gonna happen, don't you?" George said, as they walked across the car park. "I'll get up to go to the loo and Sid the Psychic will suddenly declare my dad is in the room."

Josh laughed. "Sid the Psychic?"

"What is he actually called?" Sean asked.

"No idea," Josh said, "but I bet it's something ordinary, like Fred Jones, or John Smith."

George shook his head and pointed at the billboard. "Try Gavril...what's that say?"

Sean squinted to read. "Gavrilovich Ovsianikov. Catchy!"

"Iz zare annee baddee zare?" Josh said, pretending to look all mysterious. George tutted.

"You promised me beer."

"Or vud you raazer ze wodka, comrade?"

George rolled his eyes. "Just get inside," he said, shoving Josh towards the door.

In the hotel foyer, Adele was standing next to a table, where another woman was sitting with pen poised over a printout of the attendees' names. Adele spotted them and waved.

"Hi," she said, smiling brightly at Sean, whom she'd never met before, but she instantly picked up on the mind-probe thing, which always filled her with fear when Josh did it. Sean switched it off.

"You must be the lovely Adele," he said, swapping in the good old Irish charm. He shook her hand and kept hold of it a moment longer than was necessary. She giggled and slowly withdrew.

"Yes. Sean, isn't it?"

"It most certainly is," he confirmed.

"Thanks ever so much for stepping in," Adele gushed. "The other person had to, err, back out." She smiled nervously. The dropout was Sally-Anne—still in rehab and looking set to stay there indefinitely, or for as long as they'd put up with her. She was enjoying the rest and relaxation, not to mention the opportunity to spend *Henry's* money, far too much.

"No problem at all, Adele," Sean said warmly.

The woman at the table had been searching her list and finally found Sean's name—pencilled in next to the crossed out 'Sally-Anne Reeves'. She put a tick next to it, then looked at Josh.

"You're not Gavrilovich then, no?" he asked. George nudged him. "Well, I just thought…"

"Josh Sandison and George Morley," George told her. "It starts at seven-thirty?"

Both women nodded.

"Cool," he said, glancing at his phone: it was only ten past seven. "We're going to wait in the bar. Are you both all right for a drink?"

"We're fine, thank you, George." Adele indicated to the half-full glasses on the shelf behind her.

"OK. See you in a bit." George grabbed Josh's arm and steered him away. He was clearly in one of 'those moods', whereby anyone could end up the victim of his tormenting. As they headed along the corridor towards the bar, Sean glanced at George and gave him a subtle wink. Hopefully, with the two of them here, they might be in with a chance of containing the worst of it. They entered the bar room and Josh veered off towards the toilets.

"What d'you want to drink?" George called after him.

"Coffee, if they've got it," he called back.

"I don't mind driving, if you want to have a pint," Sean suggested. Josh gave him a thumbs-up and disappeared into the Gents'. The other two men went to the bar, where Shaunna and Krissi were currently being served. Sean did a double-take.

"Shaunna!" He leaned across and kissed her cheek. "How lovely to see you!"

"Sean," she acknowledged with a smile and returned the kiss. "This is my daughter, Krissi," she introduced. Sean stepped back to look at her.

"My word!" he said, stunned by the attractive, dark-haired young woman standing before him. Even though Shaunna had explained that Krissi was in her twenties, he'd still imagined her as a gangly, spotty teenager. He quickly recovered, though. "A pleasure to meet you, Krissi," he said.

"You too," she replied warily, looking from her mother to Sean. George was also watching on, intrigued; he coughed to get their attention.

"Hey, George," Shaunna smiled.

"You know each other?"

"Yeah. Only recently," she explained. "We met in the milk bar a couple of weeks ago and ended up sitting together, because there was nowhere else to sit." She didn't mention the heart-to-heart, nor the burger afterwards. "How do you know each other?" she asked instead. The question was directed at George, but Sean answered it.

"Oh, me and Joshy go way back," he said.

"Joshy, huh?"

"Yeah," George said, "but I wouldn't try calling him that, if I were you."

Shaunna grinned mischievously, although she had no intention of trying really. She shook her head in wonder. "What a small world!" she said. The bartender finished their drinks order; she paid and passed Krissi's drink across, then turned back to Sean. "How are you doing, anyway?"

"Yeah, I'm just great. You're looking well yourself," he said, glancing around him. "You're not with the err…"

"Husband-ex-husband? No, I'm afraid not."

"The complete and utter…" George started, but didn't finish the sentence. Shaunna patted his arm.

"He didn't do it on purpose. He got called back to the studio to re-film a scene."

"Oh, well I suppose I'll have to let him off," George said begrudgingly.

"Where's Josh?"

"He went to the loo. He was just terrorising the woman sat with Adele."

"That's Cheryl. She runs the café in the gym. They organised this together."

"Ah, right," George said.

Sean's eyes suddenly lit up. "Do you know, I've just had the most fantastic idea." He addressed Shaunna: "Let's not tell Josh that we know each other."

George looked at him doubtfully. "He'll see straight through you."

Shaunna flicked her hair back confidently. "I reckon I can pull it off."

"Well, we're about to find out," George said, as Josh came back across to them. Sean was busy ordering the drinks, which gave Shaunna time to assume her cover. Josh didn't suspect a thing.

"Have you been introduced?" he asked her, nodding in Sean's direction.

"Yeah. Sean, was it?"

"That's right. We teach the counselling course together."

"Oh, OK. So he's a therapist too?" she asked, convincingly feigning ignorance.

"I am," Sean leaned back and confirmed. George quickly turned away.

"Mum," Krissi interrupted, "I'm just gonna visit the Ladies'."

"Good idea," Shaunna said, glad for a temporary escape. "I'll come with you." They headed off.

"Crap." Josh patted his pockets. "I've left my phone in the car. Be right back." He left too. George examined Sean, and was still doing so when he turned to hand him his drink.

"Husband-ex-husband?" he asked.

"Yeah. Let's just say we were sat together for quite some time."

George took a mouthful of beer, but Sean still spotted the look.

"All entirely innocent," he assured him. "We talked, that's all. Soph and I are still trying to sort things out."

"It's none of my business."

"Of course it's your business. Soph is your friend. You care about her and she cares about you too. Shaunna and I just talked."

"Fair enough," George accepted. "But so you don't accidentally drop yourself in it, Kris—the husband-ex-husband—is also part of our friendship group."

Josh was on his way back.

"Thanks for the warning," Sean said.

A moment later, Shaunna and Krissi emerged from the Ladies'.

"Adele just texted to say we're to go in now," Shaunna explained. "And we can take our drinks with us."

Sean was still waiting on his coffee.

"You go on," he suggested. Josh nodded and the four of them departed for the room on the first floor, where most of the guests, or, perhaps more aptly, audience, were already sitting, in rows, chatting to each other and eagerly eyeing everyone new who entered the room, which was something between a conferencing facility and a small theatre. There was a row with five vacant seats almost exactly in the centre, and Josh led the way over. Adele was at the back and stood on tiptoes to look over the heads of the other people. She waved. Shaunna waved back, then turned to George.

"How're we doing?" she whispered.

"All good so far," he whispered back.

"What's that?" Josh asked.

"See? Someone cares enough to make sure I'm OK," George said. Josh gave him a sickly grin.

"It's not like you're going to end up playing Russian Roulette, although…I never thought of that. Maybe it's all a façade and he's actually some Cold War relic, come to pick off enemy spies, one by one, by slowly driving them as mad as he is, with stories of long-dead relatives coming back to haunt them."

George blinked slowly and turned back to Shaunna.

"See what I mean?"

She laughed.

Sean came into the room and all heads turned to follow him, as he walked across the front, spotted Josh and the others, and came over. The mass disappointment was tangible. He sat down next to Josh.

"What did I miss? Anything?"

Josh looked at him in disbelief, although if he'd left it any longer then he would have missed it, as no more than ten seconds later, a short, yet rotund man walked in, and assumed a position at the front. Apart from his dishevelled mane of thick, silver hair, he looked so normal that hardly anyone noticed at first. Slowly a hush fell over the room.

"Good evening," he said in a very non-Russian accent. In fact, it was more Yorkshire than anything. "Thank you all for inviting me here this evening. My name is Gavrilovich Ovsianikov, but it's a bit of a mouthful, so most people just call me Gary."

Shaunna had been sipping her drink when he said this and swallowed hard. George looked down at his feet, so he didn't get caught up in the potential explosion of giggles, although it was going to be tough to keep it up. Josh and Sean were already so absorbed in studying the man that they apparently hadn't heard what he'd said.

"Now, a lot of mediums like to make a big show out of it, try and get a bit of banter going, but I'm not into that at all. What I will ask of you, though, is this: if someone comes through for you tonight, and you don't want me to channel them, just let me know and I'll leave you be. Is that OK?"

Lots of nodding heads.

"Great. So without further ado, I've got someone here who's something to do with this lady down the front." He looked at a woman on the front row. "He's telling me his name is Don. Does that mean anything to you?"

The woman shook her head.

"He's showing me a push bike. Don, or—"

A murmur in amongst the second row. His eyes were immediately on them.

"I know about the push bike," someone said.

"Right." He looked back to the woman at the front. "I'll return to you in a minute, petal, all right? There's definitely something around you, this

Don's telling me." He looked thoughtful, puzzled, then switched back again. "So I'm getting that there was an accident with this push bike. The chain? Am I right?"

Mutterings in the affirmative.

"And he's showing me a little boy. He's hurt himself."

"Yes."

"Did he get knocked off his bike? Is that what it is?"

"Yes."

"Oh. It's tragic, that. And he says he wasn't ready to go."

A cry from the second row.

"He says you were with him, in the hospital?"

Now a sob and further murmuring.

"And he's so happy you were there. Are you his mum, sweetheart?"

The voice was sympathetic. Josh and Sean watched and listened, their eyes flitting between the man performing at the front of the room and the woman falling to pieces in the second row. She was nodding, her face buried in her hands.

"Oh, it's so sad, this. But he says…he says you're not to worry. He's not in pain and he wants to say thank you for staying with him in hospital. And that he loves you and wants you to get on with living now. All right? Do you understand?"

The woman continued to nod and sob.

"All right, sweetheart." He addressed the woman sitting next to her. "You look after her there," he said, then back to his first attempt. "Now then, I'm still getting this name Don," he frowned. "It could be Dan, but, no I'm sure it's…" He trailed off and lifted his head, looking to the back of the room, where loud whispering could be heard. Josh sighed.

"Here we go," he said quietly to Sean.

"Is this something to do with you, my dear?" Gary asked, still looking at the back row.

"I know a Dan," Adele said. Shaunna, Krissi and George all immediately turned to watch her. Sean and Josh looked at each other and rolled their eyes.

"Right," Gary said. "So what I'm getting is—oh, right." He was watching Adele carefully as he spoke. "But it's not Don—Dan, is it? No it's not him who's here, love. Dan's still with you, isn't he? This is another man—an older man. Have you lost your dad?"

Adele nodded.

"It was quite recent, wasn't it?"

Adele nodded and sniffed. Josh snorted.

"And was he involved in an accident, love?"

Adele shook her head.

"Right. Well he's saying he was ready to go, love, and he's at peace now. But he says…" Gary paused, as if listening to a voice through an earpiece. He nodded. "He says tell Dan to look after my princess."

At that, Shaunna and Krissi started whispering frantically. George turned to Josh and frowned. Josh shrugged.

"Does that mean anything to you, sweetheart? Look after my princess?" Gary repeated. Adele nodded and started to cry.

"Sorry, my darling. I didn't mean to upset you."

Sean rubbed his eyes and stifled a yawn. Josh didn't quite accomplish the same. As convincing as it sounded, everything they'd heard so far could be readily explained through conventional means. And he was getting bored. Unfortunately, his fidgeting had brought him to Gary's attention, and now he could feel those eyes burning into him. Well, this could be fun, he thought. He looked up and gave psychic man a wan smile. He nodded slowly and returned the smile.

"You don't believe," he said. "Did they drag you along this evening?" He looked to Shaunna and Krissi. "Did you, ladies? I bet he fought you all the way. I'm right, aren't I?"

Shaunna giggled, but didn't give any other response. Gary turned his attention back to Josh.

"So, I've got here your…mum and your dad. They both left you…when you were young. Is that right?"

Josh nodded once. He was trying so hard not to give anything away; he could feel George's eyes on him and he wanted to signal to him to stop staring, but he dared not look at him. The medium shifted his gaze from Josh to George and back again.

"Your mum's glad you've found happiness at last," he said. "She's been worried about you."

Josh fought to stay still. He wanted to fold his arms, and realised that the harder he tried not to, the greater his need would become, but he mustn't do it. If this man was going to convince him at all, then he was going to have to do much better than that, and on his own. He *would not* give anything away.

"She was there with you," Gary continued. "All the way through university. She was right by your side, your mum. Did you know that?"

Josh shrugged and tried to steady his breathing. Even though he didn't believe in any of this, it was still affecting him, and his heart was thumping, fast and hard.

"I'm going to leave it there, all right?" he said. Josh released the breath he'd been holding very slowly and quietly. George reached down to get his drink and deliberately steadied himself with a hand on Josh's thigh, then glanced up at him as he sat up again. Josh gave him the slightest of smiles. Gary moved on.

The rest of the first half of the 'show' went past in a bit of a blur for Josh, who couldn't quite shake off the emotional state he'd got himself into. He was a bit cross about it, because he'd always believed he was above falling for their tricks, but, he kept reminding himself, these guys were professionals. Their skills-set was just the same as his and Sean's. However, he and Sean had integrity, perhaps even a little too much of it at times. If he were to assume that there was no life after death, and he'd yet to see evidence that could convince him otherwise, then these so-called psychic mediums were fraudsters, confidence tricksters, and no less unscrupulous than Rob Simpson-Stone. In fact, what they did was worse, for they preyed on the hopeless and the desperate. Some people spent hundreds of pounds, visiting one psychic after another, in the hope of hearing that one message that would tell them conclusively their much missed loved ones had made it safely to the other side.

When the interval came (Gary called it a 'breather'), Josh and Sean headed for a table in the farthest corner of the hotel bar, while the others bought drinks. Their discussion was general and academic in nature, starting with an update on the situation with Kevin Callaghan, not that anything had changed. Alice and Bill were still resolute; Hadyn was making excellent progress, but didn't want to talk about Callaghan; James was working long hours. Sean was fully aware that he was obsessing over it merely to distract himself from his and Sophie's current estrangement and everything that went with it. When they'd exhausted that subject, they moved on to arguing out the morality of Gary the Russian medium, with Sean suggesting that if he truly believed he was communicating with the dead, then it wasn't fraudulent at all, although both he and Josh knew of people who had been sectioned for admitting to much less.

"For instance, Sean said, "there's a patient in at the moment, and you just can't have a conversation, on account of the voices. You have to shout your damn head off to be heard over the top of them."

"And our friend in there is no doubt an equally good fit for the criteria," Josh contended.

Sean hummed thoughtfully. "You're right—of course—but it's about function. Can he continue with his day-to-day activities? Yes. Can he hold down a job? Yes."

"Is he a danger to others…"

"No," Sean interrupted. George, Shaunna and Krissi arrived with the drinks and sat on the stools opposite.

"Danger doesn't necessarily have to be physical," Josh argued.

"True enough," Sean said. "But were any of these people brought here against their will?"

"You're still defining force in physical terms."

"I see what you're getting at. Psychological force can be just as dangerous."

"Just as dangerous? It's a far more lethal weapon. You're playing with the mind, to the point where all alternatives have been stripped away."

"That would be so, in certain contexts."

"It's the case here, also."

"I disagree. If we were talking about a grooming process…"

"Which we are."

Shaunna was listening to the discussion, her eyes shifting from one to the other, like watching a very slow game of tennis.

"They're always like this," George said to her quietly.

"That's perhaps a little tangential to where we started," Sean said.

George cupped his hand around his mouth.

"My point——" Josh began to respond.

"Even if they agree with each oth…" George stopped, having realised that Josh was looking at him. "What?"

Josh shook his head. He picked up his drink and took a gulp, then continued.

"My point, as we acknowledged in our report last year, is that when a person's ability to make an objective judgement is distorted by bereavement, they can not possibly be deemed capable of giving rational, informed consent. The same is true of those who seek out the 'wisdom' of psychics."

"Not so," Sean said, shaking his head vehemently. "As you just said, the people here were not sought out by the psychic. They made a free choice to attend."

"How is it free choice? Someone who is emotionally compromised does not make a free choice. They are motivated purely by affect."

"Is that not always the case?"

"Unmediated affect. They can't resolve their difficulties themselves, so they look to a psychic, who tells them what they want to hear. Then they go to another psychic to substantiate what they've been told. It matters not if, by some quirk of coincidence, they both say the same thing. Either way, the bereft become trapped in a cycle, reinforced by the relief they experience each time they receive reassurance that their loved ones are peering peacefully down on them from the other side of the Pearly Gates."

Josh stopped talking and took a deep breath in preparation to continue defending his position.

"Well," Sean said. "I don't know what to say."

Josh's mouth fell open.

"You've fairly nailed it there, Sandison."

"Surely you're not going to give up that easily?"

209

Sean shrugged. "Who am I to argue with the pure, observable logic of behaviourism."

Josh breathed out heavily through his nose, then started to laugh.

"Balls," he said. "I hate you, Tierney. You're a git." He clanged his glass against Sean's coffee cup and they both slurped, then sighed, at exactly the same time. George tutted.

"Huh?" Shaunna said.

Josh smiled apologetically. "Sorry," he said. "Sean and I went to university together and we had this lecturer who believed that everything could be explained through behaviourism."

"Huh?" Shaunna said again.

"Basically," Sean said, "it's a way of saying that all behaviour is learnt through giving rewards for that which you want, and not rewarding what you don't want."

"Like when I give my dog a treat for sitting when I tell him to?" Shaunna asked.

"Exactly!"

"Not that my dog does anything that I tell him to."

"Which is the problem with behaviourism," Josh said. "Most animals exhibit a certain amount of free will when it comes to these things. Humans, for instance, sometimes see straight through it and make a decision not to comply. On the other hand they may choose to go along with what's expected of them, not because of the 'reward' on offer, but because they have the capacity to reason it through and decide it's worth their while in the longer term."

"But other animals wouldn't be able to do that?"

"Depends on the animal."

"OK, so if I tell Casper to sit for a treat, but Kris has got a cheese sandwich, then he's going to choose to wait for a bit of cheese sandwich and ignore me?"

"That's the one," Sean said.

"But surely he's just choosing one reward over another? He likes cheese more than dog treats, and knows if he begs for a bit of the cheese sandwich, then he's gonna get it."

Josh looked at Sean and nodded.

"She's got a point there," he said.

"She has."

Shaunna rubbed her hands together. "I like this psychology stuff. Tell me more!"

Adele was on her way over to them.

"Gary's ready for us again," she called as she approached.

"Saved by la belle," Sean said.

"For now," Shaunna grinned.

They picked up their drinks and followed Adele back across the bar, Sean and Shaunna walking in front. Josh watched their backs as they talked.

"They're getting on well, considering they've only just met," he said to George.

"Um, yeah, I guess they are," George mumbled. Josh looked at him out of the corner of his eye. George turned away and spoke to Krissi.

"What d'you think of tonight?" he asked her.

"It's interesting," she said. She knew he was trying to cover up, but she couldn't think of a single thing to add to this. Josh shook his head and said no more on the matter.

Back into the 'theatre' then, for the second act. Once again, Mr. Ovsianikov headed straight in, and it was essentially more of the same: an alleged visitation from some poor young woman's long dead twin, who told her she'd find the missing key to unspecified locked receptacle in her bedroom drawers, followed by a tender plea for forgiveness from a mother who let down her family terribly, by leaving both father and children when she selfishly suffered a fatal heart attack at the shockingly early age of thirty-two. Josh glanced around the room, counting heads: sixty people, and at this rate, eight messages sent and received, at most. It seemed cold reading was only marginally more successful than cold calling, and his mind started to drift along this train of thought. Perhaps that's how Gary recruited his 'spirits' prior to the show; a quick call of, "Is there anybody there for anybody here?" then lined them up on some mystic telephone switchboard, although he must have lost one of his heavenly connections, for he never returned to the woman on the front row.

"We've reached the end of our time here this evening," Gary said, looking rather weary, if truth be told, but then, Josh thought, hadn't Kris always said that acting was exhausting? "So I'd like to thank you all for coming along. Please help yourself to my cards here at the front. I offer private readings by appointment. Maybe see you all again."

The audience started clapping. Josh leaned across to Sean, but Sean spoke first.

"Surely he'd know?" he said.

"That's exactly what I was going to say," Josh laughed. They joined in with the clapping, then it subsided and people started putting on their coats and picking up their belongings, some of them stopping to thank Gary on their way out.

"You ready?" Josh asked George and Shaunna.

"Yeah," Shaunna said. "Another drink before we go?"

George nodded. "Sure. Why not?" Josh and Sean seemed amenable to the idea.

"I'm going to head off, Mum," Krissi said. "Jason's meeting me outside, so I'll see you at the weekend." She kissed Shaunna's cheek.

"All right, hun." Shaunna gave her daughter a quick hug and waved her off, before the four of them made their way from the room. As they approached the door, Gary nodded and smiled at each of them in turn, then put out his hand and touched Josh on the arm. Josh stopped. The others had continued to walk on. Gary kept eye contact with him.

"That friend of yours," Gary said, "the one who won't go to the hospital?"

Josh scrutinised the man's face. They were equally matched and he couldn't read him. The man kept his focus.

"So you're a sceptic. That's a good thing. Keeps us lot on our toes," he said. "But whether you choose to believe what I say or not, your friend needs to see a doctor."

Gary broke the eye contact and began gathering the remainder of his business cards.

"It won't make any difference in the end, of course."

Josh stood his ground.

"It's incurable," Gary said. He turned back to face Josh. "But she doesn't have to suffer the way she is doing. She's a martyr. You need to convince her that she doesn't have to be, and convince them to forgive her." He walked past Josh and touched his arm again, but said no more. Josh watched him leave, then went down to the bar to join the others, trying not to think about what he'd just been told. He paused in the doorway, watching Shaunna and Sean from a distance, and decided to visit the Gents' first. He needed to try and flush the psychic's words from his mind.

George was just drying his hands and turned to see who had come in behind him. "Where did you get to? I was just about to go looking for you."

Josh didn't reply. Instead, he grabbed George's still-wet hand, pulling him into the toilet cubicle. He put his arms around him and kissed him tenderly, then snuggled against him. George pulled him close.

"What's that for?" he asked.

"I just needed a hug," Josh said.

"You OK?"

"Yes, sort of. I'll explain when we get home. It's to do with Jess."

"Ah," George said.

"I've just been..." Josh stopped talking. They heard the door to the toilets open, then somebody whistling as they unzipped their fly and started to pee. Josh looked at George and stifled a giggle. They waited with breath held, listening for the rezipping. The door outside opened and closed again and the whistling faded out; they were alone once more.

"Of course," Josh said, as he stepped out of the cubicle, "if you let me hug you in public, then we wouldn't end up looking like we're cottaging."

George couldn't think of anything to say in his defence, so he just gave Josh another quick kiss before they stepped back out into the bar.

"It doesn't mean I don't love you," he whispered.

"I know," Josh said. They went over to join Shaunna and Sean.

"I've just been explaining humanism to Shaunna," Sean said.

"Oh, you poor thing!" Josh gave her a sympathetic smile. Shaunna smacked him on the hand in mock chastisement.

"I think it sounds really interesting, actually," she said. "So, let me see if I've got this. Self esteem needs are about independence and prestige, feeling like you're valued?"

"That's right," Sean confirmed.

"And only when you feel valued can you go on to self actualise?"

"Correct."

Josh sat back with his arms folded and watched the two of them.

"I see," Shaunna said. George picked up his glass and started studying it. The whole interchange was clearly rehearsed, and a lead-up to their finale and reveal.

"But enough of this nonsense," Sean said. "I didn't come out for the evening to work."

"Of course," Shaunna smiled. "Sorry."

"Oh, no need to apologise," he said. "Why don't you tell me a little about yourself?"

"You're the psychologist. You tell me."

"Is that a challenge?" Sean asked flirtatiously.

"If you want it to be," Shaunna counter-struck.

"Well, let's see now." Sean pretended to study her. "You're married, or maybe divorced. No. Separated. But you still live with him, is that right?"

"Yes," Shaunna said in greatly exaggerated surprise.

"And Adele, over there, is your best friend."

"Wow!" Shaunna shook her head in 'amazement'. "How did you know that?"

"Who knows? Maybe there's something to this psychic stuff after all," Sean said very seriously, but with a twinkle in his eye.

"Surely you don't believe in telepathy?" Shaunna asked.

"Why not?"

"Well, because Josh doesn't, and you're both psychologists, I just thought…"

"How about we try a little experiment," Sean suggested. Shaunna shrugged. "I'm going to ask you to think of a word, all right? You type it on your phone, and I'll try to guess it."

She took out her phone and opened up a blank text message. "No cheating," she told him. He covered his eyes and turned away. She typed

213

the word and showed it to George. "I'm done," she said. Sean turned back and studied her face for a few seconds.

"Hmm. Tricky," he said. "Is it—no, that's silly." He shook his head and laughed to himself. "Is it Freud?"

"Oh my God!" Shaunna exclaimed. She turned her phone around to show Sean that the word on-screen was indeed 'Freud'. Josh picked up his drink and took a large mouthful.

"Want to try another?" Sean asked. Shaunna nodded over-enthusiastically. Once again, Sean hid his eyes, whilst she typed on her phone and showed it to George.

"Let me see that," Josh said. He read what she had typed and nodded. "He'll never get that."

"What's your wager, Sandison?"

"I don't know. Let's see." Josh drummed on his chin while he thought. "How about I cook dinner for us at the weekend?" He took out his own phone, as if to check his calendar.

"I'm going to Ireland with Soph."

"All right then. Next Wednesday?"

"You're on."

"And if you don't get it, fair and square, then it's dinner at your place."

Sean nodded his acceptance of this. Josh smiled to himself, so confident that he'd never in a million years 'guess' what the word on Shaunna's phone was, because it was two words—another name, and one that he wouldn't automatically associate with her.

"OK, I'm going to go with—" Sean pressed his fingers to his temples, making a big deal out of rubbing them and screwing up his eyes, as if concentrating really hard. He almost looked constipated. Finally he blurted, "Cordelia Kinkade."

At the exact moment Sean said this, his phone vibrated across the table and he picked it up, feeling all smug, knowing that he'd 'guessed' correctly. He unlocked the screen. There was a text message, and it read:

I had you at behaviourism.

Sean locked his phone and laughed. "They can see straight through it," he said, recalling their earlier conversation.

"And decide it's worth their while," Josh grinned. "I believe that game goes to me, Doctor Tierney."

"Sandison, you're a git."

"That may be so, but I'm a git who's coming to dinner at your house next week."

214

DEMONS
Friday 17th–Tuesday 21st March

With just the end stall left to rake, George took a moment to rest, leaning his back against the freezing cold concrete wall of the stable block. He shivered and swallowed, trying not to vocalise how painful it was, knowing that it would make it hurt more. He'd had this many times before. Strep throat, as they called it on the ranch, or bacterial tonsillitis, as it was called here: he'd been plagued by it his whole life, any time he'd been feeling stressed or under the weather for a while. He felt a cough building, fought to suppress it, failed, bawked and cried out. Jake stuck his head out of the stable door.

"Bloody hell, George. Go home, mate!" he said. He'd already told him once, having seen how pale and shivery he was when he arrived for work, but George was a fighter. He'd inherited his stubbornness from his mother. However, even the most mule-headed of individuals would be hard-pushed to keep fighting when faced with a fever and a throat full of pus.

"OK," he relented. "I'll just spread this straw, then make a move."

"No you won't," Jake told him sternly. "Go and wait in the café. Get Hannah to make you a drink. I'll give you a lift shortly."

He was too ill to argue and struggled up to the café, where Jake's daughter, Hannah, took one look at him and immediately poured him a mug of soup.

"It's clear vegetable," she said, bringing it over and placing it in his hands. "I strained it, so it's just liquid."

"Thanks," George stammered, shivering so violently that some of the soup jumped over the rim of the mug and was slowly dribbling down the side towards his hands, although Hannah had added some cold water to thin and cool it. George lifted the shaking cup to his mouth and sipped carefully, fighting to swallow.

"I get tonsillitis all the time," she explained, "and the soup helps. More than anything else does, anyway. Do you think you could cope with some painkillers?"

George shrugged. His throat felt as if it were crammed full of shards of glass. Hannah brought over a packet of codeine.

"They're only tiny," she said, popping two of the very small, white pills onto his upturned palm. He put one on the back of his tongue and took a

215

mouthful of the lukewarm soup, bracing himself. One down, one to go. The second pill got stuck in his throat and made him gag. He fought the impulse with everything he had, knowing that he'd end up vomiting. He took another mouthful of soup and swallowed quickly; the pain tightened like a barbed wire necktie. The door to the café swung open and Jake came in, leaving a trail of straw across the recently brushed tiled floor. Hannah tutted at her father.

"You'll have more than a bit of straw to worry about tomorrow," he said; he still backtracked and wiped his feet. "They reckon it'll carry on snowing into the first half of the week, as well. You'll be in the best place, mate," he told George.

"I should be all right by Tuesday," George croaked.

"You weren't in next Wednesday or Thursday, were you?" Jake asked. George shook his head. "I'll see you a week today then, if you're well enough, that is. Are you ready?" George took the mug over to Hannah and she went to take it off him. He shooed her hand away, rinsed it with boiling water and stuck it in the dishwasher. She smiled gratefully. They both knew the drill: as fellow tonsillitis sufferers they appreciated how easy it was to pick up the infection, particularly if you were susceptible.

"Hope it passes soon," she said. She watched him follow her father out to the Land Rover and wearily climb up into the passenger seat.

It was only a five minute drive from the farm to the village, but feeling the way he did, it could have been a trip to the other side of the world. Relieved, but by this point unable to speak without retching, George just waved his thanks then shuffled his way up the path to the house, every step a massive effort. Josh was at the university today, and Blue hadn't had his walk yet, not that there was anything he could do about it. The young dog greeted him by gently putting his head against George's thigh, and went outside to do his business in record time, completely aware that his human was sick. George filled a glass with water and went up to bed, just about getting his jeans off before he fell under the duvet and passed out.

He came to and peered blearily at the fuzzy numbers on the clock: 5:45. It was dark. He closed his eyes again.

It was daylight; the bright, white, silent kind of daylight that only exists after snowfall. He tried to swallow, lifted his head, looked around. He was on his own, but he could hear conversation downstairs. Josh. He was on the phone, talking about—

"Hey."

Josh's voice. George opened his eyes and squinted, attempting a smile.

216

"Tonsillitis?" Josh asked. He nodded. "You need to try and drink this." Josh held up a glass containing a couple of inches of cloudy liquid. "It's soluble cocodamol. Ellie said it'd help."

George tried to pull himself up the bed, but his arms were too weak and it hurt. Oh, God, it hurt. He ached everywhere. Even his fingernails.

"Lift up again," Josh instructed him. He lifted his head and felt pillows being stacked behind him.

"OK?"

George nodded. He took the drink and tried to swallow some. It wouldn't go down. He was going to throw up. Like a flash, Josh positioned a bowl next to him and he spat into it.

"I hate this," he said, unable to voice more than a whisper.

"I know, ma moitié," Josh said, holding George up until he finished retching. George closed his eyes, registering that this was the first time ever Josh had called him by a pet name, or that's what he assumed it was. Josh didn't even seem to be aware that he'd done it and George was too sick to question it out loud. He attempted the cocodamol again, this time with some success, and lay back.

"Can I get you anything?" Josh asked. George swallowed and winced.

"No, I'm OK," he mouthed silently.

Josh nodded and smoothed his hand over George's head. His eyelids drooped shut and Josh pulled the covers up around him, then returned downstairs, where he'd been all night, working through a research proposal that the chair of the ethics committee had passed to him yesterday. He picked up his handwritten notes and wandered through to the kitchen, put a cup under the spout of the coffee machine, turned the dial and pushed the button, all without any conscious effort. He picked up the cappuccino and wandered back to the lounge, where Blue was asleep in front of the fire. They'd need to go for a walk soon, and it was still snowing. However, the reluctance to go outside resided with the dog, not Josh. He was in the mood for a good, long hike through the fields. He loved the fresh snow and didn't care that it was still coming down. In fact, aside from it being upsetting to see George so ill, he was also disappointed, because he'd have gladly gone out walking with them at five o'clock this morning, had George been going to work.

He picked up the remote control, switched on the TV and flicked backwards and forwards through the channels. There was nothing that took his interest. He switched the TV off again. It was too quiet. He started to fidget. He picked up his phone and sent Sean a text message: "Are you up yet?" Less than a minute and no response later, he called Sean's mobile phone.

"Hello?" Sean answered.

"Did you get my text?"

"Yes. I was just typing a reply."

"Oh. Sorry. You up?"

"Obviously," Sean said dryly. "I'm at the airport."

"Oh shit," Josh said, to himself, although still with the phone to his mouth, so Sean heard him.

"What's up? You sound stressed."

"I'm fine. Did you read that research proposal?"

"Not yet. I'll read it on the plane. You sure you're all right?"

"George is sick. He's got streptococcal tonsillitis."

"Sounds nasty."

"He gets it all the time. Or he used to, when we were at school."

"Oh, right, so. I think we're ready to board."

"Have a good trip," Josh said. He hung up. He'd forgotten Sean and Sophie were going away for a couple of days. He looked at Blue, who sensed his eyes on him and lifted his head, yawned and curled up again. Josh crossed his legs and sat with his chin on his hands, drumming on his cheeks with his fingers. He needed something to do. He got up, drank his coffee in one gulp, took his cup out to the kitchen, and opened the back door, standing for a few seconds and watching the snow flutter down. It was quite mild, considering. He stepped outside and picked up a handful of snow from the patio table; the furniture had been left behind by the previous owner and was quite attractive, under all that snow. He scooped up some more and compressed it against his palm, smoothing it into a hard, round ball. A smile slowly spread across his face. He took another handful of snow and compacted it against the ball, then some more, and put the ball down, rolling it into the six inch blanket on the ground, it becoming bigger and bigger as it gathered more snow. Round and round the garden he went, in a chaotic spiral, until the ball was almost two feet in diameter. His hands were burning with the cold, so he used his foot to shove more snow around the base of what was about to become the snowman's body. He repeated the process to make a head and carefully placed it on top of the body, after which he went inside, retrieved his old scarf, along with a carrot and two sprouts from the fridge, and adorned the snowman's neck and face. All he needed now was a mouth. He stood with his arms folded, trying to think of what he could use. A brainwave hit; he returned to kitchen and tipped half a dozen frozen peas into his hand. A couple of minutes later he stepped back to admire his work. Blue stretched lazily at the back door, watched him for a moment, then plodded back to the lounge.

Josh reciprocated the smiley pea mouth grin, patted the snowman on the head and went inside, only then realising that he was actually rather cold. He rubbed his numb hands together in an attempt to get the blood running back through them—never easy at the best of times—and wondered what he could do next. Watch a film, maybe? He went through the catalogue of his mind, trying to think of one that he fancied watching. His hands were starting to warm up now, although his feet were not, and his shoes were so wet that they squelched. Time to take the dog out, then come back and change into dry clothes. He grabbed his coat and Blue's lead.

"Come on, sleepyhead," he called. Blue did as he was told, although he wasn't even slightly enthusiastic about it. "We'll make it a quick one," Josh assured him as they stepped outside, the snow settling in big white spots on the dog's back. "You look like a Dalmatian in negative," Josh said, as they trotted off down the road towards the park. They'd been walking for less than five minutes when Blue stopped for the first time and lifted his paw off the ground, looking very sorry for himself. Josh frowned and inspected the paw. In between the pads was a lump of hard ice, the result of snow compacting underfoot. He carefully pulled the ice away, then checked the other three feet. All well, they continued on their way, stopping every so often for Josh to repeat this action, as necessary.

In the park, a gang of local teenagers were engaged in snowball warfare. Josh and Blue kept to the perimeter, staying behind the trees as far as was possible. It was fascinating to watch the battle strategies, with each side having their own hierarchy, an older boy shouting commands to his troops—a group of four lads ducked behind the roundabout. Meanwhile, the enemy was led by a tall, lanky girl in a chunky, bobbly sweater, who was manoeuvring her soldiers into position through silent hand signals, as they crawled on their bellies, leaving trails in the deep snow. Blue had moved on, and Josh followed, watching battle commence once again, the lads behind the roundabout taking an absolute battering. By this point the snow was coming down heavily and the wind was starting to blow drifts of white powder up into his eyes, making it difficult to see much at all. He called Blue back to him and they continued home in the same stop-start fashion, stepping into the warm hall and both shaking off the snow. The house was silent; George was fast asleep and didn't even stir when Josh staggered and fell against the bed as he struggled to remove his wet socks. He pulled on some dry ones, went downstairs and made another cappuccino, then resumed his position on the sofa. Now what? The vacuuming needed doing, but it would have to wait until George was awake and well enough to stand the noise. He could clean the bathroom. That was a quiet job. Or maybe the oven. He picked up his cup and went back to the kitchen, opening the oven door and peering inside. They'd bought some oven cleaner a while back, and he took the spray bottle out of the cupboard, squinting to read the tiny, printed instructions on the back.

"Use when oven is warm. Simply spray on, making sure all surfaces are coated, leave for twenty minutes, and wipe with a clean, damp cloth. Hmm. Sounds easy enough."

Josh lit the oven and shut the door again, taking the time it took for the oven to warm up to admire his snowman, who looked decidedly more well-built than he did an hour ago. The snow was really coming down now, in huge, white blobs that thudded lightly as they hit the kitchen window, before slowly sliding down to join the several inches already accumulated on the sills. The oven was nicely warm, so Josh turned it off and sprayed inside, coating all five surfaces, then closed the door and returned to the lounge to wait out the twenty minutes. It stretched before him like an eternity. He switched on his laptop, loaded a game and pretty soon got bored with that. He tried another game: same effect. He opened 'chat', but quickly realised he didn't want to 'chat' with anyone and closed it again. Another five minutes. He put his laptop on the table and wandered back through to the kitchen, put some bleach down the sink, wiped over the coffee machine, spent a moment contemplating colour schemes for a new kitchen and tried to visualise what it would look like with the extension. That done, he watched the oven timer slowly tick through the last two minutes and opened the door; the ammonia fumes knocked him backwards.

"Jesus!" he cursed, waving his hand in front of his face. "Didn't mention that in your stupid instructions." He found an old tea towel and dampened it under the hot tap, then started to wipe the inside of the oven. Had he been properly paying attention, he'd have noticed the *WARNING: IRRITANT. CONTAINS AMMONIA. Use in a well-ventilated area and wear rubber gloves.* As it was, he was well into cleaning the soapy residue before he realised that it was burning his hands.

"Bugger," he said, rinsing them under the tap, which instantly eased the burning, but only if he kept them in the running water. After five minutes of this and still they stung, he withdrew one hand, took out his mobile phone and dialled Eleanor's number. He left it on the draining board on loud speaker and swapped hands.

"How do I treat ammonia burns?"

"Why? Who's got ammonia burns?"

"Me, you goon."

"Where?"

"On my hands. I was cleaning the oven."

"Why didn't you put rubber gloves on first?"

"Because I'm an idiot? What can I do?"

"Run them under the tap."

"I'm doing that."

"That's all."

"For how long?"

"Until the burning stops."

Josh sighed and quickly pushed the button to hang up. It was his own fault. He was going to have to finish the job, somehow, too. He turned off the tap and tried to ignore the stinging in his fingers, and the fact that the skin had turned white all around his nails, grabbed a pair of rubber gloves from the cupboard under the sink, growling at the oven cleaner spray bottle, as if it were to blame for his stupidity, pulled the gloves onto his hands and soldiered on. Half an hour later, he peeled the gloves off in relief. He heard noise upstairs and made George some blackcurrant squash.

"I brought you a drink," he said, taking it to him and putting it down on the bedside cabinet. George had been to the bathroom and thrown up. He looked slightly better than he had done first thing this morning.

"What's the smell?" he whispered huskily.

"Ammonia," Josh said. "Oven cleaner."

"You cleaned the oven? Why?"

"Because it needed doing."

George closed his eyes. The oven didn't need cleaning, certainly not with ammonia. It was brand new when they moved in, only four months ago, and got cleaned every time it was used.

"How're you feeling?" Josh asked.

"OK," George murmured carefully. "Codeine is good."

"You can have some more in an hour or so. Do you want anything to eat?"

George frowned.

"Thought I'd ask. I'll leave you to sleep. I'm going to clean the bathroom, so just bang on the wall or something if you need me." Josh got up and walked towards the door.

"Josh?" George called after him, his voice coming out as a strangled groan.

"Yes?" Josh turned back. George smiled feebly.

"Doesn't matter," he said and lay down again. There was nothing he could do about it. Ride the storm.

He slept fitfully, waking every so often and checking the clock, uncertain whether it was day or night, because it was dark and he was in bed alone. At one point he awoke to find a glass of water and some of the same small codeine pills Hannah had given him. He took them and drifted off again. The next time he came round after that it was daylight, and he could hear the shower running. The taste in his mouth was disgusting, making him feel sick. He pushed his legs off the bed and sat up, swaying with the effort. He took a sip of water, swallowed—a little less painful this morning, maybe—

but the water came back and he staggered from the room, just making it in time. He collapsed over the toilet and vomited what little there was to vomit. After a minute or so of retching he sat on the floor, leaning against the wall, his eyes streaming from the pain and exertion. The shower curtain was pulled the full length of the bath, no movement from behind it. He crawled the short distance across the bathroom floor and peered around the edge of the curtain.

"Josh?"

No response.

"Josh. Get up."

He was kneeling, naked, under the lukewarm running shower, his forearms crossed and clasped tightly against his chest, his eyes closed. George pulled the curtain back.

"Get up!" he said more urgently. "Come on, please?"

Josh started to sob. George felt his legs give way and slumped, with his back to the bath, clinging to the lip. He felt his own tears starting to well. He couldn't do this, not when he was so sick himself.

"Please get up," he pleaded, his voice breaking. He started to gulp, squeaking with the pain. He slid down onto the floor and cried himself into unconsciousness.

***

When he awoke again, he was still lying on the bathroom floor, covered with a duvet, a pillow under his head. Josh was sitting against the door, watching him. His face was streaked with tears. George stretched out a hand and Josh took it. Neither of them spoke. Minutes passed. Neither moved, paralysed by sickness. Eventually, cramp pushed George up and he pulled his foot towards him.

"This can't happen again," he said. Josh nodded.

"I know."

***

The next twenty-four hours were very difficult, and if the possibility had existed, George would have phoned his mum for help. She was the only person he could think of that he wanted right now; the only one who would be able to cope with the pair of them being ill, the dog needing to be exercised. Her refusal to possess a phone left him with no other option: he called Kris. Josh went berserk.

"He can't come here. He can't see me like this," he shrieked. It was the most he'd said since Saturday.

"So stay upstairs," George said. "Blue needs to go for a walk. You can't do it. I can't do it…"

"I can do it," Josh protested. "I'll just go and get my coat now." He got up and left the room. George put his head in his hands. He knew what was coming.

"Oh, no." Josh stood in the middle of kitchen, staring, disbelieving, at the mess and devastation. He had no recollection of any of it, not until now, and as it all came flooding back to him, his knees buckled. This had to stop. George appeared in front of him, his hands stretching down to him.

"Come here," he said gently. Josh shook his head.

"I need medication."

"We can talk about it later. Let's just go and sit in the lounge for now."

"This isn't fair."

"Joshua, get up and come with me." This time George said it more sternly.

"It's such a fucking mess." Josh started to cry.

"It'll clean. Now get up! Kris is going to be here any second. Do you want him to see the kitchen looking like this?"

That did the trick. Josh stood up and walked away. George closed the kitchen door and followed him back into the lounge.

"I'm sorry."

George shrugged. He still felt too sick to deal with this properly, but he was on the mend now. He'd be more or less back to normal by tomorrow—Tuesday, as he'd predicted—and the likelihood was that Josh would be too. Four days of hell, then straight back to life as usual. There was a knock on the door. Josh bolted upstairs. George went to let Kris in.

"Hi," he smiled weakly.

"Hi. Ooh." Kris stopped and looked at George's sunken eyes and pale, waxy skin. "Don't take this the wrong way, but you look like death."

"I feel pretty grim, to be honest," George said. "And I feel better than I did."

Kris stepped inside. "What is it? Flu?"

"Tonsillitis. Josh has—a bug, of some sort."

"Ah. Nice timing! Funny how it always happens like that. The gods obviously have a very cruel sense of humour." He paused to rub Blue's head; the dog was very pleased to see him. "Still, at least it's stopped snowing now. The roads are clear in town." George hadn't so much as looked out of a window in days, so it could have been six foot thick for all he knew. "Anyway," Kris continued, "Shaunna's waiting outside with Casper, so we'll get going. We'll take Blue back home with us, give you a couple of days to get better, if you like."

"Would you mind? That'd be wonderful."

"Sure. You'd do the same for us." Kris waited for George to attach Blue's lead and opened the door. "Come on, Blue." He gave George a quick hug. "Give me a call when you're well enough, OK?"

"Thanks, I will." George watched them walk away down the path, then waved to Shaunna before he shut the door. Josh had come part way down the stairs and was sitting on the fourth step from the bottom. George leaned on the end of the banister rail, exhausted.

"You need to go back to bed," Josh observed.

"I do. Come with me?"

"OK."

They spent the rest of the day cuddled up under the duvet together, watching old films and taking turns to get drinks and make toast. They ordered in a takeaway for supper—hot curry, to kill off the last of the strep, George said. Then they slept right through to Tuesday morning. Sean was taking Josh's university session for him, to give them time to get everything straight again, and all things considered, it really wasn't that bad; just a little accident with an exploding bottle of oven cleaner, several ruined baking tins and a pan of pasta congealed into one solid, gloopy lump. George took it outside and bashed it against the bin, where the pasta landed with a satisfying 'thwock'. He looked away, disgusted and still feeling a bit nauseous from the infection, in the process noticing the melting remains of the snowman. He shook his head and half laughed to himself. It could have been a lot worse. But if he had any choice in the matter, it wouldn't happen again.

Aries

Snow-white and sacred is the sacrifice
That Heaven demands for what our heart doth prize:
The man who fears to suffer, ne'er can rise.

DEAR FRIENDS
Friday 24ᵗʰ March

They were sitting in her mother's lounge, the silence of the room a stark peace that neither wished to breach, but breach it they must. Outside, as if volunteering a call to action, a blackbird sang its soaring song. Jess passed the card across to Josh. He closed his eyes.

"You know what this is," she said. Josh may have nodded. She couldn't be sure. "If you think this is the wrong way to go about it, please…" She couldn't bring herself to make the offer. It was the only way she could do it. Josh blindly grasped for her hand. She found him.

"Before I read, tell me your plan." He was seeking objectivity, distance.

"I'm going to wait until after the weekend, let them read, give them time for it to sink in. Then I'll give permission to ask questions, be angry, pretend it's not happening."

Josh opened his eyes again and examined the picture on the front of the card. It was a print of *The Enchanted Garden*, by John William Waterhouse, the painting left unfinished on his easel when he died—of cancer. They had once visited an art gallery, just to see that unfinished painting.

"I nearly chose Ophelia," Jess said.

"The one in the meadow?" Even in the awfulness of the moment, he had to fight the smile.

"God, no. She looks like she's just had an orgasm. The one where she's sitting on the bough of a willow tree, looking all thoughtful and spiritual."

"I think this is a much better choice."

"Yes, I thought I'd rather be remembered as unfinished," she said. "And I still think he looks like you." She nodded at the card.

"He does not!"

"He does. He's definitely got that Gallic look about him. It's the nose."

"He really doesn't look like me." Josh examined the man in the painting again, though he'd done so many times before. "He's got black hair for a start. And he's wearing a hat. When have I ever worn a hat? Never!" Always the same justification. Jess laughed, listening to him.

"So," Josh said. He took a breath, then let it go. "I guess I'd better read this thing." His heart quickened, yet his whole being felt as if it had ground to a complete halt. With massive effort, he moved his thumb and opened the card.

It was handwritten. He hadn't expected that. The message, he'd assumed, would be the same for each of them, although quite why he'd thought that he couldn't explain, for he had not taken this emotional shortcut himself. And the handwriting: it was beautiful. Jess wrote in a free-flowing cursive style, with great, swooping curves and delicate vertical lines ascending to meet the imagined horizontal guides of handwriting books from days gone by. The dots were precise and uniform, the spacing so even as to give the illusion that the page had been spawned by a hot metal press. The longer he gazed upon the words, the clearer they became, phrases emerging from the swirling splendour, sliding into one another to form sentences, then paragraphs, the beauty of their delivery lost to that most dreadful news they brought forth.

***

Dear Josh,

Forgive me for personalising this only insofar as I have used your name, and taken the trouble to write by hand. This should make it clear that I have not done this 'the lazy way'. Rather, I feel that it will work best if you all have the same information. It will save confusion, and disagreement, later.

Enclosed with this card you will find envelopes containing three other documents, entitled, 'Advance Directive', 'Power of Attorney', and 'Last Will'. I give these to you as my closest friends.

After several months of trying to hide from the truth, on Thursday, 16th March, I finally accepted the counsel of the wise, and agreed to attend the hospital. On Monday, 20th March, I did exactly that, and was given the results of tests conducted before Christmas. I have Stage 4B ovarian cancer. This is the most advanced stage of the cancer, meaning it has spread to other organs; in my case, my liver. It is incurable.

I have already spoken to the consultant about my treatment options, and a Macmillan nurse is coming this week to discuss with me the types of support I want, and need, at this time. The term they use for this is 'palliative care'. I would never presume that you would take on any of this care, but the nurse at the hospital said that supporting family and friends is as important to them as supporting the patient. I felt it was necessary for you to know this.

My treatment: the oncologist has sorted out the bleeding for me, so now it's straight on with the chemotherapy, to slow the progress of the tumours. They don't like to answer that question: 'How long have I got?', and redirect it into all kinds of statistics on surviving to the five year mark. But, I asked, realistically, how long? It's all guesswork on their part. Months was the measure of the answer I squeezed from them. Months, along with a caveat about treatments, and results, and healthy eating, and positive outlook, and so on, and so forth…

I am not ready to answer your questions yet, but I will be soon. Talk to me. Come and visit me. I want us to go out for coffee, or to the pub, to enjoy birthdays - all of those things we have always done, because I am still me. I'm just me with cancer. Treat me the same as you always do. Shout at me if I'm being a selfish cow. Mock me if I do something superlatively ditzy. Hug me if I'm sad. Hug me if I'm happy. In return, I will try not to die on you too soon.

All my love, forever and always,
Jess

Friends, you and me.
You brought another friend,
And then there were three.

We started our group,
Our circle of friends,
And like that circle -
There is no beginning or end.

***

He closed the card. She waited as long as she could before she spoke.

"Should I leave it? Tell them instead, when I'm ready?"

It weighed hardly enough, the card, not to carry such words; the smoothness of its pressed pulp flatness barely registered beneath his fingers.

"Of course, I still need to talk to Ellie." She spoke to fill the bloated moments, even though it was a consideration that would soon become fact. "You know? About the offices and the lease—give her time to consider what she wants to do, discuss it with James."

Josh opened the card again.

"And I'm going to stay with my parents for now, until they go on holiday, but I want to try and get back to normal, as much as I can."

A frown, to conceal and obscure; that was all he offered.

"So I should give them the cards then, like I planned?"

"That we would do, we should do when we would," he recited quietly. He held the card against his chest. "And then this should is like a spendthrift sigh, that hurts by easing."

"A straight yes or no would suffice, Joshua."

He smiled gently, sadly, and at last found the word.

"Yes."

SHADOWS
Saturday 25ᵗʰ March

"Mrs. Moreau? Can you hear me?"

She tried to roll onto her side, but found she was unable. Her arms felt so—so something. The word eluded her.

"Call 999," the voice said. She recognised it, couldn't place it. It was as if it were all only half spoken.

"Hello?" Another voice now. "Ambulance please…"

The string of questioning began. The passer-by paused to ask the postman the postcode of the property outside which they were standing, surrounded by neatly pruned rose bushes within clumps of dwarf narcissi, a line-up of yellow petal heads nodding in silence as they waited for the parade, and she strewn across the threshold, neither in nor out.

"Mrs. M…" The passer-by looked to the postman again. He held up the undelivered letter. "Moreau." The passer-by spelled it out as commanded. "She's collapsed and can't get up." Another set of questions. Airway clear? Yes. Breathing? Yes. Conscious? Yes. Other symptoms? "Yes," the passer-by said snippily. "We think she's had a stroke."

***

Kris clipped Casper's lead to his collar and quietly left the house. Everyone else was still in bed, which was typical, even on a day such as this. They took the shortcut across the park, cutting ten minutes and half a mile from their walk, although it was a means to an end only; after all, it was Saturday morning, and they were heading for the woods, to meet George and Blue.

***

"Can you hear…bed now…kin?"

An arm appeared in front of her, and then a face. She could barely see a thing, a ring like the hood of a coat obscuring the vision of her left eye, her right eye part-closed, and try as she might, she couldn't get it to open.

"Could you please say it again?" she asked.

"Oh. Do…English?"

231

She tried to shake her head, frowning to indicate she didn't understand. Were it not for the dreadful noise they were making, she'd have believed she was alone, for she could only hear them now that they had moved out of her line of sight. The door to the room slammed so loudly.

"We…interpreter…Spanish, not…"

And then another face, and a voice—female.

"Mrs. Moreau…Anglais?"

She tried to respond again, but still they did not seem to understand. It was all becoming too frustrating.

"Hey, it's…no…cry."

The woman—a nurse—wiped the tear from the side of her face, but a further one escaped and ran into her ear. It itched so, and she could not lift her hand to tend to it.

The nurse next to the bed recorded the blood pressure reading on the chart. "Have we been able to contact next of kin yet?" she asked the other nurse.

"Not yet. The postman seemed to think there's a grandson lives nearby."

"What a shame, poor love." She moved towards the door. "I'll go and do room two."

***

"Good morning," Kris called cheerily as they entered the gateway to the woods.

"Good morning," George said, slightly quieter than usual, but with a smile nonetheless. His throat was almost back to normal, although he was still feeling a bit run down. The weather wasn't helping much, considering it had gone from six inches of snow this time last week, to a couple of days of typical early spring weather, with a bright, warm sun and clear sky, followed by today's overcast and muggy outlook. The dogs were happy whatever the weather—in Blue's case, with the exception of snow—and went tearing off through the trees as soon as they had been liberated from their leads.

"How are you?" Kris asked. "Better?"

"Much, thanks. And how are you? Excited?"

"Getting that way. I know it's probably a big deal to everyone else, but it doesn't feel any different from doing radio stuff, to be honest."

"Really?"

"Yeah. Go in, rehearse, record. Go home again. Same job, different studio. Although I got recognised by someone when we were in the supermarket the other day."

"The shape of things to come?"

"I hope not. That's only from the trailers! This time next week I might have to wear a disguise. A stick-on beard and a pair of big sunglasses."

George laughed. "It's just as well I won't be here then. I'm on a course."

"You'll have to remind me nearer the time, or I'll be standing at the gate wondering where the hell you are."

"I'll text you when I get on the train."

"Yeah, how do you do that?"

"What?"

"Just remember things like that, because I know for sure that you'll remember to send that text."

"I don't know. I just do. It's no different from you remembering your lines."

"No. I suppose you're right."

They spotted a woman with two spaniels walking ahead of them and picked up their pace.

***

Josh went tearing straight through the deserted main reception of the hospital and onwards down the corridor, veering off at the 'Assessment Unit' sign. He rang the bell on the ward door and waited. He peered through the safety glass panel; a couple of nursing staff were sitting at the workstation, acting as if they hadn't heard him. He rang the bell a second time and one of them glanced over. He smiled hopefully. She came to the door.

"Sorry, sir, but visiting isn't until this afternoon." She was polite, but clearly unhappy about having been disturbed from her paperwork.

"I received a call from the ward manager," he explained. "My grandmother has been brought here."

The nurse frowned. "Do you know which room she's in?"

"No idea, sorry."

"What's your grandmother's name, please?"

"Jeane Moreau."

"One moment." The nurse went back inside the ward and spoke to another member of staff—a senior doctor, Josh assumed, as she wasn't wearing a uniform of any sort. The nurse came back and let him in.

"She's in room one. There's a nurse with her, so just let her know who you are." The nurse returned to her workstation, leaving him to find his own way.

His grandmother opened her eyes, as best she could, at the sound of the door, although she could barely see. Josh moved closer.

"I don't understand what they are telling me. They won't explain why I'm here, or what's happening. What's happening?" She rambled on in

French. The further into what she was saying she got, the less sense it made, with words missed or substituted in error.

"Are you Mrs. Moreau's grandson?" the nurse asked him.

"Yes, I am."

"Presumably you understand her?"

"Sort of. She's not making much sense."

"Joshua, where is the, err, the teacher?" his grandmother asked.

"We've been struggling to explain what's going on, and obviously she can't tell us if she's in any pain, or how she's feeling."

Josh's understanding of French was excellent, but he didn't speak it well. Even so, he spoke to her in French now.

"Are you in pain, Grandma?"

"A little. My head hurts. I can't lift my arm. Is it a..." She searched for the word.

"They don't know what's wrong and they have to ask you questions, but you need to answer in English."

"What do you mean? What is this?"

"The nurses don't understand you. Talk to them in English," he repeated.

"Stop it!" his grandmother said, her left eye wide with panic, her right eye still sagging and out of her control. Josh went over and held her right hand.

"Grandma, can you squeeze my fingers?"

She only half caught what he asked of her, but made enough sense of it to make an attempt.

"Are you squeezing?"

"Yes!" She started to cry.

"Can you understand what I'm saying to you?" he asked in English.

"Yes, I can understand, but you miss some," she replied in French.

"Repeat me," he said, then again, in English. "I have a cat whose name is Claude." She tried to say the words, but they wouldn't sound. She closed her eyes and the tears oozed out of the corners. "It's OK, Grandma." He returned to French now. "Just try one more thing for me. Say this: I have a cat whose name is Claude." She repeated it back and was mostly accurate, but missed out the word 'cat'. Josh turned to the nurse.

"She's usually fluent in English and French," he explained. "She says her head is hurting, and she can't lift her arm. She was unable to squeeze my hand." He turned back to his grandmother.

"Move across so I can see you," she said, motioning with her left hand. He did so and sat facing her.

"Grandma, can you see how many fingers I'm holding up?" He held his left arm out, away from the bed.

"No," she said. Slowly he moved his hand across in front of her.

"Yes. Three," she confirmed.

"OK, good." He switched to his right hand and repeated the procedure. She interrupted straight away and correctly stated the number of fingers.

"She's lost some of her right visual field," he told the nurse. "She can only see directly in front of her and from this point, she can't see at all." He lifted his hand to indicate. "She can understand some of what you're saying to her, but she's only processing certain words, and thinks she's responding in English."

"That's a new one on me," the nurse said. "I've been working with stroke and brain injury for fourteen years and I've not come across this before. We'll need to try and get an interpreter in."

"I'm happy to interpret."

"I'm afraid that's not permitted."

"I understand. Is someone on their way?"

"Unfortunately not. We have no-one here who can speak French."

Josh rubbed his hands over his eyes, trying to contain his frustration. "So perhaps I could do it in the interim?"

The nurse frowned thoughtfully. Her patient was becoming anxious and had a right to know what was going to happen, but it contravened hospital policy. She gave Josh a sympathetic smile and continued writing on Mrs. Moreau's chart as she spoke. "I appreciate your concern. However, it needs to be a specialist interpreter. We're going to have to explain the procedures and run some tests while we scan her brain."

"I see," Josh said. "I presume you mean cortical activation measurement using fMRI?" The nurse stopped writing and examined him. "I'm a psychologist, so I do know a little more than the average layperson, and if I don't understand, I'm big enough to say so."

***

George had arrived home to find an empty house, which he expected. However, an hour on, he was beginning to worry, as Josh was usually home by now, and his mobile phone was going straight to voicemail. He made the lunch, and left it in the kitchen whilst he showered and changed into his work clothes. After being off for four days, he'd offered to work the Saturday late and he was going to have to leave soon. He tried Josh's phone again; still voicemail, and likewise on the surgery landline, which meant he'd diverted calls to his mobile, and therefore also meant he'd finished for the day.

***

"We're going to take Mrs. Moreau for her scan shortly, Mr. Sandison," the doctor explained. "We'll transfer her by ambulance to the neurology centre, and she will remain there after the procedure for any treatment. The procedure is quite painless…" Josh allowed the registrar to continue with her explanation of how an fMRI scan worked, nodding at the appropriate junctures. At the end, he turned to his grandmother and translated for her.

"OK?" he asked.

"Yes."

"I just need to go and call George to tell him."

She seemed confused by this.

"My fiancé, Grandma."

"Your fiancé, yes," she repeated back, although it was clear she didn't recall that they were engaged.

"You know George."

"Yes," she said. "Your friend from school."

"And now we live together."

"He went to America," she stated. Josh nodded. "How long since he came back?"

"Two and a half years."

"Ah, yes," she said. He could tell that she was aware of the memory loss and was trying to cover it up.

"Don't worry, Grandma. It will all come back," he assured her, although it was by no means certain that she'd even pull through. "I won't be long," he said, then gave the edited highlights to the doctor, in English.

The ward had a no mobile phones policy, so he had to go outside, and was almost out of the building before he had a signal. He clicked on the most recent missed call to return it. George's phone rang out, then went to voicemail, so he left a message to explain what was going on, and returned to accompany his grandmother in the ambulance.

***

George picked up the message a couple of minutes later, but didn't feel he could ask to leave, having already been off sick for most of the week, so he continued with clearing the barn, all the while worrying about Josh's grandmother, and Josh. He'd mostly recovered from his 'episode' last weekend, but they still needed to talk properly about getting some kind of contingency plan in place. Josh also had yet to make a decision about the university job, and the two issues went hand in hand. On the plus side, they'd had quite a productive discussion about how stressful it had been for George, and he'd been honest about how worried he was leaving him on his own next weekend.

236

George was so preoccupied by his thoughts that he didn't notice Jake until he was right in front to him.

"When you're finished here, you can clock off," he said.

"I've not done the pens yet."

"I'll do them. You've done everything else. And I can see you're bothered about something. What's up?"

"Ah, it's nothing really," George attempted to deflect. Jake gave him an enquiring look. "Josh's grandma's in hospital. He thinks she's had a stroke." George moved towards the forklift truck as he spoke, in readiness for shifting the last of the hay bales down to the stables. Jake stepped in his way.

"Get gone," he said.

"I'm not going to be able to do much at the hospital," George justified.

"It's not up for discussion. You've worked for me for nearly six months, and taken four days off, and that was because you were told to."

"But I only came back in yesterday."

"But nothing. Go!" Jake continued to block George's passage to the forklift and stared him down. George sighed.

"All right. Cheers, Jake. I'll make it up to you."

"I know you will. In all honesty, I've never had a grafter like you before, but you're a stubborn so-and-so too. Now scram!" Jake patted him on the back, then more or less saw him off the premises.

***

The suddenness of the shaking didn't just wake him up, it startled him to such an extent that five minutes on his heart was still racing. They were taken from the waiting area, to sit in a small side room and await the arrival of the consultant. Damned insomnia. Josh rubbed the inner corners of his eyes and took a deep breath, hoping to re-oxygenate his brain.

"You OK?" George asked.

"Yeah," Josh yawned. "Tired."

"And stressed."

"True." The door opened and Josh fought off another yawn. The consultant nodded an acknowledgement and remained standing. He had the scan images in his hand.

"Your grandmother has experienced an intracerebral bleed, caused by a dissecting aneurysm. We're going to operate this evening, to relieve the pressure and repair the damaged blood vessel. There doesn't appear to be much in the way of permanent damage, so we're optimistic for a good outcome."

"What does that mean?" Josh asked. "Good as in she'll probably survive, or good as in she'll recover function?"

"Both, Mr. Sandison. Be assured that whilst the procedure is risky, we perform it quite frequently. However, I do also need to discuss with you the potential genetic risk, given that your mother also died from a ruptured aneurysm following surgery."

"I understand." Josh's voice was calm, although both he and George were panicked by this possibility.

"In the event that we find any abnormalities, we would operate if necessary, prescribe preventative treatment and advise on changes to your lifestyle."

"Will you automatically send me an appointment, or should I speak to my GP?"

"We can arrange that here. Any further questions?"

That was the cut-off. The consultant was done and they followed him out of the room, then went up to tell Josh's grandmother what was going on. She was much more settled here than she had been in the hospital, helped along by one of the nurses currently on duty having quite a good grasp of French. They'd also given his grandmother a mild sedative, but she seemed to understand why they were going to operate and what would happen during the surgery, so now it was just a case of waiting for the surgeon to be ready.

***

"I'm going to the gym," Dan said as he opened the door to leave.

"What? Now?"

"Yes, now."

"Shaunna and Kris will be here in an hour."

"So? I'll be back before it's on."

"But…" Adele scowled. She couldn't think of a single reason why he shouldn't go, other than the one reason why he was going.

"See you later." The front door closed behind him.

***

"Text from Jess," Kris said, handing his phone to Shaunna. She read it aloud.

"Hi Kris. Good luck for tonight. Will be watching with Mum and Dad. We're so excited!" Shaunna handed his phone back. "Wonder how she is?"

"Josh went to see her yesterday, George said, and she looked terrible apparently, but the bleeding's stopped. She's having her first lot of chemo this week."

238

"Poor thing. I hope she doesn't have as bad a time of it as Mum did." Shaunna continued wiping the kitchen cupboards as she spoke. "The nausea was the worst part and she was so dehydrated. She just couldn't keep anything down. Those pills they gave her never worked either. Still, it was a few years back. Maybe there's all new treatments now." She rinsed the dishcloth and hung it on the drainer, still keeping her back turned. "It doesn't seem that long since she went. Weird. And yet so much has happened that it should feel like a lifetime."

Kris watched her carefully, listening to what she was saying. She was right; it was exactly ten years to the day that her mother had died—an anniversary she'd acknowledged briefly at Christmas, but hadn't mentioned at all since. To look back on it now, it felt like just a couple of years had passed, yet they had been through so much, and as he recalled the things that had happened, time seemed to stretch, becoming longer, and longer. Krissi's twenty-first birthday, the paternity tests, the stabbing, the affair, the breakdown, the break-up—they had been through it all together. They had shared in the pain, and the joy, and now? He was making his debut in his first major TV role on the anniversary of his mother-in-law's death, whilst Jess began her battle against cancer, Josh and George awaited the outcome of Josh's grandmother's surgery, Dan and Adele tried to come to terms with the loss of their baby, and Shaunna pretended that all was well when it was not. She turned to face him and he held out his arms. She fell into them and buried her face in his shirt. He smoothed her hair and rubbed her back, holding her close, hating that she was hurting so much, but taking something from the fact that she still needed him, that he could still offer her comfort.

Ade appeared in the kitchen doorway. They made eye contact and Kris smiled briefly to indicate everything was under control. Ade nodded and wandered away. He was lost, and, he knew in that moment, he had lost. He should leave. He'd realised some time ago that this was so. He wasn't ready to do it of his own free will, would rather take every last moment with Kris and throw away his pride than walk away. This bond they shared, Kris and Shaunna and their friends, was so strong that it repelled intruders, like an electrified fence, keeping *them* all inside. At New Year, when they attended the party at Eleanor and James's new house, he had wondered how James had broken through, even considered asking him if there was a secret that he had not been told, a key to his entry and acceptance into the fold. They talked of Adele's ex-husband, who had failed to achieve the same. And then there were others, and he had dared to hope that he, like James, was exceptional. Now that hope was nothing more than the final wisp of smoke from an extinguished candle. He should leave.

***

The visitors' lounge was precisely what they had expected: six low chairs with beech arms and firm cushions upholstered in slate blue-grey polyester. A tiny television screen adorned a bracket affixed to the centre of one wall, and a small, blind-covered window offered a drab view of the building opposite. Josh sat on the far side of the small table and picked up one of the magazines. Home furnishing. He put it down again, absently turning his attention to George, who was fiddling with the remote control, trying to figure out how to turn on the TV. A couple of minutes later he handed it over to Josh, who pressed a button and the TV instantly came to life. George huffed.

"There's a vending machine downstairs. I'll go and get us coffee," he said. Josh nodded his acceptance and picked up the magazine again. Now, even though he knew his perception of time was somewhat skewed, he was quite sure that insufficient of it had passed for George to have made it to the ground floor and all the way back again, but the door opened anyway. Josh glanced up and smiled at the woman as she came in. She returned the smile uneasily, then sat at the far end of the room. She took out her phone, checked the screen, and put it away again. She sighed, fidgeting in her seat. She looked over at Josh, then put her hands over her face.

"Oh, I'm sorry," she mumbled tearily through her fingers.

"Don't apologise," Josh said gently. "It looks like you're having a difficult time." She nodded, but couldn't get it together to vocalise a response. He kept his attention half on her and half on the TV, where the continuity man had just announced that *Shadows* was coming up after the break.

"Do you want a distraction, or to talk about it?" Josh asked. She laughed in relief.

"Distraction sounds wonderful."

"This programme that's about to start? One of my friends is in it."

"That's exciting," she said, with flat affect. She took a tissue from the box that someone had thoughtfully left on the window sill. "What's it about?"

"It's a crime drama set in Manchester, and that's pretty much all I know."

George returned with the drinks and smiled an acknowledgement at their new companion. He sat down and passed Josh his drink.

"My son collapsed today and he's in a coma," the woman said quickly. The threat of more tears stopped her from elaborating further. She switched subject. "What part is your friend playing?"

"He's a detective inspector," Josh said, and looked to George for the name.

"Mark Lundberg?" George suggested.

240

"Yes, that rings a bell." The opening titles began: a black screen and dark music formed by long, deep notes that overlapped discordantly. As the tempo increased, the screen started to fill with vague images that gradually came into focus, of police officers making arrests in city streets that could have been anywhere in the UK, but then Manchester's gay village came into view, and the camera took them along Canal Street. The footage was shaky, as if being taken by someone as they ran. The music was fast and bassy.

"That's where Silhouetto performed," Josh said, recognising the outside of the club; the name of it had been covered over in the video production process.

"So it is," George muttered nervously, hoping that it would be enough to stop Josh from further revealing that they had visited a gay club, although generally when he started on one of these things there was no holding him back. For once, Josh picked up on it and said no more. Now the titles were rolling over the top of the footage—some of the actors they had heard of before, some not, and finally 'Kristian Johansson', with a bit of footage including him.

"Oh my God, oh my God!" Josh gushed excitedly. George watched him and laughed. "That is so awesome!"

"That's your friend, I assume?" the woman asked.

"Yeah, that's him," George confirmed.

"He looks so different on-screen," Josh said, shuffling forward on his seat, as if that might somehow afford him a better view. He pulled at George's sleeve and let out a little squeal of excitement. "Kris is on TV, George. Look!"

***

The reaction in the Jeffries' lounge was along the same lines, but without the volume control on the shrieks and squeals. Adele kept shaking Kris by the arm and pointing at the TV.

"You look so sexy in that suit," Shaunna said, then, realising what she'd just said, shoved a handful of popcorn in her mouth.

"You do too," Eleanor agreed. "Loving the tie especially."

"D'you think the Kris Johansson Fan Club could pipe down a bit over there?" Dan said. "Only at this rate I'm gonna have to turn on the subtitles." He was sitting on the floor, with Little Shaunna on his knee. They'd just sat through the opening scene, where a man ran into an alleyway and got brutally clubbed to death, with Dan doing his best to distract his daughter so she didn't see. Cut to DI Mark Lundberg getting out of his car and talking into a mobile phone. As soon as little Shaunna heard Kris's voice, she turned and looked at him, then at Dan, her forehead crinkled into a frown. She got up and toddled over to the wall on which the

TV hung, and tried to see behind it. She was completely bewildered and went and hid her face in her dad's t-shirt.

***

"Better?" Jess's mum asked her. Jess rested her back against the extra pillow and nodded. Her mum sat down again. "What did I miss?"

"Nothing yet," Jess's dad said without taking his eyes from the TV. "They've called in all the senior CID for a conference."

The screen displayed a large room, with around a dozen people all sitting and watching a slideshow of horribly maimed bodies.

"This is Aaron Devling," the officer at the front of the room told his colleagues.

"That's the guy who got murdered at the beginning," Jess explained. Her mum mouthed an 'oh'.

"Last seen alive on March the sixth, leaving the club with this man," the officer continued. The slideshow moved on, this time showing an image of a living person, a good-looking young guy with jet black hair. "We have yet to trace his whereabouts." The slideshow screen became dark. "It will not surprise you to hear that we suspect the offences are linked." The camera panned around the room, settling on the different faces of the 'officers' within, all listening seriously and intently. When it came to DI Lundberg, however, he appeared distracted, more concerned than his colleagues. The scene moved on, the officers leaving the room with their various instructions to coordinate information from their prior investigations. DI Lundberg held back to speak to the officer at the front of the room.

"David," he began seriously. "Aaron Devling. Where was he found?"

"I'm not sure." The other officer—David—started checking through notes on a laptop screen. "Next to the bins at the back of The Grapevine. Why d'you ask?"

"Just curious."

David shrugged. "The back of one club down that way is much the same as any other. Men making the most of…"

"I knew him," Lundberg interrupted abruptly.

The first ad break. Jess's mum picked up the empty mugs, ready to refill them.

"I bet that's the one he had the affair with," she speculated.

"In the first episode?" Jess asked, incredulous. It was a long time since she'd watched a Saturday night drama series.

Her dad nodded. "Hook 'em quick. That's how TV works these days. If they don't get the viewers from the start, then it's axed. Like that show you used to watch."

"Which one?"

"The one about demons, or was it vampires? I don't know."

"Anyway," her mum interjected, "I still think it'll be him."

"I can always ring Kris and ask," Jess suggested. Her dad looked at her in horror.

"Ruin the surprise? No. We'll wait and see."

"Unless it gets the chop before episode two," her mum qualified. "Then you can ask him."

***

"You nailed the accent in the end then?" Dan remarked, as he and Kris returned from the kitchen with more drinks.

"A bit of coaching and a lot of practice."

"I didn't think you knew anyone from Manchester."

"I didn't. George introduced me to his mum and her friend Pauline."

"George's mum's from Manchester?"

"Yep." Kris said no more, as it was clear George was uncomfortable with people knowing about his mum, and it wasn't his place to say anything, not even to Dan. However, there was something else that he needed to tell him. "Just a word of warning. You might want to avoid watching episode three."

"OK," Dan said. "Understood."

***

After his earlier burst of excitement, Josh was now quiet and subdued, his mind flitting between worrying about how his grandmother's surgery was progressing and staying focused on the TV.

"It's a shame this is on at the same time as bingo," George thought aloud. "I'd love to know what my mum thinks of his accent."

"Pauline's recording it," Josh said.

"Oh?"

Josh immediately realised his mistake and got up. "I think I might go and get another coffee. That wasn't too bad for a vending machine." He looked across to the woman, whose name was Liz, they had established. "Would you like anything, Liz?"

"No thanks. I'm fine," she said. Josh nodded and turned away.

"I'll go if you like," George offered.

"No, no." Josh quickly fled. George watched on through narrowed eyes.

"Are you two together?" the woman asked after Josh had gone.

"Err…"

243

Over the years they had each individually been asked that exact same question so many times, and whilst repeatedly answering 'no' had been both painful and infuriating, it was somehow easier. However, this was the first time he'd been asked since the answer became 'yes', and his delay was not because he was considering lying about it; more that he'd had it drummed into him his whole life that the world was a violently homophobic place—had seen often that this was so. He felt cornered and it was ridiculous. He was big enough to look after himself, if it came to it, and could probably take any verbal abuse that came his way, so he only had to answer the question. Nothing to lose. Everything to gain. A tiny step in the fight against homophobia; one almighty leap into the feared and unknown for George.

"Yes," he said at last.

Liz nodded. "Thought so. You're so in tune with each other."

"Yeah," George said, although it was more a sigh of relief. "We've known each other since primary school."

"Incredible! And how long have you been together?"

"Since last September."

Liz nodded again, but didn't comment; the ad break came to an end. The *Shadows* splash screen displayed and then they were straight back into the action: a chase, on foot, down Oxford Road, presumably, based on the road signs. Josh returned with the vended drinks: a coffee for himself and a hot chocolate for George.

"Everything OK?" he asked.

"Yep."

"Any news?"

"Not yet. I don't suppose they'd tell me anyway."

Josh sighed and sat down.

"I'm probably speaking out of turn here, George," Liz hedged, "but do you always assume the worst of people?"

He looked a little shocked by the accusation.

"I don't mean it as a criticism, just an observation."

Josh looked from one to the other of his companions; he had no idea where this had come from.

"I just asked if you were together," Liz explained, then turned her attention to George. "And it took you about five minutes to answer."

"It wasn't that long," he protested. "Was it?"

"It was almost an entire ad break."

"Ah," he said quietly.

"Look, I can't even begin to imagine what it's like to be the victim of other people's hateful bigotry, but I think you might be overdoing it a little on the self-preservation."

244

"I understand what you mean," George argued, "but with all due respect, our friend Kris?" He nodded at the TV screen. "He got bullied all the way through school for being gay, and we went to what was generally considered to be quite a progressive high school."

"But the way I see it, you are far better placed to challenge those kinds of attitudes than your friend."

"How so?"

"You're just a normal guy, doing normal, everyday things. Like this, for instance. I'm guessing you haven't told the staff here that you're partners?"

"No," Josh confirmed; it had been for George's sake that he hadn't.

"So how would they know, George? Unless you tell them, they will assume at best that you are brothers, but more likely just friends, or anything else that denies you the right to get through this together."

George stared into his hot chocolate. He knew she was right, because it wasn't just about being gay. It wasn't *even* about being gay. It was about the people who depended on him: his mum, and Josh, yet in trying to keep them safe, he was possibly doing them more harm.

"I'm not suggesting you start marching the streets with a freedom flag," Liz said, "but just think what you're missing out on. The world's not so awful a place, really. When my son collapsed today, so many kind people went out of their way to help him—people he didn't know, strangers, who didn't judge him, even though many choose not to see him, because he's lived on the streets since he was seventeen—his choice, if you can call it a choice, but I love him just the same."

The door to the visitors' room opened and a doctor Josh and George hadn't seen before came in and smiled gently at Liz. It was apparent that it wasn't good news. She nodded and followed him from the room, taking her belongings with her. It was the last they saw of her.

***

"When you said you were in a TV series, you didn't actually mention that you were the main character," Andy said as the end credits rolled.

"Didn't I?" Kris asked, keeping his face downturned. No-one had yet passed comment on what they thought of it, and he dared not ask. He was prepared for bad reviews in the press, but from his friends? His ego might not take it.

"No." Shaunna poked him in the side. "You didn't!"

Adele sat motionless, her mouth hanging open in awe. "So that other DI, Louisa Summers—is she involved with you, err, I mean your character?"

"No," Kris answered cautiously, as the truthful response would have been 'not yet'.

245

"Oh, OK. They just seemed to have a bit of a thing going on between them," Adele said. "I wonder if anything will come of it, but then, you're happily married. I mean, your character is." She frowned, trying to figure it all out in her mind. Kris gave her a hug.

"Adele, you've just made my day!"

"Have I?"

"Yes, you have."

Eleanor tutted and got up to hug him. "It was awesome, Kris. I can't wait for the next episode. Any chance of a few plot spoilers?"

He laughed. "None whatsoever. It's written into my contract."

"Aww. You can trust us," Adele tried.

"You're kidding, right?"

"What if we make our own contract, swearing us to secrecy?"

"Nope!"

"Meanie."

"Yep."

***

"Eh, Paul, how about a bit of a nightcap at yours? Get that telly programme on the go."

"Aye, alright then, Iris."

The two women bustled through the alley leading from the bingo hall, back up in the lift to Pauline's flat, and settled in with a cup of tea apiece.

***

"Mr. Sandison?" The doctor appeared before them.

"Err, yes," Josh slurred. He'd been asleep for a while.

"Would you prefer to talk somewhere more private?"

"No, it's fine," Josh confirmed. The doctor glanced at George. "He's with me."

The doctor nodded. "Your grandmother is in recovery, and the surgery went very well. We're going to keep her on a ventilator and sedated, just for a couple of days, to give her time to recover."

Josh sagged in his seat and automatically grabbed George's hand.

"She'll be brought back up to the ward shortly. I'll ask the nurses to keep you informed."

"Thanks," George called as the doctor retreated from the room. Josh exhaled shakily.

"This is just so awful," he said. "How much more have we got to go through?" George put his arm around him, releasing the tears.

246

"Hey. She's going to be OK, the doctor said," he comforted.

"I know," Josh sniffed. George pulled him close and stroked his head. Ten minutes on, a nurse came in to find them in exactly the same position. Josh had fallen asleep again.

"Is he OK?" the nurse asked.

"Yeah," George smiled. "He sleeps when he's stressed."

"Just to let you know, Mrs. Moreau is back on the ward now. She's sedated, but you're more than welcome to pop in and see her, for your own peace of mind."

"OK. Thanks." George gently nudged Josh awake and they went to see his grandmother. She looked so serene.

"We'll keep her unconscious until Monday, so don't worry about coming in tomorrow, as she really won't know you're here."

Josh leaned over the bed and kissed her porcelain forehead. "Good night, sleep tight, Grandma," he said, in French.

***

"What d'yer reckon then, Paul?" Iris asked.

"Aye. Not bad at all, that. Same time next week?"

"Yeah. Why the fuck not? Ta-rah, Paul."

"Night, Iris, love."

***

Kris and Shaunna arrived home to find Ade sitting in the living room, reading a book.

"Hi," Kris called on his way to the kitchen. Shaunna went upstairs to change into something more comfortable.

"Hi," Ade called back.

"Want a drink?"

"Sure." Ade came up behind Kris and kissed the back of his neck. "You were awesome."

"Thanks." Kris was past pretending that everything was OK between them, but he didn't want to hurt Ade. He turned and smiled, allowing him close.

"What's up?" Ade asked.

"Nothing. Why?"

"You seem edgy."

"Do I?"

"Yeah. Didn't they enjoy it?"

"They?"

"Your friends. Dan, Adele…"

"Oh! Yes, they enjoyed it. Adele was trying to get me to divulge the storyline."

"Did you crack?"

"No. I'm not allowed to!" He sidestepped to get the cups and Ade moved away.

"I would've liked to have come with you tonight," he said quietly.

"Why didn't you say so?"

"I didn't feel I could."

"Ade, it's not like…" Kris stopped.

"It's not like what? That you're pushing me away?"

They held eye contact for several seconds. Shaunna walked into the kitchen and passed between them. Ade shifted his gaze to the floor.

"Did you see it?" she asked him.

"Yes. I was just asking Kris if you enjoyed it."

"Yeah. It was really good. Especially that bit where you pinned that bloke up against the wall and he spat in your face."

"That was disgusting to film," Kris said. "He actually had to spit in my face and it took us four takes to get it right. The poor guy must've drank a gallon of water in the process."

"It looked so real. You had that full-on angry glare you get."

"What full-on angry glare?"

"The one when you're, well, full-on angry!"

"I don't get angry."

"Pah!" Ade said.

"See?" Shaunna laughed. "It's not just me who thinks it, so it must be true."

"Yeah, that's right. Why don't you just gang up on me."

Shaunna gave Ade a wink. "We intend to. We're gonna make you tell us the plot."

"No, you're not."

"Yes we are." She advanced on him and tickled his sides. His arms instinctively stiffened and trapped her hands. She wriggled her fingers.

"I won't break," he laughed.

"You will."

"Will not. I am strong."

"Not as strong as I am," she taunted. He still hadn't released her.

"I'm gonna head on up to bed," Ade said. He backstepped out of the kitchen. They didn't even notice.

MILK BAR REVISITED
Monday 27th March

"Why are you sitting out here?"

Shaunna approached the chrome tables and chairs adorning the pavement in front of the milk bar, where Sean was sipping at a drink, and shivering.

"Last time I went in there, a strange woman came and sat at my table," he grinned.

"Ha! Come on. It's bloody freezing." She went inside and he followed, a bit of the homeless stray about him. "Do they do hot drinks?" she asked him. He shrugged. "Is that not a hot drink?"

"It may have been, once upon a time."

Shaunna tutted. "What hot drinks have you got?" she asked the girl behind the counter, who had been waiting patiently on smiley standby.

"We have Hot Chocs in a variety of flavours—the banoffee is my favourite—plus we have hot milkshakes. Strawberry cheesecake, peach melba, apple crumble and custard…"

"Apple crumble and custard?"

"Yes. Or there's blueberry pie."

"Hmm." Shaunna frowned thoughtfully and glanced at Sean's glass. "What've you got?"

"The banoffee hot chocolate. It came highly recommended."

"Yes," said the girl behind the counter. "It's my favourite."

Sean raised a solitary eyebrow and tried not to smirk.

"I think I'll go with the apple crumble," Shaunna said, then turned to Sean. "You want another?" He slurped and nodded at the same time—no easy feat, as he discovered when the gloopy last dregs of his very chewy Banoffee Hot Choc dribbled down his chin. He tried to suck them back up into his mouth, but it was too late. Shaunna laughed at him. They retired to their table. Yes, indeed. One visit and it was already *their* table.

"So I watched a bit of that crime drama nonsense," Sean said, blasé.

"OK?" Shaunna queried.

"Yes, I suppose it was. He's not a bad little actor, that husband-ex-husband of yours."

"Huh? Oh yeah." Shaunna was distracted by the two young men sitting across from them, both sucking hard at their straws and experiencing the same lack of success she had encountered on her first visit here. "Why?"

"Why what? Suffer the pain of the yoghurt not-smoothies?"

"No. Why give a compliment and make it sound so condescending?"

"Did I?" Sean pretended to be surprised. "It was unintentional."

"Hmm. Says you."

Their drinks arrived.

"They're quite hot," said the Milky's maid. It was written on her apron: Amy, Milky's Maid.

"OK. Thanks." Shaunna carefully pulled the glass close to her and put her hands around it. Amy the Milky's Maid wasn't wrong. Shaunna moved her hands away. Amy placed the second glass down.

"Thanks." Sean used the paper napkin to manoeuvre it along the table.

Their 'maid' nodded politely and returned to her position behind the counter.

"Yes, so was it well received?" Sean asked.

"What?"

"The TV show? Did the reviewers like it?"

"Yeah, I think so. We don't talk about it."

Sean gave her an enquiring look.

"It's his job. If he worked in telesales he wouldn't come home and tell me all the ins and outs of it."

"I take your point. But it's not exactly your run of the mill kind of occupation, is it?"

Shaunna shrugged. "He's always been an actor. It's pretty run of the mill to us."

Sean accepted this. "And how are you doing?"

"Yeah. I'm doing OK. You?"

"Fine, fine. What've you been up to?"

"Not a lot. Working, mostly."

"Me too." Sean tried his drink. Still too hot. "Shall we start again?"

Shaunna laughed dolefully. "Yeah."

"And how are you doing?"

"Awful. You?"

"Feckin' terrible. What've you been up to?"

"Worrying about a friend who's just been diagnosed with cancer. You?"

"Worrying about becoming a father, amongst other things."

"When's it due again?"

"Twenty-fourth of August. It's my wake-up call."

"I wouldn't be too eager to wake up yet. Plenty of time for that after the baby's born."

"Of course. You're well versed in these matters."

She looked doubtful. "A long time ago."

"Does it change?"

"No. I guess not."

"And Krissi is utterly stunning."

"Hands off! She's too young for you."

"If I was going to be doing any hands-on, it would be with her mother."

"Oh, you're too charming."

"I've heard it said before." Sean smiled and patted her hand. "I hope you know that much as you are an incredibly attractive woman, I would do nothing to further complicate our already overly complex and trying lives."

"I know, Sean. You don't need to explain." Shaunna smiled and her eyes twinkled with fun. "I'm really enjoying the innocent flirting, truth be told."

"Good to hear. I'll be sure to keep at it."

"You do that." Shaunna withdrew her hand to try her drink again. It was a little cooler now, and absolutely delicious. "Mmm. That is one hell of a drink."

"Nice, is it?"

"It's like liquid dessert. Minimum effort, maximum pleasure." She took another big slurp and slithered down her seat. Sean laughed.

"What isn't there to like about liquid dessert?"

"My sentiments exactly." She watched him for a moment, and he watched her.

"Go on. Ask," he said in that know-it-all way he sometimes had about him, though she had realised last time they met that it was mostly an act.

"If you can guess correctly what I want to ask, I will buy the next round."

"D'you think I'll be wrong?"

"I can't see how you would get it from one look."

"All right, you're on." He dragged it out, knowing it was worth it, because he was completely confident in the correctness of his assumption. "So, taking a wild guess, I'd say that in all probability, what you're most curious about, thus what you probably want to ask me, is how well I know your man Joshy."

"Agh! How do you do that? In fact, how do you both do that?"

"Telepathy, I told you." Sean winked.

"No, seriously. How do you do it?"

"People are consistent, and therefore predictable."

"It's psychology?"

"Yes, it's psychology. You've no doubt come across the 'think of a vegetable' mind trick?"

"Nope."

"All right, well here goes. I'm going to write down the name of a vegetable." Sean took a pen out of his pocket and turned his hand palm inwards. "And you're going to guess what it is." He wrote on his hand. "OK. What is it?"

"Erm." Shaunna frowned in thought.

"Don't think, just say it."

"OK. Broccoli?"

Sean laughed. "Trust you to be ever contrary." He showed her his hand, with the word 'carrot' scribbled on it. "More than eighty percent of the time, people will say 'carrot'."

"So why didn't I?"

"That's the bit psychology's not so good at. We look for common trends, the 'normal' patterns of behaviour. The only time we look at the exception to the rule is when we're trying to fix it. Make it 'normal', if you will."

"Are you saying I'm abnormal?"

"Not at all. You're unusual though, that's for sure."

"Unusual I can deal with. But anyway, don't try and waylay me with your vegetable trickery. Tell me about you and Josh."

"Ah, you properly caught me out there. As you know already, we went to university together, and we shared a house from second year onwards. We had some great times." Sean smiled as he allowed himself to reminisce a few.

"And some not so great," Shaunna observed.

"Yes. That's right enough. Studying is hard. Sharing your living space is hard also. Put them together and you're going to fall out every now and then."

"Neither of you struck me as the kind of man to get all worked up, until I listened to you at the psychic night, which was very entertaining, by the way. Far more so than Gary the Russian! And I must admit, you got me hooked on psychology. Josh doesn't exactly share his trade secrets, so I've never really given it any thought before."

"He always was one to keep things close to his chest."

"Like his feelings for George, for instance?"

"Amongst other things, yes. But we should leave Joshy be now. He'd be bloody furious to know we've been talking about him." Sean emptied his glass and pushed it towards Shaunna by way of a hint. "I'll pay for them, you order them. I'd like what you've just had."

"I don't mind paying for them," Shaunna said. "Now I have a husband-ex-husband with TV star money."

"You can tell me all about it when you get back."

She smiled wanly at him and went to order the drinks. When she returned, he attentively held her gaze.

"I think Kris and Ade are on the brink of breaking up," she told him. "Which is awful, because Ade loves him, and I can see how much he's hurting. Like on Saturday, when we got back from Adele's, he was trying so hard to be part of what we have—our friendship group—but Kris won't let him. It's like—oh, I don't know really. Like he doesn't think it will last, so can't see the point in making the effort, and it's more or less been that way since the get-go."

"And did you have it out with him about the baby idea?"

"Not really. Well, not at all. We rarely get any time to ourselves when Ade isn't there, which suits me just fine, as when we're alone, Kris gets too close, you know? Not just physically, either."

"You don't want him to."

"I don't want to think about it, not at the moment. It's hard enough trying to deal with Jess, and Josh's grandma, and then there's…"

"I'm sorry," Sean interrupted, "Jess who?"

"My friend Jess—the one with cancer?"

"Yes. Is she friends with Josh too?"

"Yeah. We've all been friends since school."

"Not Jess Lambert?"

"Yes. Oh God. Of course! You must've been at the same uni. Did you know her? I didn't think, Sean, I'm so sorry."

"Hey, don't worry about it. Why would you?" Sean rubbed his chin thoughtfully. "Is it serious? Stupid question," he admonished himself. "Of course it's serious. It's cancer. I mean what stage is it at?"

"I don't know much, other than that she had minor surgery a couple of weeks ago and she was having her first chemo session today."

"That's quick," Sean thought aloud.

"Josh is closer to her than I am. You'd be better asking him. If she's going to tell anyone…"

"Yes, but we already established that Josh doesn't share." Sean tried to push the thought from his mind. There was no point speculating; maybe he would try asking Josh, just on the off-chance. He changed the subject. "OK, so I know Josh, and Jess; I've met Adele, and I know George, of course. Then there's you, and the husband-ex-husband. Is that everyone in your friendship group?"

"Nearly. There's also Ellie, and then there's…"

Shaunna paused for Amy the Milky's Maid to deposit their drinks on the table, and they both nodded their thanks.

"And then there's Dan and his older brother, Andy. Dan and Adele are together. Andy was sort of with Jess, but isn't anymore."

"Andy." Sean eyed her carefully. "Oh, now there's a spark."

"What? I don't think so!" She could feel her cheeks getting hotter and hotter. Sean continued to watch her. She sighed. "Andy is Krissi's dad, that's all."

"That's all?"

"Yes. It's not like that."

"Not like what?"

"Like anything. It was an accident. A one night thing. Well, maybe a two night thing, but whatever. There's nothing going on between me and Andy." She picked up her drink and sipped it, keeping her eyes averted.

"Come now, Shaunna. I thought we were getting on better than that."

"We were. I mean we are. It's just, well, Andy's looking for a relationship. I'm not. Can we talk about something else?"

"Sure. What would you like to talk about?"

"You said you were worrying about other things too. You want to talk about that?"

"Oh, why not? It's quite an interesting story, actually."

Shaunna picked up her glass and settled in to listen.

"A few months back, I got a call from a colleague who works for the prison service. She'd been treating an inmate who was serving a life sentence for murder. He killed himself."

"Oh, how sad."

"Quite, although it happens more in prison than in the outside world. Sadder still, it looks like he was innocent, and this colleague of mine—and I'm trusting you not to breathe a word here—she passed the guy's case notes on to me, telling me she thought there was enough evidence in them to re-open the case."

"And is there?"

"Well, it's all hearsay, of course, because it's my colleague's record, not his own firsthand account. And I knew the guy before he went down. He was nice enough, but very mentally unstable. The police thought he was responsible for attempting to murder me too."

"Someone attempted to murder you?"

"It's not as glamorous as it sounds, and to be fair it could well have been my own doing. There were painkillers in my kettle, and I sleepwalk, not that I keep painkillers in the house, but maybe Soph—well, anyway, the thing is that there were other witnesses, but they're not willing to come forward, and they'd need to in order for the police to even consider investigating again."

"But surely, if you knew they'd got the wrong man, you'd come forward?" Shaunna asked rhetorically. "I know I would."

"It's not so straightforward, I'm afraid. See, the victim left a fair bit of money in his will. He'd been having an affair and fathered a son, who's since inherited that money, making him a likely suspect for the murder, except he didn't know the victim was his father until after the murder. Unfortunately, his biological mother and his adoptive father are the witnesses I mentioned, and my colleague's notes suggest the son also may have seen something."

Shaunna was listening to all of this, making the connections in her head, but she didn't say anything. Indeed, she was trying her very hardest to give nothing away, but the story was striking too many familiar chords. She sipped at her drink. Sean continued.

"Of course, if I knew the boy, I could approach him directly, see if he'd be prepared to go to the police, but I don't want to upset things further. He's been through enough already." Sean paused and studied Shaunna for a moment. "What is it?"

"You sound very keen to re-open this investigation. I'm just wondering why."

"Miscarriage of justice."

"No. It's more than that. It excites you."

Sean shrugged. "Yes, I'll admit that it does excite me. It's not that interesting a job, being a psychologist. Most of the time all I do is recommend treatment programmes and the nurses do the rest."

"So is the murderer still out there?"

"Assuming my colleague was right, yes, he is."

"And is the son at risk?"

"Potentially. It's hard to say without knowing the motive."

Shaunna stirred her drink, disturbing the apple pieces so that they swirled around the glass for a moment, then sank to the bottom once again.

"Do you believe in fate, Sean?"

"What makes you ask?"

"How long have you lived here?"

"About eleven years."

"Why did you move here instead of somewhere else?"

Sean frowned, puzzled by the question. "It was the first full-time position that came up."

"Did you know that Josh and Jess lived here?"

"I knew they came from around here, but I didn't know whether they'd moved back after graduating. As I say, the job came up, and it was a nice enough place, so I took it."

"Would you say that was fate?"

"Priming, mixed with a pinch of coincidence, I'd say."

Shaunna chewed her thumbnail thoughtfully and watched the two young men get up, leaving their glasses and empty chocolate wrappers on the table. The 'maid' went over and cleaned up as soon as they'd gone.

"Do you know who owns this place?" she asked.

"Can't say I do."

She turned to face him. "Jason Meyer," she said. "It's part of Campion Community Trust."

255

He nodded slowly, but avoided looking at her. He studied his glass.

"He and Krissi are flatmates," she continued. "And the Ellie I mentioned? You might know her as Eleanor Brown, née Davenport? Your innocent murderer was her lunatic ex-husband, I believe?"

Still Sean didn't speak, and was making more of a deal than he needed to of mixing up his drink.

"She's been Josh's closest friend for a very long time."

Sean nodded, having decided to own up, although he still wasn't prepared to resume eye contact. "Yes. I know her. Well, I say know—I met her up in Newcastle once or twice, and we've worked together a few times in a professional capacity. There's that small world for you again."

Shaunna smiled. "Yeah. I think I've seen bigger marbles. Anyway, what I was going to say is that Jason's a really nice guy. A sensitive soul, but got his head screwed on. I've known him a good few years, and the one thing I can tell you about him is that he's the sort of person you can count on to do the right thing." She waited for Sean to look up. "So," she said, "I'll ask again. Do you believe in fate?"

Sean smiled. "Yes," he said. "I think maybe I do."

DOG PEOPLE
Saturday 1st April

Josh stretched out his arms and legs, poking George with his toes. He was sat on the side of the bed, putting his shoes on.

"Sorry," he whispered, "I was trying not to wake you."

"It's OK." Josh sat up and rubbed his eyes. "What time is it?"

"Quarter to six."

He yawned and flopped back into the pillows, spread-eagled, his fingers dangling over the edge of the mattress. A cold, wet nose poked against his hand and he patted the bed. Blue jumped up and snuggled close.

"You're going to regret that later," George said. He watched as Josh and Blue curled up together, the dog's paw resting on Josh's shoulder, their faces close together, staring into each other's eyes.

"At least we'll both have someone to cuddle tonight." Josh kissed the head of the soppy, young German Shepherd dog; he was quite a size now, but a considerate bedfellow who kept to his side. George smiled. He'd been so worried about leaving Josh on his own for the weekend. Now he could see that he wasn't alone after all.

"He's going to miss his walk with Casper. Maybe I'll suggest to Kris we rearrange it for tomorrow. I should be back by about half past five, six at the latest. It'll still be light by then."

"Damn. I'll have to go shopping on my own," Josh joked. Blue licked him on the chin. "I'm doomed, Blue. What am I going to do?" The dog mouthed gently at Josh's hand, then snuggled into the crook of his neck and snuffled contentedly.

"You can always leave it till Monday, and we can go after work," George suggested.

"No, I'll be all right, although I think I might do it online. In fact, don't worry about Kris. I'll take Blue for his play date today."

"OK. Cool. It'll probably do you good."

Josh could only make out George's outline against the light coming through the curtains, but he could see he was still fretting. This would be their first night away from each other.

"Hey," he said, poking him with his toes again. "I'm going to be fine." George sighed. Josh rubbed his foot against the bottom of George's back. "I'll miss you though, if that makes you feel any better."

"I'll miss you too." George got up and collected his phone, then walked around to Josh's side and bent to kiss him. Josh grabbed him by the t-shirt and pulled him down on top of the duvet.

"I love you," he said.

"You know, I might just change my mind and get back into bed." He was only half joking, although Blue now had his eyes tightly shut, pretending to be asleep, and the train was going to leave in an hour, whether George was on it or not, so he reluctantly pulled away. He kissed Josh again, then kissed Blue. "Love you," he said. Then he was gone. Josh checked the time—it was 5:52—and went back to sleep.

***

"Good morning!" Kris called, with a smile and a certain amount of undisguised surprise, as Casper led him through the gate into the woods, eager to greet his friend.

"Good morning," Josh responded. He unclipped Blue's lead and gave him permission to go and play. Kris was still battling to release the dozy Labrador, who was now lying on his back, tail wagging frantically, with Blue standing over him.

"George having a lie-in?" Kris asked. The two men stepped off together; Casper righted himself and tore off through the trees, with Blue lolloping lazily behind.

"He's on an animal husbandry course," Josh explained.

"Ah yeah. He told me last week. How's your grandma doing?"

"OK. She's on the mend from the surgery, but we're going to have to look at nursing homes. She's lost a lot of her mobility and speech." They didn't talk of Jess. Not yet. That time would come. "How's your week been? Paparazzi hounding you yet?"

"Actually, it's been OK. I got a bit of hassle at the studio when I went to do that interview on Tuesday, but they've left me alone pretty much."

"Yes. I saw that. It was quite interesting listening to you being a TV star."

"Ha, yeah. It's just another of the many roles I play in this life."

"And very convincingly, I must say," Josh complimented.

"Why, thank you," Kris smiled, taking a mini bow. Josh laughed and shook his head.

They continued along the winding path, every so often catching a glimpse of the two dogs, alternating in which of them was doing the chasing and being chased. It was a beautiful spring morning, the air filled with the scent of new cherry blossom and melodious blackbird song. Josh inhaled deeply and sighed. Kris glanced at him and grinned.

258

"It's fabulous, isn't it?" he said.

"It is!" Josh agreed, surprised by just how much he was enjoying being out in the fresh air, dog-walking, in *wellies*! It wasn't the first time he'd been out walking with Blue; after all, it was only a couple of weeks since he was dragging the poor dog around in a snow drift, although he was doing his best to forget about that weekend, other than to marvel at the wonder of British weather—that it could be below zero and blizzardous, then a fortnight later be as warm, sunny and verdant as this. So: their first proper walk together without George. Apart from a couple of trips to the beach, the wildest the terrain ever got was the gravelled footpaths around Farmer Jake's, not like this incredible, rambling meander through woodland. In the distance there was a staccato tapping sound and Josh paused to listen. The noise stopped, then started up again.

"Woodpecker," Kris explained.

"Wow!" Josh said, his eyes widening in wonder. "I don't think I've ever heard one before."

"Well now you have."

They walked on, mostly in silence, with Josh intently examining his surroundings, occasionally pointing out things which Kris was ashamed to realise that he took for granted—the very last of the snowdrops bobbing their heads to the tune of the light morning breeze, the deep green shoots of new bluebells pushing their way through last season's mulch, the unfurling bracken—all of these incredible changes taking place before his eyes, and he, who dared to call himself an artist, rarely stopped to consider their beauty. Sometimes all that was needed was a fresh perspective.

Blue had become bored with playing chase and fell in alongside his human companions, leaving Casper to run after a grey squirrel, as it chanced staying at ground level a little longer, safe in the certainty that the big yellow dog was no match for its speed and cunning.

"We used to see red squirrels here," Kris said, "and we often see foxes. There are hares too. I saw three of them, across the fields, last year. I know it sounds obvious to say so, but they really are unbelievably fast."

Josh was listening and taking it all in without a word. The magnificence of the English spring had stilled not only his tongue, but his thoughts also. His brain, always run ragged with theories and ideas, interpreting feelings, uncovering meanings, over-thinking how he was feeling himself and worrying about those he loved—it had stopped. All of it. The relief of having his mind fill instead with the fragrant, glorious silence of the morning astounded him. He looked down at Blue, loyally walking at his side. Blue looked up into his eyes and Josh felt his heart swell with love.

The fourth member of their group was by this point trailing far behind, but after he'd spent several minutes standing at the foot of the tree that had been the squirrel's final escape route, Casper gave up and rejoined the party, ready to partake of his number one favourite pastime: Frisbee fetching. Kris dutifully pulled the toy from inside his jacket and launched it like a discus, so that it spun off, travelling a good distance along the path before it landed. Casper ran after it, skidded to a halt, picked it up, plodded back and stopped in front of them.

"Leave," Kris commanded. Casper let go and watched intently as Kris repeated the action. All the while, Blue trotted along beside them.

"You can go play too," Josh told him. He looked up as if to say, "I am too sensible for this silliness."

"He'll usually have a play once we get to the spring," Kris said. "Casper drops the Frisbee in and Blue fishes it out again. It's hilarious."

"Hmm. Especially when he comes home. Mud everywhere!" Josh rubbed the dog's head. For such a young animal—not quite seven months old—he really was surprisingly well-behaved and didn't make that much of a mess in the house.

"Does it drive you mad?" Kris asked. "The mud and hair and stuff?"

Josh shrugged. "I don't care. George, on the other hand, can't stand it. Normally, the minute the pair of them get back from the woods, he baths Blue and then spends the best part of the day vacuuming and mopping and wiping down the walls."

"Really? I always thought you were the fussy one."

"Are you serious?" Josh looked at Kris and he winked. "Yes, you're right," Josh agreed, "I am a bit of a fusspot at times, but he's just as bad—worse, in fact, because he's always like it."

They walked on, stopping every so often to politely converse with other dog owners, many of whom were familiar with Casper and Blue; likewise, Kris knew their dogs by name and the human interactions were entirely focused around their beloved pets—newly discovered best walks, different diets being tried, visits to the vet, their most and least favourite treats—all recent events of significance to canines. Josh was absolutely fascinated by these interchanges; it was unchartered territory for him. Better still, there was no hidden agenda, no unconscious intent, no underlying dialogue. The words were what they were: honest and from the heart. These people truly adored their dogs, and it would seem in return that the animals had granted them the greatest gift: the chance to just be themselves.

A little further along, they came to the spring and a spaniel suddenly appeared from nowhere, an enormous stick—more of a branch—clenched in its jaws. It bounced on past, spraying Kris and Josh with water, then dropped the stick at the feet of a woman standing on the bank.

"Morning," Kris greeted her.

"Morning," she called back. She hoisted the stick into the spring, where another spaniel that had been wading around in the shallows now leapt into the deeper water and grabbed one end. With an almighty splash, the first spaniel flung itself off the bank and took a hold of the other end, and the pair of them played tug of war. Josh watched on, amused and enthralled by their antics. By this point, Casper had joined them and had a grip on the middle of the stick, trying to wrestle it away, at the same time as keeping his head held high above the water. The spaniels pulled the stick down and Casper bobbed under the surface, emerging a second later in a frenzy of excitement that saw him racing up and down the opposite bank, shaking his head so vigorously that the spin of his ears formed a translucent halo. Blue had gone over to greet the woman and she was baby-talking him.

"Where's your dad today?" she asked.

"He's on a course," Kris answered on the dog's behalf.

"Ah," the woman said. "Poor baby Blue. Bet you're missing him, hey?" She rubbed his ears and he pushed his head against her hand. She addressed Kris now. "How's Casper's tummy this week?"

"A lot better. We figured out what caused it. He's been stealing the fat balls we put out for the birds."

The woman grimaced. "No wonder he had a bad tummy then. I watched *Shadows*, incidentally."

"Did you?" Kris asked reticently.

"I did. It was ever so good." As she turned her attention from Kris to her dogs, she gave Josh the most fleeting glance. He was used to this; unless they had given him prior permission, people's sensing of his ability to read them often caused discomfort, although on this occasion he had slightly misinterpreted the woman's reaction.

"By the way," Kris said, picking up on his curiosity, "this is Phyllis."

"Hi," Josh acknowledged her.

"Hello," she smiled back.

"Phyllis, this is Josh—George's partner."

"Oh." She frowned, clearly puzzled by this news. "I've always assumed you and George were together."

Kris shook his head. "Nope."

She became a little flustered. "Sorry," she said to Josh. "That sounded terrible. I didn't mean to imply—"

"Don't worry. It's fine," he assured her.

"So," she looked down at Blue, "you've got two dads to take you on walks then, lucky boy." He cocked his head on one side at the mention of 'dad'. Casper clambered his way up the bank and pushed between Blue and Phyllis. "Yes, you're a lucky boy too," she said to him, laughing. He wagged his tail, although it looked more like his tail stayed still and his body wagged,

261

the way he was wiggling about. However, he was also fickle and ready to get back to playing fetch.

Kris threw the Frisbee and Casper caught it in mid-air, then promptly dropped it in the water. Blue immediately sprang into action and jumped, from standing, right into the middle of the spring. He scooped up the Frisbee and gracefully carried it back to Kris, dropping it at his feet. Kris picked it up and threw it again. Casper caught it, dropped it over the edge and Blue rescued it, and so on it went. Josh couldn't believe what he was seeing.

"I love the way they do that," Phyllis laughed.

"That is pretty impressive, I've got to admit," Josh said.

"Yeah, for about the first five times, maybe," Kris groaned. Phyllis gave him a sympathetic smile.

"Well, I'm going to head back. My daughter's home for the weekend and she's brought a term's worth of washing with her. Whoops! There goes a Saturday!"

"Nice," Kris said dryly. "Don't work too hard."

"I'll try not to." Phyllis moved off. "Still, at least there's something good on TV tonight—I may even open a bottle of wine! See you both again." She smiled as she passed them by; a few seconds later her two spaniels followed.

"See you," Josh replied.

"Bye, you two," Kris said, running his hand along the backs of the two soggy dogs as they paused on their way past. "Bye, Phyllis."

They watched as she wandered off along the path, her dogs trotting along behind her. She was precisely how Josh had imagined her to be when George mentioned 'the woman with the spaniels': green wellies with beige pants tucked into brown, woolly socks, green waterproof jacket—every bit the middle class woman of semi-rural England. He'd lay money on her being a retired teacher.

"You're in your element, aren't you?" Kris observed, pulling Josh back from his analysis.

"I am. But you know the best thing about it? Everyone here is so—genuine."

"What d'you mean?"

Josh thought for a moment. "It's like you drop the act. Be who you really are, instead of constantly worrying how you will be perceived by others. You say what you actually feel and think. It's so refreshing to only have to listen to the words."

Kris picked up the Frisbee and removed the slimy greenery tangled around it. He threw it to Casper, who kept hold of it, this time running further along the bank before he dropped it. Josh and Kris walked on behind him until they came to an arched wooden bridge, where they crossed over the spring to a small picnic area with two tables. They sat at the one nearest to the bank and took turns at throwing the Frisbee, as dictated by Blue.

"While we're talking about dropping the act, can I be frank with you?" Kris asked.

"I suppose, but remember I'm not one of you Dog People," Josh replied cautiously.

"Meaning what?"

"That I reserve the right to refrain from going entirely au naturel."

"Yeah, I wasn't going to ask you to get naked," Kris joked, but he understood what Josh meant, because that was what he wanted to talk to him about.

"Does it bother you?" Josh asked.

"You and George?"

"Yes."

"No. Not really. Not you and him being together. Not at all."

"Kris! Stop qualifying, or you'll have me wondering whether you're telling me the truth!"

"It's the truth, I promise you." Kris felt a little uneasy about having this conversation, but he'd wanted to speak out forever and the chance might never come again. "What does bother me is that it took you so long."

Josh didn't respond to this, or not with words, but Kris picked up on the flicker of a reaction, because here, in these woods, he was the one with the power to read people, and for all of Josh's resistance to going 'au naturel', it was contagious. The shield he held between himself and the world at large kept slipping away from him, and while he was considering whether he should try and get a tighter grip or just throw it away for Casper to drop in the spring, Kris seized the opportunity.

"I was jealous of you at school," he confessed. Josh stared at him in disbelief. "You were quiet and studious, unbelievably clever—everything I wasn't, although that wasn't what made me jealous. Even if I'd been just like you, I doubt it would have made any difference, because George always cared more about you than me. All the time we were together he talked about you—the things you used to do together, your plans for the weekend, where you were going to apply for uni. He could hardly talk about anything else, and it made me feel like I was second choice."

Josh was taken aback. This was not how he remembered their school days at all. True: he'd always been the quiet, studious one, until he got to sixth form, where he discovered that not only did he have opinions, but he was allowed to state them, and it made him cringe to think how pompous and self-opinionated he had been on occasion. There was a certain irony to Kris's confession, though, for this was the time when his own jealousy started, as he watched his peers falling in and out of love at a startling frequency, while he remained on the sidelines, wondering when he would catch them up. However, it meant little that George had often talked about him; they'd been friends for so long, and back then spent a great deal of their leisure time together.

"He used to talk about you a lot too," Josh said after a few minutes' reflection. "You definitely weren't second choice. He felt very betrayed when you got with Shaunna. He loved you. He still does."

"Yeah, I know. But you know why he felt betrayed, don't you? It wasn't because I was with someone else."

"No. It was because you were with a girl."

"And he still won't accept it. When Shaunna and I split up, he was there for me all the way, but I can't help thinking it was because he thought I'd been 'pretending to be straight' all those years."

"Well, you know George. Everything's black or white with him, although he's getting better."

"That's true," Kris said thoughtfully. "You don't think I was pretending, do you?"

"No. Whatever badge you want to wear, it doesn't alter the fact that you love Shaunna."

Blue was having a bit of trouble freeing the Frisbee from where it had caught on a tree root, and they paused their conversation to watch as he tried different ways to free it. Eventually, he waded to the other side of the tree and tugged until the disc slid out into the water.

"Clever boy!" Kris called. Blue came bounding over, looking very pleased with himself. He dropped the Frisbee and Kris threw it again.

"When he properly fell in love with you," he said, picking up the conversation where they had left it, "I was devastated—for him rather than for me. I made my decision and didn't regret it, but I knew how hurt he was. He needed to be with someone who would look after him, someone he could trust, and because you were in the closet, I knew there was no way…"

"Whoa! Let me stop you right there!" Josh swivelled around to face Kris across the picnic table. "In the closet? How in God's name did you reach that conclusion?"

Kris leaned on his hand, pinching his septum between his thumb and forefinger to aid his concentration. He was going to have to be very careful how he worded this.

"OK," he began, "I love George too, but not in 'that way', in case you're wondering. He was my first boyfriend and he is still the closest friend I have, next to Shaunna, but I fucked that up. However, that's by the by." He took a deep breath and made eye contact. "Because I knew. I knew you'd been in love with him since sixth form, but you didn't do anything about it."

"Ah. I see," Josh said. Kris shook his head. Josh frowned. "I don't see?"

"Oh, you see just fine—with twenty-twenty vision, unless it's anything to do with George!"

Josh laughed. "I can't argue with that."

"I'll tell you when I first realised you were in love with him. You know the barbecue for Shaunna's eighteenth?"

Josh tried to piece together the remnants of memory of that barbecue. What he could remember was that it was in the garden of Shaunna's parents' house, which was full of fruit trees and water features. Her mum was an exceptional gardener who could grow anything—a trait she had passed on to her daughter. There was a greenhouse full of tomatoes and Josh recalled that she had picked a crop just for the barbecue, which pleased him immensely, because he loved fresh tomatoes. His grandma used to grow them and teased that he would turn into one if he kept on eating them the way he did when he was younger. However, as for remembering anything about George at that barbecue: two months after the sixth form ball? He was well into the throes of denial by then.

"I can't recall much about it," he admitted.

"Let me jog your memory. I was trying to be 'the dad', flipping burgers, whilst keeping a three year old away from a barbecue, as well as checking everyone had a drink and making sure Shaunna was happy. You know the drill. And wise-ass that I am, I burnt myself. Pretty badly too." He held up his left hand and showed Josh the outer edge, where there was still a faint scar. Josh winced in sympathy. "So," Kris continued, "Shaunna's dad took over the barbecue and George took me to the kitchen to run my hand under the tap."

"Ohhh," Josh said slowly. He closed his eyes and smiled self-consciously. Now he remembered.

"Yeah." Kris waited until he opened his eyes again. "I don't think I've ever seen anyone blush as bright pink as you did then, although you're not far off it now. But in answer to your question, no, we were not back together, because I really was in love with Shaunna."

"OK," Josh said, accepting this explanation. "I'm not suggesting you're lying to me here, but if you knew how I felt, why didn't you tell George?"

"I wasn't going to out you. You'd never have coped with it. You'd have probably denied it."

"I wasn't in the closet."

"So why then? See, the barbecue was the first time I saw it, and I knew that he was also in love with you. At first, I thought it was because you didn't know that he felt the same way, not that it was public knowledge, or anything like that. He did tell me eventually and I tried to downplay it, because there you both were, every time we'd come home from uni, whenever and wherever we went, pretending that you were 'just good friends', with this incredible spark of energy between you. It was like watching lightning and waiting for a crash of thunder that never comes. After he told you how he felt—God, that was a tough year, with you up in Newcastle much of the time, and him—well, he was heart-broken. He went off to the ranch and you'd changed so much, acting like you didn't care anymore. Then he came back and there it was again, as bright and fully charged as ever."

Josh had switched to over-attending to the dogs, because he was finding this most disconcerting. Kris had never been this good at reading people. Sure, he did it on a surface level for his work, but that was all.

"I'm sorry," Kris said. "I didn't mean to embarrass you."

"No. It's fine. It's just that I try and keep myself to myself and now you're telling me you've been able to see right through me for the past twenty years."

"Only when it comes to George. That's why I took notice. Otherwise, you're still as deep and mysterious as ever." Casper and Blue had resorted to grazing and were happily tucking in to a very lush patch of grass over by the other picnic table. "I did tell him, you know, after he came back from the States and you both obviously still felt the same way. He didn't believe me. I suggested he should just ask you outright, but he kept making excuses—he was trying to sort out somewhere to live, too busy with his course, or you were working—anything to avoid confrontation."

"Yes, that sounds like George," Josh said. "I saw an email he sent you which I assumed was about this, trying to blackmail you into going on James's stag night."

"Yeah. It didn't work."

"No, although it did prompt us into talking. Actually, that's not strictly true. The reunion—" Josh paused, because what happened before and during the reunion was responsible for forcing them to finally own up to their feelings, but Kris had made George's evening very difficult by kissing him in front of everyone and he didn't want to get into a row over it, particularly as he was more on Kris's side in this than he was on George's.

"By the way, I must also apologise for my behaviour at the reunion," Kris said. "It was all in a good cause."

"I've seriously got to get out of these woods," Josh muttered. "You're blessed with some kind of supernatural power here, I swear."

"Don't like getting a taste of your own medicine, hey?" Kris teased. Josh raised an eyebrow and Kris winked mischievously. "As I say, I'm sorry. It didn't mean anything."

Josh patted his arm. "Don't worry about it. You probably know already that you upset George, although I understand why you did it—trying to prove no-one really cares these days."

"Erm, I think he might have slightly misquoted me there," Kris said. The dogs were done grazing now and the two men headed back the way they had come. A rabbit ran across the path in front of them. Casper momentarily thought about chasing it then changed his mind, exhausted from his extended play in the spring. Blue was back at Josh's side and clearly considered himself a cut above anything as undignified as running after rabbits. They continued on in silence for a while before Kris spoke again.

"What I actually said was, 'Let's see if anyone cares.'"

Josh stopped walking. Kris turned back to face him.

"You meant me."

"I did mean you. I saw you standing outside the loos, then you were gone, and when you came back again I thought, 'sod it'. I've kept quiet long enough. So I kissed him to provoke a reaction. And I got one. Oh boy, did I get one! He went ballistic!"

"Suzie Tyler upset him."

"No, I mean after he found out you saw us. He was livid. He phoned me on his way home from the jazz club and bawled me out."

"Ah. That was most likely my fault. I told him I didn't care that the two of you kissed."

Kris nodded to signify his understanding, although he was looking a little confused. Josh caught up with him again.

"I don't care, incidentally," he said, "though I did at the time, so don't go trying it again, will you?"

Kris smiled. "I wouldn't dare."

They were almost back at the gate and both dogs stopped to have their leads re-attached. The walk had been highly enjoyable for all four of them and Kris said as much as they prepared to part company. Josh was tempted to ask if it would be OK for him to tag along occasionally, but decided against it. Kris and George needed their time together and he shouldn't covet this. However, the unasked question left an open pause at their departure that begged to be filled.

"What did you mean about you and Shaunna?" Josh asked.

"About me fucking it up?"

Josh nodded.

"The affair. This relationship with Ade. It's not what I want."

"What do you want?"

"I want to be allowed to desire her the way I used to. I still love her so much."

"Then tell her." Kris swallowed hard and looked away. Josh brushed his arm. "Tell her, Kris. Don't live in the closet. It's dark and lonely. I know."

"But you said you were never in the closet."

"Well, the thing is, IKEA sell lots of different models of bedroom furniture. I thought you'd know that better than anyone, what with you being from Swedeland, and all."

Kris laughed lightly. "Yeah. That's true. They do." He nodded. "OK. I'll talk to her."

"You do that. Thanks for this morning. It's been really, really good.

"It has. Enjoy the rest of your weekend."

"You too."

BF—FE?
Sunday 2nd April

In the beginning...

Studious, sensible, immature loners, their friendships from childhood in flux, as those they held dear began to change in ways they could barely comprehend. Two high school students, facing the first major decisions of their academic life. They needed someone; across a form room filled with the strangers who had not so long ago been their peers, Joshua Sandison and Eleanor Davenport found each other.

Looking back on it now, as he sat at 'their' table, in the Thai restaurant that had, in its previous incarnation, been Eleanor's pizza restaurant, Josh concluded it was not that remarkable. Eleanor was brilliant: even at thirteen, she exuded an intellectual elegance that most fail ever to achieve. In part, he could appreciate that their pre-high school education had much to do with it, for Jess too possessed this quality, whereas he, equal on all government means of measuring, had been less rigorous, perhaps even sloppy, by comparison. Sloppy, but always on time: he glanced at his phone; it was gone six o'clock.

The problem then, was this: how to address their differences without making it personal, when it was, to him, a very personal matter, one which he had only faced up to relatively recently, and certainly wasn't comfortable brandishing on the battlefield. And he knew that both points of contention were intrinsically linked in Eleanor's mind. This was about the sanctity of life, the upholding of God's law. Catholicism. Dogma.

Ten past six: the door opened and Eleanor came trotting towards him.

"Sorry," she said breathlessly, "James got back late."

"You could've sent me a message, or something."

"True, but it's only ten minutes, after all."

Josh refused to be drawn further on this petty point. "I've ordered a combined starter, and my main course."

"What is it?"

"A prawn platter of some sort. I didn't take much notice."

"OK." She glanced the length of the restaurant, in search of service. "They haven't changed it much, have they?"

Josh looked around him, not for the first time. "No."

"The seats and tables are still the same." She smoothed her hand across the familiar bench seating, feeling the crinkle of the vinyl below the lime green velour façade. "I wonder if they've done anything to the kitchen?"

A waiter came over.

"Madam: here's a menu. Can I get you a drink?"

"Just a glass of Coke, thanks."

"Sir?"

"I'm fine, thanks, for now."

Polite nod. He departed. A thick, palpable fog of silence descended.

"Are we actually going to talk, or…"

"Or what, Ellie? Carry on ignoring it, and hope it goes away?"

She took a deep breath, steadying herself with hands against a table lip.

"Your main course, madam?" the waiter intervened.

She scanned the menu, pointed to an item. The waiter smiled, nodded, retreated. She returned to the matter at hand.

"Why are you being like this? I don't understand."

"Because you're wrong, about Kevin, and Sophie."

"What in God's name has what happened to Kevin got to do with Sophie? I barely know the girl."

"Woman."

"Sorry?"

"She's a woman. Don't belittle her decision by referring to her as if she were a child."

"That's not what I meant, and you know it."

"Really?"

She shrugged. "All right, you might have a point, but it wasn't conscious."

"Now it is."

The starter arrived. Round one. Ding, ding.

"The thing is," he said, lifting a shrimp, still in shell, from the inner circle of the platter, "the two issues are related, and as you so rightly blasphemed: 'in God's name'."

She likewise took a shrimp and pulled off its head. "In essence, yes. Each is the taking of a life. But then Sophie kept the baby, didn't she?"

"That's beside the point."

"How is it?"

"We're here because we disagree. Because we disagree to such a significant extent that our friendship is in disarray, and will remain so regardless of whether Sophie Spyris safely delivers her offspring. And, you know, I've already had this discussion with Sean, who just can't quite shake off the chains of indoctrination, even though he's not been to church since he was fourteen."

"So he wanted her to keep the baby."

"No. He wanted her to not be pregnant."

"So he thought she should have terminated."

"No. He wanted her to not be pregnant!" Josh selected another shrimp. "But he also respects her right to choose."

"Which should be an informed choice, as I told George."

"Employing a pro-lifer as an abortion clinic receptionist does absolutely nothing to inform women of their choices. You were out of order, shouting at George the way you did. He was standing up for Sophie."

"And who will stand up for her baby?"

"She was nine weeks pregnant."

"The human soul exists from the moment of conception."

"So what about your contraceptive pill?"

"What about it?"

"Am I right in thinking that if it doesn't prevent fertilisation, then it causes spontaneous abortion?"

"OK, I'll concede that one, although contraception in all its forms is against Catholic teaching."

"However, we're not talking about Catholic beliefs in general here, are we? We're talking about *your* beliefs."

"Which on this occasion coincide directly with the Church. The bible is quite clear…"

"Yes," Josh interrupted, "but even the Catholic Church considers it less a rule book than a set of guidelines these days."

She ignored him and continued: "The bible is quite clear. The Law of God is written into the heart of every human, knowable by reason…"

"Don't paraphrase a pope to me and pass it off as the bible. I've read the bible."

"Have you ever been assessed for autism spectrum disorder?"

"And don't make this more personal than it needs to be! I've got an eidetic memory, not autism, not that it matters either way."

"But maybe it does. See, from where I'm sitting, there's a distinct lack of empathy here…"

"Empathy with whom? With you?"

"You don't even attempt to respect, let alone understand my beliefs."

"Are you telling me you feel so strongly about this that my empathy with you should over-ride that which I feel towards Sophie, or Sean?"

"No, but I'm supposedly your best friend. Well, second best these days."

Josh picked up a piece of the lollo rosso garnish, tearing it to shreds as he observed her, trying to ascertain if her last remark was intended to be so cutting. If it was, then it changed everything and this wasn't about a simple difference of opinion after all. He asked her outright.

"Are you jealous?"

"No."

"Are you sure?"

"That's ludicrous. Of course I'm not. Now who's making it personal?"

"I wasn't. I was just…" He sat back and sighed. "I was just making sure."

"Well, I promise you this has nothing to do with jealousy," she said, then added, "not of George."

"Then who?"

"Sean. A little."

He ran his fingers through his hair, put his hands behind his head and stared up at the ceiling, as he had done many times before.

"They changed the light fittings," he observed. She glanced up.

"So they did." She examined their almost virgin starter. "Look, I accept that in some situations abortion is morally and medically appropriate. Can we leave it at that?"

Josh shrugged back into the corner of the seat. "OK, I suppose."

"It's a compromise."

"Of sorts, but my point still remains. It's Sophie's decision to make. If her own beliefs were the same as yours, and she'd made the decision to keep the baby on that basis, then I would accept the decision as the correct one, not because it is based on religious principles per se, but because they are *her* principles."

"Are you finished with this?" the waiter asked.

"Yes."

"Yes, thanks."

He nodded and took it away.

"What main course did you order?"

Josh thought for a moment. "Chicken with coconut and green chillies."

"Sounds nice."

"What did you order?"

"Don't know, to be honest."

Josh laughed. It wasn't entirely hollow, but it would take more than a main course to fill it. The food was delivered soon thereafter. Seconds out. Round Two.

"I've got a letter," Josh said, extracting a sliver of chilli from beneath its cool coconut duvet. "It's from Kevin."

Eleanor endeavoured to harpoon a chilli of her own. She failed and used her fingers.

"To you," Josh clarified.

She picked up her drink. "Chillies are hot."

"Yes." He chewed on.

"What does it say?" she asked. "The letter."

"Do you want to read it? I've screened it, of course, and it's fairly benign, for the most part."

She nodded slowly. "Yes, I think I do."

He took it from his pocket and passed it across the table.

"Which bits do I need to look out for?"

"The end is possibly the worst."

She nodded again, even more slowly. She unfolded the paper—two pages, written on both sides. It began:

Dear Ellen…

"Why?"

"He always did call you that, didn't he?"

"It was a poor joke. A poorer one now. He's not even here to see my reaction."

"Perhaps he's watching?"

"I doubt there are windows in hell."

Dear Ellen,

Before I go any further, I must apologise for everything. Please believe me when I say that my concern for your safety was paramount, even though the benefits of hindsight and a good psychologist mean I appreciate that this is not how it would have appeared at the time.

Since last we spoke, I have been diagnosed with schizoaffective disorder. It would seem, though I am stable now, that the Biddiscombe case caused me to have some kind of psychotic break. Not surprisingly, I recall very little of that time, other than the pervasive misery of depression. I tried to call you and left countless voicemail messages. I just needed to talk to someone who would understand what I was going through. I believed that you were such a person. Again, in retrospect, I can see how my repeated calls could be perceived as harassment.

"Oh, shit."

Eleanor picked up her fork and scooped some food from her plate to her mouth.

"What is it?"

"Kev tried to call. He had my old mobile number and it was out of service."

"So the voicemails?"

"I never received them. Do you know what this Biddiscombe case is that he mentions?"

"Not yet. Sean's trying to find out."

She took another forkful of food and continued to read.

I'm not really sure of what happened next, other than that I needed to somehow keep working, but with my registration suspended, my options were limited. It wasn't the money. As you know, it was never really about the money. I could have worked in a fast food restaurant, like you, if it were only about the money. However, my parents were desperate for me to retread my sister's and their footsteps. Medicine. There were no other options offered to me. And I love being a doctor.

I made myself available for charity work, and I was truthful. I told them my registration had been suspended; I reported to the interim panel, but the GMC seemed in no rush to push on with the investigation. In the mean time, I was happy to do whatever I was legally allowed to.

By this stage, the police were investigating, and the charity got wind of it. Before I knew it, I was being arrested for practising with no licence, but I did not. I have been many things in my life, Eleanor, but I am not stupid. The guy from the BMA has been fantastic throughout - we were at uni with him - Callum Grady? He corroborated what I'd said all along: CPR is first aid, not medicine, so at worst I had committed ABH, if indeed I had committed as much as that.

Eleanor paused and frowned. "CPR? ABH?"

"Ah, we have been able to find out about that. Kevin performed CPR on a guy who collapsed at a car boot sale, and broke two of his ribs. The man died in the ambulance, and his family involved the police. Initially, the police said they were going to try and get the case dropped."

"It's pretty common for CPR to cause broken ribs."

"That's why they were going to drop it, but then they found out about the suspension."

"This is completely—" Eleanor breathed out heavily.

"Read on," Josh prompted. "It only gets more absurd."

By this point, I was sick of Newcastle; there was nothing for me there, so I went back to Hull, following Callum's advice to keep the GMC updated on my whereabouts. I got involved with the local hospice, driving patients to and from the hospital for their treatment. It gave me much to think about, and a lot of time sitting around to do it. I made a decision: when the investigation was over, I was going to enrol for training in palliative medicine, because I was still optimistic that they would find in my favour.

You know what my parents are like, so it will come as no surprise to you that I didn't tell them what was going on. Unfortunately, one day when I was at the hospice, Callum called and spoke to my father. I got the third degree.

"His dad's a dreadful bully," Eleanor said. "He'd have hit him."

Josh didn't pass comment.

274

So, I moved on. I had no choice. I went back up to Durham and stayed with friends, just trying to keep myself together. This was when things really started going downhill, and they put up with me for as long as they could, but I was quite sick. I was prescribed anti-depressants - they totally knocked me out, although I hadn't realised how much they were affecting my visual acuity. I crashed the car into a wall. Luckily I was on my own, and I wasn't badly hurt, but apparently I took myself to A&E and caused one hell of a commotion, shouting about how I was a doctor and criticising the nursing staff. I don't recall any of this, which is probably as well.

Eventually, after a few weeks of subtle hints from the friends I was staying with, they told me bluntly. I needed to leave. They had young children and it wasn't healthy for them to see someone in the state I was in, so I headed down to Lincoln, to stay near Callum. He arranged a room for me in a local bed and breakfast and put me in touch with a counsellor, who reminded me of Josh. It must be something about their training. Talking to the counsellor did help a little, and on my more lucid days, I could see that it was just a run of really bloody bad luck, but other times I was starting to think that someone was pursuing me. These thoughts still return, and the psych here in the prison has been great at helping me to stay in touch with reality, but back in Lincoln, the real world just slipped away.

"I need to try and get hold of Callum Grady."

"I spoke to him last week. He said he couldn't tell me anything, but he was prepared to talk to you."

"I'll call him tomorrow."

I was terrified that the police were looking for me and I went 'on the run', working my way down to you. I rented a bedsit in the town centre, and tried to get some sense of routine back into my life. I registered with the local hospice to do some voluntary work - just sitting with people, offering a bit of company, which was where I met Sean Tierney. I told him I remembered seeing him once up in Newcastle, recalled you talking about him when we were studying, but hadn't realised you lived near each other. He said that he only knew you through a mutual acquaintance, but what a coincidence it was that we should meet up at the hospice. Of course, this only exacerbated the paranoia, and I started to fear not just for my own safety, but yours too.

"Oh God," Eleanor said. She folded the letter and put it down next to her plate. The food was cold.

"Have you reached the end?" Josh asked. She shook her head.

"No, but I can see how it's going to end already."

"Yes. Kevin commits suicide."

"Don't be smart," Eleanor snapped. "I mean before he was arrested." She took a mouthful of the cold food and grimaced in disgust. For what it was worth, Josh had hardly touched his either.

275

I was aware that my mental health was precarious, and I didn't want to see you while I was in such a mess, so I decided - and believed it to be a rational decision - to keep watch on you, to make sure the people who were after me didn't find out who you were and endanger you too. I needed to get close to you, but not arouse your suspicion, because they must not know who you are. I have to keep you safe.

So, I contrived to meet your friend, Jess Lambert, for a drink. The date turned into a second date, and then a third, but she cancelled at the last minute, and I reasoned that she had realised who I was. I went to see her one last time, under the guise of trying to talk her into going on another date, and planted the microphone in your stairwell. Don't worry. It's no longer working. In fact, it stopped working before I was done with my surveillance. I guess that's what happens when you buy cheap foreign rubbish.

"So there's still a hidden microphone in the offices?"
"Keep reading, Ellie."

The one in your lounge kept working right up until the day I tried to call you, to warn you about them - about him. I've done my best to cover my tracks, and I wish I could say with certainty that the others do not know where you live.

The stress was immense. When you were at work, I knew you were safe, and at home I could keep a constant vigil. I didn't sleep for weeks, and I could do little to keep tabs on you in between. Overhearing Sean Tierney talking to Josh on the phone was a godsend, because I knew you were still in contact with Josh and saw a lot of him, so I broke into Sean's house to plant the third, and final microphone - they seemed such a bargain at the time.

"How does this happen to someone?" Ellie asked. Her face was paled in horror at what she was reading. "You met Kev. You know what kind of person he was. He was so reasonable it was infuriating."
"Well, I..."
"Just like you, in fact. Always so cool and calm, when the world can be at war all around you."
Josh examined his drink to avoid eye contact.
"Maybe that's why I fell for him," Eleanor reflected, "because he was like you."
"I hope you're not suggesting I'm psychotic."
She laughed and shook her head.
"No. I'm not. Neurotic, maybe."
"Would you like to order any desserts?" the waiter interjected.
"Not for me, thanks," Eleanor smiled at him, as he removed their almost full plates.
"Could I have a coffee, please?" Josh asked. The waiter nodded politely.

"Certainly, sir."

Eleanor waited until he'd left before she continued. "Joking aside, Kevin was no less reasonable or stable than you, which is what makes all of this so completely unfathomable."

Josh shrugged. "That's the thing with mental illness, though. You can't see it. For all you know the waiter could have debilitating depression, or anxiety. Or both."

"Yeah, I suppose no-one would know about my...past just by looking at me."

He needed to steer them back on track.

"Whatever the Biddiscombe thing is, it sounds like it was the trigger for Kevin's illness."

Eleanor nodded thoughtfully. She turned to the final side of the letter.

When I saw him in Sean Tierney's house, that was when I knew that I had to get to you, to protect you. That was when I knew for sure that he was a part of this. He is dangerous, Eleanor, you must believe me. I tried to get you away from him, but you wouldn't listen to me. The knife - it was for self-protection. I would never have hurt you.

If you choose to ignore this letter, I will understand. After all, I'm not the man I was back in Newcastle. I'm not the man you knew. These days I barely even recognise myself. But at the very least, for your own safety, talk to somebody about this. The murder I confessed to I did not commit. I have nothing left to lose. You have everything.

I would never have hurt you. I hope you know that. It is James that you should fear.

My best wishes and regards,
Kevin

Eleanor remained still, holding the letter in front of her, after she had finished reading. Josh could tell she had finished, for she was staring at a point beyond the page itself. He waited to see if she would snap out of it and when she didn't, he gently touched her hand. She jumped. He smiled an apology. She closed her eyes, rubbed the bridge of her nose with her finger, and breathed, slow, steady, deep breaths. Josh watched and waited. He was good at it—he'd been doing it a long time, although never for her. She bustled from one conversation to the next, rushing into statements, often with an almost careless sense of abandon, charging off into the next thing she simply had to say, her previous words left hanging with no space to respond in between.

"Why did he kill himself?" she asked, finally. It had been ten minutes or more since she'd finished reading. Josh took a breath, prepared to answer, but she continued onward: back on form.

"That's what I expected. Dear Ellen, I'm sorry, but here are the reasons I have decided to end it all. Yours, Kevin. Not this rambling lunatic making allegations against my husband."

"Surely the reason is in there, if you…"

"He's my baby's father, for heaven's sake!"

Josh resumed staring at the light fitting above.

"We did all this. It was done with. Finished. James is innocent. So why?"

Josh made eye contact with her, but still chose not to answer.

"Are you going to say anything?" she asked. She was angry, frustrated, confused. In pain. The waiter walked past, giving them a courteous nod. "Excuse me," she said, "but can I see that dessert menu?"

"Of course, madam."

"Do you actually want dessert?" Josh asked.

"Two shrimps and a few shreds of chilli," she defended. "No, I don't want dessert, but I'm hungry, and I'm stressed and I…"

"Let's go and eat fish and chips," Josh said. He beckoned the waiter and settled the bill.

***

"It's quite a nice evening," Eleanor remarked, as they strolled through the park, picking at chips wrapped in paper. The sun had not long passed the horizon and the scent of cut grass filled the air.

"Yes," Josh agreed, "it's very nice."

"What do you think?" she asked. He frowned, seeking clarification. "Of what Kevin said about James?"

"I think he believed it. The question is why."

"Isn't it obvious? Because he was insane!"

"Perhaps that's all it is."

"All it is? He killed himself. Is that not proof enough?"

"No. It's too easy." Josh paused at a bench and sat down. She remained standing, leaning against the railing.

"How can you say…"

"Shush, Ellie."

She let out the rest of the sentence as a breath.

"What I mean is it's convenient for us to dismiss what he says as the product of an unsound mind. Less convenient is the possibility that as Kevin's mental health improved, so too did he begin to comprehend that the injustice served upon him still threatened those he loved."

"He killed himself, Josh! Doesn't that nullify everything he said?"

"And there we are again. Right back to square one. Kevin Callaghan was a good Catholic boy, so therefore he must have been mad."

She screwed up the chip paper and threw it in the bin.

"Sit with me, Ellie." Josh patted the bench. She looked away. "Please?"

She sat.

"Thank you." Josh spoke quietly, largely out of fear that raising his voice would send his temper wildly out of control. He took her hand and smoothed it with his fingers. Neither looked at the other as he continued to speak.

"My experiences have led to me having very strong views on suicide and its rightness, or wrongness, that have nothing to do with the destruction of life, or the failure to perform one's obligations. Nor do I think that a certain degree of insanity is required in order for someone to pursue that path. I appreciate it is difficult to accept that sometimes the decision a person makes to end their own life is rational and measured. And before I go any further, I'm not saying that James is guilty of anything, or that Kevin was not sick. There is something very wrong here, and we need to know what it is, but we're getting nowhere, going around in these infernal circles. Kevin was very sick. It was why he confessed and pleaded guilty to a murder that he knew nothing about. As for his suicide? He'd lost his career; he'd lost his family; he'd alienated the one and only friend he had left. It would've made less sense if he'd chosen to continue serving his sentence, if he'd chosen to live.

"Unfortunately—for us—he didn't. But he can still tell us what he knew. He's left so much evidence. The problem is trying to extract reality from within the delusion; the fact from the fiction that he had been living for the best part of a year. Something he saw led him to believe that James was guilty."

Josh stopped speaking and turned so he could look at her. She leaned her head against his shoulder. "I don't want to fight with you, Josh."

"Nor I with you. You can't change my mind, and I can't change yours, but since when did it start to matter so much?"

She shrugged. "Since we got all grown up?" she speculated.

Josh put his arm around her and kissed her head. "Forgive the cliché, but grown up doesn't have to mean grown apart." He lifted his free hand and held it up, little finger extended. Eleanor smiled, then hooked her little finger with his, as they sat, together, and watched the night slowly slide across the sky.

THE CHRISTENING
Sunday 9th April

As soon as they were finished in the church, George sprinted home to exchange his Sunday Best for his usual jeans and t-shirt. Two hours in a suit and tie was about his limit, and he returned to find that the others had done likewise. Poor little Toby was still donning his christening gown, looking like a rather sullied floating little ghost, dressed from top to well past toe in embroidered white lace. A dollop of chocolate pudding and a scowling grandmother later, he too was back in his usual attire and racing around the garden on his hands and knees, trying to catch up with his older brother and cousins.

The service had gone just as expected. George had followed, with a certain sense of bewilderment and hypocrisy, the lead of his fellow godparents in committing to foster the faith of the Church, when he had only the vaguest notion of what that was. Worse still, the cylindrical wax effigy of 'Jesus as the light of the world' dripped and burned him, and short of shoving his hand in the font, which he didn't think would be particularly well received, he had little choice but to suffer the blister that had now popped from the tender web between thumb and forefinger. Not even 'kisses better' from Oliver and Josh were helping, particularly as the latter refused to wait for the priest to leave first.

"Oops. Missed!" he said, kissing the back of George's hand instead. George smiled nervously and went off to play football with Oliver.

"If memory serves correctly, I recall you accompanying young Eleanor to mass quite a few times over the years," Father McGrath remarked to Josh.

"Yes," Josh confirmed. "Your memory is accurate. I'm quite partial to the occasional sermon and soul-cleansing."

The priest ignored this and continued: "I had hoped that we might one day bring you into the fold. I can see that it is most unlikely now."

The two men watched on as Toby crawled into Oliver's path, sending his older brother flying headlong into the net. George quickly scooped Toby up and cuddled him until he was over the shock, kicking the football back to Oliver at the same time.

"George is going to be an exceptional godparent," Father McGrath observed, then added, "considering."

"For a protestant, you mean?" Josh asked facetiously. The priest gave him a look that was part smirk, part smile, and shook him by the hand; soon after, he said his goodbyes to the numerous guardians, by genetic or religious determination, of the newest member of the flock.

So that's where they were up to: a post-christening drink in the Browns' significant back garden, while the children and George played football, and the adults discussed the prospects for a good summer. Indeed, the afternoon was a promising pre-empt for glorious days ahead, with the sun bright and strong on this early spring day. Not a cloud in sight, and the tall panelled fencing afforded an excellent windbreak.

"I'm going to pop to the supermarket," Eleanor announced. "Get some bits and bobs of barbecue food." Dan's and Andy's faces instantly lit up. "And cook it in the oven," she said. The brothers slumped in their chairs again. Eleanor laughed. "Too many children around to barbecue safely," she explained, "and men!"

"I'll come with you," Dan suggested. "Pick up some more beer, if everyone else is up for it?" He got no complaints, so they departed, returning a short while later with far too much food and beer for the relatively small gathering of family and friends. Out of Eleanor's siblings, only Charlotte, Ben and Peter remained, the others having headed back homewards to prepare for another Sunday evening before school and work in the morning. Jess had gone with her parents straight after the service, as the first chemotherapy treatment had left her easily fatigued; the grandparents had left not long after the priest, although that meant there were still thirteen adults and five children to cater for. Josh followed Eleanor inside and helped her load burgers and corn cobs onto trays.

"Do you really need an oven of this size?" he asked, opening one door of the enormous range.

"Only when the family all descend at once. My mother suggested we do Christmas here this year."

"Rather you than me."

"Yeah. Think I might move into a three bedroom semi between now and then."

Josh laughed and took a beer from the box Dan was emptying into the fridge, a process that was taking a lot longer than it ought, because every time he went to put a bottle away, someone took it from his hand.

"It seems a pretty decent area," Dan remarked as Eleanor reached past him to retrieve the salad dressing.

"It is," she concurred. "The houses are all the same size as this, so you have to be quite well off to afford them, or have a massive family."

"Bragging again, Doctor Brown?" Josh said. It was meant as a joke, but had apparently been interpreted as a criticism, for Eleanor didn't respond.

Instead, she collected a pile of plates and took them outside. Dan and Josh looked at each other.

"Touchy subject?" Dan asked.

"Not that I was aware of," Josh said, puzzled. He watched her through the kitchen window, as she engaged in a quick and stilted conversation with Charlotte, who shook her head, then got up and walked towards the kitchen, calling back to her older sister over her shoulder. She arrived inside a moment later.

"I'm to tell you that it's nothing to do with us," Charlotte said to Josh. He raised his hands in query. "I don't know either. She's been cranky all day. I thought it was this whole christening thing."

Josh rubbed his chin thoughtfully. "Yeah, you're probably right. Do you know what you did to upset her?"

"No idea. One minute we were talking about my new job, the next..." She shrugged.

"You've got a new job?"

"Yep!"

"Congratulations!" Josh gave her a hug.

"Thanks."

"What doing?" Dan asked.

"Marketing manager for a media company. I start two weeks on Monday." She had been made redundant from her last job just before Christmas. "So, anyway, that's what set *her* off this morning. Accordingly, I'm a 'lucky cow' who 'keeps landing on my feet'."

Josh was watching Dan out of the corner of his eye, as he fought with the final box of beer bottles, huffing and snorting, but not making any progress. He handed him a pair of scissors.

"Yeah," Charlotte continued, "even though this 'lucky cow' is now on five grand less than she was this time last year, with all the same financial commitments as before. But enough about me." She turned back to Josh. "I hear you've moved house."

Andy came in for a beer and took the one in his brother's hand. Dan snarled.

"We have," Josh said. "We're in a little terraced house now."

"Right out in the sticks," Andy chipped in.

"We're not that out in the sticks," Josh protested.

"*We*, as in...?" Charlotte asked.

"George and me."

"Oh, right. So you're still sharing a house, then?"

"Erm, yes," Josh confirmed.

Charlotte nodded slowly. "And at the risk of getting my head bitten off, dare I ask if..."

Josh swigged at his beer to hide his smile, and watched her, whilst she tried to gauge how he was going to take the question. Andy and Dan listened on in amusement.

"Go on," Josh prompted.

"Are you and George together now?"

Josh started laughing.

"What's funny?"

He didn't respond. She flapped her arms, as was the way of the Davenport women under duress to defend their position.

"It's just that all I've heard for years is 'Josh this' or 'George that', and I noticed at Ellie's wedding you looked a lot more comfortable with each other, but—you know what? Forget I asked."

"You are so like your sister, Charlie, d'you know that?" Josh grinned.

"Charlie? Nobody's called me that since I was about twelve!"

"It suits you," Andy said.

"How so?"

"Dunno. Charlotte sounds snooty and you're definitely not snooty. Charlie's more down-to-earth, approachable. Fun."

Charlotte smiled. "Thanks. I do kinda miss it."

"Anyway," Josh said, "in answer to your question, yes, George and I are together." He held out his hand to show off his ring.

"No way! Congrats!" She lifted his hand and examined the white gold band more thoroughly. "That's gorgeous. Blue topaz is my favourite gemstone." She pulled the silver chain around her neck free from her shirt to show off the uncut topaz pendant hanging from it.

"That's really pretty," Josh said.

"So when did you finally get together?"

"Just before Ellie's wedding, actually."

"Awesome! And have you set the date for your big day yet?"

"No. We're in no rush. I can't believe Ellie didn't tell you."

"I've only been back a few weeks."

"Ah, yes, that's right. How was Brisbane?"

"Hot. Busy. Expensive. No jobs there either, not that I went with the intention of looking."

"You'd consider emigrating?"

"Possibly. To be honest, it's not much different from any other big city."

"Ooh, I don't know," Andy contended. "It's very clean."

"True. And the people are more polite than in most."

Andy nodded in agreement. "I was in London a few months back."

"Tell me about it!" Charlotte groaned. "How rude?"

"I hear ya."

Josh and Dan looked at each other.

"So yeah," Charlotte continued, "as cities go, Brisbane's OK, but it's the coast that keeps on luring me back. The surfing's superb."

"Oh, yeah," Andy said dreamily. "Incredible beaches."

"Yeah. Gotta be seen to be believed," Charlotte agreed, a wistful look coming over her face.

"I'd love to go again," Andy said.

"Did you get down to Snapper Rocks at all?" she asked.

"Did I ever! I like Duranbah way better. Not as many tourists."

"True. Or autograph hunters. I loved Cudgen Reef, though I didn't go out."

"Oh, I'd forgotten about Cudgen Reef! I met this great guy there…"

Josh and Dan edged towards the door.

"…who was going right down the coast…"

They stepped outside and left the surfers to their paradise.

Back in the garden, Ben was holding court, telling some long-winded story about the time when Peter—the youngest of the Davenport siblings—removed his nappy and then proceeded to pee in his dad's tea cup. The adults and Oliver thought it was hilarious. Peter, meanwhile, was doing a very poor job of trying to stick the tabs of Toby's nappy, which wasn't entirely due to his own failure, even though it was only the second time ever he'd changed a nappy. Mostly it was because Toby wanted to get back to playing with his cousins, who were kicking the football at a fence panel, and had been doing so for quite some time. At the next thud, Eleanor stormed down the garden and confiscated the ball.

"Can't you get your children in order?" she shouted at Ben, then stomped off towards the kitchen.

"Who's rattled her cage?" Ben asked.

The other adults resorted to quiet mumbling amongst themselves. George looked at Josh and raised his eyebrows.

"Yes, all right," Josh sighed, understanding George's unspoken suggestion that he go and see if she needed to talk about it. He went to find Eleanor.

"So, George," Ben said, now he was done picking on his brother, "what's this I hear about you making an honest man of our Joshua then?"

George turned red.

"Or have I got that wrong?"

"Um, no." George didn't know what else to say.

"Ben!" his wife, Jo, said. "You've embarrassed the poor guy."

George smiled nervously and resorted to peeling the label from his beer bottle, grateful that the conversation had quickly moved on to Kris's TV show. He felt a tug at his sleeve.

"Dorge?" Even though Oliver could now say 'George' perfectly, he still liked to call him this. "Can I be your best man? Pleeaasse?"

"You're always my best man, Ollie," George said. Oliver grinned at him. "You wanna play more football?"

"No thanks." Oliver stretched his arms high in the air for effect. "I'm tired." George picked him up and sat him on his knee.

"Tell you what," he said, "when Josh comes back, we'll tell him our secret plan." He whispered into Oliver's ear and the little boy nodded enthusiastically.

"What should I put these burgers on?" Josh asked, quickly placing the hot oven tray on the side and shaking his hand.

"That plate," Eleanor said, nodding to indicate. Charlotte and Andy were now sitting at the table in the adjoining dining room, going through each other's online photos, presumably of surfing, judging by the occasional exclamations of 'Sick!' and 'Extreme!'. Eleanor glanced over at them and snorted.

"What?" Josh asked.

"Some help would've been nice," she sniped under her breath.

"Right," he said firmly. "Come with me." He grabbed her by the arm and led her into her own living room. "Sit." She sat. "What's the matter?"

"Nothing," she lied.

"You were perfectly happy, until I made that remark before."

"Agh! Why do you always have to go looking inside my head?"

"I didn't need to. You had a go at Charlotte too, and Ben. So come on." He folded his arms and waited.

"OK. Fine," she relented. "They've called the auditors in at The Pizza Place."

"Right?" The tax year had just ended, so Josh didn't think this was a particularly odd thing to occur.

"Apparently, there are 'financial irregularities' that have been brought to their attention."

"By whom?"

"James doesn't know, but they've been grilling him all week. They even demanded to see our personal accounts—bank details, mortgage documents—everything."

"Why would they need to see your personal accounts?"

Eleanor sighed. "They wouldn't say, but it's been terrible. James is so stressed, not that you'd know to look at him. He's been in Birmingham by seven every morning, and it's way past ten before he gets home again. I told him to stay there, but he said he didn't want to. He's hardly slept a wink all week, and I still haven't been able to get hold of Callum Grady. I feel like everything's falling apart."

"Oh, Ellie, bless you. Why didn't you say something?"

"Because we were barely talking as it was, and you were worrying about your grandma, and then there's Jess. Besides which, I'm always dumping my troubles on you."

"We're friends. That's what friends are supposed to do." He crouched in front of her and took hold of her hands. "Is there anything I can do to help?"

She shrugged. "I don't think there's anything anyone can do."

"If that changes, just say so. OK?"

She didn't respond.

"OK?" he prompted.

She nodded. "OK. Thank you." She attempted a smile. "Best go get those burgers sorted," she said with rather less enthusiasm than she'd had for the idea earlier.

"It won't take us long if we do it together," he comforted. They returned to the kitchen just in time to help Andy and Charlotte take the last of the food outside; they'd taken care of everything. Eleanor gave Charlotte a hug.

"Sorry. I've been foul today."

"Yeah, sis, you have, but no matter. You OK now?"

"Better," Eleanor said. She caught hold of Josh's hand as he walked past; he turned and smiled at her. They went to rejoin the others in the garden.

As soon as Josh sat down, Oliver climbed onto his knee, which wasn't something he did very often, as their attachment was by proxy. He studied Josh's face very carefully, then picked up his hand and did the same with his engagement ring.

"What's up, Ollie?"

"It's a secret," Oliver replied, and put his finger on his lips.

"Ohhh," Josh said slowly to indicate his understanding. George shook his head and smiled.

"I think we can tell Josh, Ollie."

"Um, OK," Oliver said, in exactly the same way George always said it when there was something he was excited about but didn't want anyone to know.

Josh looked from one to the other of the secret keepers. "So?"

Oliver turned and lifted Josh's hair from his ear and Josh leaned closer. There was a lot of indecipherable hissing as Oliver whispered.

"Pardon?" Josh laughed. Oliver sighed in childish exasperation and tried again.

"Sps-sps-sps-sps-sps…best man."

Josh moved away and rubbed his ear.

"Did you get it?" George asked. Josh shook his head. "Me and Ollie want to start planning our wedding."

Josh gasped dramatically. "Ollie! Are you going to marry George?" Oliver rolled his eyes.

287

"No, silly. *You're* going to marry Dorge. I the best man."

"Oh! Phew! You had me a bit worried there."

"I'm going to marry Shabina," Oliver explained, then clarified, "when we've growed up a bit." James heard this declaration and laughed.

"Oh, no. Not Shabina again. That's all he's talked about for the past two days."

Josh smiled. "Ah, young love," he said philosophically, then turned to George and Oliver. "OK, you two, tell me more about this wedding."

"Well," Oliver began purposefully, "when Daddy and Ellna got married they couldn't have fetti, because the man who cleans the church said no, and me and Dorge were very pointed about that, weren't we, Dorge?"

"Yes, Ollie, we were very pointed," George repeated, trying not to laugh.

"And at the park Dorge said that the leaves were like big fetti, and I said when Josh says he wants to marry you, you should say yes, but only if you can get married in the park."

"OK," Josh said to show he was following so far.

"But Dorge said that the leaves only fall in the park in the autumn, and Mrs. Beavis says that too, so you're getting married in the autumn next time it comes, which first it's spring, then it's summer and after the summer holidays it's the autumn, and then it's winter and it's Christmas." Oliver grinned broadly, very pleased with himself for knowing all of the seasons in order.

"I see," Josh said.

"You can think about it," Oliver told him. "And tell Dorge later."

"Thanks, Ollie," Josh smiled. The little boy's expression was so serious. "But it's OK. I don't need to think about it." Oliver blinked at him expectantly. "I think it's an awesome idea." Josh looked from Oliver to George as he said this.

"Good," Oliver said. He slid off Josh's knee and went to see if he could talk Eleanor into giving him his football back.

"Are you sure?" George asked, still holding eye contact.

"Yes," Josh said very certainly. "Are you?"

"Need you ask?"

"Well, I just thought it might be a bit too 'out' for you, that's all," Josh tormented. George ignored it.

"So, autumn then?"

"Autumn then," Josh repeated.

Andy's face suddenly appeared between them, grinning.

"Party on!" he said.

"I reckon we should have a game of footy to celebrate," Dan suggested.

"Cool," George agreed, "but can we eat first? I'm starving!"

"Figures," Josh laughed. He waited whilst everyone else loaded food onto their plates, then got himself a burger. George's excitement was only barely contained and he kept taking hold of Josh's hand, then letting go again so he could pick up the over-stuffed burger he had concocted, interspersed with gabbling away about whatever came into his head.

As people came to the end of eating, Dan assumed the role of one of the team captains.

"We should do Davenports versus Rest of World," Charlotte suggested.

"Fine by me," Dan said. "Saves arguing over who's playing on which team."

"All right," Charlotte said, "so I s'pose I'm gonna have to put up with you in goal." She poked Ben in the arm.

"Hey! Why are you captaining the Davenports? I'm the eldest!"

"Actually," Eleanor interrupted, "I am, but I'm not playing, and I say Charlotte's captain."

"You girls always gang up," Ben protested.

"Not at all. She's a better player than you. It's about time you got over it."

"So," Charlotte said loudly, "Ben in goal, Peter—you can be our back four, George up front…"

"Hang on, hang on," Dan said. "George isn't a Davenport."

"Close enough for rock and roll," Ben said.

"No way are you having George!" Andy said.

"Err, I'm sitting right here, you guys," George said.

"And who says I don't want to play?" Josh added.

"Do you?" Charlotte asked him.

"No," he grinned.

"Or me," Adele said. Shaunna gave her a look.

"Seriously?"

"What do you think?" Adele giggled. "In these shoes? Can you imagine?"

"I'll play," James offered. Charlotte looked surprised, because her brother-in-law really didn't strike her as the sort of man to play football, but she recovered quickly.

"OK. Cheers, James. Right then, so that's Ben in goal, me up front, James midfield, Peter defending. Who else? Jo?"

Jo shook her head. "Count me out. I'm lousy at ball games, unless running away from the ball is any use to you?"

"It's always worked for me," Kris grinned.

"So you're not playing either?" Dan asked.

"Nope. Cheerleader all the way." Kris waved his hands in the air as if holding pom-poms, and started chanting, "Rest of World! Rest of World!"

"It's not very catchy, is it?" Andy observed.

"How about Circle United?" George suggested, keeping his face as straight as he could.

"I like it," Shaunna laughed. "I reckon we go with that."

"You're not playing," Dan told her.

"What d'you mean, I'm not playing?"

"You can be a cheerleader, with Kris."

"I'm not bloody well cheerleading!"

"She's gonna have to play, bro," Andy pointed out. "Or we'll be a man, I mean a person down before we even kick off."

"She's a...*she!*" Dan said.

"Well spotted," Shaunna snapped, getting annoyed.

"All right," Eleanor said, "how about Shaunna plays for us, and James: you play for...*them.*" She thumbed dismissively at Dan and Andy. Kris waved his arms in the air and chanted, "Circle! Circle!"

"Shut it, Johansson, or I'll pull rank," Dan told him. Kris just did it more.

"That sounds like a decent arrangement to me," Charlotte said, eager to get on with their four-a-side match, now she'd realised the advantage was with them. Ben wasn't that great a footballer, but Peter wasn't too bad. However, Dan had seriously underestimated both the talent and effect of she and Shaunna as their opposition, and as they strolled across to the park, they got straight into planning their strategy. Ahead of them, 'Circle United' were doing likewise: the Jeffries brothers defending, George up front and James in goal. Adele, Jo and Eleanor had stayed back at the house with the children, other than Oliver, who was currently sitting on George's shoulders and had duly been designated the job of 'referee'. Kris and Josh were going along to watch, just for the fun of it, but were also 'assistant referees'; in other words, Josh, who knew nothing whatsoever about football, was going to keep an eye on the time, whilst Kris was going to employ his limited expertise to guide the ref in the event of any foul play, of which there was likely to be a fair bit.

"Of course," Josh whispered to his fellow cheerleader-cum-linesman, "you do realise that Shaunna was on our primary school team, but she hardly ever got a game, because of a certain captain's sexism?"

"Yeah, she told me that. She's pretty good too, from what I've heard."

"And Charlotte played for the women's national Under 21s."

"That's brilliant!"

"Yes, I think us Circles are about to get our asses kicked."

"Although we've got George. He's bloody amazing."

"Is he? I've never seen him play."

"Ooh, I have," Kris said. "Lots of times. Mm-mmm."

"Oy!" Josh elbowed him. "Don't you ogle my fiancé!"

Kris laughed. "You'll be ripping his clothes off the minute you get home, I guarantee it."

They arrived at the park, and the team captains flipped a coin. Davenport Rangers, as they were now called, won the toss and decided to kick off. Oliver blew the whistle and Josh started the stopwatch on his phone: fifteen minutes each half. Shaunna kicked the ball and Dan intercepted immediately, taking it all the way up to the other end of the half-sized pitch, where Peter slid in front of him in a failed attempt to steal possession. Dan passed to George and George turned to see if he had a clear shot, surprised to find, given the size of their teams, that there was no way he could sneak the ball through. He passed back to Andy, who crossed to Dan, then back to Andy, but Peter kicked it away. Shaunna got it on her left foot and dribbled back to Charlotte, the Jeffries men still making their way up the pitch. Charlotte tried her luck, but James kicked it straight back out again. Shaunna got it, ran it around Dan and passed to Charlotte. Andy was now marking Charlotte closely and was between her and the goal, so she passed back to Shaunna, which proved to be a good move, and was part of their strategy, knowing as they did that Dan wouldn't tackle a 'girl'. Unhindered, Shaunna ran the ball up the left hand side and took a shot. Dan got a touch on it and it went rolling off across the park. Oliver looked to Kris.

"Corner," Kris said.

"Corner," Oliver repeated loudly. Charlotte arrived back with the ball and took the corner, sending it soaring over Andy's head; Peter got it and passed to Shaunna. This time, Dan was on her right away and as she tried to pass to Charlotte, he headed it away to George. It was just him and Ben now, like old times. George afforded himself a second of smugness and aimed for the top left corner of the net. The 'crowd' went wild. Circle United 1; Davenport Rangers 0.

Ben threw the ball out and Peter got it halfway up the pitch, before Dan decided to get him back for his early sliding tackle, and took him down. Oliver blew his whistle and marched across, with hands on hips. Josh and Kris watched on from the sideline, laughing at their miniature head ref and his finger wagging. For his part, Dan looked shame-faced and went off with his head down to await the throw-in. Peter threw to Shaunna, and with Dan still sulking, she continued, unmarked, for several yards, but then Andy came charging across. She quickly kicked the ball away, but was unable to see around him and now Dan had possession again. Charlotte expertly got the ball from him and she was off. There was no stopping her. This time James didn't stand a chance, as she kicked it hard and fast right into the centre of the net. The 'crowd' went wild again. 1-1.

"Who's side are you on?" Dan shouted across.

"Everybody's!" Josh and Kris said together.

"How long left?" Kris asked.

"Erm." Josh had been completely absorbed by the game, and had to unlock his phone to check. "Four minutes," he said, then went straight back to watching, as Andy ran the ball past the halfway line and took a long shot. Ben caught it and threw it to Peter, who kicked it straight on to Shaunna, then on to Charlotte, who turned and planted it in the back of the net.

"Disallowed!" Dan shouted.

"If that's disallowed, then so's yours," Charlotte argued.

"Why?"

"Because you headed it to George."

"And?"

"If we're playing by five-a-side rules…"

"How would *you* know?"

"I beg your pardon?" Charlotte was right up in his face.

"Oh no," Josh said. "There's only one thing worse than a Jeffries brother riled."

"Hmm," Kris frowned.

They were still yelling at each other, and Charlotte was shoving Dan in the chest. Dan had his hands raised in mock surrender. Everyone else knew better than to get involved.

"Should we, err, intervene, do you think?" Kris suggested hesitantly.

"No need." Josh nodded towards Oliver, who was blowing his whistle loudly and marching towards the warring captains.

"Sin bin," he said loudly to Dan.

"But ref…" Dan began. Oliver pointed off-pitch and Dan stomped away.

"Time, ref," Josh called. Oliver blew his whistle again and the teams jogged over to the sideline.

"Wow, Ollie!" George said, rubbing the little boy's head. "You really know your stuff!"

Oliver turned and gave him a very stern look. George gulped and stepped away.

"That's you told," Josh laughed.

"Yep." George leaned closer and whispered: "Although I think the ref might have been a tiny bit lenient with his Aunty Charlotte."

Dan was standing on his own, sulking. Andy glanced over at him and decided to keep his distance, instead going to talk to James, who'd seen a lot more action during the first half than Ben had. Meanwhile, the Rangers' players were in a huddle at the far end of the pitch, with Charlotte's arms flaying wildly as she discussed their tactics for the rest of the match.

Back into position then, for the second half. Andy's hair was damp with sweat, and judging by the attention he was paying to some of the opposition, it had little to do with the exertion of the game itself. With Dan in the sin bin for another two minutes, Andy kicked off, which is to say he dribbled the ball around Charlotte, headed off down the pitch and passed to George, who sprinted away and scored from well outside the area. Kris went wild. Josh just stood staring.

"What did I tell you?" Kris said.

"Oh God. I'm so in love."

"Oh God, you're such a girl!" Kris laughed, pushing him playfully.

The ball was back in play again, as was Dan, and he wasted no time in gaining possession, his off-pitch break affording him a new resolve that culminated in a goal of his own, putting United 3-2 in the lead. However, no sooner had he scored than Peter right-footed it on to Shaunna, who'd spent an entire two seasons' worth of games sat on the bench, having to look at that smarmy face. Now she was going to have him. She stuck her toe right in behind the ball and paused to watch as it sailed past James's outstretched left hand and he fell, almost in slow motion, to the ground.

"Yeeesss!" she shouted and punched the air. Charlotte came over and they hugged, jumping up and down together—an action that proved rather too much for Andy, who didn't even see James throwing the ball in his direction and as a result it struck him in the side of the head. He staggered, dazed, and fell over.

"Get up, soft arse," Dan shouted as he charged past in hot pursuit of Charlotte, who had the ball once again and was closing in dangerously. She hooked it in with her left foot and it rebounded off James's chest, straight back out to Dan, who turned on the spot and kicked it away to Andy, who was only halfway to standing, but somehow managed to send it on to George, already at the halfway line, and now sprinting with the ball, unmarked. A deft thwack with the side of his boot and Circle United were back in the lead, with less than five minutes until the whistle. Ben threw the ball out to Peter, who once again passed it forward to Shaunna, who was being blocked every step of the way by Andy, thus had to pass it back to Peter, then back to Ben and out again, this time straight to Shaunna, who got around Andy by running very wide and thumped it in Charlotte's direction. Dan kicked it away, back to Andy, with Shaunna marking him so closely that he could smell her perfume, mingled with fresh sweat. He went to take the ball from her and she nutmegged him, leaving him to stand and watch as Charlotte homed in on the goal, once again sending it soaring past James. Four all, with a little over a minute on the clock.

Now it got racy, with both team captains dead set on winning, even though the rest of the players would have been more than happy to run down the clock. The strikers were both still fresh, because Charlotte still played on a regular basis and whilst Dan and Andy were fitness fanatics, they didn't have the regular outdoors physical work that George enjoyed. Peter, Ben and James were flagging, but Shaunna was running on pure adrenaline, so when Ben saved George's next attempt and threw the ball out to Peter, she was up there, ready to take possession and that's exactly what she did. George went after her and cleanly tackled her to get the ball back, then headed away with it, only for Shaunna to turn around and repeat the action. The pair of them continued in this fashion, until Shaunna broke away and kicked the ball out of play. The whistle sounded and George and Shaunna high-fived as they made their way off the pitch.

"Penalties?" Charlotte called across to Dan. He nodded in agreement.

"No!" came the cry of the other six players and the referee. Dan and Charlotte glared at their respective team members as if they had committed some great mutiny.

"Face it, Jeffries, you got beaten by girls," Shaunna said to Dan as they headed back to Eleanor's.

"We drew!" he retorted.

"Yeah," Charlotte justified, "but only because we were brought down by the male contingent of Davenport Rangers."

"Hey, I resent that," Ben complained. Charlotte looked at him darkly.

"I think we all played brilliantly," Peter said, trying to stop any inter-sibling trouble before it began.

"Yeah, we did," George agreed. He was walking next to Josh, with Oliver, now freed from his responsibilities, swinging between them.

Josh glanced across at George. "I think you should join a pub team, or something," he said. "So you get to play more often."

"Ha!" Kris scoffed. "You mean so you get to watch him play more often!"

Josh giggled and turned pink. George looked from one to the other.

"What did I miss?"

"Nothing," Josh mumbled.

Kris clasped his hands under his chin. "Oh, he's so dreamy," he said, fluttering his eyelashes. Josh stuck out his tongue at him.

"Ah," George said, grinning. There was no point in protesting. He was a bit of a wow on the football pitch, not that he was one to gloat, but he'd learned long ago to just enjoy the post-match adulation.

"So," Andy said, handing Charlotte a bottle of beer; they were back in Eleanor's kitchen and on their return walk had discovered that they both supported the same local team. "How d'you fancy meeting up before the match next week?"

"Sounds good to me."

"Awesome."

Oliver came tearing through the kitchen and disappeared up the stairs. Andy and Charlotte listened to the thud-thud above, then he came running down again. He skidded to a halt in between them.

"I'm going now, Aunty Charlotte," he said.

"OK, Ollie." She stooped to hug him. "Thanks for being a very fair referee today.

"Yeah." Andy agreed. He held out his hand for Oliver to give him five. Oliver returned the gesture, then ran off into the garden, where James was waiting, car key in hand. He gave Eleanor a kiss.

"See you tomorrow night," James said.

"Give me a call. Let me know how it's going."

"I will."

James and Oliver made their way out to the car.

"Don't forget, Dorge," Oliver shouted back. "Give me a call. Let me know how it's going."

"OK. Will do," George replied, laughing.

"What's that about?" Eleanor asked.

"Wedding planning."

"Whose wedding?"

"Ours."

Eleanor gave the slightest of nods.

"We're going for autumn some time," George said. "Probably whenever Ollie's on half term from school. When's that?"

"Last week of October, usually," Shaunna answered.

"Oh, that's good, so…" George took out his phone to have a look at the calendar, thus didn't see Eleanor's troubled frown, but Josh did. He made a quick getaway, under the guise of using the bathroom, in order to get his feelings in check, because it had reignited the anger and resentment he'd been feeling towards her since Christmas, when he'd called to tell her about their engagement. At the time, George suggested it was only because she wasn't first on their list of people to notify, and that she was still reeling from playing only a passing role in their reconciliation, but it was more than that. For as much as they had disagreed on the morality of abortion and suicide, he could appreciate her point of view on these matters. Regardless of whether it came from some great omniscient being, or was merely a chance coming together of 'star stuff', life was a gift to be cherished and put to good purpose. As for the sinfulness of homosexuality—he knew the Catholic church's stance, and Eleanor's particular take on this, given that they'd argued it out countless times before. It was a stalemate he did not want to revisit, especially now, with all that was going on. But at some point, unless

Eleanor suddenly experienced a complete religious meltdown, they were going to end up having one almighty fight.

For now, though, Josh had successfully reined in his thoughts and emotions and returned to the garden, pausing to get beer on his way through. Charlotte and Andy, were once again sitting at the dining table and having a very giggly conversation; the connection between them had been apparent all day, and in fact, Charlotte's personality wasn't massively different from Bertie's, or any of the other women Andy had dated over the years, with the exception of Jess, which was the root of why they had never made it as a couple romantically. Jess had told Josh that she and Andy had chatted about her current health situation, but from the way he was behaving, one could be forgiven for thinking he didn't know a thing about it; perhaps the flirting with Charlotte was a coping strategy. Whatever, Josh had lingered far too long at the fridge, pondering these possibilities, and Andy had started to occasionally glance his way; he headed outside and resumed his seat next to George, who was still browsing the calendar on his phone. Meanwhile, Dan, Adele and little Shaunna were preparing to go home, as were Ben, Jo and their children, although in their case, 'home' was one more night with Mr. and Mrs. Davenport senior, and Peter decided to leave with them. Eleanor saw them all out, no longer able to conceal her yawning.

"It's been a very long day," she explained apologetically to those who remained. It was also getting a little on the chilly side in the garden, so they moved into the kitchen to finish their drinks.

"It's been a lovely day, though," Shaunna said. She was carrying Toby, who looked ready to fall asleep, settled against her shoulder and gently pulling the curls of her hair straight, then releasing them, fascinated by how they sprang back again.

"Yes, it has," Eleanor agreed. She started filling the sink, piling the baking trays next to it in preparation.

"Here," Josh said, "I'll do that."

"I'll give you a hand," George offered. Eleanor shrugged.

"Thanks. I'll go and give Toby his bath then."

"I don't mind doing it," Shaunna said. "In fact, I'd love to."

"OK. So I'll..." Eleanor began. Kris shook his head and pointed across to the dining table. "Whatever it is you think you're going to do, I'll do it. You go and sit down."

"Well, I was gonna go to the loo, actually," Eleanor grinned, "but seeing as you offered."

Kris laughed. "Can't do that one for you. Sorry!" Eleanor patted him on the shoulder and went off to visit the other bathroom. Kris glanced over to where George was now washing the dishes and Josh was drying. "How did you end up with the short straw, when you volunteered first?" he asked Josh, getting another tea towel so he could help.

"I'd rather dry up," he explained dismissively.

Charlotte and Andy chatted on, although they were doing so whilst collecting the remaining plates and glasses from the garden, and were a long time returning from their 'one final check'.

"Your godson is going to bed," Shaunna shouted from upstairs.

"OK," George said. "I'll be up in a sec." There were only a few plates left to wash.

"I'll do those," Kris offered. George dried his hands on the tea towel and went to kiss Toby good night. Josh and Kris continued in silence. Eleanor was on her way back down.

"By the way," Kris said quickly, "I've told Ade."

Josh nodded in understanding. Eleanor arrived next to him and smiled. "Thanks."

"No problem. We'll get going soon."

"Yes. So will we," Kris said. "I'll just pop and use the loo first." He left.

"What d'you think of that?" Eleanor asked Josh, tilting her head in the direction of the window, through which Andy and Charlotte could just about be seen in the evening's dwindling light. Although they couldn't hear what was being said, it was clear that Andy was telling Charlotte about some sporting misadventure or other, for it involved a physical demonstration and they were both laughing. When he was done, he moved closer.

"I've seen worse pairings," Josh observed. "In fact they go very well together."

"They're not a pair of wing chairs, Joshua!"

Josh laughed. "How long's Charlotte visiting for?"

"She starts her new job in two weeks' time, so hopefully no longer than that, although…" She watched ruefully, as her sister put her arms around Andy and kissed him on the cheek. They started strolling towards the house.

"I wouldn't worry. It's not going to get too serious in that short a time."

"Hmm. I'd like to say I share your optimism." Eleanor stopped talking, as Andy and Charlotte appeared in the kitchen.

"I'm off now, Ellie," Andy said. He gave her a hug. "Thanks for a really great day."

"That's quite all right. I'm glad you've enjoyed it."

"Yeah, I have. Have you?"

"It's been brilliant, actually, but I'm knackered, so…" Shaunna and Kris arrived back downstairs and she gestured to shoo everyone towards the door.

"Don't feel you need to beat around the bush," Josh joked. They watched from the doorstep as Andy left with Kris and Shaunna to walk home.

"I'll give you a call in the week, if I haven't heard from you first. OK?" Josh said, giving Eleanor a hug.

"Thanks. I'm sure it'll be just fine."

Josh waited for George to come back down, then they too headed off homewards, although in a taxi, as they now lived too far away to walk. Eleanor flopped wearily onto the sofa.

"You want a cuppa?" Charlotte shouted from the kitchen.

"Please," Eleanor shouted back. She was asleep before the kettle came to the boil.

HOMECOMING
Monday 10ᵗʰ April

Jess closed the front door on her parents, utterly thrilled to be back in her own house once again, and determined to recover as much of her independence as possible. The first lot of chemo was done with, and it had knocked her out for a few days—almost the entire two weeks, in fact—but she was feeling OK today. Second chemo treatment tomorrow, and nurses coming in every day, just to check all was well, or as well as could be expected. She'd cope. Of course she'd cope.

***

Andy opened another bottle of beer. The silence was complete, out here, at the far end of the garden, away from the house and the noises of motors and heaters and idiot brothers. Already today—and it was only two o'clock in the afternoon—Michael had broken a stack of plates when he reached behind them for a bowl and shoved the whole pile onto the floor, lost Len a job when he threw his phone out of the door, and made their mother cry by telling her that she was too old to wear a bikini. In her own house. He was a shit of the highest order. He needed dealing with, but Mum told Andy to keep out of it, which was why he was sitting under the pagoda at the bottom of the garden with a bottle of beer, the card from Jess on the seat next to him, the writing smudged by raindrops, but not teardrops. Not yet.

***

First nurse visit done, and it was a bit of a palaver, trying to work out what was expected of her, with the nurse trying to reassure her that there were no expectations. Now to 'potter', as her mum liked to call it. A bit of light housework, get rid of the dust from the lounge that she hadn't sat in for quite some time—could it really have been before Christmas? Certainly, it was long enough for it to feel unfamiliar. And uncomfortable. She moved from the chair to the sofa, then back again. Too much pain! What time did she take those last pills? Only three-thirty? How can that be? She turned on the TV, stuck on a film, and fell into a fitful sleep.

"Bro?" Dan waited for Andy to pick up the card so that he could sit down. "I've just seen Len. He was ranting on about his phone. Something about it falling in the pool?"

Andy raised an eyebrow.

"Said you were out here. Not a bad day, as it goes. Pretty warm. Tell you what, though, I'm suffering for that game of footy yesterday. My legs feel like lead."

Andy tipped the empty bottle to his mouth and sneered at the lack of liquid.

"Well, this is a riveting conversation. You gonna talk to me?"

"Mike."

"What about him?"

"The phone."

"That was Mike, was it?"

"Yep. Did you see Mum at all?"

"She was in the pool."

"What was she wearing?"

"A swimming costume? How the fuck should I know?"

"I need more beer."

"Aren't you meeting Charlotte later?"

"How d'you know that?"

"She asked Ellie to call me, because you weren't answering your phone."

"It's in the kitchen."

Dan sat back on the bench and tuned in to the birds. He frowned. "What's going on?"

"Put it this way. If I go back in there, I'm gonna kill him. No two ways about it."

"Because of Len's phone?"

"Amongst other things."

"Because of Jess?"

"Amongst other things."

"What other things?"

Andy got up and walked away.

Quarter to five: Jess woke up, moaned out loud, though no-one was there to hear it, shifted gingerly in the chair and tried to stand up. Her left leg wouldn't comply. She sat and waited for the feeling to return, fully expecting it to transform into pins and needles. It didn't. Was this the nerve damage they'd warned her about? If she'd had her phone or her laptop to hand she could've checked. After all, she was past caring what the internet told her now. The reality *was* the worst case scenario, and it didn't get worse than that. She tried wiggling her toes. No joy. This could make for an interesting week.

But the dead leg thing—other people said it didn't happen until after their second treatment; perhaps it was the pressure on the nerves. She was guessing. Everyone was different. That's what they'd said. Regardless, it was time to try and stand up. She pulled herself forward, pushing her arms against those of the chair, shuffled, flopped her useless left leg and positioned her foot manually, put her working right leg next to it, and stood up. Then fell down.

***

"What's Mike done to upset Andy?" Dan asked. Their mother continued on her way to the other end of the pool, as if she had not heard the question. Back up again to the top, not so much as a glance at her youngest son, then down again to the far end, and back. Dan moved along the edge and crouched, in wait of her next arrival.

"Mum?"

"You know what your brothers are like. They're always at it."

"There's more to it than that." He watched as she turned and swam away. "I'll go and ask Mike then, shall I?" She just kept on swimming.

Back inside the house, Andy was in 'his' room, Michael was sitting at the kitchen table, a newspaper spread in front of him, to his right previous editions of the same in a dishevelled pile under a heap of balled socks. Chocolate wrappers, a paint tray, and a half-empty cold cup of tea completed the collection.

"How much shit?" Dan asked in disgust and disbelief.

"What?" Michael said. "It's only a couple of papers."

"And the rest!"

"I'll move it in a minute, all right? She send you to have a word, did she?"

"*She* being Mum? She didn't say anything at all. What've you done to Andy?"

"Nothing, that I know of. Why? Is he having another hissy fit?"

"You do know about Jess, I take it?"

"Jess as in the ex-girlfriend who two-timed him for a con artist, or are we talking about another Jess here?"

Dan looked up above him and worked hard to keep his hands free and loose. *Deep breaths. Don't retaliate.*

301

"Jess has been diagnosed with terminal cancer."

"And what?"

That was the trigger. The papers and socks went hurtling across the kitchen, closely followed by the paint tray. Even in his rage, Dan avoided the mug of tea. Disrespectful to their mother, and he was better than that. He was better than Michael, who now had the decency to look a little afraid, with his youngest brother's hand around his throat, his breath in his face.

"Go for it," he goaded, believing that this would save him, at the same time as winding Dan up to the point where he broke, only to spend weeks seething in silent rage at what could have been if he hadn't 'done the decent thing' and walked away. That's what Michael believed. How frail and lacking in substance belief can be.

***

"There you go, hun." Shaunna put the cup of tea on Jess's bedside table. Jess stuffed the tissue against her nose.

"Thanks," she mumbled through the soggy paper.

"No problem. You took those pills, didn't you?"

Jess nodded.

"And you've got your phone here?" Shaunna checked as she said this. The phone was on the bed, next to Jess's right hip. "How's your leg now?"

"OK," Jess said, still tearful.

"Do you need anything else before I go?"

"No. I think I've got everything."

"All right. Ellie said she'd call in once Toby's in bed, make sure you're comfortable. I'd stay, but—"

"Thank you. I don't know what I would've done." Jess started to cry again. Shaunna went over and hugged her.

"When I've been and sorted my dad I can come back. How about that?"

"No. Don't worry. I'll get my head together and I'll be fine. It was just with my leg, and it being my first day on my own. I thought I'd be OK, but I'm not, and now..." Jess's words fell away into further sobs.

Shaunna could feel the process of acceptance starting within her friend. Writing the letter to them all hadn't touched her; she'd done what she needed to do. Now, at the point where from most illnesses it would be the start of recovery, all Jess could see was the beginning of the end.

"OK. I won't come back tonight," Shaunna said, "unless you call me, and you must call me if you can't cope. I can be here in less than ten minutes. I know you want to get back to normal as much as possible, so I'll leave it at that. How does that sound?"

"Great." Jess picked up her tea and sipped it. "What time is it now?"

"Just gone six. Ellie will be here between half seven and eight. Kris said he'll phone when he gets off the train at nine, just to make sure you're OK."

"I'll be OK."

"And if you're not, what are you to do?"

"Call you," Jess said. "I will. I promise."

"Good. I'll see you tomorrow, unless you phone before then." Shaunna gave her a kiss and headed off to see her dad, whose dementia was at a point where he probably wouldn't remember whether she'd been or not, but the mask was ready to slip.

***

"Why the fuck didn't you just let me kick the shit out of him?"

Dan was pacing up and down the atrium, trying to shake off the pain now registering in his knuckles. He had hit Michael so many times and so hard that Len had to take him to hospital, although for a while it looked as if he might refuse to. Fortunately—for Michael, but not for anybody else—Andy had heard the chair go over, and flew down the stairs, pulling Dan off and throwing him to the ground. He had learned the hard way that assuming Dan had calmed down before he had actually calmed down was likely to result in significant injury, so he sat on him, pinning him to the floor by the arms, until Len and their mother got Michael out to the car and away. Andy attempted a gradual release of Dan's left wrist: he didn't try to hit him, so he slowly climbed off. And then came the knee to the balls.

"Bastard," Andy shouted, more at himself for not realising this was what would happen. He got him every time.

"You know what he said, don't you?" Dan asked.

"Of course I bloody know. He's been at it for days. Anne's filed for divorce. It's nothing against me, or you, or Mum, or Len."

"And d'you think they'd be so fucking understanding if it was you treating everyone like they're shit on your shoe? You've got every fucking right to be angry, but no! Mike's got 'anger issues'. Anger issues my fucking arse. He's just a knobhead. You know it. I know it."

"Yeah. Alright, bro. I get it."

Andy was sitting on the second from bottom stair of the leftmost of the twin staircases, with his head down, rubbing his temples to stave off the headache caused by beer in the afternoon and too much stress. He was supposed to be meeting Charlotte for a pint, and she was coming here, so there was no getting out of it. That gave him an hour to try and calm Dan down enough for him to drive home safely, or drive him home himself and hope he got back in time.

Twenty minutes forward: the pacing had stopped, and they were both in the kitchen, drinking orange squash, courtesy of their mother, who was making dinner around them, the only words spoken an occasional 'excuse me' as she edged past. She too was wondering how best to get Dan out of the house before Michael returned from the hospital. She'd not seen him this angry in years, but she'd heard what had passed between them. He'd been egged on.

"I'm going," Dan said, getting up all of a sudden. "I don't want to stir up any more bother." He kissed his mum on the cheek, bumped fists with Andy and left. Andy met his mother's gaze and they both sighed.

"What time are you going out, love?" she asked.

"In half an hour. We're only going to the pub."

"'We' being?"

"Charlotte. Ellie's younger sister."

"Oh, that's nice. A date, is it?"

"Mum!" In spite of being almost forty, Andy still shuffled on his seat in embarrassment. His mother laughed.

"Dinner won't be ready for another hour. Do you want something to eat before you go? I can make you a sandwich."

"No, I'm fine, thanks, Mum. I'm not hungry, to be honest." Andy got up and gave her a hug. "I'm gonna go shower and change."

***

Tuesday morning: the first thing Jess did was wiggle the toes on both feet. All working. She stayed where she was, taking a moment to appreciate the wonder of being in her own bed, in her own house, with her own things. She stretched out her arms, her fingers brushing against her phone. She sent Shaunna a text message to thank her for coming to the rescue last night, then carefully got out of bed, testing her legs for weight-bearing before she moved into open space. All well, she walked very carefully to the bathroom, showered, and returned to the bedroom without falling over. Her body had successfully survived the chemotherapy, and recovered just in time for the next dose of poison.

***

Andy was last up, though first awake. He'd listened to the sound of his mother preparing to go shopping, Len lamenting having to take her, Michael demanding she bought protein shakes, doors slamming, much cursing, then peace once again. Assuming the coast was clear, Andy put on his shorts and went down to the pool. A few quiet lengths to clear his head.

He grabbed an apple juice on his way through, left his towel on a lounger and made a shallow dive into the soothing blue water. The perfect temperature—just cool enough to register, but not so cool as to require any effort to stay warm. He swam, up, down, up, down, how many lengths he didn't know, for he wasn't counting, then flipped over onto his back and floated, adrift on the surface of his mind.

The pub last night: Charlie—as they had decided she would now be known—had kicked his ass at pool. He thought she probably would, and he didn't care. It was great to go out and spend time with someone without all the added complication of trying to win, or wondering where the night might lead. Good, simple fun.

A splash. A wave across the pool, washing over his face and startling him. Andy righted himself.

"Alright, *bro*?" Michael sneered as he ploughed past in an unnecessarily violent crawl, the splashing caused by his arms repeatedly hitting the water extending as far as Andy's towel on the lounger. Andy pulled himself up onto the edge of the pool and sat, watching his idiot older brother turn at the far end and head back. He stopped, pushed his wet hair from his face and grinned, sickly sweet. "Good date last night?"

Andy didn't respond. He got up and started to walk away.

"She wasn't giving out then?"

Andy picked up his towel.

"Not that it stopped you in the past, huh? Guess it's all down to Dan now, to keep the Jeffries family line going, so long as they can keep one alive."

Andy leapt back into the pool and grabbed his brother by the hair, pulling him down under the water. He waited long enough for Michael to start panicking and thrashing around, then pulled him back up again, pinning him against the edge of the pool, an arm against his neck, head bent right back over the lip. Andy looked down on him, hatred seeping from every pore, which only served to escalate his fury further—that Michael could get to him like this.

"The only reason I'm not gonna kill you is Mum," he growled, then released him and moved away, before his temper obliterated the one last shred of conscience standing between him and a life sentence. Michael coughed and rubbed his neck.

"What the fuck is with you two?" he said. There was fear in his eyes. Andy got out of the pool once again, picked up his towel and walked away, not even noticing that Len was standing in the kitchen. He'd dropped their mother off at the supermarket and returned home just in time to see what had taken place. He strolled slowly into the conservatory and stood, hands in trouser pockets, waiting for Michael to turn his way.

"A month," Len said, quiet, calm, menacing.

Michael laughed, a mix of mocking and nervousness. "A month what?"

"Out."

Len turned his back on him.

"Where am I s'posed to go?"

Len shrugged.

"You can't kick me out."

"I just did, sunshine."

End of discussion.

***

Wednesday morning: no sleep, nausea, diarrhoea. Andy went running in an attempt to sweat it off. Jess called the Macmillan nurse.

***

Thursday afternoon: Jess had been asleep for the entire day, drifting in and out of unconsciousness just long enough to realise three things. First and foremost, she didn't want any more chemo. If she had only months left, then she wasn't prepared to waste them on days spent feeling like she was going to throw up, whilst not being able to on account of the anti-emetics, followed by days of semi-conscious half-numbness, huddled under a duvet with the heating on full-blast. Secondly, she couldn't do this on her own. Thirdly, she missed Andy. She called him up. No answer.

***

"Come on! It's not even that heavy!" Dan taunted his brother.

Andy grimaced and pulled on the handles of the chest fly. He was done.

"You bottler!"

"Yeah. You can stop now. It's a crap machine anyway. Think I'm gonna go back on the cross-trainer for ten."

"Suit yourself." Dan added another twenty kilos to the fly machine and sat down, watching his brother set up the cross-trainer. Andy took out his phone and plugged in his headphones as he started to step. He paused, pressed the screen and lifted the phone to his ear. Dan couldn't hear the conversation over the gym's booming dance track, but he could see Andy's facial expressions changing—concerned frown, smile, laughter, curiosity, concerned frown again. Andy hung up and set off once more on the cross-trainer. Dan went over and got on the next one along.

"Looked intense."

"Huh?"

"Phone?"

"Oh. Yeah. It was Jess."

Dan pulled back on the handles and settled into a leisurely pace.

"She had the second lot of chemo on Tuesday and she's feeling like crap."

"Yeah?"

"Yeah."

"Got any plans for tonight?"

"Nah."

"You should take her out for a meal."

"Who? Jess?"

"No, Charlotte."

Andy knew what Dan was trying to do, and he wasn't going to play along, apart from which he'd been out with Charlotte twice this week already, and they were going to the football together on Saturday, so there really was no need for Dan to push the issue.

"Gonna pop round and see her when we're done here," Andy said.

"Who? Charlotte?"

"No," Andy laughed dryly. "Jess."

"Fair enough."

"Meaning?"

Dan said nothing.

"You think I should just ignore her? She's…" Andy couldn't finish the sentence.

"It doesn't change what she did."

"True. But as Josh said, we've got to move on."

"Josh wasn't there with you in Kathmandu."

Andy didn't pass comment. Dan was right, but there was no point holding on to the past. He couldn't keep hating her, and if it had been anyone other than Rob Simpson-Stone, he'd have forgiven her in a heartbeat, but then he'd always found it easier than his brothers did to forgive and forget. Well, forget.

"I just think a bit of self-preservation is in order," Dan said. "She knows you're a pushover, and she'll use it against you."

"She's sick!"

"And you'd still be running at her beck and call if she wasn't."

Andy stepped off the cross-trainer. "I'll see you later," he said. He grabbed his towel and water bottle and walked away. Dan didn't try to stop him.

BLACK HOLE SON
Saturday 15ᵗʰ April

BLACK HOLE STUDIOS
Grand Opening: Saturday 15th April 7pm

Crimson Cemetery
Gods of War
James Dean's Not Dead
The Late Poets
Raven Heartspill
Santa Venera
Carnival Queen
Roach Reunion
and many more...

Recording, Rehearsal and Performance Spaces
Excellent Rates - Discounts Available

A Campion Community Trust Project
For more info, contact stu or jason @--

Krissi peered over Jason's shoulder and re-read the poster that had been pasted on billboards and blank walls all over town for the past month, with an ad in the local press two weeks running.

"I still think you should've toned down the death metal," she said. Jason folded his arms.

"Not enough indie for you?"

"Not enough indie for anyone!"

Jason ignored her and wandered back into the main studio, where Stu was trying his best not to get in the way of the lighting technician—someone that both men had been 'friends' with since college, who was brilliant at what he did, but was one of the most irritatingly smug and boastful individuals they'd ever known. Luckily, they only had to put up with him today, because he'd come in to set up and run the lighting for the show, then after that they were on their own, and even though the rig and desk looked complicated, it wasn't really that different to operating the mixing desk in the recording studio. Now, Tony—the lighting technician—stood in the centre of the stage and cast his eye up and along the array of impressive equipment adorning the lighting bar. Stu sauntered to the back of the studio, and stopped next to Jason.

"He's driving me mental," he muttered out of the corner of his mouth. "He's been going on all day about when he did this show, or that TV programme, or worked with some famous band or other. I know, Tony. You're awesome. Now shut the fuck up."

Jason smiled. "He's not gonna let me forget he's doing this for free, either. That's all I get whenever he talks to me."

"Yeah. Tell me about it," Stu said knowingly. They watched on as Tony jumped down from the stage and jogged the few feet to the desk. He pushed a couple of buttons, and the stage was suddenly bathed in blinding white light.

"Couple of presets," Tony shouted back to them, and played with his desk, setting off the moving lights in a chasing pattern that ran all around the room, lighting up Jason and Stu as it passed over them. He watched them, nodding superciliously. "You like?"

"Yeah. That's pretty cool," Jason said with his usual lack of overt enthusiasm; even if Tony hadn't known that he was always like this, he was too thick-skinned to be bothered by it. He changed the settings and the lights returned to the stage, where the beams of white were picked out by the smoke that had been pouring out of the machine for the past couple of minutes. It did look impressive, particularly to the band members now arriving to do their soundchecks.

"Best get back to it," Stu said, shaking hands with one of the musicians. Jason nodded.

"Give me a shout if you need any help."

"Will do," Stu called as he headed for the stage.

***

Seven o'clock: the place was crammed full of people of all ages, all in gig-going attire. Those bands with merchandise had stalls set out in the reception area, and were doing a roaring trade, as was the vending machine and Jason's apprentice technician, who was at present enhancing his woeful customer service skills through the exchange of cash for confectionary and canned soft drinks. Meanwhile, Krissi was yet again running off copies of the pricelist and Jason was giving guided tours of the rehearsal rooms and recording studio. Even his well-practised sullenness was being put to the test by the level of excitement he was feeling. This had been his dream for so

310

long, but he never imagined it could happen for real. When he was sixteen, his band trudged around from one place to the next, begging nights in the church hall, or cramming themselves into parents' garages, only to be moved on again and again. What they wouldn't have given to have had somewhere like this to rehearse, or better still record their 'amazing' new songs, before they were lost in a history of bitter band break-ups that may never have happened if they'd had the space to grow. As he took the final group through to the control room, Stu informed him through his earpiece that Crimson Cemetery were preparing to go on stage, and he fought to contain his smile, for this was the band that emerged from those embryonic days, and he felt like their time had finally come. He led the group of assorted musicians and audience members out of the room and headed back for the auditorium.

Of course, the down side to all of this 'dreams come true' stuff was that he had to formally welcome everyone, and it really wasn't his forté. However, he'd rehearsed and he was keeping it short and to the point; let the music and venue speak for itself.

"Good evening. Thanks everyone for coming. What an awesome crowd!" He paused as they cheered for themselves. "We've got a great line-up for you tonight, all local bands, performing a mix of covers and originals. First up, will you put your hands together for Crimson Cemetery."

The crowd whooped and applauded, and Jason moved to the side of the stage, relieved to have made it through his short opening announcement. His fellow trustees had now also arrived, and were standing at the very back of the auditorium, conspicuous in their shirts and slacks, in a room filled with people all wearing black jeans and t-shirts. Dan kept a finger in one ear, hoping to retain some of his hearing; James was wearing the ear plugs he used when flying. And somewhere in amongst the 'moshing youth', Andy and Charlotte were doing an excellent job of blending right in, so much so that Dan was still trying to spot them ten minutes into the opening act, who were probably great, if you were into that kind of thing. Actually, he thought they were appalling, and the sub-bass was starting to make his joints ache. He nudged James and indicated they should go and be elsewhere, not that he envisaged finding anywhere within a five mile radius that was any quieter. Both men headed for the outside door, and stepped into the fresh air, amazed by how little they could now hear.

"Either I've gone deaf, or that sound-proofing really is as good as they claimed," Dan remarked. James nodded.

"It is most effective," he agreed, for whilst they could still hear the music, it was no louder than the noise coming from an average pub on an average Saturday night, which was the level they had been hoping to attain, but didn't anticipate they'd reach it. A moment later, Jason followed them out.

"What d'you think?" he asked; no fighting the smile this time.

"Of the music?" Dan queried.

"No," Jason laughed. "I won't even bother asking that question. The noise level. Pretty excellent, we thought. We came out during the soundcheck and couldn't hear a thing. Best get back in there." He left again.

When Dan offered to source the sound-proofing material, Jason had been adamant regarding his requirements, to the point of rudeness at times, as Dan tried to persuade him to accept alternatives on which he could negotiate a better price. But he was insistent that this was the stuff they needed, and he was right. He'd done it once again—proved that he knew exactly what he was doing; he *would* make Campion Community Trust work. And whilst Dan was reflecting on how impressed he was, James was imagining how proud Alistair would have been to see all that Jason was achieving. With each new venture, the young man's confidence grew exponentially, no longer the restless, directionless soul that his adoptive father had pushed into jobs that he hated, and dragged to board meetings, imposing responsibilities on him that he had neither the expertise nor willingness to see through. Jason Meyer had at last come into his own.

A lull in the music signified a change of band, and Dan and James were just about to return inside, when they saw Bill Meyer pulling up into the car park in his vast silver-grey Volvo estate. They waited for him to park up.

"Good evening, gents," Bill greeted as he approached and shook hands with first James, then Dan.

"Good to see you, Bill," Dan said. A cheer from within the building was followed by a loud, wailing yell through the speakers, and then thrashing guitars.

"How's it going?"

"Extremely well," James replied. "The place is filled to capacity."

"We were just about to go and listen from upstairs," Dan said. Bill nodded, and followed them inside. He hadn't visited since January, when the building was still very much an empty shell of a warehouse, with little more than a stage and a few hanging cables, so he was genuinely overwhelmed by what he encountered when he stepped inside, and not just by the wave of noise that almost blew him back through the doors. The merchandise stalls were still set up along the outer wall of the 'foyer'—a passage that was about eight feet wide, and ran along the back of the performance studio, which was where the gig was taking place. At the end of the reception was an iron staircase, and they climbed this to the first floor, where there was another smaller reception area with a few seats, and access to the toilet cubicle, outside which a short queue of young, long-haired people were waiting. They all smiled politely and said hello to the three men as they passed by on their way to the control room, for this was the quietest

312

place in the building. They went in and shut the door. Dan switched on the lights, illuminating the recording studio on the other side of the glass screen. It was empty, of course, other than a couple of microphone stands.

"I'm not staying," Bill explained, once he'd recovered enough from the shock to speak at all. He looked close to tears, which was unlike him.

"Yeah. I think I might head off home soon myself," Dan said. James nodded in agreement. They weren't needed here.

The three men chatted for a while about the Trust and Jason's next project, although this was 'his baby', and he wanted to dedicate as much time and money to it as he could. He'd been very honest about this, and in their last meeting, James had agreed to take on responsibility for corresponding with a group of local residents who wanted to apply for funding to set up a housing collective. With the investigations going on at The Pizza Place, he was glad for the distraction. So far the auditors had found nothing, for there was nothing to find. However, he had a strong inkling he knew who it was who had given the tip-off that something untoward was going on, and also why they had done it. A couple minutes later that inkling rose to a certainty, when Dan excused himself to go and see if he could locate his brother, leaving James and Bill on their own. Bill stared into the empty recording room as he spoke.

"I hear you've been having some trouble down in Birmingham," he said. James raised an eyebrow; it was a motion that remained unseen by his associate.

"Yes, that is so, although I am confident that the ordeal is all but over," he replied carefully. "It is a shame the informant chose to remain anonymous. I would very much have liked the opportunity to speak with him about his concerns, and reassure him that all is well. I would not imagine his intent was malicious."

Bill turned to face James and nodded. "It's certainly been my experience that these kinds of things are instigated by well-meaning people trying to protect the innocent, so perhaps you're right, James. Now, I must go and congratulate my son on his achievements this evening, and get back to his mother, before she yet again feeds my dinner to her spoilt, fat Lhasa Apso." He shook James by the hand and left without another word.

***

Outside, in the car park, leaning against a wall, a young man stood, repeatedly stretching and curling his fingers, trying to get a grip on his rising panic. Four hours so far; he took the alcohol rub from his pocket and applied it once more to his stinging, raw hands, then set off on a circuit of the perimeter of the building, determined that he would go back in. He needed to do this, to go in there and stand with *his* people, listening to *his* music. He would do this.

Bill Meyer sidestepped to avoid a collision, and watched the man march on, staring directly ahead; he tried to place where he'd seen him before, but couldn't. By the time the engine of the Volvo roared to life, the man was out of sight and Bill had forgotten all about him.

LOVE HEARTS
Wednesday 19th April

For the second year in a row, there was to be no group celebration of George's birthday, which was quite normal in the general scheme of things, given that the only reason he'd been cajoled into a meal out the year before that was due to it being his first birthday since returning to the UK. He wasn't really one for big celebrations, as his mum never had the sort of money required for parties. Thus, whilst it was usually because he refused to go out, on this occasion it was out of sensitivity to Jess's situation, not that any of them felt much like celebrating. It had been an awful year so far, and it could only get worse.

So, George got up and went to work, as usual. With the lambing more or less finished, Farmer Jake's was ready to fully open its doors to the public for the summer, and George had taken on responsibility for the pygmy goats, who liked Sophie rather more than they liked him, but the risks to her and the baby were considered unacceptable, not that she had intended to continue working here once the festive season was out of the way. Aside from that, the smell still made her retch, even though the morning sickness had long since passed. George didn't mind having to deal with them, but they did have a penchant for getting under his feet, which meant cleaning out and feeding them always took a lot longer than it should. Eventually, with much shoving and nose poking from the four little goats, George managed to fill their food buckets, three of them now chomping away noisily, whilst he tried to dodge his way through the gate without little Bo following, but she was too quick and too clever for him. She butted the backs of his knees, his legs buckled, and the next thing he knew, she was skipping away across the yard.

"Bo, come here," he called after her—uselessly, as regards her doing as she was told, but not entirely so, as at the very same moment, the gate over the other side of the yard opened and Blue entered, immediately springing into action. He silently slinked along the fence, unseen by the tiny black and white goat, and circled back, so that she moved in, towards the pen, as he manoeuvred back and forth in an ever diminishing arc, shifting her closer and closer to the gate that George was holding. The two of them carefully watched each other and Bo, waiting for the optimum moment, and at the last second Blue darted to the right, forcing her towards George. He opened the gate, she bobbed back through it and he closed it quickly behind her. He looked across the yard to the big farm gate, and smiled.

"You couldn't have timed that any better if you'd tried," he called as he walked over to Josh, Blue falling in step beside him.

"I don't know why you don't just bring him in with you in the mornings," Josh said.

"I've thought about it, I must admit."

"He's better than you at looking after the animals. Those goats are too cute."

"Yeah, they are. And they know it." He glanced back at the goat pen, where Bo was peering dolefully through the bars of the gate. "So, to what do I owe this very lovely and unexpected pleasure?"

"Well, I thought, seeing as it's your birthday, and all, and we just happened to be passing this way…"

"Really?"

"No, not really. We went and got you a present." He put his hand in his jacket pocket and pulled out a packet of Love Hearts sweets.

George grinned and took them from him.

"I saw them in the newsagent's and thought of you," Josh explained.

"Uh huh? Wanna play?"

"Now?"

"Why not? I'll take my break and we can go for a walk."

"OK." Josh came through to George's side of the gate, following him across the yard. "Properly play, you mean?"

"You know what they say. There's a first time for everything." George popped his head around the door of the café to let Hannah know he was taking his break, and then he, Josh and Blue wandered up into the paddock, to sit and watch the Shetland ponies, who hadn't yet realised that they had human company, and that they were armed with sugar-based treats.

The Love Hearts Game. From the time Josh and George first started playing together outside of school, they would go to the shop near Josh's house and buy a packet of the sweets, each printed with a short, sappy phrase, and share them, making up sentences including whatever was on the sweet. When they were older, they would walk up to the fields by the local stables (and later still, where George's horse, Maggy, was in livery), and also feed them to any of the animals who came over. The horses loved them, although they were always careful not to give them too many. Like it wasn't good for humans to eat a lot of sugary foods, the same was true for their equine companions.

At first, the game was entirely innocent; just two little boys, sharing their pocket money purchases and practising their creative language skills, back when the phrase 'KISS ME' provoked little more than a giggle and, if enacted, a pretence of disgust as the recipient wiped the kisser's spit from wherever they had planted their lips. However, as they matured, it became more meaningful and began to evolve; by the time they were nearing their teens, there was far greater emotional intent behind what they said and did, certainly from George's perspective. Josh, for the most part, had merely learned to emulate the behaviour of his peers, and realised in later years that this was when he had honed his people-reading skills, for whilst he didn't fully understand how it felt to be sexually attracted to or romantically involved with someone, he could spot the signs in others from a mile away.

Many of the messages the sweets bore were funny, or innocent, so didn't cause either of them too many problems. For instance, it was fairly easy to come up with something amusing to say that included 'BLUE EYES' or 'CRAZY' without it becoming too personal. More troublesome were the messages like 'BE MINE', 'LET'S KISS' OR 'I WANT U', particularly as the final version of the game worked like this: you took the next Love Heart out of the packet, and had to choose whether the other person was to 'do it', 'say it', or 'horse it'—a forfeit, whereby a horse or pony of their choosing got the sweet. As George's best friend, Josh had always known he liked boys, therefore George would happily divulge his feelings if given a 'say it', such as 'I want to ask so-and-so if he will BE MINE'. Josh would imitate this, and didn't discriminate in his choice of recipient for his 'say it'. If George ever questioned in his mind why that was, he didn't voice it.

The very last time they played the Love Hearts game was just before they went away to university, hence was also the last time that Josh saw Maggy alive—not long after he and George had secretly fallen in love, or, at least, it was a secret from each other, but everyone else appeared to have figured it out way back. Needless to say, they each clocked up quite a few 'horse-its' on that occasion. Josh remembered now, with stark clarity, one or two of the phrases they had encountered during that game, where he came so close to telling George how he felt, like when he got 'FIRST LOVE'…

**

"I have known you since I was eight," Josh said.

"Seven."

"No. Eight."

"Seven," George insisted. "I was just turned eight when I went to your school, so you were seven."

Josh huffed to hide his frustration, the moment lost. He went for a slight change of approach. "All right. I have known you since I was seven and you have never told me who was your 'FIRST LOVE'."

George didn't answer straight away. He was too busy stroking Maggy.

"It's, erm…" he began. "I, err…"

"Sorry." Josh realised he'd embarrassed him.

"It's OK."

"I should've just gone for a horse-it."

George smiled nervously, seemingly relieved to be let off the hook, and Josh assumed the answer was Kris. A few turns later, the same phrase came up again, and this time they didn't hesitate in passing it off as a forfeit. Josh's hand shook as he held it out to Maggy, the tiny round sweet in the middle of his palm, his only chance to say something before he left for university, eaten by a horse. How often he had wondered what might've been, if only George had asked him that question.

From George's point of view, that game looked much the same. A run of sweets and lies, as his heart sank further and further: 'BE MINE', 'MY BOY', 'KISS ME', 'IT'S TRUE'—their equine friends thought it was their 'LUCKY DAY'! When the game was all but over, George gave Josh a purple Love Heart bearing the words 'FOR KEEPS', with a promise that whatever happened when they each went their separate ways in September, their friendship would be for keeps, forever. Josh had put the sweet in his pocket and kept it ever since.

***

Now George held out the packet to Josh and he closed his eyes, feeling around for the rim of the first sweet. He found it and pulled it free, cautiously opening his eyes. "Do it," he said very seriously. For a moment, George was concerned, until he read it.

"'HOLD ME'. That's no challenge," he smiled. He took hold of Josh's hand. Josh put the sweet in his mouth and held the packet so that George could take the next one. He read it and huffed.

"That's rubbish," he said. "Horse it?" He held it up to Josh.

"'CHEEKY BOY'? That is rubbish. Horse it."

George put the sweet to one side and pulled out the next one. He grinned. "Do it."

Josh read 'HUG ME' and did so. One of the ponies was heading their way; he released George so he could offer it the 'CHEEKY BOY' sweet. It seemed quite happy with that and had a good nosey around to see if there were any more treats to be had.

"He is a cheeky boy too," George said, patting the fat little grey pony on the flank. It wandered off again. "Your turn."

Josh took the next sweet and passed it to George. "Say it."

"Umm." George thought for a moment. He wasn't feeling very creative. "I can't believe after all this time that you are 'ALL MINE'?"

Josh shrugged. "OK. That's a pass, I suppose."

George gently pushed him away. "Let's see you do better," he challenged, taking the next sweet and holding it up for Josh to read without looking at it himself. "Say it."

"Easy. The best part of falling out for ten years was when we finally got to 'MAKE UP'." He smiled and acted all coy and cute. George laughed.

"Very sweet," he said. Josh likewise held up the next one without looking first. George read it. "Snap!" He hugged Josh, as per the written 'HUG ME' instruction.

"I once figured out the probability for getting the same message twice," Josh said.

"I remember," George groaned, waiting for the next command. Josh glanced at it and wrinkled his nose.

"Horse it."

"That's one each." George passed the 'KEEP COOL' sweet to a little black pony that was standing very close, along with the other four in the paddock; a queue of tiny horses scuffling and impatiently awaiting their turn.

"I hope there's a few more duds, for their sake and ours," Josh remarked, backing off, with the grey pony snorting in his face. He pushed against the side of its nose and it moved away.

George took out the next sweet: 'I'M SHY'. "Say it or horse it?" he asked.

"Just horse it, for goodness' sake," Josh said, getting up. "I think I might go and stand on the other side of the fence."

"Good idea," George agreed. He fed 'I'M SHY' to a very unabashed black and white pony, as they walked back to the stile. Josh took out the next sweet along the way, and passed it to George, his hand shaking with the anticipation.

"Say it."

"I have loved you since I was…"

"Eight," Josh interrupted. He couldn't stop himself from smiling. "But was I the first?"

"Yep," George said. He hopped over the stile and grabbed Josh's hands, pulling him over and kissing him. "You were most definitely my 'FIRST LOVE'."

"Awesomely sweet. And worth waiting twenty-one years for. You're in the lead now, I'd say."

"Cool," George grinned. He hoisted himself up and sat on the wooden fence. Josh leaned against his legs. George took out the next sweet and read it, then passed it to Josh, who kissed him.

"Hey! I didn't say what you were supposed to do with it."

"Sorry, I just saw the word 'lips' and figured you'd want me to 'do it'."

"It doesn't even make sense, 'TRUE LIPS'."

"Well, it's done now, unless that wasn't true enough?" Josh stretched up and kissed him again, taking the packet from him at the same time. They were nearly halfway through and only three horse-its so far, although they decided to make that four, with the repeat of 'MAKE UP'.

"Adele wears too much," George said after the little grey pony had snaffled the sweet from him. "See? I could have kept my lead, no problem." He unwrapped the next sweet. "Say it."

"I am for 'EVER YOURS'," Josh said. "Too easy. On that point, I have another letter for you at home. I wrote it this time last year."

George looked worried.

"It's fine," Josh assured him. "You'll like it, I promise." He took the next sweet and held it up. "Say it."

"It's my birthday. I think you should 'SPOIL ME'."

"Spoil, or ruin?"

"That's not so sweet. That's kinda dirty."

"Well, the choice is yours."

"Hmm. Tempting. I'll think about it." George took the next sweet out and mouthed 'yeesss' to himself, punching the air the way someone does when their team scores. He held it up to Josh, a little too far away for him to read it. "Say it," he commanded, his eyes twinkling. "You are mine, am I yours?"

"I have loved you since I was..."

"Seven," George finished. "Not eight. Seven, Joshua. But was I the first?"

"My 'FIRST LOVE'," Josh said, reaching up and placing his palms on George's cheeks, "and my only."

"OK. That is sweet." George leaned down and kissed his head, snuffling in his hair. It smelled of coconut. "That's very sweet. Now we're heading into statistical improbability territory. Am I right?"

"Well, it's low, yes." Josh started trying to figure out the odds of getting the same message twice, in each of two different packets bought by the same two people twenty-one years apart. George attempted to interrupt this thought process with another sweet. It was the third 'HUG ME' in the pack, but Josh wasn't paying any attention.

"Assuming all things are equal," he said.

George shook his head, but let him continue.

"The probability is approximately nought point nought, nought, nought, nought, nought seven, or one in 150,000. But..."

"Oh, man. What did I do?"

"It stands to reason that they make more with phrases containing the word 'love' than any other, so there's a positive bias..."

"Joshua."

"Also, there are more phrases now than there were then, plus…"

"Joshua!"

"Other extraneous variables that are impossible to predict with any certainty, such as differences in the mass of…"

George kissed him and he instantly stopped talking. "You're such a boffin," George murmured, their faces close.

"Boffin?"

"Yeah." George fed the 'HUG ME' sweet and the one after (which simply read 'NEAT'), without looking, to the pony nuzzling in his hand. He was still staring right into Josh's eyes.

"I don't know whose turn it is," he said, slowly drawing away.

"Me neither." Josh continued to stare up at him. George glanced away to read the next sweet in the packet and suddenly remembered something that he'd intended to ask, but had completely forgotten about until now.

"You know when I had tonsillitis?"

"Mmm?"

"You called me a pet name."

Josh examined the sweet in George's hand. "I didn't call you 'SWEET HEART', did I?"

"I don't think so. It was French. Ma…ma…something beginning with 'm', I think."

"Ma moitié?"

"Yep! That was it!"

"I called you ma moitié? I don't recall that. Well you are, although it's normally used by men when referring to their wives."

"Why? What does it mean?"

"It means—I could tell you anything and you wouldn't know if it was the truth," Josh grinned mischievously.

"You could. But I think you owe me, seeing as you basically just called me a girl."

"No I didn't! As Sean said, you're definitely all man."

"Did he now?"

"Yeah."

George tickled him in an attempt to glean more information. Josh giggled and wriggled, but stayed exactly where he was.

"And obviously gay," he added.

"Am I?"

"I have no idea. You're just you, but I don't think he meant you were camp, or anything like that."

"Why on earth did he say it, then?"

"He was trying to allay his jealousy of you and Sophie."

George nodded. "Yeah, OK. Anyway, you were telling me what ma moitié means."

"Oh, yes. That's what we were talking about, wasn't it?"

"So?"

Josh looked away into the distance, his lips pursed.

"I can always check on a translation website," George told him.

"If you can figure out how to spell it," Josh teased. "I'll save you the trouble and just tell you. It means 'my half', which is to say I would be incomplete without you."

"My half," George repeated. He smiled. "I like that."

"I like this too," Josh said, holding up a Love Heart, containing the words 'KISS ME'.

"You do, huh?"

"I do."

"I'm guessing you don't want to horse it?"

"Just do it, Morley!"

"OK," George grinned, "if you insist." He bent down and gave him a kiss, then took the next sweet out. "I'm going to give this next one to…"

"Me," Josh said, and took the sweet from him with his lips.

"Because you're 'MY HERO'?"

"No. Because that was only the fourth purple one in the pack and they're my favourites."

"Oh, you're 'TOO MUCH'," George laughed, holding up the next sweet.

"Or maybe," Josh pulled another one free, "it's 'JUST YOU'?"

"That was terrible," George said. He gave the next one—'MY DOLL'—to his favourite Shetland pony, who was actually called Dolly, so that worked quite well, and also gave him a break from coming up with corny lines. There were two left: one orange, one yellow. They took one each.

"You go first," Josh said, "it's your birthday."

"OK." George turned the sweet over. "I'm feeling a bit sick."

"Oh dear. Too many sweeties?"

"Nope. I think I've got the 'LOVE BUG'."

Josh groaned and allowed George to feed him the sweet.

"Never mind," Josh said, as George grabbed the last one from him, and his fingers, with his lips. "Even if you throw up, I still 'LIKE YOU' anyway."

"Only 'like'?"

"Who am I to argue with the dictations of sugar and food colouring?"

George jumped down from the fence and straightened his jeans, pretending to look hurt.

"Ma moitié, je t'aime!" Josh gestured dramatically with his arms. He grabbed George and kissed him once on each cheek, then, more tenderly, on the lips. "Je t'aime," he repeated seriously. "Bon Anniversaire."

George grinned. "Thanks. I love you too."

***

Dear George,

Sometimes, a cigar is just a cigar.
Sometimes, a water chute is…

How long can I keep stopping myself from falling?

Happy Birthday.
I love you.

Ever yours,
Josh

Taurus

Rejoice, my friend, if God has made you strong:
Put forth your force to move the world along:
Yet never shame your strength to do a wrong.

THIS LAST NIGHT
Sunday 23rd–Monday 24th April

23:59
Andy: So tomorrow's the big day!
Charlie: Yeah.
Andy: You excited?
Charlie: A little.
Andy: Only a little?
Charlie: A lot. Can't wait.

00:03
Charlie: It's been an awesome two weeks.
Andy: Agreed! Hope I haven't been too miserable.
Charlie: Of course not!
Andy: I have, haven't I? Sorry.
Charlie: Don't be. You've been fun! How are you feeling?

00:08
Charlie: Andy?

00:09
Charlie: Still there?
Andy: Yeah.
Charlie: OK.

00:11
Charlie: I shouldn't have asked.
Andy: It's fine.

00:15
Andy: Don't want to do it.
Charlie: I know.
Andy: Just got to get on with it.
Charlie: Yeah.
Andy: Still don't want to do it.
Charlie: You crying?

Andy: My words getting wet?
Charlie: Wish I could…
Andy: I know.

00:17
Charlie: But we've had fun, haven't we?
Andy: Yeah. My knees are too old for this!
Charlie: Mine too!
Andy: Still, gave the old snowboard a good airing.
Charlie: True. Dry slopes totally suck.
Andy: Ha. Yeah.
Charlie: And if you need to talk, ever, you know where I am.
Andy: Yeah. Thanks.
Charlie: Promise?
Andy: Promise.
Charlie: OK.

00:25
Charlie: Got to go. It's late.
Andy: No worries.
Charlie: Got to be up in five hours.
Andy: OK.

00:27
Andy: Thanks Charlie. Take care.
Charlie: You too. Night night. Sleep tight. x
Andy: Night. x

***

"Why are you still up?" George rubbed his eyes and yawned. "You do know it's half past twelve?"

"Yes," Josh said, and wheeled himself back from the computer so George could see what was displayed on-screen. He crouched down and squinted at the document.

Monday, 24th April
Dear Professor Belling,

Many thanks for taking the time to meet with me during the past few months. I am more than satisfied with the outcome of these discussions. To re-cap what we have agreed:

- I will work for the university on a pro rata basis, equivalent to 0.8 of a full time contract.
- My employment will be as a senior lecturer, teaching across undergraduate and postgraduate courses, as pertinent to my academic specialism. I am contractually obliged to continue to contribute to the research excellence of the university.
- I will also engage in the supervision of undergraduate dissertations and postgraduate theses, again, as commensurate with my level of qualification and academic expertise.
- I will no longer be responsible for providing counselling services to students in my present capacity.
- Where it is deemed appropriate, I will continue to serve on the ethics panel.
- I am permitted to use my office for the equivalent of one day per week for the purposes of continuing my private counselling work.
- I will be moved to a new office in The Faculty of Social Sciences building, on the first floor, in order that I am able to work closely with Doctor Tierney.
- I will be permitted to work from home as and when I am not specifically required to be present on campus.

Assuming that we are in agreement regarding the points identified above, and the offer is still made as per the terms and conditions of the contract, I would be happy to accept your offer of employment, commencing from August this year.

Yours sincerely,
Josh Sandison.

George finished reading and nodded. "Are you sure?"

"What do you mean, 'am I sure'? You've been pestering me to do this for months!"

"Yes, but is it *your* decision?"

"It's *our* decision. We're getting married in the autumn, remember?"

"I know, but it's still not really anything to do with me. What I mean is you need to do what's right for you and if you're not sure, then you shouldn't do it. We've got enough money coming in, and if the counselling…" Josh reached up and put a finger against George's lips.

"It is what I want to do, George." He released him and pulled him close. "Shall we go to bed now?"

"I was already there," George said, allowing himself to be steered back to the bedroom. "You're not going to tell them about—you know what, are you?"

"No. I think I've built in enough flexibility so I don't have to."

"But what if one of your lectures coincides with an episode?"

"Then they'll be in for a very interesting lecture! Now will you please stop worrying?"

George got back into bed and waited for Josh to do the same, then cuddled up close.

"I don't want to keep going on, and I'm not necessarily saying we discuss it now, in fact I'm not suggesting that at all, and now I sound like you, so…"

"George, you're doing it again."

"I know. Sorry. We still need to talk about telling everyone else."

"It's going to have to wait."

"Why?"

"Because of Jess."

"Is that an excuse?"

"Yes."

"OK."

"Good night, George."

"Good night, dearest."

Josh started laughing. "Don't!"

"Why not? If you can call me ma…ma—whatever it was…"

"Ma moitié."

"Yeah, that, then I need…"

Josh kissed him. "Shush."

MAKING PLANS
Monday 24th April

Dan grabbed Andy's bags and followed him outside, shoving them into the back of the 4x4.

"Now, if there's anything at all that you need, call me." Andy's mother hugged him and kissed his cheek.

"Thanks, Mum. For everything," he said, returning the kiss and slowly withdrawing. The way he was feeling just now he'd rather have liked to stay inside his mother's embrace forever more, but there was nothing to be done.

"Tell you what you can do," Dan said, accepting his own hug and kiss. "Kick that lazy-assed eldest son of yours into touch. He's taking the piss."

"Yes, Daniel, thank you. He'll be gone soon enough."

Dan looked at her doubtfully. There was no way she was going to throw him out. She was too soft on him; always had been. In fact, the only one she'd ever been tough on was Andy, perhaps because he was the middle child.

"I'll give you a ring later," Andy called, as he climbed into the passenger seat.

"All right, love."

Dan got in and started the engine, and their mother waved them off. Andy climbed out to open the gates, waited for Dan to drive through, closed them and got back in again.

"Alright, bro?" Dan asked, watching him as he fastened his seatbelt.

"Yep," Andy confirmed too breezily. They headed out onto the main road, down to the first set of traffic lights, where Dan signalled left and turned into a side road. He stopped the engine and turned to face his brother, putting an arm across his shoulders. Andy had his face in his hands, his whole body shuddering as he took a battering from wave upon wave of despair.

"I know I said you were a pushover," Dan said, "and I'm sorry. I was wrong. What you're doing takes real guts." He swallowed back his own tears. "And, err, if there's anything…"

Andy nodded and sniffed, unable to convey in words how grateful he was for the support. What was more important right now, however, was that he pulled himself together before they arrived at Jess's. She didn't need to see him like this. It wouldn't do either of them any good.

Dan waited a couple of minutes more before re-starting the engine, then swung a deft U-turn and headed back up to the traffic lights to continue the journey into town. It was a dreary, drizzly day, where everything felt sticky and damp; too warm for coats, too cold to be without. Inside the 4x4 it was temperate and arid, the air conditioning quietly humming away, audible, unusually, due to the absence of music. Every so often, the full extent of what was happening would hit Andy again, his stomach lurching queasily at the prospect of what lay ahead.

As they pulled up outside the house, Jess's mum was on her way out to her car, another woman standing in the doorway, laughing and saying something muted by the closed windows. Dan glanced across at Andy, but didn't speak, knowing that they had reached the point where they would need to keep their emotions in check as much as possible, although he could still sense the sorrow. It was as oppressive and abundant as the humid air that rushed in when Andy opened the door. Dan watched him make his way over to Jess's mum and hug her, then followed at a distance.

"Hi, Mrs. Lambert," he greeted casually. She smiled.

"Hello, Dan. How're you? Haven't seen you in ages. You're looking well."

"Thanks. You too. Have you been away?" He had noticed the natural golden tan and was pleased that it gave him something to say.

"Yes. Got back from Florida last week. We thought we'd better take our hols early this year, what with…well, anyway, the weather was glorious. I must get this shopping inside before the ice-cream melts."

Dan and Andy watched her lift the hatch of her car and took bags from her, before following her inside and depositing them in the kitchen.

"Where is she?" Andy asked, noting the empty lounge.

"Having a shower. She only got back from the hospital half an hour ago. The chemo makes her feel grotty, she said."

Andy nodded his understanding. "I'm gonna take my stuff upstairs. I'll see if she needs anything while I'm there." Dan threw the keys across and Andy returned to the car, leaving his brother with Jess's mum. The silence of these two relative strangers filled the room, interspersed only with the crinkling of plastic supermarket bags.

"Shall I put the kettle on?" Dan suggested.

"Good idea." She'd put away all of the food that would spoil and went to stand by the back door. She lit a cigarette. "I was going to give up," she explained. Dan filled the kettle and switched it on. He gave her a sympathetic smile. "I still should, really, but what's the point? Have you ever smoked?"

Dan shook his head. "Never. More by luck than judgement. A lot of my friends took it up at school, but it didn't really appeal."

"No. A good thing it is too. I know Jess smoked when she was younger. She tried to hide it, of course, but even I could smell it on her uniform. I asked her if she smoked once, expecting her to lie and deny it, but she just owned up. Funny girl like that, she is."

Dan prepared cups, occasionally glancing across at Jess's mum. It was difficult to find anything to talk about that didn't involve references to life, or death. In the end everything did.

Jess's mum drew hard on the half-smoked cigarette and dropped it to the patio, crushing it with the toe of her canvas pump; she dressed much more casually than her daughter; today she was wearing turquoise cargo pants cropped to just below the knee, and a white cap-sleeved t-shirt with a tiny printed logo. As she bent over, her t-shirt rose up, revealing a tattoo of a single daisy in the small of her back. She picked up the obliterated filter with its singed tobacco hair and walked over to the outside bin to dispose of it.

"Coffee or tea, Mrs. Lambert?" Dan called.

"Steph," she said, reappearing in the kitchen.

"Steph," he repeated.

"Tea, please." She fished in her handbag for chewing gum. Andy came back inside and ran straight up the stairs.

"You want a drink, bro?" Dan shouted after him.

"Yeah. Tea, if you're making it." Andy headed straight for his old room, where Jess's mum was currently staying, and placed the largest of his bags, containing his everyday clothes and toiletries, against the wardrobe doors. He'd left most of the superfluous stuff—his dinner jacket, ski boots and the like—at his mother's. No point bringing them back here; he wouldn't be staying long enough to need them. Once again, his stomach twisted at the thought, and he pushed it as far to the back of his mind as he could. Jess was still in the shower, so he went into her room and sat on the bed, looking around him at all of the boxes of pills and medical supplies. Part of him marvelled at the newness of this experience, not that it was one he would ever have sought, but, perhaps, that would be the way he could get through it. After all, it was no different from the work the overseas volunteers did, or those who worked in hospices here at home. They must take some sort of solace, gain some satisfaction from it.

"I didn't know you were here." Jess appeared in the doorway, her head wrapped in the purest white towel, a white towelling robe draped loosely around her. Andy smiled.

"We only just got here. Dan's entertaining your mum downstairs. I came to see if you needed anything."

Jess slowly lowered herself onto the bed beside him.

"No, I'm fine. I just need to sleep." He moved so she could lift her legs up. She lay on her side, and put her hand under her cheek. "This chemo is going to kill me before the cancer does."

Andy couldn't think of anything to say. He had so many questions, but they all seemed so inappropriate and he doubted he'd get through asking even the first of them without a return of the tears. This thought in itself made his eyes itch and he turned away so that she couldn't see.

"Come and lie with me," she said sleepily. He sniffed and shook his head. "It's OK to cry."

He shuffled his way around to the other side of the bed and carefully slid across next to her. She lifted her head and put it on his chest, smoothing his cheek with her palm.

"Let it go," she whispered. He grasped her, trying not to squeeze too hard. "It's all right, now," she soothed. He sobbed, unable to catch his breath or any sense of reason. This was it: the tsunami of grief he had held back, as powerless as Canute.

Downstairs in the kitchen, Dan and Steph conversed politely, trying to pretend and wishing they couldn't hear. Dan's heart was breaking for his brother, for Jess, for her mum, and for himself. They'd known for a month—the term 'palliative care' featured prominently in all their browsing histories—but still the realisation was a staggered process and today it was their turn to finally face the truth.

It was quite some time before Andy made it back downstairs, his eyes swollen and red, blotchy-faced and ragged.

"Steph," he smiled feebly at Jess's mum, "she said to pop in and see her before you go home."

Jess's mum nodded and straightened her top, then went upstairs.

"Tea's gone cold," Dan said. He couldn't look at him, not without risking treading the same path into inconsolable anguish.

"Yeah, never mind." Andy picked up the mug and swigged it down in one go, grimacing. "Ugh." He rinsed the mug under the tap. "The treatment's really getting to her. She says she wants to stop it."

"Why?"

"She doesn't want to lose her hair."

"That sounds about right," Dan laughed. Andy joined in. It was forced and they both knew the real reason. The chemotherapy was there to slow the growth of the tumours, not to cure her. She was going to die; it was only a matter of when.

"We need to talk to Josh and George at some point soon," Andy continued. "They're why she agreed to the chemo. So she could see them get married."

Dan continued to nurse his empty cup, unable to speak or make eye contact, even though his brother was watching him.

"And as it turns out," Andy said, "if you just let go it actually doesn't feel so bad, once you stop yelling like a baby."

Dan put his hand up to cover his eyes, for a moment holding on to what little emotional control he had, but then submitting. He cried in silence, his whole body shuddering; as it subsided, Andy passed him a piece of paper towel.

"Cheers," he said, sniffing loudly and wiping his eyes. "This really isn't my style, bro, you know?" He sighed and studied the tiles on the wall opposite, more tears escaping from the corners of his eyes.

"I know. Don't worry. Your reputation's safe."

Dan patted him on the back. "We need to draw up a rota," he said.

"For what?"

"To give you and Steph a break from time to time. You can't be here doing this on your own."

"Just keep the business afloat. That'll do me."

"That goes without saying, but you're gonna need more help than that."

"Well, there's nurses and carers coming in regularly, so we should be all right."

Dan shook his head. "Not that sort of support." They could hear Jess's mum moving around upstairs, getting her things together in preparation to go home: the first shift change of many was about to take place.

"I'm gonna give Josh a call in a while, set the ball rolling, OK?" Dan asked, although he'd have still done it even if Andy had said no.

Soon after, Jess's mum went home, for the first time since her holiday in Florida, and not before making Andy promise to phone if she was needed. It was Monday and he was 'in charge' until Thursday, then she would take over the care again until next Monday, and so on. Or that was the plan.

JEFFRIES AND ASSOCIATES
Thursday 27ᵗʰ April

Josh watched Adele bustle past with a serving bowl. She placed it on the mat at the far end of the centre run of the enormous rectangular dining table. Dan remained clutching a second serving dish of the same design—white porcelain with a delicate silver detail around its circumference—biting his lip and frowning heavily.

"For the love of all that is!" he snarled, suddenly slamming the dish down and shaking his burning hand free of the hot oven glove.

"That doesn't go there," Adele said.

"I don't fucking care!" He retreated to the kitchen. Adele lifted the dish—without the aid of an oven glove—and repositioned it in the centre of the table. She afforded herself a satisfied smile.

"What else? Oh, yes. Wine." She trotted off after Dan. Josh and George glanced sideways at each other.

"They'll settle down in a minute," Andy muttered quietly, or as quietly as was possible, given the loudly hissed argument taking place in the kitchen. None of the three men were particularly worried; after all, they'd been watching the pair of them bicker for more than thirty years.

"I don't mind telling you, Andy, but this feels a bit strange," Josh said, following Adele's movement back and forth through the gap of the open door. She was fighting to free a cork from a bottle and refusing absolutely to pass the task to Dan.

"Why? You've been here for dinner loads of times."

"Yes, but not like this."

"You mean because of Jess?"

"I suppose that's partly it, yes, although I was talking more about this particular combination of 'us'."

"Ah, I get you," Andy said.

"I don't," George frowned. Josh took his hand.

"When you were in the States, Ellie and I used to come round for dinner quite often, and Shaunna and Kris would usually be here too." He moved in closer and whispered. "Even when Dan and Adele weren't together."

"Ah, OK," George grinned. "Bet that was fun."

"It was interesting, that's for sure," Josh said. Andy laughed.

"Yep. That's one way of putting it."

He couldn't pass any further comment, because Dan and Adele had returned, and seemed marginally less unfriendly than when they left. The wine bottle was open, and Dan looked smug; evidently Adele had relented.

"Everyone got a drink?" she asked. George and Andy both lifted their beer bottles to check they had enough for now, which they did. Josh glanced into his empty coffee cup, but said nothing. Dan disappeared with the cup before Josh even had a chance to protest. He returned a moment later, sat down, then got up again, having left his beer in the kitchen. Finally he returned, put his beer down firmly and pulled in his chair.

"Help yourselves," Adele said. George didn't need telling twice. He put three of the new potatoes on his plate, making a decision there and then to come back to them once everyone else was done. They smelled delicious, and he could resist no longer. He put one in his mouth, sat back and gave out a sigh of sexual proportions. Adele and Josh giggled.

"Good, are they?" Andy asked.

"Heavenly," George said. "What've you put in the butter? I'm getting a hint of garlic—not too overpowering, either—a touch of sage. And thyme?" Adele nodded. "It's that other…" He picked up another potato and nibbled at it. "It's got a kind of sweet and sour thing going on, like—white wine?"

"Close," Adele said. "It's Champagne vinegar."

"Ah, man. These are—" George sighed again. Andy offered him a piece of skillet-fried pork and he nodded enthusiastically. Andy put it down on his plate and left him to his savour his potatoes.

"Anyway," Josh addressed Adele, "whilst I adore your cooking, although clearly nowhere near as much as some other people…"

"You have *got* to try the potatoes," George urged.

"I will, in a minute," Josh laughed. He turned back to Adele. "You said you wanted to talk to us about something?"

"Yes, though not me. Them." She pointed at Dan and Andy. "I was just being the corresponder."

"Correspondent," Dan corrected.

"Whatever," Adele snapped.

Josh quickly got some of the potatoes before George ate them all.

"It's about Jess's chemo," Andy said.

"Right?"

"She wants to stop it. It's making her really sick, and the next dose will probably be enough for her hair to start falling out."

"So why hasn't she stopped it?" George asked.

"Erm." Andy felt uncomfortable just coming out and saying it. He also wasn't sure he could say it. *Because she doesn't want to die before you get married.* He put the words in his mouth a few times, trying them without uttering them. He looked to Dan for help.

"She's holding out to see you get married," Dan said. "She knows you were talking about an autumn wedding, and if she stops the chemo now, she might not be well enough to enjoy it."

Josh put down his fork and sat back, silent and thoughtful for several minutes. Everyone else continued to eat.

"Why didn't she talk to us about it?"

"Because she's hellbent on not being a burden," Andy said. "She wants everything to continue as normally as possible."

"But she must know we'd be OK with moving the wedding forward." He turned to George to check. "We are OK with it, I assume?"

"Yeah, of course we are!" he confirmed through a mouthful of tarragon sautéed mushrooms. "Although the best man's gonna be pissed."

"Best man? Dan asked.

"Oliver," Josh explained.

"You mean I get another wedding off?"

"Yes." Josh laughed at Dan's reaction. "Are you pleased about that?"

"Pleased? It's the best news I've had in years!"

With the difficult bit done, the dinner continued quite jovially. Adele and George shared favourite recipes, whilst Dan and Josh engaged in their usual posturing. Andy joined in where he could, but he was having to work hard to stay chirpy, and gladly tended to little Shaunna on the multiple occasions she was awoken by the sudden increase in volume of the discussions going on around the table. For dessert, Adele had made a blueberry fool, topped with roasted almonds, and home-made amaretti biscuits on the side. George wasn't sure about the combination, until he tasted it.

"Oh God!" he said. He turned to Josh. "I'm sorry, but I'm dumping you for Adele."

Josh laughed. "That's high praise indeed." Adele looked proud enough to burst.

"Mmm," Andy agreed. "That is pretty special. I like amaretti biscuits."

"Me too," Josh said, "although I've only had them with coffee before, and never home-made."

"They're really very easy to make," Adele dismissed. George was immediately attentive. Dan and Josh rolled their eyes.

After dessert, they took their drinks over to the sofas to discuss what they were going to do about the wedding.

"We can go to the register office after I finish work tomorrow," Josh suggested. "Just go with whatever the first available date is."

"There's a notice period, I think," Andy said.

"How long?"

"Not sure."

"Sixteen days," Dan told them, then busied himself with selecting a new music playlist. Josh nodded.

"So that would make it the week commencing the fifteenth of May, which is when the counselling course finishes."

"I'd rather leave it a bit longer," George said.

"Why?"

The other three people continued to chat quietly around them.

"I need time, to talk to Ollie about it, and then there's my mum, and...it's a bit, um..."

Josh took his hand. "I understand, and I think you're right. Plus, we've still got to sort out my grandma's house. But you know it won't be a big public affair? Just us and a few friends."

"That's what I mean."

"It'll be fine," Josh said gently. George smiled and nodded.

"Yeah. It will, won't it?"

The next day, at two o'clock on the dot, George met Josh at the university so they could go straight to the register office. The clerk checked their documents and went through the available slots.

"OK, there are two on Thursday the eighteenth of May."

"What do you think?" Josh asked George. The fact that he didn't answer right away was a response in itself. "What about June?" he asked the clerk. She had a look.

"Busy month," she said. "Nothing until the nineteenth, at one o'clock."

They looked at each other and nodded.

"We'll take it."

THE BEST MAN
Monday 1st May

Bank holiday Monday: Josh dropped George at Eleanor's, then headed onwards to his grandmother's to begin the house clearance. Neither was looking forward to what the day held, but there was no use delaying. These things must be done.

"Hi, James," George smiled and stepped into the hallway, immediately getting ambushed by a very excited four and a half year old.

"George," James acknowledged. He seemed very serious, and a little withdrawn, even for him. The company investigation was to blame, George guessed, but he couldn't ask in Oliver's presence. He followed James through to the kitchen, Oliver already gabbling enthusiastically about the wedding and Shabina and football.

"Hey, Ellie," George said, giving her a hug. "I need to tell you something, but I need to tell somebody else first." He tilted his head in Oliver's direction as he said this.

"Is it to do with your dinner at Dan and Adele's?"

"Yeah."

"OK. You staying for a drink?"

"No. I'll do that when we get back."

Oliver ran into the garden and collected his football.

"Come on, Dorge." He went tearing off down the hall to the front door. George shrugged.

"See you later," he said to the adults. Oliver was waiting for him outside, and held his hand as they walked to the park.

There were quite a lot of children out playing, not surprisingly, as it was a warm day, although in typical English style, the sky was overcast, and there was a definite threat of thunder on the horizon. The football pitch was already in use, so they wandered over to a vacant patch of grass beyond the play area, where Oliver set down his ball and kicked it. George kicked it back, trying to focus on both his thoughts and actions at the same time. He'd had a few ideas on how to approach the issue, although it was about much more than the wedding. Oliver's only experience of someone dying was when Eleanor's patient had died during their time in Wales last year, which he understood simply as something that had made Eleanor very sad, and he was at an age where the concept of death was likely to be impossible for him to comprehend. Sean had suggested telling him in clear, literal terms, which would undoubtedly lead to lots of questions, and George didn't know how he was going to deal with this, but figured that allowing Oliver to see how he really felt probably wasn't such a bad thing.

"After we've played football," George began, "we need to do some of the planning for the wedding."

"OK," Oliver said, running after the ball and kicking it back to George. It went right over his head and he had to jog a fair distance to retrieve it. They carried on like this for ten minutes or so, before Oliver decided he needed a rest, although the puffing and panting was all an act, because he was eager to talk about the wedding, and had also seen the ice-cream van pull up at the gates to the park. They walked across and on the way, George started the discussion for real.

"You know Jess, don't you, Ollie?"

"Mmm—" Oliver scratched his head and pursed his lips together in thought. "She looks like Shabina's Barbie doll. Not the one that looks like Shabina. The nother one, with blonde hair."

"OK," George laughed, assuming they were talking about one and the same person. "Well, Jess is very poorly, Ollie, and she's not going to get better."

"She can go to the doctor and they give her medicine," Oliver reasoned.

"That's a very good idea, and most of the time doctors can fix people, like when they fixed your leg last year. But sometimes the doctor doesn't know how to make somebody better."

"Like Jess?"

"Yes. Like Jess."

"Is she going to die?"

"Yes."

"When?"

"Nobody knows. But she's getting more and more poorly every day."

"That's very sad."

George couldn't tell if any of this was going in. They had reached the ice-cream van now and he bought them each a '99', then they went and sat on the grass by the duck pond, watching a female duck and her five fawn ducklings visiting the people dotted around the perimeter, on the lookout for tidbits.

"Why do people die?" Oliver asked. George thought about what Sean said: the questions can seem profound, but they probably aren't.

"Because their bodies are broken and they can't be fixed," he answered.

"Is Jess's body broken?"

"Yes. On the inside."

"She breaked a bone?"

"No. She's got cancer."

"What's cancer?"

"Well, our bodies are made up of lots of tiny things called cells, and they all have jobs to do, like when your leg got better, your body made new bone cells to mend the bone. But when someone gets cancer, some of the cells go bad and stop the good cells from doing their job."

"I not got cancer?"

"No, Ollie, you haven't."

"I catch cancer off Jess?"

"No. It's not like colds and tummy bugs. It just grows inside the person who's got it."

"Why?"

"I don't know, Ollie. It just happens, and sometimes the doctors can fix it, but sometimes they can't."

Oliver stayed quiet after this, and was holding the tiniest end of his cone in his hand.

"I give this to the ducks?" he asked.

"Ducks don't eat ice-cream, silly Billy," George said lightly.

"What do ducks eat?"

"Insects, fish, berries, lots of things."

"Not bread?"

"Nope."

"I tell my mummy that. She says they like bread."

"Ah," George said cautiously. Now this was even more tricky to negotiate. "Lots of people think ducks like bread, but it's very bad for them."

"It give them cancer?"

"No, but it gives them a poorly tummy."

Oliver got up and put the end of his cone in the bin. George was still sitting on the grass. "You sad about Jess, Dorge?"

"Yes," George nodded, feeling his eyes start to fill with tears. Oliver watched him for a minute, then walked over and put his arms around his neck, holding him tight. George let out a sob.

"Poor Dorge," Oliver said. "It's OK." He rubbed George's head—quite roughly—then stepped away. "So we got to not do the wedding in the autumn?"

"We've got to do it sooner, so that Jess can come."

"OK." He picked up his football and tried to put it under his arm, then held out his hand.

"Come on. We go and play and you can splain."

George let Oliver 'pull him up'.

"When you want to get married?" he asked.

"June the nineteenth," George told him.

"When is June?"

"Next month."

"Next month? That's very very soon, Dorge." He started marching across the park, 'dragging' George behind him.

"I thought we were going to play football."

"We not got time now. We got to do planning."

"I'm sure we've still got time for some more football, Ollie."

"No." Oliver shook his head and kept on going.

"No?"

"No. I the best man."

"Oh, OK. I suppose that means you do know best."

"Yes, Dorge. So stop dawgling or we going to be late!"

"Oh, man," George muttered under his breath. Oliver dragged him all the way back to the house and flung open the door.

"Ellna, we got to do planning for the wedding right away," he said, casting his football aside and running straight up the stairs. Eleanor watched in bewilderment, as Oliver returned with his sketchpad and pencils and spread them out on the table. "You sit there," he said to George, indicating to the next chair along. George did as he was told.

"You want tea, or beer? Or something stronger?" Eleanor asked him.

"Err—" George waited for Oliver to slide the sketchpad in front of him. He handed him a green pencil.

"You do the writing," he said.

"Tea's fine," George said quickly. Eleanor nodded. She was behaving very oddly too.

"You do the date at the top, please," Oliver said. George started to write.

"You OK?" he called across to Eleanor.

"Yes," she said, then left the kitchen.

"You done it?" Oliver asked.

George nodded.

"OK. What we do next?"

"We stop panicking!"

"I not panicking, Dorge. I excited. What time you want to get married? You can write it down."

George wrote down 'one o'clock'. The pencil lead snapped. Oliver sighed and took it from him. He dug out his sharpener and twisted it around the end of the pencil.

"I can do it," he said. George watched him struggle on for a minute or so, then he sighed again and passed it over. The kettle came to the boil and Eleanor returned. She made the tea and put it on a mat across the other side of the table.

"Can I talk to you for a sec?" she asked.

344

George nodded. "Won't be long, Ollie."

Oliver glared at him. George followed Eleanor into the living room, where James was sitting, working on his laptop.

"I've got to be honest about this," she said, "but it's against my beliefs."

"What is?"

"Gay marriage."

"OK."

"I just needed to tell you. I love you both dearly, but I don't understand why you want to get married."

"Because we love each other?"

"Yes, but why do you need to get married?"

"I'm sure I just answered that." George frowned.

"Can't you just live together?"

"Why did you and James get married?"

"Because we wanted to start a family."

"So if we decided to adopt…"

"That's the thing, isn't it? You can't *naturally* start a family."

"I, err…" He didn't know what else to say.

"For the record, James doesn't agree with me," Eleanor said, folding her arms and glowering at her husband, then turning her attention back to George. "And I'm not going to stand in your way, but I needed to tell you. That's all, really." She left the room and went back to the kitchen. George looked at James and shrugged.

"I tried reasoning it through with her," James said. "She's quite adamant that the bible teaches that it is wrong, therefore it is wrong."

"But Buddhists are OK with it?"

"Buddhist teaching focuses solely on the quality of relationships, and tolerance and respect. Eleanor will not be persuaded, but as she says, she is not going to stand in your way."

"Yeah, I think I'll leave her to Josh to deal with."

James nodded. "A wise move."

George turned to leave, then turned back. "Just to forewarn you, I might've upset Ollie's mum by accident." James raised his eyebrows, part in query, part in surprise that George could be capable of upsetting anyone. "I told Ollie that feeding bread to ducks was bad."

"Ah," James said. "Yes that will indeed set the cat amongst the pigeons." He smiled at George. "Or, perhaps more aptly, the ducks. Do not worry, my friend. These things happen."

James seemed rather pleased that doubt had been cast on the parenting expertise of his ex-wife, but no more was said, so George returned to the kitchen, where Oliver had made significant progress during his absence, albeit in infant hieroglyphics.

"We going to need these things," he explained, pointing at the drawings. "These are wedding rings, and a car to go to the church, and a…"

"We're getting married in the register office, not the church."

Oliver continued undaunted. "And this is the flowers. You don't get bridesmaids, cos you both grooms. And you got to have a cake, and foods, and a party, and a honeymoon."

"I'm going dizzy just thinking about all these things, Ollie."

"It's OK, Dorge, I got it. You tell me what things you like and Ellna will help, won't you, Ellna?"

"Erm, well, I'll try, Oliver, but…"

"You got to go to work," Oliver sighed. "I know." He looked at George and frowned. "You ring Shaunna's mummy on your phone, please? I talk to her."

George had no idea what to do. He was stuck between Oliver's desperation to do this and the impracticality of him being able to do so, given that he wasn't even five yet. He took out his phone and brought up Adele's number, then passed it across to Oliver.

"Thanks." Oliver pressed the 'call' button without the need for instruction. He slid off his chair and walked towards the back door, the phone against his ear. George and Eleanor looked at each other, utterly baffled.

"Hello?" Oliver said, as he headed out into the garden. "Is that Shaunna's mummy? This is Oliver Brown. I got to talk to you about the wedding…"

BREAKSTUFF
Wednesday 3rd May

Josh stood in the centre of the empty living room, slowly rotating on the spot, observing the ghosts of the furniture in the wallpaper he had hung for his grandmother a year after he returned from university. He felt a great sense of accomplishment that the house was almost clear, but a greater sense of sadness that this, the place where he grew up, was to be theirs no more. So many tangible reminders of memories now departed in backs of vans, taken away to be given or sold to others. Still more were stashed within crates and boxes, hidden from sight until such time as he could stand to look on them again. This room was now devoid of all but the wallpaper; no point in staying, he moved on to his grandmother's bedroom.

The bed still remained, for it was brand new, and of an excellent make. She had slept on it for less than a month when the stroke felled her in the hallway—a moment tattooed into the carpet by the gush of blood from the gash on her shin as it collided with the aluminium door frame. The estate agent decreed that the carpets could stay. They would appoint a cleaner and no doubt add it to the bill later. And so: this bed. It was going to Eleanor's, to take up residence in one of the two guest rooms, to be enjoyed by countless Davenports for years to come, while his grandmother suffered a bed slept and urinated on by countless others, until such time as she recovered some mobility. Social workers. He never did get on with them especially well. But he was not going to allow himself to sink into this. He could feel it pulling at him, the darkness. He was avoiding his old room for that very reason. His phone vibrated and gave him some focus; a temporary distraction.

On our way now. Ellie x

Well, he thought, isn't that nice? Two days ago, she declares him a sinner, but she's prepared to accept his charity still.

Other than the bed, this room too was clear, which left only his room. He approached, put his hand around the doorknob and took a deep breath. He heard the front door open, held the breath a little longer.

"Hi."

Footsteps around the downstairs rooms, echoing in spite of the carpets.

"Where are you?"

"Up here." He let the rest of the breath go. George came up the stairs.

"You've done it all."

"Almost."

"Ah. The dreaded bedroom," George said with a grin.

"Glad you think it's funny."

"I don't. I'm trying to jolly you along. You been squeezed lately?" He was referring to the twenty-four hour blood pressure monitor that their practice nurse had attached to Josh's arm that morning, as a follow-up to the clear MRA scan, mainly to put his mind at ease. He'd been checking the readings—all normal so far—concluding that if he could get through today without them fluctuating, he could get through virtually anything.

George put his hand over Josh's and turned the handle. The door cracked open.

"Have you been in here at all since then?"

"No."

There was a knock at the front door.

"Ellie."

George closed the bedroom door again and went downstairs. Josh braced himself.

"Hey, George," Eleanor greeted him, stepping inside. Her father was right behind her.

"George," he acknowledged.

"How's things?" George asked. The usual round of pleasantries carried them up the stairs. Josh stepped aside, to allow Mr. Davenport access. He was experienced in these matters and they would take their directions from him.

"All right then. Josh and Ellie: if you can get that mattress down and stick it in the hall. George and I can bring the base, get it in the van first."

"OK," Josh said, but it isn't the easiest of things, to coordinate your efforts when you're not talking to each other, which is to say that they had not yet had words and had both realised that saying nothing was the easiest way to avoid doing so. However, it could not last forever. With much grunting and griping, they finally leaned the mattress against the wall downstairs, and went into the living room to keep out of the way, listening to Eleanor's dad and George communicating sensibly as they negotiated the corner at the top of the stairs and slowly manoeuvred the cumbersome but not especially heavy divan base downwards.

"George told me what you said," Josh mumbled quietly, believing that in so doing he could deliver his viewpoint without it escalating further. He felt the squeeze of the blood pressure cuff on his arm and ignored it.

"It's just how I feel," Eleanor said in a slightly louder voice, but still little more than a muttering really.

"Is it? Or is it what the Church tells you to feel?"

"It's what *I* believe."

"For what reason?"

"Marriage is about family."

"Where within the bible…"

"I'm not doing this, Joshua. Marriage is a sacred institution. The union of one man and one woman, for procreation. There is nothing wrong with gay relationships…"

"And yet that is the aspect of homosexuality that is clearly condemned by the bible."

"The act itself is the sin, but the Church is against unjust discrimination in all its forms."

"So your discrimination is just?"

"Marriage is one man and one woman. What you will have is not a marriage."

"Why? What makes it any less of a marriage than what you have?"

"We have Toby."

"And Shaunna and Kris? Was their marriage less of a marriage because Krissi was not the result of *their* union?"

"Of course not."

"And the straight couples who choose not to have children, or can't have children. What about them, Ellie? Their marriages are presumably worthless too?"

"They could still naturally reproduce, because they are male and female. You and George…" She stopped short of saying it: that it was an unnatural union.

"Marriage is about love and commitment. We've waited long enough to make that commitment, and you have been there all the way. Now you're telling me that you think this is wrong? I never had you down for a narrow-minded, unthinking fool, Ellie. You're so clever. How can you be so utterly bloody stupid about this?"

"That's what you think, is it? My beliefs are stupid?"

"No. I think you're stupid for not questioning the bullshit you've been fed all your life."

"Oh, so it's my parents as well?"

"Don't you dare! This is, once again, about *your* beliefs. Not your parents' and not the Church's either. It's your interpretation, because let's be honest, if we go down the route of 'the bible says this' or 'the bible says that', then the bible says that raping a woman is preferable to homosexuality. Is that what you think too?"

"I can't win, can I? If I say it's my beliefs, then you'll belittle them for being mine and mine alone. If I say they're based on the bible, then you'll claim I'm condoning rape!"

"Or you can stop being such a dogmatic bitch and think for yourself for once."

"You know what, Josh? You're right. If you're saying it's wrong to speak up for marriage, to stop it from being morally degraded by some nonsense plea for equality, when gay marriage is not and can not ever be equal to real marriage in God's eyes, then you're right. I'm an unthinking, dogma driven automaton." She moved away towards the door.

"And you would leave it like this?" Josh shouted after her.

"Oh, go to hell."

"When I do, you'll be right there beside me."

She slammed the front door.

Driven by an instinct from the past perhaps, though he'd never been prone to tantrums, Josh flew up the stairs and into his old bedroom, picked up the first heavy object he could lay his hands on—a book, naturally—and threw it hard at the wall, followed by another, and another, until every single book from the shelf was strewn, pages splayed, spines cracked, across the bed and the floor. Next went the piggy bank received on opening his first bank account, a piece of quartz from a primary school trip to Derbyshire caves, a ship in a bottle his dad had given him for his sixth birthday, a hand, staying his arm from behind.

"Stop it."

He fought for a few seconds, then relented. He collapsed. George held him close, waiting in silence for the rage to subside, to be replaced by tears, then silence once more. His next comment could well have been interpreted as an attempt to steer Josh away from the desecration of his friendship with Eleanor, but it was a truthful expression of George's unrelenting shock at the view that had met him when he came into the room; a room that Josh himself had not entered since he officially left home.

"It's like a time capsule," George said, as Josh moved away from him, trying not to see. He took the blood pressure monitor from his pocket and checked the last measurement: still normal, incredibly. George walked across to the bed and started picking up the pieces of glass from the bottle. He carefully lifted the ship, now fractured at its midpoint, and placed it on top of the smooth quilt.

"I wanted to start from scratch," Josh explained, acknowledging the things of his childhood, wondering how he might now find the will to part with them for real. "If I'd taken them with me, then I would have kept returning to them. I needed to move forward, but I couldn't throw them away, so I left everything as it was."

"Didn't your grandma try and get you to sort through it all?" The thin coating of dust indicated she'd continued to clean in here, right up until her stroke.

350

"She did at first, but she didn't need the room. I think she realised that it was a kind of safety net." Josh picked up a snow globe and shook it, momentarily mesmerised by the motion of the white specks swirling around the tiny bronze Eiffel Tower inside the sphere of glass.

"I'm going to get a dustpan," George said. He stopped by Josh on the way past and kissed him tenderly on the forehead. "Don't break anything else while I'm gone," he joked lightly. Josh tried to smile, but decided it was best if he stayed perfectly still and awaited George's return before he attempted to start sifting through his belongings. If he viewed it rationally, there wasn't that much stuff: the books, a few trinkets, some photo albums and a couple of ring binders of lecture notes from university. There was also his music collection, which he now possessed in digital form, and he felt confident that he could part company with their physical counterparts without causing himself too much distress. He heard George coming back up the stairs and walked around the bed to where his old stereo once stood. Other than his clothes and his 'survival kit', it was the only thing that he had taken with him.

"Do you know something?" Josh moved to allow George to pass and spoke whilst he cleaned. "Apart from my dad, my grandma and me, there's only one other person I've ever allowed in this room."

George finished brushing the glass into the dustpan and put it to one side.

"I couldn't stand it," Josh continued. "Everyone else seemed to have their friends around all the time, and I wondered how they coped with people in their private space. Pyjama parties? What the hell are they about?"

George smiled. "You've never been to a pyjama party?"

"Not unless sleeping rough at the ranch counts."

"Yeah, I suppose it kind of does."

"Have you?"

"It's more a girls' thing to do. Boys have 'sleepovers'. I stayed over at Kris's a few times, in the treehouse. And we nearly had one, didn't we?"

"But not in my room. We were going to camp out."

"Are you comfortable with me being in here now?"

Josh sighed.

"I mean, if you want me to go and wait downstairs while you sort things out, I'm OK with that."

"No." Josh sat on the bed and picked up one of the books, straightening the crumpled corner from where it had hit the wall. "I need you to be here." He was struggling to cope, with the room, and the house, and his grandmother's stroke, and Jess's illness. And Eleanor. George sat on the other side of the bed and leaned back so he could look at him.

351

"We're in your bedroom, and no-one's home," he said, his eyes twinkling with mischief. Josh managed to smile this time.

"No way, Morley. The bed's full of dust, and there's probably glass splinters everywhere."

"Shame." George stood up again. "Right. I'm gonna go and get a couple of boxes from the car. We can have this clear in an hour, take the bed to the recycling centre, be home for seven. What d'you say?"

"I say, yes, so long as we can get a takeaway on the way home, and also…"

George paused at the door.

"I love you," Josh finished.

"I'm sure a bit of dust won't hurt…"

"Boxes," Josh commanded. George huffed.

"Boxes," he said and went downstairs.

After that, they made short shift of clearing the room and arrived home a little before seven. George put the boxes up in the loft, whilst Josh fed the dog and emailed the estate agent to tell them the house was clear. By the time George returned to the lounge, their Indian takeaway was laid out on the table and a film was all ready to go.

"You OK?" he asked Josh as he sat down next to him.

"Yes. It's quite a relief, actually. Thank you."

"For what?"

"For being there, and for being here."

"Where else would I be?"

"You know what I mean." It was an indirect reference to Eleanor. George leaned forward and broke the edge off a poppadom, dipping it in the mango chutney.

"She'll come round," he said. Chutney was slowly descending from the poppadom and Josh put his head on George's lap, intercepting the drip with his mouth.

"Right now, I don't care one way or the other. We're getting married and there's nothing she can say to change that."

"I'm very glad to hear it. On that note, are we gonna get wedding rings?"

"I don't know. I'd never worn a ring before this one, and I can't see me wearing two."

"My dad gave me a ring."

"Did he?"

"Yeah. It was a gold signet ring with a tiny diamond chip in it, not that I ever wore it. When he left, I told Mum she could sell it to help out with money."

"Did she swear?"

George laughed. "I can't remember. Probably. It wasn't worth selling, so she told me to keep it and put it away somewhere, because one day I wouldn't hate him so much. She was wrong." George shook off the feeling. "Anyway, what I was going to say was we could just exchange our engagement rings again."

Josh nodded. "I think that's perfect."

"Cool." George shuffled forward as far as he could and Josh moved to get up. "No, don't," he said. "I can reach." He stretched and grabbed the rest of the poppadom. Josh passed him the pot of mango chutney and they somehow shared it between them without moving. "What are we going to do about our names?"

"Morley-Sandison?" Josh suggested.

"Or Sandison-Morley? That's better, but it's one hell of a long name."

"Josh Sandison-Morley," Josh recited. "Josh Morley-Sandison. Or we could just stick with our own names?"

"Yeah. Let's go with that."

Josh reached across and picked up the other poppadom. "We also need to decide on vows."

"They have standard ones, don't they?"

"Yes, but there's so much more I want to say."

"So say it."

"That's not what I mean. I denied how I felt about you for so long. Now I want to tell the world."

"Do I get a choice in this?"

"Of course you do!" Josh sat up, causing a landslide of crumbs to tumble to the floor.

"It's just—well, what if you say something that, um…" George stuttered to a stop and held his finger up so that Josh would give him the chance to finish. "Why is it, when I try…" He sighed. "The words are here!" He pointed at his head, frustrated.

Josh took his hand and squeezed it in reassurance. "You could try writing them down, then you can read them—like a script. In fact, I've just had a thought."

He left the room and returned a moment later with his tablet. "We can have prompts." He opened the browser and showed George a website he'd been looking at for inspiration; it suggested starting with the same lines and writing individual vows based on these.

"This way we both have some idea of what to expect, but can still surprise each other."

"That could work." George pondered for a moment. "Yeah, OK."

"Yes?" Josh said. "Really?"

"Yes, really. But can we eat now, please?"

Josh began speaking as if making a public address: "What I love most about George is his blatant oral fixation. He is *obsessed* with food!" The blood pressure cuff started to tighten around his arm.

"Hey, you suggested the takeaway!"

"And if I hadn't?"

"Um, well—OK. Am I obsessed with food?"

"No. You do lots of physical labour, therefore you need lots of calories." Josh put his hand under George's t-shirt, running his palm over the firm, lean, muscles. "And as Sophie's birth partner, I suppose technically you're eating for two," he said, bending to kiss his belly. It rumbled in response. "I may have to collect further evidence, after we've eaten."

"Uh huh? And what I love most about Josh is *his* blatant oral fixation..." A kiss on the lips stopped him this time. The blood pressure cuff released its grip.

"Guilty as charged," Josh murmured, then moved away to check the readings. He laughed in disbelief. "I don't know. I have a screaming row with Ellie and it stays exactly as it is, yet you can get a rise out of me." George glanced at the display.

"Snap," he said.

"Are we talking about blood pressure?"

George grinned. "That too."

FIXING A HOLE
Thursday 4ᵗʰ–Sunday 7ᵗʰ May

Once the chemotherapy drugs left Jess's system, and with the pain and bleeding under control, she felt better than she had since Christmas. Thus, by the time it came around to her mum's next stay, they had talked it through, and decided that it made more sense for Andy to move back in permanently, rather than pack up and return to his mum's for four nights a week and risk further trouble with Michael. Steph was more than happy with this arrangement, because she was struggling to sleep at all, so the three of them agreed that she would continue to come during the day, freeing Andy to get on with some work, go to the gym, or just go and be somewhere else, and then she'd go home at night.

Over the weekend, Andy was trying to keep out of the way as much as possible, to give Steph and Jess time together. Saturday morning, he took little Shaunna to the park, then went to his mother's for a swim. She and Len were away until Sunday evening, and Michael was doing his usual trick of staying in bed all day, the sound of his TV audible in the atrium downstairs. At the first sign of movement, Andy got his stuff together and left, walking back into the town to eek out his time away, his mind wandering ahead of him, imagining every terrible outcome to this living nightmare. He was paying little attention to where he was going, for he had jogged and drunkenly traipsed these streets forever. He stopped to check his phone: still only three in the afternoon, and he was hungry; no surprise therefore, that his subconscious had deposited him outside The Pizza Place.

"Hey, Andy," Krissi greeted him. "You OK?"

"Not bad, thanks. You?"

"Yeah. I'm good. What can I get you?"

"Pizza, and lots of it."

Krissi laughed. "OK. Takeaway?"

"Nah. I'm gonna sit in. Jess's mum's at hers for the weekend and I'm trying to give them some space."

Krissi found him a table and left him with the menu. "Give me a shout when you've decided what you want," she told him.

"OK. Cheers." He sat down and opened the menu, but he wasn't reading it. He wasn't thinking about anything. He was just in a kind of daze. At least when he was with Jess, it gave him something to do, a way of occupying his mind. Without that, his brain seemed to have ceased functioning.

"Decided yet?" Krissi asked.

"Huh? Oh. No. Not yet."

"Tell you what," she suggested. "I'll choose for you."

He nodded. "Yeah. OK."

She took the menu from him and went through to the kitchen, where she told Wotto to make one of his extra-large house specials with extra toppings, stuffed crust—the works.

"Got a special visitor, have we?" Wotto asked.

"Yeah. Very special," she said. She returned to the front counter, watching Andy, in between seating customers and processing payments. He didn't even notice. He looked so desperately sad that she had an almost uncontrollable urge to hug him, but it would be weird. Yes, he was her biological father, but he wasn't her 'dad'. He was Andy—her parents' wayward mate, as she'd told him at the time, although he wasn't acting very wayward just at this moment, and it was hurting her to see him, sitting so quiet and still, in a world entirely of his own. Wotto sent through that his pizza was ready, and she went to collect it from the kitchen.

"Thanks," she said, picking up the enormous pizza tray. Wotto put his hand on her arm.

"Look, boss. It ain't my place to say, but you gotta do what feels right, you know what I mean?"

She continued to look at the pizza in her hands for a moment, then met Wotto's gaze. "Yes. Thanks." He gave her his best beaming smile and she somehow smiled back.

"There you go." She put the pizza down in front of Andy.

"Whoa! Just as well I'm hungry!" he said, his eyes growing wide and round at the sight before him. She sat opposite.

"What you up to tomorrow?" she asked. He shrugged.

"Dunno. Haven't thought that far ahead."

"Yeah. I suppose that was a silly question, really. When have you ever thought that far ahead?"

Andy looked up, about to protest, and she winked at him. He pulled a slice of pizza free. "You want to share?" She accepted and took a slice from her side.

"So I was thinking," she said. She took a bite of the pizza and immediately started fanning her mouth with her hand. He was doing exactly the same.

"Hot," he said.

"Very," she agreed and tried to carry on, regardless: "Tomorrow, how about you and me get on a train and head on out to the theme park?"

He swallowed hard and looked around for a drink, but he hadn't ordered one. Krissi went to pour a couple of Cokes. She brought them back and he glugged thirstily, then sat, attentive, waiting for more.

"That's all," she said. "You're the only person I know who loves them as much as I do. I've been working too hard. You've been working too hard. We should do it."

"I've not been working that hard."

"Err, I think you'll find you have! Don't forget, what you're doing for Jess, Mum did for my grandma when I was younger. She was totally exhausted."

"Look, Krissi, I…"

"No. You look. You've spent the past two and a half years doing everything you can to try and fix your mistakes, and I kind of understand why you think you need to, but I kind of resent it too. Before that, Mum did it. Sooner or later, you both need to realise that I'm not your mistake. I wasn't planned. So what? Lots of kids aren't planned. But how many of them get to be brought up by nine parents?"

Andy sat back and examined her face. She was being completely sincere.

"Eat!" she ordered. He gave her a playful salute and picked up another piece of pizza.

"This is good pie," he said.

"Pie?" she queried. He gave her a big, cheesy grin. She rolled her eyes and got up, ready to return to work.

"I'll come back when you're finished eating to sort out train times and stuff."

"I didn't say yes," Andy argued. She held up her hand.

"I'm not *asking* you," she said. He watched her, as she greeted the family who had just arrived and found them a table, then turned and glared at him—just like her mother. He quickly got on with eating the rest of his pizza. When she came back she patted him on the head.

"Good boy. Well done." She picked up the empty pizza tray and started to walk away. "Nine-thirty at the station," she called over her shoulder. "Don't be late." She disappeared through the kitchen door, leaving him no opportunity to protest further. He smiled to himself, left what he hoped was enough money for his pizza, and went home.

***

"That is one awesome coaster," Andy said, as they staggered away from their third ride of The Tartarus. "What next?"

"Burgers?" Krissi suggested. Andy nodded and they headed for the closest fast food franchise. It was a gorgeous day, with just the perfect amount of sun for wandering around in the open air, and they sat at a picnic table with their burgers and milkshakes.

"Last time I came here was for my twenty-first," Krissi said.

"Last time I came here was…" Andy thought for a moment and shrugged. "I don't know. Longer ago than that. The Tartarus wasn't here, I know that much. And Space Station Theta had only just been built."

"We should go on that next," Krissi enthused. "It's a classic ride."

"A classic! Now I feel old."

"Nah. You're not old."

"Forty next month. That's old!"

"You've always seemed younger than the others, like my older brother. Same with George."

"Yeah, I can see what you mean."

"And Adele's always been like one of those funny pretend-posh aunties who leave lipstick on your cheek every time they visit."

Andy laughed.

"Whereas Jess always felt like a real aunty, you know? Like she was Mum's older sister."

"Not sure if she'd like that much, though I always thought Josh and Ellie acted a lot older than the rest of us."

"Yeah," Krissi agreed. "Ellie still does. Josh has totally changed."

"D'you think so? He seems the same as ever to me."

"He's more fun than he used to be."

"And Dan?"

"He's like the distant father. He thinks he's in charge of us all, but clearly he's not."

"No. Your mother is."

"Yep. You'd better believe it." Krissi became quiet and thoughtful for a moment and then smiled to herself. "Then there's Kris."

"He *is* your dad," Andy said. Krissi nodded.

"Yeah. He is. So anyway, are we gonna do this Space Station thing?"

"Yeah, why not?" Andy slurped the last of his milkshake. "After all, it's a classic."

Krissi grinned and linked arms with him as they took off across the theme park together. Whilst they queued for the ride, she asked him about his mum and Len, whom she had seen in passing at Dan and Adele's engagement party, but not spoken to. Andy came clean and explained that he'd only told his mum about her on that day, so she had been waiting for a formal introduction, and until such time as it was granted, refused to take action herself. The queue had moved on quickly, and they put this conversation on pause to take their seat in the carriage, which was like a waltzer, but on a track running around the dark enclosure, luminous planets and projections of galaxies and stars swirling and spinning around them. Every so often, the track would drop steeply downwards, and the carriage would tilt and spin as they rounded a corner, both of them swaying together to one side or the other in order to spin faster. For all that it was a 'classic' ride, in that it didn't scare the living daylights out of its passengers, it was a fun ride too, and they were both giggling and dizzy when they emerged, blinking, into the daylight once more.

"Now what?" Krissi asked.

"Ice-cream," Andy said. Without thinking, he grabbed her by the hand and pulled her through the crowd towards an ice-cream kiosk. Only when they stopped did he realise what he'd done.

"Sorry," he said, releasing her hand as if it had suddenly become too hot to touch. She shrugged.

"What ice-cream you getting?" she asked.

"Dunno. I'm thinking…" He glanced at the vast array of flavours available. Krissi stood next to him, also trying to decide.

"PBJ!" they both said at the same time.

"Ha ha! The Jeffries genes strike again," Krissi laughed.

"That's a crazy ice-cream flavour."

"Yeah, and I reckon if we got Dan and Shaunna here, they'd both choose it too. In fact—" Krissi took out her phone, took a photo of the ice-cream display and posted it online, with an instruction to Dan. She and Andy made their purchases and wandered off across the theme park, eating their ice-creams and chatting about the day so far, which was sadly nearing the end. Some of the rides were already starting to close up, and the shutters were down on the burger place they had stopped at earlier. Krissi's phone bleeped and she took it out. She grinned and held it out to Andy.

"Insane!" he said, shaking his head and laughing. Both Dan and little Shaunna had chosen the PBJ ice-cream, although his niece's choice was based on the cartoon parrots on the carton, rather than the flavour itself, and in any case she was too young to eat peanuts.

"One last ride?" Krissi said as they neared The Tartarus, which had a sign up stating the same.

"Yeah. Let's do it!"

When they finally reached the end of the double ride that they'd been given, Andy gave Krissi a hug, and this time didn't follow it up with an apology.

"Thanks," he said. "This has been one of the best days of my life. In fact, it might even have been THE best day."

"Really? Wow! After all the amazing things you've done?"

"Yep. After all the amazing things I've done."

"Cool. Now I feel super-important."

"And so you should," Andy told her. "Which reminds me. Weren't you supposed to be getting a promotion?"

"Err, yeah. I was."

"What happened?"

"Wotto happened." She blushed. "There's nothing going on, but…"

Andy nodded. "I get you."

"It's between you and me, that one."

"No worries," he assured her.

They left the theme park and took the short walk back to the train station, both flopping into their seats, exhausted, but still buzzing with the adrenaline of a day's frivolity and junk food. The train moved away from the platform and Krissi turned to look out of the window.

"So," she said. "I'm thinking before we go home, we go visit the grandmother I don't yet know."

Andy watched her and waited, but as always there was no more.

"OK," he said. "I'll just text to check they're back." He did that and received a reply a moment later to confirm that they were. He took a deep breath and exhaled slowly.

"You worried about it?" Krissi asked.

"Yeah. Crapping myself." He tried to make it sound jokey, because he was feeling quite nervous, but also excited. When he'd told his mother last October, it hadn't been well received; however, so much had changed since then that he knew it was going to be all right. For the first time in his life, he was proud to be a dad. He was proud of Krissi; so proud, in fact, that the words passed through his lips as he thought them. She smiled.

"Thanks," she said. "That means a lot."

They continued the rest of the journey in silence, neither speaking until they were standing inside the atrium, with Andy listening in an attempt to locate where in the significant house he might find his mother.

"The conservatory," he said, stepping off and indicating that Krissi follow, down the corridor, past the kitchen and through to the vast glasshouse, where his mother and Len were laid out on loungers, both of them armed with large tumblers of whisky on the rocks. As soon as Len saw them approaching, he made his excuses and left. Andy's mum got up and gave Krissi a brief, friendly hug, then stepped back so that she could look at her properly.

"Good God!" she said, glancing from her grown-up granddaughter to her son and back again. She couldn't believe that people hadn't realised earlier that this young woman was Andy's daughter. Admittedly, on an average day, when Krissi was in her formal work attire, with her hair tied back, she didn't look quite so much like him, but with her hair down and the pair of them looking a little windswept and tanned from their day in the sun, there was no mistaking the genetic association. A couple of minutes forward, Andy's mother was still staring at her. Krissi just smiled.

"Mum!" Andy appealed. She shook herself out of it.

"Sorry," she said, "but, well. You can work it out for yourself. It's lovely to meet you properly, at last. Would you like a drink?"

"I'd love one, thanks."

Her grandmother beckoned her over to the lounger next to her. "Andrew, go and get drinks for Krissi and yourself. In fact—" She finished the rest of her whisky and gave him the glass.

"What d'you want, Krissi?" he asked.

"Just a Coke?"

He nodded and went to the bar, of which there were two, the closest being just the other side of the door to the conservatory.

"So, Krissi, I don't want to put you on the spot, but I'd love to know more about you."

"Erm, well, I…" Krissi frowned. "What do I call you?"

"Barbara is fine, lovey."

"OK. Barbara. I work for a pizza restaurant—The Pizza Place. I've been there for nearly two years now. And I've got a flat just outside the town centre, which I share with my friend, Jason."

"Andrew tells me you're twenty-three."

"Yes. That's right."

Andy returned, having heard all of what had been said so far. "She doesn't just 'work for' The Pizza Place. She manages a restaurant."

"Golly!" his mum said. "That's quite an achievement." She stopped short of making a comparison to Andy's lack of success, which she'd have done in the past, but at the moment she had the utmost respect for what her middle son was doing. He'd turned out well in the end, even if this beautiful young woman was evidence that he hadn't always made the best choice. But that was by the by. "And how's your mum doing these days? Is she well?"

"Very."

"Is she still a hairdresser."

"At the moment, but she's talking about going back to college in September."

"Is she?" Andy asked.

"Yeah. Don't know what she'll be studying, though."

Andy sipped at his bottle of Coke—a traditional-style glass bottle—quietly pondering this news.

"I love the pool," Krissi said, taking the moment to look around her. "That must be so brilliant to have."

"It is," Barbara confirmed. "It was part of the reason we bought this place, although it was in a bit of a state when we got it, but it's getting there, slowly."

The sound of someone talking loudly inside the house now floated out to them. Andy closed his eyes and took a deep breath.

"No trouble," his mother warned. Andy nodded to confirm that he would be on his best behaviour.

"Mum?" Michael shouted as he came into view. "Where've you put my keys?"

"I haven't put them anywhere."

"Well, I left them on the table and they're gone, so someone must've moved them."

"Try looking under all your other junk, Michael."

"For fuck's sake." He stormed off, not a word to anyone else. Krissi looked at Andy and he raised an eyebrow.

"That's Mike, by the way," he said. She laughed. A minute later Michael walked back out, his keys in his hand, picked up his phone from the glass table next to them, and left again.

"Sorry, Mum," his mother shouted after him. No response. "You know what this is about, don't you?" she asked Andy, then went on to tell him. "This is because Leonard's given him his marching orders. He hasn't paid a tap while he's been here, and refuses to help out. The final straw was when he started that fight with you and your brother. And the language that comes out of his mouth is appalling. I don't know where he gets it from."

"I do," Andy said under his breath.

"Yes, all right, Andrew." Their mother's second husband, to whom they referred as 'Dad the Second', swore all the time and was around for most of their adolescence. "So," she concluded, "Leonard decided enough was enough."

"Good for Len."

"He's going this week."

"He says."

"Oh, he's going. I'm sick to the back teeth of listening to him moaning on about how bloody awful..." She stopped and patted Andy on the arm. "Anyway, you know what he's like."

"Yeah. And it'll be awesome to have the house back to yourselves."

"True, although you weren't so bad to have around really." She smoothed his cheek with her palm and he smiled.

"Well, I guess we'd best get going, or Steph will wonder where I've got to." He stood and gave his mum a hug. "Thanks for the drinks, and stuff."

"Thank you for bringing Krissi to visit." His mum got up to see them out, and hugged Krissi again, but this time it was a family hug. "It's really lovely to meet you. You must come back soon. Bring your swimming costume and use the pool, whenever you like. Once we've got rid of Michael, we're going to fit a gym as well."

"Cool," Krissi said.

"Super-cool!" Andy said. "You kept that quiet, Mum."

"Yes, well, we don't want to give him any reason to stay, now, do we?" They wandered back through to the atrium and stopped to exchange hugs one more time.

"Thanks for the drink, Barbara. It's been great chatting to you. I'll definitely visit again," Krissi said, then followed Andy outside.

"Hang on," Len called. He threw a set of keys to Andy. "I'll send one of the lads to pick it up tomorrow."

"Cheers, Len. Which one is—" Andy looked at the keys and a huge grin spread across his face. "Are you sure?"

"Yeah. See you later."

"Thanks." Andy tossed the keys into the air and caught them with his other hand. He and Krissi waved back at his mum and Len and walked across to the garage; it was quite a trek, given the size of the house and the deep gravel they had to trudge through to get there. Andy pressed the button and the garage door slowly rose, revealing the shiny black Ferrari inside.

"Oh my God. No way!" Krissi started bouncing up and down.

"Yes way," Andy said. She tutted. "Too old school?" he asked.

"Yeah," she laughed as she climbed in the car beside him. "But who doesn't love a classic?"

MADNESS
Monday 8th–Saturday 13th May

Monday: back to normality, and over the days that followed, the new routine quickly took shape. Jess would get up and eat breakfast, returning to bed after a couple of hours, where she'd stay until around lunchtime, get up again, sit downstairs or out in the garden for a while, have a lie down late afternoon, then sit and watch TV for the early part of the evening. Andy worked around her, stopping to make lunch, or watch TV with her, or to make drinks for visitors. The nurses came and went. The hours did the same. Still the events of the past two and a half years hung over them, ignored, pushed to the back of conscious thought, deemed too destructive and impossible to resolve. But at some point they were going to have to deal with them; the following Saturday it looked like that time had finally come.

Steph had gone home a couple of hours earlier, and Andy had been watching football on the TV in the lounge, or rather, the TV was tuned to a sports channel that was showing a football match, and he could probably, at a push, have given a report on the score—no, he couldn't, but he might have been able to guess with some accuracy at which two teams were playing—but his mind was nowhere. He was trapped in limbo, the emotions swirling around his head in a massive, explosive broth of frustration, sorrow, regret, desire; he couldn't even comprehend what this was. It was some kind of madness, of that he was sure, because in all of his life he'd never felt like this. When Kris stabbed Dan, he'd felt anger, guilt, vengefulness, one emotion tumbling after the other, but not all at once. When he'd faced Shaunna, again he'd been angry, with himself, yet there was a sense that he could somehow undo the damage. Even with Jess and Rob, there was sadness, loss, and yes, more anger; minor grazes compared to this. His entire existence, following his instincts, doing whatever the moment dictated, had been lived by letting those emotions wash over him and then watching them leave. He didn't experience remorse. He didn't get confused. He just rode the wave and paddled on. But this was beyond his control. He couldn't get a hold of any of it; nor could he let it go.

Upstairs, Jess was sleeping. She'd had a restless night, been in too much pain to properly settle, and now, in the early evening, with the sun at its brightest so far this year, she was in a deep, deep sleep, unaware of the turmoil that was sending Andy into a crazed frenzy in the room below. He got up, went out into the garden and perched on the edge of the patio table, trying to home in on something he could make sense of. He was here, with Jess, before it was over. It had been over since last September. That much he understood. Yet, he was here again now, for her, and he didn't begrudge her that. He'd already seen the end, lived through the end, come out the other side, because it hadn't been that awful. Of course, this trial that he faced—that they all faced—was going to be beyond horrendous. The next few months would take every ounce of strength they had, and for what? All those years they had stayed together as friends. All of them. Through relationship break-ups, lies, secrets, moving away, coming back together. The nine of them: The Circle. What a pointless, shitty name that was. A circle could expand and contract, but it was always whole; eternal.

And then it came to him. All of a sudden; a bright dawning light of realisation. He was lonely. He needed somebody. Something. He didn't want to be here, going through this pretence of loving someone, even though he knew that this was what he had to do. It didn't matter how often they had fought. It was useless to get worked up over her betrayal of their friendship for a quick and meaningless fling. He didn't need to love her. He just needed to make sure that she felt loved, to stay afloat until the sun faded, for her. But to do this, to somehow find the strength to see it through, before this madness sucked him under then left him washed up on a desolate beach somewhere, he needed to love for real, and to be loved.

He took out his phone and scrolled through his contacts. Should he call, offer the truth, beg to be heard? Beg to *be loved*? Or should he stay silent, hope that this moment would pass and all would be as it was once more? Bullshit. It would never be the same again. He pulled up a number and hit 'call'.

"Josh? Dude, I really need to talk to someone. I'm going out of my mind. Can I make an appointment to come and see you?"

"Yes, sure. Actually we were just on our way round for a visit, so we can sort it out while we're there."

"It's not that urgent, mate."

"Really?"

Silence.

"We'll see you soon."

The line went dead. Andy's knees gave way.

***

They sat in the car outside, watching for a sign of life within. Josh didn't want to ring the bell and disturb Jess, for he was quite certain that Andy would have called without her knowing. After five minutes spent observing the still, quiet house, they got out and peered through the front window. The TV was showing football highlights, interspersed with the rambling wisdom of aged pundits, smarming and smirking, as if they could still swagger onto the pitch and win the match in the final seconds. But there was no sign of Andy. They walked around to the side gate and George peered over the top. He nodded and lifted the lever. The gate resisted. He reached over and pulled the bolt clear. The gate swung open. They stepped inside, spotted Andy, sitting with his back against the wall, his head in his hands, his knees bent up. George stepped over his feet and went inside to take up the vigil. Josh knelt before Andy and waited.

Thirty minutes, thirty-one, thirty-two; the kitchen wall clock was visible through the open door, its electronic, battery-powered slow click-click a flatulent, dull pulse fizzling away almost before it reached them. Still Josh waited.

Forty-three minutes: Andy lifted a hand away from his face, lifted his head from his knees, raised his eyes to the skies and sighed, the whole of his being trying to escape in that breath, to fly away free with the circling gulls high, high up above.

"I was thinking before," he said, "when I was watching the football. One time we were playing a cup match and I got badly fouled in the area. I took the penalty and played nearly the entire second half with a torn hamstring."

"Impressive," Josh remarked.

"Yeah." Andy slowly closed his eyes and opened them again, making eye contact. "And I got to thinking *why*. Why can't I do the same thing with all this crap in my head? Block out the pain, like I did with the hamstring?"

"You can, up to a point."

"But I can't. I've tried and it just won't fucking go away." He ran his hand over his hair and tugged at his crown, as if to prove that there was no escape hatch.

"After the game, what happened to your hamstring?"

Andy didn't answer.

"I don't know much about sports injuries, but I'm guessing it took a lot longer to heal than if you'd stopped playing when you got injured."

Still nothing.

"OK. What I can give you is this."

Andy blinked; catatonic attentiveness.

"Control. But you have to be willing to work with me."

"Can't you just make it go away?"

"For now. And when it comes back, it might break you."

"Do it."

Josh shook his head. "Believe me when I tell you that this is not what you need. Look, I'm no expert. But I know someone who is. My colleague, Sean:

he works at the hospice. He uses lots of different techniques to help people cope with extreme emotional distress, but they don't work by blocking it out. He helps you to think about things differently." He watched Andy as he spoke. "It's about getting control, not hiding from it." He was falling apart.

"I can't do this," he said. "I can't do…" His feet, in spite of the non-slip soles of his baseball boots, slipped away. His soul collapsed.

"I can ring Sean now. He'll be at home." No response. Josh laid his hand on Andy's arm. Andy grabbed onto it and held on, a singular thread of sanity binding them together. "OK," Josh said. He slowly pulled away and took out his phone. It was ringing as he made his way back out onto the street, but Andy called him back. Sean had answered immediately. "Can you hold on a sec?" Josh asked.

"Sure," Sean said.

Andy looked up into Josh's eyes, pleading, desperate. "I don't want to talk to anyone else. Please? You can help me."

Josh sighed and nodded. "OK. But I'm going to get some advice first."

He continued on his way and explained to Sean what was going on: that Andy was after suppression. Did he think it would work? Sean was reluctant to say yes—understandably—because he didn't consider his achievements a success. Was he aware of the dangers? Was he truly aware? A few months, Josh reasoned, nowhere near as damaging as decades, and it did work. It was a success. Wasn't he still here, now? Sean partly conceded, but remained resolute; it was friendship that counted; friendship, and accepting that some things we can not change. The victorious supporters cheered in the background. Josh hung up.

"Three two on penalties," George reported back to Andy. "Your boys held out well."

"Didn't know they were playing," he replied, for the sake of politeness. He was lost.

"We're going out for a while," Josh explained. George nodded and watched them leave, then quietly closed the front door behind them.

"Andy?"

George turned back, startled by the white-robed wraith gliding towards him.

"He's popped out." He recovered quickly. "I'm afraid you're stuck with me." He smiled.

"I just came to get a drink," Jess explained, "and to tell him to turn that bloody telly down."

"Ah, well. It's over now." He switched off the TV.

"Who won?"

"No-one."

ACHIEVEMENT, UNLOCKED
Tuesday 16ᵗʰ May

It was the final week of study for the first batch of counselling diploma students, and if Sean and Josh were completely honest, they were a little bit sad it was almost over. Sean had delivered his last session yesterday; today it was Josh's turn: two hours of wrapping up, submitting logbooks and selecting a sample of folders for moderation purposes, then an afternoon in the Students' Union bar. George was going to join them later, he said, and he was really excited to see his ex fellow students all successfully passing their course. He had no regrets for dropping out; his only worries about doing so had revolved around losing contact with Sophie, but that wasn't going to happen for at least another three months, or ever.

Josh was logged into the university network, whiteboard loaded with his very brief and showy presentation, if for no other reason than to prove that he could do it if he wanted to. Five to eleven: Sophie walked in and smiled.

"Morning," he greeted her in his academic persona.

"Good morning, Josh," she said, edging along the front row of seats. This was the smaller of the two lecture theatres and a good size for their class, which had only nineteen students, leaving them plenty of space to spread out. Sophie was also glad to have moved from the seminar room where their sessions had been during the first year, as there was no way she could have fitted a six month pregnancy bump in behind the attached desk. She'd had enough problem when she was pre-pregnancy size and couldn't imagine ever being that slim again.

Dead on eleven o'clock, the first glut of students arrived, mumbling greetings at Josh as they climbed the slight rake and took seats nearer the back of the room. He watched them, with arms folded, fascinated; they were all the same.

The final cohort typically arrived about five minutes later, one of them coming over and placing a takeaway cup on the desk next to Josh. The student nodded an acknowledgement and Josh smiled at him.

"No sugar?" he asked.

"No sugar," the student confirmed.

"Cheers." Josh remained seated, sipping at his coffee, waiting for them all to settle into their seats. As the last of them opened their files, without moving from his chair, Josh picked up the remote control and dimmed the lights. The whiteboard display faded to black and for a moment they were in total darkness. The sound of a clock's ticking steadily filled the room, followed by the gradual appearance of a digital countdown on the whiteboard: large, stark white numbers, 1:53:50, followed by a blur as the hundredths of seconds whizzed by. The ticking was now joined by a steady heartbeat, so loud and bassy that it resonated through the body of each and every student.

Josh got up and moved around to the front of the desk, perching on the edge as he spoke, slowly and deliberately.

"In less than two hours, you will leave this room as a fully qualified counsellor. You will be responsible for the wellbeing of other people. Vulnerable people, who will place their lives in your hands."

The door to the lecture theatre opened a few inches; Sean squeezed through the gap and leaned against the wall. Josh continued.

"They will seek your wisdom and objectivity. You will be deemed omniscient, messianic even. They will come before you, believing you hold some great truth about the human condition—their condition."

As he spoke, the screen changed, the countdown clock now in the bottom right, whilst the faces of the founding fathers of modern psychotherapy cross-faded one into the next—Van Eeden, Freud, Adler, Jung, Erikson, Maslow, Rogers, Ellis, Beck, and others—tracing a path through the decades.

"As we have looked to the great scholars of our science over the past two years, willing them to bestow on us their wisdom, so too will your clients look to you. They will expect the impossible."

The faces faded away now, replaced by blurred artistic impressions of war, death, famine, celebration, victory, love, and still that heartbeat persisted, a barely detectable increase in tempo making the students feel uneasy, though most could not fathom why.

"Your greatest disservice to the people who rely and depend on you would not be to offer them the impossible…" Josh paused in his narration as the heartbeat began to slow, the countdown now returning to its previous central position, looming vast and painfully bright over the blackness. Josh waited for the heartbeat to stop before he spoke again. "But to believe that you can."

He turned on the lights, the white on black of the on-screen countdown now in negative. The students blinked and squinted against the sudden brightness. Josh over-rode the impulse to do likewise and continued his delivery.

"Of course, it is not quite so immediate as I have indicated this morning. In a few moments we'll go through the process of applying for accreditation, but it is precisely as I suggest: a process. A mere formality. You have accrued a wealth of knowledge and experience. Indeed, many of you already accept payment to undertake the duties for which you will duly receive certification. And you can rest assured that Doctor Tierney and I do not grant your qualification lightly.

"At times you may have found us to be objectionable, offhand, impatient, arrogant. We do this to bring out the best in you, and you have risen to that challenge. You have, without exception, excelled in the work you have produced, the experiences you have documented. However, do not believe for one second that the arrogance and conceit we have enacted before you grants us the right to abuse our position of power and authority. For the greatest powers we possess are compassion, empathy and humility."

Now the clock faded from view, replaced by a page from a dated university prospectus. Mostly it contained blocks of text, under various subheadings, arranged around photos of an unknown institution and its students. Josh clicked the remote control and the projection zoomed in to the photo at the centre-right of the page; it was of a research lab filled with undergraduates, too small for them to be recognisable, all facing the psychologist standing before them. The image zoomed in further. It was heavily pixellated, and Josh used the laser pointer to pick out two of the students at the back of the group. He shone the red light on the dark-haired figure to the left. Sean squinted and attempted to focus, then laughed quietly. The students murmured. Josh then indicated to the blonde-haired figure on the right, although everyone had already realised it was him.

"No letters after our names, nor titles before them; no strings of publications, proven track records, commendations. Just two undergraduates amongst many tens, hundreds, thousands, tens of thousands. We were then, as we are now: nothing special."

Josh blanked the screen and stayed quiet for a moment or so, to allow all that he had said to filter through.

"The rest of what we need to do today is procedural. Ticking boxes, completing forms, signing off, selecting samples. Get used to it." He stepped away from the desk, towards the raked seating. The students followed his every move. He paused again. "OK. Logbooks first, I say. Get the really tedious bit over and done with. The sooner we get to the bar, the better." He released them from his formal presence. Some sighed audibly. Sean casually strolled across with his hands in his pockets, although his expression gave away how impressed he was by what he had just seen. Josh *was* something special. That's why he'd asked—nay, begged and blackmailed him to come and teach the course.

"I'll start at the back," he offered.

"Great," Josh said. They'd be done much sooner if they did it together and he loathed checking their logbooks, but the students needed the evidence for their accreditation and it had to be right. Being the perfectionist that he was, Josh had essentially taken responsibility of them for the second year of the course, thus they were all well and truly up-to-date; similarly, both he and Sean were confident in their random selection of folders for moderation, although other course leaders may have been tempted to cheat and select the two they knew would be best.

As Josh and Sean made their way up and down the room respectively, they noticed a small group of students midway who were huddled together, far more interested in a magazine than their current task. Josh shot them a warning glance, but didn't investigate further. If he got to them first, then he might try and find out what it was that had them so unusually distracted. As it was, Sean got there before he did and even though the magazine had been quickly hidden away, he was much nosier, so just asked outright.

"Erm, well," the female owner of the magazine mumbled nervously, "I bought this on the way here, and…" She took it out of her bag and passed it to Sean. It was bent open at a full two-page photo spread, bearing the headline, "*Shadows* Star's Secret Wife". It took Sean a few seconds to examine the pages and a few more before it dawned on him what he was looking at.

"The husband-ex-husband!" he said, exhaling sharply and shaking his head in disdain. "Those bastards are a rash on the arse-cheek of humanity."

Josh frowned. Granted, Sean tended to be a little more laidback with the students than he was himself, but even so, with his professional switch engaged, this exclamation was uncharacteristically coarse. Sean looked up from the magazine pages and across to Josh, then moved towards the door, taking the magazine with him and jerking his head to indicate that Josh follow.

"What's up?" he asked, stepping onto the draughty corridor outside. Sean waited for the door to close and passed him the magazine. He looked over the images, read the headline, then looked over the images again, this time stopping to examine each one in detail, squinting to read the 'witty' captions.

Photo #1: DI Lundberg proves he's got the moves.
Photo #2: Roger that.
Photo #3: And that.
Photo #4: Wouldn't mind a bit of that either.

Josh started to laugh—a dry, humourless expression of his disbelief at what he was seeing. He read the brief paragraph at the bottom of the second page.

Kristian Johansson, AKA *Shadows'* DI Mark Lundberg, sure seems to love his method acting. Seen here with no less than four separate love interests, we're wondering just how many more you've got in the closet, Inspector?

p.s. the redhead's his wife...

"Oh, for fuck's sake," Josh said, slamming the magazine into a paper recycling bin. He walked away, putting his hands to his head, raking his fingers through his hair. Sean retrieved the magazine so he could return it to its owner. Josh paced up and down the corridor.

"How the fuck do they do it?" he asked Sean. "That," he thumped the page, his fist landing more or less on the bottom left image, "was an early Saturday morning, about six weeks ago."

Sean examined the photo. It showed Josh with his hand resting gently on the arm of the other guy—Kristian Johansson, presumably—and they were gazing right into each other's eyes.

"It looks pretty intense."

"Yes, it was. But it was about Shaunna."

Josh took the magazine from Sean again and studied the photo of Kris and George. It too was taken in the woods, and showed them hugging. To anyone who didn't know them, it would look like they were romantically involved, but it was no different from any other time they were together, in the company of friends or alone. Above the picture of Kris and him was one where Kris had his lips to Adrian's ear, and again, the facial expressions portrayed great emotional intensity. And then there was the photo with Shaunna, a beach shot with no inclusion of Casper in the frame, which would have been the reason why they were both staring dreamily into the distance. For all of these snapshots being an invasion of Kris's and their privacy, Josh had to admit that the photographer was impressive. He couldn't even remember touching Kris's arm when they were out with the dogs the weekend George was away, but recognised by their location as it having been taken towards the end of the walk.

"Do you want to say anything to that lot?" Sean asked, nodding in the direction of the classroom. "Or shall we just move on and leave them speculating?"

"I don't know, to be honest. It makes no difference to me, but you know how George is. He's going to hit the roof."

"All right. How about you give him a call and warn him. Meanwhile I'll neutralise any gossip."

Josh nodded. "Thanks."

"See you in mo," Sean called back as he returned to the lecture theatre, where there was an instant and complete silence. He looked over the group and raised an eyebrow.

"You'll be wondering about this photo of our esteemed two-I-C? Well," he laughed, "who would've thought that he'd have famous friends? But let's have a bit of respect, folks, all right? Just because Josh knows this guy," he waved the magazine in front of them, then gave it back to the student, "doesn't mean he's going to be hunting down autographs for anyone. And I know I've no need to remind a bunch of top class professionals like your good selves that confidentiality is king. So," he advanced to the last person whose logbook he had been checking, "let's get back to it, shall we? Good."

A couple of minutes later, Josh came back. He hadn't been able to get hold of George, but had spoken briefly to Kris, whose agent had already called to tell him about the article, and he was devastated, not so much for himself; he knew when he chose this career that with success came a certain loss of privacy, and if it were only his own, then he'd have been more than happy to accept the publicity. Josh reassured him that he was OK with what had happened, and didn't blame him, but the other three were an entirely different matter. Now Kris was going to have to face Shaunna and Ade and tell them about the photos before someone else got there first.

Soon after one o'clock, they all headed to the Students' Union for a post-course celebratory drink. Sophie and Sean were still a little awkward with each other in social situations, but because all of the other students were there too, they seemed to be getting along OK, although she chose to sit with her classmates rather than Sean and Josh. Sean had offered to drive so he had a reason to refuse offers of Guinness without having to make up excuses, which meant Josh was on the lager; an hour forward, he'd only had one pint and nothing to eat. He was standing at the bar, checking his phone and waiting to buy a bar snack of some sort when George arrived, walked right up to him, put his arms around his waist, pulled him close and kissed him fully on the lips. Josh closed his eyes and blushed.

"Oh good grief. Please tell me you didn't just kiss me in front of all my students."

"Yeah, I did," George grinned. "Although as of one o'clock this afternoon they're no longer your students."

"But they might be again in September."

"True. Still, if you'd rather they believed you were involved with that dreadful man-whore, Kristian Johansson..."

"Ah. You've heard."

"Kris phoned before to let me know, and then Adele called, then Shaunna, then Pauline, and then Wendy collared me on the way in." Wendy was the student who had been passing the magazine around in class that morning.

"Are you OK?"

George shrugged. "Not much point in me getting all het up about it after the event, is there? But you know the pic of Kris and Ade? That was taken when Kris was telling him it was over."

"Oh no."

Josh finally got the opportunity to buy some peanuts and ordered George a drink at the same time. As they walked over to where Sean was sitting, a group of students commandeered George.

"Won't be long," he said. Josh rolled his eyes and returned to Sean. He sat down next to him. Sean sniffed.

"You've not taken up smoking again, have yer, Joshy?"

"No, but I might need to change my cologne. I think I preferred it when people kept asking if George and I were together!"

Sean laughed. "Everything all right?"

"Better than expected, actually." Josh was still somewhat surprised by how well George was dealing with it. The campus was safe though, compared to the real world. Twenty minutes or so later, when George finally escaped from his old classmates, he came over, sat next to Josh and took his hand. Josh glanced at him, spotted the mischief twinkling away, and decided not to challenge it. Once the students had finished whispering excitedly amongst themselves about one of their course leaders and his boyfriend, things settled down, and the afternoon went by quite pleasurably, with some of the more sensible people pausing from their drinking to order in pizza, then going out in dribs and drabs to receive their delivery and eat. Josh was still hungry, so when his coffee-bringing student was on the phone to the pizza delivery place, he made a beeline for him.

"Can you order me a cheese garlic bread while you're at it?" he asked.

The student nodded; he was listening to them reading back his order. "Yep, and a cheese garlic bread," he said. They spoke again. "OK, cheers." He hung up. "Half an hour," he told Josh.

"Great. Oh, and thanks for all the coffee, by the way." The student smiled at him.

"Thank *you*," he said, his words loaded with the sincerity of emotional expression that only alcohol can endow. "I've learnt so much from you, Josh. How d'you keep it all in your head?"

Josh smiled, slightly bashful. "Dunno. Big head, I guess." The student— the best-looking of three all named Asif—laughed and picked up his pint. Josh looked puzzled. Asif shrugged by way of asking why.

"I assumed you were Muslim," Josh explained.

"Ah. Nah, man," he said, suddenly with a laddish air about him. "My family are though. I'm an atheist."

Whilst this interchange had been taking place, Sean had also wandered off to chat to students, and Sophie had gone to sit with George. She'd bought a copy of the magazine and they'd been looking at the article, but then George's attention had switched to watching Josh and Asif talking.

"He's not," Sophie said.

"He is. Look." George nodded in the direction of Josh's feet. His toes were pointed at Asif, his left foot slightly forward. Sophie shook her head.

"It doesn't mean anything." They continued to watch, as Josh laughed and then touched Asif lightly on the arm as he reached for his pint.

"And that?" George asked her.

"Oh, for heaven's sake."

"You're telling me he's not flirting?"

"So what if he is?"

George huffed and picked up his drink, all without taking his eyes off Josh, who finally became aware that he was being watched. He excused himself from his conversation and went over to George.

"Hey," he smiled and sat down opposite.

"Hey," George responded brusquely.

"What's up?"

"Nothing."

"I've just ordered a garlic bread." George nodded. Josh frowned. "Are you sure you're OK?"

"Fine."

Sophie subtly nudged him with her elbow. He attempted a smile.

"So what's Asif up to these days?" he asked.

"He says he's got two days a week as a counsellor at a school with a high proportion of pupils from Asian backgrounds."

"Oh, right."

"He can speak four languages. Did you know that?"

"No, I didn't know that."

"Well, he can." Josh eyed George carefully. "Anyway, what've you been talking about? Babies?"

"Nope."

Sophie breathed out through her nose. Josh looked to her for help.

"He thinks you were flirting with Asif," she explained.

Josh nodded slowly. "I see." He sipped at his drink thoughtfully. "I wasn't."

"I told him that."

George still wasn't convinced. Josh moved around the table and sat next to him.

"He's a student, George. Come on!"

George scowled a moment longer, but he had to relent. There was no way that Josh would flirt with a student—not on purpose. His professionalism wouldn't allow it.

"OK." He gave him a watery smile by way of confirming that he really was OK, or would be soon, and changed the subject. "Kris sent me a message before, offering to come in and say hi to your students. What d'you think?"

"I think that would be awesome," Josh said, because he was secretly delighted to have a famous friend, especially now he was sure George wasn't upset by the magazine feature.

"Cool." George took out his phone to reply to Kris. "They were filming some of the final episode on location yesterday," he continued to speak whilst typing, "in that club where we saw Silhouetto."

"Silhouetto?" Sophie asked.

"The naked dancers."

"That's right. I remember you telling me."

Josh blushed. George laughed.

"I've watched a video of them online since, and they're actually very good."

"And very naked," Josh said. Now he was the one getting grumpy.

"You can't see anything," George justified. He picked up his phone and checked it. "Kris said he's coming down as soon as he's finished shopping." He addressed Sophie. "You haven't met Kris yet, have you?"

"I haven't met any of your friends."

"You've met Dan, Andy and Ellie."

"I mean *properly* met. It's a bit difficult to strike up a conversation in a hostage situation."

George laughed. "Well, I think you'll like him."

"Is he anything like his character?"

"Um, a little, maybe…"

"Ha!" Josh interrupted, although not intentionally.

"He's not that much like him."

"Swedish guy living in England, married to a woman, but attracted to men…"

"He's not a policeman."

"So he's actually Swedish?" Sophie asked.

"Yeah," George confirmed. "He moved here when he was three, though, so he hasn't really got an accent, as such. A Swedish accent, I mean. Nor a Mancunian one."

Sean had come back over to their table and just caught the end of their conversation.

"Who are you talking about?"

"The husband-ex-husband," George said. "He's coming for an impromptu autograph signing."

Sean nodded, but didn't pass comment. He hadn't met Kris either, but he'd spent enough time chatting to Shaunna to conclude that he didn't much like him, and was trying his best to hide this fact from his companions—not the easiest thing to accomplish, given who they were—his genius psychologist housemate from university, and his partner, who was probably the most well-balanced and empathetic man he'd ever met, and the woman who was carrying his child.

And that was when it hit him.

"Soph. Can we talk?"

"What, now?"

"If possible."

"OK." She got up and followed him from the bar, back to his office. He unlocked the door, cleared the chair. She sat. He sat.

"Soph, I'm sorry."

"What for?"

"Everything. I've not been here for you these past few months, and I should have been."

She shrugged. "Apology accepted."

"How've you been keeping? Are you OK?"

"I'm very well. You?"

"Fine. And the baby?"

"The baby's great."

"You're six months along now. Have I got that right?"

"Yes."

"Oh, good. Do you know if it's a boy or a girl?"

"No. I told them I didn't want to know, but if you want to know…"

"Oh, no. I'm fine not knowing. I just wondered."

"Sean." Sophie reached across the desk and took his hand in hers. "Tell me what you want."

"I don't know," he said. "It just sank in. When I was sitting in the bar? That in there," he nodded at Sophie's bump, "is my son, or daughter." He shook his head. "I can't comprehend it."

She got up and walked around to his side of the desk, and placed his palm on her belly.

"Wait," she said. He stayed perfectly still. "There. Did you feel that?"

Sean smiled. "That's incredible. Does it hurt? Is it uncomfortable?"

"Sometimes it can be a bit uncomfortable, but it doesn't hurt."

"And have you decided on the kind of birth you want and things? I'm sorry. I don't know enough to ask the right questions."

"George is going to be there."

"That's good." Sean nodded. "Yes, that's good."

"I think we should go back now, don't you?"

"OK. Just—just one more thing, Soph?"

"Hmm?"

"What about us? Can we try and work it out?"

Sophie smiled and kissed his cheek. "Let's play it by ear. How about that?"

"That will do me perfectly," Sean said. He locked his office again and they returned to the bar, where Kris had just arrived and was talking to Josh at the bar.

"So that's him, then?" Sean said to George.

"The husband-ex-husband? Yep."

"He looks thinner off TV."

George glanced at Sean; he was smirking. "For a straight man, you're a very accomplished bitch."

"Why, thank you!" Sean laughed. "What's he like, really?"

"What do you see?"

"A perception skewed by what Shaunna has told me."

"So look again."

Sean watched Kris and Josh conversing. Every so often Kris would touch Josh on the arm, and Sean would sneak a look at George to see if he was reacting to it, but he wasn't.

"It doesn't bother you?" Sean asked after five minutes of this. George looked puzzled. "The touching."

"No. That's just Kris. He's one of those touchy-feely types. That's the thing with those pictures in the magazine. He's always hugged and touched people when he talks to them."

Sean continued watching. "And the eye contact. Everyone who's approached him he's given good eye contact."

A group of students were now gathered around Kris and were going through Josh in order to ask for autographs. It was obvious that Josh was enjoying it as much, if not more than Kris. Sean was frowning, still struggling to cast off his preconceptions, in spite of the new evidence.

"He's a good guy," George told him. "I'd vouch for him any day." Kris hugged the person whose notebook he had just signed and looked over to George. He smiled. George smiled back.

"You were together once?" Sean asked. George laughed.

"Tuned in at last?" he said. Now Sean laughed too.

There was a lull in the autograph signing and Josh gestured to Kris to follow him over to where George and Sean were sitting.

"Kris, this is Sean Tierney. Sean, this is Kris Johansson."

Kris smiled and gave Sean some of that 'good eye contact', holding out his hand.

"Lovely to meet you," he said.

"You too," Sean replied, shaking the offered hand.

"Thanks for inviting me down here. It's all still a bit of a novelty for me, signing autographs."

"And finding your photo in trashy magazines?"

"Yeah. I couldn't believe it when my agent told me." He looked at Josh and George apologetically. George got up to visit the toilets and put his hand on Kris's back as he passed by.

"It really is OK," he assured him. Kris put his hand on top of George's and smiled up at him.

"Thanks," he said, the relief evident in his tone. He watched George as he walked away, then turned back to Sean. "Shaunna's told me a bit about you."

"Has she now?" Sean tried to make his response sound light-hearted. He was quite surprised she'd mentioned him at all, given the nature of their conversations.

"Only a little. So you teach the counselling course with Josh?"

"Yes, I do."

"You teach full time?"

"No, I'm a clinical psychologist by trade. Work at the hospital and hospice."

"Oh, wow. That must be so rewarding. And quite hard to cope with at times too, I'd guess."

"You'd be right about that. Have you always been an actor?"

"Yeah, I have, although mostly radio, so I've been able to stay anonymous until now."

Josh's glass was empty again.

"I'm going to the bar. Anyone need a drink?" he asked.

"I'm fine, thanks," Kris said.

"Me too," Sean confirmed. He waited until Josh had gone. "Right, Kris, I'll be brief. I don't usually interfere, but it's clear to me that you and Shaunna need to sort things out between you." Kris moved back on his stool, trying to create some distance.

"You've only just met me. I'm guessing Shaunna's been talking to you about it?"

"No. She doesn't talk about you, but she *tells* me. The thing is this." Sean pointed to his eyes. "You see here." Then he lightly touched the side of Kris's head. "I see here, and what I see is two people who need to be honest with each other. Honesty's a good thing." Sean glanced past Kris, to where George was now standing next to Josh at the bar, with his arm around him, their noses almost touching. Josh was pretending to resist and George was smiling impishly. Kris turned to look too and couldn't believe what he was seeing. He shook his head and turned back to Sean.

"George is never that open in public."

"Damned paparazzi," Sean said, nodding towards the magazine Sophie had left on the table, open at the photo spread. "Still, as they say, the camera never lies. Now, I'm sorry to desert you, but in order to thwart self-accusations of hypocrisy, I must go and talk to the mother of my unborn child. It's been great to meet you, Kris, the husband-ex-husband."

"The what?" Kris said.

Sean turned and gave him a wink.

"Honesty's a good thing. Just remember that."

Gemini

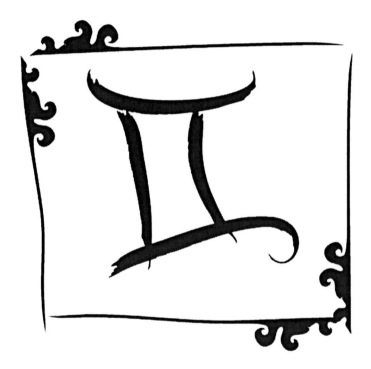

Bitter his life who lives for self alone,
Poor would he be with riches and a throne:
But friendship doubles all we are and own.

ROTATION
Wednesday 24ᵗʰ–Sunday 28ᵗʰ May

"Hiya," Shaunna called, dropping her bag in the lounge. Jess was standing in the kitchen, a teabag dangling from her fingers.

"Hi," she called back. Today she was dressed, in light, non-restrictive clothes, but they were at least clothes, not a nightshirt and socks.

"How're you feeling? You look loads better."

"Yeah, I am, thanks. Well…" People don't get better when they're dying, Jess thought.

"You'll have to take whatever good days you get, if you're planning on staying with us a while," Shaunna said. It sounded callous, but it wasn't intended to be. She'd nursed her mother to the end, and it was a truth that she had realised during those final few months: that the truth itself could not be denied, because the end would come regardless and it made the little things so much more significant, the tiniest of joys more important than ever. Together they had sat in the garden and watched bees and butterflies for hour upon hour upon hour, hardly daring to stir, for fear of disturbing their beautiful toils. They had listened to the birds in the early morning, and to their absence at midnight, talked of everything, and nothing at all. When the darkest days arrived, they were brighter for the time they had shared together while they still could.

"What was that pain management thingy you were talking about?" Jess interrupted Shaunna's reminiscence.

"Acupressure."

"Like acupuncture?"

"Basically, but without needles. Josh says it's all in your head, but they use it at the hospice and it works for a lot of people. I'll bring my book with me next time. It's got all the pressure points in it and we can figure it out."

"Or we could walk to your house in a little while and get it?"

Shaunna thought for a moment, visualising the route and marking off in her mind the places they could stop so Jess could rest. "OK," she agreed. There was the sound of movement above them.

"Andy's up," Jess observed. He'd been having trouble sleeping for weeks. Now it seemed he couldn't get enough. "I'll go and get my shoes and tell him what we're doing. In fact, he can have my cup of tea. Ooh, I'm quite excited to be going out!"

385

Shaunna watched Jess shift weightlessly away, almost floating up the stairs. She'd lost so much weight it was frightening, and Shaunna could appreciate that the others may be having quite a time coping. She heard the toilet flush, the bathroom door open, then close, then footsteps on the stairs, heavy this time.

"Hi." Andy came into the kitchen and picked an apple out of the fruit bowl. He examined his first choice, decided it didn't fit and swapped it for another.

"Hi," Shaunna responded. He bit into the fruit and grimaced. She laughed. "Toothpaste and apple doesn't go, does it?" He shook his head and shuddered. "How are you doing?"

He bit into the apple again.

"I'll ask another time," she said.

He walked past her and opened the door, glancing outside at the bright, sunny morning. "It's a nice day."

"Yes, it is."

"If you need me…"

"I won't."

"But if you do…"

"Andy," Shaunna said sharply, "have a rest, for God's sake. I know it's tough for you to step aside, but as Josh said, you've got to let us help. For you and for us. And I'll look after her, I promise."

"But…"

"But nothing." She grabbed him by the scruff. "If you say anything else I'll…" Their faces were close. Too close.

"You'll what? Break my nose?"

"Worse."

"Ohhh," Andy tried to mock, but he was laughing. "I'm sooo scared!"

"Just watch it," she warned, releasing him and smoothing his t-shirt. She glanced up into his eyes, their faces still only inches apart. They heard Jess making her way down the stairs. Shaunna quickly kissed his cheek and moved away. A blush spread outwards from the spot where her lips had touched.

"OK," Jess said brightly. "I'm ready."

Shaunna nodded at Andy. "We'll see you later."

"Give me a ring if you…" he started.

"Shut it," she called back as the front door closed behind them. He scratched his head, took another bite of the apple and went back to bed.

They set off at a steady, but leisurely pace. The sun was warm and it was a glorious day. Jess was enjoying the chance to be outside, and away from Andy. She knew he was doing it for her, but he was being so over-protective, not allowing her to so much as cook a meal, and it was driving her crazy. However, she didn't know how to address it without upsetting him; since last weekend, he seemed somehow to be different, like he was operating on automatic, a robot going through the motions, and talking to him was an utterly unnerving experience. It was almost as if his body was there, but his mind was elsewhere, and she could understand that it was what he needed to do to deal with this. Perhaps he thought it was what she needed. It was impossible to tell, and unless he let her in, there was no way of asking the question.

"Penny for them," Shaunna prompted, glancing sideways at her friend. Jess shook her head non-committally and shrugged.

"I was thinking about Andy. He's doing this weird coping thing, where he talks the talk, but there's no-one home."

"Yeah. I noticed that," Shaunna said, then realised that Jess was slightly out of breath. "Did you need to rest?" Jess slowed to a stop.

"I can't decide," she said. She frowned, but didn't say anything else for a while. "I'm not sure if I've accepted it, or I've just pushed it out of my head, but I'm kind of OK with it, you know?"

Shaunna watched her without speaking, her eyes offering response and encouragement to continue.

"When I resigned from the CPS, it suddenly dawned on me that if I died tomorrow, then I'd have achieved absolutely nothing. And I set up the business, and it's the best thing I ever did. It's not like I'm going to be around to miss it for much longer, so I've no regrets."

They moved off again. Still Shaunna remained silent.

"Andy's been a good life coach in that regard," Jess continued. "All those times I yelled at him for going off on a whim, or not thinking through the consequences of what he'd done before he did it? I've been just the same, and it's downright irresponsible, but I'm not sorry. Not even for what happened with Rob last year."

Shaunna's eyebrows raised involuntarily.

"Yes, I know," Jess admitted. "It was selfish and unfair on Ellie and the rest of you. I'm not saying I don't care about any of that. What I mean is that if I hadn't done it, I'd be wondering now, what if? What if Rob and I had got together? Would we have got married? Had kids?"

"I see what you mean," Shaunna conceded. "Did you ever want to start a family?"

"No. Career girl all the way. I made that decision back in primary school. I was going to be a lawyer."

"That's serious advance planning!" Shaunna joked.

Jess smiled. "It was because of Daisy—the pain I felt must've been nothing compared to what my mum and dad went through, but it hurt

387

sufficiently for me to realise that I would never be strong enough to cope with something like that."

Shaunna nodded thoughtfully. "I can remember my mum coming home and telling me about Daisy, but you've never talked about her, so I didn't like to say anything. She died in the summer holidays, didn't she?"

"Yeah. Between third and fourth year of juniors. Seventeenth of August, it was. And your mum was amazing. She really looked after me. She was such a brilliant teacher."

They had arrived at Shaunna's house now, and Jess leaned on the wall whilst Shaunna retrieved her key from her pocket; Casper was barking and snuffling at the other side of the door.

"I'll just go in and grab the dog," Shaunna said, pushing her way inside. She got hold of Casper's collar and pulled him back so Jess could go in without being bounced at. However, she quickly realised that it wasn't necessary, for as soon as Jess stepped into the hallway, Casper stopped wriggling to break free and very gently put his nose against her hand.

"I think you've seriously underestimated his intelligence," she said, following Shaunna through to the kitchen, with Casper walking quietly at her side. He stood by and waited for her to sit down, then sat next to her. No tea towels, no ridiculous wiggling around the floor on his back. He just sat. Shaunna shook her head in disbelief.

"I think you might be right," she said, already filling the kettle, "although I was starting to question it after his performance in Wales last year."

"I wonder what he'd be like as a PAT dog?"

"What's a PAT dog?"

"Pets as Therapy. They visit hospitals and hospices." Jess's eyes glazed over and she looked away.

"What's wrong?"

"The hospice. The nurse who wrote up my care plan mentioned it, for respite and later reference, she said."

"Have you been and had a look?"

"No. Nor do I intend to. But anyway, maybe you could see about registering Casper, and have a chat with Sean about who you'd need to speak to."

Shaunna turned and stared at Jess, horrified. "Sean?"

"Yeah. Sean Tierney? George said you knew him. He works at the hospice."

"I know, I just…bloody George! I hope he hasn't said anything to Kris."

"Why? Are you and Sean involved?"

"Good heavens, no! We're just friends, and I did tell Kris we'd been introduced at the psychic night, but, well, let's just say that I may have been a little more open with Sean than Kris would appreciate."

"Ah. I understand." Jess watched on as Shaunna finished making the tea and brought it across to the table. "Sean and I had a bit of a fling back at uni."

"Yeah. I mean, I didn't know that, but he told me he knew you from uni, and I'm actually not that surprised."

Jess laughed. "I don't quite know how to take that."

"In a good way," Shaunna assured her. "He's got something about him that I can't put my finger on. Kind of deep, and mysterious. A sense of underlying danger. I can see how he'd be exactly your type. Anyway, I'll just pop and find that book while I'm thinking about it." She left Jess deep in thought, and in Casper's capable paws, returning a couple of minutes later with the book.

"I've just realised," Jess said. "The last time I sat here was when Andy told you he was Krissi's dad."

"So it was!"

Shaunna found she was smiling at the thought of it. How much things had changed since then.

"You're so strong," Jess said, not quite out of the blue.

"Not really," Shaunna dismissed. "Sometimes you just have to take whatever life throws at you, make the most of it."

"I wish I had your strength, Shaunna, I really do." Jess put her head down and sighed heavily.

"Aww, hey." Shaunna shuffled her chair closer and took Jess's hand. "You *are* strong, and I know this is your battle, but it doesn't mean you have to do it on your own. It's OK to need people, and also to know that they need you. Of course we will miss you when it's your time to leave, and sometimes we're going to behave in all kinds of selfish ways, because it's tough for us too, but you will never be alone. We're The Circle!"

Jess tried to laugh but the tears kept on rolling. Shaunna wiped them away with her thumbs.

"It's such a lonely fight," Jess said, "and I feel so selfish saying that, because I know you're all here for me, but I'm in here on my own. It's like—I don't know. Being the knight who's sent to fight the dragon in a faraway land, knowing that everyone is on his side, but he's completely alone. Except I'm not coming home." She gasped and fell against Shaunna. "I'm so frightened. How do I do this?"

Shaunna held her tight and stroked her hair back from her face, her own tears flowing down onto her neck. After a while the sobbing quieted; Shaunna lifted Jess's hair, like a mother about to make plaits for school. She spoke slowly and carefully.

"Every single one of us is standing right beside you. We can't slay the dragon for you, but we will be there with you to fight it, to the very very

389

end, and if you ever drop your sword…" She turned away, but there was no attempt to hide that she was crying. Instead, she opened the cutlery drawer and reached inside. The sunlight coming through the kitchen window glinted off the object she now held in her hand and Jess looked up.

"You can borrow my butter knife." It was the most sincere promise in the world.

Jess started to laugh, then Shaunna did too, and soon their laughter had dried up all the tears. Shaunna swept her hair over her shoulders and went in search of tissues. When she came back, Jess hugged her.

"Thanks."

"You're welcome." She sat down again and picked up her tea.

"Can I keep the knife? Just in case I need to butter a dragon."

Shaunna smiled. "Of course you can. And if you lose it, or it gets blunt, I've probably got a melon baller somewhere."

***

"Thanks everyone for coming," Adele said, smiling brightly at the people gathered in front of her. "Before we begin, can I check you've all got your notepads ready?"

"Notepads?" Andy asked. Everyone else turned away from him a little. Adele sighed loudly.

"Yes, Andy. How else are you going to remember what you need to do?"

"I'll just keep it in my head."

"Just as well it's a big one, hey, bro?" Dan grinned.

"You know how people keep telling us we look like twins?" Andy reminded him. Dan straightened his face again.

"If you're quite finished, Mr. Jeffrieses?" Adele said, then looked puzzled whilst she considered whether the plural was correct. A general murmur of conversation swelled. Jess coughed and immediately the other five people in the room started to fuss around her.

"Oh, would you stop!" she laughed. "I was clearing my throat for Adele's benefit. Adele, over to you!"

"Thank you, Jess. Now, as we all know, Josh and George have booked their wedding at the register office for the nineteenth of June, and they think they're just going to have a quiet little gathering of friends, followed by a couple of drinks, and then go home." She paused, fully expecting everyone to start talking again, and when they didn't, she smiled and made a satisfied little 'hm' sound to herself. She pressed on.

"A few weeks ago, I received a very anxious call from the best man, and we've had a couple of discussions since. He's asked for our help, because he's in Birmingham, and, well, he's only four. So, what we are proposing is that we give them the kind of wedding they deserve. I mean, it took them all this time to get together, how can we possibly let them do it their way?"

"Yeah," Dan agreed. "At the very least they should have a wedding car."

"And a reception," Kris stated. "You've got to have a wedding reception. Who goes straight home when they've just got married?"

"Then they'll need a honeymoon as well," Andy said, already browsing his very own mental brochure of perfect honeymoon locations.

"And a cake," Jess added. "It's a shame Ellie's not here, or we could get her to ask her mum to make one."

"I can do that," Andy said.

"What? Make a wedding cake?" Adele asked. He looked at her disbelief.

"No. Ask Mrs. D. if she'll make it."

"Mrs. D.?" Dan enquired.

"Yeah, bro. Me and Mrs. D. are 'like that'." Andy crossed his fingers to signify.

"We'll need to figure out a guest list," Shaunna said, moving things on. She frowned. "I don't think they've got that many friends. I mean, they never go out, unless they're with us."

"Sean might know," Jess suggested.

"Yeah, that's true," Shaunna nodded, then shut her mouth quickly.

"I've got his phone number," Jess said, covering up, as neither of them knew that Kris and Sean were already acquainted. "I'll send it on to you, Shaunna, so you can chat to him."

"Cool. Thanks."

"All right then," Adele announced in a bright, loud voice. "So, to re-cap." She glanced down at her tablet. "Dan: you're going to arrange a car…"

"Hold up. Since when?"

The girls started laughing.

"Since we all just volunteered," Kris explained.

"Balls," Dan grumped, although he was actually perfectly fine with it. However, if he didn't complain, Adele would think he had a problem.

"If I may continue," Adele said. "Dan: car. Kris: you're going to book a venue for the reception. Try the hotel where we had the psychic night and mention my name. I'm sure they'll help us out."

"Okey dokey," Kris said. He typed into his phone.

"Andy: talk to me about this honeymoon."

"Yeah. I've got a couple of ideas I can go with. I'm thinking they'll want to take the dog with them, and won't want to be gone too long, so it'll have to be in this country. Can I come back to you on it?"

"Of course," Adele permitted with an oh-so-sweet smile. She was having the time of her life. "And do let me know how you get on with Mrs. Davenport regarding the cake."

"Will do, boss," Andy grinned.

"Shaunna: can you get onto this guest list, please?"

"Of course, hun."

"I think that's everything." Adele tapped her nail on her teeth, her eyes moving down the screen as she read through her bullet-pointed list.

"I don't want to be the fly in the ointment here," Jess said, "but they are seriously going to protest about this honeymoon. We need to cover all our bases—I can hear Josh now! 'I've got nothing to wear! I've got people to see!' You know what he's like, and George is nearly as bad."

Everyone hummed thoughtfully.

"OK, how about this?" Shaunna suggested. "When I phone Sean, I'll ask whether he can cover Josh's appointments for a few days."

"Fab," Adele said. "Dan, could you pop and see Jake at the farm and fill him in?"

"Bad choice of words, that," Andy joked. Dan glared at his brother.

"I will," he said.

"Excellent." Adele pushed a button on her tablet and several phones around the room beeped. "That should be an email from me outlining what we've discussed. We'll arrange another meeting for some time next week. Thanks, everyone."

***

"Evening shift coming through," George called, wheeling the chair into the hall. Jess glanced through the lounge doorway and frowned.

"I'm not getting in that thing," she said. He looked hurt.

"Why not?"

"For a start, you don't have a licence."

"That's a good point."

"Or insurance."

"I'll just have to make sure I don't crash."

"Where are we going, anyway?"

"Pub quiz."

"Excellent." Jess got up. "I think I can manage without the chair though."

"OK. I'll walk with you to the car, then come back for it, just in case."

"Andy?" Jess called out to the kitchen. "Do you want to come and do this pub quiz?" He walked into the hall, drying a glass with a tea towel.

"Do you want me to?"

"It's up to you. It'd be fun to have you there, but if you need to have some 'you time'—"

Andy thought for a moment. "OK. I need to shower, so tell me which pub you're at and I'll come down in a while. How does that sound?"

"Cool," George answered. "We'll be at The Red Lion in the village. Knowing what they're like, the quiz won't start for another hour or so yet. See you later."

***

"So, is there a sports round?" Dan asked, taking a seat at the next table along from where Josh was currently sitting on his own.

"Hey, Dan. Come to join the A-team?"

"Nope. We've got our very own team," he said, as Shaunna sat down next to him. "We're ready to kick some serious pub quiz ass."

"There is no way you're going to beat us," Josh gloated.

"Is that right?" somebody said behind him.

"Ah, crap." Josh sighed.

"Famous last words there, Joshy." Sean put his arm around Eleanor. She gave Josh a smug look, then went to sit with Shaunna and Dan.

"What are you doing here?" Josh asked.

"I believe, in the business, it's called 'phoning a friend'," Sean grinned. "Or friends, in fact."

"Speaking of which," Jess said, coming up behind Sean. He smiled at the sound of her voice and turned to greet her. Luckily, he'd been warned that she'd lost a lot of weight, and had enough experience at the hospice to know what to expect, so he didn't even notice, or if he did, he hid it very well. He put his arms around her and hugged her.

"It's fantastic to see you, Jessie," he said, withdrawing slightly to give her a kiss.

"You too, Sean. You're looking good." She gave him a once-over. "Really well. Are you well?"

"The best I've been in a long time," he said sincerely. "And how about you? Are you doing OK?"

"Better than OK. These guys don't give me any choice in the matter." She smiled at her friends. Andy put drinks down in front of Dan, Shaunna and Eleanor, then sat opposite Josh.

"What've you done with George?" he asked.

"He went to get another drink about a quarter of an hour ago. Wasn't he at the bar?"

"Not that I saw."

Josh frowned. "I'll go and have a look for him, just follow the trail of donkeys' hind legs." He took a quick swig of his orange juice and headed off towards the back of the pub, slowing as he passed the bar, to check that George wasn't standing in front of somebody else. Still not catching sight of him, he went into the men's toilets, and found them to be empty. He took out his phone and had his number up ready to call as he came back out, and spotted him, standing at the door to the beer garden, talking to another man. Josh slowed to a halt and listened hard, trying to tune in to what they were saying. He couldn't make out the words, and stepped back out of sight to watch, initially in an attempt to lip-read, but found he wasn't watching the man's lips at all, because a sudden wave of jealousy had washed over him, almost enough to make him physically sick. And for as much as he could see that there was nothing untoward going on, the other guy was good-looking, young and clearly very interested in everything George had to say. Worse still, George was doing little to put him off.

"What's up?" Dan asked, edging past to go into the Gents'. He looked to see what Josh was looking at. "He's one of Aitch's lot," he said.

"He's in the police?"

"Yeah. Can't think of his name. Graham something or other, I think. Decent bloke, anyway."

Dan disappeared into the toilets, leaving Josh on his own once again. George had just realised how long he'd been chatting, and patted the other man on the arm, then turned to go back inside. He didn't spot Josh immediately, because he too had turned away and was walking quickly to try and get back to the table before George saw him. Needless to say, this didn't happen, and George glanced at him as he resumed his seat, so concerned about the way he was behaving that he didn't even notice Eleanor, Shaunna and Sean sitting at the next table along, until Shaunna spoke to him.

"You OK, George?"

"Huh? Oh, um, yeah. I'm fine. What're you all doing here?"

"Came for the quiz. Andy phoned Dan, and, err, I was there, so…"

"And Sean?" Josh asked.

"I asked him," Shaunna said.

"And I asked Eleanor," Sean explained. "We were having a meeting."

"At eight o'clock on a Friday evening?"

"Yes!" Eleanor snapped. She gave Josh a look that would have silenced him even if they had been on speaking terms, and in the current climate sent a chill right through him. He picked up his drink and tried to get back into the spirit of things by starting a highly contrived conversation about films with Andy. As it happened, when Dan returned from the toilets, he spotted the look in Josh's eye and decided to try and resolve the problem for him.

"Alright, mate?" he said, clapping George on the back as he stepped past to get to his seat.

"Yeah. Not bad. You?"

"Got no complaints. Saw you chatting with DS what's-his-face before."

"Farrar," George said. "Graham Farrar."

394

"That's it," Dan nodded. "I couldn't for the life of me think of his name. I didn't know you knew him."

"I don't, really," George said cagily.

Dan didn't know what to say to that. So much for defusing the situation.

"Nice little pub, this," he opted for as a change of subject, and it was a good choice. It was an old coaching house on the main road through the village where Josh, George and Sean lived, so was effectively their 'local', and the conversation switched to discussing the authentic interior, with its whitewashed, rough plaster walls and exposed oak beams, the extensive range of traditional ales and pleasant, chatty atmosphere. All the while, Josh continued to watch George, trying to control the jealousy that had once again set his heart racing. He got up and made a quick dash for the toilets. Seconds later, George arrived.

"Hey, what's the matter?" he asked.

"How do you know that Graham guy?"

"He's the one who arrested me after the incident in the park."

"I see," Josh said.

"What do you see, exactly?" George felt a slight bristling of the hairs on his neck.

"Oh, George. Don't be like that."

"Don't be like what? He recognised me and thought he'd give me an update on what happened."

"OK," Josh mumbled, although it still wasn't.

"The dog that got attacked pulled through, but lost one of its front legs. That's kind of good news, isn't it?"

"Yeah."

"So what's the problem?"

"I haven't got one. As you say, he was just giving you an update."

"And yet you've made yourself sick with worry?"

"Jealousy. I'm sorry. It's not that I don't trust you, I promise."

"So what, then?"

"It's…" Josh took a deep breath and turned away. George nudged him.

"Hey."

"I'm sorry."

"I think I know what it is. And it's fine. Well, it's not, but I understand."

"Do you?" Josh asked doubtfully.

"I love *you*. That's all you ever need to know. OK?" Josh didn't respond. George nudged him again and he smiled.

"Yes, OK."

"Good. Now let's go win this quiz." He gave him a quick kiss and they went back outside.

"You know we've got no chance, with Ellie and Tierney on their team?"

"And you and Jess on ours? We'll wipe the floor with them."

"Ever the optimist!"

"Yep!" George grinned. They got back to their table and Josh gave Dan a nod of thanks. Dan gave him a swift half-wink in acknowledgement.

"Right," Sean said, rubbing his hands together. "Let's bring it home." The quizmaster left their answer sheets and pens and Eleanor immediately took charge of theirs, whilst Josh was 'given' the position of scribe on the next table along; that is, the other three members of the team knew he'd sulk and complain all night long if he wasn't doing it. At the exact same moment, he and Sean each put their mobile phones down in the middle of their tables.

"What's that about?" Andy asked.

"No cheating," Josh said.

"If we win, we do so fair and square," Sean told his teammates. Dan was the only one to protest, but he still went along with it.

"We're evenly matched," Shaunna said, looking around her team, and then across to the others, and she was right. On their table, the intellectual contingent was Sean and Eleanor, with Dan able to answer anything of a sport or business nature. Likewise, on the other team these roles were fulfilled by Jess, Josh and Andy respectively, whereas she and George offered a wealth of general knowledge and common sense. Or that was the theory, anyway.

"Good evening, ladies and gents," the quizmaster's voice came over the pub's sound system. "And welcome to tonight's quiz, brought to you by yours truly, with a little help from the internet."

George leaned across to Shaunna. "Where's Kris tonight?" he whispered.

"Chat show," she told him.

"Oh." George frowned. "I can't believe I forgot."

"It's OK," Josh said. "We're recording it." George looked relieved. It would have been the first time he'd missed one of Kris's TV appearances; they were all still so excited about having a famous friend, watching every quiz show, chat show and breakfast TV interview Kris's agent pushed his way—it was safe to say that at the moment the Great British TV viewing public couldn't get enough of Kristian Johansson.

"We've got eight rounds, and you can play your joker to double your points on anything but the music round," the quizmaster continued.

"Which round d'you think?" Eleanor asked. They all pored over the quiz sheet, with its eight sections, each printed with a title and ten numbered lines underneath. The same process was happening at almost every table in the pub.

"Dogs could be a good one," Andy suggested.

"Maybe," George said, "although we've done this quiz a few times and it's unlikely to have anything to do with dogs."

"I know a fair bit about science fiction," Sean said.

"About time you owned up to being a fraud," Josh sniped at him in jest.

Jess took the sheet from him. "I think we go for General Knowledge. That's got to be straightforward enough."

Josh shrugged. "OK. General Knowledge?" The other three team members nodded; their opponents had opted for A Man's World.

"We need a team name," Eleanor said. "How about…"

"Brains and Brawn," Shaunna interrupted. Sean laughed.

"I like it."

"Which one am I?" Dan asked with a grin.

Josh scoffed and turned back to his team. "They should be called Superiority Complex. Bloody know-it-alls."

"Complex Superiority?" Jess suggested. Andy nodded.

"That works."

Josh and George shrugged indifferently, but had nothing better to offer.

"Round One: Cryptic," the quizmaster announced, so they stuck with it. "Any jokers on Cryptic?"

And they were off. On previous occasions, when George, Josh, Sophie and Sean had played the quiz, they'd come to realise that the Cryptic round was potentially the hardest of all, although it could, like tonight, end up being the easiest. It consisted of ten cryptic clues on a specific topic; in this instance, it was football teams. The only one that stumped the football fanatics of Brains and Brawn was 'White birds spot city', which Complex Superiority answered immediately, although they couldn't figure out 'Workers, smart with sun-god', which pleased Eleanor no end, because she'd got that one all by herself. Safe in the knowledge that they were heading into Round Two on a level pegging of nine out of ten, Shaunna raised the joker for Brains and Brawn.

"Round Two: A Man's World," the quizmaster began. "The clue's in the name of the round. All your answers begin with 'man'."

"That's us ballsed," Dan groaned.

"We'll be fine," Shaunna asserted.

"Question one: a hard brittle greyish-white metallic element, atomic number twenty-five."

"Or not," she muttered.

Everyone looked quietly puzzled. George sat with his arms folded, giving the others a chance.

"Question two," the quizmaster said. George tutted.

"One is manganese," he whispered in Josh's ear. Josh scribbled it down, shielding the sheet with his free hand.

"A variety of beet cultivated for cattle food."

Again, Brains and Brawn had no idea. Meanwhile, all eyes were on George. Josh handed him the pen so he could write the answer: mangel. It continued this way, with Eleanor getting a few because they were related to medicine or mythology, as in the case of mandible and manticore, but by the end of the round, George had aced the paper, and Eleanor was still looking at four blanks.

"Round Three: Connections..." On it went, with both teams performing at around the same level for this and the Dogs round, which was, as George had predicted, nothing to do with dogs, but essentially the same set-up as the 'man's world' round. On the music round both teams had the same problems identifying the tune based on the intro, given that they were all about the same age, although Andy got quite a few of these that other people didn't know. Whilst the music round played, Jess went to the toilet, stopping to talk to Shaunna at the bar on her way back.

"Did you get much sorted?"

"Yeah. Sean's given me a list of names of students and staff at the university that know them quite well and he's more than happy to pick up the therapy stuff for a few days."

"Cool. Andy said earlier that he's provisionally booked a hotel."

"And Kris booked the room for the reception too," Shaunna confirmed. "You had any joy?"

"Not yet, but never fear. Your secret personal shopper is here." The women laughed and high-fived, then returned to their respective teams for the second half of the quiz.

"I was just saying to George," Josh recapped as Jess sat down, "the Science Fiction round is next, and he knows quite a bit about science fiction. I think we should play our joker on that."

"Yeah. I don't see what we've got to lose. We're already ahead of Brawns and Brain."

Andy laughed. "Go for it. I know a bit about *Doctor Who*."

"That's interesting." Josh was a little surprised to hear this, because he was something of a fan himself, but wouldn't have thought it of Andy.

"Yes, he does." Jess beckoned Josh closer. "And *Star Wars*, and quite a few dodgy programmes I can't even tell you the name of."

"What are you saying about me?" Andy asked her.

"Nothing," she grinned and acted innocent.

"Decision made, then," Josh said.

"Round Six: Science Fiction," the quizmaster declared. "Any jokers?"

Jess waved their joker above her head.

"All righty," the quizmaster acknowledged. "Question one: which part did Deforest Kelley play in the TV series *Star Trek*?"

Now, where Sean didn't care that the other team members might perceive him to be a geek for knowing the answer, George did care, so he held back for a few seconds, pretending that he had to think about it.

"Come on, George!" Josh said, pen poised over the designated space on their answer sheet.

"Question two," the quizmaster continued.

"It's Doctor McCoy," George admitted, as if confessing to a terrible sin.

"Who played the third incarnation of the Doctor in the TV series *Doctor Who*?" the quizmaster asked.

"John Pertwee," Andy mouthed at Josh. George took the pen off him and wrote it down.

"I knew that!" Josh protested.

"Yeah, but you're writing too slowly."

"Question three: what was the name of the computer in the cult TV series, *Blake's Seven*?"

George gave Josh an enquiring look, mixed with a smirk. Josh sighed and relinquished command of the answer sheet.

"Question four: in *Star Wars Episode Four*…"

Josh folded his arms and looked away, whilst Andy hissed the answer at George. Jess shook her head in dismay.

"Question five: To date, how many different incarnations of *Star Trek* have there been?"

George scribbled the answer down, and on it went, right through to the tenth question, all answers present and correct.

"Good choice of joker," Shaunna called across.

"Thanks," George replied, hastily pushing the answer sheet back to Josh.

"Next up: Science Fact," the quizmaster moved them along quickly.

"I'm surprised you didn't choose this as your joker," Josh said to Eleanor. She gave him a quick smile, but didn't respond otherwise. In the event, none of the questions were above high school science level, so both teams performed well on this and the last round: General Knowledge. At the end they switched papers with other teams and Dan and Andy went to the bar.

"What d'you think of that Sean Tierney bloke, then?" Andy asked.

"Seems decent."

"Yeah." Andy was non-committal. "He was there the night Ellie's ex had her in the car."

"Was he? I don't remember."

"Him and Josh were both pissed and Sean buggered off—left the rest of us to deal with it."

"Hmm," Dan said, trying to recall. "Was that his girlfriend then? Sarah? Sara? Something like that. The one you were getting all up close and personal with."

"I wasn't getting all up close and personal," Andy protested. "And her name's Sophie."

Dan raised an eyebrow. "I take it you're not too fond of Sean, then?"

Andy shrugged. "As you say, he seems decent enough."

"But?"

"I'll leave it with you, bro," Andy said, patting his brother on the back.

Dan nodded. "Fair enough." They arrived back with the drinks just as the quizmaster announced the results.

"Thanks for playing The Red Lion quiz tonight, folks. First prize is a whopping ninety quid. Our winners, for the third week running…"

"Bloody cheating so-and-sos," Sean said.

"…with eighty-five out of a possible ninety points, are The Crash Test Mummies."

Whoops came from a table at the back of the pub, where sat a group of middle-aged women, including the leader of the parish council.

"So unfair," George moaned. "You should let us use our phones."

"No!" Sean and Josh said together.

"In second place, with eighty-two points, Complex Superiority."

"Woo-hoo!" Jess shouted, then more quietly: "What do we win?"

"Two free drinks each," George said.

Andy shrugged. "Better than a kick in the teeth."

Dan glanced over. "That can be arranged," he offered.

"In joint third place, with seventy-eight points, Them in the Corner, and Brains and Brawn."

"Oh, well, that's not so bad," Shaunna consoled the rest of her team. They didn't look especially convinced. "We could always come again next Friday," she suggested. "Have a rematch."

"Actually, me and Dan were chatting about this the other day," Andy said. "With my birthday being so soon after the wedding, we were thinking of having a joint celebration next week instead."

"Not a rematch, though, hey, bro?"

"Why not?" Andy joked. Dan glared at him, but then the glare morphed into another expression: the expression of a challenge accepted.

"I'm game," Dan said. He looked to the rest of his teammates and their opponents on the next table. "What d'you reckon?"

Shaunna shrugged. "Sounds good to me."

"Me too," Josh agreed.

"What do you think, Jess?" Andy asked.

"I think I could cope with that."

"Awesome. That's sorted then." Andy nodded at his brother and Dan gave him a subtle wink in response, because that was only half the story. The other half involved Andy's lack of enthusiasm for celebrating his fortieth birthday with Jess being sick, but some things are best left unsaid. Instead, he allowed her to start interrogating him about presents, all the while wondering why, when he was sure she said she'd bought it already.

Across the table, George was wiping the condensation from his glass, and listening to Jess and Andy having their conversation about shirts. It wasn't very interesting, but he was pretending he hadn't noticed that Josh was staring at him and had been for quite some time. Eventually he couldn't help it and started to smile.

"What?" he said, still focusing on his glass.

Josh shook his head. "Nothing. Just you."

"Huh?" George turned and met his gaze, seeing the answer right there, in the deep blue pools of his eyes. Jess and Andy continued to talk in the background, and had seen what was passing between their two teammates. It was so beautiful that it sent a shiver down Andy's spine and he was struggling to keep on with the random nonsense he was concocting on the spot. Jess took hold of Andy's hand and gave it a quick squeeze to confirm that she could feel it too. For a few minutes more, Josh and George continued their silent communication, a connection beyond the comprehension of the rest of their friends, the rest of the world. At the far side of the next table along, a best friend looked on, a dilemma rising up through her, spilling into her conscious thoughts. It took so much effort to tear her eyes away, and when she did she met with Sean's piercing gaze. She picked up her phone from the pile in the middle of the table.

"I need fresh air," she excused. Sean watched her leave.

"Is she OK?" Shaunna asked.

"She'll be fine," Sean said. "So, did the husband-ex-husband mention we exchanged greetings?"

"No! When was that?"

"At the university the other Tuesday. He came to sign autographs."

"Oh, right. He's not mentioned it. I mean, I knew he went up to the uni—I was with him when George texted—but not that he'd seen you."

Sean nodded without comment.

"And do you still hate him?"

"What makes you think I hated him to start with?"

"You told me," she said with a grin. Sean shook his head and laughed. He'd noticed that a certain Jeffries brother was trying, but failing, to ignore them and decided to attend to it.

"So, Andy," Sean called over. He waited for Andy to properly look his way. "You did a grand job of those loft stairs."

"Thanks."

"I was thinking about getting some installed myself. How much would it set me back?"

"Depends."

As this conversation commenced across their group, Shaunna's phone vibrated itself off the top of Sean's, both still in the middle of the table. She picked it up, read the text message and walked around to Jess to show her the screen.

JUST GOT OFF PHONE FROM ELLIE. SHES ON BOARD. A X

Jess nodded and smiled.

"What's up?" Josh asked.

"Nothing. Why? Did you want to go home?"

"Not unless you do," he said, knowing he'd been deliberately silenced, but with absolutely no clue why. Jess didn't want him to start second-guessing, so she quickly quashed his curiosity.

"She should've come with us," she remarked to Shaunna. "I'm sure Alice would have been happy to babysit, if she'd asked."

"True. Oh well, maybe we can persuade her to come next Friday."

What they were saying did have an element of truth to it, for Shaunna had suggested to Adele that she come and join in the quiz, and she made her excuses—too much planning to do for the wedding, no babysitter, and so on—but the reality was that she was terrified everyone would think she was stupid.

"OK, people," Eleanor said, coming back in to retrieve her bag. "I need to get going." Shaunna bustled over and gave her a hug.

"Thanks, Ellie. We wouldn't have come third without you."

"Glad I could help," she smiled. "Jess, I'll see you tomorrow. Night." She gave a general wave to the rest of them and left. Josh unflared his nostrils, and for a while the conversation continued as before, but then Jess started to flag and they all made tracks, Sean having arranged for Andy to pop round when he had the time, to measure up and quote for loft stairs. It was a very convincing cover story.

***

"Why are you looking at men's clothes?" Josh put the cups down on the bedside table and left the room again.

"Andy's birthday present," Jess called after him. "What are you doing now?"

"Cleaning the wash basin."

"Why?"

"Because there's toothpaste and shaving stubble all round the taps."

"Oh, OK." She kept open the current page, displaying a variety of linen shirts in cool summer colours, and opened a new window over the top. "You don't have to do that, you know."

"I do. It's horrible."

She sighed. There was no point trying to talk him out of it. This was how Josh performed his 'shifts': a mix of completing any household cleaning that had been overlooked by Andy, making cups of coffee, and in between chatting about whatever came to mind. With the exception of the cleaning, it was how they'd always been, and she was very grateful for it. But today she really needed him to come and sit down.

"Are you going to be much longer?" she asked.

"No." She heard the toilet flush and he appeared in the doorway, his hands red from being submerged in cold water and bathroom cleaner. "I'm done now. Men are quite disgusting."

"Erm, aren't you one of those men folk?"

"Yes, but George and I don't count." She understood what he was getting at. Both he and George had been raised as lone children by strong, independent, single women, and as a consequence would never dream of so much as leaving up the toilet seat.

Jess brought up on-screen the shirts she'd been looking at and showed him. "I wanted to ask you what you think of these?"

"For Andy?"

"Yeah. I've been trying to get an answer out of him for weeks about what he wants, but he's 'still thinking about it', so I thought I'd just buy him some clothes. I know it's a bit crap, but I'm kind of limited in my options."

Josh looked over the shirts and frowned.

"I'm not sure they're Andy's style, but I don't really take much notice."

"Would you wear them?"

"Maybe. If they had long sleeves."

"Like this one?" Jess clicked on a link and showed him.

"That's really nice. How much is that?" He squinted at the price. "Do people pay that much for shirts? It's only a square of cheesecloth with a hole in the top!"

Jess laughed. "It's a bit more intricate than that." She loaded a different page. "Then there's these linen trousers." She passed him the laptop again.

"Hmm. Andy's not really a trousers kind of guy. Jeans in winter. Shorts in summer."

"I thought you didn't take any notice."

"I'd have to be blind not to notice those legs."

Jess gave him a questioning look.

"Yes, all right. Andy's got a fine pair of pins. Muscly, well honed, not too hairy." Jess grinned at him and he blushed. "I can look, can't I?"

"You can. I'm just surprised to hear that you do."

"They are nice trousers, regardless." Josh passed her laptop back. "And how many hundreds of pounds were they?"

Jess tutted. "It's fascinating," she said, "the different styles people adopt. Do you think it reflects their personality?"

"Up to a point, I suppose."

"Like Kris, for instance, with his flamboyant printed shirts, and Dan with his perpetual white shirt and black pants, always casual yet professional."

"So, would you describe yourself as emotionally open and out-going?"

"It's not entirely inaccurate."

"OK. And what do my clothes say about me, Doctor Lambert, pop psychologist extraordinaire?"

"That you're very guarded, with a common sense take on life."

"D'you know, you might be onto something here," Josh tormented. She ignored him and continued.

"Whereas George is down to earth and open in most respects."

"Down to earth, yes."

"I did say 'in most respects'. You'd never catch a glimpse of him topless in public."

"No. Although he does sometimes wander around the house topless." Josh let out an unconscious, contented sigh.

"Nice view, is it?"

"Oh yes. He's kind of—perfect." He smiled and went a bit mushy. Jess laughed and nudged him with her knee.

"Shame he hides it in baggy t-shirts, hey?" she said.

"It's certainly a shame for everyone else."

"Maybe you should buy him some more fitted t-shirts? He might wear them if you did."

"He probably would, but I hate clothes shopping, and when he goes he just comes back with more of the same." Josh drank the rest of his coffee and got up. "So what d'you fancy for lunch? Do you want to go out somewhere?"

"I'm quite happy here today, thanks. A salad would be lovely though."

"All right. A salad it is." Josh headed downstairs, leaving her to finish her online shopping. Now that she knew what she was buying, she was done in no time at all.

TWO MINDS
Monday 29ᵗʰ May

The shop bell tinkled. Josh waited for the buzzer to sound and braced himself as he pushed the door open, the bright white light and its myriad reflections off myriad shiny objects instantly making him squint.

"Ah, good afternoon, sir. Back so soon?" The jeweller was perched on a high stool at one end of the counter, a magnifying eye piece clamped in his eye socket, his already absurdly long fingers appearing longer still in their white cotton gloving.

"Hello," Josh returned the greeting cautiously.

"Be with you in a moment, sir," the jeweller explained, each word snapped out concisely, each consonant delivered hard, tees with tongue thrust against the teeth, vowels stretching one word until it met with the next.

"No problem," Josh muttered. He busied himself with attending to his favourite cubed display cabinet, on this occasion exhibiting a stunning collection of pearls clasped in red-gold claws or dropping from fine rose-hued strands, so perfectly arranged that it was like glimpsing into the depths of some fantastic coral reef. A parody of himself he might be, but this guy really knew what he was doing.

"Now then, sir." The jeweller's voice beckoned his attention. Josh about-turned. "One hopes your presence signifies repeat custom, rather than dissatisfaction."

"Erm, yes," Josh confirmed. So much for laughter being a social phenomenon. What good was it going to do him now to burst into uncontrollable fits of giggles? He focused on the matter in hand, or rather, on hand. He took off his ring. "This is just an initial enquiry," he said and paused. The dilemma raging in the mind of the man before him was quite incredible to behold. He was so drawn to the ring that he would have been right at home in a Tolkien novel, yet his desire to excel in customer satisfaction kept his gaze centred on Josh. In spite of his obvious awareness that he was being analysed, the jeweller appeared completely unperturbed. Intriguing. Mesmeric, even.

"Sir?" he prompted.

"Right. Yes." Josh quickly rallied his senses. "As you may recall, last year I purchased a ring from you that is very similar to this one."

He held out the ring as evidence. The jeweller's pincer digits plucked it from his grasp, his other hand searching blindly and locating a pair of half-moon, gold-framed spectacles, which he duly propped on the end of the long, thin slope of his nose. His entire being looked as if it had been stretched out of proportion, elongated like a reflection in a fairground hall of mirrors.

"Indeed, I do, sir. Your purchase was of an emerald setting, was it not?"

"Yes, it was." Josh nodded and kept nodding, watching his ring being twisted this way and that, securely yet seemingly precariously perched between the man's pipe-cleaner fingers.

"Sir might like to state his requirements a little less cryptically," the jeweller remarked. Josh caught a trace of humour flicker across his face.

"That would help, wouldn't it?" he smiled. "I was wondering whether it's possible to swap some of the stones from this ring with some of the emeralds from the one I bought."

"Absolutely, sir." The jeweller took off his glasses and handed Josh his ring back.

"Excellent." Josh returned it to his finger.

"Will that be all, sir?"

"Yes. Thank you," Josh said. "Thank you." He turned and walked towards the door, waiting for the catch to be released. The buzzer sounded and he pulled the door handle. "Incidentally, your display is beautiful," he added.

"Why, thank you, sir. Good day to you, sir."

Josh paused a moment to watch the jeweller return to his prior occupation, then stepped outside and closed the door behind him. He slowly blew air out of his mouth and started the walk back to the car.

Well, it hadn't been as bad as he'd expected. The past two times he'd visited, he'd ended up snorting with laughter, although on both occasions he'd been in the company of people who didn't assist much when it came to controlling such urges. The first time it was George, who tried his hardest to keep a straight face, and the more serious he became, the more difficult it was for Josh to contain his giggling fit. The second time he wasn't with anyone, but there were two other customers who were having the same difficulty. Anyway, he'd got the answer he was hoping for, so now he could ask George what he thought.

FLAT
Tuesday 30th May

Josh unlocked the car as he approached, got in, stuck the key in the ignition, put on his seatbelt, turned the key, released it, turned it again, released it and exhaled.

"Crap," he said. He tried again: nothing. It was completely dead, only the slight click of something in the engine compartment trying its best. He took out his phone and brought up his mechanic's number.

"Hi, Lee, it's Josh. Don't suppose you've got ten minutes to come and jumpstart the car?"

"Sure. Where are you?"

"Not far from you, actually. I'm parked outside the tower block, next to the burnt-out wreck."

"Oh!" Lee sounded surprised. "I'll be with you in five," he said. He hung up.

Josh passed the short time examining the wrecked remains, trying to identify what kind of car it had once been. It must have been smaller than his car, because the chassis was much shorter. Otherwise there was no way of knowing what it was. The sound of a van pulling up on his other side drew his attention, and he smiled across at Lee.

"Thanks. You're a star."

"No problem," Lee said. He got Josh to try the ignition again, with the same outcome, and nodded knowledgeably. "Did you leave your lights on?"

Josh frowned. "I don't think so." He checked the dial to find that it was set to halfway between the 'automatic' and 'on' positions. "Yes, you're right, as usual."

"So, what brings you to this neck of the woods?" Lee asked as he opened the bonnet of Josh's car and connected leads to his battery.

"Visiting someone," Josh said, then quickly qualified: "A client."

Lee looked doubtful. "Wouldn't have thought there'd be anyone in there who could afford a therapist. Not without a psychiatrist forcing them to see one, anyway."

Josh didn't respond to this. He knew about Lee's upbringing, but it wasn't appropriate to say, so he kept quiet and watched on as Lee started up his van, then left it running and returned to the car, giving the battery a couple of minutes to pick up charge.

"I'll give it a quick check in a mo, to make sure it's nothing more than it getting run down from your lights," he explained. He leaned on his van and glanced up at the block of flats. "I used to live there. Bloody horrible place, it is."

"Really?" Josh tried to sound surprised.

"Yeah. Damp, cold, the electric's always going off. It needs demolishing. Should've been knocked down years back, but the council couldn't be arsed to spend out. They think it'll just fall down by itself. It might yet. Try that again now."

It took Josh a moment to realise that this last part was an instruction. He turned the key and the engine immediately roared to life.

"OK. I'll just give that a look-see," Lee said. He collected a meter from his van and went around to the front of the car, where he fiddled about for a couple of minutes, then came back to the driver's door. "All looks fine." He disconnected the jump leads from the battery and closed the bonnet. "Should be good to go."

"Thanks again," Josh said.

"No problem. See you soon." Lee got into his van and with a wave he was gone.

TWO HEARTS
Thursday 1st June

The shop bell tinkled. George waited for the buzzer to sound and pushed the door open, instinctively lifting his hand to shield his eyes from the brightness of the lights inside.

"Hi there," he smiled at the jeweller. The man unnecessarily straightened his tie and smiled back—a plastic smile; it could even have been a plastic tie, given the precision of its knot.

"A good morning to you, sir. How may I help you?"

"I came in a few months back, I don't know if you remember?"

"Yes, sir, I do. To purchase a ring set with blue topaz."

"That's the one." George took off his own ring and passed it across the counter. "I was wondering what the chances are of switching a couple of the emeralds from this with the blue topaz. I think they're about the same size."

"They certainly appear to be, sir, you're quite right." The jeweller picked up his magnifying eye piece and positioned it in his left eye socket to examine the ring more closely. "It will make for an intriguing combination." He handed the ring back to George.

"I hope so," George said, returning the ring to his finger. "How long would it take to do that, if we decided we wanted to go ahead?"

"Just a few days, sir. I would prefer to tend to it myself, therefore at the beginning of the week, if that is convenient for you, sir?"

George nodded. "That's great, thanks." He turned and walked back towards the door, pausing to watch the glass cube of pearls in rose gold make a full rotation.

"They're beautiful."

"It certainly does seem to be a very popular display, sir," the jeweller said. "I don't envisage that any of those particular pieces would be to sir's requirements?"

"Not really, no," George smiled. This guy was very astute. OK, he'd bought a man's ring, so in asking if the stones could be swapped between that one and his own, he'd effectively outed himself.

"It is rare to find men's jewellery set with pearls. However, if sir was interested in..." The jeweller stopped, having noticed George's discomfort. "I'm terribly sorry. That was dreadfully forward of me, sir. I'm not generally in the business of canvassing for sales. I must apologise most profusely."

"No problem," George said carefully. He could feel the giggles squirming their way up his throat and was not going to give in to them. It would be so embarrassing. He gave the jeweller a quick smile and completed his journey to the door, waiting out the eternal two seconds it took for the buzzer to sound. "Thanks again," he smiled and quickly stepped out into the walkway of the shopping mall. A successful trip, all in all. Now he just needed to see what Josh thought of his idea.

PERFECT MATCH
Friday 2nd June

The Red Lion pub. The Friday Night Quiz. The rematch, with added support.

On the Brains and Brawn team were the original four members: Eleanor, Sean, Shaunna and 'birthday boy' Dan, although his birthday was two days ago and he was hoping it wouldn't get mentioned. Also playing were James and Kris, the latter of whom was enjoying not being the centre of attention for an evening. Adele insisted she wasn't officially part of the team, to keep the numbers even on both tables, for across the way were the six members of Complex Superiority: Josh, George, Jess and Andy as per the original line-up, with Sophie, 'brought out of temporary pregnancy-induced pub quiz retirement', and 'visiting parents for the weekend', Charlotte Davenport.

Now everyone had arrived, Dan and Andy went to get the first round in; Dan looked over to their tables to remind himself of the drinks, and made eye contact with Charlotte. She nodded a friendly acknowledgement, but he spotted the competitive gleam; he smiled in return.

"Shame Bertie's in Africa, or you could've had the full set," he joked.

"Funny," Andy retorted sarcastically. "Although you're overlooking a couple there."

"Ah. Of course. What was she called again?"

"Danni," Andy reminded him, unnecessarily. He took the first few drinks over, then came back for more.

"That's right," Dan said. "Short for Danielle. I'll tell you what, bro, they were some fantastic tattoos she had—wonder if your name's on there somewhere now?"

"Yeah, yeah."

"And then, of course, there was Rachel."

"Let's just forget about her, shall we?" The 'relationship' with Rachel lasted one date and a fortnight of phone calls, where she persistently informed Andy that it was 'love at first sight' and didn't believe him when he gently informed her that the feeling wasn't mutual.

"At least she had a woman's name."

Andy laughed. "D'you know what? I hadn't noticed. Maybe that's the key."

"The key to what?"

411

"Happy relationships."

"But you're still single."

"Yeah, and I'm also still on speaking terms with Danni, Bertie and Charlie."

"Fair enough," Dan conceded. They returned with the rest of the drinks, just as the quizmaster was making his way around with the answer sheets.

"D'you think we'll get lucky with the rounds again?" Andy asked, as he resumed his seat next to Jess.

"No such thing as luck," Josh said, making sure he was turned away from Sean as he said it. He followed it up with a subtle wink in Andy's direction; the reason became clear soon after.

"You're not going to insist on that no phones nonsense again, are you?" Eleanor asked.

"It's not nonsense," Sean argued. "It's about the value of victory."

"I agree with Ellie," Kris said. "If everyone else is gonna use their phones, why shouldn't we?"

"Because we don't need to," Josh told him. "We are above cheating."

"But we're not cheating," Shaunna justified. She paused whilst the quizmaster delivered their sheets and took their entry money. "We're levelling the playing field."

"We don't need to," Josh repeated. "We're already at an advantage to everyone else here."

"That sounded really arrogant," Sophie said, "but I understand what you mean."

"Did it?" Josh asked George. He shrugged indifferently. He, Andy and Dan had no intention of involving themselves in this discussion.

"Well, well, what do you know?" Sean had the quiz sheet in his hands and had just started reading over the round titles.

"What?" Eleanor asked. Sean passed it to her and she read it out loud. "Law and Order, K9, Extreme Sports—is he having a laugh?"

Josh smirked into his drink and waited for Eleanor to read on, because he hadn't intervened just for his own team's sake.

"Oh, hang on," she said. She stared at Josh. He turned his back. George looked from one to the other of them, trying to work out what was going on. Eleanor passed the quiz sheet back to Sean. He read through the remaining rounds and grinned.

"Sandison, you're a..."

"I assume we can stick with our 'no phones' policy?" Josh interrupted.

"Absolutely!" Sean agreed. They could hear the Crash Test Mummies grumbling and arguing over which round they disliked least for their joker, whereas both Brains and Brawn and Complex Superiority were somewhat spoilt for choice.

"How did you do that?" George whispered to Josh.

"I didn't do anything," he replied, also whispering. "I merely pointed out to Ron—that's the quizmaster, by the way—that I'd overheard customers complaining about the same team winning every week."

"Really? That's all you did?"

"Well, I may have given him some ideas for interesting rounds at the same time. And I was very nice to him."

"You mean you psyched him."

"Persuaded."

George rolled his eyes.

"So, thoughts on a joker?" Jess asked.

"I think the birthdays boys should choose," Charlotte suggested.

"Cool," Andy said. He picked up the quiz sheet and glanced over the categories. "That's easy then. If Extreme Sports is what it says it is?"

"Even if it's not, it's going to be about sport," George reasoned.

"OK. Let's go with that," Andy decreed.

On the other team, Dan was still frowning at the sheet. "I dunno," he said. "That Jack of All Trades round could be anything."

"Grease Lightning?" James queried. "That must surely be about automobiles?"

"Knowing this quiz, it'll be about the weather in Athens," Sean joked, and he had a point.

"We've got time to think about it, anyway," Shaunna said, "unless anyone thinks we should go for Law and Order?" That was the first round.

There was a loud murmuring of 'no' around their table, although it was nothing compared to the continued grunting of the Crash Test Mummies.

"Good evening, ladies and gents," came the quizmaster's voice, as usual amplified by the speakers, "and once again, welcome to our Friday night quiz. It's great to see so many of you in again. For those of you who are new, or a bit forgetful, a quick reminder of how it works. We've got eight rounds, and you can choose to double your points on any round other than the music round, by showing your joker. Without further ado, let's head straight on with Round One: Law and Order. Any jokers?" There was general mumbling all around the pub, but no jokers. "All right then. Questions all relate to famous figures in Law, factual or fictitious. A nice easy one to start you off. Question one: which famous detective duo lived at 221B Baker Street?"

Adele was busy buffing her nails and intermittently sipping at her wine. The answer was hissed around their table, and she glanced across to see what Eleanor had written.

"I knew that," she whispered excitedly.

"Question two: by what nickname was the criminal Albert de Salvo better known?"

Again, there was the hissing of potential answers around the table, but some disagreement over the correct one. Adele was pretty sure she'd watched a programme about him the previous week, but she didn't like to say. Eleanor had written down the New York Bomber. Adele nudged Shaunna.

"I think it's the Boston Strangler," she whispered.

"Are you sure?" Shaunna asked.

"No. Just leave it," Adele said.

The rest of the round consisted of the same kind of questions—the identity of the Demon Barber of Fleet Street, the real name of Black Dahlia, and so on—and Adele found herself in the same dilemma twice more, but she chose only to share her thoughts with Shaunna, knowing her friend would not ridicule her if she was wrong. However, the questions had got her attention, and she entered the second round, Jack of All Trades, with a new enthusiasm. She even put her nail buffer away.

"Round Two: we're looking for the surnames of famous Jacks," the quizmaster explained.

"Bet you're gutted," Dan said to Kris.

"Why?"

"No DI Lundberg questions in the first round."

"Ah, yeah," Kris nodded dolefully. "When I star in a pub quiz, I'll know I've made it for real." Both men laughed, then quietened down for the next set of questions.

"Question one," the quizmaster began. "Which Jack wooed the women of Eastwick?"

Kris leaned in and whispered loudly to Eleanor. "Nicholson."

"I think the whole pub heard you then," she said.

"Oops!" He grinned and put his hand over his mouth.

"Question two: which famous Jack found a successful career in teaching after being fired by his own band, No Vacancy?"

Again, Kris came up with the answer right away, but this time whispered quietly, and with his hand in front of his face, having been reminded by Shaunna that Josh was quite adept at lip-reading, and Complex Superiority looked clueless for a while, but then it came to Andy in a flash and he grabbed the pen from Josh to write it down. Josh squinted to read the writing and nodded.

"Of course!" he said. The round continued in much the same way, with Kris getting the answer to every question, and more or less straight away, whilst Complex Superiority muddled through. Round Three didn't go much better for them, given that 'Beauty and the Beast' turned out to be mostly about fashion, much to Adele's delight. From the first question, which asked for the name of the designer who introduced the Little Black

Dress, she was on a roll and aced the round for Brains and Brawn, just going to prove that 'brains' aren't everything. On to Round Four, and Complex Superiority were finally in with a chance, for it was a picture round, with the pictures consisting of ten photos of dogs of different breeds. They were told that this round would run straight into the music round, so Josh and Charlotte went up to the bar to buy the drinks, leaving George to answer the questions for their team, whereas it was down to Shaunna and Kris on the other team, and a couple of the rarer breeds had them really stumped. Dan and Andy had both gone to chat with a group of men they'd employed as crew a while back, and Sean was visiting the toilet, so in the absence of the competitive elements of their teams, the K9 experts pooled their knowledge; in other words, George gave Kris and Shaunna the answers.

The bar was busy and it took a while for everyone to be served, but as people started to return to their tables, the quizmaster announced that he would play the clips for the music round twice through, and it was as well, for George had taken a large mouthful of beer just as the first clip started and he spurted it out with such force that it completely soaked the answer sheets on both tables. Furthermore, he was so completely helpless with laughter that he couldn't even explain what he'd found so funny. There was one other person who knew, and he was trying very hard to preoccupy himself with cleaning up the mess that George had just made, his face burning bright red, desperately hoping that the moment would pass unseen. The clip in question was from the Aerosmith song, "Love in an Elevator", and by the time the beer was cleaned up, Josh had realised exactly why George was laughing so much. People had also started to notice how sheepish Andy was looking and one by one turned their gaze from George to him. Andy covered his face with his hands, although he was laughing, because it was more funny than embarrassing.

"I'm gonna get you back for this, Morley," he said. He looked around at the dozen pairs of eyes burning into him and sighed. "OK. It's like this. When I was in Glasgow before Christmas, I was on my way up to my hotel room, when the lift got stuck between floors, for two hours."

"Two hours?" Shaunna repeated. She looked at him sympathetically. "That must've been awful."

"Yeah. It was a bit of an ordeal, especially as it jammed right next to a vent for the hotel's central heating system. By the time they got us out it was like a sauna—no exaggeration."

"Us?" Dan asked.

"Me and Bertie," Andy explained. Dan nodded, a smirk slowly working its way onto his face.

"Who's Bertie?" Jess asked.

415

"The one I told you about? She went to Africa to teach English."

"Oh yeah." Jess was satisfied with that, although that still left several of the others, including Shaunna, in the dark. Andy glanced ruefully at her and pressed on.

"So, we're there in this lift, and we had to strip off. I was wearing a suit, and Bertie was in blacks and whites. It was roasting. She took off her tights and top, and I was gonna strip to my boxers, but the zip got stuck on my trousers, and my hands were slippy on account of the sweat, so Bertie was trying to help me unzip my trousers, and she pulled the zip and it, err..." Andy winced at the memory and the rest of them got the idea, the men in their midst all now donning similar facial expressions, apart from George, who knew how this ended, so was still giggling away to himself, stopping every so often to dry his eyes.

"Anyway," Andy continued, "between us, we managed to free me from the zip. I was bleeding quite a lot, and I'm a bit of a wimp when it comes to my own blood, so I was trying not to look, whilst Bertie applied pressure to the wound, and she went to pick up her shirt to use it as a compression dressing, because my shirt was over the other side of the lift. As she turned away, she caught her hair around the hook on the waistband of my trousers. The lift started up again and the doors opened on us, me standing there topless, with my trousers undone, her half-naked, and with her hand around my you-know-what and her face in my crotch."

Other than Adele, who looked horrified by the whole saga, everyone else was now in a similar state to George, and it was some time into Round Six: Medicine Men, before they regained control. Shaunna wanted to ask Adele why she didn't think it was funny, but every time she tried to speak, she started laughing again, so gave up in the end, assuming she hadn't understood, although it was quite the contrary. There had once been an incident in the department store changing rooms, where a man almost bled to death following a zip-trapping, and she didn't find it funny in the slightest.

The Medicine Men round turned out to be yet another good one for Brains and Brawn, with Eleanor and Sean between them knowing every single famous contributor to medical science that they were asked to name. The sick irony of being the only member of Complex Superiority to know that the first female winner of the Nobel prize was Marie Curie was not lost on Jess, and in the end she had to jolly the rest of them along by making light of it. Now they were into the final two rounds, and both teams still had their jokers to play. Complex Superiority were sticking with their first choice of Extreme Sports, which was the very last round, but Brains and Brawn couldn't decide between that and Grease Lightning.

"It's your call, Dan," Shaunna said.

"Why me?" he protested. "I don't know anything about pub quizzes. And if we lose, it'll be my fault."

"We're not going to lose," Sean asserted. "We might not come first, but we're definitely not coming any lower than second."

"That's as good as losing," Kris said, knowing how competitive his friend was.

"What do you think, James?" Dan asked. James shrugged.

"Toss a coin?" he suggested. It was as good a means to choose as any. Sean stood up and withdrew a ten pence piece from his pocket.

"All right. Heads we go for Grease Lightning, tails, Extreme Sports." He flipped the coin, but he didn't catch it. Instead it landed on the table, on its edge, and stayed right where it was.

"No way!" Shaunna said. "I bet you couldn't do that again if you tried."

Dan shook his head in disbelief. "Ha! What are the odds?"

"One in six thousand," Josh answered, knowing it was a rhetorical question and also that this was the correct answer. "It's known as a flipistic singularity," he explained.

"And can the smart Alec over there also tell us what Grease Lightning is about?" Dan asked, the usual rivalry now sparking between them.

"Genius, not mind-reader," Josh retorted. He picked up his pint and took a slurp. Dan's neck muscles bulged and George glared at Josh. "But it's probably your safest bet," he said, then gave George a quick smile. Whether he was telling the truth or not, it was decision time.

"Round Seven," the quizmaster began. All seven members of Brains and Brawn looked to each other in panic. Dan shrugged.

"Fuck it." He picked up the joker. "It's only a pub quiz. It's meant to be fun. What d'you reckon, bro? Does it suit me?"

Andy looked at the card with the joker hat on it that Dan was holding above his head and grinned.

"Nah, maybe something with bells on?"

And so, they headed into the round, quickly discovering that Josh's advice had been sincere and good, for the questions were indeed about automobiles, with Dan easily answering those relating to supercars, and James picking up the ones about classics. By the time the round was over, they were confident that they had full marks.

"Our final round this evening: Extreme Sports," the quizmaster said. George had been curling the corner of their joker between his thumb and forefinger, and needed a nudge from Sophie before he realised he needed to hold it up. Here, Andy and Charlotte came into their own, firing off the answers so quickly that Josh could hardly keep up with writing them down, and they'd been right again; all of the questions related not to extreme sports, but to extreme sporting events—deadly Formula One accidents, freakily high final scores in football matches, the record for the longest volley at Wimbledon, and so on. At the end of the quiz, they all swapped papers and marked the answers from other teams, with optimism running high on both tables, as they listened to the correct responses and judged the papers in front of them accordingly. Adele couldn't believe it when she heard that Albert de Salvo was in fact the Boston Strangler, and wished she'd had the guts to speak up. They handed the marked answer sheets back to the quizmaster, and James and Kris went to the bar.

Josh and Adele exited the adjacent toilets at the same time and Adele smiled awkwardly, trying to avoid eye contact. It was a reaction that Josh was used to getting from her, although not usually to this extreme, and he immediately tried to ease her discomfort.

"Have you enjoyed tonight?" he asked.

"I have. I didn't think I would."

"Why not?"

"Because I'm not that bright."

"You're much more clever than you think you are."

"I'm really not." She turned and made fleeting eye contact with him. "Can I tell you a secret?" she asked.

"Of course."

"I, err…" She giggled nervously, then became serious and looked down at the floor.

"Is it about reading?" Josh prompted. She nodded. "You struggle with it, don't you?"

"Yes," she confessed. "I can read and write, just…"

"Not as well as you'd like to be able to."

She nodded again. "That's why I messed about at school, and why I left without sitting most of the exams. It was so difficult for me. And sometimes, when I'm trying to understand stuff, Dan makes fun of me. He doesn't know how hard I try, but it makes me feel so stupid. I'd love to go back to college, like Shaunna, and…" She sighed and turned away, biting her lip. She looked almost ready to cry.

"Hey," Josh said gently, putting his arm around her. "Firstly, you are *not* stupid. Think how many of those questions you knew the answer to when no-one else did."

"It's just a silly pub quiz," Adele dismissed.

"Perhaps, but most of the people in here only know the answers because they look them up on the internet. You had the answers in your head."

"See, that's what I mean. I wish I could write them down. And I've always wanted to read books, but all those tiny words—it makes me feel dizzy trying to concentrate."

"But that doesn't make you stupid. The other thing I was going to say is that school and college isn't like when we went. There's tons of support for students who find reading and writing hard. One of the students who just passed the counselling course is dyslexic and the university loaned him an audio recorder to make his notes. If he'd had to sit written exams, they'd have arranged for someone to be his scribe and write his answers for him."

"So I could go back to college?"

"Of course you could! You'll have to tell them the truth about the problems you have, but I'm sure they'd give you lots of help. What do you want to study?"

"Oh, I'm not sure. I haven't really thought about it properly. The gym job's great and everything, but—I just don't know. What if I mess up?"

"You won't. Just go for it, Adele."

She looked at him and nodded.

"You've got nothing to lose. And if I can help you, I will."

"Thanks," she said. She gave him a quick hug and kissed his cheek, then looped her arm through his as they returned to their respective tables, where Dan was doing something on his phone, Sophie and Andy were chatting away on their table, and James was talking to Charlotte. Most bizarrely, Kris and Sean were laughing and joking together. Shaunna and Jess had passed them in transit to the toilets, but Eleanor was missing, and once again George was nowhere to be found.

"Do you know where he's gone?" Josh asked Sophie.

"Outside with Eleanor," she said.

"Oh." Josh sat down, thinking he'd rather have been told he was talking to that police officer guy from last week. He certainly wasn't going to be heading out there to join them, of that he was quite sure. Instead, he listened to Andy and Sophie's conversation while he waited for George to return.

"I still say pregnant women are beautiful," Andy stated.

"OK. Convince me," Sophie challenged.

"You glow."

"I'm too hot."

"You're all—feminine and soft."

"Fat, with water retention."

"Your hair is all thick and shiny."

"Needs washing and cutting."

"And so natural."

"I couldn't be bothered to pluck my eyebrows or put on any make-up."

Andy raised his arms in mock despair. Sophie laughed, then winced and shifted position.

"Plus I keep getting kicked in the bladder." As she said this, a small wave of movement chased across her abdomen.

"That's so awesome," Andy said, unable to take his eyes off her belly. Josh glared at him, willing him to look over, because Sean was now watching them, and appeared to be ever so slightly irritated, which wasn't like him at all.

"Thanks for your patience," the quizmaster's voice came through the speaker so loudly and suddenly that Josh jumped. "I just had to verify the prize for tonight's quiz."

George and Eleanor came back in and resumed their seats. Josh glared moodily at George, who gave him a reassuring smile in response. Shaunna and Jess dodged their way past the quizmaster and sat down.

"The kitty tonight stands at a record one hundred and five pounds, so I'm going to keep you in suspense a little longer, and give you the results in reverse order."

"I can't stand it when he does this," Sophie grumbled, "and I'm desperate for the loo."

"Maybe we came last," Josh consoled.

"I think I'd rather wet myself!"

"In ninth place, with forty-five points, the Hard Hats."

The men Dan and Andy had been talking to earlier all cheered and clanged their glasses together in a toast.

"In eighth place, with fifty-one points, Mr. Ballroom Blitz himself!" There was general applause and the 'newbies' on their teams looked to see what all the fuss was about.

"He does this quiz solo every week," Sean explained, pointing to the lone man at a table at the rear of the pub.

"The man at the back," Shaunna said, realising the meaning of his 'team' name. He was red-eyed and lolling, and looked like he'd had far too much to drink to score a singular point, let alone fifty-one of them.

"In seventh place, with fifty-nine points, In First Place."

"Huh?" Adele said.

"Their team name, hun," Shaunna explained.

"What is?"

"In First Place."

"I don't get it." Adele frowned, then thought about it, then giggled. "I get it," she said, very pleased with herself.

"To complicate things further," the quizmaster continued, "in sixth place, with sixty-one points, Last As Usual."

Shaunna turned to explain to Adele, but she put up her hand.

"I got it already," she grinned.

"In fifth place, with sixty-six points, Them In The Corner."

There was a bout of booing from the team members themselves, because they usually ranked in the top three. They turned and glared at Complex

Superiority. Josh shrugged at them apologetically. He really didn't want to upset the locals. Well, most of the locals.

"In fourth place, with seventy-four points, Pass The Salt Vicar."

"Who thinks of these team names?" Kris asked, glancing over at the fourth place team, which did, in fact, include the vicar.

"OK, people, this is it," Josh said, rubbing his hands together. He was desperately hoping to hear that the Crash Test Mummies were in third place.

"It was very close here at the top," the quizmaster said, dragging it out even longer.

"Come on!" Sophie said, jiggling on the edge of her seat and trying to keep her knees together.

"You struggling, Soph?" George asked sympathetically.

"Fucking right, I am," she snapped at him, but he didn't take it to heart. He was quite used to it by now.

"In third place, with eighty-six points, Complex Superiority."

"Thank Christ," Sophie said, and wobbled off to the toilets as fast as she dared.

"Bugger," Josh said, a little deflated, but not yet defeated, for there was still hope.

"In second place, with eighty-seven points," the quizmaster said, glancing from the Crash Test Mummies to Brains and Brawn, but giving nothing away.

"Much as it pains me to say this," Josh told Sean, "I hope you're about to wipe the smile off that bloody woman's face."

"Are you ready for it?" the quizmaster asked.

"Yes!" came the cry from all over the pub.

"In second place, it's…"

"I'm going to go and…" Sean started.

"The Crash Test Mummies."

"Yee-hah!" Shaunna shouted.

"Which means we have brand new champions tonight, with an incredible eighty-nine out of ninety: Brains and Brawn."

There was much applause from around the pub, because Josh had been telling the truth when he'd informed Ron The Quizmaster that people were getting fed up with the Crash Test Mummies winning every week, and the fact they'd been beaten was all the sweeter for it having been done without the aid of mobile phones.

"Well done, guys," George said.

"See?" Shaunna nudged Adele. "Next time speak up. We'd have got full marks if you had!" Adele smiled. This night had been just the confidence boost she needed.

"How's that for a birthday present, bro?" Andy asked. Dan nodded.

"Yeah. Pretty decent."

"It gets even better than that," Shaunna said. Charlotte had sneaked off, and now returned, carrying an enormous, rectangular cake, decorated as a football pitch, with two Subbuteo players standing in the centre circle. Shaunna had already cleared a space, so that Charlotte could put it down.

"Penalty shootout," she grinned. "No cake till you both score." Andy and Dan looked at each other and rolled their eyes at exactly the same time. They moved across to take their positions, one at each end of their edible pitch.

"You go first," Dan suggested. "Age before beauty." He grinned.

Andy tutted. He positioned the ball as best he could on the tiny pitch, then flicked his player. The ball went straight in the net.

"You didn't even try and save that!"

"Nope. I want to eat cake," Dan said. "Plus, he's not a proper goalie, is he?"

"Fair enough."

"Why not?" Josh asked.

"No stick," came the response from Andy, Dan, George, Shaunna and Charlotte.

"Oh. Silly me for not realising!" Josh remarked wryly.

"It's OK, I didn't know either," Adele placated, "and I'm part of a winning quiz team."

"You are too," Josh said. She smiled proudly.

"What do they mean, no stick?" she mouthed at him.

He shrugged and mouthed back, "I have no idea." George shook his head and sighed.

"I'll explain later," he said.

Andy waited for Dan to position his player, then he sat back and watched. Right at the last second, he moved his 'goalkeeper' to intercept and the ball rolled off the side of the 'pitch'.

"Aw, come on!" Dan complained. "I want cake!"

"Yeah, but I've got to beat you at something tonight."

"For fuck's sake," Dan laughed. They moved their players back to the other end, and Andy took his second shot. 2-0.

"Right. Don't even think about it," Dan warned, as he lined up the ball for his next attempt. Andy raised his hands, and kept them raised until after Dan had flicked his player. The ball went wide and landed in Shaunna's wine. She plucked it out, wiped it on her top, and passed it back to Andy.

"This is lunacy," Dan said, watching Andy score his third penalty. "Can't we just cut the damned thing?" he asked. Charlotte folded her arms and shook her head.

"Nope! You know what they say about revenge being sweet?"

Dan sighed and prepared to take his next shot. One goal. That's all he needed. It really wasn't that difficult. He took aim, flicked his player, and finally planted the ball in the net. There was much cheering, and Charlotte handed the knife across. Dan left it to Andy to make the inaugural cut, then they let George do the rest, because he was sat closest.

"Cheers, everyone, for an awesome birthday night out," Dan mumbled through a mouthful of cake.

"Agreed," Andy said in the same fashion. "It's been great fun. Same time next week?"

"No!" came the resounding reply. After all, they still had a wedding to plan.

AS ONE
Monday 5th June

They were sitting in the car at traffic lights, neither having yet shared the details of their separate trips to the jeweller who had sold them Krissi's bracelet for her twenty-first birthday and each, individually, their engagement rings. And being a man of great integrity, the jeweller hadn't mentioned a thing about it to either of them.

"Can we pop to the mall?" Josh asked. "I want to have a look at those new controllers." George eyed him suspiciously.

"Why? What's wrong with the ones we've got?"

"Oh, nothing. The new ones are apparently a more ergonomic design."

"Um, OK." George agreed hesitantly.

"Stop worrying."

"I'm not!"

"Lies." Josh pulled away from the lights. Every time he suggested buying something new it resulted in an interrogation. Understandable, really.

"Actually," George said, trying to make it sound inconsequential, "while we're there, can we pop to the jeweller's?" Josh's heart leapt into his mouth.

"I guess. Why?"

"I want…a watch."

"A watch?"

"Yeah."

"Why didn't you say so before your birthday?"

"I only just decided."

Josh tutted in disbelief. Neither of them spoke after that, until they'd parked up and were on their way to the lift.

"So, what kind of watch do you have in mind, sir?" Josh said, pronouncing each word with short, snappy syllables.

"Don't! It's already bad enough!" George pushed him into the lift.

"Not a watch for *her*, is it, sir?"

The doors closed and George put his arms around him and kissed him, only releasing when the lift slowed and the 'lift voice' announced "doors opening". He stepped away and grinned.

"There. That shut you up," he said and walked away, Josh following in a daze. "You want to go to Gadget Heaven first?"

"No. Let's go and look at watches."

They made their way to the jeweller's, pushed the doorbell and waited. A few seconds later the buzzer sounded and they went inside. The jeweller was dealing with another customer, but looked up in acknowledgement. Josh turned away to study the cube, still displaying the rose gold and freshwater pearls.

"He looks happy to see us," he remarked out of the side of his mouth.

"Indeed," George replied. "You could say he is almost ecstatic with delight."

Josh closed his eyes and held onto the giggles with every bit of willpower he had, trying to think sad thoughts, just to stay in control. George winked at him and watched the other customer leave. She didn't appear to be having quite so much of a problem.

"Good morning," Josh said, pushing George towards the counter.

"And a good morning to *you*, sir," the jeweller smiled broadly at Josh, then at George.

"Hi," George returned the smile coyly.

"How can I help you today, sirs?"

"He wants to buy a watch," Josh said quickly, on George's behalf.

"A watch, sir?" The jeweller looked surprised, although only mildly, to hear this.

"I, err…" George began. He frowned.

"I'll give you a moment, sir," the jeweller offered with a barely perceptible wink, unnerving George further. "One of my pearls seems to have escaped." Josh's eyes widened as he watched him take out his keys and head for the glass display cube.

"Did he just…" he started to whisper to George.

"Yes," George hissed back. He was toying with them, except that so far each believed it was directed at them personally.

As they engaged in their hushed dialogue, the jeweller continued to make minor adjustments to the display, surreptitiously removing a couple of items and placing them in his pocket.

"No way!" George said loudly.

"Yes. We've done it again," Josh responded. They both started laughing. Josh turned to the jeweller. "OK. We're ready now," he said, then added, "sir." He grinned at him. The jeweller nodded and returned behind his counter.

"We're getting married in two weeks," George explained, understanding now why the jeweller had made the remark about the pearl, which was a bit rude, in retrospect, but achieved precisely what he had intended.

"Congratulations, sirs," he said solemnly.

"So should we give you our rings now?" Josh asked. He stepped a little closer to the counter and leaned over it, supposedly examining the glittering bracelets and bangles within. George glared at him. Josh was looking directly at the jeweller, but with his head bowed, fluttering his eyelashes.

"Absolutely, sir. I think that is an excellent idea," the jeweller replied, still with a serious expression, and a glint in his eye. George looked from one to the other and felt his hackles rise. His fiancé was flirting. *Flirting! With the bloody jeweller!*

"Awesome. Here's mine. Sorry, my hands are a bit clammy," Josh said. He smiled as he pulled his ring off and gently placed it on the jeweller's palm, then nudged George. "Give him yours."

"Huh?"

"Give him your ring, George!"

"Oh, yeah." George took off his ring and thrust it at the jeweller.

"Thank you, sir," the jeweller smiled. George nodded briskly; not the slightest danger of him getting the giggles today.

"When will they be ready?" he asked.

"End of business, the day after tomorrow, sir."

"My, you don't waste any time," Josh said. George walked off to look at the watches. He didn't actually want a watch. He'd never owned a watch in his life, although he'd always rather liked the old-fashioned pocket watches.

Josh waited for the jeweller to fill out the receipt for their rings. He tore it from the pad with a flourish and held it out, pincered between his index and middle fingers.

"Thanks," Josh smiled and took it. "Would you like to come?"

George slowly turned around and his gaze met with the jeweller's.

"To our wedding?" Josh added, in case it hadn't been clear to begin with. "We'd love to have you there."

The jeweller's eyes remained locked with George's for a few seconds longer, then he turned to look at Josh. "Oh, I don't know about that, s…"

"We really would like you to," George said. He came back over to the counter. He sort of understood now, although he was still jealous and mad as hell.

"Well, I, err—I don't know what to say, sirs," the jeweller stammered. His eyes clouded over and he shook a white, cotton handkerchief from his pocket. Josh tutted.

"Just say yes. Or yes, sirs, if you like."

"Yes," the jeweller replied. "Thank you."

"Cool," George nodded. "That's settled, then. We'll bring you an official invitation when we come back for our rings." He moved to leave. "Come on, Joshua," he said, his chirpy tone belying how he was feeling. Josh followed him.

"Just one moment, sirs," the jeweller called them back. He reached into his pocket again and removed the objects he'd collected earlier, then opened a drawer in the counter. "I hope you don't mind, but I selected a little something that I thought you might like, by way of congratulation, and to express my gratitude for your repeat custom and frequent commendation."

They watched as he polished the objects, unable to see what they were, and placed them in two boxes. He gave them one each.

"If I have made a dreadful misjudgement, then please do feel you can exchange these gifts for something more to your tastes," he added, a touch nervously, Josh thought.

"Thank you," he said.

"Yeah, thank you," George repeated, feeling a bit guilty now.

"Don't open them here," the jeweller told them, but the request came too late and he made himself busy with cleaning the counter, polishing away fingerprints that only he could see.

"Wow!" Josh said.

"This is…" George lifted the pocket watch out of the box. He turned to look at Josh, who was staring in awe at his cufflinks, which were of the same design and materials as the watch: brushed chrome, with inlaid rose gold and faux mother of pearl.

"How did you know?" George asked, but then it dawned on him, the connection between the jeweller and Josh that he'd failed to spot earlier.

Josh shook his head. "We can't take these. We don't even know your name!"

"Vincent," the jeweller said quickly. "I believe that resolves your dilemma, sir?"

Josh looked him in the eye and established that the gifts were non-returnable. "Thank you, Vincent. So you will come, then? To the wedding?"

"Absolutely, sir. I'm already planning an outfit." Momentarily he had dropped the façade and Josh seized the chance.

"Good. Just one other thing, while we're at it," he said. "He's George. I'm Josh. We'd be delighted if you'd stop calling us sir."

The jeweller nodded and smiled. "Consider it done," he paused for effect, "sir."

Josh pretended to glower at him, although there was no pretence from George, whose eyes were glowing greener than usual just now. They said their goodbyes and Josh followed him out of the shop, aware that George was in a bad mood, but not of the reason for it.

"That's so nice of him," Josh said as they headed back to the car.

"Nice, yeah," George grumped.

"What's the matter?"

"Nothing at all."

"Really?"

"If you discount the fact that you were flirting with someone else—again, *and* right in front of me."

"Flirting with…?"

George didn't respond.

"Well?" Josh prompted.

"The jeweller, obviously."

"I was not flirting with the jeweller!"

"You were." George walked on ahead and held the door open. Josh stepped past him.

"I really wasn't." He pushed the button to call the lift. "Was I?" He looked genuinely shocked.

"Don't pretend you didn't realise."

"George. I didn't realise," Josh said sincerely. "That kind of, erm, oh God."

George tutted. The lift arrived and they stepped inside.

"You seriously didn't know?"

"No. I'm sorry. It won't happen again. Actually, that's a stupid thing to promise. How would I even know if it did?"

"When you get home from work, I'll explain it to you. Flirting 101."

"Might be useful. That's really very dangerous. Do I do it a lot?"

"Nope. Ignoring your inadvertent flirt with Asif, I've only ever seen you do it with two other people."

"Who's that then?"

"Ellie."

"You're kidding me."

"Why do you think I used to get all flustered and jealous?"

"I flirt with Ellie? Are you sure?"

"Yep."

"Why would I flirt with Ellie?"

"I dunno. Maybe because it's safe?"

The lift stopped and they got out.

"You didn't get your new controllers," George said.

"It was a ruse."

"I figured as much."

"Ruse gold," Josh said and started giggling. This too was a ruse, because he was a little alarmed by what George had told him.

"That's really not that funny," George remarked as they climbed back in the car.

"I know. Sorry." Josh put his seatbelt on and started the engine. "Who's the other person?" he asked, slowly reversing out of the space.

"Guess," George said.

"Is it you?"

"If only!"

"Kris?"

"Nope."

"Shaunna?"

"Definitely not."

"Just tell me!"

"All right then. It's Dan."

Josh stalled the engine.

IF
Monday 19th June

3:33 a.m.

Dreams can stretch time, into forever.

3:34 a.m.

Or flash by in less than a blink.

4:38 a.m.

The first: a walk down the aisle of a jumbo jet, undertaken by a stewardess in typical 1970s attire—pillbox hat, puffed cravat, pencil skirt, smile-painted, too-red lips. She walks, all eye contact and carefree tosses of the head. But for the spotlight on her eternal journey, the plane is in darkness, the blinds shut, the bright white interior dulled grey, the beeps and bongs of seatbelt warnings...

The second: he is playing outside and everything is big, hazy, hot, the grass of the meadowy expanse up past his knees, naked knees, for he is in shorts. The smells: the scent of evening primrose, stock—he is uncertain how he knows these things—and in his hands the most enormous, sweet, soft tomato. It takes both hands to lift the vast fruit to his mouth. The skin breaks; juice and pips trickle down his chin onto his shirt...
"Joshua. Where are you?"
His mother's voice. He hears her in English, though she is speaking French.
"Joshua! Are you ready? Oh, no, no, no!"
She looks at his tomato juice soaked shirt and shakes her head.
"Come," she says, "we will change your clothes. You must be smart, and handsome."
She scoops him up in her arms and carries him off, up the meadow, through the garden and towards the house. Yet they do not arrive. They walk, and they walk, and the house stays just where it is.

Josh lay perfectly still, on his back, for several moments, allowing the sweet, oblique memory of the dream to ebb away. The feeling still remained. He got up and made a coffee, then cautiously ascended the stairs to the loft, gathering the photo albums they had brought home from his grandmother's house. He climbed back into bed and sat, coffee in one hand, flicking through the pages with the other.

A little before six o'clock, George awoke suddenly and sat up. Josh looked at him in puzzlement. He turned and rubbed his eyes.

"What you doing?" he yawned.

"Good morning to you too!"

George smiled sleepily and stood up, stretching as he plodded off to the bathroom. He returned a few minutes later, still looking very sleepy. He picked up Josh's empty cup, went downstairs, returned again armed with two full cups, and got back into bed.

"Your photos," he stated.

Josh nodded and put down the album he was currently browsing to pick up the first one. He flipped open the cover, revealing a single picture positioned in the centre of the first page. "My mum," he said. George took the album from him and studied the small photo, sepia tinted by age. It was of a slender woman, with sandy blonde, shoulder length hair and a creamy complexion. He glanced at Josh and back at the image of his mother.

"She's beautiful," he said. "You look just like her." He pointed to the large, stone house behind her. "Where is this?"

"France. Eygalières. I think that's where it was." Josh turned to the next page: two photos here, of his parents on their own, then of his parents with him, held in his mother's arms; he was no more than eighteen months old, and his hair was white blonde. His father was darker, heavily set, with facial features clearly defined even though the photo was distant and slightly blurred. He traced the outline of his parents with his finger. "I had a dream, about my mum. She'd dressed me up to go somewhere and I dripped tomato juice all down my clothes. She was really angry, but she didn't shout at me." Josh remained quiet after this, allowing George to turn the pages and examine the photos within. They were all of his parents and him, with a couple of his grandmother: meals taken outside, sitting around a large, wooden table bleached ash-grey by the hot provincial sun, of him sitting on his mother's lap, or his father's, all smiling at the camera. Many depicted the meadow Josh had seen in his dream, although he could not have stated with conviction whether his ancient memory of the place originated in these photos or reality.

"I remember hardly anything about them," he said. "Sometimes, I used to look at these albums and imagine my grandma had made them up, found the photos in a junk shop and planted them in my room—for what purpose?

432

I couldn't say. But that's why I never talk about them, because they don't seem real. Sometimes I catch a scent hanging in the air, and with it a feeling that I'm missing something, someone, and eventually I realise it's her. Or I'll hear a song, and I'm transported back to being small, so small, sitting in the passenger seat, trying to see over the dashboard, and I hear that song the way it sounded in my dad's car, but him? I can see in my mind's eye my grandma, with the phone in her hand, when they called to tell her that he had died, and she cried, and I understood that he was dead. I understood what death meant, but the only sadness I felt was for her, because she was sad."

"Do you miss them?" George asked.

"No. I miss the idea of them, but I never really knew them well enough to miss them." Josh closed the album and placed his palm against the cover. "You know I don't go in for any of that spiritual nonsense," he justified before he ventured any further, "and it's likely the dream was because I'd been thinking about them, but it's made me feel, for the first time in my life, that they're more than just memories, like they're close by."

George took Josh's hand and kissed it. "What do you think they would make of us?"

Josh shrugged. "I don't know." He smiled. "But your mum—"

"Ah, yeah," George sighed. "My mum."

"I'm going to ring Pauline later," Josh said, and only partly in fun. "Get her to go round and remind her to take out her rollers."

"Hey, you never know. Today might count as a special enough occasion."

Josh laughed. "I hope so." He put the photo album on top of the others and turned so he could look at George. "I mean this most sincerely, I couldn't have wished for a better mother-in-law."

"Yep," George agreed, "she's definitely enough mother for the both of us!"

***

A couple of hours later, Sophie arrived with a poster tube containing the properly printed version of George's vows, which she wouldn't allow him to see.

"I really could do with a quick rehearsal," he pleaded.

"Ta-da!" she said, pulling a rough copy from inside the tube. "Here's one I made earlier." She handed it across. "You have a read-through and I'll go and make us a drink." She headed off for the kitchen and called back. "Where's Josh?"

"Gone to get his eyes tested."

"He's what?" The incredulity took her voice a tone higher than usual.

"Yeah, I know." George rolled the paper the other way to stop it curling back on itself. That was going to be a trial this afternoon, he realised, as he fought with it a second time, then pinned it down on the coffee table with a coaster at each corner. He read under his breath:

"When I first saw you, you were standing behind your chair, pretending to be invisible, glancing up furtively to see who the newcomer was. That newcomer was me." He ran out of breath. "Damn. Soph?"

"Yep?" She reappeared in the doorway, holding her hands beneath her belly and fidgeting. "Need a wee. Go on."

"It's OK. It's not urgent." She nodded her gratitude and waddled up the stairs. George freed the sheet of paper from the coasters. It was a little flatter now. He took it to the kitchen with him and finished making the tea, then returned with one cup at a time as he tried to read, but kept running out of breath before the end of the paragraph. He put the second cup on the table and sat down.

"OK. Breathe," he said. He scanned over the words and started again.

"When I first saw you, you were standing behind your chair..." he heard the toilet flush, "...pretending to be invisible, glancing up furtively..." Sophie came back down the stairs. "Can we mark some pauses in?"

She shrugged. "I don't see why not." Slowly, she lowered herself onto the sofa.

"You OK?"

"Yep. Just need to give birth now. Well, not right now—I can't believe I've got to endure another two months of this. Ow!" She put her hand on her side. "Braxton Hicks," she explained. George placed his palm on the top of her rock-solid bump.

"Man, that's gotta be a pain."

"Man, it is!" she said. "Anyway. Tell me where you want these pauses and I'll mark them on the official edition." She took out the original and George passed her a pencil and a book to lean on, which she tried resting on her belly, but it kept slipping sideways. She shuffled along to the end of the sofa and balanced the book on the arm. "OK. I'm ready."

"OK. The first one," he re-read the first paragraph, "before 'That newcomer was me.'"

Sophie's eyes moved as she read, then she stopped and marked the sheet. "Got that."

"All right. Next one." George hadn't got any further. "Hang on, I'll need to read it out to tell you."

Sophie picked up her tea and balanced it on top of her belly.

"I saw a beautiful, shy, intelligent boy," George read, "with eyelashes so blonde and eyes so blue—did I really write this?"

"Yes, you did."

"I don't remember this bit."

"Well, I may have taken a bit of editorial licence, I'll admit, because what you actually said was, 'His eyelashes were so damned blonde they were like rays of sunshine, and his eyes! Oh, Soph, they were so sad and so blue it made me want to cry.'"

"I did not say that!"

"You did!" She took out her phone and played back the recording. George blushed and hid behind the paper. "Although," she said, "in your defence, you had drunk an entire bottle of rosé."

"Oh, fine," George relented. "Right, so 'I saw…blah, blah, blah…so blue, and I knew, from that moment, that I wanted to spend the rest of my life with that boy.' Pause there. 'For that boy was you.' And there."

Sophie marked the pauses where indicated and lifted her cup, as a wave of motion made her whole belly move from left to right.

"Doing somersaults again. I'm sure this baby's gonna be a gymnast."

George watched, fascinated. They'd done all the feeling first kicks and stuff months ago, but this was some kind of wonderful, and he felt so truly privileged to be a part of it.

"The next bit then?" Sophie prompted.

"Err, yeah." George turned back to his words. "OK: 'You are my best friend, because you are my everything.' You know he'll have the whole 'ma moitié' thing in his vows, and all I've got is a cheesy 'you are my everything'."

"Is it the truth?"

"Yes."

"Then it's not cheesy."

"It sounds so—oh, I don't know. I can't get it right. I need to say more, but…" He shrugged despondently.

"You're not seriously thinking of rewriting these now, are you? We've only got another four hours, and no wine!"

"Wine? It's not even nine o'clock yet! And anyway, the registrar would have to approve them. It's just—" He scrunched up his face and huffed, still not happy with what he'd written. "Never mind," he said, turning his attention back to the paper. "Stick a pause after 'everything'. Then, 'You are my beginning, my end and all that is between, because I can not remember my life before you.' Stick another pause there. And then just leave the last bit. I can do the love, cherish and honour without thinking."

"Are you sure?"

George laughed. "I've been rehearsing my entire life!"

"OK." Sophie marked in the last pause. "All done?"

"Yep."

435

"Cool." She rolled the scroll and put it back in the tube.

"I'm glad we got that thick paper. I'm a nervous wreck!" George held up his shaking hands by way of demonstration.

"A few hours from now it'll all be over bar the shouting."

"Yeah," George sighed. He went over and kissed her cheek, hugging her as well as he could around the girth of seven months' gestation. "Thank you, Best Woman," he said.

"My pleasure."

***

On his second attempt, and with much puffing and panting, Josh cleared the lift doors with the wheelchair. Jess looked up into her friend's face; he was swearing under his breath and sucking the finger that he had just sandwiched between the chair handle and the wall.

"Seriously, anyone thinking of opening retail premises should have to complete a week of pushing a wheelchair around them first," he said, snagging the next corner as they turned right and headed into the shopping mall.

"That's actually not a bad idea," Jess agreed. She wasn't quite central on the seat and the steel tube of the arm was pressing against the bony protrusion of her hip. "They should also make them sit in the damned things for a while." She shuffled herself sideways and exhaled breathily. "So, optician's first, is it?"

"Yep."

"OK." She was going to leave it at that, but found she couldn't. "Why are we doing this today?"

"Because."

"Because?"

"You know falconry?"

"Yeah?"

"You know the way the bird's wings flap frantically as they come in to land on their handler's arm?"

"Yeah?"

"That's how I feel today."

Jess laughed. "Are you freaking out?"

"Erm, a little bit?" They approached the doors of the optician's—one of those vast, brightly lit, supermarket style places, with an express service, not that this was why Josh had chosen it. He'd gone online, typed 'optician' and the name of their town into the search box, and this was the first place that had come up. The online booking system offered him an appointment for nine o'clock this morning, so here he was.

"Joshua Sandison," he informed the woman behind the counter. She checked her computer screen and asked him to confirm his details.

"OK, Mr. Sandison. Please take a seat. The optician will be with you shortly." Josh parked Jess at the end of the row of chairs and did as instructed.

"When did you last get your eyes tested?" Jess asked.

"Ooh," he said, frowning and pretending to think. He tapped his finger on his lips. "Err…"

"Joshua?"

"It was, well, it was probably…"

"It was ages ago."

"Yes," he admitted. Jess rolled her eyes. "Put it this way: I was still at university."

"You mean to tell me you've gone all these years without wearing your specs?"

"I only need them for reading."

"You only *needed* them for reading. You probably need them all the time. They might even say that you're not safe driving."

"For your sake, I hope you're wrong." He nodded at the wheelchair. "Can you imagine how much damage I could do pushing that thing all the way home?"

"We'd have to get George to come and pick us up."

"You've got no chance." The door opposite where they were sitting opened and a man came out, followed by the optician, Josh presumed, from her formal attire, and glasses with frames and lenses so thin they were almost invisible.

"Joshua Sandison?" she called.

"Guess I'm about to find out," he said. He got up and followed the woman into the room. To pass the time, Jess took out her phone and opened the webpage she'd bookmarked previously; she'd been reading people's stories about staying in a hospice—something she still hated the idea of. Here she was, a thirty-nine year old woman, a professional woman, who had lived on her own almost all of her adult life. Hospices, she'd believed, were not for people like her. They were for old people, or people in their final days. OK, so, she'd accepted that she wasn't going to be here forever, but she wasn't going anywhere yet. She wasn't ready to give up and go to the hospice, to die. Not even reading these stories of people living with long-term illnesses, people of all ages and walks of life, was enough to convince her that it was the right place for her. She put the phone away again and switched her attention to the antics of the people around her, choosing frames and having glasses fitted. It was quite amusing to watch the faces they pulled at themselves, pouting and turning sideways, so engrossed in their decisions that they'd lost all awareness of those bearing witness to their gurning. It was quite a trial, choosing frames, though, even if there was still something exciting about the prospect of getting new glasses—until the disappointment set in of not being able to find frames you like as much as the old ones. She was due an eye test herself next month. Next month: it was a long, long way off. And would it be worth the expense? That probably wasn't the kind of 'positive thinking' the oncologist was talking about, but it was a valid concern, nonetheless.

"If you go over and choose your frames, then see one our assistants, they'll go through it with you," the optician said as Josh exited the room.

"Thanks," he replied, then to Jess: "Hardly changed at all. Left eye slightly worse. Right eye exactly the same."

"Even with all that straining at your laptop and reading in the dark, *without* glasses? Impressive!"

"You know they're old wives' tales, don't you?" he said, steering her over to the racks of frames labelled 'For Men'. He selected one of the pairs closest to him and put them on. He looked at Jess. She screwed up her nose. He put them back.

"It's true," she argued. "If you don't wear your glasses, you damage your eyes further."

"No, you don't. You just make them tired." He found another pair, this time with silver wire frames. He peered through the scratched fake lenses. Jess shrugged indifferently.

"Surely, if you're making your eyes tired then that strains the muscles and causes damage?" she said.

"Not so. Here. Keep hold of those a minute." He gave her the silver frames and picked out some black ones of the same design. He examined his reflection. "Good grief," he said and quickly put them back where he'd got them from.

"So all those eye exercises are pointless too, then?"

"Yep." He picked up some of the 'frameless' glasses similar to the ones his optician had been wearing. He put them on. They had very narrow lenses and were almost completely hidden by his hair. He nodded at his reflection and turned to Jess.

"They suit you," she said. "I'm not convinced though."

"How about these instead?" He picked up another pair—massive, round and bright blue. He put them on and blinked rapidly through them. She laughed.

"I meant by your argument, not your choice of frames."

He grinned and put the blue frames back. "You can't change the shape of your eye just by wearing or not wearing glasses." He was bored now, and settled on the 'frameless' frames and the silver ones Jess was still holding, as the shop had a perpetual two-for-one offer, according to the sandwich board he'd narrowly missed on his way in.

"So why do more people wear glasses these days?" Jess persisted; Josh pushed her chair over to a table, as indicated by one of the assistants.

"It's not causal."

"Say what?"

"It's nothing to do with there being more computers, is what I mean."

"So why then?"

"Because they're more readily available, perhaps? You know, more opticians, cheaper frames, free prescriptions for people on low incomes, et cetera?"

"Yeah, all right," she conceded, mostly because the assistant was already sitting down, waiting to deal with Josh. The woman gave him an absurdly bright and enthusiastic smile, considering she was only selling glasses.

"The optician mentioned you were considering contact lenses?"

"Yes, I was," Josh confirmed, "but then she talked me out of it, so I'm just going to stick with the glasses and have a think about eye surgery."

"All right then. And these are the frames you've chosen?"

"Yes." He resisted the urge to pass sarcastic comment on the pointlessness of the question.

Over the course of the next twenty minutes, the frames were measured, as was Josh, and the assistant tapped away at her keyboard, interspersed with him explaining to Jess what the optician had said about contact lenses and how they could damage your eyes if you wore them too much. This was news to him, although he'd always thought it probably wasn't healthy to deliberately stick foreign objects in your eyes, which was why he'd opted for squinting at smallprint all these years, rather than endure the pain of surgery, or acknowledge his own vanity as regards his refusal to wear his glasses.

"That's everything then, Mr. Sandison," the assistant said with another of her exuberant smiles. "Now, we can process the wire frames by the end of today, but I'm afraid it could take up to two weeks for the others." She blinked at him meaningfully.

"There's no rush," he said.

"OK. Are you paying by card?"

"Yes," he confirmed, trying not to look too horrified at the total cost currently displayed on-screen. He stood up to pull his wallet from his pocket, except it wasn't there. "Damn," he said. He sat down again. "I think I must've left it in the car. I can tell you the numbers, if that's any good?"

Before she got as far as responding, which only would have been to tell him that they needed the card itself, Jess had already taken out her credit card and handed it over.

"Thanks," Josh smiled guiltily.

"No problem. You know that's the real reason why you brought me with you today."

"I'll transfer it to your account later."

"Before or after the wedding?"

"Erm…"

The assistant handed Jess her card back. "You're getting married today?" she asked. Josh nodded. "Congratulations," she said, once again accompanied by the vast toothy grin.

"Thanks," he responded, surprised to find himself returning a similarly vast and toothy grin. He felt his stomach lurch, suddenly so unbelievably excited. His heart was racing. "Wow! I'm getting married!" He looked up at the clock. "In less than four hours, I'm going to be a married man. How awesome is that?"

Jess tutted, then laughed. The assistant passed her the receipt and smiled once more.

"Have a lovely day," she said, addressing them both.

"Oh, no. *We're* not getting married," Josh explained. He took out his phone and unlocked the screen revealing the photo of George that was his background image. It was one where he'd caught him off-guard, and kept clicking away whilst George tried to grab the phone from him, so he was laughing and his eyes were sparkling bright green. He showed the assistant. "That's my fiancé," he said. She studied the photo for a few seconds.

"Mmm," she said appreciatively, "Shame he's taken." Josh smiled.

"Yes, he's all mine." He gave the assistant a wink and she afforded him one final superbright, toothpaste ad smile, then he and Jess left, heading for the nearest coffee shop for breakfast. It was a little after ten in the morning.

"It's amazing how 'out' you are," Jess said. Josh put the cups on the table and sat down.

"What makes you say that?"

"You don't care, do you? If that woman in the optician's had suddenly gone on a huge homophobic rant, what would you have done?"

"Lodged a formal complaint and taken my business elsewhere. But I knew she wasn't going to do that."

"Really?"

"Yes. I'm quite good at judging people," he said with a grin.

"Other than best friends who don't agree with gay marriage?"

"No comment."

"Have you still not made up?"

"Nope. And I don't think we're going to, either." He sighed and started playing with his coffee cup.

"I can't believe she's being like this."

"I can. Ellie's got her reasons, not that I agree with any of them, but you can't undo nearly forty years of indoctrination." Their toasted sandwiches arrived and they sat eating in silence for a few minutes, before either spoke again. Jess had been watching him carefully, noting the occasional flicker of emotions unchecked as they registered and passed.

"You're not sad about it. How come?"

Josh finished his current mouthful and put his sandwich down. "Because she's the same as she always was. It's me that's changed, or rather I speak out about it these days, because it matters now. Back in school, when you and George were off chasing boys, we used to spend hours and hours debating religion, and it was never personal. When she realised Pete was gay, she adjusted her views a little bit, but before that—see, Kris, she could cope with, because he 'turned out right in the end'. George, she concluded, missed out on having a father around, although when you meet his mum later you'll realise that he hasn't missed out at all. Regardless, Ellie decided it was because of some kind of lack in his life, rather than that he was immoral or evil. I think she expected that one day he'd just grow out of it. Then Pete hit puberty and she sort of accepted that people don't get to choose. But she's always thought acting on it was wrong. As for getting married: that's a non-starter." Josh smiled remorsefully. "We can't fix it."

"Hey," Jess said. She reached across and took his hand. "You'll figure something out. I'm sure of it."

"Maybe." He picked up his sandwich again, but didn't eat any yet. "I hope you know you're not here just because Ellie and I aren't speaking."

"The thought never even occurred to me," Jess assured him.

"See, we only became as close as we did because we didn't fit in at school. George was always, *always*, my best friend." Josh studied his sandwich. He needed to prepare himself for the rest of what he wanted to say, for in the back of his mind was a fear that the chance would never come again. "There haven't been many people in my life who have stuck by me, through the good and the bad. It's one of the hardest things to do, to be there for someone who's going through a difficult time. I push people away, and most, understandably, are glad of the chance to escape. Ellie's one of them. I'm not saying she's never been there for me, but when things are really bad, she can't cope. No control, see? That's all it is. But you, Jess; you've always been there. Even when I told you to leave me alone, you wouldn't bloody do it!"

Jess smiled. "Yes, I remember you were very insistent."

Josh laughed, then became serious. "I was so ill, Jess."

"I know. You ended up in hospital, didn't you?"

Josh paused a moment, then nodded. "Twice."

"I thought so. Sean wouldn't tell me anything, just that you'd gone 'away', but you weren't at home and you weren't with Ellie, so…"

"He was—is—incredible. I love that man so much, even if he does drive me to distraction. And he still won't explain why he decided to take a job here, of all places." He looked at her suspiciously. "Wasn't anything to do with you, was it?" She shook her head.

"No. We swapped contact details and everything, but the quiz night was the first time I'd seen Sean since you did a bunk."

"I didn't do a bunk. I moved out." She stared him down. "Oh, all right. I did a bunk, although somehow he always knew where I was living, like he was keeping tabs on me, which is why I don't buy his defence that fate delivered him here the year after George went to America. That's what made me think you might've told him."

"What was there to tell? You weren't in love with George, remember?"

Josh grinned. "So, when did you figure it out?"

"There was nothing to figure out. As you say, George was always your true best friend. It's impossible to be that close to someone and not be in love with them."

"Which makes it even more of a tragedy that it took us so long to get together." The regret washed over him and he closed his eyes in an attempt to block it. Jess reached out and touched his arm.

"Hey. You were never apart," she said gently. "Not really."

"I suppose you're right."

"Did Sean know about you and George?"

"No. When I told him last year he seemed genuinely surprised."

"Well, maybe he's right then. Maybe fate did bring him here. Some things are just meant to be, aren't they?"

"Yes," Josh laughed. "That's what people keep telling me. You should talk to Sean, you know. About the hospice? He won't push you into anything, and he'll be honest about what it's like, whether it's right for you."

Jess shrugged and turned away from him.

"So anyway." He changed to a slightly lighter tone. "I *am* going to return the favour and be here for you, as much as I can. That's a promise. None of your 'I don't need anyone' nonsense."

"Thanks," Jess accepted.

"And thank *you*. For always helping me to see clearly, in more ways than one. You ready?"

"Are you?"

"Oh yes," Josh said confidently. "I'm so ready."

***

442

Adele and Eleanor were frantic, although they were keeping it to themselves rather convincingly. Everything was done. The room was decorated. The car was ready and waiting. The cake had been delivered two hours ago. The food would arrive at two. James had given the boys a bath and they were both playing quietly, ready to put on their suits at the pre-ordained time. Alice was dealing with little Shaunna, and had reported that Andy had printed off all of the reservation information for the hotel. The suitcases were packed and in the back of the 4x4. Kris had booked the taxi, ready to pick him up, then go and collect Iris and Pauline. Shaunna was meeting Adele at the nursing home to accompany Josh's grandma. There was absolutely nothing left to do. And they were frantic.

"OK, Ellie. Go get yourself ready," Adele suggested. "I'll finish up here."

"Thanks, Adele." Eleanor hugged her, which was uncharacteristic. "We're a formidable team."

"You bet!" Adele said, patting her back and feeling decidedly uncomfortable. Eleanor drew away and wiped her eyes.

"Oh. How silly," she gulped. Adele immediately pulled a clean tissue from her jeans pocket and passed it across. Eleanor dabbed at her eyes and sniffed. "I can't believe they're actually getting married. After all this time."

"Have you changed your mind?"

"No, but they're going to do it whatever, and Josh is my…" She started to cry. Without thinking, Adele put her arms around her and slowly steered her over to a seat.

"Hey, now, shhh. It's all right."

Eleanor sobbed away for several minutes, trying every so often to get the tears in check, and failing. Eventually, with much gasping, she was able to speak.

"Am I a bad friend for thinking it's wrong?" she asked. Adele shook her head.

"Of course you're not. Your beliefs are very important to you, and there's nothing wrong with that."

"Yes, they are." She nodded emphatically, but at the same time she was beginning to register a sense that whilst they were important to her, they were not worth losing her friendship with Josh for. With this thought in mind, she blew her nose and pulled herself together again.

"Better?" Adele asked.

"Yes, thank you." Eleanor took out her phone and walked towards the door. "I'm going to ring Josh, see if he's OK with me popping in before I go home. I've got some serious apologising to do."

"OK. I'll just check the tables and head off too. See you later." Adele followed her to the door and watched her leave, then wandered back into the room, singing to herself.

***

Eleanor knocked and waited. She knocked again. Still no answer. She raised her hand to knock a third time and the door opened. Josh stepped to one side and gestured for her to come in, all without a word. She followed him into the living room, where a still of a cartoon racing game, paused mid-action, was displayed on-screen. George was sitting cross-legged on the sofa.

"Hi, Ellie," he greeted cheerily.

"Hi," she replied. Josh indicated to the chair and she perched on the very edge of the cushion.

"You're getting married in less than two hours," she said.

"Yes," he confirmed, as if it were a question, rather than a statement of fact.

"And you're sitting around playing games?"

"Yes, we are."

"Aren't you worried you're going to be late?"

"Are we?" he asked George. He shrugged and shook his head.

"I don't think so. Are we?"

"The thing is—" Eleanor began. "Forget it. I didn't come here to lecture you. I don't even know why I think I would need to."

"OK?" Josh prompted her for an explanation.

"I'm sorry," she said. "I can't change the way I feel or my beliefs, but it doesn't matter. You love each other and you want to get married. I want you to be happy, and enjoy your day, and I've been selfish, and I'm—sorry." She stood up and moved towards the door. Josh watched her and would have let her leave, but George gave him a look that forced him into action, which was probably a good thing. He was only going to regret it if he let her walk away.

"Ellie."

She stopped, but stayed facing away from him. He walked over to her.

"Ellie. Look at me."

Slowly she turned around. He watched her a moment, smiled and nodded. "Thank you."

"For what?"

"For apologising." She moved towards him and he opened his arms. "I'm sorry too," he sighed, pulling her close, "because there's no middle ground this time." He sounded defeated.

"I love you," she said. "That's the only thing that matters today." She leaned against his chest. He kissed the top of her head.

444

"And I love you, although you smell of cheese and onion crisps, which isn't very fetching." She laughed and moved away.

"I'll see you soon."

"You will." He walked her to the door and watched her leave, then shut it behind her and returned to the lounge.

"Right, Morley." He grabbed his controller and sat down next to George. "This cup is mine."

***

George came running down the stairs, trying to fasten his trousers at the same time.

"Hold on, hold on!" he shouted at the third round of hammering on the door. He flung it open.

"Alright, mate?" Dan grinned.

"Err, hi," George said self-consciously.

"I know it's a bit early, but Adele thought the way the pair of you are about getting to places on time, if I left it any later than quarter past, then you'd have already set off. I hope you don't…ah." Dan looked away, having realised that he'd disturbed them. "Sorry." He blushed—not something he did often. "I'll just wait in the car."

"Thanks," George said. He closed the door and turned back. "Well that wasn't embarrassing at all!" Josh burst out laughing.

"I realise this is a unique occasion, but I think maybe we should just give up on the whole nookie in the daytime thing."

"Oh, I don't know," George said, shuffling him back against the wall and kissing his neck. "It's kind of exciting, don't you think? Getting caught in the act."

"Well, yes, but…" Josh tried to push him away. "Seriously! George? Dan's sitting outside. In fact, why is Dan sitting outside?"

"Don't know. Don't care," George murmured. "Please?"

Josh sighed, feigning reluctance, and led him back upstairs. "You'd best hurry up."

"Ha ha," George replied.

***

"So whose car is it?" Josh asked, smoothing his hand across the plush back seat of the shiny, new convertible.

"My mum's. Unfortunately the Ferrari's gone in for a service, but this is pretty decent. Two-fifty brake horse power, the nought to sixty's not great, but it drives well."

445

"Right," Josh said distractedly. "Ferrari, did you say?"

"Yeah, nice car, although it's the FF, obviously, and Len's a boring old bugger, so he opted for the black. Plus, it doesn't have one of these." Dan pressed the touchscreen in the centre console. It chimed and lit up.

"Oh, now you're talking." Josh leaned forward to get a better look. George started making snoring noises and slid sideways. Josh grabbed his hand and pulled him upright again.

"Internet, media centre, 3D SatNav, all voice command."

"Nice!"

"Yeah." Dan stopped talking, because his mouth was about to run away with him, and he'd nearly told him that the SatNav in the 4x4 was all programmed and ready to go. Adele would've had his nuts on a platter for that.

Not long after, he pulled up outside the register office. "You get out, and I'll go find somewhere to park."

"Cheers, Dan," George said. He patted him on the shoulder. "You're the best-looking chauffeur I've seen!"

"Hey, I'm just glad not to be best man!"

Josh started walking towards the building, looking back to see why George hadn't yet caught up with him.

"What's the matter?" he asked. George continued staring ahead of them. Josh turned around. "Ah," he said, surprised to see the crowd of people standing there, waiting for them.

"So much for a quiet wedding," George muttered. He took Josh's hand. "Shall we?"

"Oh, I suppose so," Josh replied with a grin.

They walked across, towards their friends, family and select others who knew them best, all there by invitation, though not from the couple themselves.

"You're late, Sandison," Sean beamed.

"It's only ten to one!" Josh protested.

"That's what I mean!"

George gave Kris a hug, then Shaunna. "Who do we have to blame for all of this?" he asked.

"Adele, with a little last minute assistance from Ellie."

Josh had already found Adele, trying to hide behind everyone else. He narrowed his eyes and examined her. "So, any more surprises in store?"

She giggled and started playing with her hair.

"Don't make me go in there," he said, then spotted his grandma to Adele's right.

"Grandma! How did you get here?" he asked in French, taking hold of her hands.

446

"Your friends, Adele and…" she shrugged.

"Shaunna," Adele told her. His grandma nodded to confirm this.

Josh grinned and gave Adele a hug.

"Ooh, Josh!" she squeaked.

"Adele, you're amazing. Thank you." He kissed her on the cheeks.

"That's my son-in-law," Iris was explaining unnecessarily to James. "Or he will be half an hour from now. Your lads, are they?" She nodded at Toby, in his pushchair, and Oliver, who was standing in front of it, completely awestruck.

"Yes," James said. "This is Toby." Toby looked up at the sound of his name and gave Iris his best smile. "And that's Oliver." Oliver stayed where he was and continued to stare.

"Hey, Ollie," George called, making his way over. "Don't you look smart!"

"I got a waistcoat." Oliver pulled his blazer open to show it off.

"So you have! Very snazzy!" George gave Pauline and his mother a hug and a kiss. "You OK?" he asked.

"Aye. I'm fine, love. Are you?"

"Yeah, I'm OK. A bit nervous."

"Is she your mum?" Oliver pointed at Iris.

"Yes, she's my mum."

Oliver nodded, a look on his face that said, "I thought so." Iris grinned at him and he grinned back.

"George!" Josh called and beckoned him over. "It's time."

"OK." George turned and smiled at his mum. "See you in there," he said.

"Alright, love," she replied. She fussed with his lapels and smiled up at him. "You look very handsome."

"Thanks, Mam. I love you."

She watched as he walked over to Josh and they both went inside.

"Paul? Got an 'anky there for us, love?" she sniffed.

***

They had discussed the order of the ceremony with the registrar, and opted to do all of the official bit first, so as soon as everyone was crammed into the room that was barely big enough to contain their closest friends, never mind double that number, the registrar headed straight into her standard greeting.

"Good afternoon, everybody. I'd like to welcome you here to the register office for George and Josh's special day." She went on to introduce herself and the man sitting at a table across the room, who presently opened out the

447

large, hardback, register in front of him. The rest of what followed was the mandatory, legal notice about declarations of lawful impediments, all undertaken very seriously with not a murmur passing within. Josh could feel his pulse thudding against his collar, and George's hands were slipping apart with sweat. Then, just as the registrar drew breath to continue, a noise startled everyone in the room. The door opened and a man squeezed through the gap.

"Sorry," he whispered, a hand raised apologetically as he tried to seat himself inconspicuously. The guests all looked horrified. Josh frowned, as he watched the tall, tanned, incredibly broad-shouldered man edge along the back wall. He seemed vaguely familiar, but Josh couldn't place him, and looked to George, to find that he had the hugest grin on his face. Josh shrugged in query.

"Ray," George mouthed.

"Excellent timing, sir," the registrar said with a smile, easing the pressure. Everyone laughed quietly in relief and mumbled to each other; she waited for a moment to allow things to settle before she went on with the legal stuff—the meaning of marriage, both legal and solemn, followed by the official declarations and contracting statements, which only required that they repeat the words after she'd said them. All very easy so far, but the time had arrived to share the vows they had written. They'd decided that Josh would go first, because he was supposedly more confident speaking in public, not that he was feeling that way just now. The registrar stepped back slightly to give them space, and Josh swallowed a couple of times, trying to lubricate his very dry throat.

"Hey," he said, making eye contact with George.

"Hey, yourself," George said back. His eyes were sparkling emerald green; they took Josh's breath away. After a moment or so he took in a gulp of air, and began.

"When I first saw you, I wondered—why? 'Twelve free chairs in the classroom,' I thought, 'so why has he chosen to sit at *my* table?' After all, I was just the quiet kid in the corner who didn't speak to anybody." He shook his head and laughed lightly. "And as you settled in, it made even less sense, for it soon became apparent that you were one of the popular boys; you were good at football; you could stand up for yourself; you'd never turn your nose up at the opportunity for a bit of innocent mischief. Yet you were so sensitive, and kind. I saw, and still do see in you all the things I wish that I could be. Self-confident, generous, compassionate, creative. You give with no expectation to receive. And you have such strength. So why did you choose to sit at my table? Why did you choose—me?

"To this day, I don't know the answer to that question. Sometimes the 'why' isn't so important. Some things just *are*, perhaps because they're meant to be. I suspect the fact that we're here now, thirty-one years down the line, means we were always meant to be. Thirty-one years." Josh paused and put his hands in his pockets. He glanced at their friends. "Pity someone didn't tell us sooner."

Some smiled; most were too entranced to do anything other than watch and listen. Josh turned back to George and held his gaze, falling into the deep, wonderful, wonder of it.

"I've lost where I was up to," he said. "It's those eyes. Every time I look into them, I fall even deeper in love with you. Amazing. I've known you since I was…" He stopped speaking, but continued to gaze at George. Their friends watched on, unsure of why Josh was suddenly quiet. But George was smiling. He knew why.

"Seven," he said, completing Josh's sentence.

"Not eight?"

George shook his head. "Definitely seven."

Josh took George's hand in one of his own and turned it palm upwards.

"And you've been my best friend ever since. Why? Well, I can answer that one. You are my best friend, because…" Josh freed his other hand from his pocket. He held, between his forefinger and thumb, a tiny, pastel-shaded, cylindrical stack. He removed the top from the stack and dropped it onto George's palm. "You were my…"

George looked down and saw the Love Heart sweet in his hand.

"FIRST LOVE," Josh said. As he continued to speak, he delivered each of the messages in sweet form. "IT'S TRUE, and today I promise to LOVE YOU, and ONLY YOU, FOR EVER. Because you are MY ALL."

He closed George's hand around the Love Hearts, but kept hold of it, lifting it to kiss it, his lips lingering against George's fingers. "Ma moitié," he whispered.

They both remained quiet and still for a moment longer, then Josh released George, although it took him longer again to remember what he was supposed to do next. He put the sweets in his inside pocket, exchanging them for the weighty roll of cream paper and something else.

"You know that thing we do? Where we go to say the same thing at the same time? Or I buy an engagement ring, and you buy an engagement ring, and they're almost identical? Yeah, well, this is for you." He opened Josh's hand and placed the singular Love Heart in the centre of his palm. "It's to go with the other one I gave you," he explained. Josh lifted the sweet so he could read the word printed on it: YOURS.

"Yours. For Keeps," George said. "I guess I could've left it at that, but…" He sighed. "Here goes."

Carefully, he pulled off the ribbon and freed the roll of paper, surprised to find that his hands were still. They weren't shaking at all. He stretched the scroll straight and held it up before him, as if he were about to read an ancient declaration of governance, then took a deep breath to steady himself—out of expectation rather than necessity, he realised, once he'd done it. He looked up from the words, to Josh, whose expression was painted with expectancy, his breathing paused, waiting. George smiled and his eyes twinkled. Josh remained serious, the slightest nod of his head encouraging, urging him on. George looked down to the words again: not so much to say, really. He scanned over them, the intention to pre-load them into his brain. Josh watched, waited, his own eyes following the movement down through the lines etched on that opaquely mysterious paper. As George reached the bottom his face broke into a grin and he glanced to Sophie, sitting a few feet away.

"Yeah, I guess so," he said. Her smile tipped the tears off the precipice of her cheeks. George turned back to face Josh, scanned the first line of his script and made eye contact again.

"When I first saw you," he began to orate, "you were standing behind your chair, pretending to be invisible, glancing up furtively to see who the newcomer was." He paused, as indicated. "That newcomer was me. Oh, screw it!"

He stopped speaking and bit his lip, deep in thought. This wasn't what he wanted to say. Not now he was here, standing before a registrar, as his friends and his mum bore witness to the moment he had dreamed of for what seemed like forever. Not when he was about to publically declare his feelings, to once and for all be free of the ropes with which he had bound himself; to finally marry the man he loved. Because for as much as they were his words, they seemed so artificial, contrived, sculpted. He released the top of the paper and it sprung neatly back into a roll. He shook his head in dismay at the unfairness of it.

"First time ever I know what I want to say and I'm not allowed to say it." He gave the registrar a watery smile. She watched him for a moment, then smiled back her approval.

"Yes, that's fine," she confirmed.

He nodded in thanks and inhaled until his lungs could take in no more air, slowly turning to face Josh once more. Josh met his gaze, concern registering in his eyes, along with an implied intention to try and help him out. George gently pressed the tip of his index finger against Josh's lips. They were so soft and warm—and silent! He let out some of the enormous breath.

"No know-it-all remarks from you today," he said. He heard their friends—The Circle—laugh quietly. Slowly, he moved his finger away and took Josh's hand in his own, studying it momentarily. The words were still all there, and in the right order, but he wanted to say them so desperately

450

that he knew they would gush forth in a babbling stream if he didn't slow himself right down. Josh gently squeezed his hand, prompting him to continue. George looked up and a tear escaped.

"I love you, Joshua, do you know that? I love you so much that it just keeps on knocking the words right out of me. And then it came to me, reading what Sophie helped me to write," he looked down at the coiled scroll, "that I'd been doing it all wrong. That what I really needed was a different way to tell you, maybe charcoal, or oils, or watercolours. And then I could paint what you mean to me, the promises I make to you today and every day. I would choose crimson, and rose…" He brushed his fingers across Josh's cheek and it flushed with colour. George smiled. "Maybe a little more crimson than rose," he said. Josh lowered his head, and his hair flopped over his face. George waited until he looked up again before he continued, so he could focus on the incredible blueness of his eyes. "And I'd paint the endless dawn, slowly fading into the cerulean blue of an eternal sky." He lifted a stray lock of hair away from Josh's face, ran it through his fingers. "Raw sienna, orange and vermillion for sunrise, a radiant halo stretching across the horizon of forever. *Our* forever.

"You are my dawn; my sunrise; my horizon. You are my eternal sky. All that I am and all that I have I share with you, because it is you. Whatever happens that will always be true. For better, for worse, in sickness, in health, I promise to love and to cherish you, and only you. Hell, I'd even promise to obey you, if that's what you asked of me. Because I, George Morley, am so in love with you, Joshua Sandison. You *are* my everything."

George stopped and nodded resolutely, then glanced sideways at the registrar.

"Did I get it all?" he asked. She smiled.

"Yes, I think you probably did."

George looked back at Josh in time to catch him silently mouthing, "Wow!" and smiled, with relief, in part, but mostly because he was so happy that he couldn't help it. He heard Eleanor sob and rolled his eyes. Josh giggled. The registrar gave them a moment before she continued.

"We have now come to the part of the ceremony where George and Josh have chosen to exchange rings."

There was a sudden flurry of movement, the sound of feet scampering across the carpet, then a thump, as Oliver tripped and fell flat on his face, his hands clenched so tightly that his knuckles were shiny white. He quickly righted himself and charged forward, stopping between Josh and George. The registrar looked down at the breathless little boy.

"Here they are," he panted. He held out both hands, the glistening metal bands balanced on the topmost of his upturned palms. "Sorry, Dorge. I muggled them up."

"Thanks, Ollie. It's OK. We'll figure it out," George assured him. Oliver straightened his jacket and returned to his seat, where Eleanor hugged him tightly and James rubbed his hair.

"Hey," Andy whispered to Dan, "I reckon you've been permanently replaced there, bro."

"And I could think of no-one better to take the torch," Dan whispered back.

The friends fell silent, watching on as Josh and George exchanged their rings, having first established which was which, now that they were identical, other than one being slightly larger than the other. Vincent had done a beautiful job of them, even polishing and re-presenting them in identical ring boxes. He looked so incredibly proud and emotional, sitting at the back of the room, next to Cordelia, the pair of them sniffling and sharing a packet of tissues. If ever there was a friendship in the making, here it was.

"What is it they're doing now?" Josh's grandma whispered to Adele, and not really so much of a whisper.

"Exchanging rings," Adele whispered back.

"Uh," she said. "Do homosexuals do that?"

George's mum heard the word 'homosexual', for it was the same in both languages, and tutted. Josh heard her too and screwed up his eyes.

"Yes, they do," Adele confirmed solemnly, taking hold of Mrs. Moreau's hand. "Hush now."

"Uh," she said again, but that was all.

With their rings now in place, the registrar smiled and made the final declaration, but Josh and George didn't hear a word of it, until the end when their guests started clapping and the registrar touched them both on the arm.

"You may now kiss," she said.

And so they did, although they were smiling far too much for their lips to make proper contact. All that was left was to sign the register, and they both suddenly had the same change of heart, not that it made any difference there and then, but for some reason they felt the need to make the decision before they signed.

"Which way round?" Josh asked.

"Yours first," George said.

"You sure?"

"Yeah."

They signed the register and that was it. George and Joshua Sandison-Morley stepped into the midst of their family and friends, officially together, at last.

WHEN
Monday 19ᵗʰ June

By the time they reached the wedding reception that they didn't know they were having, Josh and George had given up trying to hold back their tears at every new and entirely unexpected surprise their friends thrust upon them. They were also both feeling a little bit drunk, having only eaten breakfast and then each downed two glasses of Champagne in quick succession. Adele brought them a 'pre-buffet taster', to help them slow down; after all, they had a five hour journey ahead of them, not that they knew anything about that yet, and it was only just after two in the afternoon.

The reception was in a different room to that in which the psychic evening had been held a few months earlier. This one Adele had decorated, with pale cream carnations in tiny, deep green vases on each table, and heart-shaped foil green and blue balloons, for she had picked up some time ago on the colours of the stones in their rings, and also their significance. She was so pleased with herself for this that she smiled every time she glanced up at the helium filled hearts floating above—exactly what she was doing when Josh touched her on the arm.

"Thanks for everything," he said, hugging her. "Again!"

"Aww, that's OK," she smiled. "I've had the best time doing it. And your grandma is so lovely."

"She didn't give you any trouble?"

"Not at all. She was ever so tired though and went straight to bed when we took her back. It's so sad that they can't get a nurse who speaks French. She was telling me how lonely she is."

Yes, she is. And it might even help her to recover too."

"Can you do that from a stroke?"

"A little. I've seen people regain some of their language understanding with speech therapy. I don't think she'll get her English back, but, well, there's not much I can do about it, other than visiting and taking her out to different places, keep stimulating her mind. They're very good in the nursing home, but they're so busy and there's never enough staff."

"I wouldn't mind visiting and taking her out sometimes," Adele offered.

"You've done enough."

"No, I'd love to do it."

He examined her face and saw that it was the truth. He nodded.

453

"Thanks, Adele. You're fab." He hugged her again, then released her. "Right, I need to go and find George."

"Over there." She pointed across the room to George and Ray, standing together, talking and laughing. "Ray's such a nice person. When we were at George's ranch, he showed me around the stables."

"Did he?"

"Yeah. He offered to teach me to ride too. Dan didn't like that idea very much."

Josh laughed. "No, I can imagine! I'll see you later."

Adele gave him a little wave and watched as he walked across to George and Ray. George turned and gave Josh the biggest smile when he saw him approaching; Adele sighed with happiness, then went straight back to rechecking all was in order.

"Josh, you remember Ray?" George asked.

"I remember an online chat in the middle of the night," he said. Ray smiled and nodded.

"I remember that too."

"And something about a horse called—Star?"

"Ah yeah. She's a real cutie-pie these days. We have her working with the kids with problems. You know? Disabled kids, sick kids with cancer, that kind of thing. She's so calm and balanced, like she just totally connects with them."

"Wow. That must do the children so much good."

"Yeah," Ray agreed, his enthusiasm lighting up his eyes in much the same way as George's did his. "We had this great guy working with Star and some of the more troublesome horses. He had a special gift for bringing them round."

"Yes," Josh grinned, "I think I might have seen him in action once or twice." George smiled bashfully and Ray laughed.

"It sure is our loss," he said, giving George a wink. "I guess the call of the heart was stronger, huh?"

"Guess so," George said.

"I have to say," Josh remarked, "I didn't know you did any of that on the ranch."

"We just started the past couple of years. Rodeo rehab. It's pretty awesome. You should come visit again some time, see what we've done with the place. We've given it a real good makeover," he looked at George, "with the money you gave us."

Josh stared at George in amazement. George just shrugged and looked embarrassed.

"Oops," Ray cringed guiltily. "Sorry, G."

"Hey, it's OK," George assured him.

"Well I'm gonna get another beer. You guys OK?"

"Yeah, thanks," George said. He waited until Ray was at the bar, then turned to Josh and took hold of both of his hands. "It's nothing bad, I promise."

"So why didn't you tell me?"

"Because I didn't want to talk about it back then. When I came home for Krissi's birthday, I was still fighting it so hard. Selling the ranch to Joe and Ray—I knew I was doing it because I kept hoping you'd change your mind about us."

"But you could've kept the money."

"I didn't want it and you wouldn't have understood that. You'd have pressured me to keep it, or invest it, and I'd have done so because you told me to. And I didn't want it. When you're young and you're poor, you think money will make you happy. It doesn't. If you've never been without, you think being poor will make you miserable, and it does, but it's not the end of the world. It's just—I don't know. I needed to move on, get closure."

"From Joe?"

"More from my dad than Joe. Mum always said his money was a curse, and she was right, because I gave it all away and look what happened!" He pulled Josh close and kissed him. "Can you believe this?"

Josh shook his head. "No. I'm having a problem taking it in, to be honest. I think I've lost my touch. How in God's name did they do all this without us knowing?"

"Dunno, but it's the best thing ever. Well, the second best, anyway." He kissed him again. "I love you, Mr. Sandison-Morley. Man, that's a mouthful!"

"And I love you, Mr. Sandison-Morley." Josh paused, thoughtful for a moment. "Yes, it is. Whose silly idea was it again?"

"Ours."

"Oh, yes." Josh grinned, although his smile quickly faded when he noticed who else had just arrived.

"What?" George asked, looking worried.

"How brave are you feeling?"

"Why?" George went to turn his head to see what Josh was looking at, but Josh turned him back again. George frowned. "Is it that bad?"

Josh watched over his shoulder. "It's not horrendous, but—well, you'll just have to see for yourself."

George slowly scanned the room until he spotted who Josh had been talking about. "Ah," he said. "You know we haven't spoken since we were about eighteen?"

"He still might not recognise you."

The man had spotted them and waved. He was on his way over.

"Hi, Lee," Josh called as he approached.

"Josh," Lee acknowledged. "Congratulations." He shook hands with Josh first, then George. "You kept that quiet."

"Yes. Or at least we tried to, but our friends took over the arrangements and this is what we got. Thanks for coming."

"No problem, mate. After all the work you've sent my way, it's the least I could do. Plus, as I said to your friend Sophie when she invited me, who doesn't like an early dart?"

"True enough," Josh laughed. "I believe there's a free bar too."

"Good to hear," Lee said distractedly. He kept glancing in George's direction, almost as if he were checking a rear view mirror. It was clear that he'd recognised him, but didn't know what to say and, given that fact, was now struggling to find anything to say at all. Seeing as there was little point in introducing them to each other, Josh was a little stuck himself.

"I'm, err, gonna go and get a, err, pint," Lee stuttered eventually.

"All right. Catch up with you later," Josh smiled. He watched Lee wander off, dazed. George exhaled slowly.

"What do I say to him?"

"I have no idea."

"I'm gonna have to say something." He stepped away and shrugged, then followed Lee over to the bar. Lee gave him a quick smile and turned away again.

"Hey," Kris said, appearing next to Josh. "Enjoying yourself?"

"Kind of," Josh mumbled. "See that guy at the bar?"

"With George?" Kris squinted at the two men, still standing side by side and looking very uncomfortable. Lee turned his head slightly towards George and said something. George nodded. "Who is he?" Kris asked.

"Lee Johnson—my mechanic," Josh said. Kris nodded once, but was none the wiser. "AKA Jono?"

"Jono? Oh! *That* Jono!" Kris started laughing. "George dumped me for him."

"Really?"

"Not for long though. Well, I say not for long—did you know, he's got a…" he whispered the rest of the sentence into Josh's ear. Josh's mouth dropped open. Kris nodded emphatically. "Oh, yes. Gemma Spiller's a very lucky girl."

"Who?"

"His missus. Over there." He nodded to a woman standing near the door, talking to Adele.

"Brunette Bob!" Josh exclaimed. "So that's her name."

"Yeah. What fun!" Kris said. "Think I might go over and introduce myself." He grinned and headed off towards the bar, coming up behind and

456

between George and Lee. George stayed a while longer, then excused himself and returned to Josh.

"Well, we've said hello now. So unbelievably awkward."

"I'm not surprised! Kris just told me about Jono's, err, hidden talent?"

"He didn't? Oh God." George covered his face with his hands. "It's not actually that well hidden either." As he said this, Lee turned in their direction, and now he knew about it, Josh couldn't help but notice. Lee gave him a brief smile and raised his pint. Josh returned the smile and put his head down quickly.

"I'm never going to be able to look him in the eye again."

"Which eye?" George asked with a wink. Josh started laughing, and probably would have continued to laugh for quite some time after, were it not for the barman clanging the 'last orders' bell to get everyone's attention.

"Ahem," Adele said loudly. She was balanced very precariously, standing on a chair and leaning on Shaunna's shoulder. "I'd like to ask the grooms, if they wouldn't mind, to do a bit of a speech."

"Didn't you just know this was gonna happen?" George muttered.

Josh sighed, then cupped his hand around his mouth and shouted across the room. "Dan, it's over to you, mate." Everyone laughed.

"Actually, if I could say a few words." Dan stepped forward. The room fell silent. "I just want to say what an honour it is to finally be celebrating the marriage of two of my best and oldest friends. I don't know how many of you are aware of this, but we became classmates back in primary school, when clever-clogs over there put us all to shame with his perfect scores in spelling tests, and filled the reading corner with books none of us could read. Just as we got over that kick in the ego, this new kid arrives and wipes the floor with us on the footy pitch. In fact, a certain G. Morley still holds our high school record for the most goals scored in a season." There was applause, and Dan waited for it to stop before he continued. "You're one hell of a striker, George, and I'm proud that I can say I've played on the same team as you, mate—football team, that is." Everyone laughed again. "And Josh," Dan made eye contact with him across the room and smiled. He tried a couple of times to speak, but each time felt a lump form in his throat. Andy came to the rescue.

"I think what he's trying to say is thanks for putting up with all his strops over the years."

Dan pretended to scowl at Andy, then smiled and nodded to say he was right. There was more clapping, during which Josh noticed a significant group of students from the counselling course arrive. He glanced witheringly at Sean, who just smiled at him in response.

As the applause died down, Shaunna started chanting, "Speech, speech, speech," and George hid behind Josh.

"I'm doing it, then?" Josh asked. George nodded. Now all eyes were on them.

"OK, well, first up," Josh began, "that mischief I mentioned earlier? Adele: do you remember that time when your pumps ended up on the roof of the dining hall?" She nodded and Josh thumbed over his shoulder at George. "And Shaunna's incredible shrinking skipping rope?" George turned away so that he had his back to Josh. "Also, there was this one occasion when…well, you get the idea," Josh said. George turned around again and grinned. Josh took a hold of his hand and looked into his eyes adoringly, and it was truly how he was feeling. "Over the past few months, all of our closest friends…" George spoke into his ear, "The Square, did you say?" George whispered again, "Hexagon? I don't know. What shape…" George said something else. "Oh, of course. The Circle." There were multiple groans from the seven other members of their friendship group, and Josh waited for this and the general noise to stop before he continued. "Our closest friends have spent the past nine months telling me how they all realised, independently and in some cases a very, very long time ago, that George and I were in love, which, I'll be honest with you, folks, freaks me out more than a little. And then you go and put on this incredible wedding celebration for us, and we didn't suspect a thing. Now, either I'm out of practice, or you're all getting far too adept at covering your tracks." He eyed them all suspiciously, then smiled. "Whichever, thank you so much for everything. We're having a wonderful day, and we hope you are too. Thank you."

Everyone started to clap and cheer, and then called for George to also make a speech. He looked to Josh for help to get him out of it, but Josh just shrugged.

"Imagine they're horses, or something," he said. George raised an eyebrow.

"Horses?"

The room was quiet again now, and he looked around at all the faces staring at him in anticipation.

"Horses," he repeated and shook his head. "You know, I don't do this public speaking thing very often, or at all, in fact, so I'll just keep it short." He pulled the roll of paper on which his vows were printed from where it was still stashed in his inside pocket and waved it at Sophie. "OK. Two things: firstly, if anybody ever asks again if Josh and I are together…" At this point, anyone who had ever asked either of them that question started to laugh, which pretty much left only the barman and Lee Johnson not doing so. "Secondly, I want to thank a few people, without whom we wouldn't be here now. The Circle," he said, raising his glass to them. "Love you guys." He waited for the general toasting to finish before he went on. "And to Soph

and Sean: words can not...what I mean...agh! Thank you. That's all."
People lifted their glasses again, and Sophie and Sean, who were sitting at
the same table, nodded in acknowledgement. "Also, I'd like to say a massive
thank you to Mrs. Kinkade, as well as apologising for the pumps, and the
skipping rope, and, um, for soaking your chalk in water and then putting it
back under the blackboard."

She looked at him sternly, then started to laugh.

"Seriously, thank you for not judging us. I think the world's finally
starting to catch up with you, Miss."

She smiled at him tearily and drew a star in the air with her finger.

"Finally, I need to..." George made eye contact with his mother and
couldn't go on, but he was determined he was going to say this, so he stayed
where he was, swallowed hard and let the tears that had already fallen roll
down his cheeks. He took a breath and tried again. "My mum," he said, and
indicated to her with his hand. She met his gaze and smiled. He started to
cry. She tutted and rolled her eyes and he tried to laugh it off, but couldn't
and had to turn away. Josh pulled him close. There was a communal
'ahhhh'.

"Do you want me to do it?" Josh asked him quietly. George shook his
head.

"Give me a minute."

Josh kept hold of him and waited. George gulped and wiped his eyes on
his sleeve.

"OK," he said. He cleared his throat and started over. "My mum'll tell
you I'm a soft shite, which I'm obviously not," he joked. Everyone laughed,
as much to encourage him along as anything. "What more can I say? You
all think you've got the best mum in the world, but you're wrong." He
paused to breathe and blink back the tears. "Because she's sitting right
there." He made eye contact with her again, and saw that now she too was
crying, which set him off properly, so the rest of what he said was delivered
interspersed with sniffs and gulps.

"I know we've not had it easy, and how hard you've worked to give me
a good life. I hope I've at least achieved a few things that made it all worth
the effort, and that I can one day make you as proud of me as I am that
you are my mum. I love you, Mam. Thank you." And with that, he
collapsed against Josh and sobbed uncontrollably. His mum got up, made
her way over and hugged him tight. There was another 'ahhhh' and
everyone applauded loudly. Adele came tottering over and cupped her
hand around Josh's ear. He nodded and raised his voice to make the
announcement.

"Adele says the buffet is open, so thanks once again to all of you for being
here this afternoon. Please do go and help yourselves to food. Enjoy!"

The conversations slowly resumed, as people wandered over in dribs and drabs to collect food, or to go and chat to George and Josh. Andy wheeled Jess across and George bent down to hug her.

"That was so lovely," she said. His mother had remained standing next to him.

"Thanks," George said, still feeling quite tearful. "Mum, this is Jess."

"Hello, love," she smiled.

"And this is Andy."

Andy smiled and shook Iris's hand.

"Pleasure to meet you," he said courteously and with that little sparkle of Jeffries' flirtatiousness. Iris gave him a demure smile in return.

"Dan's your brother, I take it?"

"Yep," Andy confirmed.

"They're not twins," George and Josh said in unison and started laughing. Iris gave them one of her 'old-fashioned looks'. Andy laughed too.

"People generally assume we are," he explained. Iris nodded. She turned to George.

"I'm goin' to get Pauline, go for a quick cig."

"OK, Mum. See you in a bit."

"You will, love." She reached up and gave his chin an affectionate pinch. "And I'm always proud of you," she said, then quickly turned away. They watched her waddle off across the room, back to her place to collect her handbag and her friend. Andy clapped George on the back, but didn't say anything. George gave him a wink.

"I'm gonna go get another drink," Andy said. George nodded.

"Think I'll come with you." The two of them went to the bar, leaving Jess and Josh alone.

"Are you enjoying yourself?" she asked.

"I am. Especially the not being bullied by Ellie bit." They both laughed lightly at this. It was the truth: aside from the advantage of the organising being mostly of Adele's doing, the continued disharmony between them meant Eleanor was keeping her distance, for which he was kind of glad, although it still hurt, and he didn't want it to bring him down. He pushed it from his mind and smiled at Jess. "And are you enjoying yourself?"

"Yes," she said. "Yes I am. I'm shattered, mind you. Personally, I blame eye tests at the crack of dawn."

Josh laughed. "You know if you need to go home that's fine by us."

"Ha!" She tried to look offended. "Not a chance, Joshua! I've got this little beastie, so I'm here for the duration." She lifted the hem of her shirt to reveal the bag containing the syringe driver for her pain relief.

"That's really cool. You can't even see it under your clothes. But seriously, Jess, if it gets too much…"

"Listen here, Sandison." He coughed to correct her. "Which is it? Morley-Sandison?"

"The other way around."

"Right. Listen here, Sandison-Morley—bloody hell! Are you sure?"

"Too much?"

"You tell me. You're the one who's gonna have to fit it in boxes on forms and stuff. Anyway, I'm staying to send you off, even if it sends me off at the same time."

"Send us off where?"

"Figure of speech. That's what you do after someone gets married."

"I see." Josh narrowed his eyes.

"Don't start," Jess laughed.

"Is there something you want to tell me?"

"Nope."

"Really?"

She looked away and studied a nearby balloon.

"I'm sure it would help…"

"Pack it in!" she warned jokingly. He grinned. She shook her head at him. "All I'll say is that we aren't done with you yet."

Josh continued to pretend to glare at her a moment longer, but she wasn't giving in.

"Anyway," she said, changing the subject, "I had a quick chat with Sean earlier. He's going to arrange a tour of the hospice for me."

"Excellent. You know they've got a pool and a gym and all sorts?"

"I'll try and keep an open mind then." Andy and George were on their way back over.

"What's that?" Josh asked, taking a beer bottle from George and nodding at Andy's glass.

"Coke."

"You not drinking?"

"No, mate. I'm still on antibiotics for that insect bite."

"Oh, right."

"What insect bite?" George asked.

"Bites, I should say. Mozzy, or something," Andy explained. "Got stuck in my boxers."

"Ooh, nasty," George sympathised.

"You'd better believe it." Andy glanced around the room. "Food queue's gone down. Think I'll go get some. What d'you want, Jess?"

"Whatever," she said. Andy nodded and went off in search of food. Josh examined her and raised an eyebrow. She pursed her lips.

"Here, Dorge." Oliver came running across to them. He handed George a tiny quiche.

"Thanks, Ollie."

"Ellna said the best man's got to look after everyone, and you're busy circle-eighting, and I got foods for you and for Josh, but I dropped the plate."

"Oh dear." George stifled a chuckle. He glanced up and saw Eleanor watching them from across the room. He tapped Josh on the arm. "Won't be a mo," he said, and went over.

"Hey." She got up to give him a hug. "You OK?"

"Yep. Just wanted to come and say thank you."

"It was almost all Adele's doing, so there's really no need."

"Yes there is," George countered. "We appreciate it, *both* of us, even though one of us is too stubborn to admit it."

"You don't have to speak on Josh's behalf. This is my fault, not his. I shouldn't have said what I did."

"And neither should he, but anyway, it's done now. It'll sort itself out."

"I hope so," she said sadly.

"I know so," George told her.

She looked at him doubtfully. "Have you seen your cake?"

"Only briefly. Adele said your mum made it."

"Yeah, she did," Eleanor confirmed. She frowned. "She's coming up for half an hour when Dad finishes work, to give you your wedding present."

"OK." Now it made even less sense. Eleanor saw his reaction.

"Yeah, I know. I don't understand either. If she knew about Peter she'd go completely nuts, but she's genuinely happy for you and Josh. I had a huge row with her too."

"Look, Ellie." George took her hands in his. "If it's what you believe, then it's what you believe. It doesn't matter what Josh, or your mum, or anyone else thinks."

She closed her eyes in an attempt to stop the tears.

"Really, it doesn't," he assured her. She nodded and gave him a hug.

"Thanks," she said, "but I'm going to be having a long, hard think about it all. It's clearly me who's out of touch with the rest of the world, and I'm trying, George, I really am, it's just…"

"I know." He gave her one final hug. "And I honestly do believe it will fix itself, in time. But enough of this nonsense. I'm starving, so I'm gonna get some food." Eleanor tutted and raised her eyes knowingly.

When he got there, he found that James was helping Oliver to load up an empty silver platter with two of everything.

"The best man said the grooms need food," James explained.

"The best man's right about that," George laughed, rubbing Oliver's head. Oliver looked up at him and grinned. "Thanks, Ollie. You're the bestest best man, *ever!*" That just made him grin all the more.

"Ah, there you are, George." Cordelia approached him, trying to be dreadfully serious and teacher-like. Without a second thought, he gave her a hug and kissed her cheek, then realised what he'd done. He stepped back and blushed. She took hold of his hands and looked up at him, holding eye contact for many seconds before she spoke.

"I haven't seen you for such a long time," she said. "I was telling Vincent all about you before—how worried we were that you might struggle to make friends, starting a new school so late on, and not even at the beginning of the year. How wonderful that you and Joshua found each other. And your vows! I was listening to you both and thinking," she nodded, "yes—these are my boys. Little Joshua Sandison and his love of words, and his best friend, George Morley, always such a gentle, creative child." She gazed up at him again. "*My* boys," she repeated. "I am so proud of you." She paused to peer over her glasses at him. "In spite of the wet chalk."

A voice spoke close to her ear. "Told you it wasn't me, Miss." A smile spread across her face and she released one of George's hands, exchanging it for Dan's.

"Daniel, dear, I see you're still tormenting that poor girl."

"'Fraid so, Miss."

"Oh, well. Not to worry. She always did give as good as she got. I hear you have a little one?"

"Yes, we do, although she's with her nana this afternoon."

"Congratulations, Daniel. And what did you name her?" As she asked this, Adele and Shaunna came over, arms linked, and giggling.

"I'll give you three guesses," he said. She turned to see what he could see.

"Now, girls. I do hope you've not been up to any mischief."

The pair of them stopped giggling and stood almost to attention.

"No, Miss," Shaunna said. "We've done all our work, *and* tidied away too."

"Very good, Shaunna," Cordelia laughed. She accepted a hug from each of them, and embarked on the same conversation about their children as that which she'd just had with Dan. Whilst this was going on, Andy came back for more food, arriving just in time to hear Shaunna getting flustered trying to answer questions about Krissi. He gave her a wink as he shuffled himself between Dan and Cordelia.

"You might want to record this, Mrs. K., because I'm about to own up to being naughty, of my own free will."

She looked from Andy to Dan, and shook her head.

"You look even more alike than you did as children," she observed. "So what is it, Andrew, dear? Did you bring sparklers to the party?"

He immediately turned to Dan.

"Hey! Don't blame me," he protested. "They all know it was you!"

"I'll never break!" Andy grinned. "Anyway, what I was going to say is that Shaunna's awesome and beautiful grown-up daughter is my daughter too, not that I can take any of the credit. I only wish I could!"

Shaunna smiled at him. "Thanks, although you do have to accept some of the responsibility for how she turned out. In fact, you all do."

Cordelia looked around the people standing before her, at once seeing them as the adults they were and the children she had known. It was making her quite sentimental.

"It's been wonderful to see you all," she said, "but I really must return to my new friend Vincent." She leaned in towards George. "We have so much in common—did you know, we both have degrees in fine art?"

"I didn't even know you studied art, Miss!" George said, incredibly impressed by this.

"Yes, indeed I did. I've always been surprised you didn't pursue that path yourself. And we both went to the same university. Now what are the odds of that?"

"No idea, but I know someone who can work them out for you."

Cordelia laughed. "Speaking of which, do remind that husband of yours he promised you'd both visit soon. Let's hope he doesn't keep me waiting quite so long as he did you. I'm afraid I have neither your youth nor patience."

With that, she gave them each a pat on the head and went back to Vincent to share the bottle of red wine they'd been enjoying prior to her extended leave of absence.

When Iris returned from her 'quick cig', which in fact consisted of chain-smoking four cigarettes in a row and still wasn't quite sufficient to stave off the emotional onslaught, she noticed Eleanor sitting on her own, and went and sat next to her.

"George tells me yer a doctor," she said.

"Yes, I am," Eleanor confirmed.

"Good job, that, bein' a doctor. Rewardin'."

"Yes."

"And bloody 'ard work, I would think." Iris folded her arms. "Lot of pressure on yer."

"Yes, there is."

"Aye." Iris adjusted her position. "Makin' fast decisions, and you've got to get it right first time, eh?"

Eleanor's eyebrows raised slightly, but she didn't respond.

"It's as well not everythin' in life's like that, eh, love?"

"No. That's very true," Eleanor said. The pause made her feel very uneasy. After all, she'd never met George's mother before, although she was quite sure she was getting a ticking off.

"Listen," Iris turned and looked at her. "Georgie said you've got yer knickers in a knot about him and Josh gettin' wed."

"Did he?"

"Aye, he did, love. But, as I told him, it takes some of us a bit longer to weigh things up, you know what I mean?"

Eleanor closed her eyes and nodded.

"Specially you clever-uns," Iris continued, "cos there's more to think about, in't there?"

Eleanor opened her eyes again and smiled. "Yes, Mrs. Morley. You're absolutely right."

"Aye, sometimes I am. Anyhow." She slowly eased herself to her feet, groaning with the pains of age. "If Georgie asks, I was tellin' yer about me bunions. Ta-rah, love." She patted Eleanor on the knee and left her alone once more.

Over the next hour, a few more guests arrived; with needing to have the reception early for various reasons, not least so Jess could enjoy it, many were coming straight from work, including Wotto and Krissi, who had left Karen and the assistant chef in charge, and were both fretting about it. Jason was with them, and stayed for about twenty minutes, then left again to go and set up the studio for a recording session. A select group of staff from the university also dropped by to offer their congratulations and leave cards, as well as Jake and Hannah from the farm, accompanied by Damien and Amelia—two young students who worked in the café during the holidays. Josh watched Amelia give George a card from her and Damien, whilst Damien stood by, giggling coyly. He was a very clever young man, destined to achieve great things, but George made him nervous and the more nervous he became, the more camp he acted. Amelia, on the other hand, was very sociable and seemed entirely at ease talking to anyone and everyone. She grabbed Damien by the arm and dragged him over.

"Congratulations," she smiled at Josh.

"Thanks," he said, accepting her friendly embrace.

"You both look lovely."

Josh smiled and adjusted his sleeves self-consciously, catching a glimpse of his cufflinks in the process. He was also caring for the pocket watch, as George had discarded his jacket and tie right after their speeches. He was now open-shirted, with a plain white t-shirt on display, but he still looked— perfect. Josh tore himself away and returned his gaze to Amelia.

"I study psychology at sixth form," she said.

"Is that A Level?"

"Yeah. It's really interesting. It's my favourite subject."

"It's a good subject to study. Are you thinking of doing it at uni?"

"No. I was going to, but I'm not very good at the academic stuff. I'm applying to train as a nurse."

"OK, that's cool. And psychology's useful to that, too."

"Yeah, that's what my teacher said. I was thinking about mental health nursing, but I'm still looking into it."

"What about you, Damien?" Josh asked. "What career have you got in mind?"

"Either veterinary medicine or biomedical science of some sort. I've been talking to George about Aberdeen, as they offer quite a good range of biomedical courses." He blushed as he said this and Josh fought the urge to smile.

"That's awesome. So I'm guessing you're studying the natural sciences?"

"Yes," Damien confirmed nervously.

"Good stuff," Josh said. It felt unbelievably good to know that his *husband* was the object of this good-looking young man's attraction, even if there was a twenty year age difference between them. Of course, Josh couldn't see past his own feelings to make an objective judgement, but others had pointed out that it was the combination of the qualities he had mentioned in his vows, and George's rugged handsomeness that made him so appealing—to everyone. It was also the reason for Josh perpetually questioning why George had fallen in love with him, when he could essentially have taken his pick. So, along with his own sense of wonder, he also felt a bit sorry for Damien. It's not a nice feeling to have a crush on someone unobtainable, or, indeed, that you think is unobtainable, as had been his reality for a very long time. Damien and Amelia were still standing nearby, engaged in a hushed conversation, with him vigorously shaking his head in response to her whispered suggestions.

"By the way, there's food over there," Josh told them, trying to put them at ease, "and the bar's free, so go and make the most of it."

"OK. Thanks." Amelia once again led Damien away by the arm. Josh shook his head and smiled. They reminded him of Ellie and himself when they were in sixth form, although he'd never been that tactile, nor she that confident, but watching the pair of them, tormenting each other, and the obvious trust and mutual respect between them, made him a little nostalgic, and sad. He allowed his gaze to drift from the two young people to Eleanor, to find she was watching him too. She got up and walked towards him, keeping her eyes fixed on his all the way. When she finally arrived, she threw her arms around him.

"I'm so, so sorry. I was wrong, and I said some appalling things. I wish I could turn back the clock."

"You can't," Josh said, "but it's OK. You know what they say? What doesn't kill us…"

She kissed his cheek. "I was out of order, Josh. I really am truly sorry. And I take it all back. There's nothing wrong with gay marriage. How can *this* be wrong?"

"That's not what it says in the bible."

"True, but as a wise man once told me, it's probably more of a guide book than a rule book, and some of it needs bringing up to date." She smiled at him. "As do I."

"Well, I'm pleased to have been the one to drag you into the twenty-first century, even if you did kick and scream all the way." She play-smacked his arm and he mouthed an 'ouch'. "And for the record, I am also very sorry for what I said, especially for calling you—what I called you. I'm so ashamed that I can't even bring myself to say it again."

"Which name specifically? The narrow-minded fool or dogmatic bi…"

"That one," Josh interrupted and blushed. Eleanor laughed and hugged him tighter.

"Apology accepted, although you were right."

Dan appeared next to her.

"Alright, Ellie. I'm off to see a man about a dog."

"Okey dokey," she replied. "See you soon."

Dan nodded at Josh and then left.

"What the hell was that about?" Josh asked.

"Wait and see," she said, cryptically tapping the side of her nose. "I think it might be almost time for you to cut your cake."

"OK," he agreed happily. He wasn't worried what they did to him anymore, and it was a very strange feeling. "I'll go find the husband," he said with a grin. Eleanor tutted and went off in search of Adele.

He met George halfway across the room, in the middle of an expanse of floor where there were no tables, nor people standing around chatting.

"Hi," George smiled and put his arms around him.

"Hi, yourself," Josh smiled back.

"You want to dance?"

"Slow dance, you mean?"

"Yeah. You know, like a first dance."

"There's no music." That wasn't strictly true, although it was too quiet to be heard over the conversations taking place all around them.

"So what d'you think?" George started swaying in time to an imaginary rhythm.

"As long as you're sure it's not too 'out' for you?" Josh teased. George pulled him closer still and they began to slowly circle together.

"When the song finishes," Josh said, "we've got to go and cut the cake."

"Uh huh," George sounded, nuzzling into his neck. "You smell so sexy," he whispered.

"Thanks. So do you."

"How d'you know?"

"Just guessing." Josh laughed and kissed him. "You smell good, though."

By now they'd gathered a bit of an audience, but they didn't care, and carried on dancing for a minute or so longer, before the sound of Adele coughing into her hand signalled that it was time for them to cut their wedding cake. Eleanor's mum had arrived just before their dance: it turned out that there were, in fact, two tiers to the cake, and she had come with the second one, which was yet another surprise. She checked that her miniature grooms were correctly positioned and stepped away. Josh and George approached, hand in hand, and both stopped, amazed.

"Are we not allowed to have any secrets?" Josh asked.

Adele giggled and stood on tiptoes so she could whisper in his ear. "You're not the only one who watches people," she said.

The top tier of the cake, which they'd already seen, was square and iced in plain cream—the same colour as the carnations on the tables—with a tiny, fondant stack of Charles Dickens' books in the centre, the two grooms sitting back-to-back on top of them. The bottom tier was also cream, but round in shape, and decorated as a giant Love Heart, with the words 'JUST MARRIED' and 'JOSH AND GEORGE' written in the palest turquoise within the turquoise outline of a heart. Josh felt the tears welling and before he could do anything about it, Adele put her arms around him; the floodgates opened.

"Oh, Adele," he cried, and that was as much as he could manage. Mrs. Davenport watched on, satisfied that it was a job well done. George gave her a thumbs-up in case there was any doubt, and just as soon as Josh recovered, they got on with the official cutting of the cake.

"I'll make sure everyone gets a piece," Adele said. "You go and say your goodbyes."

"Why? We're not going yet, are we?"

"Err—" Adele glanced behind them, and they turned to see Dan and Andy standing casually, with Blue. George raised his hands in query.

"You two ready?" Dan asked.

"Ready for what?"

"To go on your honeymoon," Andy said.

"What?" they exclaimed together.

"I'm at work tomorrow," George said.

"You're not," Jake decreed.

"And what about my clients?" Josh asked.

"All taken care of, Joshy," Sean assured him.

"But we haven't got any stuff packed, or…" Josh began.

"So," Jess said, "do you think this linen shirt would suit Andy?"

"You sneaky..." He started to laugh and looked at George. "Looks like we're going on our honeymoon."

"Yep. Where to?"

"Cornwall," Andy said. "You'll love it. The place is perfect—gorgeous little bay, picturesque views, stunning wildlife, beautiful sandy beaches where you can sit and read or paint or whatever, rock pools, waves—awesome waves. They get breakers of up to..."

"Yeah, I think they get it, bro," Dan interrupted. "And there's a hotel right on the beach where even the hairiest of guests is welcome," he said, patting Blue on the head.

"You'd best get a move on," Eleanor prompted. "It's a five hour journey."

"Five hours and twenty-three minutes," Adele corrected. "In the current traffic."

"What d'you reckon?" Dan said to Andy. "Do it in four?"

"Depends if you're gonna let me do the driving."

"You'll be there before dark, whatever," Kris said.

"If Andy's driving, they'll be there before they've even left," Shaunna joked.

"You know that doesn't actually work," Josh said. Everyone groaned and George nudged him.

"We won't be there at all at this rate! Come on, dearest." He tugged Josh by the hand.

"Don't even go there," Josh warned jokingly, allowing himself to be led outside, to where Dan's 4x4 was fully fuelled and loaded up with their new luggage. Dan opened the back and Blue jumped straight in. George attached the dog's harness and closed the door, then climbed in the back seat, next to Josh, who was sitting and silently shaking his head in wonder.

"There's a takeaway cappuccino in the cupholder," Dan pointed out. "Hopefully it'll keep you going until we get to the motorway."

"Pfft," George said. Josh stuck out his tongue.

"All set?" Andy asked them.

"Yep," George confirmed.

"All right then. Let's go!"

Slowly, Dan pulled away from the kerb, giving the newly weds time to wave to all of their 'family' and friends, now congregated outside the hotel to send them off.

"Oh my God!" Adele started to giggle when she saw the back of the 4x4, and its 'Just Married' banner. "Who did that?"

Eleanor and Jess looked at each other and shrugged.

"Not me," Kris said. "Dan told me if I stuck anything to his car he'd 'rip me a new one'."

"Yeah, well," Shaunna smiled, brushing her palms together, then slinging an arm around Adele. "Let's just call it payback, shall we?"

"For the pumps and the skipping rope?" Adele asked as they made their way inside once more.

"And the glue sticks."

"And holes in jumpers."

"Not to mention the smartass comments."

"Or the correction fluid."

"Matches spent on the bench."

"Disappearing ribbons."

"Stinkbombs in desks."

"Plastic spiders…"

"Real spiders…"

The Story Continues in...

Breaking Waves

Your invitation to join Josh and George
on their Cornish honeymoon.

A short summertime romance with sun, sea,
strawberries and much soul-searching.

and...

In The Stars Part II
(Cancer–Sagittarius)

The Circle is in flux. It's been a hectic six months and as the
friends head into the heat of summer, more trials await that
will truly test the bonds of friendship.

And just who did kill Alistair Campion?
Could the answer be in the stars?

Hiding Behind The Couch Website:
www.hidingbehindthecouch.com

www.debbiemcgowan.co.uk
www.beatentrackpublishing.com

Lightning Source UK Ltd.
Milton Keynes UK
UKOW02f0918290316

271079UK00002B/464/P